Kneeling in front of the big stone hearth, Chance had a roaring blaze going in minutes.

Kate walked over as he came to his feet. "It's obvious you've had a lot of practice at this." For a moment, they stood there staring at the flames, then Kate felt his eyes on her and slowly turned to face him.

"I've had a lot of practice at a lot of things," he said softly, roughly. Something shifted in his features, turning turbulent and hot. The kiss he claimed wasn't the soft, gentle, tender kiss she expected. It was a fierce, taking kiss that left her breathless and yearning, a wild, reckless kiss that made her legs begin to quiver and her heart beat like a drum. His mouth moved over hers as if this moment was more important than drawing his next breath, and suddenly she found herself feeling the same insane sensation.

She kissed him back with a recklessness foreign to her until now, her nails digging into his shoulders, her breasts aching, her nipples swelling. They strained toward the front of his denim shirt, rubbing, moving, the friction exquisite, drawing a moan from her throat.

Books by Kat Martin

HOT RAIN

MIDNIGHT SUN

DEEP BLUE

THE SECRET

Published by Kensington Publishing Corporation

THE SECRET

KAT MARTIN

ZEBRA BOOKS
KENSINGTON PUBLISHING CORP.
http://www.kensingtonbooks.com

ZEBRA BOOKS are published by

Kensington Publishing Corp.
119 West 40th Street
New York, NY 10018

All Kensington titles, imprints, and distributed lines are available at special quantity discounts for bulk purchases for sales promotion, premiums, fund-raising, educational, or institutional use.

Special book excerpts or customized printings can also be created to fit specific needs. For details, write or phone the office of the Kensington Special Sales Manager: Attn.: Special Sales Department. Kensington Publishing Corp., 119 West 40th Street, New York, NY 10018. Phone: 1-800-221-2647.

Zebra and the Z logo Reg. U.S. Pat. & TM Off.

ISBN-13: 978-1-4201-2881-9
ISBN-10: 1-4201-2881-7

First Printing: March 2001

10 9 8

Printed in the United States of America

Chapter One

Kate Rollins cast a nervous glance at the glowing red numbers on the digital clock on her desk. Ten P.M. She should have been home by six.

She darted a look at the tall corner windows of her seventh floor office. It was black as sin outside, no sign of a moon, any stars obliterated by the bleak gray overcast and the downtown LA smog. She didn't like working so late, being one of the last people to leave the building, didn't like the eerie sound of her own footsteps echoing down the empty marble-floored halls.

She didn't like walking out onto the dark, deserted sidewalk, especially not tonight. Not when she had promised her twelve-year-old son, David, she would take him to the new Schwarzenegger movie that was playing at the cinema. But her boss had called just before five and insisted on a change in the ad campaign she was presenting to Quaker Oats, one of her biggest clients, first thing in the morning.

Finished at last, Kate slid her ballpoint pen back in the top drawer of her desk and rolled back her chair. Determined to say goodnight to David before he fell asleep, she collected her leather briefcase, slung the strap of her Bally handbag over her shoulder, and headed for the bank of elevators waiting down the hall.

In the lobby, she waved to the deskman, said a quick goodnight to the security guard next to the revolving door, and walked out onto the sidewalk. The night was damp and still, the March air cold and sticky, heavy with the smell of car exhausts and throbbing with the distant blare of horns. Knowing the area could be dangerous this late, Kate nervously hoisted the strap of her bag a little higher on her shoulder and started walking down the sidewalk to the parking garage around the corner where her Lexus was waiting.

As she made the turn, she spotted the entrance down the block that descended into the garage. She had almost reached it when she heard a sound behind her, someone running down the sidewalk. More than one person, she realized, her pulse kicking up, beginning a worried beat inside her chest. Two young men, both wearing bomber-style leather jackets, Hispanic, perhaps, with their black hair and olive skin.

At the high-pitched squeal of tires, one of them glanced back over his shoulder, and she saw a low-slung, iridescent-green, '62 Chevy sliding on two wheels around the corner. The men caught up with her at the same instant the car roared up beside them.

A hand swung out the open window.

The stubby, blue-metal barrel of a pistol appeared.

Kate never heard the shot. Instead, as she started to run, she felt only a searing, white-hot pain in the side of her head, saw the ground rushing up to meet her, then her eyes rolled back and the world fell into darkness.

Chapter Two

The wail of the siren awakened her for an instant in the ambulance. Fifteen minutes later, Kate woke up on a fast-moving gurney, her head pounding in agony, the metallic smell of blood in her nostrils. Two green-gowned orderlies, shouting orders as they rushed her down a narrow white corridor, shoved the gurney through swinging double doors marked in bold red letters, SURGERY.

She couldn't guess how many hours had actually passed before she awakened what must have at least a full day later. She heard the steady beeping first, a comforting rhythm she latched onto, fixing her senses there, using it to ground herself.

She was lying on a narrow bed, chrome railings protectively locking her in, a plastic tube down her throat, a needle stuck into her arm, wires attached to her chest and forehead. She wore a white cotton nightgown that bunched around her legs, trapping them uncomfortably. She couldn't muster the strength to free them.

A faint hum entered her consciousness, and the whoosh of air rushing in and out of some machine. The pounding in her skull began again, swelling until it was nearly unbearable. A nurse arrived, plunged a syringe into the shunt in her vein and the pain began to recede. She slept for a while then awakened to the muted sound of voices, and distant, muzzy fragments of conversation.

" . . . drive-by shooting . . . "

" . . . still looking for the guys . . . "

" . . . miracle she's still alive . . . "

Male and female voices, fading in and out, leaving snatches of conversation that began to fit together like the pieces of a puzzle. Eventually she heard enough, remembered enough, to know what had happened. To know that a shooting had occurred and a bullet had ripped into her head.

Technically, one of the doctors said, she'd been dead on the operating table for almost ten minutes. Her heart had completely stopped. Her breathing continued only by the mercy of a respirator. For a few brief moments, she was no longer a living human being.

Kate had no doubt it was true.

Lying in her narrow bed in the intensive care unit of Cedars-Sinai Hospital, with monitors beeping and needles stuck into her arms, Kate knew deep down inside, where her heart pounded erratically and the blood pumped with sluggish rhythm through her veins, that during those vital moments in surgery, everything in her existence, everything she had ever believed had drastically changed.

She concentrated on the hum of a nearby machine,

the repetitive sound soothing in some way. She had read about such occurrences, when people died and were brought back to life. A *near-death experience*, it was called.

It had certainly been that and a whole lot more. Whatever it was called, it was something so profound, something so utterly amazing she would never, for the rest of her life, be able to forget it.

Kate closed her eyes and let the memory return, as crystal clear as it was during the time it had occurred. Lying on the operating table, she had heard the distant, muffled urgency in the voices of the doctors and nurses, felt the last few, erratic beats of her heart. Then her body suddenly shifted and she started drifting upward, floating away from the commotion below, toward the ceiling above her head. For a moment, she hovered there, confused, disoriented, looking down on the five green-gowned doctors and nurses working over the still form on the table. She could hear them very plainly.

"She's going into vee-fib!" someone shouted, the bleeping from the machine beside her changing to a steady hum.

"We're losing her!" one of the nurses called out.

"Get those paddles over here!"

She watched them a moment more, feeling so light, so completely unfettered.

Realizing that the person on the operating table must be she and if it were true, that she must be dead.

Then she started drifting upward again, right through the roof of the hospital, up above the city. The view was spectacular, like looking out the window of an airplane, seeing all the sparkling lights below.

If I'm dead, she remembered thinking, how can I possibly see? She started moving faster, faster, out into the darkness. It should have been cold, but it wasn't. A pleasant, warm nothingness surrounded her, comforted her, kept her from being afraid. The thick, penetrating blackness took the shape of a tunnel and she was drawn into it, carried upward through the darkness toward the tiny white pin-dot of light she could see at the end.

The light grew bigger, brighter, more pervading, until she was swallowed by it, became part of it. A soft, yellowish glow at first, it grew to the purest hue of sparkling white that she had ever seen.

My eyes should be hurting, she thought, but then she remembered that she had no eyes, had no real body. Looking down at herself, she could see the light streaming through her transparent form, glowing in every molecule of her being. She reached the end of the tunnel, came fully into the light, and a magnificent landscape appeared. Plants and flowers, shrubs and trees, in scarlet and emerald and purple, the purest, most vibrant colors that she had ever seen.

Shapes began to appear. They were people, she realized, recognizing her mother first among the others, looking younger than she had at thirty-four when she had been killed in the auto accident. Beautiful and vital and glowing with the same bright light that enveloped them all. She didn't see her father, but she hadn't seen him since she was two years old, and though she'd occasionally wondered if he might have passed away, she supposed he probably hadn't.

Other familiar faces appeared, her fourth grade teacher, Mrs. Reynolds, looking radiantly healthy and content; a young man who had worked with her at the office and died unexpectedly of a heart attack.

Another face appeared, a woman with the first hint of gray in the long, dark brown hair she wore pulled back in a bun, an attractive woman she had never seen but somehow looked familiar.

Her mother was smiling and though she didn't speak, Kate somehow knew her thoughts. *I love you. I miss you. I'm sorry I left you.*

More thoughts intruded, thoughts that compelled her to think about her life, about what was really important and what wasn't. About how the years sped past and you had to make the most of them.

One thought overrode all of the others. *It isn't time for you to be here. Someday you'll return, but not yet. Not yet.*

But she didn't want to leave, not now, not when the light was pouring through her, filling her with joy, with a complete and utter rapture unlike anything she had ever known before. Not when every cell in her body sang with it, pulsed with it.

No! she thought, *I want to stay!* She reached toward her mother, tried to resist the pull, the feeling of being drawn backward, but she was powerless to stop it.

A last thought reached her, a disturbing thought that came from the lady who looked familiar but wasn't. She was trying to tell her something. It was important. Urgent. It was a dark thought about pain and fear, nothing like the warm, pleasant thoughts she had received from the others. Kate struggled to decipher what it was, but it was too late.

She was plummeting backward away from the light, hurtling through the tunnel, spinning through space, moving even faster than before. With a sharp wrenching pain, she slammed back into physical awareness. For an instant, she lay there stunned, feeling the steady pumping of her heart, the tingling of her skin. She was alive and breathing, her mind whirling with thoughts of what had just occurred.

Then the black void of unconsciousness engulfed her once again.

Days passed. Kate drifted in and out of consciousness. She stirred in her narrow bed in the ICU, the sound of a woman's voice pulling her from slumber. When she opened her eyes, she saw her best friend, Sally Peterson, standing next to the bed.

"You look like hell, kiddo. But then, I doubt anyone who gets shot in the head is going to look much better."

Kate felt the faint pull of a smile. Her throat felt scratchy when she tried to speak. "How long . . . how long have I been in here?"

"Four days. I came to see you yesterday. Do you remember?"

She thought for a moment and the memory surfaced. She smiled with a measure of relief. "Yes . . . I do."

"Good girl." Sally moved closer to the bed. She was taller than Kate, who stood just a little over five-foot-two. She had straight blond hair while Kate's was thick and curly and a deep dark red. A thirty-three-year-old divorcee who ate compulsively when she suffered from stress, Sally had put on twenty pounds in the five years they had been working together at Menger and Menger, the advertising agency where they were both employed. But she was bright and hard working, and the best friend Kate had ever had.

"They're going to move you into a regular room tomorrow," Sally told her. "The doctor says you're responding to the surgery very well. They say you're going to be as good as new and out of here sooner than you think."

"Yes . . . Dr. Carmichael . . . told me." Kate moistened her dry lips. "Is David . . . ?"

"Your son is fine." Sally poured water into a paper cup and held it to her lips so she could drink. "Your husband is bringing him in to see you a little bit later this afternoon.

She rolled her eyes upward, toward the bandages covering all but her face. "Did they . . . shave my head?"

Sally laughed. "Ah—a note of vanity. She must be feeling better. Just a small circle above your left ear. They have such great techniques these days. Not like the old days."

Kate relaxed back against the pillow. It was silly to worry over something as trivial as the way she looked, but somehow she felt better knowing her appearance hadn't changed. It was perhaps the only thing about her that hadn't.

"Is there anything you need?" Sally asked. "Anything I can get for you?"

"Nothing I can . . . think of. But thanks for . . . coming."

Sally set the cup back down on the tray beside the bed, reached over and squeezed her hand. "I'll be back again tomorrow. That old bat, Mrs. Gibbons, will have my head if she thinks I'm tiring you too much."

Kate worked up a smile. Her eyes felt heavy. She let them slide closed. Her head ached and the bandages around it felt thick and uncomfortable. She heard Sally slip out of the room and the door softly close. As she drifted back to sleep, her mind returned to what had happened to her during the surgery, to the glorious place she had been, a place filled with light and joy. Kate wondered if the place might be heaven.

She thought of the familiar/unfamiliar lady and wondered who it might be. *What was she trying to tell me? What had she so desperately wanted me to know?*

Then she wondered if any of it had even really happened. Or if it were all some sort of fantastic dream. It didn't feel like a dream. Nothing she had ever experienced had ever felt more real.

As she drifted into a fitful sleep, Kate knew she wouldn't rest until she knew the truth.

Chapter Three

The April rains came. Not much as storms went, just a light spattering that barely moistened the earth, a little wind, then the sun popped out again. Kate heard the knock she had been expecting and hurried to the front door of her condo. She opened the door for Sally Peterson, who stood out in the hall.

"You ready to go?" Sally asked.

"Almost. Are you sure you don't mind driving me? I know it's a lot to ask."

"Don't be silly. I needed an excuse to get out of the office, anyway. If I had to sit there and listen to that obnoxious Bob Wilson bragging about another one of his conquests I would have put a gun to my head." Sally's eyes flashed toward Kate. "Sorry. I didn't mean—"

"It's all right," Kate said. "Hopefully, I'll be able to

joke about it myself before too long." It was Friday, three weeks since the shooting. Sally was driving her to Westwood, to see a doctor named William Murray. Murray was renown for his work on NDE—the medical term for near-death experience.

"I hope I'm doing the right thing," Kate said, leading Sally into the kitchen where she had left her purse.

"You told me this has been bothering you. You haven't been sleeping like you should. I have a feeling it's even worse than you're saying."

Kate sighed. "I can't get it out of my head. I dream about it at night. I think about the shooting, but mostly I think about the light and the people I saw. I need to understand what happened to me. I need to find out if it was real."

"Then you're doing exactly the right thing."

"What if this guy turns out to be some kind of quack?"

"You said he had a very good reputation. You got his name from the psychology department at UCLA, for heaven's sake. He can hardly be a quack."

"I suppose you're right. It's just that . . . This is really hard for me, Sally."

"I know it is. But maybe this guy will able to help you make some kind of sense of all this."

"God, I hope so." Kate walked into the kitchen. Like the rest of the condo, it was ultramodern in style, with stark white walls, black granite countertops, and expensive brushed-chrome appliances. It wasn't really her taste, but the location was one of the best in downtown LA and the price had been right. She had always meant to remodel. "Before we go, there's something I want to show you."

Sally sat down on one of the stools around the circular granite-topped breakfast table. "What is it?"

"Remember when I first told you about my experience? How I described the light and told you about seeing my mother and the others?"

"Telling me you saw your dead mother isn't something I'm inclined to forget."

Kate smiled. "Then you remember the other woman I mentioned, the one I didn't recognize but who somehow looked familiar."

"Yeah, what about her?"

"I was up in the attic the other day looking for some of my old high school yearbooks and I ran across a box of my mother's things I had stored up there. I forgot I even had them. I was only eighteen when she died. At the time, it was simply too painful for me to look at them. When I found them, I got to thinking ... the woman I saw must be someone I know or am somehow connected with, since the others were all people I remembered. I thought maybe I'd find something in the box that would help me figure it out."

Sally stared at the yellowed, dog-eared photo Kate held in one hand. "Don't tell me you found a picture of the woman you saw in the light?"

Kate sat down at the table across from her, slid the faded, black and white photo in Sally's direction. "I know it's hard to believe. I found this in the driver's license compartment of my mother's wallet, wedged behind her license. I should have guessed who the woman was when I saw her, but I'd never met her, never seen even a picture of her, and I just didn't put it together."

Sally studied the faded photo. A woman and a young girl stood side by side. The younger woman, dressed in bell-bottom jeans and a long-sleeved turtleneck sweater, looked a lot like Kate, but she was more slenderly built.

Her breasts were small and pointed, while Kate's were round and full, Kate's hips more curvy than slim. The woman's nose was straighter and not turned up at the end like Kate's.

"I assume the younger one is your mother," Sally said.

"That's right and the other woman—that's my grandmother, Nell Hart." In the photo, Nell looked about the same age as she was when she had appeared in the light, an attractive woman with a few streaks of gray in her thick, dark brown hair. "They look a lot alike, don't you think? That's the reason she seemed so familiar. When she died she would have been much older, but all the people appeared much younger there."

Sally glanced up from the photo, her expression full of disbelief. "You're telling me this is the woman you saw the night you were shot?"

"I remember her face as clearly as if she were standing here with us right now."

"And before that, you never knew what she looked like? You'd never even seen a photograph of her?"

Kate shook her head. "She and my mother had a falling out when Mama was only sixteen. My mother rarely talked about her. She told me once that Nell kicked her out of the house when she found out Mama was pregnant. Apparently Nell didn't like my father. She said he was no good and forbade my mother to see him. My mother, of course, being my mother, immediately ran off and married him. Jack Lambert took off two years later, so in a way my grandmother was right. But Mama never went back to Montana, and she and my grandmother never saw each other again."

"Your mother lived in Montana?"

"She was born there, but I gather she couldn't wait

to leave. Mama hated the country. She was a city girl through and through. She loved the nightlife . . . and the men. I guess that's why she ran away."

Sally stared down at the photo. "Your grandmother hasn't been dead all that long, has she? It seems like you mentioned something about an inheritance of some kind."

"She died about two months before the shooting. I didn't hear about it until three weeks after her death. I got a letter from a lawyer named Clifton Boggs. Boggs said Nell had left her property to me, since I was her only living relative. I have no idea how he knew where to find me. As far as I knew, Nell and my mother never made contact. At any rate, the estate isn't much. A farmhouse on eighty acres and a small cafe."

"Where exactly is it?"

"A little town called Lost Peak."

Sally grimaced as if Lost Peak, Montana must be the end of the earth. She set the photo back down on the table. "You said the woman in the light was trying to tell you something."

Kate nodded. "That's right. I think it was really important. I wish I knew what it was."

"I hate to say it, Kate, but odds are, you're never going to find out." The corners of her mouth tipped up. "At least not in this lifetime."

Kate flashed a smile of amusement. "Maybe not. At any rate, I need to talk to someone about it."

"And that's exactly what you're going to do." Shoving back her chair, Sally hauled herself to her feet. "Which means we'd better get going. You don't want to be late for your appointment."

As it was, even with the traffic, they arrived exactly on time. Sally parked her dark gray Mercury Sable at the curb, and they walked up Gayley Street to the doctor's office.

When they pushed through the door, Kate was pleasantly surprised to find the place had been decorated in the best possible taste. If Murray was a quack, he was a very successful one. Comfortable, gray leather sofas rested on plush burgundy carpet. A granite-topped coffee table sat in front of the sofa, a sign that read NO SMOKING perched next to a stack of carefully chosen magazines.

To Kate's relief, she only had to wait ten minutes before the nurse called her in.

"Kate Rollins?" She nodded.

"I'll be right out here if you need me," Sally said as Kate walked past her into the wood-paneled office and closed the door.

"Thank you for seeing me on such short notice, Dr. Murray."

"I'm glad we found a way to fit you in." He was a slender man in his mid-forties with short, dark brown hair and hazel eyes. His smile seemed sincere as he poured her a cup of coffee and seated her in an overstuffed chair in front of his desk.

"All right, Mrs. Rollins, why don't we just begin? I read about the shooting several weeks back. Anyone who watched the news was aware of it—and that it was a miracle you survived. I also saw a recent article in the *Times.*"

Kate inwardly grimaced at the reminder of the article that had been written about her "trip to The Other Side."

"Since my specialty is the study of NDEs," the doctor went on, "I presume that's why you're here. If that is the case, the easiest way to start is simply for you to tell me about it."

Kate took a steadying breath, her fingers wrapped securely around the coffee mug she held in her lap. For the next half hour, she told Dr. Murray what had happened the night she was shot.

"It isn't something I can simply put behind me," she said when she was finished. "It changed me, Dr. Murray. It changed everything I believed. The doctors at the hospital say it was only an hallucination, but I don't think that's true."

She told him about the photo she had found and that her grandmother had turned out to be the woman in the light.

"Surely what happened must be real. There's no way I could have known her, yet I recognized her immediately as the woman I had seen."

The doctor sat forward in his chair, his elbows propped on his desk. "Believe it or not, your story is fairly typical—and during the course of my research, I've heard nearly five hundred of them. Most people don't realize how often this phenomenon occurs. The Gallup Poll reported thirteen million people claim to have had a near-death experience."

Kate's eyes widened. "Thirteen million?"

"That's right. And I know what happened to you after you told people about it. There were those who looked at you as their last, desperate hope while others saw you as the nearest thing to Satan. The truth is you are simply one of millions who have taken some sort of unfathomable journey. I like to think if it is as kind of an enlightenment, if you would."

Kate ran a finger around the rim of her cup as she considered the doctor's words. "I've been reading everything I can find on the subject. From what I gather, the medical community isn't convinced it's real. They've come up with a number of theories to explain it. I read one that proposed it was simply the result of a dying brain."

He nodded. "There are those who are convinced that in an NDE, the dying person isn't traveling toward a beautiful afterlife; they believe the neurotransmitters in the brain are simply shutting down, creating a lovely illusion. The pattern, they believe, is the same for anyone facing death. The question is, if that is so, why would the brain be programmed that way in the first place? And it doesn't explain the small percentage of people who have a negative experience."

"I gather there are some who do."

"That's right. Mostly people carrying some sort of guilt, or are, perhaps, attempting suicide. What happens to them is almost exactly the opposite of the joyous emotions you felt."

"I've read other explanations."

"The temporal lobe theory, perhaps?"

She nodded.

"It's true that some features of a typical NDE can occur in certain forms of epilepsy associated with damage to the temporal lobe of the brain. Proponents of the theory believe the stress of being near death can stimulate the lobe. But the usual results are sadness, fear, and feelings of aloneness. Not what you've described at all."

"What about lack of oxygen? That's what my doctor told me it was."

"Yes, well, did your doctor happen to mention that the hallucinations produced by an oxygen-starved brain are extremely chaotic, more like psychotic delusions? They're completely different from the tranquility, peace, and calm you encountered."

"So you believe what happened to me was real."

"It doesn't matter what I believe. What matters is what you believe."

"It felt real. It still does. I wish I knew for sure." Kate looked off toward the window. The clouds were all gone. Another sunny day in California. She wondered what the weather was like in Lost Peak, Montana. "I keep thinking about the people I saw ... thinking about my grandmother. If it really happened, whatever she wanted me to know seemed crucial in some way."

"People have returned from The Other Side with all sorts of messages—everything from warnings of impending global disaster to personal communications from loved ones. Perhaps she wanted you to do something for her. Perhaps she wanted to warn you."

"Warn me?" A little shiver ran down Kate's spine. "Ever since this happened, I've been trying to recall the details of those last few moments. The feeling I got from her seemed so cryptic, and somehow very frightening, out of synch with everything else that was happening. This may sound crazy, Dr. Murray, but I keep thinking it had something to do with her death. I don't exactly know why I feel that way, but I do."

The doctor drummed his fingers on the desk. "It's possible, I suppose. As I said, I've encountered any number of different occurrences."

Kate sighed and shook her head. "I never wanted any of this. I wish I could just forget it, but I can't."

"In time, the memory will begin to fade. I can't promise you it will completely disappear. Occurrences such as these are often life-changing. People come away with a completely new perspective. They see things more clearly, understand what is important in life. If you're lucky, perhaps that will happen to you."

Kate mulled that over, thinking that in a number of ways it already had.

She stood up from her chair. "Thank you, Dr. Murray. You've been extremely helpful. I'm glad I came."

"If you ever need me . . . if there's anything else I can do, don't hesitate to call."

"I won't." But she didn't think it would happen. Speaking to the doctor had helped to clarify her jumbled, uncertain thoughts.

Now that she had a better understanding of what she had experienced, Kate had other, more important things to do.

Chapter Four

Two months passed. Two months, and not a day went by that Kate didn't think about the night she had died. As Dr. Murray had said, in those few brief moments, she had seen herself, seen her life in a way she never had before. She had discovered what was important, and been given a second chance to do something about it.

Standing in the entry of her condominium, Kate pulled a soft gray cashmere cardigan over her suit, and eased her curly, shoulder-length dark red hair out from under the collar.

"You're leaving?" She couldn't miss the anger in her husband Tommy's voice. "I don't believe it. I thought last Sunday was a fluke."

"I told you I was taking David. I asked you to come with us, but you said that you were too busy."

"I *am* too busy. Too damned busy to waste half the

day sitting on a pew in some damnable church." At the age of thirty-two, three years older than Kate, Tommy Rollins was tall and thin, with angular features and straight brown hair that nearly reached his shoulders. They'd been married since she was seventeen, when Tommy was the lead singer in the Marauders, a local rock band, and Kate was head cheerleader, pregnant after the second time they made love in the back seat of Tommy's old Ford coupe.

She'd thought then that she loved him. Now, she wondered how she ever could have been that stupid.

"I tell you, Kate, I think that bullet did more to your brain than punch a hole in it. You've been acting half crazy ever since the shooting."

"I don't see how taking my son to church on a Sunday morning is acting half crazy."

"Oh yeah? Well, it isn't just church and you know it. You used to like to party. Man, when we were first married, you could outdrink half the guys in the band. Now you hardly even drink a glass of wine. You're really turning into a bore, Kate. You know that?"

"You're right, Tommy—I don't drink like I did when I was twenty. I have an important job with a ton of responsibilities—something you couldn't begin to understand—and I have a twelve-year-old son to take care of."

"Yeah, well, what about those crazy books you've been reading?" Tommy sauntered past his electric guitar case, open and sitting on the camelback sofa she had saved for months to buy after they'd moved into the condo. A rush of air scattered the pages of the latest song he'd been trying to write. He stopped at the pile of books neatly stacked on the small, antique French writing desk in the corner.

"Look at this crap." He held up the leather-bound volume that sat on the top. *"Beyond the Light: Finding the Spirit Within."* He grabbed another. *"Life After Life.* Here's a hot one—*Return from Tomorrow: Is There Life After Dying?* What a load of bullshit!" With an angry grunt, he swept his arm across the desk, sending the whole stack crashing to the floor.

Kate bristled but made no move. The books might not have the answers to all of her questions, and she might not find the comfort she sought in church, which up until now she had rarely attended, but she had to explore every possibility. Considering what she had experienced, she was doing the best she could.

"I don't like it, Kate. I didn't marry some religious fanatic and I don't want to be married to one now."

Kate glanced down the hall, checking to be sure that David was still in his room. "I'm hardly a religious fanatic. But I have to admit you have a point. Maybe you haven't changed all that much in the past twelve years, but I'm a different woman than I was at seventeen. Our marriage was a mistake from the beginning and both of us know it. For David's sake, I've stayed when I should have gone. I've put up with your infidelity. I've ignored the tantrums you call your artistic temperament. I've supported you, hoping you would finally grow up and make something out of yourself. But as of this minute, Tommy, I'm through with all that."

She drew in a steadying breath and plunged ahead, determined to take the course of action she should have embarked on long before this. "I didn't mean to do it this way, but the fact is, I want a divorce. I should have gotten one years ago, but I wanted David to have a father. Since you've never really been there for him anyway, I don't really see that it matters anymore."

Tommy's face turned the shade of a pickled beet. He opened his mouth to argue, but the sound of his son's voice cut him off.

"Mom?" David stepped out into the hallway. Seeing the worried expression on his face, Kate's chest tightened. She hadn't meant for him to hear. She would call back the words if she could, but it was too late.

She forced herself to smile. "It's all right, honey. Your father and I have some things to work out, that's all."

"Yeah," her husband said snidely, "like getting a divorce—which, by the way, is fine with me."

David's thin face turned pale. "What are you guys talking about? You aren't really getting divorced, are you?"

The worry in his eyes made her throat close up. With his slender build, hazel eyes, and straight brown hair, David was a smaller version of his father. But unlike Tommy, her son was sensitive and vulnerable. He had always been shy and a little withdrawn, exactly the opposite of Tommy, who was at his best when he was belting out a hard rock tune in front of a hundred people. Kate didn't want to see David hurt and yet, now that she had finally taken the first step, she knew she had done the right thing.

She walked toward her son and leaned over to hug him, but David turned away. Kate's heart squeezed painfully. Lately, he'd been growing more and more distant, arguing all the time, getting bad marks in school. Last week he had even been sent to the principal's office. Kate prayed the divorce would make things better not worse.

"We'll talk about all this after church, okay?" Pulling his navy-blue jacket off a hanger on the back of a chair, she held it out for him to put on. "We'd better get going. We're going to be late if we don't hurry."

David didn't budge. "I'm not going to some stupid ol' church. I'm staying here with Dad."

Tommy flashed a look of triumph. "That's right, kid." He turned a mocking glare on Kate. "You go on to your damnable church, Kate. David and I are staying right here. There's a ball game on. That's better than listening to some stupid preacher yapping about hell and damnation."

Anger made her cheeks go hot, but Kate knew better than to argue. She had already crossed one line—a very important one—and she didn't intend to go back. The next step would take careful thought and planning, but she was determined.

Everything had changed the day of the shooting. For the last few years, she had simply existed, trapped in a rotten marriage, catering to a husband she merely tolerated, working twelve hours a day in a job that left no time for her son.

In a single instant of clarity, she had seen the years of her life slipping away, seen the damage she was doing to the child who needed her so badly—and found the courage to do something about it.

Tomorrow she would start the divorce proceedings.

The day after that, she would begin the rest of the changes she planned to make.

It would take a little time to prepare, to make the necessary arrangements, but Kate believed she owed it to herself—owed it to her son—to make something out of the life that had been returned to her the night that she had died.

* * *

The days seemed to drag, but a month had passed since his mom had filed for divorce and they had moved out of the condo into a small apartment. Tonight it was clear and cool, the Monday night traffic lighter than usual.

David Rollins' jeans made a faint brushing sound as he eased the stairwell door closed and crept toward the pillar in the lobby. His tennis shoes squeaked on the polished floor and he stopped dead-still, praying the security guard hadn't heard.

His heart was pumping, his palms felt clammy. He plastered himself against the pillar and waited for the guard to get up and make his rounds as he did each night, David had discovered, around ten P.M.

As soon as the man was out of his chair and starting down the hall, David made a break for the door, shoving it open and racing out onto the Hill Street sidewalk. It was a school night, past time he should be getting ready for bed, but his friends, Tobias Piero and Artie Gabrielli, were waiting. Artie had his hands stuffed into the back pockets of his baggy jeans. Toby had his bill cap on backward.

"Hey, man," Toby said, "we thought you might not get out of the house. You know how your old lady is about stayin' home on a school night."

"Yeah, well, she thinks I'm asleep in my room. I figure what she doesn't know won't hurt her."

Artie just laughed. "I knew you wouldn't let us down. Toby's scored some weed, man. Tonight we're gonna howl."

David had only smoked marijuana a couple of times, and all it had done was make him dizzy. But Toby and

Artie thought it was cool, so he guessed he would try it again. It was a warm, dark night, with only a sliver of moon, but it was too smoggy to see any stars.

The three of them started off down the block, talking about Mr. Brimmer, the history teacher who had kept Toby after school for writing the F-word on the blackboard in big chalk letters, but they hadn't gotten more than a couple of feet when a fat guy in a windbreaker, jeans, and Reeboks walked up.

He slowed his pace to match David's. "Hey, you're Kate Rollins' kid, aren't you?"

David looked up at him warily. "Who wants to know?"

"Listen, kid, I'm Chet Munson with the *National Monitor*. We'd like to do a story on your mom. If you'd be willing to cooperate, it would make you a nice chunk of change."

"Hey, man, cool!" Toby said.

"Bullshit," said David. "You leave my mother alone." He set his jaw, hoping he looked tough, but inside he was feeling a little bit sick. He'd read the story about his mom in the newspaper, her trip to "The Other Side." A small column hidden on a back page of the *Times*, but that was bad enough. The *National Monitor*—jeez—that would be awful. He could just imagine his mother's picture plastered all over the cover of one of those stupid magazines they put beside the checkout stands in the grocery stores. The kind with headlines like HALF MAN, HALF ALLIGATOR FOUND IN FLORIDA SWAMP. OR WOMAN ABDUCTED BY ALIENS — GIVES BIRTH TO THREE-HEADED BABY. David shuddered to think what the kids at school would say if they read about his mother in a paper like that.

The reporter still walked beside him. "All right, then, just tell me a little about heaven. Your mom's been there, right? What'd she say about it? Did she see any angels? What did they look like?"

"I don't know anything about it," David said, which was more or less the truth, "and even if I did, I wouldn't tell a scumbag like you."

Artie punched him in the shoulder. "Don't be a chump, man. So your mom's a little spooky. What of it? If you can make some cash—"

"Forget it," David said. He turned to the reporter. "Get the hell outta here, man. And don't come around here bothering me or my mother again, you hear?"

The fat man shrugged his shoulders. "Okay, kid, but sooner or later, I'm gonna get the story anyway. When I do, you're the one who'll be the loser." The guy in the windbreaker jammed a card into the pocket of David's jeans. "Call me if you change your mind." With a glance at the other two kids, he turned and jogged back toward the blue Chevy van that was parked at the curb.

"What an asshole," David mumbled.

"I think you shoulda done it." Toby lifted his baseball cap then settled it back down on his head, hiding most of his dirty brown hair. "We coulda bought some great weed with that kinda cash."

David didn't answer. He was still thinking what would happen if the *National Monitor* really did do a story about his mother. His friends had teased him ruthlessly after the article in the *Times*. Most of them thought it was a load of bull.

"Hey, I got an idea," Artie said. "Let's go down to the parking lot on Fifth Street. Sometimes somebody leaves a car in there after the attendant's gone home. If they do, sometimes the keys are still in it."

"Cool!" Toby said. "Let's go."

David bit his lip. "I don't know if that's such a good idea. What if we get caught?"

"We ain't gonna get caught," Artie promised. "I've done it a couple of times already. We'll just go for a little ride then bring it right back."

He didn't really want to. He didn't even know if Artie could drive. Still, he didn't want to go home yet. If he did, he'd just lay there thinking about his mom on the front page of the *Monitor*, imagining all kinds of horrible stuff.

"All right," he finally agreed. "Let's go." It was something to do, better than worrying about the newspapers or missing his dad. The truth was he missed his mom, too, since she always worked so much. Yesterday she had quit her job the way she'd promised. Maybe things would be different now, but he wasn't really sure. And he hated the weird stuff she'd been doing lately—getting divorced, saying they had to move.

God, he'd like to kill the sonofabitch who shot her in the head.

"So . . . I guess you had a pretty exciting night last night." Sitting in the kitchen of Kate's small apartment, Sally accepted the mug of coffee Kate set in front of her on the inexpensive oak table Kate had recently purchased. She had moved in the day escrow had opened on her condo, the sale part of the preliminary divorce settlement that she had made with Tommy.

She sighed as she poured the last of the coffee into her cup and walked over to brew a fresh pot. She had told Sally about David's joy ride in a stolen car and that he had spent the night in juvenile hall.

"It was awful, Sally. The place was unbelievably cold and sterile. And the kids . . . they all seemed so hopeless. The matron treated me like I was Ma Barker and David was a member of the gang." She shook her head. "I still can't believe it . . . not my David. But it happened. And I'm afraid it could happen again."

"Maybe it's good they were hard on him. Seeing what it's like when you commit a crime might be exactly what he needs. Maybe it'll straighten him out."

"I hope so. I don't think I can take something like that again."

Sally took a drink of coffee. "What about Tommy? How are things going with him?"

"You know, at first I actually believed he was going to be decent about all of this. Then he hired some fancy lawyer. Yesterday he threatened to sue me for custody of David—not that Tommy really wants him. I reminded him he had no means of supporting a child. I mentioned the times he'd been arrested for possession of marijuana when he was younger. All it did was make him mad. The only way I could convince him to leave us alone was to agree to pay him alimony."

"Alimony! Are you kidding?"

"In a bizarre way, I suppose it makes sense. Tommy hasn't earned a nickel in years. He'll need time to get back on his feet."

Sally made a rude sound in her throat. "Like he isn't coming out of this whole thing smelling like a rose? He gets half the money from the sale of the condo, doesn't he? The property you bought with the money you earned working sixty hours a week? The one you've been making all the payments on?"

Kate refilled Sally's mug with the freshly brewed coffee, refilled her own, and returned the pot to the burner.

"Doesn't seem right, does it? But you know what, Sally? I don't really care. All I want is to finally be rid of him."

"I don't blame you. He's been a pain in the ass for years. Besides, you've got to do what's best for David."

Kate's heart twisted. *David.* She could hardly believe the troubled, sullen youth her son had become. Part of it was the divorce and losing his father—not that Tommy had ever really been much of a one. Part of it was her job and the demanding hours it required. Some of it was the way her life had changed since the shooting.

Kate shook her head. "A lot of what's happened with David is my fault."

"A lot of people work long hours, Kate. With Tommy unemployed you really had no choice."

"It isn't just work. It's all the changes I've made. Getting a divorce, moving out of the condo, quitting my job." She smiled. "I'm finished with the last of the projects I started. I've already given them my notice."

"I figured you had. I can't say I'm happy about it but I really don't blame you."

Kate reached for the copy of the *LA Times* that lay open on the table. "On top of all that, take a look at this." She shoved it over to Sally.

"What? Not another one of those horrible stories?" Sally smoothed the newsprint and began to scan the columns in search of the article Kate referred to. Halfway down the page, she spotted it. " *'Woman Tells Tale of Life After Death. Gives Dying Man Hope.'* Oh, God." Sally blew out a breath and started to read. For several long moments, she said nothing, then she muttered a curse at the reporter who had been so malicious.

"I can't believe it. This is the second time in the past three weeks your name's been in the paper. The last one made you sound like some kind of saint. This one makes you sound like a certified nut case." She tossed Kate a disappointed glance. "I thought you weren't going to say any more about your experience."

"Mr. Langley was so afraid of dying," Kate said. "He was such a dear little man. You remember him, don't you? The grocer who owned the store down the block from the office? I heard he was sick and I stopped by the hospital to see him. When I saw him lying there, I thought maybe if I told him what I saw the night I was shot it might make things easier for him."

"You're such a pushover, Kate. If someone asks for your help, you can't ever seem to say no."

Kate glanced away. "I know."

"So what happened to poor Mr. Langley?"

A chill swept through her. She curled her fingers around the mug, trying to absorb the warmth. "He died two days later. I hope what I said helped to comfort him in some way."

Sally sighed. "I hope so, too."

Kate stared off toward the window looking down on the small grassy park where David played basketball after school. "God knows what the kids in junior high will say to David when they see it. Kids can be so cruel."

She set her nearly untouched mug of coffee on the table in front of her. "I've got something to tell you, Sally."

"Oh, oh. I don't like that look."

Kate just smiled, thinking how much she was going to miss her friend. "You remember the day you drove me to Westwood to see Dr. Murray? We talked about the property my grandmother left me."

"I remember. I presumed you were going to sell it."

"I was. I've never even been to Montana. I thought,

what in God's name would I do with a business out in the middle of nowhere?''

"Has my hearing gone bad, or is there a ring of past tense to that?"

"I'm not selling it, Sally. Not now. Not with everything that's happened and my worries about David. I've decided I'm going to move there. A lady named Whittaker has been running the place since my grandmother decided to retire, but apparently the woman is getting too old for the job. My timing couldn't be better."

Sally's blond brows pinched together. "I don't know, Kate. Lost Peak, Montana? Good Lord, it *snows* there. It doesn't sound exactly like a trip to Newport Beach."

"No, it doesn't, thank God. It sounds like a place with good old-fashioned values, a place where the late news isn't filled with rape and murder, where innocent people don't get shot in the head just walking down the street. I won't be making anywhere near as much money, but my hours will be my own, and I'll have a lot more time to spend with David."

Sally sighed. "I suppose, when you get down to it, that's all that matters."

Kate agreed wholeheartedly. David needed her. He needed a place with families who cared about each other. He needed to get as far from gang wars and juvenile delinquency as he possibly could.

The more Kate thought about it, the more eager she was to leave. She had no relatives; she was an only child. And Tommy's parents were a lot like Tommy, spoiled and self-centered, with little time for David. The school year would soon be over. Except for her friends, there was nothing to keep her in LA.

Kate tried to imagine what she might encounter in Montana. She had never really thought of herself as a country girl, but recalling the eye-burning LA smog, the frustrating traffic snarls, her concrete and asphalt existence, the idea was more than appealing.

It would mean a drastic change of lifestyle for both of them. It wouldn't be easy, yet Kate found herself looking forward to the challenge.

Sally took a drink of her coffee. "That day we went to see Dr. Murray . . . you said your grandmother was trying to tell you something. That isn't the real reason you're going, is it? You're not on some sort of mission to discover what Nell was trying to say?"

"I'm going because it's the right thing to do. I've got a chance to start over, to give David and me both a new life. If I happen to learn a little about my grandmother while I'm there, what could it hurt?"

Sally scowled, knowing Kate's curious nature only too well.

"Look on the bright side—now you'll have an excuse to visit Montana. You always said you wanted to learn to ski."

Sally rolled her eyes. "Skiing's one thing. Grizzly bears are another."

Kate just laughed. Still, she couldn't help wondering what she might learn about Nell Hart, once she got to Lost Peak.

And she thought that faraway Montana might just be the answer to her prayers.

Chapter Five

There were a lot of places a guy could be in the world, but as Chance McLain stood on the banks of Beaver Creek at the base of the snow-capped Mission Mountains, he watched the frothy water rushing over the slick, mossy rocks and thought that Montana had to be the best of them.

Which is why it made him half crazy to see the dead fish floating on the surface of the stream, to know that Consolidated Metals was up to its old tricks, and arsenic waste from its gold mining operation was pouring into the creek.

Damn, why couldn't anybody stop them? Probably because Beaver Creek ran mostly across the Salish-Kootenai Indian Reservation and no one really cared. No one but the Salish, that is.

Maybe being part Indian on his mother's side was the

reason Chance felt so strongly about it, but he didn't think so. He believed any man worth his salt who knew the damage Consolidated Metals was doing to the environment would be damn mad about it. Unfortunately, knowing it and proving it to the people who mattered weren't the same thing.

The sound of heavy, rubber-soled boots crunching on the rocks along the bank drew his attention. "I saw a nice white-tail buck up on the side of the mountain, but I couldn't get a shot." His best friend, Jeremy Spotted Horse, stopped at the edge of the creek beside him. They were hunting elk on the reservation, meat for Jeremy's freezer, since he had a wife and two kids to feed and his job at the lumber mill didn't pay all that much. They hadn't seen any elk, or even much sign, but a nice fat deer would do almost as well.

"You seen anything?" Jeremy asked.

"Yeah, I saw something, all right." Chance squatted on his haunches beside the creek. "Take a look at this."

Jeremy stared down at the water, caught the glint of silver that had once been a beautiful rainbow trout. Now its mouth stood open and its eyes were cloudy, staring up at the clear Montana sky but never seeing it again.

"Damn! Those rotten bastards are at it again."

"Somebody's got to stop them before they wind up killing half the fish in Montana—and God only knows what else."

"Easier said than done." Jeremy sighed and scratched his head. "We've had half a dozen meetings about it, talked to them till we're blue in the face. You can see how much good it's done."

"Every time I see that sonofabitch Barton, it's all I can do not to punch him out."

"You do, you'll wind up in jail for assault. Lon Barton's one of the richest men in the state and his father's richer than that. He's got the best lawyers money can buy, and you aren't one of his favorite people."

Chance grinned. "That, my friend, is my one claim to fame."

Jeremy slapped him on the back. "Well, you had better leave Barton alone, ol' buddy. And on an equally important subject, I'm getting hungry. We can try our luck again in the morning. In the meantime, let's go get something to eat."

"You got it, Kemosabe."

Jeremy laughed, enjoying the joke they had shared since they were kids. Chance the Lone Ranger. An only child whose mother had died when he was three and a father who mostly ignored him. Jeremy his faithful Indian sidekick.

They headed down the mountain to the place where Chance had parked his silver Dodge pickup, opened the doors, and slid onto the sheepskin-covered seats. Chance stuck the key into the ignition and fired up the powerful V-10 engine. "The Lost Peak Cafe is the closest place around."

"Perfect. I can already taste a piece of Myra's apple pie."

Chance drove the pickup onto the gravel road leading down from the mountain. He passed the open field at the edge of town where a hundred years ago the assayer's office had been, splashed through a couple of mud puddles, and pulled up in front of a low-roofed, battenboard building that sat on the only street in town. Climbing out of the truck, they stepped up on the wooden sidewalk in front of the Lost Peak Cafe.

Chance halted in front of the door, staring at the

Gone Out of Business sign that hung on the screen as if it were a venomous snake. He shoved back his black felt hat, hardly able to believe it.

From a few feet away, Jeremy softly cursed. "Well, that damned well puts a thorn in our plans," he grumbled.

Chance just scowled. He'd been coming to the Lost Peak Cafe since he was a boy, driving into town with Ed Fontaine, the owner of the ranch next door to his father's place, or occasionally with the old man himself, though as bad as he and his dad got along, he'd tried to forget most of those times.

"I can't believe it." Jeremy looked into the darkened interior of the cafe. "The place was practically an institution. Mrs. Whittaker didn't say anything about closing it down the last time we were in."

"I guess once Nell was gone, some of the fun went out of it for her." The two old women had been best friends since they were girls. When Nell had wanted to retire, Aida Whittaker had taken over running the place.

"I guess that's probably it." Jeremy thumped a finger against the offensive sign. "We'll have to drive twenty miles more just to find a place that's open."

"Yeah, and so will everyone else in Lost Peak." Which wasn't saying much since there weren't that many people who lived in a place most folks saw as little more than a grease spot in the road.

"Damned shame about Nell," Jeremy said. "She was a good ol' gal. With her dead and buried, I guess I should have figured Aida would eventually close the place down. Somehow I just never really believed it would happen." Jeremy was shorter than Chance, his complexion even darker, but both of them were broad-shouldered and black-haired, though Jeremy's hair was long and straight while Chance's was shorter and slightly wavy.

"Times change, Jeremy. Besides, you never know. Maybe somebody will buy it. There are worse places to live than Lost Peak."

Jeremy laughed. "Maybe for people like you and me. We look out there and see the snow on those mountains, see the whitest clouds God ever put on this earth, and think we've cornered a little bit of heaven, but the average guy only sees the ice in the winter and the bugs in the summer."

"Maybe so. I guess we'll just have to wait and see."

"So, what do you think? Shall we head on into Arlee or skip breakfast altogether? I know you probably got a lot to do at the ranch."

"We've got things pretty well under control right now. Besides, now that you got me thinking about it, I'm damned hungry. The Lone Eagle's the next closest spot. The food isn't all that good but it's better than nothing."

"I'm sure gonna miss Myra's apple pie," Jeremy groused, speaking of the cafe's long time cook.

"You can say that again," Chance agreed as they turned and headed back to his pickup.

But more than that he would miss the two old women he'd been so fond of. He didn't get into Lost Peak all that often, but whenever he did, he tried to stop by and see Nell and Aida. After Nell's death, Aida had started talking about moving to Oregon to live with her daughter and son-in-law. Apparently, she'd finally done it. He hoped she would be happy there.

"As long as we're heading north," Chance said, rounding the truck and jerking open the driver-side door, "we might as well stop by and see that lawyer, Frank Mills, up in Polson. See what progress he's making with Consolidated Metals. We can tell him what we ran across today and give him a little nudge in the right direction.''

"Yeah," Jeremy agreed, sliding into the passenger seat. "I suppose we oughta go see him ... even if it probably won't do a lick of good."

Chance clenched his jaw. "We'll find a way to stop them. If this lawyer can't do it, we'll hire one who can."

But Jeremy didn't look convinced, and deep down, neither was Chance. With a last disappointed glance at the locked door of the Lost Peak Cafe, he shoved the Dodge into reverse and backed out onto the street.

Chapter Six

Lost Peak, Montana. Population 400. When the lawyer had called it rustic and out of the way, he'd made the year's biggest understatement.

A gas station with an out-of-date pump that also sold hunting and fishing gear sat next to a grocery store with an old-fashioned Coca-Cola sign in the window and sagging plank floors. There was a beer bar with eight barstools and a slightly uneven pool table; Dillon's Mercantile, a store that held an astonishing assortment of nearly obsolete merchandise; and Kate's own little slice of paradise, the newly refurbished Lost Peak Cafe.

No, Lost Peak wasn't much of a place in the overall scheme of things, not when you'd once lived in a deluxe condominium in downtown LA, but Kate was convinced it was also quite possibly one of the most glorious, most scenic spots on the face of the earth. In fact, sometimes when she looked out the restaurant windows at the snow-capped mountains across the valley, she thought that the problems that had brought her to Lost Peak were an odd sort of blessing.

"Mornin', Kate. Didn't hear ya come in." Myra Hennings, the cook and the woman for whom Kate still thanked God every day since arriving a little over a month ago, stood behind the gleaming stainless steel griddle, waving a greasy metal spatula like a band leader's baton.

"Sorry I'm late, Myra." Standing behind the long Formica counter on the other side of the pass-through from the kitchen, Kate shrugged out of her nylon jacket and stuffed it behind a stack of napkins on one of the shelves underneath. "The power went out and the well wouldn't work. David didn't have any water for a shower. We finally realized we'd only tripped a breaker. I'm afraid we're still pretty new at this country-living thing."

"Don't worry—you'll get used to it."

"At any rate, David missed his ride and I had to drive him to school." They had decided to enroll him in summer school. With the turmoil of the past few months, he had gotten behind in his studies, and taking a remedial math course might help him meet some of the kids in the area.

Myra grinned, showing a row of crooked teeth. "Don't worry about it—we did just fine without you. I figured you'd be here as soon as you could or you woulda called. Besides, we just got busy a few minutes ago."

A woman in her late fifties, Myra Hennings was broad-hipped and stoutly built, with hair God had lightened to gray and Myra had turned a brassy shade of blond. She was a widow with three grown kids scattered around the country and an army of grandkids. She was a hard worker and she really knew the restaurant business, but it was her warm, unflappable disposition that made her invaluable to Kate.

"Well, I'm here now and ready to go to work." Kate refastened a button that had popped loose on the front of her pink nylon uniform, tied a matching pink apron around her waist, and shoved a pin into the bun at the back of her head that held a wad of her thick dark red hair. "Just tell me which orders go where and I'll get them on the tables."

But Myra wasn't listening. She was staring through the pass-through, across the Formica counter into the dining room. "God, if I was only twenty years younger ... " A wistful smile lifted the sagging skin along her neck. "Isn't that the most gorgeous hunk of man you've ever seen?"

There wasn't the slightest doubt whom Myra meant. Kate watched the tall, black-haired man return from the pay phone and slide into one of the pink vinyl booths in front of the window. She hadn't been out on a date in years, hadn't been the least bit interested in a man, hadn't even noticed one. After Tommy, she wasn't sure she ever would again. But this man, dressed like a cowboy but looking more like an Indian, was impossible to miss.

"Who is he?"

Myra's pale eyebrows shot up. "Are you kidding? That's the owner of the Running Moon Ranch, one of the biggest spreads in the county. His name's Chance McLain."

Of course it was. It seemed like every guy in Montana had a name like Rex or Chase or Cody. "Who's the guy with him?" Six inches shorter, even darker-skinned but not as athletically built, with black hair hanging down in a single long braid, the man was obviously a Native American. Living so close to the Salish-Kootenai Reservation, Kate had seen a number of them around.

"That's Jeremy Spotted Horse. Chance is part Indian on his mother's side. He's got lots of friends on the rez. Tries to help them as much as he can." Myra slid a platter of steak and eggs, a side of biscuits, and a tall stack of pancakes heaped with crisp fried bacon across the stainless steel shelf. "As a matter of fact, this is their order. You might as well take it on over."

Kate didn't miss the sparkle in Myra's eyes. The woman was the town's resident matchmaker. What she didn't know was that Kate wasn't in the market for romance—not anymore. Her single bout with love had been a disaster. She wasn't interested in men, now or any time in the future. She had a son to raise and a business to run. She had left her past in LA, found a place where she and David could start over, and she hoped her troubles were behind her.

One look at Chance McLain, with his hard good looks and lean, rangy build, and it was clear the man was nothing *but* trouble.

Still, he was a customer and she had a job to do. Balancing the plates in one hand as she had learned to do working her way through college, she grabbed the coffeepot and started across the room.

Chance leaned back in the padded booth and stretched his long legs out beneath the gray Formica table. The restaurant wasn't fancy, not by a long shot, but the pink ruffled curtains at the windows and the wood-framed samplers Nell Hart had stitched gave it a certain homey charm. And the food was always good. He'd been damned glad when the place had reopened.

His mind slid back to the times he had come to the cafe as a kid and Nell always managed to save him that last piece of hot apple pie. Smiling at the memory, he jumped when Jeremy nudged his leg, signaling that the food had arrived and reminding him to get his elbows off the table to make room for the plates.

He looked over at the steaming platter of buckwheat pancakes the waitress was setting in front of Jeremy, and his eyes fixed on a pair of size D breasts straining against the front of a pink nylon uniform. One of the buttons popped open just then and he caught a glimpse of pale skin and frilly white lace.

Chance sat up a little straighter in his seat. He knew he was staring; he could feel his face heating up. His body tightened, and under the table, he felt the first stirrings of an arousal.

Damn!

Maybe it was the fact that the woman he'd been seeing for the past three years was a model, slender and fashionably small in the bosom department. Or maybe it was just that she'd been away in New York for the last three months and he hadn't slept with anyone else, as he usually did on occasion.

Whatever it was, he found himself tipping his head back to see what the woman in front of him looked like, curious in a way he rarely was.

Soft was his first impression. Soft eyes. Soft mouth. Soft curves. She wasn't very big, maybe five-foot-two, but there seemed to be a lot of woman packed into that petite body. Her hair was a pretty shade of dark red. A curl had come loose from her otherwise tidy bun and brushed against a cheek that looked as soft as the rest of her.

This time he did go hard and he straightened in his seat, trying to get comfortable. It wasn't like him to react this way, not at all. Still, his palms itched to cup those heavy, feminine breasts, and his jeans went tighter still.

When the platter of steak and eggs slammed down in front of him so hard some of the juice spilled over the edge, Chance inwardly groaned. It was only too obvious what he had been thinking. He silently thanked God she couldn't see the heavy bulge hidden beneath the table.

Instead, she set her jaw, gave him a cool look the length of her lightly freckled nose, and walked away, disappearing back inside the kitchen.

Jeremy's soft laughter drew a muttered curse. "So . . . you like that, do you?"

Chance just grunted. "Apparently, I do. Who the hell is she?"

"Her name is Kaitlin Rollins. Old Ironstone says she's Nell Hart's granddaughter." Harold "Chief" Ironstone was the town's oldest citizen. "She and her son, David, moved into the old Hart house about a month ago and re-opened the cafe. I know you don't get out much, but I figured you'd have heard by now."

"I've been busy. I was in once since the place opened back up, but I didn't see her."

"She's a pretty little thing. Ironstone says she's a real nice lady. Her kid's kind of a troublemaker, though. Got that LA-tough chip on his shoulder."

Chance cut into his steak. He liked it cooked well-done and Myra had managed her usual good job. Then again, why shouldn't she? She'd been cooking at the

Lost Peak Cafe for the past twenty years. He was glad the new owner was smart enough to know a good thing. "How old is the boy?"

"About twelve, I think. I've seen him once or twice. He's working part-time over at Marshall's Grocery."

Chance dug into his eggs, also cooked just right. The biscuits were buttery and golden. "She married?" He hadn't meant to ask, but the words seemed to slide past his lips.

"Was, I guess. Divorced now."

"You say they're from LA?"

"Yeah, so I heard."

"I didn't even know Nell Hart had a granddaughter."

"Neither did I. I'm surprised she never mentioned it.

Chance downed another bite of eggs. "Even if Kate Rollins inherited the place, I'm surprised she didn't sell it. I can't imagine a young, single, city gal moving way out here."

Jeremy shrugged. "Ironstone says she's kinda secretive about it. Might be interesting to find out why."

It might be at that, Chance couldn't help thinking. It might be even more interesting to unbutton that row of buttons down the front of her uniform and see what the lady had hidden inside all that pretty white lace. It was an astonishing thought, considering. It occurred to him he hadn't felt such an instant attraction to a woman in years, maybe never.

"I thought you and Rachael were getting pretty thick," Jeremy said, jerking Chance's gaze back from where it had wandered toward the kitchen and reading his mind so clearly he felt the heat rise at the back of his neck.

"We are, I guess. We've always had an understanding.

We figured we'd get married sooner or later. In the meantime, Rachael has her freedom and I have mine. She's been pressing me lately, though."

"I figured she would, sooner or later."

Chance shrugged. "It's what her dad's always wanted, and marrying her would certainly be in my best interest."

"You can say that again. Once Ed's gone, the Circle Bar F will belong to Rachael. That would double the size of your spread."

"So I guess when she comes back home, we'll probably set the date."

Jeremy swallowed a mouthful of pancakes. "If that's the case, then my advice is to stay away from the pretty little redhead."

Chance glanced up, saw her bent over a table across the way, her hips wriggling as she wiped up a spill, and felt the same shot of lust he had felt before.

"You're right, Jeremy. That's damned good advice." And Chance meant to take it. But even as he finished the last of his eggs, tossed down money for the check, and added a hefty tip, he found himself thinking that surely it wouldn't hurt if he happened to stop by again in a couple of days.

Ever since the cafe had reopened, he'd been craving a piece of Myra's homemade apple pie.

"I'm sorry to have to do this, David, but for the next two weeks, you're grounded."

"Grounded? Aw, Mom."

"You deserve it, David, and you know it." They were standing in the entry of the white wood-frame house they lived in on the hill behind the cafe. It was part of the eighty-acre parcel of property, including the cafe,

Kate had inherited. With its incredible views of the mountains, and surrounded by tall ponderosa pines, it was the very best part to Kate.

"I hate this place," David grumbled. "It's the pits. There's nothin' to do and the kids are all geeks. I want to go back to LA."

Kate looked over at her son, saw the stubborn way his mouth was set, saw the tension in his shoulders. She knew he wasn't happy in Lost Peak. She had known it would take time for him to adjust to such a drastically different lifestyle, but she hadn't expected him to get into trouble even out here.

"Mr. Marshall caught you stealing a package of gum. Now you've lost your afterschool job. I thought you liked working at the market."

He shifted from one foot to the other, dragging the toe of his sneaker back and forth across the polished oak floor. "It was okay, I guess."

"Then why did you steal the gum?"

His thin shoulders went up in a shrug. "I didn't think I'd get caught."

"Oh, David."

"Come on, Mom, it's no big deal. At home everybody takes stuff. The stores are used to it. It's right in their yearly budget."

She walked over to the narrow window beside the front door, stared out at the mountains for a moment, then turned and walked back to her son. "God, I can't believe this. You actually think it's all right to steal?"

"I'd never take anything big."

Kate gripped his shoulders. He was already taller than she was. She had to tip her head back to look him in the face. "Stealing is about character, David. It's like lying. There are people who lie, people who cheat, and people who steal. They're all the same kind of person. They aren't the kind other people respect. They aren't the kind other people trust. Is that the kind of person you want to be?''

"In the city, they—"

"I don't care what they do in the city! We don't live in the city anymore and we aren't going back there again. The people who live here have good old-fashioned values. They don't lie, they don't cheat, and they certainly don't steal. That is the way I've tried to raise you. You've always been a good boy, David. Once people get to know you, they're going to like you. But you have to earn their respect, and stealing from them isn't the way to do it.''

His fist slammed hard against the wall. "You don't get it, do you? I don't care if these hillbillies like me or not. I want to go home! If you won't leave this place, I'm gonna call my dad. I can go back and live with him.''

A wave of nausea swept through her. David returning to his delinquent friends in LA. David being raised by a father who would indulge him all the way to a jail cell in some dismal prison.

"Is that what you really want—to live with your dad? In your heart, you know what he's like. He can hardly take care of himself, let alone you. He doesn't even know anything about you. You pretend he's the perfect father, but deep down you know it isn't the truth.''

David didn't argue, just stared down at the toes of his dirty sneakers.

"I love you, David. I only want what's best for you. You know that, don't you?''

"I suppose so," he muttered without looking up.

"We've got a chance to make a new life here. We can do it, if you'll only give it a try.''

David said nothing.

"I want you to go over to Mr. Marshall's store. I want you to take some of the money out of your savings bank and pay for the gum you stole. And I want you to apologize. If your apology is sincere, Mr. Marshall will know it, and maybe in time, he'll decide to forgive you."

David's shoulders slumped. "I already told him I was sorry."

"Did you mean it?" Kate found herself holding her breath.

"I know I shouldn't have taken it." Embarrassment formed small pink circles in David's cheeks. "I've only done it a couple of times. The other guys thought it was cool, but it always made me feel kind of funny."

Kate wrapped her arms around her son and gave him a hug. "That's because, in your heart, you knew it was wrong. Everything's gonna work out, honey—you'll see. Just give it a little more time."

David just nodded. When she let him go, he went up to his room and came down with a handful of change. He left the house, heading for the store, and when he came back, his shoulders looked a little bit straighter.

"I paid him for the gum. I told him I'd never steal anything from him again. He wouldn't give me my job back, though. I guess I really don't blame him." Walking past her, he slowly climbed the stairs and disappeared inside his room.

Kate sighed. It was a hard lesson, but one she hoped he'd learned. She shuddered to think what would happen if he hadn't.

Or if he was serious about going back to live with his father.

Kate despised the thought of returning; she liked it here in Lost Peak. The people she had met had been friendly and helpful, more so once they learned she was Nell Hart's granddaughter. Nell had been well liked, Kate was surprised to discover. On the rare occasion her mother had ever mentioned her, she had described Nell as a heartless, emotionless sort of woman, the sort who would toss her pregnant, unwed daughter out in the street.

But the house Nell lived in from the day she married Zachary Hart was warm and cozy, filled with a charming feeling of home. The place was in far better repair than Kate had imagined it would be. With a new coat of paint on the walls, the old carpet pulled up and the hardwood floors refinished and covered with colorful throw rugs, it was the sort of place she might have chosen over her high-rise condo if she had been given the choice.

When she had lifted the dust covers off the furniture, she was thrilled to find dozens of lovely antiques. Mixing them in with the furniture she had brought with her from LA kept the charm of the house intact, while her overstuffed sofa and chairs gave it a comfortable, slightly more modern feel.

She wondered if Nell Hart would approve. She didn't have the slightest idea what Nell was really like, but she intended to find out. Now that they were settled, Kate meant to begin her search.

Chance wheeled his pickup into a parking space in front of the Lost Peak Cafe, turned off the engine, and cracked open the door. He knew he shouldn't be there. He had commitments, even if they were more or less unspoken. The last thing he needed was to get involved with a woman.

I only want a goddamn piece of pie, he told himself. But

he knew it wasn't the truth. The sexy little redhead had been on his mind since he'd seen her that day at the cafe.

"Hey, Chance!" Harold "Chief" Ironstone sat on a rickety wooden bench beside the front door. He was there more times than not, wrapped in a blanket, wearing his moccasins and a high-crowned hat with a feather stuck in the top, looking exactly like the wooden Indians they had for sale to the tourists down at the trading post on Highway 93.

"Hey, Chief, how's it goin'?" Chance shook the old man's hand, felt the strength that remained there in spite of his more than eighty years.

He gave Chance a grin. Amazing how many teeth were still left in the old man's head. "Good day. Nice weather. You meet the new owner?"

His glance swung toward the door. "Yeah, sort of."

"Good woman. Nice boy." Chief wasn't really a chief—the Salish had tribal leaders, which wasn't at all the same—but everyone called him that and had for years and he didn't seem to mind.

Chance nodded. "I haven't met the kid. Ms. Rollins seems all right. Food's still good."

Chief patted his protruding stomach. "Yeah, especially the pie."

Chance grinned. He touched the brim of his hat. "Good to see you, Chief."

"You, too, Chance."

He pulled open the screen door, turned the handle on the front door, and walked in.

The place never changed. He was glad about that. Oh, there was a bright new sign on the roof and one out on the road that hadn't been there before. Both of them had the cafe's new logo—a picture of distant, snow-capped Lost Peak inside a forest-green circle. Aside from that, the new owner seemed to like the homey charm of the place and left things pretty much the way they were. It was cleaner, he saw, the curtains freshly washed, the wooden floor waxed to a high sheen. He liked the fact Kate Rollins hadn't made things different, just better.

He saw her as he slid into a chair at one of the Formica-topped tables in the center of the room, took his hat off and rested it on the chair next to his. He ran a hand through his hair, erasing the creases and shoving it back from his forehead.

For a few short minutes, he watched her work. She was efficient, he saw, never forgetting an order, careful to see that none of her customers were ignored. Which, he supposed, was why she walked over to him, though the look on her face said she didn't really want to.

"Coffee?" she asked, standing several feet back from the table as if she couldn't trust what he might do. Damn, he'd certainly got off on the wrong foot with the lady.

"That'd be great." He gave her what he hoped was a charming smile and turned over his cup, waited while she poured it. "You're Kate Rollins, the new owner."

"That's right. And you're Chance McLain. You own the Running Moon Ranch."

Chance's smile deepened. At least she'd asked his name. "I guess when you live in a place this size, everyone pretty much knows everyone."

"I suppose. Until I moved here, I'd never lived in a town this small."

He wanted to ask why she'd come, but he didn't think she'd tell him. Maybe the house she'd inherited was the only place she could afford to live. "We were all disappointed when Mrs. Whittaker closed the cafe. The place was sort of an institution around here. Considering the job you've done since you reopened, I think I can safely say most of the folks hereabouts are darned glad to have you."

Some of the stiffness left her shoulders. "Thank you. When I came here, I hoped the people in Lost Peak would be friendly. So far, they've all been great." She handed him a plastic-coated menu. It was new, he saw, with the same dark green, mountain-in-a-circle logo that was on the sign, but most of the items listed were still the same. As his eyes ran down the page, his mouth curved faintly at the small red hearts beside the heart-smart, low-fat items. He didn't imagine they'd be hot sellers here in Lost Peak.

"Mrs. Whittaker ran the cafe for my grandmother—Nell Hart. Did you know Nell, too?" she asked.

He nodded. "For as long as I can remember. She was even more of an institution than the cafe. We were neighbors, in a manner of speaking. Part of her property—your property now, I guess—borders a portion of mine."

She looked like she wanted to ask something else, but another customer walked in. "Take your time," she said. "I'll be back in a minute to take your order."

Chance just nodded. He watched her make her way across the floor, liking the unconsciously sexy way she moved. He had to admit he was curious about her. What was she doing in a place like Lost Peak? Even if Nell had left her the cafe, why hadn't she sold it and taken the money? Mostly he was trying to figure out what there was about Kate Rollins that made him think of taking her to bed. He only knew that he wanted to.

She came back and took his order, then continued

busily serving the rest of her customers. She returned
a few minutes later with a plate heaped with warm apple
pie and just slightly melted vanilla ice cream and set it
on the table in front of him. He could feel his mouth
begin to water.

"Man, this looks great."

Kate smiled. "Myra's a marvelous cook. I'm lucky to
have her."

"You're right about that." He took a big bite of pie,
swallowed most of it and talked around the rest.
"Nobody but nobody makes better apple pie."

The lunch hour was nearly over and the place had
begun to clear out, as Chance had been hoping it would.
Kate went up to the cash register at the front of the
restaurant to take the money from the last of her customers. A few minutes later, she returned to his table, armed
with a fresh pot of coffee.

"Warmup?"

"You bet." She leaned over to refill his cup and he
tried not to stare at those magnificent breasts. "You're
new to Montana," he said, swallowing another bite of
pie. "Have you had much chance to see it?"

"Not really. Mostly my son David and I have just been
getting settled in."

"I heard you had a boy. How's he adjusting so far?"

Kate hesitated and for a moment he thought she
might not answer. Then she sighed. "Not very well,
I'm afraid. He misses his friends—though believe me,
I don't. He feels out of place here, I suppose. He knows
how to play basketball, but he doesn't have a clue how
to fish. I imagine it's hard for a twelve-year-old who's
always lived in the city."

"Yeah, I imagine it would be." Worse than that, he
thought. He couldn't imagine not knowing how to toss

a line in the water. Or hunt, for that matter, or pack horseback into the mountains. He couldn't help wondering what kind of man the boy's father was. Maybe a lot like his own. He felt a shot of sympathy for Kate Rollins' son.

"You still closing the place on Sundays?" he asked.

She nodded. "We open at six and close at eight on weekdays. We're open till nine on Friday and Saturday nights."

"Pretty long hours."

"Not for me. I set my own schedule. One of the reasons I came here was to spend more time with my son."

He liked hearing that. He was too young when his mother died even to remember her, but he thought that he would have liked it if she had wanted to spend time with him.

"There's some mighty pretty country hereabouts. Since you haven't had a chance to see it, I'd be happy to show you around."

Her expression subtly shifted, began to close up. "As I said, my son and I are just beginning to settle in. Thanks for the offer, but I'm afraid I'll have to pass."

He fiddled with his pie, kept his eyes on the ice cream melting on his plate. "Maybe some other time."

But her lack of response said it wasn't going to happen. As he watched her walk away, he was amazed at the degree of his disappointment. Chance leaned back against his chair with a sigh, the pie getting cold though the coffee was still steaming, his appetite suddenly gone. It galled him a little that she had so flatly refused him. In his wilder days, half the women in the county had tried to get him to take them to bed and half of them had succeeded.

But obviously Kate Rollins wasn't interested. Chance found himself wondering what he might do to change that.

He left his pie unfinished, tossed a handful of money down for a tip, picked up the check, and had almost reached the cash register up front when the bell rang above the door. Randy Wiggins and Ed Fontaine, two of his best friends, appeared in the opening. Randy was a male nurse of sorts—though Ed never referred to him that way—a caregiver for a man with too much pride to admit he needed one. Holding the door, Randy waited while Ed rolled his shiny chrome wheelchair inside the cafe and let the door swing closed behind them.

Chance strode toward the slim, gray-haired man who had been more of a father than his own ever was. "I thought you'd gone to Denver," he said to Ed with a smile.

"I'd planned to. My meeting with the Cattle Association was cancelled." Ed shook the hand Chance offered. "I was on my way back from Missoula when I saw your pickup parked out front. I've got some news I thought you'd want to hear."

"Oh yeah? What's that?"

"Consolidated Metals just filed a permit to construct a new mining operation on Silver Fox Creek—right here in Lost Peak."

"Damn!"

"I knew that'd make you happy. Those bastards don't know when to quit. That lawyer, Frank Mills, the Indians hired hasn't done a blasted thing. The guy's probably on Lon Barton's payroll, just like half the judges in the county." Ed was lean and hard, wiry and tough as boot leather. He ran a ranch the size of Chance's and he did it from a wheelchair. There wasn't a man alive Chance admired more than Ed Fontaine.

"Mills is trying to get an injunction," Chance told him. "But he says we need more evidence. Jeremy wants to get some pictures of the leaks in the tail pond, but we'd have to get inside their compound to do it. We were hoping the sworn testimony of some of the tribal leaders, along with the lab results on the water would be enough."

"It probably will be. Unfortunately, that isn't going to stop them from building a new mine here in Lost Peak."

Chance heard a noise behind him. He turned to see Kate Rollins walking toward them. God, she was a pretty little thing. Not that Rachael wasn't. Rachael went light years beyond pretty. With her elegant cheekbones and silver-blond hair, Rachael Fontaine had graced magazine covers all over the country. She was model-thin, with a set of legs that went all the way up to her neck. She was stylish and sophisticated in a way Kate Rollins never would be. He wondered how he could be attracted to two such opposite women.

"I'm sorry to interrupt," Kate said, "but I couldn't help overhearing. Now that I live here, I consider myself a member of the community. From now on, what happens here in Lost Peak affects me, too."

"Ed Fontaine and Randy Wiggins, meet Kaitlin Rollins, the new owner of the cafe."

"A pleasure, Ms. Rollins," Ed said, extending a gnarled, weathered hand that had seen fifty years of hard work. Kate gave him a warm smile and shook it, a firm, confident handshake, Chance noticed, that made Ed look at her a little differently than he had before.

"Ma'am." Randy tipped his hat in her direction.

Kate smiled a greeting then returned her attention to Ed. "I gather this mining operation wouldn't be the best thing that could happen to Lost Peak."

"From your standpoint it might not be too bad. It would probably bring in more business, if that's what you're after. Families would start moving in; the town would probably grow."

Chance could have sworn her face went a little bit pale. "I like the town just the way it is," she said in a voice as firm as her handshake. "I wouldn't be living here if I didn't."

He smiled at that. He liked it the way it was, too. As far as he was concerned, Montana was the last best place. He wanted it to stay that way.

"Consolidated Metals isn't known for its environmental consciousness," Chance told her. "Their mine on Beaver Creek has had more than twenty-four water quality violations, including half a dozen cyanide spills and acid mine drainage problems. They can't put in another heap-leach mine here now—thanks to a recent change in the law—but they're trying for an appeal even as we speak, and knowing them as I do, if they start an operation in Lost Peak, sooner or later, they'll pollute Silver Fox Creek, one of the prettiest little fly fishing streams in the country."

"What can we do to stop them?" Kate asked. Her eyes seemed greener than they had before, and he thought they held a spark of determination.

"I suggest we hire an attorney of our own," Ed said, "preferably one who can't be bought."

"Good idea," Chance agreed. "Got any idea who might be the best man for the job?" Pulling his wallet from the back pocket of his jeans, he tossed down enough bills to pay for the pie. Kate punched the amount into the register and handed him the change.

Ed scratched the back of his head. "We could talk to Max Darby, or maybe Bruce Turnbull. I've had dealings with them before."

"All right, and while we're at it, a private investigator might not be a bad idea. Maybe he can uncover something about Consolidated that might be useful."

"If there's anything I can do to help," Kate said, "I hope you'll let me know."

Chance smiled down at her. "Thanks for the offer. We're going to need plenty of help getting the word out, letting people know what the company's trying to do. We might just take you up on it."

"Getting the word out is my specialty. I was in advertising before I came here."

"You sold advertising?"

She gave him the same tight smile she had given him the last time he'd come in. Chance cursed himself for the ground he'd just lost.

"You might say that. I was vice president of Menger and Menger, a big ad agency in LA. We worked on everything from political campaigns to breaking out new food products for companies like Quaker Oats. In comparison, I don't imagine getting the word out on Consolidated Metals to the people in Silver County would be too tough a job."

Chance inwardly groaned. If there was one thing Ed had taught him it was not to make snap judgments. When he glanced at his mentor, the older man's eyes were twinkling, saying, *See what happens when you do?*

"Sorry. I guess I just didn't expect a corporate bigwig to be running a cafe in Lost Peak."

"*Retired* corporate bigwig," Kate corrected, and he

could see that she was enjoying herself. "And to tell you the truth, I like my change of occupation. It feels darned good not to have to answer to anyone but myself."

"Well, we're happy to have you on our team," Ed said. "We'll keep you posted. And you can be sure we'll take you up on that offer to help."

While Randy held the door, Chance wheeled Ed out to his Chevy van. Randy pushed a button and the lift gate at the rear hummed as the metal platform dropped down.

"We've got to keep on this thing," Ed said, referring to Consolidated's project.

"No one knows that better than I do." Chance rolled Ed's wheelchair onto the lift gate then waited as it hoisted the older man up.

"Have you heard from Rachael lately?" Ed called down to him from the back of the van.

"Not for a couple of weeks. She's busy with that new modeling contract. They've been shooting on location all over the country. I imagine she'll call when she can."

"I imagine she will." Ed sighed. "What that girl needs is a husband and babies. Think about it, Chance."

Chance only nodded. He rarely thought of Rachael, Ed's daughter, when she wasn't around and she hadn't been around much lately. He ought to feel guilty, and maybe he did, a little.

But the hard truth was, the only real guilt he ever felt came from putting Ed Fontaine in that chair.

Chapter Seven

It was five minutes till closing. The late July sun had succumbed to clouds and rain, and the cafe had been empty for nearly half an hour. While Myra finished up in the kitchen, Kate sat down in one of the empty booths, took out her notepad, pulled out the pencil stuck behind her ear, and began to list the information she intended to gather about Nell Hart.

Now that the restaurant was running smoothly and the house was in order, she was determined to get underway. Unfortunately, she wasn't exactly sure where to begin. The best way, she figured, was simply to amass as much data about the woman as she could get her hands on.

Birth Certificate, she wrote. She'd get a copy of both Nell's and her mother's at the Silver County courthouse in Polson.

Death Certificate. While she got the certificate on her

grandmother, she might as well obtain a copy of Zachary Hart's, as well. Kate's long-dead grandfather had died when Kate's mother, Celeste, was only six. Since her mother could barely remember him, Kate knew nothing about him, either.

Copy of the will. She'd been notified by mail of her inheritance. It hadn't occurred to her to ask the lawyer for a copy of the document. She would try the Recorder's Office first, since one of her customers had told her wills were often a matter of public record. If not, she could write to Clifton Boggs. Either way, a copy should be easy enough to get.

Boxes in the attic. There was a ton of old stuff up there she had noticed when she had moved in. She had picked out a few of the smaller antiques to use as accents throughout the house, but she hadn't gone through the stacks of papers and boxes of clothes that were still up there. It would be interesting to see what she found.

Call Aida Whittaker. Nell's longtime friend might have general information that could be useful. She underlined the words, having meant to phone the woman long before this.

The bell above the door jingled. She looked up just in time to see Chance McLain walk in. He peeled off his rain slicker, slapped his low-crowned black Stetson against the leg of his jeans, and started walking toward her. Kate's stomach fluttered. She felt the oddest urge to run.

"I know you're closed," he said before she could say what she was thinking. "I've been on the road most of the day. I thought you might still have the coffeepot on. I could sure use a cup before I head the rest of the way up the hill."

Kate nodded. "No problem." She could hardly ask him to leave, as wet and tired as he looked. And wet and tired as he looked, he still looked unbelievably good.

He stood at the table till she returned a few minutes later, a steaming Styrofoam cup in her hand and a lid to go with it.

"It's thick enough to cut," she said. "With the storm, business has been slow. We haven't made a fresh pot for a while."

"I'm used to it that way. Long as it's hot, it'll do me just fine." He reached into his pocket for the money to pay her, but Kate raised a hand to stop him.

"This one's on the house."

He smiled. "Thanks." He reached down for the cup, saw her list sitting next to it, and his straight black brows arched up in silent question.

"I'm trying to gather some information on my grandmother," she explained, though it was hardly any of his business.

"You ever meet her?"

Kate shook her head. "She and my mother . . . didn't get along."

He blew across the top of the coffee, carefully took a sip. "I'm surprised to hear it. Everyone liked Nell."

"So I've been told." But Kate wasn't convinced. From what her mother had said, Nell Hart was cold and selfish, more concerned about what the neighbors might think about her unwed daughter being pregnant than she was about her daughter's welfare.

"Half the county showed up at the funeral," Chance was saying as he set the cup back down. "We all felt bad about the accident. The old gal had plenty of life left in her. She died way before she should have."

She died way before she should have. The words echoed through her head and Kate's legs started shaking. She must have swayed toward the Styrofoam cup because it suddenly tipped over and red hot coffee splashed across the table. Chance leaped out of the way just in time.

"Oh my God! I'm so sorry!" Kate turned and raced for a towel then rushed back to sop up the mess she had made. "Thank heavens you moved so quickly. I nearly scalded you."

"It's all right—no harm done." He stared down at her with those intense blue eyes of his. "Was it what I said about Nell?"

Kate finished wiping up the coffee then sank down in one of the captain's chairs around the table. "It just came as such a surprise. It never occurred to me that her death had been anything other than natural causes. Nell was seventy-two. Mr. Boggs, her attorney, mentioned her sudden death. I just assumed Nell died of a heart attack." She looked up at him. "What sort of accident did she have?"

Chance sat down across from her, looking uncomfortable in his role as the bearer of bad news. "Nell slipped and fell, that's all. She hit her head on a corner of the sideboard in the dining room of her house. It could have happened to anyone."

But it didn't. It had happened to Nell Hart. She had died before she should have. Did her premature death have something to do with the mystery Kate was determined to solve?

If there really was a mystery.

If any of what had happened the night of the shooting was real.

"Are they . . . are they sure it was an accident?"

Chance eyed her strangely. "Everyone assumed it was. There wasn't any evidence of foul play. No one broke into the house or anything—at least not that I heard anything about."

Kate bit her lip. She was probably being ridiculous. Probably. "I'm sure you're right. It's just that . . ." *That I saw her after I died and I think she was trying to tell me something. Get real, Kate.*

"Just that what, Kate? Do you have some reason to think it might have happened otherwise?"

She summoned a nervous smile. "No, of course not." She got up from the chair, picked the Styrofoam cup up off the floor, and started for the kitchen. "I'll get you another cup. You're probably more than ready to get home."

Chance said nothing, just stood up from his chair and waited for her to return with another cup of coffee. This time the lid was already on.

"Thanks, Kate." She watched him walk to the door and pull it open. He paused and turned to face her. "That offer's still open. I'd love to show you around."

Kate shook her head. She didn't want to go. Chance McLain was trouble and she already had her share of that. Man-shy, she guessed. Her mother had definitely had bad luck with men. After Jack Lambert and her own husband, Tommy, Kate figured she and Celeste were pretty much alike. And Chance McLain was just too damned attractive.

"Thanks, anyway," she added as he settled his hat back on his head, grabbed his wet slicker off the coat rack, and headed out into the storm.

The bell rang as he left. The rain picked up. Heavy

sheets pounded against the windowpanes as she sat back down at the table, shoved Chance McLain's tall image out of her mind, and returned to her list.

Sheriff's office, she wrote, though she wouldn't have thought of that before.

Coroner's report. She wasn't sure she could get a copy, but she could try. She might have started into this thing a little slower than she had intended, but with Chance's innocent revelation, she was ready to move a lot faster now. And perhaps in a more specific direction.

She had an odd hunch about all of this. A feeling she was right, that the darkness and fear she had sensed in Nell Hart's presence had something to do with her death.

Kate meant to find out what it was.

Kate shoved open the glass door leading out of the County Recorder's Office in Polson, the Silver County seat. She was armed with a copy of her grandmother's will, a copy of the deed to the property she had inherited, as well as the document by which Zachary Hart had first acquired the eighty acres back in 1949.

A deed recorded in 1975 showed Nell's purchase of the Lost Peak Cafe from a man named Jedediah Wheeler thirteen years after Zach had died.

Kate paused on the sidewalk, shuffled through the papers to the copy of Nell's birth certificate. A quick calculation said her grandmother had been forty-six when she bought the cafe—three years after she had tossed her daughter out in the street.

At a cursory glance, none of it looked particularly

useful, but she had to start somewhere. She was reading
the first page of the will, trying to decipher the legalese,
wondering who else might have received an inheritance
and thereby benefited from her grandmother's death
when she stepped off the curb onto busy First Street. A
horn blared. At the same instant a big hand shot out
and gripped her arm, jerking her out of the path of a
speeding black Toyota.

"Jesus, Mary, and Joseph! What the hell were you
thinking? You damn near got yourself killed!" Fierce
blue eyes bored into her. Chance McLain still gripped
her arm.

"Sorry." The heat of embarrassment washed into her
cheeks. "I guess I should have been paying more attention."

He let her go, but made no move to leave. "You've
gotta be more careful. This time of year, the place is
crawling with tourists. Most of them are so busy gawking
at the mountains around the lake they haven't got a
clue what's going on."

Right now she didn't have much of a clue herself.

"So . . . what are you doing in Polson?" he asked,
both of them still standing on the corner. He was more
than a foot taller than she was. Counting his hat and
boots, taller than that. She had been trying to ignore
him since the first time she had met him. Every time
she saw him, it was a little bit harder to do.

"I'm gathering some of the information I told you
about. I'm on my way to First American Title. The
recorder said I could get plat maps of the land I inherited. After that I'm going back to the sheriff's office."

"The sheriff? What for?"

"I've asked them for a copy of the accident report

that was turned in the day Nell died. The clerk says I'm not allowed to see it. I'm hoping the sheriff will be a little more cooperative. Unfortunately, he isn't in."

Chance studied her with those discerning blue eyes that had a way of making her stomach flutter like a feather in the wind. "I get the feeling there's more to this than simple curiosity."

"That's ridiculous," Kate countered a little too quickly. "I just feel like . . . well, like I'd like to know something about her. We are, after all, related." Before he could raise another question, she changed the subject. "What about you? Polson's a long way from Lost Peak."

A corner of his mouth tipped up. "Everything's a long way from everything up here. You get used to it after a while. I came to see a lawyer named Mills. He's supposed to be getting an injunction to halt Consolidated's mining operation on Beaver Creek, but so far he hasn't done squat."

"Why not?"

"That's exactly what I'd like to know."

"How's the campaign to stop the new mine coming along?"

"Actually, I've been meaning to stop by and talk to you about that. Ed asked me to find out if you'd be available some night next week. He thought you might be willing to give us some suggestions how to get this whole thing off the ground."

"I'd be more than happy to do that."

"Great." They had reached the door to the title company. Chance held it open while Kate walked in. "There's a great Mexican restaurant over on the river— the El Rio? After you're finished, maybe I could buy you some lunch."

Lunch with Chance McLain. Oh God, did she dare? *It's only lunch,* a little voice said. But her stomach was still misbehaving every time he looked at her, and she found herself shaking her head. "I'd love to, Chance, but I've just got too much to do."

Something moved over his features, disappointment, or maybe determination. "All right, then I guess I'll give you a call, see when we can set up that meeting."

Kate just nodded. Her heart was beating a little faster than it should have been. Her palms had begun to sweat. God, she couldn't remember meeting a man who could do that to her. Had Tommy ever had that kind of effect on her? She didn't think so. If he had, surely she'd be able to recall.

Kate waited for the copies of the plat maps, and returned to the sheriff's office. Since he still wasn't in, she would have to come back to Polson another day. The sheriff was also the coroner, so she would have to pursue that topic later as well.

It was late afternoon by the time she returned to her car, tired but only a little discouraged. She had yet to go over the information she had gathered, and next time she would call for an appointment with the sheriff before she drove all the way into town.

She had just pulled out of her parking space, her mind on the drive back home, when she spotted a big silver Dodge pickup turning onto the road behind her. Chance waved when he saw who it was.

Kate waved back and kept on driving.

Chance slammed his palm against the steering wheel of his truck. Damn! The woman was beginning to drive him crazy. He had come to Polson to order some feed and see Frank Mills. The tribal council had asked him to stop by on their behalf, to inform Mills they would be holding a special meeting in regard to the problems on Beaver Creek. If he didn't get that injunction in the next few weeks, they'd be looking to hire another lawyer.

He hadn't expected to see Kate Rollins. He certainly hadn't expected to find her about to commit suicide on the corner of the street! He almost smiled. He was damned glad he'd shown up when he did. He only wished she'd been a little more grateful.

Chance gave up a frustrated sigh. There was something about Kate Rollins. Something that intrigued him. He wasn't sure what it was, but he wanted to find out. Driving down Highway 93 back toward the ranch, he could see her shiny white Lexus on the road a couple of cars ahead of him. He couldn't believe she'd said no to him again. He couldn't seem to charm her, no matter what he did. Hell, maybe she just didn't like him.

He chewed on the thought for a while, but somehow it didn't seem to fit. He wasn't fifteen anymore, mooning over the head cheerleader. He wasn't imagining things. He could feel the pull of attraction between them. He was sure Kate felt it, too.

Why then, did she go to such lengths to avoid him?

Both of them were unattached adults. They were responsible people who knew their own minds. Why not let nature take its course? If that meant winding up in bed, what was wrong with that? It was obvious Kate wasn't looking for a permanent relationship and neither was he, but a little physical enjoyment never hurt anyone.

As tense as she sometimes seemed, it would probably be good for her.

Thinking of her softly feminine figure and those round, voluptuous breasts, Chance had no doubt that it would be good for him.

Chapter Eight

The weather remained clear, just a few puffy clouds floating over the pine-covered peaks. Kate tucked in the clean sheet she had just put on David's bed and plumped the feather pillows.

Fortunately for her, he had always been fairly neat. Not perfect, but he kept his CDs carefully stacked so he could find the one he wanted, and his "treasures," as Kate secretly called them—Sammy Sosa's home run baseball caught at Anaheim Stadium, the plaque he'd gotten for winning the fourth grade spelling bee, the shells he'd collected on Malibu beach, and half a dozen other objects—sat evenly spaced on the top shelf of his bookcase.

He wasn't that great about picking up his dirty clothes, but he usually made his bed in the mornings and Kate was happy with that.

Carrying the load of dirty sheets, she stepped out of the room into the hallway, heard the phone ringing, and hurried downstairs to answer it.

"Hello, is this Kate Rollins?" a familiar voice asked.

"Dr. Murray?"

"Kate. I had a bit of trouble getting your new number. Apparently the one you left with my secretary was only temporary. Then I remembered you had also left your friend, Sally Peterson's number. I called and she gave me this one. I hope that was all right."

"Of course it was. It took a while to get the phone hooked back up at the house. It's good to hear your voice, Dr. Murray."

"I wish I was calling just to chat, but unfortunately a problem's arisen, and I thought you'd want to know."

A chill swept through her, a premonition of something she wasn't going to like. "A problem? What sort of problem?"

"A reporter came to see me . . . a man named Chet Munson. He's with that sleazy tabloid, the *National Monitor.*"

"Yes . . . I know the one. Munson tried to get information from my son, but that was before we left LA. I thought by now he would have forgotten all about me."

"Apparently, he hasn't. From what he said, he's been talking to Margaret Langley." *Mrs. Langley—the grocer's wife.* "With *Embraced by the Light* and a number of other books on NDE hitting the bestseller lists, I guess he figures your story might turn into something."

"That's all in the past," Kate said. "I'm not talking to anyone else about what happened. Can't you tell Chet Munson that?"

"I tried to, Kate. I'm just not sure he's going to give up."

Her fingers tightened around the phone. "Do you think he'll be able to find me?"

"Hopefully not, but those tabloid guys are pretty good bloodhounds. So far, he just seemed to be nosing around. If nothing new surfaces, maybe he'll decide you're old news."

"Maybe . . ." But she was thinking how much she was coming to like Lost Peak. And what her neighbors would say if an article appeared in the *Monitor* about what the newspapers called "her trip to The Other Side." "Thanks for the call, Dr. Murray."

"No problem, Kate. I hope you'll stay in touch."

She nodded and said, "I will," just as the front door swung open and David rushed in. He was carrying his school books close against his chest, his head turned away from her in a way that instantly made her suspicious.

"David!" She hung up the receiver as he bolted up the stairs. "Come down here. I want to talk to you."

He paused halfway to the top, but he didn't turn.

"Honey, I know something's wrong. You're shaking all over. Come down and tell me what's happened."

A sigh of resignation whispered past his lips. When he turned around, she saw one of his eyes was black and his lip was cut and swollen. "Oh, baby, what happened?" She drew him toward her and wrapped him in her arms, pressing his head against her shoulder. Fine, silky brown hair that hadn't changed since he was a child slipped through her fingers. David clung to her for an instant, then pulled away.

"It was that Jimmy Stevens kid, Mom. He called me a wimp because I wouldn't ride his stupid ol' horse."

She wanted to reach out and hug him again, but she knew it would be a mistake. "Names can't hurt you, honey. You ought to know that by now. You have to learn to walk away from people like that."

"I hit him and I'm glad."

She brushed a piece of grass from his jacket just to have an excuse to touch him. "You were right in refusing to ride. Horses can be dangerous if you don't know how to handle them."

"You know how to ride. You said you took lessons at Griffith Park."

Though she'd been raised in Culver City, on the fringes of LA, she had always loved horses. When David was six, after she'd finished college and started to work, one of her friends had suggested they take lessons down at the stables in Griffith Park. She'd done it for a while and she had loved it. But Tommy thought it was crazy, and her job had started taking more and more time. Eventually she'd been forced to quit.

"I never rode enough to be very good, but at least I learned the basics. We rode English, though, not Western, like everyone does around here."

"Horses are stupid, anyway—I don't care what that hick Jimmy Stevens says." With that he turned and raced up the stairs only to come back down a little bit later with his old jeans on and a blue nylon windbreaker slung over one shoulder. "I'll be back in a while."

"What about your eye? Don't you want me to put some ointment on it?"

"I'll put some on when I get home."

She wanted to argue but she didn't. His dignity had already suffered enough. "Be back before supper, okay? And be careful if you're going off by yourself. This is pretty wild country, you know."

David made no reply, just headed for the back door and jerked it open, let it slam closed behind him.

Kate watched him through the window, heading down toward the stream that ran across the back of the property, her insides still churning. She wasn't sure what she should worry about the most: Chet Munson and the *National Monitor*, the mystery that still plagued her, or the continuing problems with her son.

David sat down on a rock at the edge of the stream, just out of sight of the house. It was pretty here, he had to admit. Nothing at all like LA. He had never seen a sky so blue, or one that looked so big. He had never seen clouds as white and fluffy as these, never seen mountains that stretched so high they seemed to go on forever.

Still, it wasn't home and he was lonesome. He missed Artie and Toby and the rest of the kids. If it wasn't for his mom, he'd do what he'd threatened and go back and live with his dad. But he couldn't leave his mother all the way out here alone and he knew she didn't like the city. And he hadn't forgotten the newspaper article or that fat creep, Chet Munson.

With a weary sigh, David reached down beside the rock he sat on and picked up the long, thin aspen branch he had fashioned into a makeshift fishing rod. Using the pocketknife Artie had given him for his birthday, a present he figured his friend had probably stolen, David had neatly sliced off the branches and smoothed the sides. He'd tied a length of twine to one end and bought a couple of fish hooks from over in the fishing gear section of the gas station to tie on the other end of the twine.

Every day this week after school, he'd come down here to the creek to try his hand at fishing.

So far he hadn't caught a thing.

He knew there were fish in the water—he could see them swimming in the shadows beneath the rocks. He baited the hook with one of the pine beetles he'd caught in the windowsill of his room and tossed in the line, dragging it beneath the boulders along the edge of the creek and hoping he could at least get a nibble.

An hour later, he was still trying, but he wasn't having any luck. He was concentrating so hard he almost didn't hear the stranger approaching. He glanced up at the sound of splashing water and the click of hooves against rock as horse and rider crossed the stream, the man's tall shadow falling over the rock where he sat.

"You must be David Rollins."

David hauled the line up out of the water and set the pole on the ground beside him, embarrassed for some dumb reason that the man had caught him trying to fish. "Yeah, so what if I am?"

The cowboy swung down from his horse, a pretty brown and white spotted one. He had never seen a horse like that except on TV. "I'm Chance McLain. I'm your neighbor over on the east . . . the Running Moon Ranch."

"I've heard of it," David said. He'd overheard Jimmy Stevens talking about the big cattle ranch that ran for miles along the road and all the way up into the mountains.

"My house is a couple of miles from here, but my property line touches yours, at least in this spot along the creek. I've got a crew out mending fences in this section today." He smiled and little lines crinkled in the dust at the corners of his eyes. They were the bluest eyes David had ever seen.

"Your grandmother always let us ride across her property," the man said. "It's a shortcut into town. I hope you and your mom don't mind." He must have assumed they wouldn't because he just turned around and started untying one of the leather thongs behind his saddle.

He looked even taller standing on the ground, lean and tough looking, not the kind of guy you'd want to mess with. His black felt hat was so dusty it looked gray. It occurred to David, if he'd ever imagined what a cowboy ought to look like, it would be Chance McLain.

"Hard to fish without a good rod," McLain said. "I carry one with me wherever I go." He took the lid off the silver tube he'd untied and drew out what looked like a broken fishing pole. In minutes, he had the parts assembled and a fly tied onto the end of the line.

"Ever cast one of these?"

David just shook his head. He watched as Chance McLain waded out into the water in his boots, not even worried about getting them wet, and drew out a long length of line.

It was really something to see, the way the fly waved and floated, then snapped out into the stream. He made it look so easy, like anyone could do it.

"Want to try it?"

He shook his head. He'd probably get the damned thing caught in a tree.

"I'll show you how, if you want. It takes a little practice, but once you get the hang of it, it isn't so hard."

He wanted to. His hands itched to get hold of that long, pretty rod.

"Come on. You can't hurt it. If you get it caught, I can get it undone."

There it was. His fear out in the open and the guy said it wouldn't be a problem. Chance McLain was back on David's side of the creek, putting the rod in his hands and David was letting him. It was lighter than he thought, yet it felt good in his palm, balanced just right.

"The trick is not to rush. Get the feel of the rod. Drag the line out easy and slow. Whip it over your head as if you've got all the time in the world. When the line's right at the top, make just the slightest hesitation, then let go. Throw it like you'd throw a baseball. Just let it sail right on out there. We'll try it on the grass a couple of times, then you can try it in the water."

His heart was pounding. His fingertips tingled, he wanted to do this so badly. The rod felt warm, curved just right against his hand. He whipped it, watched the line sail out and land not nearly far enough away.

"You started off smooth, but you snapped it a little too much at the end. Try it again."

He did it again, then again. Two times then three, he started to lose track. When he looked up, Chance McLain was smiling.

"You're a natural, David. Nice hands and an easy stroke. Want to try it out in the water?"

His mother would kill him for getting his shoes and pant legs wet, but David didn't care. He walked past Chance McLain out into the middle of the stream and it felt so darned good to be there. The water was running past his feet, icy cold yet it didn't really matter.

"Do it just like you did on the grass, nice and easy."

He took a deep breath, closed his eyes and tossed out the line. It didn't go too well at first, but after a while he relaxed a little and it got easier. Then the line snagged on a rock beneath the surface of the water.

"No problem. It'll come loose." McLain waded out and showed him how to untangle it by tugging it the opposite way, then he waded back to the bank. David kept waiting for him to ask for his rod back or tell him he was ready to leave, but he didn't seem to be in a hurry.

David knew he was taking advantage, that he ought to give the rod back and let the guy be on his way, but he couldn't seem to make himself quit. There was something about being out in the middle of that stream, about tossing out that fly and making it land just right on the top of the water, about the easy rhythm that was almost hypnotic. When something snagged the end of his line, nearly jerking the rod from his hands, and a big silver fish leaped out of the water, David felt a rush of excitement unlike anything he could remember.

"A fish!" he yelled at the top of his lungs. Already McLain was sloshing through the water at a run, wrapping one of his big hands around David's and helping him hold the rod steady.

"You've got to set the hook, then we'll reel him in." It seemed like hours. It seemed like seconds. One minute the fish was there, then in an instant it was gone.

McLain just laughed. It was deep and husky, kind of sandpaper rough. "Damn, almost had him." McLain grinned and so did David. "They're slippery little suckers. That's what makes them so much fun to catch."

David just nodded. It didn't matter that the fish had gotten away. It only mattered that he'd caught one.

"He was a dandy, too," McLain said. "A big German brown."

His heart was still thundering. He didn't want to quit. "It's early yet. Maybe there's time to catch another."

Chance looked up at the house. "What time's supper? You're mom'll be wantin' you home by then."

It was nearly six. Time to go in. "Yeah, I guess you're right."

"Tell you what. I got a couple more rods at home.

Since we're neighbors, why don't I loan you this one? You can practice your technique after school and try again tomorrow.''

David wondered if his grin looked as stupid as it felt. "You sure it's all right?"

"No problem. Just remember, you gotta release 'em if they're less than eight inches. And if you keep 'em you gotta eat 'em. You ever cleaned a fish?"

He only shook his head.

"I'll stop by tomorrow and show you how." He smiled. "Assuming between us we can catch one."

David just nodded. He felt funny inside his chest, as if something important had just happened, but he didn't know what it was. It was crazy, but that was the way he felt.

"Thanks, Mr. McLain."

"Chance," McLain said. "Just call me Chance like everyone else."

David nodded. Picking up the fishing rod, he started up the hill toward the house. Halfway there, he saw his mother. She was standing in the shadows beneath a pine tree and he realized that she had been watching.

She brushed at something in her eye and smiled as he walked past, but she didn't say anything. He waved at her but didn't stop to talk. He was thinking about the fish and how it had felt to have something so wild and beautiful dancing on the end of his line. How tomorrow, he'd be back at the stream, practicing with Chance McLain's rod and trying his luck again.

If that dumb punk Jimmy Stevens could ride a horse, surely he could learn to fish.

* * *

Kate strolled down the grassy slope toward the creek, where Chance McLain stood beside his pinto horse. "That was very nice . . . what you did for my son."

"Every kid ought to know how to fish."

"He doesn't have many friends here. You acted like a friend today. You'll never know how much I appreciate that."

He looked down at the braided reins he held in his hands. They were strong hands, dark and long-fingered, with nicks and scars across the back, hard working hands, she thought.

"It was nothing. The boy wants to learn—I'll teach him." He glanced up, smiled. "He's got a natural knack."

His hat was dusty, his face covered with a fine sheen of dust. Still he was handsome. "It was a great kindness. I wish there was a way I could repay you."

His eyes fixed on her face, intent now, the easy, slightly embarrassed expression gone. "Maybe there is."

She stiffened. She should have known there would be a catch. In this world, you never got something for nothing. "And that would be . . . ?"

Chance McLain grinned. "Let me show you around. I know this country as well as anyone, better than most. I'm proud of it. Let me show you the place you've come to live."

"That's it? You just want to show me around?"

His easy smile faded. "What did you think? That if I taught your son to fish, I'd expect to take you to bed? This isn't LA, Kate. People help each other out here. They have to. You'll learn that if you stay."

She felt like a fool. Of course he hadn't meant anything like that. "If I stay? Why wouldn't I stay?"

"You haven't been through a winter out here. You haven't walked through a field a million grasshoppers call home. You haven't had your sweet little housecat eaten by a coyote, or been chased by a grizzly bear. Life's hard out here, Kate. But I promise you, it's worth it. Let me show you this country and you'll see what I mean.''

What could it hurt? He wasn't asking her for a date. Dating a man like Chance McLain was a whole different thing and far too dangerous for someone like her. Forgodsake, her divorce wasn't even final. And the way Tommy had been acting lately—making threats, refusing to sign the settlement papers—she had to be even more careful.

She couldn't risk getting involved with a man, didn't even want to. But McLain wasn't interested in anything but building a friendship. So what if he was good looking? So what if she felt flushed and warm whenever he looked at her the way he had just then. The man was her neighbor. She couldn't simply ignore him. And the truth was, she needed friends just as much as David did.

"All right, you've convinced me. I'd love to see my new home.''

"How about Sunday? You can bring David along if you like.''

She relaxed even more. He wouldn't be asking David to come along if he had any sort of designs on her. "I'm sure he'd like that.''

"Good, then I'll pick you up at six on Sunday morning. The earlier start we get, the better chance we'll have of seeing some animals.''

"Animals? I thought we were going sightseeing.''

"The animals in Montana are part of the sights. If we're lucky, on Sunday you'll see what I mean.''

And so she finished working through the week, growing more and more nervous about the weekend. She should have said no. She shouldn't take the chance of spending time with a man like McLain. She knew his reputation—Myra said he had any number of women at his beck and call. As handsome as he was, it was easy to believe. But surely a single day with him wasn't going to throw her into a tailspin.

Then she remembered the effortless, graceful way he swung up on his horse, how rugged he looked in his long black duster, the way he had winked at her and grinned.

She remembered how her stomach had floated up with that grin and neatly turned over, and Kate began wishing she hadn't agreed.

Chance stood up in his stirrups, stretching the long muscles in his legs after so many hours in the saddle. They were mending fences in the northern pastures, where the graze was good and a number of cattle collected during the summer months.

He lifted his hat and let the breeze blow through his hair, then settled the hat back on and pulled the brim low across his forehead. He'd been riding for most of the day. They'd gotten a lot of work done, but again and again his mind had strayed. He kept thinking of Kaitlin Rollins, remembering the way she had looked, yesterday down by the stream.

All that dark red hair curling down to her shoulders. Big green eyes shiny with a hint of tears at the joy she had seen on her son's face because he was learning to fish. *Soft* was the word that always came to mind when he thought of her. Soft lips, soft skin. Thinking of yesterday, he mentally added, *soft heart*.

She had finally agreed to go out with him. He didn't

mind that she'd only done it because of the boy. The
attraction was there. Chance knew it. Kate knew it. It
was only a matter of time until something came of it.

He had a feeling Kate would be worth the wait.

One of his men whistled at one of the steers and his
attention returned to the task at hand. Across the way,
his foreman, Roddy Darnell, picked his way through a
cluster of white-faced Herefords and rode up beside
him.

"We got a problem, boss. You better come take a
look." Roddy had been working at the Running Moon
since before Hollis McLain had died and the spread
had gone to his son. He was bone-thin and sun-browned,
a good man that Chance felt lucky to have.

He reined his paint horse, Skates, up the trail behind
Roddy, wondering what lay ahead. It was always something in the cattle business. Too much snow. Not
enough rain. Beef prices down. And there was nothing
in the world he would rather be doing.

They stayed on the trail, winding slowly upward, the
country here more open than it was farther east. There
the Mission Mountains ran along the border of the
ranch, a nearly impenetrable string of high, forested
peaks that shot up nine thousand feet.

But here, the grass grew thick and sweet, grama and
bunch grass, buffalo grass farther down on the plains.

They stopped beside a small, meandering creek and
Roddy swung down from the saddle. Chance followed
him up onto a knoll where a side stream had formed
a pond, and both men stopped beside it.

"Jesus, Mary, and Joseph." Six dead steers lay around
the pond, their eyes glazed over, their tongues hanging
out. "Looks like it's the water."

Roddy just nodded. "The creek crosses the fence line

onto reservation land 'bout half a mile up. We followed it till we found what we were looking for. Someone dumped a load of mining sludge into a canyon up there. It was probably done some time back . . . a couple of years, maybe. Must have finally seeped into the ground water and somehow made its way into the creek."

"Long as it was flowing, it was partially diluted. In the pond, the pollution had time to build up." Chance swore foully. "No way to prove it was Consolidated, I don't suppose."

"Probably not. There were a couple of other mines in operation a few years back. Could have been any one of them."

"Could have been, but we both know it wasn't."

"What do you want me to do?"

"Fence off the pond. Move the cattle into that pasture east of here. The graze isn't as good but at least they won't die."

"What about the waste?"

"I'll call the county. And whoever needs to know on the rez."

"Maybe now we'll get some action."

"Maybe," Chance said. But he didn't really believe it. Silently, he wished Lon Barton straight to hell.

Chapter Nine

Kate always looked forward to Sunday mornings. It was the one day of the week that she could sleep in. She'd never really been an early riser, though she had done it all her life. First with a baby and working to put herself through college, later with a high-paying job that demanded hours of overtime, she'd never had any other choice.

She groaned as she slapped the alarm clock into silence at five A.M. and pulled herself out of bed, trying to imagine how she could have let Chance McLain talk her into giving up her precious Sunday sleep. Yawning, she padded into the bathroom, turned on the shower, and stepped beneath the hot water, letting the warm spray wash over her.

She felt better by the time she had dressed and headed downstairs. David was dressed as well and waiting in the kitchen. An empty cereal bowl and the crumbs from his toast sat on the counter. The fishing rod he had borrowed from Chance McLain leaned up against the back door.

"I was thinking . . ." he said. "Wondering if maybe you wouldn't mind if I didn't go with you. I thought . . . since I still got Chance's . . . Mr. McLain's fishing rod, today might be a good day to really give it a try."

An image of the hard-edged cowboy appeared, and a thread of uneasiness washed through her. As long as David was coming along, she'd felt safe. Now wariness settled over her at the thought being alone with McLain.

"I know how much this means to you, David, but I don't like the idea of you going off on your own. What if something happened to you out there?" The stream behind the house, Little Sandy Creek, was shallow and according to the locals, not dangerous. All fishermen went off by themselves, they said. It was part of the sport's appeal.

Still, it made her nervous to think of her son out there by himself.

"I'm not going off by myself. Chief is coming over. He said he'd go with me."

Old Chief Ironstone, David's only real friend. They made an odd pair, one so old, the other so young, yet knowing how lonely David had been, Kate was grateful for the old man's friendship.

"Well, he certainly knows his way around the forest. I suppose if he's going along, you'll be all right. I'm sure Mr. McLain will be disappointed, but I imagine he'll get over it."

David tossed her a look that said, *Come on, Mom, get a grip.*

"All right then, *I'll* be disappointed. At any rate, if

that's what you want to do with your Sunday, it's all right with me—as long as you're careful and don't go too far from the house.''

David leaned over and hugged her. ''Cool, Mom. Thanks a million.''

She gave him a tenuous smile. She had come to Montana determined that they would make a life here. That meant learning to live the way country people lived, doing the things they did.

She watched David escape out the back door as the doorbell rang out front. Taking a deep breath, she went to greet Chance McLain.

Wearing jeans, a sweatshirt, and tennis shoes, she pulled open the door, hoping it was the proper attire for their little adventure. The look of approval on his face said it was, and a warm feeling slid into her stomach.

''I see you're ready.'' Chance glanced toward the kitchen. ''Where's David?''

She smiled. ''My son went fishing. Ever since you lent him that rod, that's all he wants to do.''

A corner of his mouth curved up. The most sensuous mouth she'd ever seen. ''I guess that means I'm stuck with just you.''

''I guess you are.''

''Grab your jacket and let's get going. We're burnin' daylight here.''

''My jacket? It isn't that cold outside. Surely I don't need—''

''First rule of living in the mountains, Ms. Rollins. Never go anywhere without a coat. The weather's unpredictable up here. The temperature's been known to drop fifty degrees in a single afternoon. Believe it or not, the record's closer to a hundred.''

''Oh my God.''

He grinned. "No big deal—as long as you're prepared."

Kate rolled her eyes. "No big deal," she said beneath her breath, wondering, as she had more than once, if in coming here she'd gotten in way over her head.

Chance led her out to his pickup, one with an extended cab, mud flaps, and a toolbox in the back. He opened the door and helped her climb in, not an easy task, since she was so short and the truck sat so high off the ground.

She set her purse on the floor and leaned back against the seat. "I guess I'm just not built for a truck this big."

At the mention of her body, his eyes shifted down to her breasts, then he jerked them back up to her face. "I suppose I oughta get a running board," he said, sounding a little embarrassed and staring straight ahead. "That makes it a whole lot easier."

"Where are we going?" Ignoring his momentary indiscretion, Kate clasped the seat belt around her, noting with approval that Chance did the same.

"There's a logging road up through the mountains behind the ranch. There's some incredible views from up there."

Kate sat back in the comfortable sheepskin-covered seat, enjoying the ride along the forested road and the opportunity to study the man at the wheel without being seen. He drove with the confidence of someone who had done this sort of thing every day of his thirty-odd years, taking the steep turns as if they weren't there, gently braking when he needed without really thinking about it.

Pine trees lined both sides of the road, tall ponderosas, lodge poles, and cedars; birch trees and cottonwoods along the banks of the stream. White-barked aspens ran up the draws and she thought how pretty they must be when their leaves turned golden in the fall.

With July nearly over, the trees were fully leafed out and the snow had melted in the valleys. A blanket of white still capped a few of the tall, forbidding mountains that surrounded the town of Lost Peak. In the sunlight, the glistening snow appeared almost fluorescent.

They turned off the main, black-topped road and drove onto one of gravel, passing through a gate fashioned from two huge pine logs standing upright, a third forming a bar across the top. A weathered sign hung down—RUNNING MOON RANCH—burned into a thick slab of wood.

"My father was born on this ranch," Chance said. "Of course it was a lot smaller then."

"How big is it now?"

"Twenty thousand acres." He said it matter-of-factly, as if it were nothing out of the ordinary to own thirty-odd square miles of land. "My father built it up from practically nothing. Spent most of his life doing it. He died about eight years ago."

There was something in his words, something he wasn't saying. "Were the two of you close?"

He gave a sarcastic snort in answer. "I would hardly say that. I rarely saw him and that was just fine by me."

She wanted to ask him why, but she was afraid to. She didn't like the hard look that had come into his eyes.

"What about your mother?" She hoped it was a more pleasant topic.

"She died when I was three."

"I'm sorry."

Those brilliant blue eyes swung to her face. "Why? You didn't even know her."

"I'm sorry for you, Chance. You and your father didn't get along. You must have been terribly lonely as a boy."

He stared at her a moment longer than he should have, considering he was driving. Then he glanced back to the road. "You're right, I had a pretty rotten childhood. David's lucky to have a mother who cares about him the way you do."

"I'm not sure exactly what you mean."

"As near as I can figure, David is one of the reasons you came to Montana. You were worried about him getting into trouble. You figured he'd have a better chance of making it out here."

He was right on every score. She wondered how he knew. "He's a good boy. He just got a little mixed up."

Chance covered her hand where it rested on the seat. "You did the right thing, Kate. Montana's a good place to raise a child."

Kate stared down at those long dark fingers. "For David's sake I hope you're right." She could feel their strength, their warmth. It seemed to flow into her like the light that night at the end of the tunnel. It occurred to her she had never known the comfort of having a strong man in her life. Not a husband or a father. She couldn't imagine what it must be like to have a man a woman could really lean on.

Just then the brakes slammed on and his hand came up protectively in front of her, holding her in place though the seat belt worked perfectly fine. "Hang on!" he said rather belatedly.

"What is it? What's wrong?"

McLain just grinned in that appealing way of his. "Moose," he said.

"Moose? Moose what?"

"That moose there." He pointed toward the side of the road.

Kate shot upright in her seat. "Oh my God!" It was huge and nearly black, with legs that seemed eight feet tall. It lifted its massive head and stared at the pickup, the long stringy whiskers on its chin moving up and down as it chewed, then it lowered its head back to the grass and just kept on munching as if they weren't there.

"He's incredible. I've never seen anything so magnificent."

Chance seemed pleased, his eyes warming, little lines appearing at the corners. "There's a cow over there."

"A cow?" They'd passed a thousand head of cattle. Why, she wondered was this one more special than the rest?

"A female moose."

"A female," she repeated again, beginning to hate herself for it. "Yes, I see. A female moose is a cow."

"So is a female elk." He flashed another of those endearing grins. "It won't take you long to get the hang of it."

Kate sighed, her eyes still fixed on the two massive beasts on the side of the road. "I could sit here and watch them all day."

Chance laughed, and even his laughter sounded strong. "Not a chance, lady. I've got lots more to show you."

And so he did, amazing her with one incredible sight after another. Towering waterfalls that soared over the edge of cliffs, then crashed into a foamy white spray on the rocks below. Deer, elk, snowshoe rabbits. Even a coyote. They left the ranch by a back road leading even higher into the mountains and wound up at the headwaters of Silver Fox Creek.

When Chance stopped the truck at a wide spot in the road, she could see for miles out into the mountain-lined valley.

"You were right, Chance. This was well worth getting up early for."

"I'm glad you like it." He leaned back in the seat, stretching those long legs out in front of him. "Now just imagine what will happen to all of this if Consolidated Metals gets that mining permit."

Her eyes swung to his face, but most of it was shaded by the brim of his hat. "You're saying the pollution will affect not only the stream but all of the wild life around here."

"That's right. The fish and insects are food for larger game. And the heavy metals can sink into the ground water. Yesterday up in the northwest pasture, we found six dead steers that had stumbled across a pond fouled by mining waste."

"Oh, Chance, no."

The lines of his face looked grim. "Unfortunately, it's happened more than once."

"I meant what I said. I'll do anything I can to help."

"Thanks, Kate. We need people who care. Ed's been pressing me about that meeting. How about some night this week?"

She usually worked till two Monday through Thursday, so she could spend time with David. The evenings were pretty much open. "Just let me know which evening works best for you."

"Like I said before, we're glad to have you here in Lost Peak." He turned just a little and those incredible blue eyes fixed on her face. *I'm* glad you're here, they seemed to say.

Kate shifted beneath his close regard, trying to ignore

the warm, buttery sensation working its way out through her limbs. It was ridiculous. The man was simply being polite.

"Are you hungry?" he asked, dragging his gaze away and breaking the mood.

"I was too busy watching the scenery to think about food, but now that you mention it, I'm starved. Unfortunately, I don't see a deli on the corner."

Chance smiled. Reaching behind the seat, he dragged out a thermos of coffee and a bulging paper bag. "BLTs. Sort of a cross between breakfast and lunch, since it's still pretty early. These aren't as good as the ones from your place, but they're the best my cook could do on short notice."

"You've got a cook?"

Chance settled the bag in the crook of his arm, grabbed a blanket, and cracked open the driver-side door. "You'll need your jacket," he said. "This early, it's still pretty chilly up this high."

She grabbed the nylon jacket he'd insisted she bring and reached for the handle on the door.

"Just sit tight. I'll come around and get you. And yeah, I've got a cook. Pretty much a necessity with half a dozen full-time hands to feed."

She hadn't thought about what it must take to run a ranch the size of his. She was pondering the notion when the door opened up and Chance's big hands clamped around her waist. Her lifted her down with an ease that was almost scary and lowered her slowly to her feet.

Her body brushed his along the way, and she could feel the lean hardness, the strength she had felt before. She was standing way too close and this time when she looked up into his face, there was no doubt what he was thinking.

Something passed between them, something hot and turbulent, something she hadn't expected to feel and didn't want to.

"Kate," he said, the single word deep and slightly rough. Her stomach did a flip and slowly collapsed in a heap. Kate moistened her lips, determined to say something that would end the moment, but no words came out. Instead, Chance lowered his head and kissed her, a hot, wet kiss she felt all the way to her toes.

Unconsciously, her hands crept up and her fingers spread over the front of his sheepskin vest. Chance cupped her face between his hands and kissed her again, slowly and very thoroughly. She was shaking when she finally broke away.

The world fell silent around them. Her breath came out in soft, quick little puffs. Chance dragged in a long, calming breath and slowly released it. He glanced down at the scuffed toes of his boots then out across the valley.

"Sorry. I didn't bring you here for that. It just sort of happened."

Kate didn't answer. Her heart was still hammering, her body tingling. One thing was certain. Chance McLain knew how to kiss.

"I'm still hungry," he said, trying to return the light mood they had shared before, then having the grace to flush at the underlying meaning in the words. "The sandwiches, I mean. We wouldn't want them to go to waste."

Inwardly, she smiled at the subtle hint of shyness. There was a hard, rough edge to Chance McLain but there was a softness there, too, an unmistakable vulnerability. She had seen it in her son, the attempt to retreat behind a tough facade. Chance was older. He'd had a lot more practice. But if you looked hard, you could see the gentleness was still there inside him.

"We need to find a place to spread the blanket," she said, and he visibly relaxed. "How about over there?" She pointed to a big flat boulder that overlooked the valley.

"Perfect." Chance smiled. God, he had the straightest, whitest teeth. He spread out the blanket, opened the bag, and handed her a sandwich, then poured coffee into a couple of Styrofoam cups.

"I bet you use cream," he said. "I didn't think to bring any."

"I imagine I can tough it just this once."

He smiled his approval and handed her a cup. "So tell me a little about you. I know you worked for an ad agency. How'd you happen to get into that line of work?"

Kate shifted on the rock, the bite she had taken suddenly feeling a little too big. This was one of the reasons she hadn't wanted to come. Talking about the past wasn't something she was ready to do. "I was a business major in college. UCLA. I was solicited by Menger and Menger during my senior year. What about you?" she asked, hoping to get him talking instead. "Did you go off to school or just start working on the ranch?"

"I went to the U of M—University of Montana—down in Missoula. My father passed away two months before graduation. I dropped out to take over running the ranch."

"Two months and you didn't go back and finish?" It seemed impossible after the struggle she'd gone through to get her degree.

Chance just shrugged his shoulders. "I always knew

what I wanted to do. The Running Moon was all I ever thought of. I didn't need a diploma to run it." He took a bite of his sandwich, chewed and swallowed. "So why'd you come to Lost Peak? I know you were worried about your son, but you could have sold the cafe and the land, taken the money and gone somewhere else. There are lots of other places, slightly bigger towns that could have offered more of a life for a single woman."

Kate carefully wiped her mouth with the napkin he had pulled from his brown paper lunch sack. She thought of the shooting and the experience she'd had, of Chet Munson and the articles in the newspaper; of Tommy and the divorce, of her mother and Nell Hart and the mystery that had compelled her to come to Lost Peak.

But none of those were things that she could risk telling Chance.

Her hand faintly trembled and she was no longer hungry. "I wanted to get away from the city. When Nell died and left me the cafe it seemed like the perfect solution."

"I would have thought you'd have picked a town that at least had a theater and—"

"Well, I didn't," Kate snapped, setting her unfinished sandwich back down on the piece of wax paper it had been wrapped in and rising to her feet. "Listen, Chance, I really appreciate the tour, but I've got a lot to do when I get home, and I need to be getting on back."

Chance said nothing for the longest time. "All right, Kate. Whatever you say." Wordlessly, he tossed the last of his sandwich into the sack along with hers, cleaned up the mess they had made, and screwed the lid back on the thermos of coffee.

Kate felt a little guilty for ruining such a perfect morning, but maybe it was better this way. She shouldn't have weakened, shouldn't have come with him in the first place. With Tommy stirring up trouble, Chet Munson sniffing around, and David to think of, she didn't have time to get involved with a man.

Especially not this one.

She knew what kind of man Chance was. It was written in every line of his handsome face. Just yesterday she had overheard Bonnie Delaney, one of the waitresses who worked part time for her. "Chance's a real heartbreaker," Bonnie had said to one of the female customers. "He's left a string of broken hearts all over Silver County."

One look at the heat in those sultry blue eyes and she was certain it was the truth.

When they pulled up in front of the house, he turned off the engine and Kate cracked open the door, ready to jump and run like the little black snowshoe rabbit they had seen.

Chance caught her arm before she could leave. "Listen, Kate. Whatever your reasons for coming to Lost Peak, it's your business, not mine. I won't pry into your affairs again, but I'm not letting you run from me any longer. I want to see you again."

She shook her head a little too fiercely, stirring the curly hair around her face. "It's not a good idea."

"Why not?"

"Because I've got a son to think about and a cafe to run."

"Sorry—not good enough."

"Because we have nothing in common. I'm from the city. You're a country boy."

He only shook his head. "Try again."

"Because I'm just plain not attracted to you."

"Bullshit." Grabbing a fistful of her sweatshirt, he hauled her halfway across the car seat and captured her mouth in a scalding, mind-numbing kiss. She struggled for an instant, but the heat was too much, the fire too unbearably hot. She'd never felt anything like it.

Chance kissed the corners of her mouth, kissed her lips again, and she opened for him, letting his tongue slide in, feeling the hot, wet silkiness, desperately wanting the kiss to continue. She was trembling all over, damp in places that hadn't been damp in years. She heard herself whimper when Chance pulled away.

A long dark finger smoothed along her jaw. "Listen to me, Kate. I don't have the foggiest idea what's going on between us, but something damned well is. I didn't plan for it to happen. I know you didn't either, but I mean to find out what it is. I'll be in town on Thursday night. Don't eat before you close. We're going out to dinner."

He didn't give her time to argue, just climbed down from his side of the truck, rounded the front, jerked open her door, and lifted her down. He walked her to the door and waited while she unlocked and shoved it open.

"I'll see you Thursday," he said and then he was gone, leaving her staring dumbly after him.

Kate watched his pickup pull out of the driveway, feeling as if her world had somehow shifted. All she could think was *Oh my God, what have I done?*

Chapter Ten

For the balance of the day, Kate worried about the date she had made with Chance McLain—or more correctly, the date *he* had made that she had never really agreed to.

It was silly, she finally decided, ridiculous to let it upset her so much. Chance was only a man, after all. She had worked with men for years. At the ad agency, most of her clients were men. She knew how to handle them, knew how to say no without bruising their fragile egos. Of course, she'd been married back then.

Still, Chance was no different than the rest. Better looking, maybe. But a man, nonetheless. As long as she remembered that, she'd be all right. So he was taking her out to dinner. So what? She might even wind up enjoying herself.

With that thought in mind, she set to work on other, more important endeavors.

She had been meaning to call Aida Whittaker, Nell's best friend, just to see where the conversation might lead. Myra had given her the woman's number in Eugene, Oregon, where she was living with her daughter. As soon as David headed upstairs to play one of his computer games, Kate dialed her up.

"Mrs. Whittaker?"

"Yes . . . ?"

"I'm Kaitlin Rollins—Nell Hart's granddaughter? I've been meaning to call you for some time." They spoke for a while, just small talk, getting to know each other a little. Aida seemed genuinely glad to hear from her. She wanted to know how the cafe was doing since Kate had taken over and any new happenings in Lost Peak.

"I'm afraid I don't have much news. I haven't really been here long enough to get in on the gossip. I know they're trying to put a mine in on Silver Fox Creek, but a few of us are getting together to see what we can do to stop them."

"Good for you," Aida said, her voice filled with approval. "Maybe you're more like your grandmother than you know."

"What do you mean?"

"Nell was dead-set against mining up in those hills. She thought it was a shame what it did to the land and the animals. She told Lon Barton so, too—on more than one occasion."

Perhaps they felt the same about some things, but thinking of her mother, Kate knew she would never have treated her own child as Nell had treated her daughter.

"Who's Lon Barton?" she asked.

"You'll meet him. Sooner or later. His father, William Barton, is the major shareholder of Consolidated Metals. Lon runs the company for him. Both of them have more money than they know what to do with."

"Was there anyone else Nell didn't get along with? What I mean is . . . did Nell have any enemies?"

"Enemies? Good Lord, no. At least none that I know of. She and your mother had a terrible falling out, but that was years ago. I imagine you know all about it."

Only what her mother had told her, and it wasn't a pretty picture. Kate remembered her mother crying every year on her birthday.

"I wonder if she ever even thinks of me," Celeste had once said. But it was water under the bridge now, and nothing anyone could do to change things.

They talked a little longer, then Kate said goodbye, promising to call every few weeks with news of what was happening in town. The conversation had been a pleasant one. Though she had never met Aida Whittaker, she felt a certain connection to the woman on the other end of the phone. It was obvious what good friends Nell and Aida had been. Perhaps their next conversation would prove more a little more fruitful.

A few minutes after she hung up the phone it rang again. It was the voice of Ed Fontaine.

"I hope I'm not calling at a bad time."

"No, not at all."

"Chance said he mentioned getting together to discuss the campaign against the mine."

"As a matter of fact, he did."

"I know it's short notice, but any chance you'd be ready by tomorrow night?"

Mondays were always slow. She only kept the place open because there was nowhere else for the locals to go. "Tomorrow would be fine. We can use the meeting room in the back of the cafe, if that works all right for you."

"That'd be great. We'd like to ask anyone who's interested to join us. Would that be a problem?"

"I think it's a good idea."

"All right, then. We'll see you tomorrow night."

Kate wondered if the *we* included Chance, then shoved the unwelcome thought away. Why was it just thinking about him always made her nervous? It was ridiculous. This was business. The sort she was extremely good at. Whether Chance was there or not was unimportant. She could help these people who had so graciously accepted her into their community. Kate intended to do just that.

The meeting began at seven o'clock in the back room of the Lost Peak Cafe, an extension, according to Myra, that Nell had added fifteen years ago. It was used for large parties, special occasions, or just about anything where more than ten people needed to get together in a town of four hundred.

The group that showed up was an interesting mix of locals: Ed Fontaine, owner of the Circle Bar F; his male nurse, Randy Wiggins; Silas Marshall, the old rock hound who owned the grocery store; Maddie and Tom Webster, owners of the local beer bar, the Antlers, down the street; and Jake Dillon, a recently widowed man in his fifties who owned Dillon's Mercantile.

Jeremy Spotted Horse was there, arriving just as Chief Ironstone walked in. Half a dozen people she'd never met showed up as well. The last one through the door was Chance McLain.

Kate ignored the sudden Ferris wheel drop in her stomach and gave him a smile. Chance smiled back, but this was a business meeting and his manner said he respected that.

Leading the group toward the room at the back, she waited while everyone took a seat. She'd arranged the banquet tables in a U, putting Ed, Chance, and Jeremy beside her at the front of the room.

Ed began by thanking everyone who had taken the time to come and filling them in on the latest news about the gold mine Consolidated intended to develop on Silver Fox Creek.

"They're convinced they can overturn the ban on any new heap-leach mining, and if we don't do something to stop them they just might succeed. It won't be easy, but with all of us working together we can keep them from destroying Silver Fox Creek."

A mumble of uncertainty floated around the room. Going up against a huge company like Consolidated Metals wasn't going to be easy and they knew it. A few people voiced their reservations. Both Tom Webster and Silas Marshall were worried about waste pollution, but they thought the advantages the mine would bring might be worth it.

"A mine that size requires a great deal of labor," Tom said. "They'd be creating a lot of new jobs. Our businesses would grow. Hell, the whole town would prosper."

Jeremy Spotted Horse countered. "The biggest thing we have to sell around here is the land itself—the mountains, the forests, and the animals. That's what people come to see. A mine is hardly scenic—not when it creates a heap of tailings as high as a four-story building. And if they poison the streams, they'll kill the wildlife.

You might get a few more families moving in, but you'll lose the tourist business and the quality of life will turn to sh—. Well, you get my drift. The place won't be fit to live in."

Silas Marshall looked worried. "Consolidated Metals is a big corporation. I don't see how a handful of us has the power to stop them, even if we wanted to." A man in his seventies, Silas was tall and thin with a neatly trimmed beard that covered a long chin. Every time Kate looked at him, she thought of an aging Abraham Lincoln.

Chance stood up in reply to Silas's doubts. "Consolidated has a damned good political machine and the best lawyers money can buy. As Ed said, it won't be easy. That's where Ms. Rollins comes in. She's had experience with this sort of thing and she's going to help us figure out what to do."

This time he looked directly at her. She could feel those sky-blue eyes moving over her face and the air seemed too heavy to push out of her lungs. Hoping no one noticed the warm flush in her cheeks, she took a moment to study her notes and compose herself.

"As Silas pointed out, taking on a company the size of Consolidated Metals is a difficult task. But it isn't impossible either. The first thing we need to do is inform the public about the company's efforts to overturn the ban and remind them of the mine's potential dangers."

"How do we do that?" a man in the back row asked.

"To begin with, we'll go after the media, involve them on a local, regional, and national level. We'll need newspaper and magazine articles, and television coverage as well. We can print educational brochures, which we'll use when we hold public meetings. Ultimately, we'll need a website, and—"

"Hold it, Kate." Jeremy Spotted Horse held up one big hand. "How in blazes are we supposed to pay for all this?"

"Good question, Jeremy. We'll have to have a sponsor to help us—at least in the beginning. But as soon as we get organized, we can start raising money to fund our efforts."

Chance cleared his throat. "I imagine Ed and I can come up with enough cash to get things rolling." He tossed a glance at Ed and received a confirming nod from the older man.

"We can sell bumper stickers and T-shirts," Kate went on. "We can also hold fund-raising events." She started to add something more, but the discouraged look of the crowd held her back.

"Maybe Silas is right," Jake Dillon said glumly. "There's no way in hell we can do all of that."

Kate just smiled. "That's the best part—we don't have to." She handed out a printed sheet she'd typed up on her computer and copied on the Xerox machine in the upstairs bedroom she'd converted to an office. She might have moved to the country, but there were some things a city girl just couldn't live without. To Kate's mind, a modern, efficient office was one of them.

"You're suggesting we contact each of these agencies?" Ed asked.

"That's right. All of them are dedicated to improving the environment. They worked on getting the cyanide ban on the ballot in the first place. They'll be more than happy to help us, once they understand what Consolidated is attempting to do."

Chance read the list out loud. "Five Valleys Trust, Sierra Club, Trout Unlimited, John Muir Chapter, Montana Environmental Information Center, Montana Wilderness Association." He looked up from the list that went on for half a page and grinned. "With these guys on our side, Consolidated is in for one helluva battle."

"And it's a battle they aren't going to win," Kate said firmly.

Silas still looked worried. "Those guys aren't gonna like this."

"That's putting it mildly," Jeremy grumbled.

"Silas and Jeremy are right," Tom Webster said. "Not everyone is gonna be happy you're trying to stop them. Over near Yellowstone, environmentalists tried to stop the World Gold Mine from going in and things got really nasty. A couple of people got hurt pretty bad."

"Some things are worth fighting for," Chance said.

Kate silently agreed. She hadn't lived in Montana all that long, but already she had fallen in love with the place. The thought of ruining one of the country's last wilderness frontiers was simply unthinkable.

"All right, then. How does the Silver Fox Creek Anti-Mining Coalition sound?"

Several heads nodded and smiled. "Sounds good to me," Chance said, getting a rumble of agreement from the crowd.

"I think it would be best if Ed made the initial phone calls to the organizations on the list, since he's so well known in the community. I'm the logical person, I guess, to lay out the brochure. I'll need photographs, though. Is there anyone here who can help me with that?"

"I can," Jeremy said. "Wildlife photography is sort of a hobby of mine. And I've got pictures of some of the pollution problems caused by the Beavertail Mine over on Beaver Creek."

"Perfect. Does anybody here know any of the local newspeople? We can start with the problem of Chance's dead cattle. That ought to be of interest to the people who live around here.''

Jeremy's eyes swung to Chance. "What dead cattle?"

The room turned strangely silent as Chance explained the grisly sight he had found by his high-meadow pond. "Now you understand why this is so important. Instead of cows, that could have happened to somebody's kids.''

They went on assigning tasks and before they left, Kate asked them to sign a volunteer form, giving their names, phone numbers, and addresses. They were off to a very good start, she thought as the last of them disappeared out the door.

All but Chance, who stayed behind to help her pick up the empty coffee cups and dirty napkins and set them on a plastic tray. The cafe was just closing. She could hear the sound of Bonnie in the kitchen cleaning up.

"You were great tonight," Chance said once they were finished, one wide shoulder propped against the doorframe.

"I know it was a little overwhelming. Getting something like this started isn't easy.''

His eyes moved over her, lingered on her breasts. "Nothing worthwhile ever is," he said, looking back into her face. "The best things take a little effort." He wasn't talking about the campaign anymore, and a little shiver tingled up her spine.

"I wish it was Thursday," he said. "If I were bringing you home after supper, I'd have an excuse to kiss you.''

Kate couldn't move. Her heart was zinging, flying against the walls of her chest. He was standing so close she could smell his aftershave, Old Spice, she thought. Nothing fancy for a man like Chance, but boy, did he smell good.

"Then again," he said softly, "maybe I don't need an excuse." He moved with purpose, lowering his head until his mouth softly settled over hers. Her eyes slid closed and the world seemed to tilt on its axis. Their lips melded, sank warmly together, and her palms flattened out on his chest. It was as hard as steel, as solid as the wall behind her, wide bands of muscle that tightened as his arms came around her, pressing her against his long lean frame.

The kiss went on and on, nibbling, tasting, gentle, then deep and incredibly erotic. She knew she should end it, but his mouth was so warm, his lips so soft, she simply refused.

A loud noise sounded through the walls, Bonnie dropping a pan on the kitchen floor. Both of them broke away.

Chance smiled faintly. He reached down and ran a finger along her jaw. "I'll see you on Thursday," he said. She thought he might kiss her again, but he didn't. He must have realized she wouldn't have let him.

Even so, he seemed satisfied at the progress he had made, and that drew her stomach into a knot. Lifting his hat off the rack by the door, he settled it low on his forehead, touched the brim in farewell, and he was gone.

Kate's heart finally started to slow.

Sitting in his wheelchair next to Randy outside the cafe, Ed Fontaine spotted Chance walking toward him and wheeled himself in that direction. "I wondered if you were coming out—or if maybe you planned to spend the night in the cafe." He had wanted a word with Chance before he left for home. It hadn't occurred to him the boy might not be ready to leave, though thinking of the way he'd looked at Kate Rollins, maybe it should have.

"Sorry," Chance said, "I didn't realize you wanted to see me."

"Meeting went well, didn't you think?"

"Kate knows what she's doing. No doubt about it."

No there wasn't, Ed thought. The girl had done a masterful job of communicating her plans and getting the campaign off the ground. "There's a lot to do, but at least now we have some idea how to go about it."

"We're lucky to have her."

"Damned lucky," Ed said. He just didn't like the way Chance had kept looking at her at the meeting, or the way she kept looking at him. Not that they both weren't trying their damnedest not to. That's what worried him the most.

Oh, he knew Chance had an occasional affair. He figured maybe his little girl, Rachael, might have done the same thing, living in a big city like New York, but he tried not to think about that. In a way, it was probably good to for them to get their wild oats sown before they settled down and got married. He just didn't like the notion of Chance getting in over his head.

Especially not now.

He had just received a letter from Rachael today. In another thirty days, his daughter would be finished with the modeling assignments she'd contracted for. She was going to take some time off, come back to the ranch for a couple of weeks. *I can't wait to see you, Daddy*, she'd said. *And of course Chance, too.* She'd talked about her career, but said she was getting a little tired of all the travel. *Maybe it's time I started thinking about the future.*

Ed looked up at Chance, saw him staring off toward

the cafe. Inside he caught a glimpse of Kate Rollins in the light of the kitchen window.

Maybe it was time? As far as Ed was concerned it was high time indeed.

Kate got up early Thursday morning, worked on some ideas she had for the layout of the brochure, then headed over to the restaurant. Breakfast was busy, lunch was pretty much average. She'd started into the kitchen with the last tray of dirty dishes just as Myra walked out and the two of them nearly collided.

"You been doin' that all day," Myra said with a sparkle in her eye. "Wouldn't have nothin' to do with that date you got tonight with Chance McLain?"

Actually, it had everything to do with it. Ever since he had kissed her after the meeting, she couldn't get him out of her head. Now he was even interfering in her work!

"I shouldn't be going out with him," Kate said with a sigh, moving past Myra into the kitchen. "It's obvious the kind of man he is. If he has all the women you say he does—"

"I said the women all chase after him—there's a big difference. Oh, he's got his lady friends, all right—the man's only human, after all. And it gets darned lonely way out here. But Chance is a good man. From what I know, he's gone out of his way to be honest with the women he sees. He just hasn't met the right gal yet."

Kate set the tray of dishes down on the counter. "It doesn't really matter. I'm not ready to get involved in any sort of relationship. I don't think Chance is, either."

Myra cocked her head. "Sometimes whether you're ready or not don't make a damn." Hanging her apron on the peg beside the door, she turned and strolled out of the kitchen.

Kate followed her out, trying not to think about what Myra had said. "I've got a couple of calls to make. If you need me, I'll be over in my office."

"You're supposed to be off after lunch during the week or have you already forgot?"

Kate grinned. She was basically a workaholic, but she was trying hard to reform. With a wave at Myra, she left the cafe and started up the gravel road that led up the hill to the big white, two-story, wood-frame house. Upstairs in her office, she flipped open the file she had started on Nell Hart and called the sheriff's number written inside. This time she reached him.

The conversation was brief and completely one-sided.

"But surely just looking at the report wouldn't hurt anything. I'm her granddaughter. I just want to know what happened. If this happened to someone in your family, surely you'd want to know."

"I'm sorry, Ms. Rollins. The accident report is confidential."

"What about the coroner's report? Can't I at least take a look at that?"

"I'm afraid what your asking is impossible." Sheriff Conrad patiently explained the rules, which seemed ridiculous to Kate. Since it was obvious no amount of arguing would convince the man to change his mind, she forced a little politeness into her voice, thanked him for his patience, and hung up the phone, wondering what new tack she might take.

The August day was warm. A soft breeze blew in through the screen door. As she turned and headed back downstairs, she noticed a tall figure climbing the front porch stairs—Chance McLain. Her stomach did its usual barrel roll, but Kate ignored it. Their supper date wasn't until later tonight.

A hopeful thought struck. Maybe something had come up and he had come to cancel.

Wishing she'd at least had a chance to comb her hair and change out of her pink nylon uniform, she pulled open the door. Hat in hand, he stood in front of her, dressed in a white, long-sleeved shirt with pearl snaps, black lizard boots, and the jeans he always wore, though these were newer, not yet faded, obviously worn for a special occasion.

Her heart skipped. She told herself it wasn't because she was glad to see him.

"Has my memory failed," she asked, "or aren't you here about four hours early?"

Chance just smiled, opened the screen door, and stepped into the entry. He took a quick look around, assessing the newly refinished hardwood floors, the over-stuffed sofa, and freshly lemon-oiled antiques.

"The place looks terrific. I think Nell would have approved."

She didn't really care whether Nell Hart liked it or not, but she didn't say so. Like everyone else, Chance was convinced Nell was a paragon of virtue. Kate saw her more from her mother's point of view.

"If you've come about our date—I mean if something more important's come up—"

Chance grinned. "I can't think of anything more important than taking you to dinner."

Kate wet her lips. "If you're here about the campaign, I can show you what I've done so far with the layout on the brochures."

"Actually, I'm on my way to Polson. I remembered you were usually free in the afternoons. I know you wanted to go back and talk to the sheriff. I thought if you could get someone to cover for you later, you might want to come along."

Kate sighed. "I did talk to the sheriff. In fact, I just hung up the phone. Unfortunately, he won't let me see the accident report or the autopsy. I suppose I'll have to get a lawyer. Maybe there's some legal avenue I can use."

"It's that important?" He studied her face, trying to read her motives.

Kate kept her expression carefully blank. "I want to know what happened. Is that really so hard to understand?"

Chance's gaze held hers a moment more, making her want to squirm. "Maybe not. Tell you what. The sheriff—Barney Conrad—is a friend of mine. He owes me a couple of favors. If you want to come along, I can probably get him to let you read that report."

Her heart took a leap. "Do you really think he would?"

"Like I said, he owes me a couple of favors."

Kate wondered what sort of favors but didn't ask. Chance McLain was one of the wealthiest land owners in the county. That gave him a certain amount of power. He just might be able to help her.

"All right, I'd love to come along."

"What about David? Do you think he might want to come with us?"

She smiled just because he'd been kind enough to ask. Most men wouldn't have wanted to be bothered with a twelve-year-old boy. But summer school was over and since David hadn't made any new friends, he was more lonely than ever. He would probably have jumped at the opportunity to go if he had been home.

"David's off fishing with Chief. I think you've made a convert. Until you taught him how to fly fish, he was always talking about going back to LA. He hasn't said a word about it lately."

"I'm glad to hear it. I like your son." He smiled. "Almost as much as I like his mother."

Kate flushed a little, wondering if he meant it. She left him and hurried upstairs, phoned Bonnie to cover her evening shift, then changed into a clean pair of jeans, a cream silk blouse, and a brown tweed sport coat with leather patches on the elbows. She didn't want to look like a city girl, but she didn't want to look like a hayseed, either. She wrote David a quick note, pinned it on the message board in the kitchen, then returned to where Chance stood waiting in the living room.

She flashed him a sunny smile. "I'm ready when you are."

"If you're waitin' for me, darlin', you're backin' up. Let's go."

Kate grabbed her purse and walked past him out the door, her chest oddly full at his endearment. She couldn't help wondering if he called every woman that. It was a Western-man kind of thing. Undoubtedly he did. It was ridiculous to wish he had meant the word especially for her.

Chapter Eleven

Sitting on the comfortable seat, Kate watched Chance drive the busy, two-lane road to Polson with the same confident nonchalance he had shown before, handling the big Dodge as if it were a sports car instead of a truck she could barely climb into.

They made casual conversation along the way, Chance asking about David, how he was adjusting, whether or not he had begun to make friends.

Kate sighed. "He spends most of his time with Chief, which is fine, of course, certainly better than the kids he hung around with in LA. I just wish he had a few friends his own age. Now that summer school is out there's even less hope of that happening."

Chance seemed to mull that over. "He's a good boy. In time the other kids will figure that out. In the meantime, at least he's staying out of trouble."

True, thank God, but lately he seemed to be withdrawing again, spending more and more time up in his room. Still, her son was hardly Chance's problem. "What about you? You haven't lost any more cattle?"

Chance shook his head. "We've been keeping a close watch lately. No more problems so far."

They turned down the main street of Polson. Chance drove into a parking area behind a wood frame building and backed the truck up to a big metal roll-up door.

"While they load the feed I ordered last time I was in town, we can go over and the see the sheriff."

Kate waited for Chance to come around and open the door. She was usually too liberated for that sort of thing, but the truck was so high she didn't have much choice. And in truth, it felt kind of good being with a man who had old-fashioned manners.

They started walking the two blocks to the courthouse, Kate hurrying to keep up with those long legs of his. When he realized he was walking too fast, he slowed down.

"Sorry. I guess I'm not used to someone so small."

Her lips tightened. "I'm not that small."

One of his eyebrows quirked up. He looked like he was fighting a grin. "My mistake," he said with only a slight twitch of his lips.

They rounded the corner and walked up the long cement sidewalk leading to the three-story brick building that housed the sheriff's office. Chance pushed open the heavy glass doors out in front and they continued on into the lobby.

"Give me a minute," he said. "This won't take long."

Kate wandered while he spoke to the sheriff, filling the time by reading the community posters taped on the walls: The Silver County Fair and Rodeo, coming

up in two weeks, the 103rd Annual Arlee Powwow, scheduled for next Sunday; the 4-H Horse Show at the Polson
fairgrounds the end of the month. She smiled to think
how different life was up here.

"Kate?"

She turned at the sound of Chance's voice and he
motioned for her to join him.

"You talked him into it?" she whispered when she
reached him, only a little surprised.

"He didn't much like it, but he grudgingly agreed."
Chance grinned. "I told him he owed me for keeping
quiet about what happened at his bachelor party the
night before he got remarried last year."

Kate laughed. "So now I suppose I'm the one who's
in your debt."

Chance's blue eyes seemed to dance. "Maybe. If you
are, I'm sure I can think of a way for you to repay me."

Kate made no reply but her legs felt suddenly shaky.
What would Chance McLain want in return? Images of
his tall, sinewy body, naked and lying on top of her,
made perspiration bead between her breasts. Kate
walked through the door with her shoulders a little
straighter, forcing her mind to the meeting ahead.

Sheriff Barney Conrad stood waiting. He was almost
as tall as Chance, spare and fit, with brown hair and
hazel eyes. He was a man in his forties whose smile
showed a few too many teeth, but they were white and
even, his lips curved up in a friendly manner. Still, she
couldn't help thinking it was the smile of a consummate
politician.

"Ms. Rollins. It's a pleasure to meet you. Chance says
you're new to Montana. Welcome to Silver County."

"Thank you, Sheriff."

He led them into his private office and closed the

frosted-glass door. Reaching down, he picked up the manila folder lying on his desk and handed it over. "You realize these files are confidential. We don't usually share the information outside the office. However, since there are mitigating circumstances in this case, I suppose we can bend the rules just this once."

The mitigating circumstances being his behavior at the bachelor party? Kate just smiled. "Thank you, Sheriff. Since I never had the chance to know my grandmother, I'd like to find out as much about her as I can. Even the way she died is of interest." *Especially the way she died,* she silently amended, opening the file.

She had never read a sheriff's report, but it looked fairly straightforward. Case number. Date of occurrence. Name of the parties involved. Next came a description of the deceased, Nell Mary Beth Hart. *Mary Beth.* It was her mother's real name. She had changed it from Mary Beth Hart Lambert to Celeste Heart because she thought it sounded more glamorous.

It was a surprise to find Nell had shared her name with her daughter, an ironic sort of bond, since in life they had been so far apart.

She continued to read the report. The deputy, an officer named Greer, described the scene, that he had come upon a woman in her seventies, approximately five feet in height, weighing 95 to 105 pounds on the floor of the dining room of the house at 48 Sandy Creek Road in Lost Peak. It went on to give details of the accident scene and what the officer believed had occurred.

In response to a 911 call from a Mrs. Aida Whittaker, a close friend of the deceased who had arrived for a visit, I pulled up in front of the house at approximately 3:12

*pm. On entering the house, I discovered the body of a
female Caucasian personally known to me for more than
ten years to be Nell Hart. The deceased appeared to have
been dead for at least several hours. An examination of
the scene indicated she had tripped over a throw rug that
was found entangled between her feet. The subsequent
fall had apparently caused her to hit the back of her head
on a corner of the sideboard. There was trauma to the
head that resulted in a large amount of bleeding.*

*No other marks were evident on the body. There were
no signs of forced entry and no signs of a struggle.*

Kate read on, trying not to be moved by the picture
of the old woman dying alone on the floor of her home.

She cast a look at Chance. "It says there was no forced
entry. Would you know if Nell kept her doors locked?"

"I doubt it. Nobody around here does."

Kate went over the report one last time, memorizing
the details, but seeing nothing that seemed significant.
She handed back the file.

"Thank you, Sheriff Conrad. I believe I understand
what happened. Now if I could just see the autopsy
report, I'll be—"

"I'm sorry. I thought you understood. Silver County
is small and far from wealthy. In instances such as these,
where the manner of death is so completely clear-cut,
an autopsy is not performed. It saves the family a certain
amount of grief and the county a considerable sum of
money."

"But surely—"

"This is Montana, Kate," Chance gently put in. "Your
grandmother was seventy-two years old. When people
reach that age, sometimes unfortunate things happen.
We've learned to accept that out here."

Kate held her tongue. Chance was probably right. Even in the city, people had accidents all the time, some of them fatal. It wasn't unusual. It was just part of living.

So why did she feel so strongly that in this case everyone was wrong?

She gave the sheriff the politest smile she could muster. "I appreciate your help, Sheriff Conrad. I'm sorry for any trouble I might have caused."

His politician's smile slid back in place. "No trouble at all, Ms. Rollins. That's what we're here for—to serve those in need."

Chance settled a hand at the small of her back and they started toward the door.

"Thanks, Barney," he called back over his shoulder. Outside the building, they walked in silence back to the feed store. The pickup was loaded and ready when they got there. Chance paid for the feed, helped her climb into the cab, then slid into the driver's seat and closed the door.

He eyed her with a long scrutiny. "You're awfully quiet. I thought once you saw the report you'd feel better."

She tried for a smile, but it faltered. "Thanks for helping."

"What is it, Kate? Why is this so important? What is it you're not telling me?"

She stared down at her lap, remembering the gunshot that had very nearly killed her, the anguish she had seen that night in her grandmother's face; thinking of Chet Munson and the terrible newspaper stories; wishing she could tell him the truth.

Knowing he would think she was out of her mind.

"I don't know, Chance. Something about it just keeps nagging me. I can't seem to let it go."

He reached over and caught her hand, laced her fingers with his. "It's natural, I suppose, to wonder what happened when you lose someone in your family. I gather yours is pretty small. That probably makes it worse."

Kate didn't answer. She didn't really have a family, only she and David and a couple of distant cousins.

"It's almost five o'clock," Chance said with a glance at his big chrome wristwatch. "Why don't we go over to the El Rio and I'll buy you a margarita? You're a California girl. You gotta like margaritas."

She did, though she hadn't had one in as long as she could remember. She worked up a smile. "Sounds like a winner to me."

Chance fired up the pickup. They skirted the bottom of Flathead Lake, where Polson was situated, and arrived at a restaurant that overlooked the river. The parking lot wasn't full this early, but a few cars were lined up out front. A white Jeep Cherokee pulled up just as Chance opened her door and helped her down. She couldn't miss the scowl on his face.

"What is it?" She followed his gaze to the men getting out of the Cherokee.

"Lon Barton and some of his cronies. Just my luck I'd run into them tonight." His hard look said he had plans that didn't include anyone but the two of them, and Kate felt a soft, unexpected quiver of desire.

"Come on," he said. "We were here first and those margaritas still sound good." She let him take her hand and tug her toward the front door of the restaurant, beating Lon Barton and his men by several seconds. The place was surprisingly sophisticated, by Montana standards, done in bright blue and lemon yellow with light wood floors, ceiling fans, and pretty mosaic tiles, more like a restaurant she might have encountered at Newport Beach.

Chance led her into the bar off to the right, which was also done Santa Fe-style. They sat down at one of the tables along the side and he ordered a pitcher of margaritas.

"A pitcher?" Kate eyed him warily. "You aren't trying to get me drunk and take advantage of me, are you?"

His mouth edged up at the corners. God, such a sexy mouth. "No, but it isn't a bad idea. It'd be interesting to see what you're like once you let your guard down."

Kate took a sip of her drink, suddenly needing the calming effect. It was cold and frosty, not exactly like the ones she used to get back home, but not bad either. "I don't let my guard down often."

"You're telling me?" He took a sip of his drink. "The question is, why not?"

Kate glanced away, nonchalantly shrugging her shoulders. "Too much at stake, I guess."

"Like what? Or am I getting too personal again?"

She took another sip of her margarita. "You are. But in this case, I suppose you have a right to know."

"I'm listening." He took another drink, licking the salt off with his tongue. It was long and wet and slick. For a minute Kate forgot what she was going to say.

She drank a little more of her margarita. "The truth is, my divorce isn't final. Technically, you're out with a married woman."

One of his eyebrows inched up. "I don't make a habit of it. In your case I suppose I can make an exception. Since I've got you in the mood to be candid, what's the problem?"

Kate sighed. "My ex-husband. Tommy's been a problem since the day I met him. He wanted a bigger settlement, which dragged things out. He threatened to sue for custody of David unless he got it. I wound up having to pay him alimony for the next five years just to get him to cooperate."

"You're kidding."

"I wish I were."

"Not exactly my kinda guy."

"No, I don't suppose he would be. He hasn't been my kinda guy for at least the last ten years."

"So why did you stay?"

"Mostly because of David. Because I didn't want what happened to me to happen to my son. I was raised without a father and I didn't want that to happen to David. Eventually I realized having a father like Tommy wasn't much better than having no father at all."

"I always wanted a mother, but my father never remarried. He thought women were only good for one thing. Fortunately, he wasn't around all that often and I never believed much of what he said when he was."

"Then you don't believe women are only good for one thing?"

His mouth edged up. "Women are good for a lot of things. I won't deny, however, sex ranks high on the list."

She couldn't help a smile. Sex had never been high on her list. With Tommy it was simply an obligation. After she discovered his endless infidelities, it dwindled to nothing at all.

She glanced over at Chance. He was watching her in that intense way of his, and her insides melted like a warm cube of butter. What would sex be like with a man like Chance? And, God above, did she dare risk finding out?

They finished their drinks, then went in to supper.

Kate hadn't eaten Mexican food since she'd left LA. Considering they were 1,500 miles from the border, the enchiladas were surprisingly good, and the chile verde that Chance ordered was downright delicious. As a side benefit, the meat and cheese soaked up the margaritas they had drunk earlier.

It wasn't quite eight o'clock when they left the restaurant, but both of them started work with the sun, and everyone in Montana seemed to live on an early-morning schedule. They had just walked out in the parking lot when she spotted the man Chance had said was Lon Barton.

He was tall and blond, maybe a couple of years older than Chance, but instead of the corporate image she had expected, Barton wore his curly yellow hair a little bit long and sported a thick blond mustache. He was dressed in a red plaid shirt and jeans, looking more like a logger than the wealthy mine owner he was.

"That you, McLain?" Barton started walking in their direction, and beneath his breath, Chance swore softly. "I thought I saw you earlier," Barton went on. "How are things going over on the Running Moon?"

Chance's dark look returned. "They could be better. I could still have six more live cows instead of six dead ones if they hadn't drunk some of that water you polluted up on the rez."

Barton stiffened. "I didn't pollute anything. If your cattle are dead, that's your problem, McLain. It's got nothing to do with me." He turned his attention to Kate, whipping a red bill cap off his head that said LIFE IS SOLID GOLD.

"I don't think we've met." He extended a hand to Kate. It was smooth and pale, she noticed as she grudgingly shook it, not work-roughened, a contrast to the blue-collar look that marked the rest of his appearance. "I'm Lon Barton. It's a pleasure to meet you, Ms. . . . ?"

"Rollins. Kate Rollins."

"Of course. You're the new owner of the Lost Peak Cafe. I've heard a great deal about you."

"I've heard about you, too, Mr. Barton."

"Lon. Please. Over the next few months we'll be seeing a lot of each other. We might as well dispense with formalities now."

Chance eased her a little behind him. "I don't think she'll be seeing all that much of you, Barton. If you're counting on opening that mine on Silver Fox Creek, it isn't going to happen."

All three of Barton's companions moved in a little closer, the tallest of the bunch edging in front of the rest. "Oh, it's gonna happen, McLain," he said. "Whether you like it or not."

"Easy, Duke," Barton warned, but the man didn't yield an inch. He was taller than Lon, about the same height as Chance, but heavier through the chest and shoulders, his fleshy face slightly ruddy. As the old saying went, he looked like he ate nails for breakfast.

"You better keep your guard dogs on a leash," Chance warned Barton. "If you don't they might wind up hurting someone."

"Yeah," Duke said, stepping forward, "and tonight that someone's gonna be you!" He swung a heavy fist, and Kate bit back a gasp of alarm, but Chance anticipated the blow and ducked it easily.

"I'm glad you did that, Mullens. I've been looking for an excuse to clean your plow for the last two years." Throwing a quick hard punch that came straight from the shoulder, Chance's long reach connected solidly with Duke Mullens's chin. The man reeled backward and nearly went down. When he regained his balance, there was bloodlust on his face and murder in his small black eyes.

Worry for Chance rose up. She didn't want him getting hurt and Duke Mullens looked more than capable of doing just that.

Bouncing once or twice on the balls of his feet, Mullens spat in the dirt and charged back toward Chance. A couple of swift left jabs took Chance by surprise. A hard right to the jaw sent him spinning into the dirt.

"Chance!" Kate started toward him, but Barton caught her arm.

"Stay out of this, Kate. You'll only get hurt."

"We can't just let them fight. Can't you do something?"

Beneath the thick mustache, his mouth curved up. "Let 'em have their fun. They've been itching for this for the last two years."

"Why?"

"Bad blood, you might say. Duke stole one of Chance's women a couple years back. I guess he doesn't cotton much to that."

Duke stole one of Chance's women. The words made her feel slightly sick. Was that what this was all about? Jealousy over one of his past lovers? Kate made no reply, just stood trembling, watching in growing horror as the two men continued to battle back and forth in the parking lot.

By now, blood was running freely from Duke Mullens's nose. Chance had a cut near the corner of his mouth and blood streamed from above his left eye down his cheek, staining his white shirt crimson. Muttering a curse at his opponent, he swung a powerful blow that would have done any normal man in. Instead, Mullens lowered his head, rammed Chance like a bull, and both men crashed to the ground.

Chance rolled on top, getting in a few good blows before Mullens shoved him away and staggered back to his feet. Chance was ready and waiting. Ignoring the blood leaking into his eye, he shot a hard left to Mullens's stomach, followed by a blow to the bigger man's jaw. A hard final blow, and Mullens sailed backward, landing hard in the dirt. This time he didn't get up.

"That was for Sherry," Chance said, wiping the blood from his mouth with the back of his hand. He bent and grabbed his Stetson up from where it had landed on the ground, slammed it on his head, and strode toward her. Wordlessly, he gripped her arm, nearly lifting her off of her feet as he tugged her toward the truck.

One quick jerk and the door flew open. Chance swung her up on the seat. In minutes they were tearing out of the parking lot, gravel flying out behind the wheels as they pulled onto the street, headed back to Highway 93 and Lost Peak.

Kate's heart still pounded. But now that she was over the shock and fear, her trembling came mostly from anger. Even the dark red blood trailing down Chance's lean cheek couldn't cool her temper.

"All right, now that you've had your fun, the next fight you're having is with me." She turned a fierce look on the man with the tight jaw staring down the road ahead of them. "Was all of that really necessary? You had to brawl like an animal because some woman you were dating dumped you for another man?"

For an instant, his long brown fingers tightened around the wheel, then he sighed. "Sherry is only a friend. We dated years ago in high school. Since then, she's been more like a sister."

"Go on."

"Duke and I played football together on the varsity squad. He was a jerk then. He's an even bigger jerk now."

"That's hardly an excuse for battering each other all over the parking lot."

His mouth tightened. "Two years ago Sherry made the unfortunate mistake of going out with him. Before the evening was over, Mullens raped her."

The air seemed to stick in Kate's lungs. Date rape. It happened all the time. "If that's true, why isn't he in jail?"

"Because Sherry wouldn't press charges. She didn't think anyone would believe her. She'd known Duke for years. She'd been divorced for a while and I guess she got lonely. That night when Duke took her home, she invited him up to her apartment. It was two in the morning and both of them had been drinking. She wanted to make him some coffee before he drove back to his apartment. Instead, once he got inside, he slapped her around, dragged her down on the sofa, and raped her."

Kate stared at the muscle flexing in his jaw. The headlights of passing cars blinked past, one after another, throwing his prominent cheekbones into shadow.

"Even if that happened," she said a little more gently, "it wasn't your fault. You had nothing to do with it."

"Like I said, Sherry's a friend. Mullens is also the SOB who does most of Barton's dirty work. Which means he's most likely the guy in charge of the dumping that killed my six cows."

Whatever argument she had left slowly faded. She lived in Montana now. Apparently people here still handled their troubles with their fists. Opening her purse,

she pulled out a Kleenex, leaned over, and dabbed at
the blood at the corner of Chance's mouth.

She could feel his lips edging up. "Thanks."

"You're welcome." She blotted the blood over his
eye, wiped it off his cheek, then tucked the Kleenex
back in her purse.

Chance cast her a sidelong glance. "You know this
wasn't exactly the evening I had planned."

"It wasn't? And here I thought you set the whole
thing up just to impress me."

"If I had, I'd have left out the part where Mullens
knocked the hell out of me." He worked his jaw back
and forth a couple of times. "Duke throws a punch like
a mule. Good thing he's clumsy."

"From the looks of you, I'd say it's a very good thing."

He chuckled and relaxed back against the seat. They
rode the rest of the way home in silence. When they
reached her house, he walked her up to the door.

"I don't suppose you're gonna invite me in."

"I don't suppose."

"Next time I promise I'll be a paragon of gentlemanly
conduct."

"Next time? After what happened tonight? Who says
there's going to be a next time?"

His expression turned intense, his eyes so blue they
looked neon. "I do, Kate." Bending forward, he kissed
her, the softest, sweetest kiss she'd ever had. Then he
groaned and the softness fled.

His mouth took hers with utter abandon, hot and
restless, possessive now, telling her what he wanted. His
tongue slid in and heat flooded into her stomach, sank
like liquid into her core. Her legs were trembling, her
heart racing madly. She could feel the jagged cut on
his lip; caught the faint, coppery taste of his blood. She

found herself swaying toward him, going up on her toes, pressing herself more closely against his solid length.

His hands slid down, wrapped around her bottom and lifted her a little more, pressing her softness into his groin. He was iron-hard and pulsing, bigger than she thought a man could be, and straining against the zipper of his jeans. A wildfire flamed inside her. Any minute she'd go up in a puff of smoke.

Chance kissed the side of her neck, then cupped a breast, massaging her nipple until it grew stiff and tight.

"I wish I hadn't screwed things up tonight," he whispered, easing back, though she no longer wanted him to, pressing a last soft kiss on her mouth. "I had plans for you that didn't include Duke Mullens. I'll make it up to you, I promise."

Kate just stood there. After watching him brawl in the dirt like a cave man, she had every reason to refuse to see him again. Instead, the fact he had been fighting for a woman he considered a friend only made him more appealing. She had never known a man like him.

"How about Saturday night?" he asked, taking a step down off the porch. "You run the place. You can take the evening off if you want. I'd like to show you the ranch. We could have supper there."

She'd love to see it. But her common sense was screaming at her to say no. At the rate they were going, sooner or later, she would wind up in Chance's bed. She wasn't ready for that to happen. She wasn't sure she ever would be. And what about the consequences? Chance was far more experienced with women than she was with men. What if all she meant to him was a simple one-night stand?

Worse than that, what if her ex-husband found out? He might start trouble with David again.

Kate looked away. "I don't think that's a good idea."

"Why not?"

"The divorce, for one thing."

"My cook is extremely discreet. And the hands know better than to gossip. No one will ever know you were there."

"Chance, I don't know . . ."

He stepped back up on the porch, framed her face between his hands. "Yes, you do, Kate. You know what's going to happen and so do I." He kissed her, very deeply, very thoroughly, then he backed away. "But I won't press you. You can have all the time you need." He stepped down off the porch. "I'll pick you up at six. I want to show you around a little before we eat."

Kate said nothing, just watched him walk away, his long-legged strides carrying him over to his pickup.

I won't press you. You can have all the time you need. The words had a calming effect. The pressure was off. They could simply be together and have a good time.

Kate sighed as she walked back into the house. And even if he meant to seduce her it wouldn't change her mind. No matter how many times between now and then she tried to talk herself out of it, in the long run, she knew she would go.

She wanted to see him. She wanted to be with him. Dear God, she wanted him to make love to her. It was the most insane thing she could possibly do.

Chapter Twelve

Chance drove back to the ranch a little slower than he usually did, mentally hashing over the night's events. His knuckles were scraped and raw, burning as his fingers wrapped around the leather-covered steering wheel.

The cut over his eye was turning a purplish blue. His lip was cut and swollen—a fact he seemed to have forgotten when he had been kissing Kate.

He thought of her and silently cursed. Damn, he'd behaved like a fool tonight, letting his temper get the best of him. He'd had a premonition of trouble the minute he'd spotted Lon Barton and Duke Mullens. He should have climbed back in his truck and driven like a bat out of hell the other way, as soon as he'd seen Barton's car.

But the truth was, he wasn't a damn bit sorry. Mullens

had deserved a beating for what he'd done. The bastard ought to be in jail.

Chance sighed. At least the first part of the evening had gone fairly well. He liked Kate Rollins. Liked her intelligence and the grit it had taken for her to move from the city to a place like Lost Peak. He even liked the fact she kept saying no to him. Not many women did. Especially not the ones he pursued the way he had Kate.

Kate had principles, something too many people lacked these days. On top of that, she had the sexiest, most desirable little body he'd ever seen. Kate wasn't tall and svelte like Rachael. She didn't have the almost unreal beauty the haughty, I'm-the-hottest-thing-in-town manner, that had attracted him to Rachael. Kate was a down-to-earth, no-nonsense kind of female, yet she was soft and feminine, voluptuous in a way that really turned him on. He could imagine all of that thick red hair spread out across his pillow. His jeans went tight every time he thought of filling his hands with those magnificent breasts.

Chance slowed the pickup and turned off the road, pulling through the big pine gate that led to the Running Moon. He'd brought a lot of women up to see the ranch, but only a few had ever been invited into his house. It was his private refuge, his place of escape from the problems he faced every time he walked out the door. Still, for some odd reason, he looked forward to showing the place to Kate.

Chance drove up the long gravel driveway that led to the big two-story log house, pressed the garage door opener on the visor above his head, and drove into the three-car garage.

Stepping out of the truck, he paused for a moment

to look out into the darkness. The night was unbelievably crisp and clear, so black you could see every star,
and there was a whole diamond spray of them. He loved
nights like these. If he hadn't been bruised and battered
from head to foot, his clothes torn and smeared with
blood—some his, most of it Duke's—he'd have driven
Kate up to the top of Lookout Mountain and they could
have watched the stars together.

Somehow he knew she would have liked that. And he
would have liked just being with her.

Chance frowned, for the first time uneasy at the train
of his thoughts. He hadn't been this attracted to a
woman in years, maybe never. For nearly as long as he
could remember, it had been clear that Rachael was
the woman he would marry. He had known her since
she was a child, had been attracted to her since the day
she'd come home from her fancy Eastern college all
grown up and looking like she'd just stepped off the
cover of *Vogue* magazine—which was exactly what she
hoped to do.

They had dated all that summer. By the time she was
ready to leave for the modeling job she had landed in
New York City, they had reached an unspoken
agreement. Eventually, when both of them were ready
to settle down, they would marry.

In time Rachael would inherit the Circle Bar F. Their
children's legacy would be a spread twice the size of
the Running Moon.

Even more important, the marriage was what Ed
wanted, and Chance owed everything to Ed.

Marrying Rachael was the best thing for all of them,
probably even Rachael. Trotting around the world as a
famous cover model could only last so long. The fashion
industry was all about youth and beauty, and it didn't

take long before a woman was simply too old. Way before that happened, Rachael would be ready to settle down.

And he would take good care of her. Ed could count on him for that.

Chance thought of her exquisitely beautiful face, her pale blond hair, and slim, boyish figure. He tried to picture himself married to Rachael, coming home to her dusty and tired after a hard day of working on the ranch.

Instead of a tall, sleek blond, the woman who came to mind was way more petite, with clouds of thick dark red hair, and soft, voluptuous curves. A man could get lost in those curves. He could imagine their softness easing his fatigue.

Chance shook his head, uncomfortable with the image. He couldn't afford to get involved with Kate, not on a serious level. Nothing could ever come of it. He was already committed to somebody else.

Then again, marriage to Rachael was still months away, maybe even years.

Chance pressed the button, lowering the garage door, and went inside the house. He was worrying for nothing. Kate wasn't looking for a permanent relationship. She wasn't even divorced from the last guy she had married. She didn't want any more from him than he wanted from her. In the meantime, they could simply enjoy each other.

A knock on the front door interrupted his thoughts. He paused halfway up the pine staircase on the way to his room.

His foreman, Roddy Darnell, stuck his head inside the door. "Sorry to bother you, Chance. Ed Fontaine stopped by earlier. Said to tell you the court's finally granted that injunction against Consolidated for the spill up on Beaver Creek."

"So old Frank Mills finally came through." They'd had a helluva time collecting enough evidence to convince a judge, but apparently it had finally happened. "It was damned sure time."

"That's what Ed said. He thought you'd want to know."

Hoping maybe this time the judge would squeeze enough money out of Consolidated to actually pay for the spill and make them think twice about letting it happen again, Chance started back up the stairs. "Thanks, Roddy."

The man didn't budge, just continued to stand in the doorway. "You all right, Chance?"

He glanced down at the blood on the front of his shirt. "Had a little misunderstanding with Duke Mullens. We got it straightened out."

Roddy cracked a smile, which he rarely did. "Mullens could use a little straightenin' out."

Chance just smiled and continued up the stairs, his mind on Consolidated Metals. He just hoped whichever judge they drew wasn't on Lon Barton's payroll.

Turning into the parking lot, Lon Barton pulled up in front of the Consolidated Metals headquarters building at the mine on Beaver Creek. All four doors on the Cherokee swung open and the men stepped out. With a wave in Lon's direction, they set off toward their cars.

"See you tomorrow, boss." Duke Mullens started after them, heading for his Chevy pickup.

"Wait a minute, Duke. There's something I need to talk to you about." Mullens turned away from others. He looked like hell, both eyes swollen nearly closed and turning black and blue, his nose broken, and his lip puffed up. Duke had lost to McLain tonight, and he didn't like it. Lon wondered how long it would take before he evened the score.

Mullens walked toward him, joining him next to the car. "Yeah, boss, what's up?" A note of interest rang in his husky voice.

Duke was always eager to do Lon's bidding and it wasn't just the pay. The jobs he did were often dangerous and risky. Sometimes they even called for a bit of rough stuff. That was the part Duke liked best. Undoubtedly he was hoping whatever it was had something to do with Chance McLain.

In a way, maybe it did.

"The Rollins woman. From what I gather, she's the one heading the campaign to stop us from overturning that cyanide ban. I want to know everything you can find out about her."

Duke's interest piqued even more. "She's a hot little number. All that fiery red hair and those big round tits. I'd like to have a taste of that myself."

"I hear she's from LA. Give Sid Battistone a call. See what he can dig up." Battistone was a private investigator Lon had used on the West Coast a couple of times before. "And while you're at it, do a little local snooping. See if you can find out why she moved to a godforsaken hole like Lost Peak."

"You got it, boss. Anything else?"

"Not at the moment. First, let's see what we find out. Might turn out to be interesting."

Duke waved as he crossed to his pickup and climbed in. Mullens was well paid. And aside from the mess he'd made of things tonight, he was good at his job. It wouldn't be long before Lon knew everything there was to know about Kate Rollins.

He wondered what secrets she kept. And what he might be able to do with them once he found out.

Kate dreamed that night. It was a dream she'd had before, disturbing thoughts about the night of the shooting. In the dream, she was floating upward, hovering above the operating table, drifting away from her body. She rose through the darkness into a long black tunnel, heading for the beautiful light at the end. When she finally reached it, she saw the warm familiar faces of people she once knew. The smiling face of her mother, the faces of lost friends.

Nell Hart was among them, in the simple blue-print housedress she had been wearing in the photo. She was trying to speak, but Kate couldn't hear her. She was pleading, reaching out to her, trying to tell her something. It was important. Urgent.

Kate tried to touch her, tried desperately to understand. *What is it?* she silently pleaded. *Tell me what it is you want me to know!* But like the dreams that had come before, it was too late.

Kate moved restlessly on the pillow, trying to escape the disturbing images, struggling to awaken. On the edge of consciousness, a single thought formed in the back of her mind, hazy at first, concentrating slowly, until it was crystal clear.

Murder.

Kate slammed wide awake. She was trembling all over, her body bathed in icy perspiration. Her mouth felt dry and her muscles were taut as a shoestring. Her hair was a damp, tangled mass that clung to her neck and shoulders. As soon as she was lucid the dream began to fade, but this time she remembered it long enough to register her last single thought.

"Murder," she whispered into the darkness of her bedroom, shivering, though the room wasn't cold. Could it possibly be true? Was that the message her grandmother had wanted to give her? Or was it only some morbid trick of her imagination?

Kate sat up in bed, her back propped uncomfortably against the antique carved wooden headboard. Maybe none of it ever happened. No brilliant white light. No faces from the past. Maybe the whole thing was just a bizarre hoax conjured in her mind. Kate rubbed her eyes, feeling limp and drained. She glanced at the digital clock beside the bed. Only four A.M. She didn't want to get up, but she was wide-awake now and there was no way she could possibly go back to sleep.

Reaching over, she snapped on the bedside lamp, tossed back the pretty blue quilt she had found on Nell's bed when she'd first moved into the house, grabbed her yellow terry cloth robe, and padded into the bathroom.

She came out feeling a little better. Not wanting to awaken David, she picked up the flashlight she kept beside the bed for emergencies, stepped out into the hall, and flipped it on. It was dark in the house. The floorboards squeaked as she climbed the narrow staircase leading up to the third floor attic.

She'd been meaning to go through her grandmother's things since she'd moved into the house. There was simply so much to do that time had slipped away. Then yesterday a copy of the will had arrived in the mail, sent as requested from Nell's attorney in Missoula, Clifton

Boggs. Kate was almost disappointed to discover no other bequests in the will except the ones to her. No one had benefited from her grandmother's death, as she had secretly thought might have occurred.

She sighed to think of it. Left with another dead end, she was almost ready to give up the search. But the dream had prodded her, refused to let her quit. She was forced to begin again and at least take this last, final step.

It was dusty up in the attic. Kate sneezed a couple of times as her robe flapped open, sending a fine, silty spray of dust into the air. She picked her way past a stack of old chairs, a shadeless lamp, a pair of outdated cross-country skis, and finally reached the towering stack of boxes.

After Nell had died, Aida Whittaker had taken charge of her things, storing clothes, costume jewelry, and all of Nell's bills and correspondence up in the attic.

Kate dug around until she located the boxes marked TAX RECORDS, PERSONAL AND BUSINESS FILES, then she pulled up a little maple rocker she hadn't had the heart to throw away and started digging through the first box in the stack.

Given the assumption Nell was actually murdered—which was a very big stretch, since she didn't have a single shred of evidence to that effect—there had to be a reason. Who would want to murder a harmless old woman? What could anyone possibly have to gain? And if it was murder, how had the murderer managed to make it look like an accident?

Random murders happened, of course. Serial killers often tortured and killed victims they came upon merely by chance. Considering there were no signs of a struggle, it didn't seem likely. Nell Hart appeared to be a strong, self-possessed woman. She wouldn't have gone down without a fight. No, she had to have known her assailant, probably even trusted him.

Motive was the key. If she could discover the why, she could begin to work on the how.

The sun was coming up by the time she was halfway through the next to last box of aging yellow papers, and so far her search had been no more fruitful than any other of her endeavors. Shoving a mass of heavy red curls out of her face, rubbing the ache in her back that zinged clear up into her neck, Kate started though the last manila folder in the box.

There were documents inside, some of them dating back a number of years: the deed to the house, the deed and chattel mortgage—paid in full—for the cafe, a bill of sale for some cattle Zach Hart had purchased. Neither Nell nor her husband ever seemed to throw anything away.

Kate pulled out another envelope, this one tattered but not looking quite so old. There was another deed inside. It was dated April 18, 1972, ten years after Zach Hart had died and three years before her grandmother had purchased the Lost Peak Cafe. Kate did a quick mental calculation. Nell had been forty-three years old.

She took a closer look at the document. Unlike the other property her grandmother had owned over the years, this piece was held jointly with someone else. She recognized the name. Silas Marshall. Silas owned the grocery store across the street. He was the man who had been kind enough to give David a part-time job when they'd first arrived in Lost Peak. Two days ago, Silas had stopped by to see her. Apparently, he'd forgiven David for stealing the package of gum. Silas offered him his old job back and, eager for the extra spending money, David had agreed.

She liked Silas Marshall.

Kate tapped the document thoughtfully against her knee, then looked down at the printing on the front. Joint Tenancy Grant Deed. It was the kind of deed married couples often used, the sort that granted the right of survivorship. If one of the parties died, all rights went to the other party.

She wondered why her grandmother would have used that kind of deed with Silas Marshall. And why he had never mentioned anything about it. Surely it was simple coincidence that Silas was the only other person Kate had discovered who had benefited from Nell Hart's death.

She studied the legal description, saw that the land was somewhere in Silver County. She wondered where it was and whether or not it had any real value. She refused to let her mind go further. Maybe they had sold the piece years ago. Maybe the property was nothing but a worthless hunk of dirt.

Still, as soon as she finished working the breakfast shift, she'd go upstairs to her office and call First American Title. She'd find out if the property was owned by Nell and Silas at the time Nell died. If it was, she'd ask for a map showing the property's location and get the tax collector's assessed evaluation of its worth.

Wondering if she had the just found the first real clue to the mystery, Kate took the document and headed downstairs.

Two days passed before Kate had a chance to learn more. She was refilling the last lunch customer's coffee cup and contemplating what she'd found out from First American Title when the screen door swung open and Chief walked in.

Kate smiled and carried the coffee pot over to the booth where he sat down.

"Want a cup?" she asked.

Chief just nodded and turned over his heavy white china mug. Kate filled it up, but made no move to leave. "Have you got a minute, Chief? There's something I'd like to ask you about."

"Plenty of time," Chief said, motioning her toward the pink padded vinyl seat on the opposite side of the booth. Kate set the pot on the table and sat down.

"I know you knew my grandmother."

Chief nodded. His domed hat rested on the seat beside him, revealing his two long silver brands. He was the absolute cliche of a wooden Indian. Inwardly, Kate smiled to think that he probably dressed that way on purpose, laughing all the while at the reaction of the tourists.

"Did you know Nell and Silas Marshall owed a piece of property together?"

He looked pensive for a moment, then the light of remembrance came into his dark eyes. "Silas wanted to buy land next to his ranch, but he needed money. He and Nell were friends. Nell offered to loan it to him. Silas refused. Said they could be partners, that the land would make a good investment."

"Why? What was so special about it?"

"Big water. Deep well. People always need water. Made Silas's property more valuable."

"I see." But she didn't really, of course. Or maybe she just didn't want to. She was beginning to think her single clue wasn't a clue at all. Nobody would kill someone for a well—would they?

"Thanks, Chief."

"Your son. He's going to be a very good fisherman."

Kate smiled with pleasure. "Is he?"

"Caught a big brown yesterday. Catch and release, though. He had to let it go."

"That's all right. I'm sure he had fun just catching it."

"He's a good boy."

"Yes, he is." Kate took the coffeepot back to the kitchen, thinking of David, wishing some of the boys his own age would give him a chance.

Myra stood just inside the door. She grabbed a dishrag off the counter as Kate walked in. " 'Bout time for you to take off for the afternoon, ain't it?"

Kate looked over at the clock. "I suppose so. I've got those brochures almost done, but I need to finish the layout for the T-shirts. David's been helping me with them. We've decided to use the slogan, 'Silver Fox Creek—More Precious Than Gold.' "

Myra smiled. "That sounds real good."

"You're sure you'll be okay without me tonight? Saturday's the busiest night of the week. Maybe I should call Chance and—"

"Bonnie's a hard worker and the customers really like her. We'll be just fine." Myra eyed her over the top of her spatula. "How 'bout you? You gonna be all right? You ain't gettin' cold feet, are you?"

If anything, the problem was exactly the opposite. Just thinking about Chance made her hot, and in far more dangerous places than her feet. "Are you kidding? If I had any brains at all, I'd run like a scared rabbit as far away from Chance McLain as I could get."

"But you don't really want to. And I think Chance would be real disappointed if you did."

"I feel like I'm getting in too deep, Myra. I don't have time for this sort of thing. I've got a business to run and a son to think about. I didn't come here to get involved with a man."

"Chance ain't just any man, honey. I think you already figured that out."

Kate didn't argue. Chance was different from the typical, LA, pseudosensitive types she had known before. He was stronger, more sure of himself. More passionate about things that were important to him.

Perhaps that was what she liked best about him. That he cared so much. A lot of men were handsome, though rarely in such a hard-edged, virile way. But few men were as passionate about life as Chance.

Kate took off her apron and hung it by the door. She'd said she would go with him, and so far she hadn't been able to convince herself not to. Besides, when she talked to Chance, she could ask him about the land Silas Marshall had owned with her grandmother. She needed to understand what sort of well was on the property, and exactly how valuable it really was. She was sure it was another dead end, and if it were, perhaps she could convince herself to let the whole thing drop.

If she did, she would also have to live with the knowledge that very likely nothing that happened the night of the shooting was real. She hadn't caught even a small glimpse of life in the Hereafter. There was nothing after you died but the end.

The real truth was, Kate wanted to believe there was a beautiful place waiting for us after we died. She wanted to believe she would see her mother and her friends again. Solving the mystery, if there was one, would prove—at least to her—that such a place was real.

Kate couldn't bring herself to give up until she'd exhausted every effort.

Chapter Thirteen

Chance pulled up in front of the house a little before six P.M. He figured Kate would keep him waiting. It was a woman kind of thing, but he didn't really mind. He'd always felt at home in Nell's old house, even more so with the comfortable overstuffed furniture and colorful accents Kate had added since she had moved in.

He knocked on the door, heard galloping footsteps racing down the stairs.

David jerked open the door. "Hi, Chance. Mom said you were taking her out tonight."

"Sure am." He stepped inside, sweeping his wide-brimmed hat off. "That is . . . if you don't mind."

He shrugged. "It's good for her to get out once in a while."

"What about you, Davy? You gettin' out much these days?"

"Me and Chief's been fishin' some. Tonight I'm spending the night at Myra's. One of her grandkids is in town. His name is Ritchie. He's my age, I guess. We're gonna watch the football game on cable."

"That sounds like fun."

"I got my job back at the grocery store. Soon as I get enough saved, I'm gonna buy myself a rod. Hope you don't mind my keepin' yours till then."

"Like I said, I've got a couple of spares. Say, I've got an idea. Tomorrow's Sunday, right?"

"So?"

"You aren't working are you?"

"I don't start till next Wednesday."

"Well, how'd you like to go horseback into the hills? Jeremy Spotted Horse and his son, Chris, are coming along. We're heading up to Moose Lake. The place has got some really great fishing."

David's expression filled with the sort of yearning Chance had seen the day he had been trying so hard to fish. It was obvious he wanted to go. Then the yearning disappeared behind a mask of indifference, and David shook his head. "No thanks. I hate horses. They're ugly and smelly. I like cars."

Inwardly Chance cursed himself. If the boy couldn't fish, it was a sure bet he couldn't ride. "Well now, that's too bad. We got a whole string of remuda up on the ranch. Some of them need exercising pretty bad. I figured you'd be perfect for the job . . . once you learned to ride."

David set his jaw. "I don't think so. I'm not interested in horses." Turning, he started back up the stairs. "I'll tell my mom you're here." Sneakers untied, baggy jeans barely hanging on his slim hips, he pounded on up to the second floor and disappeared down the hall. Chance heard him shouting for his mother, and a few minutes later, Kate stood at the top of the staircase.

"You're early," she called down.

"Just a little. I'll wait in the living room if you aren't ready yet."

"I'll only be a minute. I just have to get my purse."

Chance nodded, not really surprised. Kate wasn't the sort to play the usual female games. It was one of the things he liked about her. She returned a few minutes later, carrying a sweater, since the weather had turned cool, a small white leather purse draped over her shoulder. She looked especially pretty tonight, in a pale blue silk blouse and matching pale blue jeans. She was wearing ankle-high English riding boots, her dark red hair tied back with a light blue ribbon.

As she came down the stairs, he watched the way her breasts bobbed up and down, rubbing against the sheer blue silk, making his groin feel suddenly heavy. Kate must have noticed the look on his face, for a faint flush rose in her cheeks. By the time she reached the bottom stair, her nipples were firm little nubs and it was all he could do not to reach out and curl his fingers around one.

Damn, he was hard already and they hadn't even left the house. He had promised he wouldn't rush her, and he meant it. But tonight was gonna be one helluva damned long night.

Clamping his jaw, he mentally formed a picture of a bald-faced Hereford, the way he used to when he was in high school, anything to take his mind off sex. It was ridiculous. He'd been with more women than he could count, but none of them affected him like Kate. Fortunately, his desperate ploy worked and he began to relax a little.

"Ready?"

She nodded and he settled a hand at her waist. Guiding her out the door and down the front steps, he led her over to the pickup.

"What's this?" Kate stared down at the gleaming length of chrome below the door.

"It's a running board." He glanced away, trying to act as if he hadn't bought the damned thing just so she could climb in and out a little easier. "I needed a set of them anyway. Thought I might as well go ahead and get them."

Kate smiled up at him. "They're great." She got in with a lot less effort than she usually did, and he couldn't help feeling pleased with himself. So she was shorter than any other women he'd ever dated. So what. With a little ingenuity, it didn't make a lick of difference.

He couldn't help wondering what it would be like to take her to bed. Interesting. Definitely interesting. He groaned to think he probably wouldn't be finding out tonight.

Kate sat on the seat of the pickup, trying to calm her jittery nerves. So he was taking her up to see his ranch. It was only natural that he would be proud of it. Having supper at his house was no big deal. He had a cook, so they wouldn't be alone. Besides, Chance had old-fashioned values and she didn't believe they included pressing an unwilling woman for something she wasn't ready to give.

The question was, how unready was she?

Very unready, she told herself. Maybe she would never be ready. Her nerves relaxed a little and they drove to the ranch making easy conversation. Chance told her the latest on Consolidated Metals, mentioning the injunction the court had granted. They talked about David, Chance telling Kate about the fishing trip he'd invited David to go on and the dislike the boy had for horses.

"He doesn't really dislike them," she said. "At least I don't think he does. Jimmy Stevens, one of the boys he met in summer school, gave him a hard time about not being able to ride. His pride was stung pretty badly. Now he won't admit that he'd really like to learn."

"How about you? You ever ridden?"

"I took lessons when I was a few years younger. I rode English, though, and I was never all that good. But I loved every minute of it. I missed it when I had to give it up."

"Why did you?"

"My job, mostly. I was working more and more hours. Whenever I did get time off, I wanted to be with my son."

"What about your husband?"

"Tommy was always too busy, too wrapped up in his band. The only mistake I made with Tommy was in not leaving him a whole lot sooner."

Chance tossed her a look, but didn't say more. He drove the pickup through the big pine gate leading into the ranch, and a few minutes later they parked in front of a huge log house. The place stood two stories high, with dormer windows in the rooms upstairs and a long covered porch out in front.

"It's a lot bigger than I imagined," Kate said. "I had you pictured in a quaint little cabin."

Chance chuckled softly. "Actually I added on to the house my father built, the place I lived in as a boy. It was much smaller. But I like room to move around in. Besides, I figured someday I'd want to have kids.''

Kate said nothing to that, but a funny little quiver moved through her stomach. She had always wanted more children. She just didn't want them with Tommy. What would it be like to have a family with Chance? Kate shook her head, dismissing the image. Chance had any number of women. If he were looking for a wife, he'd have found one long before this.

And she certainly wasn't in the market for a husband. Been there, done that, thank you very much.

Still, it was fun being with him. She felt comfortable with Chance in a way she rarely did with men.

"Come on," he said, "I'll show you around." For more than an hour, they walked the grounds of the ranch, which nestled at the base of the towering Mission Mountains. Chance took her into the barn, where his foreman, a man he introduced as Roddy, was busy shoeing horses.

"We don't shoe them all," Chance said. "The boys have been working some pretty rocky country east of here so we're shoeing this bunch to use in the rough terrain."

He showed her the equipment shed, which was a big metal building that looked more like an airplane hangar. A hay baler stood at one end, along with a couple of John Deere tractors, endless miscellaneous ranch machinery and equipment, and some sleds that were used to haul hay in the winter. They walked through what he told her was the birthing barn and Kate paused to look around.

"What's that?" She pointed to a long, metal, pole-like object fitted with several feet of chain.

"Calf puller. Sometimes the calves are too big to come

normally. The chains increase the leverage. It takes a couple of men to use it, but it helps the cow deliver her calf safely and in good health."

He explained how most of the calves were delivered in the spring. "That way they have a better chance of survival. That's also when we do the branding, spraying, vaccinating, and dehorning."

They walked outside the barn and over to one of the corrals where a group of cowhands perched on the fence, watching the men in the arena.

"Some of the hands are competing in the Polson rodeo. Team roping, mostly, a few of them are calf-ropers. That big guy sitting on the fence over there, that's Billy Two Feathers. He's Lakota Sioux. He's entered in the steer wrestling."

It was all so different from anything she was used to. It was like stepping back in time, into the frames of an old Western movie, and she found it completely enchanting. "Are you going to compete?"

"Are you kidding? After I nearly got my head kicked in a couple of times riding bulls, I finally got some sense."

Kate looked out to where the men practiced team roping, now that their day's work was through. Big, rawboned steers shot out of a long, narrow shoot, then two mounted riders charged out behind them, whirling stiff nylon ropes above their heads. "I've never been to a rodeo."

Chance's astonished gaze swung to her face. "You're kidding." For a moment she lost track of the conversation. It was amazing what those brilliant blue eyes could do.

"I'm a city girl, remember?"

"They have rodeos in LA. Even Madison Square Garden in New York."

"I suppose they do. I guess I just never thought about going to one."

Chance grinned. "I'll take you, then. The Polson fair starts in two weeks. The rodeo's the first weekend. Mark your calendar. We've got a date."

Kate smiled, thinking how much fun it would be to go to a rodeo with a real, bonafide cowboy. Even a year ago, if someone had told her she'd be running a cafe in rural Montana, having dinner at a ranch, and going to an actual rodeo, she'd have thought he was out of his head.

Chance finished his tour of the ranch and led her up to the house, making a point to take her in through the heavy, carved front doors.

Kate stopped in the slate-floored entry, tilting her head back to take it all in. "It's beautiful, Chance." Constructed of big pine logs, the walls were a soft, golden yellow. The ceiling rose two stories above wide plank floors that were covered by brightly woven rugs. A massive stone fireplace dominated the room, surrounded by comfortable leather sofas.

"The original house now serves as the kitchen and guest wing," Chance said. "I built this section—the living room, dining room, and master suite."

"From what I can see, you did a fabulous job."

"Come on, I'll show the rest." He led her down the hall to the bedrooms in the guest wing, each decorated in a Western motif, accented with Indian-woven rugs and bedspreads, antique furniture, and leather chairs. The dining room, lit by a massive antler chandelier, had a long, carved wooden table big enough to seat a dozen people. They went into a study warmed by a smaller stone fireplace that matched the one in the living room.

Kate paused beside his big oak desk, which was topped by a state-of-the art computer. "I suppose I shouldn't be surprised, but I am. Your good-ol'-boy image is shattered forever."

Chance laughed. "Frankly, I'm glad to hear it." He walked over to the computer and flipped it on, sat down in the brown leather chair in front of it, and logged on to the Internet. "Believe it or not, we have our own website—*www.runningmoon.com*. The page shows some of our prize-winning Herefords as well as a list of quarter horse stallions that are currently standing at stud. It's a good way for our clients to stay in touch, and it brings in new buyers. It's just good business."

"Yes, it is."

He logged off the Net and turned off the computer. "Don't tell me you're on the Net."

"The cafe hardly needs a website, but I'd be lost without my computer, and of course I have an e-mail address. It's a great way to stay in touch with friends."

Chance smiled. "A lady of the twenty-first century."

"I guess I am." She wandered around the study, admiring the Western art on the walls and some very good wildlife photography. "Is this Jeremy Spotted Horse's work?"

Chance walked up beside her. "Some of his earlier photography. I've got some of his more recent stuff upstairs in my bedroom."

Kate tossed him a playful glance. "And I was expecting you to say something about seeing your etchings."

Chance just laughed. Kate moved slowly around the study, looking at each of the photos. She particularly admired one of a huge grizzly bear lying on its paws in a field of yellow mountain daisies.

"He's really talented, isn't he?"

"He's definitely got a knack. Lately, he's been getting a little of the recognition he deserves, but it hasn't been easy."

"Nothing's ever easy, remember?"

Those incredible blue eyes swung to her face, turning hot as she recalled too late, the subtle inference had been about making love. He was standing so close she could feel the heat of his body, smell his Old Spice cologne.

"I'd really like to kiss you," he said softly.

Her insides curled, rolled up in a neat little ball. She had no idea what she would reply until she opened her mouth and said, "Then why don't you?"

Chance didn't wait another heartbeat. He simply leaned forward, tilted his head, and pressed his lips over hers. They were firm, yet incredibly soft, and a jolt of electricity shot through her, zigzagging out through her limbs. She found herself leaning toward him, her breasts flattening out against his chest.

Chance deepened the kiss, tasting her softly, then coaxing her lips apart and taking her with his tongue. He framed her face between his hands and kissed her more deeply, tilting his head first one way and then the other. She could feel the tension in his body, the faint tremor that ran the length of his tall lean frame. Then he drew away, ending the kiss before she was ready.

One of her hands still rested on his chest, but she had no idea how it got there. Beneath her fingers, his heart beat way too fast, and the dark skin over his high cheekbones looked slightly flushed.

Chance cleared his throat. "Why don't you make

yourself comfortable while I tell Hannah we're ready to eat?''

"Hannah? That's your cook?"

He nodded. "She lives in the cabin you saw out behind the barn. She'll get dinner on the table, then she's off for the rest of the night."

Kate felt suddenly uneasy. She had thought there would be someone in the house, but it would only be the two of them. She managed to bolster a smile. "Sounds good. I'm starved."

The heat in his eyes said he was hungry, too, but not for food. And the real truth was, she would rather have had another of his intoxicating kisses than a platter of filet mignon.

As it was, they sat down to a meal of roast beef, potatoes, green beans, and salad. It was a hearty meal, a man's sort of meal, and it was delicious.

"Your Hannah is a very good cook."

Chance nodded and swallowed the bite he'd been chewing. "She's been working for us since before my father died. I guess Hannah Evert's the closest thing to a mother I've ever had."

She appeared in the dining room a few minutes later, a matronly woman in her sixties, broad-hipped and gray-haired, a walking Aunt Bea, Kate thought.

Chance shoved back his chair and came to his feet. "Hannah, this is a friend of mine, Kate Rollins. She's the new owner of the Lost Peak Cafe."

Hannah eyed her sharply. "Yeah?"

Kate politely nodded. "Hello, Hannah." The older woman continued to size her up in a way that made her want to fidget. It was obvious she was protective of the man she had raised from a boy. Kate wondered what it took to pass Hannah's inspection.

"It's a pleasure meetin' you," the woman finally said. "I hear the food's still good down to the cafe—'specially the apple pie."

Kate smiled. "I'm lucky Myra agreed to come back. I don't know what I'd have done without her."

Hannah nodded as if she approved Kate's candor, and swung her attention back to Chance. "Dessert's on the stove—apricot cobbler. Coffee's made, too. If you need anything else, just give me a holler."

"We'll be fine," Chance said. "Thanks, Hannah." The older woman disappeared back into the kitchen and a few minutes later, Kate heard the door slam closed.

"I guess we're on our own," Chance said, looking a little uncomfortable. Endearingly so, Kate thought, and the fact it was true made her own nervousness fade.

"You don't bring women here often, do you?"

"No," was all he said. Chance refilled her wine glass with a surprisingly sophisticated Napa Valley cabernet, and she took another drink.

"Why me?"

Both of them had finished their meal. Chance relaxed in his high-backed leather chair. "To tell you the truth, I'm not sure. I respect what you've done. It took a lot of guts to give up a high-paying job and move to a place like Lost Peak. But you did the right thing—for both you and your son. I guess I wanted to share a little of what I've accomplished. Maybe I was hoping you'd approve."

Kate felt a rush of pleasure. *I respect what you've done.* How many men would ever say something like that? "You have a beautiful place here, Chance. The house. The ranch. All of it. You have every right to be proud of what you've done."

Chance seemed pleased at the words. He shoved back his chair. "Come on. There's a storm coming in. Why don't I build us a fire? We can have coffee and dessert in the living room."

"Sounds wonderful. I haven't had a fire since we moved here. I've been dying to try out Nell's wood-burning stove."

"I can tell you from personal experience, it works like a charm." So saying, he disappeared outside through a door beside the fireplace and returned a few minutes later with an armload of wood. Another trip and he seemed satisfied that he had enough. Squatting in front of the big stone hearth, he had a roaring blaze going in minutes.

Kate walked over as he came to his feet. "It's obvious you've had a lot of practice at this." For a moment, they stood there staring at the flames, then Kate felt his eyes on her and slowly turned to face him.

"I've had a lot of practice at a lot of things," he said softly, roughly. Something shifted in his features, turned turbulent and hot. The kiss he claimed wasn't the soft, gentle, tender kiss she expected. It was a fierce, taking kiss that left her breathless and yearning, a wild, reckless kiss that made her legs begin to quiver and her heart beat like a drum. His mouth moved over hers as if this moment was more important than drawing his next breath, and suddenly she found herself feeling the same insane sensation.

She kissed him back with a recklessness foreign to her until now, her nails digging into his shoulders, her breasts aching, her nipples swelling. They strained toward the front of his denim shirt, rubbing, moving, the friction exquisite, drawing a moan from her throat.

"Kate," he whispered, kissing her even more deeply,

his hands sliding into her hair. The pale blue ribbon fell free and the heavy curls tumbled loose, wrapping themselves around his fingers. She could feel his barely controlled desire and it set the blood pounding in her ears, made her burn as she never had before.

"We can't do this," she whispered as he pulled her down beside him on the big bearskin rug and angled his body over hers.

He kissed the side of her neck, the hollow of her throat above the buttons on her blouse. "Tell me why not." His mouth moved lower, dampening the pale blue silk, his breath hot where it fanned over a nipple. "Tell me, and I'll stop."

Her eyes slid closed, the pleasure so intense she felt as if she were melting. "I don't . . . don't want you to stop."

Every muscle in his body tightened. She could feel the strength of him, the power. "God, Katie, you'll never know how much I've wanted to hear you say that." Chance kissed her again, tasting the inside of her mouth, stroking her deeply with his tongue. With unsteady hands, he began to unbutton her blouse, the buttons popping free one by one.

Kate didn't stop him. What she'd said was the truth. She wanted him to make love to her. Just this once, she wanted to know the touch of a man she desired, a man who could make her feel things she wasn't even sure existed, things she had only imagined in secret, forbidden dreams.

Chance slid the blouse off her shoulders, a whisper of silk that made her skin start to tingle. A pretty white lace bra pushed her heavy breasts up into soft pale hills. Chance looked at them as if they were a sacred offering.

"Incredible," he whispered, pressing his mouth to

the narrow line of cleavage between them, kissing the rounded tops, sliding his tongue inside a lacy cup to circle a nipple. A sliver of heat rose up, forming a hot, damp curl in her stomach, and Kate bit back a sob of pure pleasure. The warmth slid downward, settled in the place between her legs, and unconsciously, she arched upward, giving Chance access to her throat and shoulders. He kissed her there, unsnapped the clasp on her bra, and tossed it away.

His gaze moved downward, fastened on her naked breasts, and the blue of his eyes seemed to glow. "God, you're lovely." Reaching out, he cupped one, lightly stroked his thumb over a nipple, watched it pucker and tighten. "And so damned sexy."

He lifted the fullness into his palm, bent his head, and his teeth closed over the stiff peak at the crest. A firm little tug sent a ripple of heat to her toes. His tongue darted out, swirled around the tip, and Kate bit back a soft moan of pleasure. Then he opened his mouth, took as much of her as he could, and hot, wet, heat enveloped her.

Kate closed her eyes and tried to stop the trembling that had taken control of her body. Chance eased back down on the rug and came up over her, kissing her deeply again. She wanted to touch him, to know the contours of his body, the texture of his skin. With shaking hands, she unbuttoned his denim shirt and shoved it away from his shoulders. They were wide and hard, with thick bands of muscle across the top. His chest was broad and muscled, and covered with a fine mat of curly black hair that arrowed down between the ridges of sinew across his stomach.

Kate pressed her mouth against his warm, dark skin

and felt his muscles bunch. She ringed a flat copper nipple with her tongue and heard him groan.

Chance cupped her face in his hand. "I can't remember wanting a woman so badly." He kissed her deeply, thoroughly, his fingers moving down to caress a breast. He took her mouth in another searing kiss and in minutes both of them were naked. In the light of the blazing fire, he was all dark skin and hard male muscle, his sex jutting forward, slightly intimidating in its size and length.

Lightning flashed outside the window. The echo of thunder followed, but Kate barely heard it. His hand found the soft red curls between her legs, and he gently began to stroke her. He seemed to know exactly where to touch her, *how* to touch her, and pleasure slammed through her with the force of a class five storm. Chance spread her thighs with his knee and settled himself between them. She could feel his arousal pulsing against her, big and hot and hard.

"Chance . . . ?"

"It's all right, darlin'." He smoothed back her hair. "I'm not gonna hurt you." A soft, nibbling, tender kiss followed, then one of raging passion as he slid himself fully inside.

He was huge and throbbing, stretching her to the limit, but the fullness only heightened her pleasure. Clinging to his neck, she began to move even before he did, straining upward to take more of him. The rhythm increased, Chance moving faster, deeper, harder, his control beginning to slip, continuing as if he moved on instinct alone.

Her body tingled, tightened, her muscles as taut as a bowstring. Two more pounding thrusts and the tension inside her snapped, hurling her into a powerful climax, her body shuddering as wave after wave of pleasure washed over her. Chance followed close behind, muscles rigid, head falling back, a low growl erupting from his throat.

He held himself above her for long, pleasure-filled seconds, then the tension in his muscles began to fade. He eased himself down beside her and pulled her firmly against his side, one arm forming a pillow beneath her head.

"You all right?" He turned and brushed his lips against her temple.

Kate nodded and smiled. Drowsiness was beginning to settle in, and a wonderful, lazy contentment. The heat of the fire kept her warm and the thick bear rug felt soft against her bare skin. Her eyelids drooped closed. Snuggling closer to Chance, she drifted into a peaceful sleep.

The rhythm of his heart finally slowed to normal, no longer tried to hammer its way through his chest. In the silence of the living room, the wind blew hard through the trees and distant lightning flashed, but the fire crackled pleasantly, casting golden shadows over the woman lying on the rug beside him.

Chance let his gaze roam over her in a way he hadn't had time to do before. The urgency, the burning need to have her, had simply been too great.

Now he noticed how smooth her skin was, how soft and womanly her body looked all over. Her breasts were large, the nipples round and plump in slumber. The dark red curls between her thighs still glistened with dampness in the light of the fire, though he'd had sense enough to use a condom.

He hadn't wanted to. He'd fought the notion of a barrier between them. He'd wanted to feel her softness, to mesh with her, be part of her in a way that had never been important to him before. He wanted to absorb her into his very skin, and the fact that he did scared the living hell out of him.

He'd thought, once he made love to her, some of his attraction to her would fade. Once he had seen those luscious breasts, once he had satisfied himself with her small, womanly body, he would regain his objectivity, his control. When it came to Kate Rollins, he somehow seemed to have lost it.

He watched her sleeping, thought how lovely she looked with all that glorious red hair in a tangle around her shoulders, and his body began to stir. Reaching out, he ran a finger over her breast, lightly circled a nipple, and watched it tighten.

She was a passionate woman, incredibly responsive, though he didn't think she realized it quite yet. He drew his finger lightly down her ribcage, circled her navel, moved lower, gently stroked the flesh partially hidden beneath the damp red curls. His arousal strengthened until it grew almost painful.

He wanted her again, wanted to take her slowly this time, had, almost from the moment they had finished making love. He moved above her, bent to nibble the side of her neck, and eased himself slowly inside her. She was warm and wet and he slid in easily, impaling himself to the limit. Her eyes sprang open on a soft moan of pleasure that made him smile. He had hoped she wouldn't be angry at his method of rousing her. When she arched her back, pressing herself against him like a lazy cat, he knew that she wasn't. Chance kissed her softly and started to move.

Chapter Fourteen

Kate awakened as the first gray light of dawn filtered into the room. The wind blew outside and a light rain pattered against the windowpanes. She listened to the sounds, for a moment disoriented, not quite certain where she was. She glanced at her surroundings: a king-sized bed made of hand-hewn logs; an antique coat rack near the door that held a heavy sheepskin coat, a dusty black Stetson, and a pair of spurs. Several beautifully framed wildlife photos hung on the walls.

Vaguely she remembered Chance carrying her up to his room.

Kate bolted upright. Good grief, she was still in Chance's bed! She should have been home hours ago. What would David think when she didn't come back until dawn? Grabbing the blue terry cloth robe hanging from a hook on the bathroom door, she jammed her arms into sleeves at least eight inches too long and quickly belted the sash. She was frantically searching for her clothes when the door swung open and Chance walked in.

"You don't have to panic. David spent the night at Myra's, remember?"

The breath she had been holding rushed out of her lungs. She sighed. "That's right, I forgot." She looked up at him with suspicion. "How did you know?"

He was carrying a breakfast tray, she noticed, spotting the covered dishes and the yellow mountain daisy in the bud vase.

"David told me. And before you get your jeans in an uproar, that didn't have a damned thing to do with you ending up in my bed. I didn't plan it. In fact, I tried my best to put the notion out of my head. Then I kissed you and, well . . . it just sort of happened." He walked to where she stood, set the tray down on top of an antique steamer trunk that sat beneath the window.

"I figured you'd want to get home before David did. I knew you'd be tired. I thought I'd let you sleep a little while longer."

A flush rose into her cheeks. *He knew she'd be tired?* Of course she was tired! They'd made love most of the night. She was also pleasantly battered and deliciously sated. Making love with Chance McLain was unlike anything she had ever experienced.

Still, it was a stupid, idiotic thing to do. Chance was the kind of man women dreamed about. Strong, handsome, virile—fabulous in bed. The kind who made you fall madly in love with them.

The kind who broke your heart.

He dragged over a chair for her to sit on and crouched down on a little footstool he brought over for himself.

"I hope you like bacon and eggs. I'm a pretty fair cook, as long as it's nothing too complicated."

She gave him an uneasy smile. "Bacon and eggs sound fine, but . . ."

Her cup was being filled with his great-smelling coffee when he paused. "But what? But you wish you were home instead of still in my bed? You wish you didn't have to face me after what we did last night?"

She turned away, hugging the huge robe more tightly around her. "I guess that about sums it up." She sighed, feeling embarrassed, yet wanting him to understand. "I've only been with one other man in my life, Chance. After I found out he was cheating, even that ended. And to tell you the truth, Tommy's idea of sex was a whole lot different from yours."

His gaze held hers and it was relentless. "Are you telling me your husband couldn't satisfy you?"

Her flush deepened to the color of a ripe tomato. "I don't think it ever occurred to him to try."

Chance's lips edged up at the corners. "I'll take that as a compliment."

Kate couldn't help remembering how soft and warm those lips had felt moving over her body. A little shiver she couldn't quite control slid through her body. She glanced away, wishing again she were anywhere but there, discussing her outrageous behavior of the night before. Last night she'd seen a side of herself she had never seen before. She wasn't sure she liked it.

"Why don't we eat?" Chance said gently, tuning in, as he seemed to have a way of doing, to the sensitive nature of her mood. "Then I'll take you home."

Kate just nodded. The sooner she finished and dressed, the sooner she could escape. She needed time to think, to sort out what she'd done. She needed to make some decisions.

They finished the meal in record time and Chance showed her where he had hung up her clothes. They left the house a few minutes later, sneaking quietly out the front door while Hannah hummed away in the kitchen.

It was silent in the truck on the ride back down the hill. Searching for a topic that had nothing to do with sex, her mind grabbed onto the question she had meant to ask Chance the night before. Somehow, once he kissed her, the subject had flown right out of her head.

"Last night ... earlier in the evening, I mean, before ... " Her face turned warm, and a corner of Chance's mouth edged up. Kate ignored it and plunged ahead. "I meant to ask if you might happen to know anything about the twenty-acre parcel of land Silas Marshall owned with my grandmother. Chief was telling me there's some sort of well on it."

"Chief was telling you that?"

She bit back a smile. "Actually, what he said was, 'Big water. Deep well.' I thought you might be able to elaborate a bit more on the subject."

Chance grunted, his expression turning grim. "I know the piece. Everyone around these parts does. I wish my father had bought the property when it was for sale years ago. Unfortunately, he didn't."

"What sort of well is it?"

"Artesian. Believe it or not, that well puts out more than seven hundred gallons a minute. More important, it comes out of a rocky strata that runs for miles in an area where it's nearly impossible to find any water."

"Chief said the well was next to Silas's property, but I don't know where that is."

"A couple of miles up the mountain on the north side of Silver Fox Creek. It's right next to the section of ground that Consolidated Metals wants to develop. That's why they wanted to buy it so badly."

"Consolidated Metals wanted to buy the property?"

Chance nodded as he steered the truck around a corner. "Yeah. They'd dug half a dozen wells up there and come up dry every time. They offered Nell and Silas a small fortune for the piece, but your grandma refused to sell. She knew what it would mean to the surrounding land and animals if Consolidated put in that mine."

"What about Silas?"

"Silas wanted to sell. He said it was only good business, considering the profit they would make. Two weeks after your grandmother died, he made a deal with Consolidated. We might not be worrying about that mine going in if he hadn't. Without water, the company had some really big problems ahead of it. Once they owned the well, one of their biggest problems was solved."

Hearing Chance's last words, the air she had been breathing froze like a block of ice her chest. She hadn't bothered to ask the title company if Silas still owned the property. She simply assumed he did. But Silas had sold the land just weeks after her grandmother's death. He'd made a huge profit in the bargain.

"Kate . . . ?"

She looked up at him, the blood draining out of her face. She felt oddly light-headed, like she might actually keel over in a faint.

Chance pulled the truck to the side of the road. "What is it, Kate? Dammit, you're white as a sheet."

"I'll be all right in a minute. It's just that . . ." *That I've finally found a motive for Nell's murder.* Silas Marshall had gained a small fortune because of Nell Hart's death. Was it possible that he could have killed her?

"This has something to do with Nell, doesn't it?"

She barely heard him. "I'm . . . I'm all right now. I need to get home though, if you don't mind."

"Dammit, Kate. I know every beautiful inch of your body. I've touched you, been inside you. Can't you trust me enough to tell me what's going on?"

The heat of embarrassment washed through her, yet his words struck a chord of truth it was hard to ignore. "Even if I told you, you wouldn't believe me."

"Try me. I might surprise you." It was said with such earnestness she had to take the chance.

She dragged in a deep breath of air, hoping to bolster her courage. "All right then. I think my grandmother may have been murdered. This morning, I think you might have helped me figure out why."

Chance's gaze was so intense she had to look away. He took off his Stetson, tossed it up on the dashboard, and raked a hand through his hair. "Christ." He turned toward her. "All right, you've gone this far. Why don't you tell me the rest?"

"There isn't anything else to tell." At least nothing he would remotely accept. "I had this . . . this hunch . . . that something wasn't right about my grandmother's death. I've been digging, trying to see if I might uncover something that proves I'm right."

"Just because a man makes a profit out of an unfortunate accident doesn't mean he's capable of murder."

"I know that. But as you pointed out, there was a great deal to gain. A piece of property 'worth a small fortune'—those were your words. And the chance to build a major gold mine."

"Nell's death was an accident," Chance said firmly.

"There was no forced entry, no sign of a struggle, no reason to think it was murder. Your grandmother fell and hit her head."

"Yes, she did. I don't have any doubt about that." She looked him straight in the face. "What I'm wondering is if someone might have pushed her."

Chance sat unmoving on the car seat while the silence stretched uncomfortably thin. Reaching toward the key, he started the engine, then drove the rest of the way to Kate's house. It was obvious she was still upset, but there was nothing he could say that would soothe her. As he walked her to the door, she thanked him rather absently for showing her the ranch, dismissing their hours of lovemaking as if they had never occurred.

Chance ignored a thread of irritation. "I'll call you later," he said, trying to sound as matter-of-fact as she had. As he started back to the truck, he couldn't help thinking about their earlier conversation. She had a hunch, she'd said. Even before she came to Lost Peak. It made not the least amount of sense, yet over the years, he often followed his own gut instincts and they rarely led him astray.

Still, murder was a very long stretch. Especially when the chief suspect was Silas Marshall. Silas was seventy years old himself. For as long as Chance could remember, Silas and Nell had been friends. There was even talk that some years after Zach had died, they'd had a brief affair.

It was all just speculation, of course. Still, it was obvious that Silas had a soft spot in his heart for Nell and equally apparent the old woman cared a great deal for him. It was highly unlikely Silas would kill her, no matter how much money was involved.

Wishing the subject had never come up, he jerked open the door to his pickup and started to climb in just as Myra's old beat-up Suburban turned down the gravel lane, returning David home. Chance silently thanked God he had gotten Kate home first or she never would have forgiven him.

The car parked behind the restaurant. Myra went inside to begin her duties in the kitchen and David started jogging down the road toward home. Before he could reach his destination, another car turned down the drive, a white Ford Taurus with rental plates on the front, passing him on the drive and stopping next to where Chance's pickup was parked. Curious who it might be, he watched the door crack open and an overweight man step out at the same moment David jogged past.

The boy took one look at the man, and even from a distance, Chance could see his face turn pale. Ignoring Chance as if he weren't there, David raced up the front walk, shot up the porch steps, and jerked open the door. "It's him, Mom!" His thin voice sounded even higher that it usually did. "That fat guy from LA. You better come quick!"

Chance sat there for several long moments, knowing he should start the engine and head back to the ranch, telling himself that whatever was going on, Kate wouldn't appreciate his interference. The guy, about five-foot-eight, wearing jeans and a Dodgers' baseball cap, climbed the front porch stairs, and Chance told himself it was none of his business.

Then he saw the look of fear on Kate's face as she yanked open the screen door, and thought, *The hell it isn't.*

Before he could change his mind, he was out of the truck and moving toward the fat man standing in front of her door.

Kate stared at the man in the jeans and sneakers standing on the porch. She saw Chance striding toward him, thought of what was about to happen, and felt her world tip precariously toward disaster.

"This is private property, Mr. Munson," she said, praying she could get him to leave before Chance could reach them. "I didn't invite you here and I want you to leave."

"I just came by to talk to you. I've had a heckuva time finding you, Ms. Rollins. I think the least you could do is give me a couple of minutes."

"And I think you should leave."

"Just a few questions, that's all I ask."

Chance reached the porch and stepped between them, pulling her a little behind him. "Who the hell are you?"

Munson's face drained of color, but he didn't back away. "My name is Chet Munson. I'm a reporter for the *National Monitor*. And you would be . . . ?"

"None of your damned business. What are you doing here? What's a sleazy tabloid like the *Monitor* want with Kate?"

Oh dear God, she didn't want him to find out. "It isn't important, Chance. I just want him to leave."

A sly look came over Munson's face, his newspaper-man's instinct kicking in as he sensed a new method of getting the information he wanted. He turned his attention to Chance. "I'm here to do a followup story on the shooting."

"What shooting?"

"It doesn't matter, Chance. I just want him—"

"Last March in LA, Kate Rollins was the victim of a drive-by shooting. She nearly died. Actually, she did die. She was dead for nearly ten minutes before the doctors were able to bring her back. It was in all the papers. That's the reason I'm here."

Chance's questioning gaze swung to her. "Why didn't you tell me?"

"It wasn't important. It—"

Munson broke in before she could finish, his expression entirely too smug. "You mean she hasn't mentioned her journey to 'The Other Side'? Why, Kate caught a glimpse of heaven—or so she claims. She talked to her mother while she was there, and of course, all of her other dead friends—even her grandmother. From what I gather, the old lady gave her some sort of message. Isn't that right, Ms. Rollins?"

Kate stared at Munson, a chill creeping over her skin. "How did you know that?"

Munson smiled wolfishly. "I've got ways of finding things out. Uncovering a story is what I'm paid for."

But she hadn't told anyone about Nell. Well, almost not anyone. Just Sally and Dr. Murray, and one of the girls at the office who had read a number of books on NDE and begged to know what had happened. Kate inwardly groaned. God, why hadn't she just kept quiet?

"Kate ... ?" She could hear the uncertainty in Chance's voice, a slightly raspy note, like a file running over stone. Her chest constricted, making the air burn in her lungs.

"I want you to leave," she said to Munson. "Now. This minute. If you don't, I'm calling the sheriff."

"Now, don't be so hasty, Kate. The *National Monitor*

is willing to pay you a very hefty sum of money. Everyone wants to know what it's like in heaven."

She was starting to shake. If she didn't get him out of there soon she was going to make a fool of herself. She released a breath but it sounded more like a sob. The instant Chance heard it, he grabbed Chet Munson by the front of his coat and lifted him up on his toes.

"Ms. Rollins told you to leave. Now I'm telling you. Get the hell off her property and don't come back. If you do, you'll answer to me."

Munson's face looked pasty white. "All right, all right, I'm going."

Chance set him back on his feet, released his hold on Munson's jacket, and brushed at the wrinkles he had squeezed in the man's lapels. "Lost Peak is a very small town. You aren't welcome in it. Not now nor any time in the future. Do I make myself clear?"

Munson staggered backward a couple of paces. "Yes, yes, perfectly clear."

"Then don't let your shirttail hit your ass on your way out of here."

Munson nodded vigorously, turned, and nearly ran to his car. The tires spun and gravel flew into the air as he shoved it into reverse, then jammed on the gas and flew down the driveway to the road leading back to Highway 93.

For an instant, Kate wished she could join him, wished the boards under her feet would open up and she could drop out of sight beneath the porch.

"Mom?" David's voice, sounding reedy and thin, floated toward her from the entry.

"It's all right, David. He's gone and I don't think he'll be coming back anytime soon. Go on up to your room."

For once, David didn't argue, just pounded on up the stairs. She thought that perhaps he didn't want to face Chance.

The truth was Kate didn't either.

He stood right in front of her, so near she could feel the tension still pulsing through his body. "You gonna tell me what the hell's going on?"

How could she? What could she possibly say? She swallowed against the thickness building in her throat and forced herself to look up at him. "Nothing is going on. That awful man left and that is the end of it. Hopefully, he won't be coming back."

"That's it? That's all you've got to say?"

She swallowed, but her throat was so tight it wasn't easy. "I . . . I really appreciate your help in getting him to leave."

Those fierce blue eyes cut into her like laser beams. "What about the shooting? What about your trip to 'The Other Side'? What about Nell?"

"What . . . what about her?"

"Come on, Kate. That's what this whole murder thing is about, isn't it? That's why you've been looking into her death. Because you think she gave you some sort of message."

Her chest refused to expand for her next breath of air. She was sure she wouldn't be able to force out her next sentence. "What happened to me has nothing to do with you. I'd appreciate it if you would just let it drop. If not for my sake then for David's."

"Just let it drop," he repeated darkly, as if she had lost her wits.

"That's what I said. Besides, it really isn't any of your business."

A muscle leapt in his jaw. "You made it my business

when you stayed with me last night. Or have you forgotten about that already?"

Forgotten? How in God's name could she forget the most wonderful night of her life? But one thing had nothing to do with the other, and it was obvious if she told him the truth, he wouldn't believe her.

She simply shook her head. "I think it would be better if you left now, Chance."

"Dammit, Kate."

Her lips were starting to tremble. She didn't want him to see. "Please . . ."

Chance swore softly, foully. "All right, fine, I'll leave, if that's what you want." Muttering something about hard-headed women, Chance stormed off toward his pickup. Kate stood trembling as he climbed in and fired up the engine, jammed the truck in gear, and tore down the long gravel drive. She watched until the truck disappeared around a bend in the road, then she turned and went back inside the house.

David came down the stairs as Kate started up.

"I can't believe that guy found us," he said. "You really don't think he'll be back?"

She could see the worry in his face and a thread of guilt filtered through her. David would be starting school in just two more weeks. If the kids found out about her trip to 'The Other Side,' they would give him nothing but grief.

"I really don't think so. Munson is a coward. He isn't going to want any more trouble with Chance."

"I hope you're right," David mumbled. He paused at the bottom of the stairs. "He isn't mad, is he? Chance I mean."

Her fingers tightened around the banister. "No, honey, of course not. He just had to get back to the ranch."

David nodded as if he accepted the tale, but she wasn't sure he believed her. "Do you care if Ritchie and I go fishing? He doesn't know how yet, but he says he'd really like to learn."

Ritchie's, Myra's grandson. She worked up a fairly good smile. "I think that's a terrific idea. I gather you two got along all right last night."

"Ritchie's way cool, Mom. He's from San Francisco, but he really likes the mountains. He says he loves to come here and visit. He even said maybe I could come and visit him in San Francisco."

"Oh, honey, that's wonderful. Why don't you see if Ritchie can stay for supper? I don't think Myra will mind."

"Great, Mom, thanks." In a flash, he was out the door and on his way to the cafe, where he was meeting his new friend. Silently, Kate thanked Myra Hennings for bringing the two boys together. Kate only wished he lived somewhere near, instead of in the city.

Continuing up the stairs, she went into her bedroom, kicked off her riding boots, and tossed her sweater on the bed. Desperate for the comfort of a good, hot bath, she headed into the bathroom, threw the blouse and jeans she had worn last night into the hamper, bent and turned the taps on the old claw-foot tub.

As she stepped out of her lacy white panties, she could smell the sticky-sweet odor of sex, and a rush of heated memories flooded through her.

God above, she had slept with Chance McLain. They had made wildly erotic, incredibly passionate love. It was the most thrilling, most exciting night of her life.

How could it have turned into such a disaster?

Feeling the heavy weight of depression, Kate forced her legs to carry her over to the tub. She tested the water and found it scalding hot, the way she liked it. She climbed in and sank down. If she closed her eyes, she could still see Chet Munson standing on her doorstep, ranting and raving about her trip to heaven, shooting off his big mouth. Now Chance undoubtedly thought she was some kind of refugee from the nut ward and she would never see him again.

Leaning back against the tub, Kate sighed into the silence of the steamy room. She had warned herself time and again not to get involved with him. Instead she had gone out with him, even gone to bed with him.

The truth was she cared about Chance McLain. More than she ever intended. She wanted to see him again. She wanted to be with him.

Chet Munson's words had undoubtedly killed any possibility of that.

Closing her eyes, Kate tried not to think of Chance. She tried not to see the disbelief stamped on his face as he had listened to Chet Munson's words, or imagine what he must be thinking about her right now.

She tried, but she failed miserably.

Chapter Fifteen

Chance slammed through the door of the Antlers Saloon, an old, batten-board building across and down the street from the Lost Peak Cafe. The place was smoky, the floor littered with peanut shells, but it had a sort of old-fashioned charm, which was why the place was still open after more than fifty years.

He sat down on one of the red vinyl bar stools in front of the long oak bar and propped a boot on the tarnished brass rail.

"Chance! Kinda early to be seein' you in here, ain't it?" Maddie Webster smiled as she wiped off the bartop in front of him. "What can I get you?"

Two or three straight shots of tequila might help, but he doubted it. And Maddie was right, it was way too early. "How about a red beer? You've got Moose Drool on tap, don't you?"

She nodded. "Comin' right up." While Maddie went to get it, Chance sat staring at the old-fashioned back bar, but not really seeing it. He didn't notice Jeremy Spotted Horse till the big Indian stood over his right shoulder.

"You look like a freight train that just got derailed."

Chance sighed. "Thanks. That's just about the way I feel."

"You're not usually an early-morning drinker. Something must be stuck real tight in your craw. Want to tell me about it?"

Chance blew out a breath, knowing he should keep silent. That it wouldn't be fair to Kate. Not that he really gave a rat's ass at the moment. "Just a little woman trouble. Nothing you can do to help."

"Yeah, well, don't feel bad. Willow got pissed off about the money I spent for a new Nikon lens. She was yelling the house down, so I left."

"She'll cool down in an hour or two. She always does."

Jeremy grinned. "Yeah, that's one of the things I love about her. She doesn't hold a grudge."

Chance thought about Kate and couldn't help feeling a twinge of bitterness that she had refused to confide in him. He took a sip of his beer, looked over at Jeremy, who had climbed up on the stool beside him. "You ever thought about what it would be like to die?"

Jeremy just grunted. "Painful."

"I don't mean the dying part. I mean the after. You know, what you might find on the other side, once you pass away. You ever try to imagine what might be waiting out there?"

"I don't have to imagine it. I've seen it. A lot of us have."

"What do you mean?"

"I'm talking about a vision quest. When an Indian seeks a vision, he travels to *Schi-mas-ket*—the land of the Great Spirit. That's where our visions come from."

"I remember when we were boys, you talked about it. Three days on the mountain. No food, barely any water. I'd forgotten all about it."

"It isn't something I'll ever forget. By the end of the third day, I was thirsty, cold, and hungry enough to eat a buffalo—raw. But the hours finally paid off."

"What happened?"

"My vision finally came. I saw my great-grandfather, Many Feathers. He talked to me for a while, then he transformed into an eagle right in front of my eyes. The two of us soared into the sky above the mountains. I remember how much we could see from up there— deer, moose, bear, huge pine forests, beautiful lakes, roaring rivers. I wanted to be like the eagle, to see everything as clearly as I saw it then, and I wanted to be able to remember. That was my quest. That's the reason I learned to take pictures."

Chance felt the oddest sensation. He took a sip of his beer and tomato juice, the only thing his stomach could handle this early in the day. "Kate says she's been to the other side. She says she saw her dead friends there. She claims she spoke to Nell Hart. She thinks Nell may have been murdered."

Jeremy blew on the cup of coffee Maddie had poured and set in front of him. "Interesting."

"You could say that."

"That's the trouble you were talking about?"

He nodded and Jeremy shrugged. "So Kate's had a vision—what's the big deal? The Salish would think that makes her a very special woman."

Elbows propped on the bar, Chance raked both hands

through his hair. "She didn't want to talk about it. She didn't think I'd believe what she had to say."

"Would you?"

"I don't know, probably not at the time. She doesn't want anyone in Lost Peak to know. I think that's one of the reasons she came here. Apparently, something was printed in the newspapers about it. It was probably hard on her son."

"Having a vision is nothing to be ashamed of."

Some of the tension eased from his body. For the first time that morning, Chance drew an easy breath. "No, I guess it isn't." He was glad he had spoken to Jeremy. He trusted him, and he knew that Kate could trust him, too.

"Maybe you should tell her that."

Chance mulled that over, feeling a little like a fool. He never questioned Jeremy's beliefs, or those of his other Indian friends. Why was it so hard to believe the same sort of thing had happened to Kate?

"I'll give it some thought." Pulling a couple of dollars out of his pocket, he tossed them onto the bar. "Weather's beginning to clear. We still going fishing today?"

Jeremy nodded. "Your place at noon. Chris has been looking forward to this all week."

Leaving his barely touched beer on the bar, Chance got up from his stool and headed for the door. "I'll have the horses saddled and ready," he called over his shoulder. "See you at noon."

By the time Kate finished her bath, she was feeling a little bit better. Telling herself she had more important things to do than mope over Chance McLain, she headed down the hall to her office and turned on her computer. She wanted to track down information, and the Internet was the fastest way she knew.

Assuming Nell had actually been murdered—still a very shaky assumption—the house was most likely the murder scene. If that was the case, there might be clues right under her nose. The police would use forensic techniques in this sort of investigation, but so far, she had nothing to take to them, only her unconfirmed suspicions. If she were going to find any clues, she would have to dig them up herself.

"All right," she muttered, "let's see what we can find out." Logging onto Yahoo, she typed in "forensic science," and let the search engine go to work.

The list that came up was lengthy. She began exploring each site one at a time, starting with *www.tncrimlaw. com/forensic* Carpenter's Forensic Science Resources. The site had its own list of suggested links: forensic medicine and pathology; forensic chemistry and toxicology; forensic DNA analysis; criminalistic and trace evidence—the sources went on and on.

She started with general forensic homepages and set to work.

Three hours later, the phone rang, and Kate had to rouse herself out of her computer trance to answer it. She recognized the whining tone of her ex-husband's voice and drew in a steadying breath.

"Hello, Tommy."

"Kaitlin—it's good to hear your voice." Kaitlin. He never called her that unless he wanted something. Kate pressed her fingers against the bridge of her nose, trying to stop the headache that had suddenly begun to throb.

"I've been wanting to talk to you," Tommy said. "I just got the final divorce settlement papers."

Now that *was* good news.

"I've been thinking, Kate. We were married nearly thirteen years. That's a lot to throw away. Maybe we got too hasty, you know what I mean? We have to think of David. For his sake, maybe we ought to call this whole thing off. Give it another try."

Her shoulders went tense. Anger bubbled like hot oil in her throat. Who was he kidding? Tommy couldn't care less about their marriage, or even about his own son.

"What's the matter, Tommy? Now that you're having to pay your own way, you just figured out how much it costs to live?"

She could hear his teeth grinding over the phone. "Always a smart ass, aren't you, Kate."

"I'm a lot smarter than I used to be, that's for sure. Smart enough to know when you're trying to con me."

"You love to put me down—you always have. I must have been crazy to think you might have changed."

Her fingers tightened around the phone. "You're crazy, all right—if you believe for an instant I'd ever consider going back to you."

"You bitch."

Kate sighed into the receiver. "Just sign the papers, Tommy. Let's get this whole thing over with once and for all."

"I'll sign the fucking papers. You can bet on that. But one of these days you're gonna be sorry." The phone clicked loudly in her ear and Kate set the receiver gently back down in its cradle. He'd mentioned David, but only because he'd wanted something. He hadn't asked about his son's welfare, hadn't asked to speak to him. She shouldn't have been surprised but somehow she was.

The final settlement papers hadn't reached her yet.

Mail took forever in Montana, but they were on their way. Soon the divorce would be final and she could put that part of her life behind her.

Returning her attention to the computer, she reached for the stack of information she had printed off the Web, then glanced at the notes she had made.

By the time she finished reviewing it all and read the books she had ordered, she would at least have some idea how the whole thing worked. She wasn't ready to tackle the job of actually searching for evidence, but sooner or later, she'd know enough to give it a try.

In the meantime, she intended to speak to the undertaker. According to one of the sites she had visited, morticians had, on occasions when no autopsy was performed, stumbled upon something out of the ordinary that they reported to police. As far as she knew, that hadn't happened in Nell's case, but it was worth a try.

She was usually off in the afternoons. A quick trip to the Dorfman Funeral Home in Polson, where Nell's body had been taken after the accident, wouldn't be much trouble. It was one more item on her list and at least worth a try.

Kate took her pile of research material, headed back to her bedroom, and settled in to read.

After a pleasant trip into the hills, Chance, Jeremy, and Chris arrived back at the ranch late in the afternoon. Though the fishing had been good and the weather had turned clear, Chance had wished a dozen times that he could go back and see Kate. He couldn't. Not yet. He was afraid she still wouldn't talk to him.

Instead, on Monday afternoon, he saddled Skates and a couple of other horses, gauging his arrival about the time he figured the lunch shift would be over and Kate would be back at the house.

Leading a couple of gentle mares, he headed cross-country, taking the trail that led to the fence line behind her house. He hoped by now Kate would be more amenable to hearing what he had to say, and bringing a horse for David was a little added insurance. Kate might refuse to go with him, but she wouldn't be able to refuse her son . . . assuming he could convince the boy to join them.

Unwiring the makeshift gate in the fence between their properties, he rode onto her eighty-acre parcel, forded Little Sandy Creek, and led the mares up in her back yard. The old hitching rail, a fixture on the property for over eighty years, still remained standing. He tied the horses up at the rail, walked over, and knocked on Kate's back door.

A few minutes later, she pulled it open. "Chance . . . ? What . . . what are you doing here?" She was obviously surprised to see him and he couldn't blame her, after the way he'd acted the last time he was there.

His eyes ran the length of her, which didn't take all that long, as short as she was, and he thought that she looked even prettier than she had the last time he had seen her. She was dressed in a tight-fitting pair of jeans that cupped her bottom the way he suddenly itched to do, and a red plaid shirt that pulled a little across her bosom when she moved. Her cheeks were bright with color, her eyes as green as the grass outside her door.

He cleared his throat and kept his eyes on her face. "I was hoping you might have time to talk. I remembered what you said about liking to ride. I thought maybe we could take off up in the hills for a couple of hours. I figured we might convince David to come with us."

She eyed him with a hint of suspicion. She might have said no if the boy hadn't slammed out the door at that very moment, looking even more surprised to see him than his mother had. Apparently, they both thought Munson's revelation had ended their newly formed friendship. Chance inwardly cursed.

"Hi, Davy."

"Hi, Chance." The boy's wary glance slid over to the horses.

"I know you haven't started working at the store yet. I thought you and your mom might want to go for a ride."

"I told you, I hate horses."

"Yeah, well, sometimes, I do, too. Especially when one of 'em's acting like a bonehead. But other times, they can sure be a lot of fun." Ignoring Kate's steady gaze, he went over and untied the little white-stockinged sorrel he had brought for David. She was fifteen years old and so gentle just about anyone could ride her.

"This is Mandy. She's got a real pleasant nature. I thought maybe you might want to give her a try."

David shook his head. "No thanks."

Damn, this wasn't going to be as easy as he had planned. Chance ran a hand along the mare's smooth neck. "She needs exercising real bad. I was hoping you would do it . . . you know, sort of as a favor."

"A favor? What do you mean? Are you asking me for help?"

"Yeah, I guess I am. Mandy's kind of a favorite of mine. I don't let just anyone ride her. I figured I could trust her with you."

David seemed to waver. Chance could read the indecision on his face. He wanted to go, but he didn't want to look like a fool. "You let me borrow your fishing rod. I suppose I owe you for that."

"Like I said, I hate to ask."

"I never learned to ride, you know." David moved closer, till he stood next to the stirrup.

"It just takes a little getting used to. With a little practice, I bet you could be really good."

David looked up. "You really think so?"

"I know potential when I see it. Here, just slide your foot in the stirrup, grab hold of the saddle horn, and you can pull yourself up." With a little boost from Chance, David found himself in the saddle. He slid his foot into the stirrup on the opposite side.

"I had to guess how long to make them," Chance said. "How do they feel? About the right length?"

"I guess so."

"Stand up. If you can stick two fingers between you and the seat, they're just about right." David did and it was.

"Good. Now here's how you rein." For the next half hour, Chance showed the boy how to make the animal turn, how to stop, and how to go. All the while, Kate stood watching, an uneasy look on her face.

"You're doin' great, Davy. If your mom says it's okay, the three of us can go for a ride."

"I don't know, Chance," she said. "Jeremy brought over some slides this morning. Some of them show that spill up on Beaver Creek. I wanted to work on the slide show we're putting together for some of the environmental groups."

Chance strode over to where she stood warily on the back porch. "Come with us, Kate, please?"

"Come on, Mom. I'm not going if you don't."

As Chance had hoped, the boy's insistence persuaded her. "All right, but I can't stay away too long."

Taking her hand, he led her over to the little mare, Tulip, an extremely manageable twelve-year-old quarter horse with a comfortable gait. He helped Kate swing up in the saddle and adjusted the stirrups a little shorter.

"Ready?" he asked. Kate nodded, but she didn't look all that pleased. Walking the animals back across the river, he led them single file through the gate leading onto his property, and up into the hills, hoping the next couple of hours would go better than the one that had passed so far.

Riding single file, Kate's little mare followed David's sorrel and Chance's paint along the narrow trail. She had to admit it felt good to be riding again, different in the heavy Western saddle, but just as exhilarating as she remembered.

They rode through dense forests and out into wide-open pastures, passing herds of white-faced steers and an occasional deer or rabbit.

An hour into the ride, Chance reined the paint up beneath a pine tree at the edge of a stream. "Cedar Creek is usually pretty good fishing." He swung down from his horse, walked over and helped David down. "I brought a fly rod. I thought you might want to try your hand while I talk to your mom."

David studied his face and a look passed between them. Her son was no fool and Chance didn't treat him like one. He took the rod Chance held out, along with a small box of flies, and walked off toward the stream.

As David waded into the shallow creek bed and began to cast his line, Chance turned his attention to Kate.

She could feel his gentle blue gaze as if he reached out and touched her.

"I'm glad you came," he said.

She was holding the reins, letting the little mare graze. "You tricked me into coming and you know it. You used my son as bait. You knew I couldn't refuse him."

His faint smile was unrepentant. "Guilty as charged. I don't think David minded, do you?"

She couldn't help smiling in return. "I think it was wonderful the way you convinced him to give it a try."

"Now all I have to do is convince his mom."

Kate waited while Chance pulled a blanket from his saddlebag and spread it out on the ground beneath the tree. He tied the horses up to graze a little way away and returned to where she sat on the blanket, her legs curled up beneath her.

"You've been awfully quiet today." He sat down cross-legged beside her, plucked a piece of long-stemmed grass, and twirled it in his hands. His fingers were long and dark and she couldn't help remembering how they had felt moving over her body.

"I didn't expect to see you again."

"Did you really think something some idiot like Chet Munson said could keep me away?"

She looked up at him. "Actually, I did."

"Because you figure if you were to tell me what happened in LA I'd think you were crazy."

"I know how bad it sounds. That's why I didn't tell you in the first place. Everyone else thinks I'm crazy, why shouldn't you?" For a moment, Kate closed her eyes, fighting the urge to climb back on the mare and ride as fast as she could back to the house.

"I want to hear your version of what happened. Then it's up to me to decide what I will and won't believe."

Kate smoothed a wrinkle in the blanket. Maybe it was time he knew. By now he knew most of it anyway. "All right, but don't say I didn't warn you."

For the next twenty minutes, she explained about the shooting, and what had happened to her the night she had died. She left nothing out, not even the part about her grandmother and the message she had only partially received.

"I realize it sounds completely nuts. But I believe it really happened." She told him about the photograph of Nell she had found. "That's how I knew who the woman was. Until I found the photo, I had never seen her face."

Chance twirled the black hat resting on one bent knee. "And you think she was trying to tell you she was murdered."

"I'm not sure. I think it was something about her death, or the way she died. I've had dreams about it since then. In the dreams, she's trying to tell me that she was murdered."

She watched his expression, waiting for the condemnation to appear. Instead, when he finally looked at her, a faint smile softened the lines of his face.

"My grandmother was a full-blooded Blackfoot Indian. She believed in the land of the Great Spirit. She talked to me about it when I was a boy. I hadn't thought about it in years. Jeremy Spotted Horse and a lot of the men on the rez have experienced visions. Sometimes it tells them things about the past or the future. A vision quest, they call it. I don't suppose it's fair to accept what they believe is real and not believe what you say."

Her throat went tight. Tears welled up in her eyes. Until that moment, she hadn't realized how badly she had wanted him to believe her. She fumbled in the pocket of her jeans for a Kleenex, but came up empty. Chance pulled a faded red bandana from his back pocket and mopped at the wetness on her cheeks.

"It's all right, darlin'. I didn't mean to make you cry."

She took the bandana out of his hands, wiped away the rest of the moisture, then handed it back. "I need to know if it's true, Chance. If it is, then everything that happened to me that night was real. I was actually there. Such a place really exists."

"I guess I can see why it would be so important. I'd like to believe there's such a place, too." He tucked the bandana back into his hip pocket. "I won't sit here and say I'm convinced Nell Hart was murdered. But if you want to dig a little deeper, I don't see anything wrong with that. And I'll help you in any way I can."

She wanted to throw her arms around his neck. She wanted to kiss him, right there under the pine tree. "Thank you, Chance. You don't know how much that means to me."

He came to his feet and hauled her up beside him. "Next time, don't be afraid to trust me. I won't let you down, Kate."

She only nodded. Chance glanced toward the river, saw David engrossed in fishing a ways upstream, and pulled her into his arms. "I keep remembering Saturday night. God, I think about making love to you every damned minute." Softly at first, then more deeply, he kissed her. Her knees were shaking by the time he was done.

"When can I see you again?" A note of urgency rang in his voice as he kissed the side of her neck.

"I don't know, I—"

"How about Saturday night? We'll go dancing. Every

other weekend, they have a Country-Western band at the Antlers. It's really a lot of fun.''

She laughed. "I haven't the foggiest notion how to dance Country-Western, but I'd love to give it a try."

"Great. Wonderful." He bent his head and lightly brushed her lips. "Terrific." He glanced to where David had just hooked onto a big silver fish. Chance cocked his head in the boy's direction and grinned. "I think he's getting the hang of country life."

Kate followed his gaze and her heart squeezed a little. "So it seems."

"We'll give him time to show off his fish and release it, then we ought to be getting on back. The first time out, you'll be sore if you ride too long."

Gathering their horses and belongings and finally rounding up David, Chance led them back to the house a little over an hour later, David now grousing that it was far too early in the day to quit.

"You won't be saying that tonight," Chance warned with a chuckle. "It takes a little while for your muscles to adjust to the saddle. If you want, we can ride again on Wednesday, after you get home from work."

"Yes!" David shot his fist into the air, and Kate laughed. Chance smiled at her and the look on his face made her skin go tingly and warm. They reined up in front of the hitching rail. David jumped down and Chance helped Kate alight.

"What time on Wednesday?" David asked.

"What time do you get home from work?"

"Five o'clock. That isn't too late, is it?"

"It doesn't get dark this time of year till ten. We can get in a couple of hours before that."

"Great! See you Wednesday, then." David rushed off, slamming into the house and leaving them alone.

"This has been wonderful, Chance. You'll never know how much I appreciate what you're doing for David."

He glanced away, looking a little embarrassed. "I like your boy. I hope I can help him learn to fit in." Holding the horse's reins in one hand, he swung up into the saddle. Beneath the worn, soft jeans, that molded to his body, muscles tightened in his thighs, and Kate felt suddenly too warm.

"Well, I guess I'd better be going," he said with what she hoped was a hint of reluctance. "I have work to do and I imagine you do, too."

She certainly did. The slide presentation she was working on, and her other, even more important project. Tomorrow she was heading into Polson. She was hoping for a miracle, she knew, something that might help in her search.

But Kate wasn't discouraged. She knew better than anyone that miracles really did happen.

Chapter Sixteen

Leaning back in his tufted leather chair, Lon Barton skimmed the file Duke Mullens had just brought in.

"I can't believe this. The damned woman was vice president of one of the biggest ad agencies in the country."

"Yeah. And from what this says, she was making big bucks in LA."

"Sid's note says she was one of the best ad execs in the business. She would have been pretty financially set if it weren't for her divorce. The guy held her up like a bandit."

"Yeah, well, it's usually the guy who gets stuck," Duke grumbled.

Lon read on down the page. Sid Battistone was thorough, no doubt about it. Then again, for what he was being paid, he'd better be. The file told him about

Kate's fatherless childhood and that her mother had died in a car wreck when Kate was eighteen. The file held a wealth of information on her no-good, worthless husband, including the drug charges Tommy Rollins had been brought up on six years ago, and the fact he had been sponging off Kate practically since the day they were married.

He read another paragraph on down the page. "What the hell is this?"

Duke moved around till he could read the file over Lon's shoulder. "Crazy, ain't it? I guess that's the reason she moved up here—to get away from the newspaper reporters and stuff, after the shooting."

Lon reached down and picked up an article that had been clipped out of the LA *Times*. WOMAN TELLS TALE OF LIFE AFTER DEATH. Lon scanned the article, more dumbfounded by the moment.

"Jesus—it says here Kate Rollins barely survived a drive-by shooting, that she died for nearly ten minutes before they revived her. During that time, she claims to have had a near-death experience. The article quotes her as saying she talked to her dead relatives on 'The Other Side.' Do you believe that? The woman must be out of her skull."

"Yeah, and guess what? She's been nosing around ever since she got here, asking questions about her grandmother. A couple of weeks ago, she went to Polson and asked to see the sheriff's report on Nell Hart's death. She's asked half a dozen customers about her. I looked up her phone records. She's even called old Aida Whittaker."

"I wonder what the hell she's trying to find out."

"I don't know, but on Sunday, a guy from LA was in Lost Peak looking for her. Tom Webster said he came into the bar, said he was a report for the *National Monitor.*"

"The *National Monitor?* Isn't that one of those goofy tabloids you find in the grocery stores?"

"Sure is."

"Find this guy—whoever he is. Find out what he knows about Kate Rollins. A person with her background, someone who really knows how to run this anti-mining campaign, could give us big-time trouble. I want that cyanide ban overturned and I'm not about to let some big-titted redhead get in my way."

"Don't worry, boss—I'll take care of it."

Duke Mullens's smile looked downright wolfish as he headed out the door.

On Wednesday evening, as promised, Chance arrived to take David riding. Kate had traded nights off, so she could go dancing at the Antlers on Saturday, which meant she was working when Chance came over, but according to David, he had brought Chris Spotted Horse with him.

"He's an Indian, Mom," David said with a far too serious face when she got home from the cafe that night, "but he's really okay. He goes to that Indian school—Two Eagle River? But he doesn't live very far from town. Chris says he likes to fish, so we're gonna go after I get home from work on Saturday."

"Honey, that's wonderful." Kate could have hugged Chance McLain. Then again, just thinking about him made her want to do a lot more than that. Her insides vaguely quivered. She pushed the erotic, highly inappropriate thoughts away.

On Thursday, Chance and Jeremy Spotted Horse showed

up at the cafe for lunch. Kate served them her secret recipe special meatloaf. Myra was great at apple pie, but Kate had a few talents of her own.

"This is phenomenal," Chance said, mopping up the gravy with some of the cafe's homemade bread. "How do you make it?"

Kate grinned. "I could tell you, but then I'd have to kill you."

Chance laughed, a deep, entirely too masculine sound. She turned her attention to Jeremy before wicked thoughts started building in her head. "Those slides you brought over were wonderful, Jeremy. I've got the entire presentation laid out. Ed's going to have copies made and take them to the various environmental agencies next week."

"That's great, Kate." The big Salish Indian wolfed down another bite of meatloaf, the special of the day. "I've got a lot more landscape stuff, if you need it."

"I might just take you up on that." She glanced at the clock on the wall over one of the booths. "You two need anything else? I'm taking off a little early. I've got something to do in Polson and I—"

"How'd you like some company?" Chance wiped his mouth with a paper napkin. "I've got a couple of errands I need to run. It would save me making a special trip." His eyes fixed on her face and her stomach did its usual little flip.

"That'd be great."

Chance stood up and tossed down money for the check. "I'll see you on the flipside, partner," he said to Jeremy, who shot him a look Kate couldn't read.

"Don't take any wooden nickels, Kemosabe."

Chance grinned and Kate laughed. It was obvious the men were extremely close friends. Kate liked Jeremy.

She was eager to meet his son, Chris, and Chance promised she would meet his wife, Willow, at the dance on Saturday night.

Leaving them in the cafe, she went up to the house, changed into jeans and a yellow cotton shirt, then returned. Chance volunteered to drive and they set off down the road to Highway 93.

They pulled into Polson less than an hour later. Chance didn't seem surprised when she asked him to stop at Dorfman's Funeral Home. He just pulled up in front as if it were an everyday occurrence and ushered her inside.

"Hello there. May I help you?"

Kate turned at the sound of a soft male voice.

"I'm Marvin Dorfman. How may I be of assistance?" He was a short, slightly pudgy man with pale, lightly freckled skin and thinning sandy hair. His smile seemed a permanent fixture on his face.

"It's nice to meet you. I'm Kate Rollins and this is Chance McLain. We came to talk to you about a woman named Nell Hart. Mrs. Hart was my grandmother. She died in January of last year."

"Mrs. Hart . . ." he repeated, his sandy brows pulling together. "Let me check my records." He disappeared into his office, and she and Chance followed through the open door. The funeral home was small, done in light woods, the walls painted a soothing shade of blue. Through another doorway, she could see a family viewing room with several rows of padded chairs and gauzy curtains in front of the area designed to display the coffin.

Kate returned her attention to Marvin Dorfman, who pulled a manila folder out of a metal file cabinet, slid a pair of those little half reading glasses onto his nose, flipped open the folder, and began to read.

"Ah, yes, Mrs. Hart. I would have remembered—I always remember the departed ones we've cared for— but that week I had come down with a terrible case of the flu. I had to leave early the day Mrs. Hart arrived. I was there in the beginning, though, to see that she was comfortably settled in."

Comfortably settled in. Kate wondered what that particular euphemism meant. "Then you did see the body?"

"Why, yes. As I said, I was there when they brought her in."

"I'm interested in knowing whether you might have noticed anything unusual about her? Was there anything you observed about the injuries she suffered that might have been inconsistent with the sort of fall that was the cause of her death?"

He frowned. "Inconsistent? You're asking if there were any additional injuries other than those caused by the trauma to the head?"

"That's exactly what she's asking," Chance answered for her.

Dorfman looked down at the file, then raised his head. "If we'd noticed anything unusual it would have been reported to the sheriff's office." He looked down again and Kate realized he was studying something in the file.

"May I see that?"

"We would prefer that you didn't. It is often painful for family members to see—"

"Let the lady have the file," Chance said, and Dorfman gingerly handed it over.

Kate looked down and sucked in a breath of air. What Dorfman hadn't wanted her to see were photographs of her grandmother's naked body, her modesty protected only by a very small towel. They must have been taken when Nell first arrived at the mortuary.

"I hope you don't find the picture too upsetting," Mr. Dorfman said consolingly. He had a soothing, reassuring way about him that made him perfect for the job he had chosen. And strangely enough, he did seem sincere. "We like to document each case. The information is strictly confidential and just for our records."

There were photos of Nell lying on her back, sides, and stomach. In one picture, Kate could see dark blood congealed on the back of her head. In another, Nell's ribs were showing, as well as her hipbones. She was a frail little woman. A stiff breeze would have been enough to blow her over.

Kate started to hand back the file when she noticed a slight darkening of the skin on both of Nell's upper arms.

"What's this?" She pointed out the area on the photo.

"The first stages of bruising, perhaps. It's a little hard to say simply by looking at the picture."

"Why didn't the sheriff's report mention this?"

"Possibly because they were beneath Mrs. Hart's clothing when the deputy first saw her. Her dress wasn't removed until she got here. The deputy would normally be in attendance at this point, but if I recall correctly, that was the afternoon the school bus ran off an icy embankment and the deputy was called away to assist before he could get here."

"If these are bruises, is it possible they occurred during the process of moving the body?"

"Absolutely not. We're extremely careful when making a removal. Besides, once the heart stops beating, it's impossible for a bruise to form."

Kate felt a chill slide through her. Whatever had happened to cause the marks had occurred before Nell's death. "Why weren't these reported?"

"Older people often bruise easily. And there was no reason to suspect foul play."

"So no one called it in."

"I don't think so. As I told you, I was extremely ill that day. I left Mrs. Hart's care in the hands of one of my assistants."

"And his name is . . . ?" Chance asked.

"Walter Hobbs."

"Is Mr. Hobbs in?" Kate asked.

"I'm afraid not. He's retired. He only comes in when we're very short-handed. That afternoon, my regular assistant was also out with the flu. There was nearly an epidemic at the time."

"Do you have a phone number for Mr. Hobbs?" Chance asked. Dorfman nodded and politely wrote the name, address, and phone number on the back of one of his personal cards. He really did seem like a very nice man.

"Is there any chance you could lend me those photos for a while?" Kate paused. "I promise I'll return them."

He hesitated only a moment. "Of course. I would appreciate getting them back, though. We like to keep our records complete."

"Thank you, Mr. Dorfman. You've been extremely helpful."

"We're always glad to assist members of the family. That's what we're here for."

They left the funeral parlor and made their way back to Chance's truck. Kate was silent along the way, her mind racing with possibilities.

"Dorfman's right, you know," Chance said gently as he started the truck and they drove off down the street. "Even if those marks are bruises, older people bruise fairly easily. Nell could have done damned near anything to get them."

"Or someone could have grabbed her by the arms and pushed her into that sideboard."

"Think about it, Kate. What are the chances your grandmother would hit her head hard enough to kill her? If someone wanted her dead, that's hardly a reliable way to go about it."

Kate mulled that over, said nothing for the longest time. Then she sighed. "You're right, I suppose. Still, it bothers me. Something just isn't right about this, Chance."

"We'll keep after it, then. I've got to see Frank Mills. We'll call this guy, Hobbs, from Frank's office."

They did, but Walter Hobbs wasn't in. Since he didn't have an answering machine, Kate made a mental note to call him again when she got home.

Waiting in the reception area of Mills' office, she stood up when Chance walked back into the room. "I don't believe it," he said.

"What is it?"

"Consolidated Metals pled no contest to the charges of environmental pollution."

"That's good news, isn't it?"

"Not in this case. They offered to pay what they considered reasonable damages, in this case twenty-five thousand dollars. A measly twenty-five thousand—and the judge agreed. That kind of money won't touch the damage to the environment that arsenic spill caused. And it isn't enough to stop them from doing it again."

"Oh, Chance, I'm sorry."

He didn't say anything, but a muscle knotted in his cheek. All the way home, he stared broodingly down the road, saying very little, answering her questions mostly in monosyllables.

When they finally reached her house, he walked her absently up to the door.

"Sorry I wasn't better company."

"I wasn't a whole lot of fun either."

"Saturday night we'll do better. Let's make a vow to forget all this crap—at least for one night."

Kate smiled. "You got it."

He bent his head and pressed a quick hard kiss on her mouth. "That'll have to do until then." He cocked his head toward the window, where David peered through the starched crisscross curtains.

"I see what you mean." A long, silent glance passed between them.

"Damn. How the hell am I going to make it till Saturday night?" Kate caught her breath as he leaned forward and kissed her again. She could feel the heavy bulge straining against his Levi's just before he turned and walked away.

Saturday seemed to drag. As soon as the lunch shift ended, Kate went upstairs to her office to call Walter Hobbs but he still wasn't home. She tried to work on some storyboard displays but couldn't seem to concentrate. Instead she made some calls to her list of volunteers and got them set up to begin a postcard-writing campaign to local politicians.

Eventually, the day slipped into late afternoon and Jeremy arrived with Chris, who was almost as tall as David but more filled out in the chest and shoulders.

His eyes were the same obsidian black as his father's and so was his hair, but Chris wore his cut short beneath his battered cowboy hat. He had high cheekbones and smooth, dark skin. Kate figured he must be the terror of the female population at the Two Eagle River School.

"It's really nice to meet you, Ms. Rollins," he said without a trace of the self-importance a lot of really attractive young boys had.

"It's nice to meet you, too, Chris."

Jeremy spoke up from beside him. "I thought I'd take them up to a spot I know where the fishing's real good. Since we probably won't get back till dark, I was thinking . . . maybe you wouldn't mind if David stayed overnight. My daughter Shannon is nearly sixteen. She's very responsible. She'll be there while her mother and I are over at the dance."

"Can I, Mom, please?"

Kate bit her lip. She didn't like the idea of the two boys staying with only a high school girl for supervision, but she wanted David to make friends, and Jeremy and his son seemed like good ones.

She looked at David, saw the hope in his eyes. He hated babysitters. He thought he was too old and maybe he was. She glanced over at Jeremy, saw something in his expression that made her think that Chance might have had something to do with this, but decided not to press it.

"Myra said she'd stay at the house till I got home, but I suppose I could tell her David is spending the night with Chris."

"Thanks, Mom, you're the best!"

"Like I said, Shannon is real reliable. And Willow

and I won't be out that late. She worries about the kids if we don't get back at a fairly respectable hour."

Kate smiled. "I guess it's settled, then." David collected his fishing gear and the little group left the house, leaving Kate to wander aimlessly, trying to pass the hours until the dance.

Chapter Seventeen

Late afternoon turned into evening. At eight o'clock sharp, Chance arrived on her doorstep dressed in his special-occasion blue jeans and a pale blue Western shirt with silver collar tabs.

"I hope you're in the mood for chicken and frozen pizza," he said. "That's about all they've got at the Antlers, but it really isn't too bad."

"Are you kidding? I'm so sick of my own cooking, frozen pizza sounds like a treat."

Chance caught her hand as she walked out the door and turned her around to face him. "You look terrific."

Kate smiled, ridiculously pleased at the compliment. "Thanks." She was wearing an outfit she had bought on a whim one day in Missoula, a navy-blue broomstick skirt and matching Indian-patterned vest, cream-colored cotton blouse, and silver concho belt. Since she didn't have cowboy boots, she was wearing her ankle-high English riding boots.

The Antlers Saloon was already packed. A weekend dance was a major occasion in a town the size of Lost Peak. The band, Rocky Mountain Mist, a mother, father, and two sons, was assembling on a makeshift stage, but hadn't started to play. A jukebox punched out Western tunes and several couples already circled the dance floor.

Kate listened to Garth Brooks singing "The Beaches of Cheyenne" and thought with amazement how much she had come to like country tunes. Myra had told her they had played Country-Western in the cafe for as long as she could remember. Somehow it seemed so right for the place Kate hadn't had the heart to change it. In the months that followed—rock and roll devotee that she was—she had actually begun to enjoy it.

Now, although she liked all kinds of music, she found herself most often tuning into EAGLE 94.5, the country station on the radio.

"Over here, Kate." Chance waved her over to a table he had commandeered in the corner away from the loudspeakers. They sat down and ordered pizza and beer.

"Now that we're settled in," he said, "there's something I've been wanting to do."

She arched a brow. "What's that?"

He leaned over and kissed her very softly on the lips. "Just that. I want you to think about that when we're dancing . . . and what I'm gonna do to you after we're through."

She couldn't seem to breathe. Her stomach did a quiet little roll and heat floated out through her limbs. She knew exactly what Chance intended to do. If she closed her eyes, she could almost feel him moving inside her. She could feel his mouth against her skin, his hands caressing . . . Her eyes snapped open. Color washed into her cheeks.

Chance chuckled softly. "You see? It's working already."

Kate tossed him a playfully indignant glance. "Don't be too sure of yourself, cowboy."

Chance just smiled. He looked like a man who knew exactly what he wanted and tonight he meant to get it. The way he kept staring first at her mouth and then at her breasts, she was surprised he didn't drag her down on the dance floor and make love to her right there.

She was growing flushed and beginning to perspire when the band began to play, firing out a Texas two-step. Chance grabbed her hand and hauled her to her feet.

"Come on, darlin'. I'll show you how it's done in Montana."

She thought that he already had, but she didn't say so. He pulled her snug against him, pressed his cheek to hers, and kind of wrapped himself around her.

God, he felt so good.

"Just follow me. I promise it isn't that tough." Oddly enough, it wasn't. He showed her the steps a couple of times, until her feet had accepted the memory. In her earlier years, she had been a very good dancer. It didn't take long to remember how to follow his lead, how to relax into the rhythm of the music and let him guide her through the movements. He moved like he did everything else, with a natural, easy grace that seemed rooted in his very bones.

By the end of the hour, she was dancing Country-Western as if she had been doing it for years. She was even able to make some of the difficult back and forth turns while they moved clockwise around the floor.

"You didn't tell me how good you'd be at this," he said, obviously pleased.

"I told you I liked to dance. Besides, I didn't know how good you were, either."

A thick black brow arched up. "Didn't you? I was kind of hoping I'd made that clear."

A flush rose into her cheeks. She knew how good he was. Damned good. And those hot blue eyes said he meant to prove it again tonight.

They took a break from the dancing when Jeremy Spotted Horse walked in. "Come on. I want you to meet Willow." As Chance started leading her back through the crowd, Kate recognized the woman as a customer who had been in the cafe a couple of times for lunch. Willow was beautiful, tall and reed-slim, with big dark eyes and ebony hair bobbed at the shoulder. She was wearing a pair of red jeans, a red-checked cowboy shirt, and boots. Beneath her thick black hair, long silver earrings dangled from her ears.

Introductions were made and the four of them sat down at the table.

"I like your son," Willow said, endearing herself to Kate in an instant. "He seems so intelligent. Like his mother, I think."

"That's a very nice thing to say. David's always been good in school, at least he was until he started running around with the wrong sort of crowd. I'm happy he's found a friend like Chris."

"Perhaps they'll be good for each other. Your David and his computers. My Chris and his love of the outdoors."

Kate smiled, liking Willow more and more. "I think

that's a very good combination." Both couples danced for a while, then the music slowed and the band played a country waltz.

"I bet you've danced this way before," Chance teased, leading her back on the floor.

She thought she had—till she slow-danced with Chance McLain. He pulled her close and she could feel him all around her, feel the brush of his jeans, the silkiness of his hair where it curled over her fingers. She could smell his aftershave and the faint, salty tang of his skin.

He pulled her even closer, flattening her breasts out against his chest. "God, Katie . . ." He nuzzled the side of her neck and little prickles of heat rippled over her skin. One of his thighs moved intimately between her legs and she could feel his growing arousal. He was hard as a stone by the time the music ended and she heard him softly curse.

"I'm not sure this was such a good idea," he grumbled, walking close behind her as they headed back toward the table. Kate hid a pleased, secret smile that she'd been able to have that effect on him. Then, just before they reached the table, she spotted Silas Marshall walking in.

He headed toward the rear of the bar, so tall he had to bend his head to avoid a rafter where the roof sloped down. He still made her think of Abraham Lincoln, but now she wondered if he was a whole lot stronger than he looked.

And just how badly he had wanted that piece of property he had owned with Nell Hart.

"I'll be right back," she said to Chance. "I've got to make a pit stop." Knowing she shouldn't, Kate meandered in Silas's direction, weaving her way through the crowd and stopping right in front of him.

"Silas—it's nice to see you."

He smiled. "It's good to see you, too, Kate."

"How's David working out? No problems this time, I hope."

"He just got a little mixed up, living in the city and all. I think he's learned his lesson."

"I think so, too."

"Too bad Nell never got the chance to meet him. I think she would have been proud of you both."

"Thank you, Silas." It was a very nice thing to say and the perfect opening. She simply couldn't resist. "Speaking of Nell, I was cleaning out some boxes in the attic and I happened to run across the deed to some property the two of you owned together."

In the light of the neon beer sign, she saw his Adam's apple bob up and down. "We owned that piece for more than twenty years."

"After Nell died, I guess you sold it."

He looked away. "My son wanted to borrow some money to buy a house. It's hard for kids to make the down payment with prices so high these days."

"Yes, I imagine it is. I gather Nell didn't want to sell."

He cleared his throat. His eyes began darting around as if he wished he could escape. "No, she didn't."

"You two were friends. I'm surprised you couldn't talk her into it."

"I tried to. It was a really good deal—a big profit for both of us—but Nell wouldn't listen. She could really be hardheaded sometimes."

Kate forced a smile. "Well, in the end, I guess it didn't matter. Once Nell was dead, you got the land, sold it, and got the money for your son."

His long face paled. He looked like he wanted to run. "I have to go. I'm supposed to meet some friends."

"Nice to see you, Silas."

"Uh-huh." He left as if he couldn't get away fast enough and Kate returned to the table, thinking of his reaction.

"I saw you talking to Silas," Chance said, eyeing her over the top of his beer.

"I asked him how David was doing."

He cocked a knowing black eyebrow. "Did you?"

"Yes, I did," she replied a bit defensively.

"Exactly what else did you ask him?"

Kate plopped down in her chair. "All right, I asked him about the property he and Nell owned together. So sue me."

"I thought we agreed we weren't going to worry about any of that tonight."

"I know but . . . Dammit, the opportunity just came up and I couldn't resist."

"Leave it alone, Kate, please. At least for tonight."

She felt like a spoilsport. He had brought her here to have fun, not look for clues to a possible murder. "You're right. I'm sorry." She took a sip of her beer. It was icy cold and a little foamy. It went great with frozen pizza. "I've already forgotten all about it."

He gave her one his sexy smiles. "Good girl."

"Come on, you guys." Willow stood up at the table. "They're playing a line dance."

"Not me," Chance said, shaking his head. "I draw the line at herd dancing. Besides, I've got to hit the head."

"That leaves you, Kate. Jeremy and I will show you the steps. It's easy, once you get the hang of it."

It did look like fun. Kate followed them out on the dance floor where no one danced with partners and half the bar lined up facing the band. She took a place between Willow and a tall, good-looking cowboy she had noticed when they first walked in. Chance had said hello to him. She remembered he'd called the guy Ned.

"They're playing 'Boot-Skootin' Boogie'," Willow said, practically hopping up and down in her bright red cowboy boots. "It's one of my favorites." It seemed to take forever to memorize the steps of the dance, but eventually Kate began to catch on and it really was a lot of fun.

Willow laughed. "You're a natural at this, Kate. It took me weeks to learn all of the steps."

Feeling pretty smug that she was catching on so quickly, Kate turned the wrong direction just then and bumped squarely into the cowboy named Ned.

"It's all right, sweet thing." He grinned. "You can bump into me anytime you like."

He really was good looking, tall and barrel-chested, wearing boots and a white straw hat. They say every woman loves a cowboy—or will. She already had one of her own, but this one was staring at her as if he'd like to eat her up and it felt darned good.

Kate laughed at something Ned said, bending a little closer so she could hear him over the music. Then she looked back toward the table and saw Chance glaring at her with a look as black as the sky outside the windows.

The music ended, but as she turned to go back to the table, Ned caught her arm. "How about a dance, sweet thing?"

She should have said no. Any other time, any other place, she would have. But from the corner of her eye, she could see Chance leaning against the wall, his arms crossed over his chest, and some little demon just wouldn't let her.

"All right." It was a two-step, thank God. And he

didn't hold her overly close. Still, by the time the tune was over and she was heading back to the table, she could see she had made a grave mistake.

"Fun's over," Chance said, "we're leaving."

Kate moistened her suddenly dry lips. "But I thought—"

"I said we're leaving. Now."

Kate didn't argue, just said goodnight to Jeremy and Willow and let Chance tug her out the door. Wordlessly, he helped her climb into his pickup, cranked up the engine, and drove out of the parking lot.

He took the curvy mountain road a little faster than he should have. Kate knew better than to ask him to slow down.

"Where are we going?" she finally got up the nerve to ask.

"Lookout Mountain."

"Where's that?"

Chance turned off the narrow road into an open area surrounded by trees on three sides and looking out over the valley on the other. He slammed on his brakes and turned off the engine. "Right here."

Kate fell silent. Her nerves were hopping, her heart pounding. When Chance jumped out of the car and slammed the door, she leaped as if a pistol had been fired.

He came around to her side of the truck, jerked open the door, and swung her down to the ground.

"All right. What the hell was that all about?"

She plucked at a piece of lint on her sleeve. "I don't know what you mean."

"The hell you don't. You did that on purpose. You were trying to make me jealous."

She tilted her head back to look up at him. "Were you jealous?"

"Hell, yes."

She guiltily glanced away. "I'm sorry. I didn't realize—"

"Bullshit. You knew exactly what you were doing. What I want to know is why?"

Kate sighed. The jig was up, so to speak. She might as well confess to the crime and get it over with. "You want the truth? All right, here it is. I've never had a man jealous over me in my life. I married Tommy when I was seventeen. He didn't have a jealous bone in his body. He couldn't care less if another man was attracted to me. I thought . . . I thought that maybe you would. I wanted to know what it felt like."

"You wanted to know what it . . . ?" He swung away from her, tore off his hat, slammed it up on the hood of the truck.

"Just once," she said. "Just once, I wanted to know."

He raked a hand through his wavy black hair. "Fine, now you know. Since you're having this learning experience at my expense, you want to know what it felt like to me?"

She opened her mouth, but he didn't wait for her to answer.

"It felt like I wanted to wipe up the floor with Ned Cummings. Ned is a friend and I wanted to knock him flat. I saw the way you smiled at him and I wanted to drag you out of there by your gorgeous red hair and put my brand on you. I wanted to make sure none of those guys ever touched you again."

He looked down at her and something hot and hungry moved in his eyes. "I wanted to tear your clothes off. I wanted to drive myself inside you. I wanted to do this."

Sliding his hand behind her neck, he dragged her mouth up to his for a hard, punishing kiss. For an instant, she tried to pull back, frightened by the violence she had unleashed, then the bruising kiss gentled, turned coaxing, and his tongue swept in. Heat roared through her, sank into every particle of her flesh. She felt dizzy, disoriented, as if she were falling off a cliff. He kissed her endlessly and she found herself clinging to his shoulders, fighting just to stay on her feet.

"It made me want you, Katie," he whispered as his mouth moved along her throat. "Even more than I did already." His hands found her breasts and he massaged them through her clothes. He shoved the vest off her shoulders, popped a button as he struggled to unfasten her blouse.

Her head fell back. He kissed her throat, her collar-bone, unhooked her bra and filled his hands with her breasts. His lips, soft and hot, so very, very hot, slid over her skin, moved lower, and he took the heavy fullness into his mouth. He suckled her, used his teeth to caress a nipple, and Kate heard herself moan.

She was shaking all over, her legs rubbery, her insides throbbing with heat. Another passionate kiss and he tugged her narrow skirt down over her hips. The elastic band made it easy. Vaguely, she wondered if perhaps this was the reason she had worn it, along with the thigh-high nylons and skimpy blue satin bikini panties she wore underneath.

He looked down just then, saw them, and his eyes seemed to burn right through her. "You want to know how it feels when you make a man jealous?" He lifted her up on the fender and moved between her legs. She could hear the buzz of the zipper on his jeans sliding down. He released himself, his fingers found her softness, and he skillfully began to stroke her.

"You want to know how it feels?" He discovered how slick and wet she was and lifted her again, wrapping her legs around his waist. "It feels like this," he said, and plunged himself inside.

Kate whimpered and clung to his neck, absorbing the fullness, the hot, hard joining.

"I won't share you, Katie. Not with Ned Cummings or anyone else." Surging upward, he filled her again, slid out and then in, again and again. Hot hard kisses, his tongue plunging into her mouth with the same determined rhythm as his body, had her trembling, teetering on the edge of release. Sensation swamped her, battered her, slammed her into a powerful climax.

Chance didn't slow, just kept on pounding until she came again, her body shivering, tightening around him. Two more deep, driving thrusts and he followed her to release.

She was sobbing against his shoulder by the time they were through, shaking with the force of her emotions. She felt his hands sifting gently through her hair.

"I'm sorry, Katie." He pressed a kiss on her forehead. "I just got so turned on. I hope I didn't hurt you."

She dragged in a shaky breath, thinking of the intense pleasure he had brought her. "You didn't hurt me."

Chance shook his head as he lowered her back to her feet. "I don't know what there is about you, Kate. I can't seem to figure it out."

But Kate was beginning to know very clearly what it was about Chance McLain that made her behave as she never had before. Heaven help her, as much a she had tried to fight it, she knew she was falling in love with him.

It was nearly two in the morning by the time Chance pulled into his garage at the ranch. Conspiring a little with Jeremy, he had known Kate would be alone tonight, and he had planned to bring her home with him again. He wanted another night of leisurely love making.

Instead he had taken her home. After what had happened at the bar and later, up on Lookout Mountain, it was clear that getting more deeply involved with Kate was something he couldn't afford to do.

Damn, what the hell was the matter with him?

Sure he'd been jealous of women before. He wasn't a man who liked to share what belonged to him. In the beginning, he'd been jealous of Rachael, but he was younger then. Over the years, he'd outgrown his raging hormones, and they had settled into a fairly open relationship. She saw other men. He saw other women. By unspoken rule, neither of them ever got involved. It worked well for both of them.

Tonight was different. He hadn't been simply jealous, he'd been completely enraged. He didn't want Kate flirting with other men. He couldn't stand the thought of her being with Ned Cummings instead of him. By the time they had finished making wild, erotic love, he had realized just how much he cared for her, how badly he still wanted her—and how damned much trouble he was really in.

He was in way over his head and he wasn't exactly sure what to do about it.

Chance climbed the stairs to his room, trying to figure out where he'd gone wrong. With other women, he'd been honest from the start. He'd made it clear he wasn't interested in a permanent relationship. On a subconscious level, he must have known if he'd been completely honest with Kate, she would never have gotten involved with him.

Christ, if he just hadn't wanted her so damned badly.

He had to make things right with her, had to tell her the truth. Anything less wasn't fair to Kate.

And it wasn't fair to him.

Tomorrow he would talk to her, explain the way things were. The way they had to be. Maybe she would understand. Kate wasn't ready for a serious relationship either. Maybe she would even be relieved. God, he hoped so. He didn't want to stop seeing her. After last night, all he could think of was making love to her again.

Unfortunately, when the phone rang at eight o'clock the following morning, it was Rachael on the end of the line.

And she wasn't in New York City.

She had just arrived at her father's ranch.

Chapter Eighteen

Kate rose late on Sunday morning, a little stiff but smiling at memories of the night. She glanced at the clock on the bedside table, saw that David would soon be home from Chris Spotted Horse's house, showered and dressed in jeans and a dark green sweatshirt.

A little after ten, Jeremy's rattletrap pickup pulled up. One of the doors swung open and David hopped out. He smiled and waved goodbye to Chris. It was clear the two were becoming solid friends, and Kate said a silent thank you to Chance.

Thinking of him, she flicked a glance at the telephone, willing it to ring. She had been hoping he would call this morning. It was such a beautiful day, perfect for the three of them to go for a horseback ride. But he didn't call, so she and David took a picnic lunch and hiked up into the woods behind the house.

A can of pepper spray rode in Kate's green canvas backpack. Since they lived in grizzly country, Chance had been adamant about the spray, sending a can home with David the night he had taken him and Chris horseback riding.

"Personally, it's hard to imagine standing dead-still in the path of a charging grizzly," Chance had said seriously, "holding your breath and waiting for the damned thing to get close enough to hit in the face with a spray of pepper. But most woodsmen say it works and it's a whole lot better than nothing."

She wondered what he was doing today and whether he might be thinking of her. Last night, as they had stood on the porch outside the house, she had apologized for her behavior in the bar, assuring him that trying to make a man jealous wasn't part of her normal routine. By then his temper had cooled and in some odd way he seemed to find it amusing.

"It's all right," he'd said. "I don't normally behave like a bad-tempered bull, myself." A corner of his mouth curved up. "But I'm damned glad Ned Cummings didn't ask for another dance."

The new week began and the weather turned cool, but business at the cafe remained strong. The profits had grown steadily since the place had reopened, partly because of Aida Whittaker's longtime reputation for good food and service, which Kate had been careful to uphold; and partly because she was a very good money manager, able to keep food costs down and the overhead low.

She had a small, comfortable income from money she had invested during her years with Menger and Menger, but the extra earnings from the cafe certainly came in handy, and it was a point of pride that the business be a viable, profitable endeavor.

Still, from the start, she had scheduled her hours so she would have plenty of time for herself and her son. Lately, after the lunch shift while David was still working at the store, she usually worked for a while on the anti-mining campaign, then dug around on the Net or read books on forensics.

In the middle of the week, she returned upstairs to finish going through the boxes that Aida had stored in the attic. She had already gone through all of Nell's papers. It was time to start on the clothes, jewelry, and personal items. After she had taken a quick look at everything, David could carry the stuff down and they could donate it to the Salvation Army.

Sitting in the little maple rocker, Kate sighed as she dug through a pile of her grandmother's garments, mostly sweaters and heavy wool trousers. A little pink, heart-shaped sachet lay in the bottom of the box alongside a pair of worn knit slippers.

She had never felt anything but antipathy toward her grandmother. The enmity between Nell and her mother had left Kate with a bone-deep dislike of her. Still, as she went through the clothes, she couldn't help wondering what Nell had really been like, and how a woman could so completely abandon her only child.

A shutter banged outside the attic window and Kate glanced up. The wind had picked up and it whistled under the sill, making an eerie keening sound. It was September now, the temperature colder, the leaves turning yellow and red, beginning to fall off the trees. David would be starting school next week, a thought less painful to him now that he had been making friends. There would be others, he had begun to believe. Thanks to

Chance, Jeremy, and Chief, the gap between the city boy from LA and the country boys in Montana wasn't as wide as it used to be.

David could fish and ride at least a little, and Chance had promised to get him enrolled in a hunter safety course.

"Are you insane?" Kate had argued at first. "I don't want my son shooting a gun. The last thing he needs is to be exposed to more violence."

"Hunting's a way of life up here, Kate. Every boy knows how to use a rifle. Even if David decides not to hunt, he needs to know how to take care of himself and his family. Every man ought to be capable of that."

Why it sounded so logical when Chance said it she couldn't begin to say, but if the day actually arrived and David wanted to learn, she knew that she would allow it.

Kate set another musty-smelling box next to the ones she'd already gone through and started on a third: long flannel nightgowns, long underwear, and thick woolen sox. The cotton bras were a size D cup, which made Kate smile. Nell was a small woman, yet it was obvious why Kate and her mother had both been born so well-endowed.

She dug through the box and found another, smaller box in the bottom. Kate lifted it out, took off the lid, and saw that it contained old letters. They were yellowed and faded, some of them water-spotted, the edges chewed by mice and bugs.

A funny, tingling sensation slipped through her, anticipation mixed with hesitation. The letters were private. They belonged to Nell. Yet Kate knew without the least amount of doubt that she wouldn't rest until she had read every one.

Two hours later, she was less than halfway through the stack. There were letters from old high school friends, correspondence from couples who were friends of the Harts, letters from business acquaintances. Reading them was like opening a window into Nell's life, seeing the sort of people she had been drawn to, discovering some of the reasons they had been drawn to her.

As always, she appeared to be a decent, kind sort of person. At least that was the way her friends saw her. Kate and her mother alone seemed to know the woman she truly was.

Kate finished the bundle and picked up another, turning it over in her hand. There were maybe a dozen letters in the bunch, the envelopes and handwriting all the same. The wide blue scroll looked masculine instead of feminine, and her pulse picked up a little. They were postmarked Walnut Creek, California, but as Nell drew out the first letter, she realized they were the work of someone living in Lost Peak. His name appeared on the outside of the envelope. Inside they were signed, *With loving regards, Silas.*

Kate's hand trembled as she unfolded the first letter and began to read. At first, Silas talked about the weather and told her about his son, a man named Milton who apparently had remarried and was "doing really well this time."

The second letter contained more of the same, just small talk between two old friends, yet it was obvious how much Silas loved his son, and though he was enjoying his stay in California he would be glad to get back to Lost Peak.

He missed his friends, he said, and apparently Nell— Nellie, Silas called her—was among them. There was a definite hint of affection in his tone, and Kate thought it was certainly possible that in their younger years, the pair might once have been lovers.

She had just finished the last of the letters—slightly disappointed not to have discovered some sort of secret information—and had plucked up the final bundle when she heard David calling from downstairs. *Tomorrow,* she silently promised, setting aside the aging envelopes, these in a faded shade of rose with tiny pink flowers in the corner.

As she hurried downstairs to her son, Kate told herself that reading the letters was merely an opportunity to look for clues.

But the truth was, she was looking for a chance to find the real Nell Hart, the grandmother that she had never known.

The end of the week arrived. Chance never called. He didn't stop by the cafe or come over to the house. Kate began to worry. The last time they'd made love had been incredible for her, but maybe for Chance it was nothing out of the ordinary. Maybe she had read him wrong. Aside from a couple of hot nights in the sack, maybe he didn't give a hoot about her.

If that was so, Kate wished she could be equally cavalier. Instead, at night she dreamed about him, dreamed of them making love, and woke up in a hot, damp sweat. One night she actually awakened in the pleasurable throes of a climax, her dream replaying the night they had made love on Lookout Mountain.

Good Lord, it was embarrassing what just thinking about him could do.

David went off to school the first of the week and Kate went to work, hoping Chance would call with some sort of explanation for his absence, but she was beginning to think that maybe their brief affair was over. She told herself it didn't matter. Men had short, heated encounters all the time; there was no reason she couldn't have one, too. So she'd never done it before. So what? But the truth was, she missed him, and not just the hot sex they had shared. She missed the sound of his voice, the warmth of his smile, the solid strength that had somehow made her feel stronger, too.

The sad truth was, Kate missed the man she had begun to fall in love with, and it wasn't going to be all that easy to get over him.

Still, she was determined to do just that. There had never been any actual commitment between them. Neither of them had talked about their feelings, and in a way that was good. She had held herself back a little, protected her heart as best she could. Knowing the risk was high, she hadn't given him that last little piece of herself and now she was glad.

Or at least she told herself she was as she worked through the morning, trying to smile at the customers, trying *not* to wonder where he was or what he was doing. She was fighting so hard not to think about him, she almost convinced herself the tall cowboy shoving through the door of the cafe wasn't Chance.

Then she realized it was, and the relief washing through her turned her legs to rubber bands.

Kate Rollins, you are in very serious trouble here.

The cafe was full. Chance waited for the first available seat and sat down in a booth at the window. Kate went over and filled his coffee mug, trying for an air of nonchalance, pretending she hadn't thought about him every day for more than a week.

"David started school today," she said matter-of-factly. "He was nervous, but I think this time he'll do okay."

Chance looked up, but she couldn't read his face. "I don't think he'll feel like such an outsider now," he said.

She pulled her pad and pencil out of the pocket of her uniform. "Ready to order?" she asked, her pasted-on smile still in place.

Chance hadn't even picked up the menu. "To tell you the truth I didn't come here to eat. I was hoping . . . after it slows down a little . . . we might have a chance to talk."

There was something in his voice, something regretful and gruff, that didn't bode well. Her stomach squeezed into a knot the size of a marble. "Sure. Probably another half an hour and I can get away."

Chance just nodded. He wasn't smiling. In fact he looked unbelievably grim. "I'll just have coffee, then."

Her mouth went dry. She began to steel herself against whatever he might be going to say. The bell above the door chimed again, admitting another customer, and she quickly made her escape. Two men walked in, Jake Dillon, the fifty-year-old widower who owned the mercantile, and a bald-headed man named Harvey Michaelson, a local who lived a few miles up Silver Fox Creek. Both of them had been doing volunteer work for the anti-mining coalition.

They sat down at a table and turned over their coffee cups.

"How's it going, guys?" Kate poured the steaming brew up to the rim.

Jake wrapped his big, weathered hands around the cup. "Pretty good, I guess, considering. We got that postcard-writing campaign off to a darned good start."

"Yeah," Harvey grumbled, "a little too good."

The coffeepot she held hung suspended above the table. "What do you mean?"

"He means we both got anonymous letters last week, warning us in no uncertain terms to butt out of mining affairs."

"You're kidding."

"I wish we were," Jake said darkly. "That's the reason we stopped by today. We figured you'd want to know."

Kate shoved down a thread of worry. "Well, we knew this kind of thing might happen. Have you talked to Ed Fontaine?"

"We took the letters over to his place yesterday."

"What about Chance?"

"Not yet."

"Well, he's sitting in that booth across the way. I'm sure he'd want to know."

The men turned their heads in that direction and shoved back their chairs. While they made their way over to where he sat, Kate served an order of hamburgers and fries to one of the customers, a big piece of pie to another, and collected money from some who were departing. She had just walked over to Chance, Jake, and Harvey when the window exploded in a shower of broken glass and a heavy object sailed into the room.

Customers screamed. Jake Dillon jumped out of the way just in time to keep from getting hit.

"Son of a bitch!" Chance was on his feet and running for the door before the big rock stopped rolling beneath one of the tables. He raced outside in time to see a big black pickup roaring off down the street. He followed it a ways, trying to get a look at the license plate, but the truck was already swerving around the corner, disappearing out of sight.

The door slammed behind him as he walked back inside and over to where Kate knelt in search of the rock.

"I didn't get the plate number, unfortunately, but it was a late-model, extended-cab Ford."

Lifting away a few jagged shards of glass, Kate picked up the rock, saw it was wrapped in a piece of brown paper like something torn from a grocery bag, pulled the rubber band away, unfolded and read the note.

GO HOME BITCH. WE DON'T WANT YOU HERE IN LOST PEAK.

Her hands shook. Twice she reread the words, an icy chill running up and down her spine. She had worked so hard to be accepted in Lost Peak. She wanted to make a home here for herself and David. She didn't want trouble with her neighbors.

Chance reached out and gripped her shoulders. "It's all right, Kate. They're just trying to scare you into quitting the campaign."

She thought of the newspaper articles in LA, the problems that had forced her to leave, and started shaking harder, the note still frozen in her hand.

"Dammit!" Chance pulled her into his arms. "It's all right, darlin'. They probably don't even live around here. They're probably just some guys who work for Barton."

She clung to him a moment, absorbing his solid strength, the warmth of his body driving away some of the fear. "Do you really think so?"

He eased her gently from his arms and took the note from her hand. "You heard what Jake and Harvey said. They both got letters like this last week."

She looked over at the men, feeling foolish for letting Barton and his goons get the best of her. "You're right.

We knew this could happen. It just came as such a surprise, and . . ."

"And . . . ?"

"And I really like it here. I don't want to have to leave."

Jake Dillon's mouth flattened into a thin, white line. "No one's forcing anyone to leave. You've made a place for yourself here in Lost Peak, and Barton and his troublemakers haven't got a thing to say about it."

Kate gave him a grateful smile. "Thanks, Jake." She turned to the handful of customers who remained in the cafe, most of them now on their feet. "Sorry for the trouble, everyone. As most of you know, we've been trying to stop Consolidated Metals from opening a mine on Silver Fox Creek." She tilted her head toward the broken window. "Apparently, we're doing a pretty good job of it."

Faint laughter arose, breaking the tension. The customers sat back down in their seats and began to finish their meals.

Kate looked back at the window, now sporting a big jagged hole where the restaurant name used to be. "I can't believe they'd be willing to go this far."

"Believe it," Chance said. "Barton wants that mine to go in. He wants the cyanide ban overturned and he doesn't like the fact that our efforts just might stop him."

Kate didn't say anything more, just turned and went into the kitchen. Pulling a broom and dustpan out of the closet, she went back into the dining room.

"We ought to call the sheriff before you clean that up," Chance said.

He was right, of course, but the idea of facing Mr. Politically Correct Sheriff Barney Conrad made her slightly sick to her stomach. "I suppose we should, but I've got a business to run. I'll call him later."

"Kate . . ."

"Please, Chance." He didn't say anything more and as soon as the last of the customers had left, she dragged out the vacuum and plugged it in.

"Why don't you let me do that?" Chance offered gently, reaching for the handle.

"No, thanks." It was obvious she was still upset and she wasn't surprised to look up and find him pulling his wide-brimmed hat down over his forehead and reaching for the door.

"You've got enough on your mind right now. We can talk another time."

"All right."

"And don't forget to call the sheriff."

Kate watched him leave with mixed emotions. Her woman's intuition was kicking in—big-time—telling her whatever Chance had to say wasn't going to be good. Another time, she could handle it.

Not today.

Not with the place in a shambles and threats being made against her.

Kate reached down and picked up the note scratched crudely on the piece of brown paper. "Go to hell, Lon Barton," she said out loud. "You're not going to scare me away."

Chance skimmed his fingers over the long, mahogany dining table, polished to such a glossy sheen he could see his own reflection. A crystal chandelier hung above it, each tiny prism alive with colored light. Fontaine House resembled a French chateau, slightly out of place on a Montana ranch, but Ed's wife, Gloria, had insisted on it. Whatever Glory Fontaine wanted, Ed made certain she got.

She'd been ten years younger than Ed, a beautiful blond grad student he met on a cattle-buying trip to Denver. Ed had fallen madly in love with her on sight and after an extravagant courtship, she had agreed to marry him. Glory moved to the ranch, gave him a daughter that same year, and became the center of Ed's world.

The sun shone each day for Glory, as far as Ed was concerned. When she died of breast cancer sixteen years later, Ed wanted to die along with her. But he had Rachael to think of. She was only fifteen, more beautiful even than her mother. Ed lavished her with attention, and it was Rachael who became the sun, the moon, and the center of his world.

"So what do you children think?" Ed's voice pulled him back from musings. Or perhaps he had simply been trying to escape.

"I think it's a lovely idea." Rachael turned the full force of her smile on him. Perfect pink lips. Perfectly even white teeth. She was tall and elegantly thin, her skin as pale and smooth as alabaster. Short blond hair, done in soft waves around her face, shone like twenty-four-karat gold in the candlelight. "What do you think, Chance?"

What did he think? He hadn't had time to think. Rachael had flown in unexpectedly a week ago and his life had been in turmoil ever since. Now Ed wanted him to announce their engagement at the party Ed was throwing in Rachael's honor the end of the week.

What did he think? Until the last few minutes, he'd expected to remain single for years. Now in a matter of days, he would be making a lifetime commitment.

"That doesn't leave us much time. I won't have a chance to buy you a ring." Lame excuse. Damn, what was the matter with him? He should be glad Ed was trying to set things in motion. He wanted a family, didn't he? Rachael was twenty-seven, her biological clock ticking away. It was time they both settled down and got on with the future they had planned.

"The ring won't be a problem," Ed said. "There's some nice stores in Missoula. Get one of them to lend you something until whatever Rachael picks out comes in."

She'd want something big and flashy, he knew. Not that they'd ever talked about it. But everything about Rachael spoke of money and class. Nothing but a very expensive diamond would do. Then again, what did he care? He could afford it. He rarely spent money on anything but the ranch.

"I think we should do it." Rachael flashed those big baby blues and smiled so wide a dimple formed in her cheek.

"What about setting the date?" Ed pressed. It was obvious he really wanted this. Chance's eyes drifted down to the heavy chrome wheelchair Ed sat in, and his insides slowly drew into a knot. For more than twenty years, he had tried to make amends for the accident that had put Ed in that chair. For more than twenty years, his guilt had festered, gnawing at his insides like a gangrenous wound, but there was no medicine he could take to make it heal.

He took a fortifying breath. There was only one thing he could do, and this was it. "I think it's a great idea. I only wish I'd been the one to suggest it."

Shoving back his chair he came to his feet and rounded the table to where Rachael sat. When she turned her face up and smiled, he bent his head and lightly kissed her mouth. "If this is what you want, too, then tomorrow we'll go look for that ring."

"Oh, Chance!" Rachael jumped to her feet and flung her arms around his neck. He couldn't help noticing how fragile she felt, all sharp edges and frail little bones, like holding a captured bird. "I don't know why we waited so long. We should have done this sooner."

He forced himself to smile. "If I remember correctly, I tried to get you to marry me years ago. You were the one who wanted a career as a model."

"True, but now I'm ready to give all of that up."

"Are you?" Chance asked, suddenly serious.

"Well, I'll still want to take a few modeling jobs, now and again. I'd get pretty bored if I just sat around the ranch all the time with nothing to do."

"But you do want to have a family?"

"Of course she does," Ed answered for her.

"Of course I do," Rachael agreed. "I've seen the world. I've modeled for every fashion magazine in the country. I've proven whatever I needed to prove." She flashed him another gorgeous smile. "But I've never been a wife. I've never been a mother. I'm finally ready for that now."

Chance gently slid her arms from where they rested on his shoulders. "When do you want to get married?"

"The sooner the better," Ed said.

"Don't be a pill, Daddy. Chance might need a little time to get used to the idea."

"He's had time. Too damned much time, if you ask me. What do you say, boy?"

"What about the wedding, Rachael? Do you want a big one?"

She smiled, rolled her big blue eyes. "Well . . ."

"Of course she does," Ed said. "And my little girl's gonna have it—the biggest damned wedding in the history of Silver County."

"It'll take a while to plan," Rachael continued, bubbling with enthusiasm. "How about six months from now? I'll need that much time to get organized."

Six months. In just six months he would be a married man. When had the thought turned so grim?

"I'm going back to the city week after next," she was saying. "I've got a couple of modeling jobs to finish. I'll have to pack everything and sublet my apartment. Then I'll come back and help with the wedding."

Chance just nodded. He couldn't help wondering what had motivated her sudden change of heart. For the past few years, Rachael's career had been all-important. Odds were, like a number of her other adventures, she had simply gotten bored. He said a silent prayer she wouldn't get tired of being a wife and mother.

"All right, then, it's settled," he said. "Tomorrow we find a ring. Saturday night we make the announcement." He kissed her very briefly on the lips. "Six months from now you'll be Mrs. Rachael McLain."

The name sounded funny on his lips. He supposed he would get used to it.

"I think a toast is in order." Ed called into the kitchen for a bottle of champagne, and one of the servants returned with a bottle of Dom Perignon in an ornate silver bucket. Ed popped the cork and poured it into chilled Waterford crystal flutes.

"To my daughter, the most beautiful woman in the world—except for her mother. And my future son-in-law, a man who is and always will be, the son I never had."

Chance felt a lump rise in his throat. Ed had been

like a father to him, and he had always known the feeling was returned, but until tonight he had never heard Ed say it.

"To the future," Chance said gruffly, and all of them took a drink of their champagne.

The evening wore on for a little while longer, plans being made and discarded, talk of the party Ed was throwing at the house on Saturday night, now officially an engagement party.

By the time he was able to leave, Chance's stomach felt tied in knots and a heavy cloud of gloom seemed to have settled over his head. In the past few days, his life had taken one bizarre turn after another and now seemed out of his control. He was marrying Rachael but he couldn't stop thinking of Kate.

He never should have started seeing her, should have stayed away from the damned cafe, as Jeremy had warned him more than once. Instead, he'd pursued her relentlessly, until he managed to get her into his bed. The only trouble was, he wanted her to stay there.

It was impossible, he knew. He was committed now. It was over between them. He simply had to find a way to tell her.

An image of Kate arose in his mind, her glorious red hair spread out across his pillow. He remembered her laughter, as sweet and rich as cream, remembered the feel of her arms around his neck as they moved in rhythm around the dance floor, her soft breasts pillowed against his chest. He had never taken Rachael to the Antlers. Rachael hated country music. She thought it was too low class.

Still, she was a beautiful, desirable woman, and any man would be lucky to marry her.

"Chance?" He turned at the sound of her voice. "You look like you're a thousand miles away."

Not that far, less than twenty miles, he figured. "Sorry."

"Randy's taking Daddy up to bed. Maybe we could go for a walk . . . or something?"

He knew what she was offering. They hadn't been alone for more than a couple of hours since her arrival at the ranch. They hadn't found time to make love, and though Rachael wasn't the passionate woman Kate was, she expected him to want her. Sex was her way of feeling desirable—and there wasn't much doubt she was that.

Still, tonight, with so much on his mind, making love to her was the last thing he wanted. "We aren't kids anymore, Rachael. I'm not about to take you out in the barn on some damned pile of hay. And I don't think your father would appreciate finding me in your bed— engagement or no."

She sighed, smoothed a hand over her short golden hair. "I guess you're right. Why don't I tell Daddy I'm staying with Sarah Davis after the party on Saturday night? He'll know it's a lie, but it lets us all save face."

He just nodded.

Rachael kissed him full on the mouth and Chance kissed her back. Her lips felt smooth and cool and he thought of another pair, fuller, hotter, softer.

"Good night, Rach."

"Good night, Chance."

I'm lucky to have her, he thought. And he told himself that over and over, all the way back to the ranch.

Chapter Nineteen

On Thursday morning, Kate got a call from KGET-TV, the local television station in Missoula. It was from a woman named Diana Stevens, one of the anchors from the news department, who wanted to do an interview about the efforts of the anti-mining coalition.

"Is it possible you'd be available sometime this afternoon?"

"Absolutely," Kate said. The media was key to any successful campaign. The more people knew what was happening, the better chance they would have of stopping Consolidated's efforts.

"We should be there around three," the anchorwoman said. As soon as she hung up, Kate phoned Ed Fontaine. The interview would go better with at least two people to talk to, and Ed was well-known in both Silver and Missoula counties. Unfortunately, he wasn't in. His housekeeper said that his daughter was there for a visit and they had gone off somewhere together.

Kate hadn't known Ed had a daughter, but she thought it was nice for Ed that she was there. Chance was next on her list. He and Ed knew the most about Consolidated Metals, the history of their abuses, and what the consequences would be if they succeeded in overturning the cyanide ban. She picked up the phone to dial his number, but something held her back. She hadn't heard from him since he had come into the cafe. He might think this was just an excuse to talk to him and she didn't want that.

Jeremy was working at the mill, she knew. That left Jake Dillon, who was handy, over at the mercantile right across the street. She had always liked Jake, more so after he had come to her defense that day in the cafe. And once he'd gotten onboard the campaign, he'd been tireless in his efforts.

As soon as the lunch crowd was gone, Kate went into the house, gathered color brochures, T-shirts, and some of the photographs Jeremy had taken of the spill, blown up into disgusting eight-by-ten glossies. One showed a hundred dead fish, floating on Beaver Creek, another showed brown, dying foliage along a scenic stretch of Big Pine River. Others showed the efforts of the Salish-Kootenai to remove the huge sludge pile dumped on their reservation that had infiltrated the water above Chance's property and killed six of his steers.

Carrying the information into the back room of the cafe, she set them down on a table they had placed in front of the storyboard they had made. A quick trip across the street to enlist the aid of Jake Dillon and she was ready.

Diana Stevens appeared exactly on time at three

o'clock that afternoon, a thirtyish young woman, well groomed in a short navy-blue skirt, matching jacket, and a pair of four-inch-heeled navy pumps. She looked so out of place in Lost Peak, Kate almost smiled.

She led the woman and her cameraman, a tall, lanky, man with long hair and a beard, into the back room where Jake was waiting. Introductions were made and the crew went to work.

"Today we're interviewing Kaitlin Rollins, the woman who has been working so tirelessly behind the scenes of the Silver Fox Creek Anti-mining Coalition, and one of her volunteers, Jacob Dillon, a longtime resident of Lost Peak."

She went on to list Kate's credentials, which were lengthy. It was obvious Diane Stevens had done her homework.

"Some of our viewers have been asking why you and your people are working so hard on this effort when there is already a law in place that bans any new cyanide mining in the area."

"The fact is, Diane, the mining industry, backed in most part by Consolidated Metals, is currently in the process of filing a challenge to the ban that was passed last year. They've made no secret of it. As you may have read, Consolidated claims the ban was illegal. They cite the 1872 mining law that gives anyone who wishes to mine, an absolute right to do so on federal public lands. Since the proposed Silver Fox mine falls within those parameters, they believe they can defeat the ban and go forward with the mine as planned. Which means, all of the work that was done by groups like the Montana Wilderness Association, the Sierra Club, the Clark Fork Coalition, and others, is in jeopardy of having been done in vain."

"Consolidated already owns the land and water rights they need," Jake Dillon put in. "If they succeed in their efforts, we'll have a brand new heap-leach mine on Silver Fox Creek."

"And more desecration like what you see in these pictures." Kate turned toward the table and the camera focused on the photos laid out on top, panning from one horrendous sight to the next.

"We don't want the sort of environmental problems that have plagued Beaver Creek and dozens of other mountain streams," Jake said. "We want to maintain the wild beauty of Silver Fox Creek."

The interview ended with Kate's summation of the efforts currently being made by the anti-mining coalition as well as plans being formulated for the future. Apparently pleased by the way things had gone, Diane Stevens left with a promise to return in a couple of weeks for an interview that included Ed Fontaine and Chance McLain.

"All in all," Jake said, smiling after the woman had departed, "it was a damned successful afternoon."

Kate smiled, too. "Thanks for helping, Jake."

"No problem. A little TV coverage now and then is good for business."

Kate's smile slipped a little at the thought. She had come to Lost Peak to escape her notoriety. God forbid, it should surface all over again.

"What do you think, Rachael?" Chance stood next to her at the counter of Bookman's Jewelers on Higgins Street in Missoula.

Rachael held up a slender hand and turned it one way and then another, making the diamond flash beneath the bright white lights above the counter. "I don't know for sure. It's hard to imagine what it's going to look like with a bigger diamond in the center."

The jeweler leaned over, turned her hand to examine the ring. "Not just bigger in the center. Each stone will be larger, Ms. Fontaine. The ring is going to be spectacular—I can definitely promise you that." It was their second trip to Missoula, the first effort having resulted in a very long day at several local stores, then thumbing through catalogs and still coming up empty-handed.

At last Rachael smiled. "I think he's right. With a four-carat diamond in the center and two-carat baguettes on each side, it should be magnificent."

For eighty thousand dollars, it ought to be, Chance thought. He wondered if Kate would have wanted a big, expensive ring, and knew with a flash of certainty she wouldn't have been caught dead in a ring the size of the one Rachael had chosen. He almost smiled, might have, if the thought hadn't made him feel so bad.

"You're happy with this one, then?" He picked up the ring she had laid back down on the counter.

"Of course I am—what girl wouldn't be? It's gorgeous—or at least the one Mr. Bookman's going to order will be." She flashed him a radiant smile, slipped her arms around his neck. "Thank you, Chance. Daddy always said you'd take good care of me."

Mr. Bookman gave them a winning smile. "In the meantime, you can wear this one until yours gets here. We have insurance, so you don't have to worry about that."

"Thank you," Chance said. Taking the ring, he slid it on Rachael's third left finger. "I guess it's official, then."

Her mouth curved into a sexy smile. "Yes, I guess it is." She leaned over and kissed him, running her tongue inside his mouth. A year ago, it would have made him want her, now all he could think of was getting her back to her father's ranch. God, he hoped his mood would be better by the time he took her to bed on Saturday night.

Rachael beamed up at him. "We're going to be so happy, darling. Everything's going to be perfect."

But nothing was ever perfect. Except maybe Rachael's perfect lips. Life was hard. Times got tough. He hoped she'd turn out to be the sort of wife who would stand by him in the bad times as well as the good.

But he didn't dwell on the notion. Whatever sort of wife Rachael turned out to be, his decision was made, his course set, fixed by the winds of fate when he was twelve years old.

For better, for worse. For richer, for poorer. For as long as we both shall live.

That's what marriage meant.

And that was the way it was going to be for him.

Friday came. The rodeo in Polson was this weekend, but Chance hadn't mentioned it again. Kate hadn't seen him all week and he hadn't bothered to call, so apparently they weren't going. Early in the afternoon, worried and missing him, she returned to the last bundle of letters in the box upstairs.

It was crisp and clear outside, the sun beating down through the trees, a perfect fall day in the mountains, yet she felt moody and out of sorts. With David not yet home from school, the house was oddly silent, just the creak of the stairs as she climbed up to the dusty attic, and the rhythmic moan of the little maple rocker she sat in, unconsciously moving to and fro.

The door of the attic remained open. She kept an ear cocked toward the phone, just in case Chance called. Reaching into the box, she lifted out the last bundle of letters. They were yellowed and brittle with age, the pale rose stationery faded to a pink-tinged ivory hue. But the faint scent of roses drifted up to mingle with the musty odors in the attic.

She settled the letters in her lap and pulled the narrow pink satin ribbon that held them together. They spread out haphazardly across her knees, and for an instant, she simply sat there staring at them.

It was obvious the correspondence spanned a number of years and, once again, all of it was written in the same hand. The handwriting in the oldest, most faded letters was finely etched; beautiful, graceful strokes of the pen when the author was younger. The script became more erratic, less legible as the years slipped past.

Kate lifted the first letters in the stack and her hand began to tremble. Though the envelope carried a stamp, it had never been mailed. And it wasn't addressed to Nell.

Every letter in the stack was addressed to Kate's mother.

Hesitant now in a way she wasn't before, Kate withdrew the first letter in the stack, the oldest it appeared, and for a moment she just held it, afraid of what she would find when she opened it. Eventually, she worked up her courage, used the edge of the silver-handled letter opener that lay in the box, and very carefully sliced open the seal.

The page was so stiff it cracked at the seams when she unfolded it. For an instant, her heart seemed to stop. She wasn't sure exactly how she knew, but she didn't have to look at the signature to know the letters were written by Nell.

Something painful squeezed inside her. Though the envelopes had never been mailed, Nell had written to her daughter, over and over again, in a vain attempt to reach her.

Kate stared down at the tiny flowered border across the top of the page and started to read.

My dearest Mary Beth,

I know this letter cannot possibly reach you, since I have no idea where you are. You've slipped away from me like sand beneath the tide; like smoke rising up through the chimney. You're gone and perhaps nothing will ever bring you back to me. But I do so long for your presence, and I find, as I write these words, that it brings me a little comfort, a feeling that in some way you are still here.

My dearest child, how I wish that we could start over, that I had never said the terrible words that drove you away, that I could wrap you in my arms and keep you and the child you carry safe. But now it is too late.

You will never know how much I regret the things I said, lashing out at you as I did, though in truth it was more in anger at Jack Lambert for what he did to my precious child than at you for falling prey to his wicked charm. But of course you couldn't know that. Where are you, my Mary, my dear little girl? Are you well? Are you safe? Does the child still grow inside you?

I agonize in fear for you, as any mother would.

I beg you, please, wherever you are, come home.

It was signed simply, *Love always, Mother.*

Kate stared down at the paper, the words blurry through the tears that had collected in her eyes. She swallowed past the thick lump in her throat, thinking of the pain in Nell's words, the fierce emotion scrawled on the page.

She opened letter after letter.

> *My dear Mary Beth,*
> *Still no word of you after all these years. How I grieve at the loss. I agonize with worry over what has become of you. Are you well and safe? Are you happy wherever you are? And what of your child? I often try to imagine was it a daughter or a son? A little boy with hints of his tall, handsome grandfather, or a little girl as pretty as you always were. How I wish I could see her, hold her just once. How I miss you, Mary. If only you could find it in your heart to forgive me.*

Kate's hand shook as she replaced the letter. Dear God, how wrong she had been, how dreadfully, painfully wrong. She thought of her mother and she couldn't help feeling a shot of anger. Why had her mother never tried to mend the rift? Why had she never returned to her home?

But deep down, Kate knew. Celeste Heart, the woman Mary Beth had become, was far too proud for that, too stubborn to ever admit she had made a mistake. Because of her stiff, unbending pride, both of them had suffered a loss that could never be regained.

It tortured her to think of the family she had never known, the grandmother whose love she might have had when she was such a desperately lonely child. Kate gently slid the letter back into its weathered, faded envelope, and opened the next.

By the time she had finished, two hours later, she knew that she'd been wrong about Nell Hart and so had her mother.

She had also discovered it was only in the last few years, after Celeste was already dead, that Nell had been able to track down her granddaughter's whereabouts, and then only by a stroke of fortune. Nell had been watching an old movie on TV and recognized her daughter in the minor role she was playing. When the movie was over, Nell had written down the name she had found on the credits.

Mary Beth Hart Lambert was now Celeste Heart.

According to the letters, Nell had hired a detective to track her down. The man discovered her death in a car wreck eight years earlier, but went on to find the daughter she had borne, Kaitlin Lambert Rollins. Unfortunately Nell had been afraid to call or propose any sort of meeting. Too many years had passed. Too much water under the bridge.

She had simply left everything to Kate, which in the end had brought her to Lost Peak.

"At least I know the truth, Grandmother," Kate said into the silence of the attic, but she felt anguished and heartsick, angry and disturbed. "Maybe the letters were the secret you were trying to tell me. Maybe they were what you wanted me to find."

If that was the case, then the mystery was solved. There was nothing left to discover, no murder involved. By the time she left the attic, Kate was more than halfway convinced it was true.

For now, she didn't want to think about anything but

the letters. Passages kept popping into her mind: *Where are you, Mary? Please forgive me. Please come home.*

At last she knew the truth about the woman who was Nell Hart, but with the truth came anger over all those wasted years.

The more she thought about it, the more upset and disturbed she became. Nell had made a mistake, spoken harsh words she regretted for the rest of her life. We all made mistakes. Why couldn't her mother have tried to understand? But Celeste never even tried to reach her. Kate felt a terrible grief for Nell.

And a piece of her heart blossomed with love for her.

The cafe was about to close. He had timed it that way on purpose. Chance pulled the pickup to a stop out in front and turned off the ignition, then sat there for a moment, trying to work up his courage.

He had to see Kate, had to tell her the truth. He couldn't put it off any longer. With a sigh of resignation, he left the truck, jerked open the cafe door and walked in, pausing next to where Kate stood totaling out the register. Her hair was pulled back in the tidy little bun she wore when she was working, but he knew how silky it felt when the pins were gone, how it fell in a riot of curls around her shoulders.

Her breasts swayed a little as she worked, two perfect globes, tipped by big, dark rose circles, he remembered. Her waist looked tiny above her gently flaring hips, and even in her simple pink uniform, he thought she was the sexiest woman he'd ever seen.

She looked up and saw him and warm color rose in her cheeks. "Chance . . ."

"We need to talk, Kate. I thought we might take a drive."

She glanced over at the clock on the wall. "David will be waiting for me at home."

"It's important."

She bit down on her lip, then nodded. "I'll ask Myra to stay with him until we get back. I don't think she'll mind."

Apparently she didn't. Kate returned a few minutes later, grabbed her navy wool jacket off the coat tree beside the door, and Chance led her out to his truck. He hesitated a moment before encircling her waist with his hands to help her climb in, a little afraid to touch her.

In two short weeks, he had almost forgotten how soft and feminine she was, how attracted he was to her, how responsive she had been when he kissed her.

Almost, but not quite.

Even the hours he'd spent with Rachael couldn't erase Kate from his mind completely.

"Where are we going?" she asked, her eyes on the road ahead.

"A place I know down the way a piece." They should have stayed right there in the cafe. He should have made it short and sweet and gotten the hell out of there. But one look at the uncertainty on her face, and he knew he couldn't do it that way. She wasn't just a quick, meaningless screw, and he didn't want her to think she was. He wanted her to understand why he was ending their relationship. More than anything, when this was all over, he still wanted them to be friends.

He pulled off the road down a short gravel lane. He'd thought about going back up to Lookout Mountain, but the memories were still too hot and fresh. He didn't dare take the chance.

He pulled the car to a stop on the side of the road, dragged a blanket from behind the seat for them to sit on, went around and helped Kate out of the truck. She seemed edgy, distracted in some way. He wondered if he was the cause or if something else was bothering her.

"I saw you on TV last night," he said, just to make conversation, "with that anchor woman, Diana Stevens, on the six o'clock news."

She nodded, looked a little uncertain. "I hope I did all right."

"You were terrific."

"They're coming back in a couple of weeks. They want to interview you and Ed."

"Yeah, well, I'm sure we'll have a few more things to say." He spread the blanket beneath a pine tree and they both sat down.

It was quiet here, incredibly peaceful. A full moon rose above the trees so they could see across the little meadow stretching out in front of them. Water bubbled over the rocks in a nearby stream.

"Anything new on Nell?" He didn't know why he was asking. It wasn't what he'd come for. He just wasn't ready to say the words that would end it between them.

Kate sighed. "Actually, there is. I think I've figured out what she was trying to tell me."

He turned to look at her, saw something dark and painful in her eyes. "What was it?"

"I found her letters, Chance. They were upstairs in the attic. Letters she had written to my mother. I always thought that Nell had abandoned her. I hated her for it. I never told you that, but it's true. I hated her for not being there when we needed her, and for treating my mother so badly. But that isn't the way it was."

She told him about her mother, how she had run away to Hollywood and changed her name. How, in her own way, Celeste had loved her, but she was so caught up in her career, so dazzled by the thought of being a star, she was rarely around and not much of a mother. She had never been more than a small bit player, but that hadn't mattered to Celeste.

Kate told him how Nell had tried to find them, how she had written letters year after year. Painful, grief-filled letters, begging her daughter to come home.

"It wasn't her fault, Chance. She made a mistake, but she was sorry. She wanted to make things right. She grieved for my mother till the day she died. All this time, I blamed her, but it wasn't her fault. It's just . . . so unfair."

She was crying by the time she finished. He eased her into his arms and she curled against his chest.

"It's all right, darlin'. At least now you know. If that was what she wanted to tell you, maybe now she can find some peace."

She looked up at him, her cheeks streaked with tears, her eyes luminous in the silvery moonlight. He wiped away the wetness with the end of his finger, felt the cool dampness of her cheek against his hand. He didn't mean to kiss her. It wasn't the reason he was here. He knew it was wrong, but he couldn't seem to help himself. He barely brushed his lips over hers and it was as if a fire had started.

"Katie . . ." he whispered, kissing her softly again. He felt her fingers sliding into his hair, trembling a little, making him tremble, too.

"Make love to me, Chance."

He shook his head. He couldn't make love to her. Not tonight. Not ever again. "We need to talk. There's something I have to—"

Her soft lips cut him off. They shaped perfectly to his, melted into them, pressed deeper. Her tongue touched the corner of his mouth, slid over his bottom lip, and he was lost.

He couldn't stop kissing her, couldn't stop touching her. Her breasts rubbed against him, round, soft, tantalizing. Her coat was open. He unbuttoned the front of her pink nylon uniform and reached inside, pulled her lacy white bra down, and her breasts spilled forward. They were pale and full, with the sexiest nipples he'd ever seen. He sucked each one, kissed them, caressed them.

He told himself to stop, promised himself he would, but Kate was leaning over him, urging him down on the blanket, tearing open the snaps on the front of his shirt. Her coat was gone. She slid her small hands over his bare chest, ran her tongue around a nipple, reached down and unzipped his jeans.

His shaft sprang free. She touched him there, stroked him, wrapped her fingers around him. He was hard, so incredibly hard.

"God, Katie . . ."

"Please, Chance, I need you. I don't want to think anymore, not tonight. I just want to feel."

"Katie . . ." Her small hands moved over him, exploring him, making his shaft ache and throb. He wanted to be inside her, wanted to drive into her until the aching stopped. He knew he couldn't. He was going to marry Rachael. Kate deserved better treatment. Hell, she would have been better off if she had never met him.

She leaned over and kissed him, pressed those magnificent breasts into his chest. His hand slid behind her neck, and he deepened the kiss, plundered her mouth, took her again and again with his tongue. Her glorious auburn hair came loose from its tidy bun. He pulled out the last of the pins and it swung down around her shoulders.

His body shuddered, tightened. He felt like he was on fire.

Just this one last time, he told himself. Just this one last time he would have her, and carry the memory with him for all of the years he would spend without her.

He framed her face between his hands and kissed her eyes, her nose, her beautiful, sensuous mouth.

"I'm crazy about you, Katie." It was the wrong thing to say, the very worst thing he could say, and he meant every word.

"Chance . . ." she whispered, bending down to kiss him again. Then she raised her slim pink nylon skirt, peeled off her panties and stockings, and straddled him there on the blanket, sinking down on him and making him groan.

God, she was incredible. So much woman, the sort he had dreamed of, once upon a time. She started to move, riding him like a stallion, all of that beautiful hair curling wildly around her face. He could feel her gripping him, teasing him, warm and wet all around him. Her head fell back. Her breasts swayed tantalizingly in front of his face. He cupped one in each of his hands.

He was close to climax, hot and so hard he hurt, but he held himself back, letting her take her pleasure, watching the expression on her face as she reached her release, then gripping her hips and driving into her, making her come again.

His own release came hard and fast, jackknifing into him, slicing through him in gut-wrenching waves. It was unlike anything he had ever experienced or probably ever would.

He pulled Kate down on top of him and waited for their heartbeats to slow. She was so small she fit neatly against his side, making him want to curl himself around her. Making him want her again.

He still hadn't talked to her. How could he do that now? Damn, he hated himself, yet he wouldn't change what had happened. Not for anything in the world.

He would wait until he got her home and they were sitting on her sofa. It would be tougher now. Kate had given him something special tonight, some part of herself she had held back from him before. He felt like a thief, but he still wasn't sorry, not when it was such a beautiful gift.

They drove home in silence and his nervousness returned. What could he possibly say that wouldn't hurt her? How could he make her understand?

Unfortunately, by the time they reached the house, Kate had fallen asleep on his shoulder. She looked like a small, soft kitten nestled there, and he steeled himself against the notion of making love to her again.

Christ, I can't tell her now.

Tomorrow he would be busy at Ed's getting ready for the party. *Sunday.* On Sunday he would come over early and explain, tell her everything, make her see that he had no choice. There was no way she could find out before then. And the timing would surely be better.

Wrapping her navy wool jacket more snugly around her, he carried her past Myra, who held open the door, into the house and up the stairs. Resisting an urge to undress her, he left her sleeping on top of the covers and returned downstairs.

"You two have a good time?" Myra eyed the row of snaps he had forgotten to fasten on his shirt and the bare chest that peeked through the opening.

Chance felt the heat rising at the back of his neck. "Yeah. Thanks for watching David."

"No problem. He went to bed about an hour ago."

Chance said nothing more, just walked out and climbed into his truck. For a moment he just sat there, wondering how the evening had gone so far afield from what he had planned. How was it that every time he was with Kate, things got so out of hand?

He dragged in a long, shuddering breath and fired up the truck. On Sunday, he'd make things right with her. He'd tell her the truth about everything, find a way to make her see why it had to be this way.

Until then, he would try not to think about how right it had felt to make love to her.

He would try. But Chance was fairly certain that he was going to fail.

Chapter Twenty

The cafe was busy that Saturday morning. After lunch it thinned to a crawl, giving Kate time to think. Too much time. Every time she thought of her behavior the night before, her face turned a flaming shade of pink.

How could I? she silently groaned. She had practically attacked Chance last night. She remembered tearing open his shirt, remembered the burning kisses, and riding him to climax. Dear God, she had never behaved so outrageously in her life!

Kate sighed as she cleared the last of the dishes off the tables. God, what had driven her to such insane behavior?

She knew the letters were the root of it. Her emotions had been in turmoil ever since she'd read them. They still were. For a few sweet moments last night, she had wanted to forget the past, forget her mother, forget Nell Hart.

She knew Chance could make her forget.

I'm crazy about you, Katie. The words were more precious than gold. She had lost herself in those words, been undone by them. She was in love with him. There was no question in her mind, not the slightest doubt. And she had shown him that love last night.

She was standing there, holding a greasy platter of half-finished eggs and wondering if he might be thinking about her, when the bell chimed over the door and Jake Dillon walked in.

"Mornin' Kate." Maybe five-foot-ten, with iron-gray hair and a slight paunch that hung over his Western buckle, Jake showed up at the cafe for lunch at least three days a week.

"Hi, Jake. I'll be with you in a minute."

He was still standing when she returned from the kitchen to take his order. Today, he obviously wasn't there to eat.

"What's up? Not more trouble with Consolidated Metals, I hope."

"No, no. It's nothing like that. I was just wondering if I might ask you a favor."

"Sure. What is it?"

"There's a big doin's over at Ed Fontaine's tonight—are you going?"

"To tell you the truth, I didn't know anything about it. I didn't get invited."

"Damn near everyone's going. I'm sure it was just an oversight, you being new to the area and all. I told Ed I'd be there, but I really hate to go by myself. Do you think you might go with me—just as a friend, I mean. Like I said, I sure do hate going alone."

Kate hesitated. She and Ed had spent hours together, working on the campaign. Why hadn't he mentioned it? She wondered why Chance hadn't asked her to go, and an uncomfortable shiver slipped down her spine. Maybe he was helping Ed with the preparations and just assumed she would be there. As Jake had said, it was probably just an oversight. Surely Chance wouldn't have invited someone else.

I'm crazy about you, Katie. He wouldn't have said that if he hadn't meant it. Chance wasn't the kind of man who lied.

"All right, Jake, I'd love to go. I can't stay late, though. David will be home alone." His birthday was coming up next week. He'd be thirteen, old enough not to have a sitter . . . as long as Kate was home early and Myra was a phone call away if he needed her.

"We'll come back whenever you say. Thanks, Kate."

Jake left. Kate finished her lunch duties and made arrangements for Bonnie to work the evening shift. Unfortunately, Bonnie couldn't come till six, which meant she and Jake would be arriving at the party a little late.

Wearing a short black Escada cocktail dress she had bought back in her fashion-conscious days in LA, a string of pearls she had saved months to buy, and black high heels, she was ready when he banged on the door.

"Damn. Lady, you look gorgeous. If this old cowboy was ten years younger, he might give Chance McLain a little competition."

It was the first time anyone had even hinted at her relationship with Chance and Kate found herself smiling, liking the idea.

"I think you could still give him competition, Jake." He did look good, in a dark brown, Western-cut suit, beige cowboy shirt, and brown string tie. He'd shined his boots till they gleamed, and he carefully stepped around the mud-puddles in the driveway as he helped her into his freshly washed Chevy Blazer.

"I've never been to Ed's," Kate told him as they drove toward the ranch.

"It's *some* place, I can tell you. His late wife had it built. You'll be surprised when you see it."

She was definitely that. The French chateau looked as out of place up on the side of the hill as a prostitute in church.

Still, it was done in good taste and immaculately tended. The party was in full swing by the time they got there, the house so crowded they could barely get in. Waiters seemed to be everywhere, imported from Missoula, no doubt, the nearest town of any size. They carried silver trays of hors d'oeuvres and champagne, which seemed to be flowing like water.

"Ed certainly knows how to throw a party," Kate said, accepting a glass of champagne.

Jake took a canape off a silver tray and popped it into his mouth. "Sure does."

They said hello to Maddie and Tom Webster, stopped a moment to talk to Harvey Michaelson, then made their way downstairs to the massive entertainment room. There was a pool table, a twelve-foot bar, and the biggest TV she had ever seen—and the room wasn't the least bit crowded. The rest of the furniture had been moved out and a dance floor set up in the middle. A makeshift stage had been erected at the opposite end.

She still hadn't seen Ed, or any sign of Chance. Her nerves began to kick up and she took another fortifying sip of champagne. *Maybe I shouldn't have come.* When Jake spotted a friend and began moving farther into the room, she lagged back, standing in the shadows of the doorway. The room began to fill up, people making their way toward the stage. A few minutes later, Ed and Chance appeared and the crowd that had gathered in front of them began to fall silent.

"Welcome, everyone," Ed said. "I hope you're all enjoying yourselves."

They all applauded. Somebody whistled.

"As some of you know, this shindig is being thrown in honor of my daughter, Rachael. She doesn't get home all that much anymore, and well, we just wanted her to know how glad we are she's here. Rachael—honey, come on up with your dad."

The crowd parted as she walked out a side door with perfect grace and made her way up the wooden stairs. She was dressed in a wispy, knee-length designer silk dress, a filmy print in shades of blue and green that had to have cost a fortune. Short blond hair gleamed like a cap of gold above a face any sculptor would love. She was stunning, quite possibly the most beautiful woman Kate had ever seen.

Her father took her hand and kissed it, then reached over and linked it with Chance's. Rachael smiled up at him. When Chance smiled back and entwined his fingers with hers, Kate's stomach seemed to turn upside down.

They were the perfect couple. Chance dark and handsome as the devil, Rachael a tall, golden angel. Kate felt sick to her stomach.

"I asked you here tonight for more than just a party," Ed said. "Tonight, I'm proud to announce there's going to be a wedding. It's official. My daughter Rachael—

after too damned long in the city—is finally coming home to marry Chance McLain.''

In the single instant of silence that fell, the champagne glass slipped through Kate's numb fingers and shattered on the polished hardwood floor. Chance must have heard it. The crowd gave up a cheer, but above their heads, his eyes locked with hers and the blood seemed to drain from his face. He silently whispered her name the instant before she turned and fled back up the stairs.

Oh dear God, dear God. Her heart was squeezing, her chest aching. Her eyes filled with tears, blurring her vision until she couldn't see where to go. She ran into a short-coated waiter and his tray went flying.

"I—I'm sorry," she sputtered and kept up her rapid pace. French doors led out to the terrace. She hurried toward them, turned the brass handles, and raced out into the night. Tears rolled down her cheeks. She ran down a winding brick path, tripped on a loose brick, winced at the pain that shot into her ankle, and kept on running.

Her legs were shaking. She was trembling all over, sick and numb, and aching. She thought she heard someone calling her name, and veered off the path into the darkness, making her way across the grass, out toward the stables. Her ankle throbbed. A cold breeze rustled through the trees and her bare skin dimpled with the chill, but she didn't really feel it.

She reached the fence around the corral and clung to the rail, her body shaking with the sobs she had held back until now. Great waves of pain broke over her. Dear God, if only she could wake up, banish this terrible nightmare that she had stumbled into, but she knew in her heart it was real.

She heard his voice, soft, gruff, distorted by something that sounded oddly like pain. "Katie ... God, I'm so sorry."

She whirled toward him and her hand cracked hard across his cheek. "Get away from me. Don't ever come near me again." She started walking away from him, heading toward the side of the house.

Chance came up beside her. "I know I should have told you. I wanted to ... I tried to, but something always seemed to get in the way."

"Something seemed to get in the way?" She stopped and turned to face him. "Like what? Having sex? I thought at the very least we were friends. I thought no matter what happened between us, you would treat me with a certain amount of respect."

"We are friends, Kate. More then friends."

"Then how could you let me humiliate myself like I did last night? How could you let me make such a fool of myself?"

"It wasn't that way and you know it."

"How was it, then? Why didn't you tell me, Chance?"

In the light of the moon, his features looked harsh and grim, his jaw so hard it appeared carved in stone. "I know I've hurt you. I was coming to see you tomorrow. I was going to explain everything. I thought, hoped, maybe I could make you understand."

"Understand what? That you were tired of your latest plaything?" Her voice broke. "God, how could I have been such a fool?" She started walking, but he caught her arm.

"You've got to listen to me, Kate. There are things you don't know, things I need to explain. I wish I had. God, you'll never know how much I wish I had."

"That's enough! I don't want to hear another word.

Go back inside, Chance—get out of my life and on with your own." She gave him a cool, bitter smile. "Your fiancée is waiting."

For the third time she started walking and this time he didn't try to stop her. As she headed into the shadowy darkness at the side of the house, a squat, silver-haired man appeared by her side, an old man, slightly stoop-shouldered, his skin ancient and weathered.

"I will tell Jake Dillon you are not feeling well and that I am taking you home."

Kate swallowed, summoned a faint, almost imperceptible nod. "Thank you, Chief."

"Wait here." He sat her down on a wrought-iron bench she hadn't even seen, and she sat there gratefully. She was freezing now and still shaking. She couldn't seem to stop the tears.

God, she hated him.

Just hours ago, she had loved him.

She thought she had known him, but she had been wrong.

And she never would have guessed how much losing him would hurt.

The weekend passed and Kate returned to work. Her eyes were still a little gritty, her skin overly pale. She knew she looked like hell warmed over.

She was standing in the kitchen, getting ready for the first of the customers to arrive, when Myra walked up beside her. "I imagine I'm ratin' pretty low on your list of friends right now."

Kate's heart sank. "Obviously, you heard about Chance's engagement. Please don't tell me you knew he was involved with someone else and didn't tell me."

"Lord no. I never would have encouraged you if I'd had the slightest notion of anything like that. I knew he used to see her a lot. I thought it was over between them. She hasn't been back in town for months, and she was never the right girl for him, anyhow."

Kate bit down on the inside of her jaw, fighting the urge to cry. "Apparently Chance doesn't see it that way."

Myra sighed. She ran a pencil into the brassy blond curls piled up beneath her hairnet and used it to scratch her head. "Somethin' just ain't right. He ain't in love with Rachael—never has been. Anytime they were together, that was as plain as the nose on your face."

"Then why is he marrying her?"

"I don't know for sure. But he and Ed are powerful close, have been since Chance was a boy. His father never gave him the time of day. Hollis McLain was always too busy building his empire. Ed was their closest neighbor and he never had a son. He sort of adopted Chance."

"Well, whatever the reason, in six months he's getting married. And he didn't even have the decency to tell me." Kate blinked back tears. She wasn't going to cry, not again. She had cried enough for Chance McLain.

"It ain't like him to do somethin' like this. Chance has always gone out of his way to treat a woman fairly. That boy musta had a powerful itch for you, Kate."

She swallowed back the lump that kept trying to form in her throat. "Well, now that I've scratched it, he can go back to his beauty queen and live happily ever after."

"Maybe he will, but I got a pretty fair suspicion his life with Rachael Fontaine is purely gonna be hell."

Kate said nothing to that. She didn't want to talk about Chance. She never wanted to think of him ever again. It wasn't going to happen. Chance was stuck in her heart like a painful thorn she couldn't get rid of.

If he was unhappy with Rachael, she couldn't care less. She wanted him to be miserable—didn't she? After the way he had treated her, of course she did.

But even as she worked taking orders and carrying plates, she couldn't help remembering the pain in those brilliant blue eyes when Chance had come after her at Ed's house that night.

Kate sighed as she picked up a bowl of broccoli soup. Perhaps in some small way, he actually had cared about her. It didn't really matter. Whatever his intentions, he had hurt her very badly.

And Kate would never forgive him.

A week dragged past. Still sleeping poorly, by the end of her shift, Kate was exhausted. Still, she knew once she got home she would start to think about Chance and she was determined not to do that.

"I think I'll go over and have a beer," she told Myra. "You want to come?"

Myra's blond eyebrow arched up. "You're goin' over to the Antlers?"

She had never gone into a bar by herself in her life. Maybe it was time she did. "Why not? I like Tom and Maddie and tonight I could really use a drink."

Myra grinned. "Now you're talkin', gal."

They finished closing up and walked catty-corner across the street. The bar was practically deserted, just a couple of locals Kate didn't know but had seen once or twice in town, and plump, good-natured Maddie Webster, working behind the bar.

"Well, hello there, ladies."

"You got one of them Moose Drools back there?" Myra asked.

"Sure do. How 'bout you, Kate?"

"A Bud Light would be great."

"You got it." Maddie brought their beers, set them on the top of the bar, and Kate took a drink. It was cold and refreshing and she could feel the slight relaxation after only a couple of sips.

Maddie wiped an imaginary spot on the bar in front of them, looking a little uncomfortable. "What happened out at Ed's . . . I guess that came as kind of a surprise."

Kate toyed with her beer mug. "You might say that."

"I can't believe he didn't tell you."

"Yeah, well if you think it's hard to believe, you ought to see how it looks from my shoes."

"You ask me, it was a pretty darned rotten thing to do."

Kate shrugged her shoulders, wishing they could talk about something else, wishing just the mention of his name didn't make her heart start to ache. "Maybe he saw her again and realized how much he loved her."

Maddie made a grunting sound in her throat. "You ever met Rachael Fontaine?"

"No."

Whatever point Maddie was making, Myra seemed to agree. "She might have a beautiful face, but there's lots of things more important than looks."

"You can say that again." Maddie wiped her wet towel in a circle on the bar. "Chance is a fool to marry a featherhead like Rachael. Not when he had the chance to hook up with a woman like you."

Kate flushed, but her bruised heart felt a little better. "Thank you, Maddie."

The heavyset woman moved down to the other end of the bar to refill the other customers' drinks. then returned and resumed her conversation. "I heard a couple days back you was asking questions about your grandma Nell."

"That's right." But she had given up that pursuit. She had found the letters, unlocked Nell's secret. Her search was at an end.

"What kind of questions?" Maddie asked.

"I wanted to know a little bit more about how she died. I wanted to know what happened the day of the accident."

Maddie made a sort of clucking sound and shook her head. "Your grandma was a doozie. We all still miss her. It was a sorry day for all of us when she died."

"How did you hear about it?"

"Aida Whittaker stopped by. She found her, you know. They'd been friends for years. It was real hard on Aida, I can tell you."

"I found some of Nell's letters up in the attic," Kate said softly. "After my mother left, Nell tried to find her. She must have searched for years."

"Nell loved Mary Beth," Maddie said. "It durn near killed her when the girl run off with that no-good Jack Lambert—meanin' no offense."

Kate's mouth inched up. "None taken." She took a sip of her beer. "I found some letters Silas wrote her. I guess they were pretty good friends."

"Better than that. Silas was in love with your grandma for years. He was real torn up when she died. He come in here drunker than a cowhand on payday, cryin' like a baby. Said he and Nell had a real bad fight that day. Said now he would never be able to tell her he was sorry."

The beer mug paused halfway to Kate's lips. "Nell and Silas had a fight the day she died?"

"That's what he said. Said he went over there to talk to her about sellin' that parcel they owned together and he and Nell started arguin'. A couple of hours later she was dead."

A feeling of uneasiness began to move through her. "I didn't see anything about that in the sheriff's report."

"Don't guess Silas mentioned it. You know how it is when you own a bar—you're everybody's confessor."

"I asked him about the accident, but he never mentioned he had seen Nell that day."

"I guess he still feels real bad about it."

Maybe he did. Maybe he felt worse than anyone knew. "You finished with your beer?" Kate asked Myra, suddenly eager to leave.

Myra deftly upended her mug. "Am now."

"Thanks for the drink, Maddie." Kate slid off the barstool, pulled her jacket on over her uniform, and waited while Myra did the same.

She had told herself this was over. She had convinced herself she was wrong, that Nell's message had nothing to do with murder. Now she wouldn't rest until she talked one more time to Silas Marshall. It wouldn't happen tonight, but sooner or later, the opportunity would arise.

She couldn't help wondering exactly what Silas would say when it did.

Chapter Twenty-one

The nights all seemed to run together. Kate tossed and turned, and Nell appeared in her dreams. She didn't remember much about them, just awakened in the morning with a vague sense that something was out of kilter. She felt tired and edgy as she watched David climb aboard the big yellow school bus and head down the road to the Ronan Middle School where he was enrolled.

Finishing the last of her coffee, she draped a sweater around her shoulders and set off for the cafe.

Twenty minutes before it was time to open, she was stunned to see a tall, lanky, dark-haired man walk through the back door into the kitchen.

Chance McLain.

Anger kept her back ramrod straight. It infuriated her to see how good he looked, freshly shaven, his wavy black hair carefully combed, sporting only the tiniest crease where his black felt hat had ridden on his fore-head. He held it against his jeans in a callused hand, and she tried not to remember the intimate things those skillful dark fingers done to her.

Country music played softly in the background, *"Easy on the eyes . . . hard on the heart."* No truer words had ever been sung.

She finally walked over to where he stood. "The cafe opens in twenty minutes. Customers usually use the front door."

"I need to talk to you, Kate."

"There is nothing you have to say that I would possibly be interested in hearing. Now if you would please just leave."

"I know you're angry. Give me ten minutes. That's all I ask. Ten minutes and I'll be out of your life for good."

"You're already out of my life." Kate turned to Myra. "Would you tell Mr. McLain I'm too busy to talk to him right now. I've got to be ready to open in just a few minutes."

"Dammit, Kate—"

Myra stepped between them as Kate walked away. "Another time might be better, Chance. Give her a while to cool off. Maybe she'll be ready to listen then."

Chance cast a last look in her direction, swore softly, and stalked away, slamming the door a little too hard on his way out.

Myra eyed her from across the counter. "You ought to hear what he has to say."

"Why? He's getting married to someone else. I'm not interested in continuing a relationship whenever his girlfriend happens to be out of town."

Myra just sighed and turned away. Tying her apron on over her uniform, she set to work.

The cafe was busy. Kate left after the lunch shift, went home and made some phone calls to a couple of environmental groups. She was working tonight, so she returned for the dinner shift. David wouldn't be waiting when she got home.

She smiled to think of Brian Holloway, the new friend that he had made at school. Tonight there was a Boy Scout meeting at Brian's house, and Brian and Chris Spotted Horse, who was also a scout, had convinced David to go.

Since it was a thirty-minute bus ride each way to Ronan, and the Holloways lived only a few blocks from the school, Mr. Holloway, who was also the scoutmaster, had called and asked if David could spend the night at his son's house.

Kate had been thrilled to agree. When David had asked if he could join the Scouts, Kate felt as if her prayers had finally been answered. He was becoming part of the community, making friends with children who came from good, wholesome families.

When the supper shift was over, Kate closed the cafe and made the short walk up the hill to the house. She frowned at the darkness surrounding it. She thought she had left a lamp on in the living room, but apparently she had forgotten. Digging out the key to her front door as she climbed the wooden stairs to the porch, she opened the door, went into the darkened hallway, and reached for the light switch.

Kate gasped as a hand shot out of the darkness and clamped hard over her mouth. A thick arm locked around her waist, dragging her back against a man's big body. She forced out a scream, but his gloved hand muffled the sound.

"You'd better keep quiet if you know what's good for you."

She clawed at the silencing hand and tried to twist free as he dragged her into the living room, but the man was at least a foot taller and probably a hundred pounds heavier than she was. *Oh dear God!* She'd always been afraid of something like this happening in the city, but not out here. Certainly not out here.

Frantically, she groped behind her, trying to scratch his face, grabbed a handful of soft knit fabric and realized he was wearing a ski mask. Her breath caught and the blood froze in her veins.

Oh God, oh God. Dragging in a steadying breath, she mentally ran over her options, which didn't take long, since she really didn't have any. There was no one around and she was too far away from the restaurant for anyone to hear her scream. She couldn't reach the phone, not even to knock it off the hook. With no one to help her, she had no choice but to try to help herself.

Kate kicked backward as hard as she could, twisted at the same time, and suddenly she was free. She unleashed a scream that would have wakened the dead, if anyone had been near enough to hear it, and started to run, but the man was on her in an instant, knocking her down before she could reach the front door, landing hard on top of her, knocking the air from her lungs.

She ignored the aching in her ribs, fought for breath, tried to drag off his ski mask, and succeeded in digging a long scratch along the side of his thick neck.

He rolled her over and slapped her hard across the face. "You little bitch. You wanna play rough?" Another hard slap and she moaned.

"I came to give you a message. You bow out of the anti-mining coalition. You don't, you're gonna get hurt real bad." Through the opening in the ski mask, she could see his lips pull up in a leer. "And just in case you might forget, I'm gonna give you a little something to help you remember."

Kate screamed as he caught the neck of her uniform blouse and ripped it open to the waist. Massive hands tore her bra in two, then he started to shove up her skirt. She tried to scream, got another vicious slap for the effort, and a wave of nausea washed over her, making her head spin. She tried to twist away from him, tried to shove him off her, but the more she fought, the more it seemed to excite him.

She heard the sound of his zipper sliding down, then another sound intruded, and his big hard body went tense. Kate started struggling again. She swallowed and tried to scream, but her mouth was so dry it came out more like a whimper.

Then the door flew open and Chance stormed in. "Son of a bitch!"

Her attacker flew off her as if he weighed less than a feather instead of over two hundred pounds. Curling herself into a protective ball, she managed to roll to her knees and shove down her skirt. Her stockings were torn. Her blouse gaped open.

In the darkness of the living room, she could hear the sound of furniture crashing against the walls. A lamp went flying. In the moonlight streaming in through the windows, she saw Chance threw a punch that sent the heavier man sliding across the floor. He was up and running in a heartbeat, slamming through the door leading into the kitchen. Running after him in the darkness, Chance didn't see the chair the man had dragged into his path. He hit it hard and went sprawling, cursed, tried to get back on his feet. By the time he did, her attacker was out the door and heading for the woods.

Chance didn't follow. Instead he whirled toward the living room, flipped the light on beside the sofa, and ran over to where she sagged against the wall, still crouched in a ball, holding the tattered remnants of her ruined blouse together.

Chance helped her to her feet, but she was shaking so hard, she wasn't sure she could stay upright. He must have realized how close she was to collapse because he swore a violent oath and swept her up in his arms.

He carried her over to the sofa and sat down with her in his lap, his arms wrapped protectively around her. She thought of his betrayal and knew she should pull away, but she didn't have the strength.

"How badly are you hurt?" he asked.

She swallowed, fought to stop shaking. "Not . . . not too bad. He hit me a couple of times. He tried to . . . If you hadn't come when you did, he would have . . . he would have . . ."

"Sssh, I know. It's all right. He can't hurt you now." He glanced around, the muscles still tense across his shoulders. "Where's David?"

"At a scout meeting. He's spending the night with a friend." Another shiver ran through her to think what might have happened if her son had been in the house.

Unconsciously Chance tightened his hold. "I wonder how the bastard knew you'd be alone."

"I'm not . . . not sure he did."

"What do you mean?"

"I don't know, exactly. He seemed to be playing this thing minute by minute as he went along. He wanted me to stop . . . stop working on the campaign."

Chance's face turned grim. "God, Kate. When I asked you to help, I never thought it would come to this."

Her eyes slid closed. She had to get up, get away from him, give up the warmth and safety she felt in his arms. As if he sensed her thoughts, he settled her onto the sofa beside him, pulled the afghan off the back and wrapped it carefully around her.

"I'm calling the sheriff." Heading for the phone, he dialed 911 and briefly told the dispatcher what had happened.

"There's a deputy on his way. It'll take a while—it always does—but he'll be here as soon as he can."

Kate said nothing. Her jaw ached and her lip was beginning to swell. Chance went into the bathroom and came out with a washcloth dampened with cold water. Kate took it gratefully and held it against her jaw.

"Where's your aspirin?"

"Upstairs bathroom."

He came down carrying the bottle a few minutes later, fetched her a glass of water, and waited while she swallowed the pills.

Kate set the glass down on the coffee table and turned to look at him. "What are you doing here, Chance? How did you happen to come along when you did?"

"I wanted to talk to you. I still do. But now is hardly the time."

Never was the time as far as Kate was concerned. She lay back against the sofa trying to ignore her throbbing jaw and the pounding in her head. Eventually headlights flashed through the glass in the front door and Chance got up to let the deputy, an officer named Winston, into the house. Half an hour later, a report had been filed, and at Chance's insistence, Myra had been summoned to spend the night.

"I don't need Myra to stay with me," Kate argued. "I'm sure he won't be back again tonight."

"If I had my way, I'd be the one who was staying. I know what you'd say about that, so Myra will have to do. It isn't negotiable, Kate."

She opened her mouth to argue, but she was simply too exhausted. And the truth was she didn't really want to be alone. Myra arrived a few minutes later and instantly started fussing.

"Poor little thing. Just ain't right. A woman oughta be safe in her own home."

Chance paused beside the door. "Tomorrow I'll stop by to make sure you're okay."

"No! I mean . . . thank you, but there's no need for you to be concerned." The last thing she wanted was to see Chance again, though she had to admit she was grateful for his timely arrival tonight. "The sheriff said they'd be keeping a close watch on the house."

"Yeah, well, that isn't good enough. Tomorrow I'm bringing you a gun."

"A gun!" She tried to sit up, but the motion made her dizzy so she eased herself back down. "I don't have the slightest idea how to use a gun."

"Then it's about time you learned." He didn't wait for her reply, just shoved open the door and stepped out into the night.

"Good thing he stopped by," Myra said, parroting her earlier thoughts.

"I don't want to talk to him. Can't you tell him that?"

"You know what he's like. Hardheaded as a mule and determined as a pit bull. He wants to talk to you. Sooner or later, you'll have to listen."

But Kate was equally determined. She was finished with Chance McLain and though she would always be grateful for his rescue tonight, she wasn't interested in hearing anything he had to say.

"Dammit, I told you to scare her, shake her up a little! That's all I told you to do!" Lon Barton paced in front of the small rock fireplace in his office.

"Yeah, well, you weren't there. That little bitch fought like a wildcat. She was asking for it." His lips curled up. "And if McLain hadn't shown up when he did, I'd have given it to her good."

Lon spun to face him. "Listen to me, Mullens. We're getting closer and closer to our goal. We don't need any more trouble with Kaitlin Rollins."

"Are you kidding? The woman was scared shitless. She won't give you anymore trouble. She knows what'll happen if she sticks her nose into mining business again."

"I hope you're right . . . for all our sakes." Lon picked up an antique flintlock pistol from the collection on the wall above the fireplace. He loved old weapons, the older the better, but they didn't come cheap. Maybe that was one of the reasons he liked them so much. "At any rate, it's time to let things cool down a little." He turned, aimed the gun, peered through the sight, then put it back in the rack. "You're sure nobody knew it was you."

"I told you I wore a mask. Even if McLain guessed it was me, he's got no way to prove it."

Lon nodded. "All right, then for now we won't worry about it. For the next few days, just lay low and stay out of trouble. Take a few days off. Make a trip to Missoula. Find yourself a woman, if that's what you want."

Duke Mullens grinned. "Sounds like a good idea to me."

Lon watched him leave and returned to his desk. Duke had gone further than he should have with the girl, but at least she was off the coalition and out of his hair. Without her, the group would be floundering in no time, far less a threat than they were before.

Lon smiled. Duke might be a bit overzealous at times, but he always got the job done. And considering what a tempting little piece Kate Rollins was, in a way Lon didn't blame him for trying to screw her.

Standing next to Ed Fontaine's wheelchair in the passenger terminal of the Missoula Airport, Chance watched the silver Delta 727 winging its way toward Salt Lake City on the way to New York. The plane disappeared into the clouds, and Chance turned away from the window, hiding a sharp sense of relief. He felt guilty for it. Dammit, in six months, Rachael would be his wife. He wanted to watch that plane depart and feel overwhelmed by a stinging sense of loss.

The way he had last night.

But Rachael was Rachael, not Kate. He and Rachael responded to each other as they had for most of their lives, with a comfortable acceptance, Rachael resigned to returning to Montana and beginning a life with him, Chance resigned to making her his wife. He cared about her. He always had. He had known her since she was a little girl and in a lot of ways she still was. It wasn't her fault he had finally discovered he wanted more from a marriage than that.

"Well, son, I guess we're on our own for a while."

Chance just nodded. Pushing the wheelchair in front

of him, he made his way out of the terminal to the passenger loading zone in front of the airport and waited while Randy pulled the van up to the curb. The electric gate lifted Ed and the wheelchair into the back, and Randy and Chance climbed into their seats in the front.

Randy was the one who brought up the subject that had been hammering away at his mind all morning.

"I heard you ran into some trouble in Lost Peak last night."

A thread of tension filtered through him as an image arose of Kate struggling beneath her attacker. Unconsciously his hand tightened into a fist. "Some."

"What kind of trouble?" Ed asked.

"Some guy broke into Kate Rollins' place," Randy supplied. "I guess he roughed her up pretty good. Might have done more than that if Chance hadn't happened along when he did."

"You scared him away?" Ed asked.

Chance nodded. "They must have seen the television interview Kate did last week. Consolidated's running scared. They want her off the campaign."

"Is she all right?"

"She was pretty shook up. I got a hunch the guy was Duke Mullens, but he was wearing a ski mask, so there's no way to know for sure."

"Then you don't think the sheriff will come up with anything."

"He had on leather gloves. There won't be any fingerprints. Unless someone happened to see him—which is damned unlikely—there isn't much hope of that." Ed didn't ask him what he was doing at Kate's house and Chance didn't offer to tell him. Nothing was going on between them—not anymore. He just wanted a chance to explain.

Since the plane left at 6:50 A.M., it was early when Randy dropped him off back at his truck. Chance drove over to Kate's house to check on her and was amazed to find no one at home. Worried that something else might have happened to her, he hurried down to the cafe.

Breakfast was pretty much over by the time he got there and lunch hadn't yet rolled around. Looking through the recently repaired front window, he saw Kate, dressed in jeans and a dark green T-shirt with the cafe logo on the front, standing behind the cash register.

Why it made him so damned mad he couldn't say. He just knew he was furious. Storming through the doors like a madman, he slammed to a halt directly in front of her.

"What the hell do you think you're doing?"

"Adding up breakfast tickets. What does it look like I'm doing?"

"Last night someone beat the crap out of you and today you're adding up tickets? You ought to be home resting, taking care of yourself."

"Well, I happen to have a restaurant to run. And for your information, I feel perfectly fine."

He caught her chin between his fingers and examined the purplish bruise, her slightly puffy lip. "You don't look fine. You look like you ought to be in bed." The minute he said the words, he wished he hadn't. Images flashed through his head: Kate's glorious red hair sliding through his fingers, her magnificent breasts spilling into his hands.

The color was high in her cheeks when he looked

down at her, and he wondered if she had been remembering, too.

"I have to be getting back to work," she said, trying to shove past him.

"You aren't dressed for work. Where's your uniform?"

"Change of policy, starting today. Jeans and T-shirts from now on." She gave him a sarcastic smile—"When in Rome . . . "—and headed for the kitchen.

Chance let her go. He felt guilty for even thinking about Kate when he was committed to Rachael, but there didn't seem to be a damned thing he could do to stop it. Still, whether Kate belonged to him or not, he was determined to keep her safe.

He caught her wrist as she sailed back into the dining room.

"Come on. There's something we need to do." He started tugging her toward the door at the rear of the cafe, but Kate jerked away.

"Are you crazy? I'm not going anywhere with you. I made that mistake before."

With a sigh, he pulled the gun from the waistband at the back of his jeans. "You're through with the campaign, but you still might need this." He showed her the .38 caliber automatic he figured would be the easiest thing for her to shoot.

"First of all, I'm not through with the campaign until we're sure that mine isn't going to go in. Second, I don't need a gun."

"First—you *are* through. I don't want you hurt any more than you already have been. Second—you may not need a gun, but it can't hurt to know how to shoot one."

"If I did, I might just consider shooting you!"

"Dammit, Kate. What you think of me has nothing to do with this. You need to be able to defend yourself."

Her mouth tightened. She might not want to admit it, but she knew he was right. She eyed the gun warily, then stiffened her spine. "All right. At least if the guy comes back, I won't be completely at his mercy."

Chance's stomach tightened at the thought of the bastard hurting her again. "If he does, you don't hesitate. You aim and pull the trigger—understand? Come on. I'll show you what I mean."

It was obvious she didn't want to go with him, and equally obvious she wanted to able to take care of herself. They went out behind the cafe to a spot on the opposite side of Little Sandy Creek where a mountainside formed a natural barrier that was a safe place to fire the gun. Chance set up targets, then showed her how to load the pistol. He made her load it a couple of times herself, then they were ready to shoot.

"Just remember—there's no such thing as an unloaded weapon. That's the reason you never point it at anyone—unless you intend to shoot."

He fired the pistol a couple of times, then handed it to Kate. "Hold your arms out straight, just the way I did, one hand wrapped around the other. Now brace your feet apart. Aim and fire."

She missed, but not by much. He set up another few targets and she fired a couple more rounds. Still not satisfied, he moved behind her. He felt her body stiffen, straining not to touch him, but her drive to master the weapon won out and she didn't move again.

"Ready?"

She held out the gun and Chance braced his arms around hers. He could feel her bottom pressing into his groin and bit back a silent curse. Kate fired again, hit the target dead-center, and Chance stepped away.

He cleared his throat, turned a little so she wouldn't see his erection. "Keep it handy. You probably won't need it, but I'll feel better knowing you've got it."

Kate just nodded. Chance said nothing more, and they walked in silence back to the cafe.

For the next full week, he stayed away. Fall was a busy time at the ranch, getting ready for winter, moving the cattle down from the high pastures to the lower ones out of the coming snows. But worry for Kate nagged at him, and his conscience nagged even more.

He had treated her badly and he knew it. She thought he wanted Rachael, that he had simply grown tired of her. Chance didn't think he would ever grow tired of Kate, and even though he couldn't have her, he wanted her to know the truth.

It wouldn't change things. Nothing could do that. But at least if she understood, in time she might forgive him.

Chance set his jaw. One way or another, he vowed, this time she was going to hear what he had to say.

Chapter Twenty-two

Kate finished the Friday lunch shift feeling better than she had all week. Her bruises had faded and no other incidents had occurred. Sheriff Conrad himself had stopped by to express his concern and assure her the department would be keeping a close eye on things. They hadn't found any trace of the man who attacked her, and it didn't look like they would, but they were going to keep trying.

Her life was almost back to normal.

Almost.

She was still a little edgy whenever she was in the house. A man had nearly raped her. It wasn't something she would soon forget. Fortunately, she had other business to occupy her mind, namely the matter of Silas Marshall, and this afternoon she had made up her mind to go see him.

Kate felt an odd tug of anticipation. Whenever she looked into Nell's death, Silas's name seemed to surface. She wanted to know the truth about what happened that day, and she was more and more certain Silas Marshall held the answers to her questions.

She was sitting in one of the booths in the nearly empty cafe, drinking a cup of coffee and planning what she was going to say when a familiar deep voice spoke up from beside her.

"It's time for us to talk."

She hadn't heard him come in. Kate carefully set her cup down in its saucer and slowly came to her feet, tipping her head back so she could look him squarely in the face.

"I told you—I'm not interested."

"Fine. Now I'm telling you—you're going to hear what I've got to say."

Kate's temper cranked up a notch. She whirled toward the last few patrons still eating their lunch, all eyes now fixed in their direction. She gave him a sarcastic smile and planted her hands on her hips. "All right. You want to talk. Go ahead and talk."

Chance glanced around, saw the inquisitive faces staring in their direction, and fury blazed in his eyes. "I'm going to say this one more time. We're going to talk, Kate. Somewhere private. After that, I'll leave you alone." He reached out and took hold of her wrist, started tugging her toward the door.

Kate dug her heels into the carpet and caught hold of the back of a chair. "I told you, I'm not going." His face darkened, his scowl so black it gave her a moment of pause.

Chance glared at her and set his jaw. "All right, fine.

I've tried to be patient. I've done everything I can think of to convince you. I can see it isn't going to work."

Kate yelped as he bent and tossed her over his shoulder, one long arm clamped around her knees, the other resting familiarly over her bottom.

"Are you insane? Put me down!"

"I intend to." He jerked open the door and walked out onto the wooden boardwalk. "As soon as we get to my truck."

Kate stopped struggling. It wasn't going to do a lick of good, and it only made her look more ridiculous. Thank God for her recent change of policy that allowed them all to work in jeans. Chance closed the distance to his pickup, opened the door, and dumped her in, then rounded the front of the truck, climbed in, and fired up the engine.

"This won't take long," he said. "But dammit you're going to hear what I have to say."

Kate said nothing, just let him drive away, recognizing the direction he was heading as the road to Lookout Mountain. They pulled into the overlook on the Flathead Valley, spread out below them in the distinctive red, orange, and yellows of fall.

"All right," Kate said. "You've dragged me up here. What do you have to say that's so important?"

Chance sighed. He took off his black felt hat and set it on the dashboard, raked a hand through his hair. "First of all, I didn't plan any of the things that happened. I didn't even know Rachael was going to be here until she called me from her father's ranch."

"But you were involved with her. You should have told me that from the start."

"I hadn't seen Rachael in months. We led separate lives. We had for years. Even when she got here, I wasn't thinking about marriage. Her father thought it was time. That's how it happened.''

"Her father? What does Ed have to do with it?"

Chance released another sigh, seemed to be struggling for words. "It's kind of hard to explain. Ed is more than just a friend. He's been like a father to me since I was a boy. His ranch borders a portion of the Running Moon. From the time Rachael was just a girl, her father expected the two of us to marry. We never talked about it, not really. We just assumed some day we would.''

"This isn't the Dark Ages, Chance. People don't have to accept arranged marriages.''

"Maybe not in most cases. My case is different.''

"Why is that?''

"Because I'm the guy who put Ed Fontaine in a wheelchair.''

There were a lot of things he might have said. This was one she hadn't expected. Her mouth felt suddenly dry. "Are you . . . are you saying it was somehow your fault that he's paralyzed?''

Chance stared out through the windshield. The blue of his eyes seemed to have faded, making them look like the sky on a too-hot day. "I was twelve years old when it happened. My father told me not to go riding that day. A lightning storm was coming in, he said. He told me to stay near the house.''

"But you didn't," Kate said softly.

"No. I did what I wanted. That was pretty much the way it was. My father was never around. There was no one to tell me what to do. When he did say something, I rarely listened. I didn't listen that day.''

Oh God. "What happened?"

"The storm came in, just like my father said. I was riding Sunny, this little buckskin gelding I liked. He was kind of skittery, hard to handle, but he was full of fire and he could run like the wind. We were in some pretty rugged country when the storm swept in, lots of gulleys and rocky ravines. It hit without much warning, a real bad one, raining like hell, wind blowing so hard you couldn't see. The buckskin stepped in a hole and went down. I lost my stirrups and went over his head. I landed on the edge of a steep ravine and rolled over the edge. I must have grabbed hold of a bush as I fell, but I really don't remember. I hung there for hours in the rain, yelling my head off, knowing it wouldn't do a lick of good. Then I heard the sound of voices, someone shouting my name."

"Your father came after you?"

Chance shook his head. "Ed came. I guess he stopped by my dad's place and realized I was out in the storm. The buckskin showed up about then, but my dad figured I'd just been thrown. He said a long walk home in the rain would serve me right for not doing what he said."

Kate bit down on her lip and discovered it was trembling. "So Ed was the one who found you."

"Unfortunately for him, yeah. He took one of his Indian cowhands along. Three Bulls could track a hayseed in a cloudburst. He found a spot where the ground was torn up, the place where the buckskin went down, then they heard me yelling. Ed tried to throw me a rope, but my hands were so numb by then I couldn't catch it."

Kate listened to the despair in his voice and a sweep of pity rolled through her. She could imagine how terrified David would have been, out there alone in a terrible storm, thinking no one cared enough to come after him.

"Ed told me not to worry, said he'd come down and

get me. He took the rope from Three Bulls's saddle horn, tied it to a rock, and lowered himself over the cliff. He helped me get a noose around my waist and Three Bulls hauled me up."

Chance's throat worked, but for a moment, no more words came out. "Before he could climb back up himself, the rock he had tied his rope around gave way and Ed fell into the bottom of the ravine."

"Oh, Chance." Her throat was so tight she was surprised he could hear her. Maybe he didn't.

"Ed came after me," he said. "And because he did, he never walked again."

Tears burned her eyes. Kate reached over and caught his hand. It felt stiff and icy against the warmth of her own. "You were only a boy, Chance. It wasn't your fault."

Those piercing blue eyes swung to her face. "It was my fault. That's why I have to marry Rachael. Because I owe it to Ed. He wants his daughter close to him and married to man who'll take care of her. He wants his land to go to sons who'll appreciate what they've been given and know how to take care of it. He knows I can give him those things."

The tears in Kate's eyes began to trickle down her cheeks. "What about you, Chance? You want to make Ed happy. Don't you deserve to be happy yourself?"

"Maybe I did. Once. Not anymore. Not since I was twelve years old."

Her throat ached. "And Rachael? Does she know how you feel?"

"Rachael's tired of life in the city. She wants to come home. She wants to marry a man who will give her whatever she wants."

"Maybe . . . maybe she'll make you happy."

He made no reply. He clamped his jaw and a muscle

leapt in his cheek. When he looked at her, there was so much pain in his eyes, her own eyes filled with tears.

Kate leaned against him, slid her arms around his neck, felt his arms come around her. She held him tightly and he held her.

"I'm sorry I didn't tell you sooner. I guess I just wasn't ready to let you go."

"Chance ..." She tightened her hold around his neck and the tears in her eyes began to roll down her cheeks. She was in love with him. The feeling was lodged in her heart and it wasn't going to go away.

Her throat closed up. It was over between them, but at least now she knew she hadn't been wrong about the kind of man he was.

And after what he'd told her, she loved him more than ever.

"I'm glad you made me listen," she said, pulling away from him, dashing the tears from her cheeks.

"I never meant to hurt you. I sorry, Kate, for everything."

She nodded, accepting the sincerity of his words. She dragged in a shaky breath of air. "It's all right. Sometimes things just happen."

"Yeah, I guess so." They sat there in silence for a few minutes more, as if neither of them wanted the moment to end. Then Chance reached for the key and started the engine. "I'll take you back now."

They didn't talk on their way down the hill. There was nothing for either of them to say.

Chance helped her out of the truck in front of the cafe and walked her to the door. "I wish things could be different," he said.

"So do I." But they couldn't be, and both of them knew it. Chance's mind was set and he wasn't going to change it. His strong sense of duty was one of the things she liked best about him. She watched him climb back in the truck and slowly drive away.

As he had promised she would, at least now she understood. She should have felt better.

Instead she felt ten times worse.

The weekend slipped past. She thought of Chance only a few times a day, resigned as she was to burying her feelings for him as deeply as she could. Instead she renewed her resolve to gather the final pieces of the puzzle of Nell's death and speak to Silas Marshall. As soon as lunch was over, she marched across the street to Marshall's Grocery.

Kate shoved through the door, listening to a bell that rang a little louder than the one in the cafe, and glanced around looking for Silas. Until she came to Lost Peak, she had never been in a market quite like this one, with its sagging plank floor, tiny vegetable counter, and frozen meat section. There wasn't a heck of a lot to choose from, but when you ran out of eggs in the middle of baking a cake or found the last quart of milk sitting empty in the fridge, you were darned glad it was there. It was a long way to the supermarket and though this was the only game in town when it came to buying groceries, Silas's prices were surprisingly fair.

She glanced around again, spotted him stacking Campbell's soup cans on one of the shelves, and started in that direction. There were a couple of customers up in front, but Carol Simmons, Silas's cashier, was handling them without any problem.

"Hello, Silas."

He glanced up, got a funny look on his face. "Hi, Kate.

You need some help finding something?" He stood up, stretching his pale, thin body what seemed like several feet above her head.

"Actually, there was something I wanted to ask you about."

His expression turned slightly wary. "What is it?"

"I was wondering ... the last time we talked about my grandmother, you didn't mention you had seen her the day she died."

He blinked owlishly, as if he couldn't figure out how she could possibly have known. "I didn't?"

"No, you didn't. I don't think you mentioned it to Sheriff Conrad, either."

He cleared his throat. "I guess ... I guess it didn't seem important at the time."

"How about the fight you two had? Did that also not seem important?"

He wet his thin lips, glanced around as if he was looking for a path of escape. "I ... I guess it didn't ... at the time."

"What was the fight about?"

"The property we owned."

"You wanted Nell to sell it ... isn't that right?"

"Yes ..."

"But she refused."

He nodded. "She didn't want the mine going in. I told you that before."

"Yes, you did. But that day you were determined to convince her. Isn't that the reason you went to see her?"

His pale face turned paper white, his eyes squinting, deep lines forming at the corners. "Yes."

"But she still wouldn't sell."

Silas swallowed. His body started to tremble. He ran a shaking had over his lips. "We argued something awful. I don't think we ever had such a row. My boy, Milton . . . he wanted to borrow some money. He'd married again, said the third time was the charm. He begged me to help him make a fresh start." He was no longer looking at her, just staring at the row of red and white cans on the shelf. "I didn't want to disappoint him. I pleaded with Nell to sell. She said she wouldn't do it—not for my no-account son or anyone else. That's what she said." He blinked and his eyes slowly filled with tears. "I never meant to hurt her. I swear it. I loved her. I can't remember a time I didn't love her."

Kate went suddenly numb. She had prodded him, goaded him to tell her the truth about that day, yet she had never believed he would actually admit he had killed her.

But it certainly sounded that way.

"Go on," she softly urged. "You argued, but you never meant to hurt her."

He shook his head and the tears in his eyes slid into the hollows of his cheeks. "I couldn't believe she wouldn't agree. Not when she knew how much it meant to me. I grabbed her and I shook her. I guess I must have shoved her backwards a little when I let go. The rug caught between her feet and she fell." His eyes slid closed, but tears leaked from under his sparse gray lashes. "There was so much blood. So much blood." He began to sob then, deep, wrenching sobs, and a surge of pity washed over her.

She shouldn't have felt it, not after what he had done, but somehow she did. Gently, she took his arm and led him through the door leading into his office, sat him down in the old oak chair behind his battered desk.

"I knew she was dead. I turned and ran to my car,"

he said, his face distorted with pain. "I never meant to hurt her. I loved her. I always loved her."

Kate just stood there, a thousand different emotions rolling around inside her head. Anger. Pity. Relief that she finally knew the truth.

Silas dragged in a ragged breath. "Go on. Call the sheriff. Let's get this over with, once and for all."

She reached for the phone, but something held her back. Silas had killed Nell, but he hadn't meant to. He had loved her, and Nell had cared about him, too. He was an old man. Would her grandmother want him to go to prison?

"I don't know if . . . I just . . ."

"You wanted to know the truth and now you do." Silas picked up the phone with long, bony fingers that trembled. He dialed 911. "Get me Sheriff Conrad. Tell him it's Silas Marshall calling. I got something important to tell him."

Kate didn't stay to hear the rest. Silas was doing what he should have done in the first place and yet, instead of feeling triumphant, she felt heartsick about it.

Half an hour later, once more back at the cafe, she saw the sheriff's Chevy SUV roll up in front of the grocery store, and tall, blond Sheriff Conrad get out. A short time later, he led Silas back to the car and helped him into the rear seat, pressing his head down so he wouldn't bump it on the door. Kate was glad to see the old man wasn't handcuffed.

Myra walked up beside her. "Darned shame, is what it is."

Kate had told her what happened. She wished she could have talked to Chance. "I wonder what they'll do to him."

Myra just shook her head.

Kate turned away from the window, dragged in a slow

breath of air. *It's over,* she thought. *It's over at last and now Nell can rest in peace.*

It wasn't exactly murder. Involuntary manslaughter, they called it. Still, an old woman's death had been the result of Silas's actions.

Kate released a weary breath. At least her own personal search was at an end. What happened to her that night in LA must have been real. Surely all of this couldn't simply have been a coincidence.

That knowledge alone should have cheered her. Instead that night, she dreamed of Nell and awakened in the middle of the night feeling more disturbed than she was before. Eventually, she was able to go back to sleep but this time she dreamed of Chance. In the dream she held his tiny black-haired infant son. They were happy. So happy.

She awakened with a smile that slowly faded as she realized none of it was real, would never be real. Chance was lost to her forever. Kate cursed her bad luck in finally finding a man she could love but never have.

At least in moving to Lost Peak she had found a home for herself and her son. She could thank Nell for that, and be content that the mystery of her death was solved at last.

Unfortunately, a few days later when an unexpected photo arrived in the mail, her doubts arose once more.

Chance sat on his porch talking to Ed Fontaine, absorbing the afternoon sun and an oddly warm first week of October. Ed had come with news of Consolidated Metals and the news wasn't good. It put a damper on what should have been a gorgeous day.

"So they've finally done it." He read the document Ed

had brought, a copy of the lawsuit filed by Consolidated against the State of Montana.

"We knew they were going to, sooner or later. It was only a matter of time."

"We've got to step up the campaign," Chance said, "make sure the public is informed. Consolidated will be bearing down, using every ounce of pressure they can muster. We need to do the same."

"Kate's already on it. She's been working—"

"Kate? Kate's off the project. You and I already talked about that."

"Yes, we did. Fortunately for us, Kate had other ideas. She says she's not going to let Lon Barton and his thugs stop her from doing what's right for Lost Peak."

Chance said nothing. He was torn between fury that Kate was still willing to put herself in danger and a grudging respect for her.

"She's an amazing woman," Ed said softly.

Chance felt a sharp stab of pain. "Yes, she is."

"You heard what happened with her and Silas Marshall?"

Chance snapped to attention once more. "No. What the hell happened with Silas?"

"Apparently Kate was convinced Silas had something to do with her grandmother's death. She went to see him and believe it or not, Silas confessed."

Chance came to his feet. "You mean he actually killed Nell Hart?"

"Apparently not on purpose. They had an argument over that little piece of property they owned, the one with the artesian well on it. Silas accidentally shoved her. Nell tripped and hit her head."

Chance sat back down, knowing how Ed hated having to look up at him. "I can't believe it. Kate was right."

"How'd she know?"

"It's a long story, I'm afraid. Suffice it to say, her instincts were right all along."

"She's no fool, that girl."

Only when it came to him, Chance thought morosely. But that was a mistake on both their parts.

"I know you've got work to do," Ed said. "I got plenty to do myself. I just wanted to let you know what Lon Barton was up to." Ed motioned to Randy, who stood over by the corral, talking to a group of cowhands. Randy waved and began walking back in their direction. He took hold of the wheelchair and started pushing it toward the van.

"Keep me posted," Chance called after them.

"I'll do that," Ed called back.

"And tell the sheriff to keep a close eye on Kate."

"Already done," Ed said.

Chance watched the van pull away, then headed out to the corral. Thinking of Kate made his chest feel tight. He wanted to see her. He couldn't, of course. He had made a commitment and he didn't take it lightly. Still, staying away from Kate was the hardest thing he'd ever done.

It'll get easier, once you're married.

But Chance wasn't convinced it would ever be easy to stay away from Kate.

Chapter Twenty-three

A warm afternoon sun shone in through the kitchen windows, forming patterns on the old oak table in the breakfast room. Down near the stream, Kate could see a doe standing beneath one of the pines on the hill. Seated across from her, Willow Spotted Horse sipped a cup of steaming black coffee.

Like David, Kate had needed a friend near her age, someone she could talk to, and in Willow she seemed to have found one.

"Chris said David joined his Boy Scout troop," Willow said, taking a drink from her mug. With the cafe running so smoothly, Kate now took both Saturdays and Sundays off. She had come to Lost Peak to spend time with her son and she had been able to do that more and more. "I hope he enjoys it." At present, the boys were upstairs in David's room, getting ready for an afternoon hike.

"He's really excited about it," Kate said. "And I might add I'm delighted myself."

Willow smiled. She was incredibly pretty with her big dark eyes, sculpted cheeks, and olive complexion. "They're really a nice bunch of kids, and Mr. Holloway does a great job of keeping them interested in the various projects."

Kate heard the two boys thundering down the stairs. "We're all set," David said.

"So I see," said Kate. "Now tell me again where you're going."

"Up the Little Sandy trail. We're taking our rods along in case we want to fish."

"And Chief is going with you?"

"He's meeting us up the creek a little ways, a spot he showed us before."

"Okay, but you'll have to be home by five."

"That's right," Willow agreed. "I'll be back to pick Chris up and he had better be here when I arrive."

"I'll be here," Chris promised. They tore out the back door, David the taller of the two and finally beginning to fill out a little.

"They're quite a pair," Willow said.

"David thinks the world of Chris."

Willow smiled softly and both of them sipped their coffee. Outside the dining room window, the local postal carrier drove up in front of the mailbox at the bottom of the lane.

"Mail's here," Willow said as his battered Buick sedan—the Lost Peak version of a mail truck—pulled back onto the road. "I'll walk down with you. I always look forward to getting the mail. I imagine, with so many friends still living in LA, it's even more so for you."

Kate smiled. Though there was never much of anything important, she always looked forward to the mail. "I have a friend named Sally. We usually stay in touch by e-mail, but she sends me cards now and then. Mostly it's a holdover from when I was a little girl. I was always hoping a letter would come from my father. It never did, of course."

"My father wasn't much of a dad, either, but at least he was there. Come on. I need the exercise."

Willow didn't need much of anything that Kate could see. She was intelligent and beautiful, and terribly in love with her husband.

"Jeremy is taking us camping this weekend," Willow said with a smile, linking her arm with Kate's. "We always pitch two tents, one for the kids and a separate one for us." A faint blush rose beneath her high, carved cheekbones. "Even with children, Jeremy insists on having our privacy."

Her soft look spoke of the love she felt for the man she had married, and an unexpected lump formed in Kate's throat.

"You're lucky to have found each other."

Willow nodded. "I know. I'm sorry about you and Chance. I know he felt differently about you than any other woman he ever dated. I thought it might work out."

Kate swallowed past the ache in her throat. "So did I."

"He's always cared for Rachael, but I never thought he would marry her."

They had reached the big black mailbox that sat on a post at the beginning of the gravel drive. Kate opened it as an excuse not to have to make a reply. She began to sift through the envelopes: a couple of utility bills, a credit card bill, a coupon flyer from the supermarket in Ronan, and a Bloomingdale's catalog, one of her few remaining attachments to life in the city. The last envelope slipped out of her grasp. Willow picked it up and handed it over.

"It's from Aida Whittaker," Kate said. "I've never met her, but I've talked to her a couple of times on the phone. She seems really nice. I wonder what it says." As they walked back up the drive, Kate carefully tore open the envelope. There was a letter inside, accompanied by a Polaroid picture.

"Good Lord." Willow paused at the top of the front porch stairs. "That's a photo of your grandmother in her coffin." She shivered. "I know a lot of people do that, but I think it's gruesome."

"To tell you the truth, so do I." As they went back into the house, Kate skimmed the letter, then read it aloud, knowing Aida and Willow were friends. It said that Aida was well and happy, that she had forgotten about the photo her daughter had taken the day of the funeral, and thought that Kate might want it. She asked how things were going in Lost Peak and if Consolidated Metals was still trying to open a mine on Silver Fox Creek.

"She and Nell were both real opposed to that mine," Willow said.

"I'll have to drop her a note, give her an update, and thank her for the photo." For the first time, Kate took a long look at the picture. The mortician had done Nell's hair and makeup, which seemed oddly wrong, a little too much blush on her cheeks, a little too dark a lipstick.

And there was something else, something she couldn't quite put her finger on.

"You knew Nell. Take a look at this picture and see if you notice anything wrong with it."

Willow studied the photo. "She never wore that much makeup."

"Anything else?"

Willow squinted down at the photo. "Her nose looks funny. Wider, and kind of puffy or something."

"That's what I thought." Back in the kitchen again, Kate left Willow at the table, ran upstairs, and got the file she had made on Nell Hart. The photos she had borrowed from the mortuary were still inside. She had made a note to herself just that morning to return them.

"Her face looks different in these," Kate said, handing Willow a photo of Nell lying on her back in the embalming room. There was another, closer shot, showing only her head and shoulders. Her nose looked perfectly normal.

Willow studied the picture. "They must have done something to her at the mortuary."

"I wonder what happened. In the pictures taken the day of the accident, her nose looks normal. In the ones taken the day of the funeral, it almost looks like it's broken. You don't think they dropped her or something?"

"Not a pleasant thought," Willow said.

"No, I don't guess it is." It isn't important, she told herself. You know how she died. But every time she looked at the photo, something nagged at her.

"I never talked to the undertaker, not the one who actually worked on Nell. His name was Hobbs. I called him, but he was never home."

"Maybe you ought to. You've gone this far, you might as well finish." Willow knew about Silas and about Kate's search to discover the truth of how she died. Everyone in town did by now. Silas was back at work, charged with involuntary manslaughter, but out on bail. No one seemed to know exactly what would happen now.

"Maybe I should go see Hobbs."

Her mind made up, for the next two days she phoned Walter Hobbs. When she finally reached him, he sounded impatient and slightly distracted, and she thought he might be pleasantly drunk.

Willow went with her to Polson, the day Kate finally convinced the man to talk to her. It was raining, a harsh October wind whistling through the trees.

"I love your car," Willow said, sitting in the plush leather passenger seat of the Lexus. "But once it starts to snow, you're going to need something more practical."

"I know it. I've been thinking about making a trade. I just haven't gotten around to it."

Though the roads were wet and slick, and the traffic slowed them down, they reached Polson on time for their one o'clock appointment. Hobbs's address on Sixth Avenue turned out to be an old gray wood-frame house with a sagging porch and a lawn that hadn't been cut all year. They walked up a broken, uneven sidewalk, trying to avoid the weeds protruding through the cracks in the cement, and climbed the wooden stairs onto the porch out of the rain.

Kate knocked and Hobbs answered, opening the door so they could come in.

"Thanks for taking the time to see us, Mr. Hobbs." She and Willow crossed a dreary living room with old-fashioned brown shag carpeting to sit on a worn brown velvet sofa with the stuffing coming out.

Hobbs fit right in, a short, overweight, unshaven man in an undershirt and baggy jeans. Though he wasn't drunk, she could clearly smell alcohol on his breath and understood why Mr. Dorfman, the mortician, had said they only rarely called him in, as they had done the day of the accident.

She cast Willow a grateful glance for coming along.

"You wanted to see me," Hobbs said. "What can I do for you?"

"Mr. Dorfman told me you were the person who worked on Nell Hart the day she died." When he didn't seem to remember, Kate handed him the photos.

"Yeah. Now, I remember."

"Was there anything out of the ordinary you noticed about her?"

"Out of the ordinary how?"

She could see this wasn't going to be easy. "For instance, if you look at those photos, you can see they look different. One was taken when Nell was first brought in, the other was taken the day of the funeral. If you look at the face, you can see she looks different in one than in the other."

"I don't see any difference."

Kate moved closer, tried to ignore his stale alcohol breath. "Look at her nose."

"What about it?"

Kate pushed past her frustration. "Why does it look like it's been broken or something?"

"Because it was. I remember noticing it after the embalming."

"I'm afraid I don't understand. If her nose was broken, why doesn't it show up in the first picture?"

"Because there wasn't any blood. The heart wasn't pumping any. The nose couldn't swell because there wasn't any blood in the veins. The embalming solution acts like a substitute. The tissues puff up just like they would have if she had been alive."

A cold chill snaked down Kate's spine.

Willow spoke the question that was hovering on her lips. "Are you saying that Mrs. Hart's nose was broken when she was brought into the mortuary?"

"That's the way I remember it, yes."

"Why didn't you report it to the authorities?" Kate asked.

"The woman took a fall. Wouldn't be unlikely she might have broken her nose."

"My grandmother fell backward. She hit the back of her head." She handed him the other photos, those taken with Nell on her stomach. "There is no way a fall backward could have been responsible for breaking her nose."

Walter Hobbs just shrugged. "Don't know what to tell you. Must have happened some other way."

Some other way? Had Silas hit her, knocked her into that sideboard? If he had, any sympathy she felt for him, any effort she might have made to help him, would be finished. She needed to talk to him.

And she intended to do just that.

"Was there anything else you remember?"

He scratched his unshaven chin. "Not that I can think of."

Kate got up from the sofa and Willow stood up, too. "Thank you, Mr. Hobbs." He didn't answer, just walked them to the door and held it open so they could go out.

"Charming fellow," Willow said when they got back into the car.

"Not very competent, I'm afraid. He should have reported that injury, but I guess, since the deputy wasn't there to explain how it happened, it's possible he simply misunderstood."

"Do you think Silas hit her? God, I can't imagine it. He's always been such a kind, gentle old man."

"He shoved her. He must have hit her, too. I can't figure out any other way it could have happened." She started the car and pulled onto the street. "I'll tell you one thing. I darn well intend to find out."

Kate was so intent on speaking to Silas, she didn't see the silver Dodge pickup parked off to the side of the market when she crossed the street and went into the store. Instead, she shoved through the glass front door, took a quick glance around, spotted Silas's long, bony frame, and marched in that direction.

"Hello, Silas."

He glanced away, up then down at the floor. "Hello, Kate."

"I need to talk to you. We should probably go into your office."

He nodded, looked resigned. "All right."

A deep male voice cut in just then. "I'm sorry to intrude, but I couldn't help overhearing." Chance stepped into the aisle from behind a tall stack of Coca-Cola twelve packs. He fixed those penetrating blue eyes on Kate and she could feel their warmth clear into her bones. "Is everything all right, Kate?"

"To tell you the truth, I'm not sure." He must have heard the anxiety in her voice. She was certain Silas had. "Maybe Silas will be able to help me figure it out."

"Mind if I come along?"

Of course she minded. She was trying her best to forget the man ever existed, but his worry was apparent, and she could use a little support in this. She turned to Silas, who started shuffling toward his office like a man being led to the gallows.

As soon as the door was closed, he turned and looked at her down his crooked, bony nose. "What is it, Kate?"

"I'm sorry to bother you, Silas, but yesterday I spoke to a man named Hobbs. Mr. Hobbs works part time at Dorfman's mortuary. After the accident, when my grandmother was taken there, Mr. Hobbs was the man who worked on her."

Silas looked utterly grim.

"I showed him a couple of photos I had and he told me Nell had arrived that day with a broken nose. Since you claim that when you *accidentally* pushed her, she fell backward, I want to know how that could have happened."

Silas looked confused. "I don't know."

"Did you hit her, Silas? Is that how she fell?"

"Hit her? I didn't hit her."

"You were angry. Nell wouldn't agree to sell. Are you certain you didn't strike her, maybe just once? One good hard punch and that poor old lady fell, hit her head, and died?"

Silas looked stricken. "No! I never hit a woman in my life!" He was shaking his head, looking at her with eyes that were bleak and filled with pain. "I swear it, Kate. I loved Nell. I deserve whatever I get for what I did to her that day, but I swear it was an accident. I never hit her." His voice cracked. "I would die before I'd ever have hurt her on purpose."

Why she believed him she couldn't really say. She only knew that she did.

"I loved Nell Hart," Silas was saying. "I loved her." He sank down in the old oak chair and buried his head in his hands. Kate felt the unwanted sting of tears.

She felt Chance's hold on her arm. "Let's go, Kate."

She nodded, let him guide her out of the office and close the door.

"How did you happen to find out Nell had a broken nose?"

"Aida Whittaker sent me a photo. I compared it to the ones we got from Dorfman at the mortuary. Then I went to see Walter Hobbs."

Chance sighed. "I don't think Silas hit her."

"Neither do I."

"Then again, I didn't think he killed her, either."

Kate thought about that and the same thought that had been nagging her since yesterday rose at the back of her mind. "Maybe he didn't."

Chance froze. "What do you mean?"

Kate shook her head. "I'm not sure yet." They passed a stack of flour sacks, sitting at the end of an aisle, and walked on past the cash register. Chance shoved open the door, and they walked out under the overhanging eaves.

"I don't get it, Kate. You believed Silas killed Nell. You got him to admit it. Now you're saying he didn't?"

"I'm not saying anything, yet. But when you look at the whole picture you have to wonder. Silas says he didn't hit her. If he didn't, who did? Which brings us back to the question—who had the most to gain? Silas, yes, but ultimately it was Consolidated Metals. With Nell out of the way, they got the well they needed and a shot at a valuable gold mine. They—or someone who wants that mine to go in—was serious enough about all of this to send a man to my house. That man tried to rape me. It doesn't seem like much of a stretch to think that same someone would go as far as murder."

Chance's expression turned grim. "I don't like this,

Kate. Not one little bit. So far your instincts have been dead-on. If you're right about Consolidated and you keep digging for answers, you could be in for some very big trouble."

Kate shuddered, knowing he was right.

"Is finding out if Nell was murdered worth risking your life?"

A shiver ran through her. Was it worth it? "There was a time I might have said no. But even then I was determined to find out if what happened to me the night of the shooting was real. Now I've read Nell's letters. I know what she was really like and how much she loved my mother and me. Now it's even more important for me to know the truth."

"What are you going to do?"

"I'm not sure yet."

Chance caught her arm. Even through her heavy wool sweater, she could feel the contact like a hot brand on her skin. "Whatever we once were, we're still friends. Friends help each other. Let me help you, Kate."

She dragged in a shaky breath. She didn't want his help; she didn't want to be near him. But she trusted him and she might very well need him.

"If I stumble onto anything important I'll let you know."

His grip only tightened. "Promise me, Kate. Promise you'll call before you do anything that might get you into trouble."

She looked up at him, thought how handsome he was, thought how much she still loved him. "I promise."

Chance let her go. "Be careful, Katie."

Kate just nodded. With a last worried glance, Chance turned and walked away.

* * *

A cold October wind whistled down through the pines surrounding the town. A dark platinum sky washed the landscape in dismal gray. At the bar in the Antlers Saloon, Chance sat next to Jeremy Spotted Horse. It was late in the afternoon. They had run into each other at the mercantile and stopped in for a beer before heading home for the night.

"I guess you heard the latest on Silas and Nell," Chance said to his friend.

"You mean Nell's broken nose? Willow's been keeping me posted. She and Kate are becoming real good friends. Willow went with her to see that guy in Polson, Walter Hobbs."

"Kate's always believed Nell was murdered. Unless Silas went crazy and punched Nell in the face, she just might be right."

"I've tried to imagine it. I can see how he might have accidentally caused her to fall, but I can't imagine him hitting her. They'd been friends for too many years. Nell would never have put up with him if he'd been the sort who would ever have hurt her."

"That's what I think, too."

"Which means Kate could be involving herself in something she can't handle."

"Yeah."

"And you're worried about her."

"Damned right I'm worried. If Kate's right and Consolidated Metals is involved, she could be asking for serious trouble." On the surface it seemed crazy. Silas wanted Nell to sell the parcel of land they jointly owned. They argued. Silas hit her. Nell had fallen and died when her head hit the sideboard.

Silas had made his deal on the land and that was the end of it.

But Consolidated Metals was also mixed up in that particular deal. As far as Chance was concerned, he wouldn't put anything past them. And now that Kate had put the notion of murder into his head, he couldn't seem to get it out.

Jeremy took a sip of his beer, set it back down on the bar. "Willow thinks you're in love with Kate."

The words came out of nowhere. Chance glanced up from his mug. "Oh yeah?"

"Know what?"

"What?"

"So do I."

Chance looked away, raked a hand through his hair. "Yeah, well, then all three of us have figured it out. Unfortunately, it doesn't make a lick of difference."

"Maybe you should talk to Rachael, tell her the truth."

"What truth? The truth is I have to marry Rachael. I owe it to her father. The truth is I'll make her a damned good husband. I'll take care of her, see she gets anything she wants—which is all that matters to Rachael. She'll be close to her dad, which both of them want; and she'll give him the grandkids he and I both want. That's the only truth that matters."

"You sure it's fair to Rachael?"

"If I didn't think so, I wouldn't do it." He sighed. "We both know Rachael isn't in love with me. Hell, neither of us were ever in love. That isn't important— at least not to Rachael. Until I met Kate, it wasn't important to me."

Jeremy said nothing, just took a long drink of his beer. One of the stools down at the end of the bar scraped against the wooden floor and Ned Cummings strode toward them.

"Hey, Chance! I didn't see you come in." He stuck out his hand. "Congratulations, man."

Chance shook. "Thanks, Ned."

"You and Rachael." He grinned. "I guess I should have figured the two of you would finally get together, but somehow I just never did."

"I'm lucky she said yes."

"You can say that again. That is one gorgeous female. And speaking of gorgeous women, since you're no longer in the market, I don't suppose you'd mind if I asked Kate Rollins out."

His body tightened like a five-pound line hooked onto a ten-pound fish. Ned didn't suppose he'd mind? The thought made him sick to his stomach. Ned Cummings was handsome and smart. He owned one of the nicest little ranches in the county. He'd be a good man for Kate. It was the last thing he wanted. "No . . . of course I don't mind."

Ned slapped him hard on the back. "Thanks, Chance." He grinned and winked at Jeremy. "I'll see you boys later. I'm going over to the café, see if I can manage to convince that little gal to go out with me on Saturday night."

As Ned strolled out of the bar, Chance's stomach clenched into a knot. It was all he could do to stay in his seat.

"Easy, man." He felt Jeremy's hand on his shoulder, and the tension eased a little.

"Sorry. I know I don't have any right, but . . . "

"But that doesn't make it any easier."

"No."

"Maybe she won't go."

"She'd be a fool if she didn't."

"Yeah, well that goes without saying. She fell for you, didn't she?"

A corner of his mouth edged up. "God, I miss her. She was really something special, you know."

Jeremy squeezed his shoulder. "Come on. I'll buy you another beer."

Chance nodded, but his mind was on Ned Cummings and what was going on across the street.

"By the way," Jeremy's voice pulled him back to the bar. "Chief says that tail pond up on Beaver Creek has started leaking again."

"You're kidding."

"He thinks there's a tear in the plastic liner. He says he's gonna try to get some pictures."

"He'd have to go onto Consolidated property to do that. I don't think it's a good idea, especially not now, with tempers running so high."

"Yeah, well you know Chief."

"First time I see him, I'll talk to him about it."

"Good idea."

They finished their beer and headed for the door. Chance walked outside just in time to see Ned Cummings walking out of the Lost Peak Cafe.

Chance bit back a curse when he saw the grin on Ned's face.

Chapter Twenty-four

Kate sat facing the computer in her office upstairs. An icy wind blew leaves against the window, and a branch scratched persistently against the outside wall. A shutter banged loudly and she jumped.

Ever since the rape attempt, she'd been more nervous, less comfortable being alone in the house. But she loved the old place and she told herself she was far safer here than she would have been in the city.

She focused her attention on the computer screen and scrolled down the page, having accessed this particular website, *www.forensicsciencejournals.com*, several times before. She had read this section, but among the voluminous material she had perused, had only retained a foggy memory of it. That memory had nagged her, building bit by bit, until finally it returned full-blown, driving her upstairs to the computer.

She pressed the print button, making a copy of the pages, picked them up, and scanned them more closely. It was a criminal case, one of several dozen she had read, a death by asphyxiation where the assailant had used a pillow to commit the murder. During the autopsy, the medical examiner had discovered that the victim's nose had been broken. It hadn't been spotted by the officers on the scene because there wasn't any blood pumping, and therefore no swelling of the tissues.

Kate read the information one last time, how the forensic experts, once they established the means, were able to track down the killer.

She studied the printed pages, her mind going over what she'd learned. "Is that what happened, Nell?" she muttered out loud. Maybe after Silas had shoved her and Nell hit her head, she hadn't died. Maybe Silas had decided to finish the job. Maybe he'd pressed a pillow over her face until she had finally stopped breathing.

But she had talked to Silas on two separate occasions and she simply wasn't convinced the man could willfully murder anyone.

Kate stared at the computer screen, her fingers tapping lightly on the keys. *What if Silas only thought Nell was dead?* He was frightened. It was obvious he had run away in terror. *What if someone came along a few minutes later, saw Nell lying there injured, realized Silas would take the blame, and killed her?*

It was possible. Not probable, but then nothing about this entire bizarre affair had been anything but wild conjecture from the start. Since that was the case, she might as well forge ahead as she had before.

Assuming someone had killed Nell by suffocating her with a pillow, thereby breaking her nose, then the dining

room wasn't the scene of an accident, it was the scene
of a murder. The entire house was a crime scene.

Kate resisted a shudder. She thought about the wonderful old house she had come to love. The place had
been repainted before she moved in, but the lovely
antique sideboard in the dining room had only been
cleaned and protected with a coating of lemon oil. The
carpet had been pulled up and the floors refinished,
but a number of Nell's antiques remained.

Including the pillows on the sofa.

The shudder surfaced full-force. Kate shook her head.
There was no way it could possibly be that simple. No
way Nell's murderer—if there was such a person—could
have simply picked up one of the pillows on the sofa
and pressed it over a severely injured Nell's face.

She turned back to the computer screen, read on
down the page.

> *Mechanical asphyxia is often marked by the appear-
> ance of petechial hemorrhages in the eye, but such a
> finding is not specific to the condition, and may be caused
> in a number of other ways.*

A petechial hemorrhage was broken blood vessels in
the eye and though suffocation often caused it, apparently an injury to the head could also be the cause.
There was no mention of such a hemorrhage in Nell's
case, but even if it had happened, it wouldn't have been
reason enough for the officer or mortician to suspect
any sort of foul play.

It might, however, help substantiate the actual cause
of death, should other factors arise. Still thinking of the
pillows, Kate made her way downstairs.

There were three throw pillows on the sofa, little

fringed affairs that Nell had sewn in petit point and Kate couldn't bear to throw away. She had never noticed anything unusual about them, no spots or stains that she could recall. She picked up the first one and examined it closely. Nothing. At least nothing she could see.

A search of the second pillow proved equally fruitless. The third appeared clean as well, except for a tiny, rust-colored smudge near a corner in the back.

It was probably nothing. The pillows were old. The slight discoloration could be anything.

Still, there had been a lot of blood on the floor that day, from the injury to the back of Nell's head. If the killer had used the pillow to end Nell's life and hadn't noticed the single smear of blood, he might have returned it to its place on the sofa.

Hurrying back up the stairs, she sat down once more at the computer. Backing up several pages, she punched up a section of the website that talked about blood detection and skimmed the page.

> *Blood spatters can help a great deal in reconstructing a crime scene. Drops falling from a low height, for example, will leave a small cohesive circle. At greater heights, the circle will be larger. Blood hitting a surface at an angle will bulge in one direction, indicating the travel of the droplet.*

Interesting, but not what she was looking for. She knew it was here, somewhere. If not on the Internet, then maybe in one of the books she had purchased. She searched the Net a little longer, then reached for the stack of books, digging through one after another, flipping open to the pages she had marked with yellow stickers.

Yes! There it was, in *The Casebook of Forensic Detection.* She reread the section on blood and the word she'd been searching for jumped out at her.

Luminol.

A very useful test for searching large areas for blood, it said, *especially if the area has been cleaned up. Invisible bloodstains react with the Luminol by luminescing. Darkness is essential.*

Kate whirled back to the computer, punched in the key word, *Luminol,* and there it was. *Luminol-16 Invisible Blood Reagent with Spray Head.* She clicked on price, ordered a bottle, typed in her credit card number, paid extra for two-day shipping, and the stuff was on its way.

Kate leaned back in her chair with a grin. City girl she might be, but there were definitely some advantages to having lived in the fast lane. She would test the pillow—and everything else in the dining room—as soon as the Luminol arrived. If the spot on the pillow turned out to be blood, she was going to go to the sheriff, find out if the blood was Nell's.

If it was, she was going to ask him to exhume the body.

She could image what smiling Barney Conrad would have to say about that.

Saturday night came and went. Kate was supposed to go to the dance at the Antlers with Ned Cummings, but she just couldn't bring herself to go. Ned was an attractive man and she liked him. She had accepted the date in the hope that going out with him might help her forget about Chance.

She was tired of remembering, thinking of Chance and wishing things could be different. She had known from the start an affair with him would probably end in disaster. She had to accept that he belonged to someone else and get on with her life.

Going out with Ned Cummings should have been a start. Ned was a big, warm, teddy bear of a man, jovial and fun-loving. Unfortunately, Kate felt not the least attraction to him. He was kind and considerate, but every time he walked into the cafe in his cowboy hat, she thought of Chance and her heart squeezed painfully.

In the end, she came up with the old standby headache excuse, cancelled her date, and stayed home.

One Wednesday, the Luminol arrived UPS. Kate carefully read the directions on the spray bottle. As soon as it was dark, she went into the dining room and set to work.

Chance heard Hannah's voice ringing across the back yard all the way to the stables. She hung out the back door, an apron tied around her considerable girth, a dishrag clutched in one plump hand. "Sheriff's on the phone! He says it's important!"

The sheriff. A fist of anxiety tightened in Chance's stomach. "I'll pick up in the barn!" he called back, walking rapidly in that direction and grabbing the receiver off the wall.

"It's Chance, Barney. What's up?"

"Kate Rollins came to see me today."

"She's all right, isn't she? I mean nothing's happened to her?" He could feel his heart, pounding hard against his ribs.

"Well now, that all depends on your definition. If you mean is she physically all right, then yes. Mentally, I'm not so sure."

"What's that supposed to mean?"

"It means she was in here spouting a bunch of non-sense about Nell Hart's death. She says the old lady might not have died in the fall—she might have been suffocated by somebody afterward. Apparently she went to see the undertaker, found out the old woman had a broken nose. I guess she found a pillow with some blood on it. She wants me to test it, see if it matches Nell's blood type."

Chance mulled that over, thinking how right Kate had been so far. "Maybe that's not such a bad idea."

"Yeah, well, if the blood type matches, she wants me to exhume the body. I'm not about to do that—not under any circumstances."

"Why not?"

"Because we already know how Nell died. Silas Marshall's confessed to killing her."

"Maybe he didn't do it. Maybe he just thought she was dead."

"And maybe it was an accident, just like he said."

"I realize Kate's theory might not be the easiest to swallow, but it just might be true."

"Forget it."

"I don't suppose your refusal has anything to do with this being an election year? If it turns out Nell's death was murder, not manslaughter, it might make the department look bad. Like maybe they should have been more careful."

"I'm telling you, Chance. This is not going to happen. You need to talk some sense into that woman, make her understand. The old lady is dead and buried. Silas will probably get a suspended sentence and that'll be the end of it. She'll listen to you. Convince her to let the matter drop."

Chance swore softly. As sheriff of Silver Fox County,

Barney Conrad wielded a lot of influence. It wasn't smart to get on his bad side. On the other hand, murder wasn't a matter the man should ignore. "Do me a favor. Run the blood test. Let me know how it comes out. In the meantime, I'll talk to Kate."

"All right, I'll go that far."

Barney signed off and Chance hung up the phone. Kate had promised to call him if anything came up. Obviously, she didn't consider going to see the sheriff important enough to bother. Or she simply didn't want to talk to him.

He couldn't really blame her.

On the other hand, she was getting into this mess deeper and deeper. One way or another it was going to lead to trouble.

In the morning he would talk to her. Like Barney said, maybe he could convince her to let the matter drop.

He told himself it wasn't just a convenient excuse to see her. Chance hoped to hell he was right.

They were busy at the ranch, getting ready for the fall roundup, collecting the remuda, putting the corrals in shape for the branding. To make matters worse, three days ago one of the outbuildings near the barn had been set on fire. Orange spray paint on the ground in front of it warned, WE NEED JOBS. STAY OUT OF MINING AFFAIRS.

Fortunately the fire hadn't caused much damage, but the point had certainly been made. It wasn't just Consolidated Metals who wanted that mine to go in. There were people who needed the jobs the mine could offer.

Damn, he knew the hardship miners faced in trying

to support their families, but the fact remained—the environment was more important. Once the land and streams were gone, there wouldn't be any more. The destruction had to stop.

By the time Chance left the ranch and made the drive to the cafe, it was late afternoon, the roads muddy and slick from two days of nonstop rain. As he passed the driveway leading up to Kate's house, his foot hit the brakes.

A sheriff's car sat out in front. Chance shoved the pickup in reverse, backed up, and turned down the gravel lane.

By the time he got out of the truck, his pulse was hammering away. He leapt a couple of mud puddles, took the porch stairs two at a time, and pounded on the door.

David pulled it open. "Chance! Boy, I'm glad to see you. Mom had an accident."

"An accident?" With a hand on David's shoulder, he urged the boy into the living room and saw Kate lying on the sofa, a bandage wrapped around her head. A trace of red seeped through, and worry hit him like a fist in the stomach.

"What the hell happened?"

Kate smiled weakly. "My brakes went out. The road was slick and I slid into a ditch."

Standing a few feet away, notepad in hand, Deputy Winston turned to face him, the officer who had come out to the house before. "She's got a mild concussion and a gash on the side of her head that took half a dozen stitches, but it could have been a lot worse. The road's real steep right through there. She could have slid off down the side of the mountain. Fortunately, she was wearing her seatbelt or likely she would have gone through the windshield."

Chance peeled off his sheepskin coat, took off his hat and tossed them over the back of a chair. Sitting carefully down next to Kate, he reached out and took hold of her hand. It felt small and soft in his, and colder than it should have been. He wanted to press it against his cheek, but settled for warming it between his palms. "Where were you going when this happened?"

"Up to Ronan. I needed a load of groceries. I thought I'd pick David up at school and take him along to help me. I never got that far."

"And the brakes just suddenly failed? That seems odd for such a new car."

"Unfortunately, that's what happened. I pushed on the pedal. Nothing. Even the parking brake wouldn't work." She gave him a halfhearted smile. "I needed a new car anyway, something good for driving in snow. I guess it's time I started looking around."

"Where's the car now?"

Deputy Winston answered. "They towed it to Trumper's Auto in Ronan."

Chance squeezed Kate's hand. "Can I get you something? A glass of water or maybe a cup of tea?"

"Tea would be great, if you wouldn't mind going to that much trouble."

"No trouble. I'll be right back." He went in and put the teakettle on, grateful for a chance to use the phone. Dialing information for Trumper's Auto, he jotted down the number and punched it in.

"Trumper's Auto, Pete Trumper here."

"You've got a car there, just towed in, a white Lexus, maybe a year or two old, belongs to Kaitlin Rollins."

"Yeah, what about it?"

"I'm a friend of Kate's. Chance McLain."

"You the guy with the silver Dodge?"

"Yeah."

"I know who you are. You had your truck in for service not long ago."

"That's right. Have you had a chance to look at the Lexus yet?"

"Sure have. Funny thing, that."

"What do you mean?"

"Looks to me like those brake lines were cut."

Dread moved down Chance's spine. "I was afraid you were going to say that."

"I gotta call the sheriff about it. I'm sure he'll want to know."

"I'm sure he will." But Barney wouldn't be happy about it, and neither was he. "Thanks, Pete."

He signed off the phone, wondering if the brakes had been cut because of Kate's work on the campaign, or if it might have something to do with Nell Hart's death.

He returned to the living room and set the mug of tea down on the coffee table in front of her. Deputy Winston had already gone.

"Good thing I had my cell phone," Kate said. "Out here, those things are worth their weight in gold."

"You can say that again."

David came over and sat on the chair beside her. "Are you feeling better, Mom?"

Kate smiled at him softly. "A lot better. I'll be fine by tomorrow."

Chance draped an arm around David's shoulder. "Come on, Davy. Let's let your mom rest a minute while we get something to drink." He had missed seeing the boy. He couldn't help wondering what Kate had told him about why he no longer came around.

They went into the kitchen. David popped open a can of Coke and Chance made himself a cup of instant coffee.

"I want you to keep an eye on your mom," he said as they sat down at the kitchen table. "Make sure she gets completely well before she tries to go back to work."

"I will."

"Good boy. It's been a while since I've seen you. I was thinking . . . you ever been to a roundup?"

David shook his head.

"We do it every spring and fall. This time of year, we'll be branding the calves we missed earlier, and cutting the yearlings out for sale. Chris and his dad will be working. I thought maybe you might like to work, too."

David grinned, obviously pleased. "That'd be great, Chance."

"In the meantime, why don't you and Chris come over some weekend? You can borrow a couple of horses and we'll go fishing like we did before."

David nodded. He looked like there was something he wanted to say, and Chance was afraid he knew what it was.

"Go on, boy, spit it out."

"I was wondering about what happened between you and my mom. Mom says you're getting married to Mr. Fontaine's daughter. I thought you liked my mom."

"I do like her, Davy. I like her a lot. Your mom and I are friends, just like you and me. Nothing's ever gonna change that."

"I was kind of hoping . . . maybe you could be more than just friends."

Chance's chest squeezed hard. "I guess, for a while, I kinda let myself hope that, too. Sometimes things don't work out the way we want them to."

"Yeah, I guess so."

Chance finished his coffee; David finished his Coke, and they went back into the living room to check on Kate.

"You still working at the grocery store?" Chance asked David.

"Yeah. I'm supposed to be working a couple of hours today, but—"

"Why don't you go ahead and go? I'll sit with your mother till you get back."

David glanced at Kate, whose eyes were about half closed. "Mom?"

She slowly opened them and her gaze swung to Chance's. "You don't need to stay. I'll be fine for a couple of hours."

"Go on, Davy. There's a couple of things I need to talk to your mom about. I'll be here when you get home."

"Thanks, Chance." He headed upstairs to get his jacket, came back down a few minutes later, and pulled open the front door. "I'll be home as soon as I can." Then he was gone.

"Myra working this afternoon?" Chance asked once the boy was gone.

"Uh-huh," she answered groggily.

"What did the doctor say about you staying here alone?"

Her eyes cracked open. "I'm not alone. You're here and David will back in a couple of hours."

His mouth edged up. He was there, but he didn't think Kate was all that pleased about it. He started to say something else but the phone rang, cutting off his words.

Kate's eyes slowly closed. "Would you mind?"

Chance strode into the entry and picked up the phone that was sitting on a marble-topped table. "Rollins residence."

A man's voice replied. "Who the hell are you?"

He ignored a shot of irritation. "My name's McLain. I'm a friend of Kate's."

"I'll just bet you are."

"You want to tell me who this is before I hang up the phone?"

"Just tell Kate I hope she's happy now. Tell her someday she's gonna regret it." The phone clicked in his ear. Chance hung up the receiver, wondering at Kate's obnoxious caller, and walked back into the living room.

"Who was it?"

"I don't know. Said he hoped you were happy now. Said to tell you someday you'd regret it."

Her pretty lips curved up. He could remember the way they melted under his and desire slid into his groin.

"That was Tommy," she said. "My divorce is final today."

He should have been happy for her and in a way he was. He forced himself to smile. "Congratulations."

Kate's smile deepened. "I can't tell you how good it feels."

From his single brief conversation with her ex, he could pretty well guess. "Does he ever talk to David?"

"Once in a great while. David is supposed to go down to LA for Thanksgiving. A few months back, he would have been looking forward to it. I don't think he is any more."

"Every boy needs a father. In time, you'll find someone—"

"Don't, Chance, please." Her glance slid away to the

back of the sofa. "Can't we talk about something besides the men in my life?"

She was right. What he was going to say was bullshit anyway. He didn't want her to find someone else. He wanted her to belong to him. He wanted to hold her, protect her, make love to her. He couldn't help wondering how her date had gone with Ned Cummings and if she planned to see him again. He knew better than to ask.

"Actually, there is something I need to talk to you about. It's one of the reasons I wanted to stay."

Her gaze swung back to his. "What is it?"

"Your brakes didn't just go out, Kate. I talked to the man at Trumper's Auto. Someone cut them."

"Oh my God." She tried to sit up, a soft moan escaped, and Chance eased her back down.

"Take it easy. You've got a concussion, remember?"

"If I didn't, I do now." She settled back against the pillow and Chance replaced the damp cloth over her forehead.

"The auto repair guy is going to call the sheriff. I'm gonna call him, too. Whoever did this is serious, Kate."

"Do you think they did it because I'm still working on the campaign?"

"I don't know. Three nights ago, someone burned one of my outbuildings. There are people who want that mine to go in. Whether they'd be willing to kill to accomplish the job, I don't know."

"There's another possibility, Chance."

He sat there stiffly. "I know. Barney Conrad called me."

A sigh slowly seeped past her lips. "It was awful, Chance. I used this stuff I found on the Internet. It's called Luminol. You can't see the blood unless it's good and dark, but when I sprayed it in the dining room, I could see splotches of it on the sideboard and down in the crack beneath the baseboard. I found it on the back of one of the sofa pillows.''

She went on to tell him how she had read a murder case where a woman was suffocated with a pillow and how her nose had been broken.

"I'm convinced that's what happened to Nell. She didn't die when she fell. Someone came along and murdered her afterward.''

"Then you don't think Silas did it.''

"No, I don't. The man simply hasn't got it in him.''

"I don't think so, either.''

"We need more evidence. We have to find out who the real murderer is.''

Chance sat down on the edge of the chair beside the sofa. "It isn't worth it, Kate. Someone tried to rape you. Today you could have been killed. If you keep digging—''

"The two things may not be related.''

"True, but there's no way to know for sure. The first thing you have to do is resign from the committee.''

She hesitated longer than he would have liked. "All right,'' she finally agreed. "I'll make a public announcement as soon as I can arrange it. We've got things well underway. You and Ed can keep the campaign rolling. At this point, whether I'm involved or not won't make much difference.''

"And what if you're right about Nell? What if someone murdered her, just the way you said. That man wouldn't have the slightest qualms about killing you, too.''

Her face paled to an even whiter shade than it was already.

"Let this drop, Kate. If you won't think of yourself, think of your son. He doesn't have much of a father. What the hell would he do if he wound up losing his mother, too?"

Kate closed her eyes and the air seemed to sigh from her lungs. "I guess I never thought of it that way."

"Well, it's damn well time you started."

She swallowed. Beneath her thick dark lashes, he could see the faint glitter of tears. "You're right. I have to think of David. I'm sure even Nell would want that."

He reached over and took her hand, wrapping it in both of his. "I know she would. Your grandmother wouldn't want anything to happen to either one of you because of her."

And neither would he, Chance thought, more worried than ever. There very well might be a killer loose in Lost Peak. Kate wouldn't be safe until someone discovered who it was. It was too dangerous for her to keep searching, but there was nothing stopping Chance.

He squeezed her hand, wishing he could lean down and kiss her, knowing that time was past.

He was determined to do whatever he had to in order to keep her safe.

Chapter Twenty-five

The phone rang in the family room. Ed Fontaine wheeled himself over to where it rested on an antique William and Mary table and picked up the receiver.

"Ed Fontaine."

"Hi, Daddy."

He brightened at the sound of Rachael's voice. "Hi, little girl. How are things going in the big city? You 'bout ready to hightail it back home? I thought you'd be here by now."

"That's what I called about, Daddy. Everything's taking longer than I expected. On top of that, yesterday I got a call from the Ford Agency. They want me for a *Vogue* cover. It's a big shoot, Daddy, very prestigious and the money's great. It would only take a couple more weeks and I'd really like to do it."

Ed frowned. "Have you talked to Chance about it?"

"I'm going to. I wanted to talk to you first. And I've also been thinking that as long as I'm here in New York, I ought to go ahead and pick out my wedding dress. I certainly won't find anything suitable in Montana. I was thinking maybe Fendi or Dior. What do you think?"

"You know I don't know squat about women's clothes. You just pick out whatever you want and have them send me the bill."

He could almost see her beautiful face smiling into the receiver. "Thank you, Daddy. You're the sweetest man on earth."

He grumbled, always a little embarrassed when she said things like that. "Chance isn't gonna be happy about this, you know. He expects you to start acting like a woman with marriage and family on her mind, instead of a career."

"I know. It'll just be this one last time, I promise. Then I'll be there to help. Which reminds me, I called Vincent St. Claire in Seattle. I got his name from André Duvallier. The weddings André does are simply the most scrumptious, most spectacular in New York. André won't come all the way to Montana, but he says M'sieur St. Claire will be happy to do it. He'll take care of everything, Daddy, and it'll turn out just perfect . . . if that's all right with you."

"You know it is. I just want my little girl to be happy."

"All right, then. I'll call Chance and tell him I'll be there a little later than we planned. I'm sure he'll understand."

But Ed wasn't so sure. Chance expected Rachael to settle down and start thinking about having a couple of kids. Dammit, so did he.

"You best not wait too long, little girl, if you want that man of yours to be waitin' when you get here."

Rachael just laughed. "Chance's been waiting for me for years. I don't imagine another few weeks will make any difference."

Maybe it wouldn't. Still, Ed didn't want to take any chances. He mentally smiled at the pun. "You just get that job done, buy that dress, and get yourself back home."

"I will, Daddy. I love you."

"I love you, too, little girl."

They hung up and Ed realized the tapping he could hear was the unconscious drumming of his fingers on the arm of the chair. There was nothing to worry about, he told himself. Once Rachael got back, everything would work out just the way they'd planned. All she needed was a man who could handle her, and he had no doubt that Chance could do that. The boy was a wonder when it came to women.

Ed rolled himself back into position in front of the TV. A game show was on and he liked to play at answering the questions. There was no need to worry, he repeated. All he had to do was leave things to Chance. Chance could handle just about anything.

Even his beautiful, self-indulgent daughter.

The first thing Monday morning, Chance pulled up in front of the Silver County Courthouse on his way to the sheriff's office. A thick gray mist hung over the Mission Mountains and lay like a blanket in the Flathead Valley, and the drive up to Polson had been slow.

He had called ahead and Barney was expecting him, but the sheriff hadn't arrived at the office just yet. The secretary, a woman named Barbara Murdock he had seen a couple of times before, poured him a cup of coffee while he waited.

"He called in just a minute ago," Barbara reassured him. "Said to tell you he's on his way." She was pretty, a woman in her late twenties—and single, Barney had told him—with thick black hair, pale skin, and a trim, sexy figure. Funny, six months ago, he would have asked her out, been looking forward to the challenge of maybe taking her to bed.

Now he looked at her and saw an attractive, desirable woman, but the thought of making love to her held none of the usual appeal. There was only one woman he wanted in his bed. Kate Rollins had brains and grit, and the sweetest little body he'd ever seen.

Unfortunately, making love to Kate was out of the question.

Chance glanced up, realized Barbara had been talking, smiling at him sweetly, and he hadn't heard a single word she'd said. "I'm sorry, I guess my mind was somewhere else." Yeah, like making love to Kate. "What did you say?" He could feel the heat of embarrassment burning at the back of his neck.

"I said the sheriff came in through the back. He's ready to see you now."

"Thanks." He walked past Barbara into Barney's private office and closed the door.

"I figured you'd show up here, sooner or later," Barney said from behind his desk.

Chance sat down in a chair across from him. "Did Pete Trumper call you?"

"Yes, unfortunately, he did."

"What do you think?"

"Someone probably wanted to scare her off the anti-mining campaign."

"Well, it worked. Kate's making the announcement today on KGET-TV. She's going to say that pressing business matters have forced her resignation. The coalition will now be run by executive committee."

"Smart move. Doesn't give them any real target. Maybe things will cool down a little."

"And maybe they won't. If Kate's right about Nell Hart being murdered, someone might have cut her brake lines to keep her quiet."

"It's possible, I suppose."

"Maybe someone's been watching her house. They could have followed her the day she came to see you. Speaking of which, how did that blood sample she brought you turn out?"

"O-negative. Same type as Nell's."

"And not very common at that."

"That blood could have splattered onto the pillow when Nell fell and hit her head."

"Kate said it wasn't a spot, more of a smudge, and it was on the back. The pillow would most likely have been sitting faceup on the sofa."

Barney tossed the pen he'd been holding down on his desk. "Dammit, Chance, what do you want me to do?"

"Exhume the body. If Nell was murdered, maybe you can find some DNA evidence or something. Maybe it'll help prove who it was."

"And maybe this is all a load of crap."

"Maybe. But until we find out for sure, Kate and her son could be in danger."

Barney still seemed uncertain. "I'll give it some thought. If we do exhume, maybe I can make it sound like the sheriff's department is willing to go the extra mile to solve a possible murder and protect its citizens."

Leave it to Barney to find a political advantage.

"On the other hand," he said. "Silver County is far from rich. If I go to the expense of digging up that old woman's body and we don't find anything, the tax payers are going to have a fit."

"I don't care what the taxpayers say and neither should you." Chance just wanted to find a way to protect David and Kate. Those brake lines could have broken just as easily when David was in the car. It was a miracle neither of them had been seriously injured or even killed. "I want to find out if Nell Hart was murdered."

"Like I said, I'll give it some thought."

Chance silently cursed. "In the meantime, how about assigning a deputy to look after Kate?"

Barney picked up his pen and began to tap it on the top of his desk. "I can't do that. We don't have that many extra men. I'll put an extra car in the area. That's the best I can do."

Chance sighed, accepting what he had already figured the sheriff would say. "Keep me posted, will you, Barney?"

"Of course."

Chance just nodded. If he did exhume the body, Barney would expect a major contribution to his reelection campaign.

It would be money well spent if what he found helped put an end to the threat against Kate.

"You seen the news?" Duke Mullens sauntered into Lon Barton's Beavertail office a little after the five o'clock shift change. "Kate Rollins resigned from the anti-mining campaign."

"I saw it."

"Looks like your troubles are over. She's quit the coalition and holed up like a scared rabbit. I told you I'd take care of things, just like I always do."

Lon walked over to the small refrigerator beneath his built-in bar, opened the door, and dragged out a can of beer. "You could have killed her with that broken brake line stunt."

Mullens just shrugged. "Well, I didn't, did I?"

Lon popped the top on his beer. "You want a Bud?"

Mullens straightened up his big body as it leaned against the door. "Sounds good to me."

Lon tossed him a can, walked back over to his desk. "Kate's off the campaign, but I heard she's still nosing around, trying to prove Nell Hart was murdered. If she proves it wasn't an accident, that Silas Marshall killed her with calculated premeditation, the court might just set aside the deal he made with us."

"What do you mean? They can't do that—can they?"

"They might. If Kate could prove Silas directly benefited by causing his partner's death. If that happened, Kate Rollins, being Nell's sole heir, could end up owning that well, and we'd be right back where we started."

"What about the money you paid?"

"Silas would have to pay it back. The court would probably award us a judgement, but that is hardly what we want."

Mullens took several swallows of beer, his neck muscles working up and down. He wiped the foam from his mouth with the back of a big, weathered hand. "That woman's a royal pain in the ass."

"True, though from what I've seen, she has a rather nice one."

Mullens grinned. "Maybe I should deliver another message, give her a little taste of what she almost got the first time. I bet that'd convince her to quit snooping into other people's business."

"Let's give it a little time, see how it all shakes out."

"I think we ought to take care of her now, before this goes any farther."

"You're awfully eager, Duke. Any particular reason?"

Duke upended his beer, drained the contents, and tossed the empty can in the trashcan, a good six feet away. "Maybe I just wanna even the score with McLain. He might be marrying Rachael Fontaine, but he's still got the hots for the redhead. Nothing I'd like better than to plow that fertile field, show Kate Rollins what it's like to be humped by a real man."

Lon stiffened. When he spoke, his voice rang with authority. "I said we're going to wait. You go near Kate Rollins right now, the sheriff'll be all over you. You get caught, he'll be thinking you have something to do with Nell Hart's murder."

Mullens grumbled a dirty word Lon couldn't quite hear. "Whatever you say, boss."

Lon nodded, satisfied Duke would do whatever he was told. "Why don't you have another beer?" Without waiting for a response, he returned to the fridge, took out another Bud, and tossed it to Mullens.

"Thanks," Duke replied a bit sullenly. There was something in his eyes Lon didn't like, but for now he would ignore it. Duke might be a little hard to control, but pit bulls had their uses.

Lon watched as Duke polished off his second beer in a matter of seconds. If things heated up any more than they were already, he might need his prize bulldog again.

* * *

The heavy white layers of cloud that had hovered over the mountains all day settled thickly around the ranch house, encompassing the log structure in a damp, misty fog. Sitting at his desk, a fire crackling in the stone fireplace in the corner, Chance pressed the telephone receiver against his ear.

"I don't like it, Rachael. You said you'd be back home by now."

"I know, Chance, but a couple of things have come up." She told him about some fancy modeling job she'd been offered, said how important it was, and that it would give her the time she needed to pick out a wedding dress.

"As soon as I'm done, I'll be back. Please say yes, Chance, just this one more time."

Just this one more time. Chance had a feeling his life would be nothing but a series of *just one more times.* "Your daddy spoiled you something fierce, Rachael."

"I know."

He sighed. Ed should have put her over his knee years ago. Chance wondered if he would be able to resist the temptation, once they were married.

"All right, go ahead. We both know you would, anyway."

"Oh, thank you, Chance." She made kissing sounds into the receiver. "Love you. See you soon."

Chance said goodbye and hung up the phone, disgusted, irritated—and wildly relieved. Dammit, he wasn't supposed to feel that way. He was marrying Rachael. Now that he'd made up his mind, he wanted to get it over and done with. He cared for Rachael, more than cared. He had known her for years, had always been attracted to her, at least he had been until he'd met Kate. There was a time he'd wanted desperately to marry her.

Things will fall into place, once she's my wife, he told himself again.

He wished to hell they could simply elope, go off somewhere and make it official. Instead, he would have to wait, to hear that little voice inside his head whispering, *Maybe you won't have to go through with it. Maybe you'll find some other way.*

There was no other way. Not for him. He was marrying Rachael and he intended to do everything in his power to make her happy. Once they were together, he would stop thinking about Kate.

Maybe he would even stop worrying about her.

Chance sighed. That wasn't going to happen anytime soon. At least not until he could be sure she and David were safe. The sooner Nell's body was exhumed and the problem resting securely in the sheriff's hands, the better for all of them.

He needed to speak to Kate, see how she was feeling, and if the sheriff had brought the papers she would need to sign to exhume the body. He hoped to hell he had. And he hoped, for her sake, the mystery she had been trying so hard to solve would come to an end very soon.

Harold "Chief" Ironstone slowly turned his head, searching the shadows of the deep pine forest, listening for the sound of human voices, hearing nothing but the sweet whisper of the wind sighing through the trees, the occasional cry of the white-tailed hawk that circled above his head.

Moving silently forward, he paused at the fence line that stretched along the mountain, disappeared into a ravine, then came up on the opposite side. He scanned the hillsides once more, but saw no one. Jamming his rubber-soled hiking boot on the lowest strand of barbed wire, he grabbed hold of another strand, and stretched the two as far apart as he could. He grunted as he bent and eased his stooped shoulders between them, careful not to release the wires until he was completely in the clear.

As a boy, there had been no fences here, nothing but mountains that climbed straight up to the sky and forests so thick and dark a man could disappear in them forever. The ground wore a carpet of moss and lichen, the earth, spongy beneath his feet, smelled of pine needles and musky decaying wood, a pleasant odor that filled his nostrils and beckoned him deeper into the forest.

Today he smelled something new. As he neared the banks of a narrow stream, he could see the bodies of a dozen dead fish, beautiful rainbow trout whose flashing silver bodies had faded to a dull pewter gray.

A few feet away, a dead raccoon lay on its side, its limbs stiff and twisted, the once-soft fur now coated by a layer of reddish, muddy earth.

Harold slung his canvas back pack down on the ground beneath a bush and pulled out the small Kodak camera he had purchased at the mercantile, a cheap one that only cost fifteen dollars and ninety-nine cents.

He had asked Jeremy Spotted Horse to lend him one, but as soon as Jeremy found out what he planned to do with it, he'd refused. It didn't matter. This one would take good enough pictures to accomplish what needed to be done.

He took several shots of the stream, then started up the hill, making his way farther onto Consolidated Metals property. The Beavertail Mine sat on the knoll up ahead. Off to one side and slightly below the main building, the tail pond sprawled in deadly proximity to the little trickling stream that fed into Beaver Creek. The only thing preventing the pond's lethal seepage was a thin plastic liner at the bottom.

Harold swore a white man's curse, the thought like bile in his mouth. Leaning over, he spat on the ground at his feet. Did no one care what happened to the land? Did no one care about the animals, the birds, or the fish?

But he knew that there were people who did care. More every day. They were beginning to see, beginning to understand all that they would lose if they continued to destroy the beauty around them.

Harold kept walking, making silent progress toward his destination. He moved among the shadows of the forest, skirting the tail pond, keeping himself out of sight.

As he drew closer, he began to hear the hum of engines, the faint sound of voices, men working at the mine. The days were growing shorter and soon the sun would drop out of sight behind the hills. He would have to hurry, make his move when the men changed shifts. Harold just hoped there would be enough light left to get a clear picture of the leaks in the pond.

Hidden in the depths of the forest, he waited as the minutes crept past. He wasn't in a hurry. He enjoyed being there in the woods, watching the way the wind moved a single blade of grass, hearing the rat-tat-tat of a woodpecker working to find its supper in the trunk of a heavy-barked tree.

Eventually, the hum of machinery slowed, marking the end of the shift. Harold waited patiently for the men to file out to their cars and drive away while others arrived to take their places. In the orderly chaos of car engines starting and doors being opened and closed, he quietly moved toward the tail pond.

Here and there, he could see fresh rips in the plastic, see contaminated water oozing sluggishly into the ground. Worried about the light, he took photos of the leaks as quickly as he could, and several photos showing the pond in proximity to the narrow little stream.

He finished the first roll of film, returned to the bush and stuck it into his backpack, loaded another roll, and returned to the pond. A few more shots and he would leave. In a couple more minutes, the light would be gone and it would be so dark it wouldn't matter.

His flash went off. Just one more shot of the stuff oozing out between those two rocks near the stream and he could disappear back into the forest. He lifted the camera, pressed it against his eye, then pain shot into his stomach and the breath burst out of his lungs. As he doubled over fighting for air, someone wrenched the camera away from his numb, shaking fingers. He saw it crash against a rock, shattering the lens, mangling the gray plastic casing. It slipped beneath the water of the gently meandering stream.

Ignoring the pain and the trembling in his limbs, Harold straightened, turned to face three of Consolidated's men.

"You're trespassing on mine property, old man." One of them, a bulky miner with thick shoulders and a dark red beard, poked a finger into his chest. "You know what happens to trespassers?"

Harold didn't answer. He wasn't sure but whatever it was, it wasn't good.

"Go get Mullens," the miner ordered, and the second man, the youngest of the group, turned and raced away.

The third man jerked him around by the shoulder. "You heard what Joe said. You're trespassin'. We don't cotton to trespassers 'round here."

Hauling back a fist, the man threw a punch that must have broken a bone in his face and slammed him into the dirt. Pain rolled over him in waves. Through a blinding haze, he saw that the man was tall and gaunt, grinning beneath a bright green John Deere baseball cap. His hands still balled into fists, he grabbed the front of Harold's jacket, hauled him to his feet, and hit him again.

"You need a lesson, Indian," the bearded man said.

"Yeah—we're gonna teach you it doesn't pay to stick your nose into other people's business."

Harold tried to climb to his feet, but his legs felt rubbery and refused to do what he told them. The gaunt man kicked him in the ribs. He heard a snapping sound, and the searing pain that screamed through his body nearly knocked him out. The bearded man dragged him up and punched him again. He could feel the blood running down the back of his throat and a knifing agony that spread outward through his chest and down his legs.

The taller man laughed, dragged him upright, and hit him again. He heard the sound of boots, shuffling through the forest as the second man returned, bringing a fourth. He recognized the sound of Duke Mullens's laughter.

The toe of Mullens's heavy boot slamming into his stomach was the last thing he remembered.

Chapter Twenty-six

David sat next to Chris Spotted Horse on a rock in the clearing next to Little Sandy Creek. They were waiting for Chief, fishing in the spot he had shown them, one of his favorites. Waiting and waiting, but Chief didn't come.

"Do you think he forgot?" Chris asked, having just returned from fishing a little way upstream.

"I don't think so. We talked about it yesterday after school." He looked up at Chris, an awful thought striking. "You don't suppose something's happened to him, do you? When we talked, he said he was going to take some pictures up at the Beavertail Mine. He said the tail pond was leaking arsenic into the little feeder stream that ran into Beaver Creek."

Chris's dark skin looked suddenly pale. "My dad told him not to go. Chief wanted to borrow a camera but my dad wouldn't loan it to him. He said it was too dangerous. He said he'd have to sneak onto Consolidated property and if they caught him, there would be hell to pay."

For all of two seconds, David stood immobile, his hand wrapped tightly around the fly fishing rod, a brand-new Orvis he had just purchased with the money he had earned over the summer. "We gotta tell someone. We gotta do something. I got a real bad feeling about this."

"Me, too," Chris said, and both of them bolted toward the trail that ran along Little Sandy Creek. They didn't slow down till they reached the clearing where David's house sat on the gently rising knoll above the cafe.

"Come on. My mom's working today. She'll know what to do."

They made their way down the hill and burst through the back door into the kitchen of the cafe.

"Well, for heaven's sake." Myra jumped out of the way, spatula in hand. "Where's the fire, you two?"

"Chief's missing," David panted, trying to catch his breath. "He was supposed to meet us up at the fishing hole, but he never showed up. Where's Mom?"

"I'm right here." She smiled as she set down a tray of dirty dishes. "Are you sure Chief didn't just forget?"

David told her the story, Chris chiming in about Chief wanting to borrow a camera from his dad.

"I know something's happened, Mom. We've got to go find him."

Kate looked down at her son, unconsciously biting her lip. Chief had never once disappointed the boys. His word was as reliable as the sun coming up. If he said he would be there, he would be there—unless he wasn't physically able.

She glanced up at the clock, saw it was nearly ten

A.M., and untied the apron she wore over her jeans. "Call Bonnie," she said to Myra. "Ask her to work the lunch shift."

"You ain't plannin' to go off lookin' for Chief by yourself?"

Kate paused. "I thought I'd call Jeremy, see if he would go with me."

"I think we ought to call Chance," David said, and Kate's stomach instantly knotted. "He's got horses. We might need to borrow them. There's lots of mountains and forest up there."

"I don't think that's a very good—"

"David's right," Myra agreed. "With Chance and Jeremy's help, you might just be able to find him. And Jeremy would probably call him anyway."

The knot in her stomach tightened even more. She didn't want to call Chance. She was doing everything in her power to stay away from him.

"I'll call him," David said before she could argue. "I know his number."

It was only a few minutes later that Chance's big silver Dodge pulled up in front of the cafe. He took off his black felt hat as he strode through the door. His eyes swung to hers, and a sweet, warm frisson rippled up her spine. She hadn't seen him since the day her brakes had failed. Watching him stride toward her, her heart pattering as if she had run a race, she could imagine how hard it was going to be to see him with another woman.

He stopped a few feet in front of her, so tall she had to tip her head back to look into his face. "David told me what happened."

She nodded, tried in vain to pull her gaze away. God

it felt good just to look at him. "He thinks Chief may have gone onto Consolidated property."

"If he did, and they happened to see him, he could be in serious trouble."

"That's what I was afraid of. We've got to find him, Chance, but I'm not sure where to start looking."

"I talked to Jeremy. Chief doesn't have a phone, so Jeremy's going to stop by his trailer." Like a number of other Salish, Chief lived in a single-wide trailer on the reservation. "He'll talk to Chief's neighbor, see if he might know something. He ought to be calling any minute."

A few more minutes passed then the phone rang, and Kate picked it up. Hearing the deep, familiar roll of Jeremy's voice, she handed the phone to Chance.

"What'd you turn up?" he asked. She couldn't hear the answer, but Chance frowned. "Okay, so that's it, then. I'll meet you there."

"What is it?" Kate asked worriedly.

"Joe Three Bulls is Chief's closest neighbor on the rez. He says Chief mentioned getting pictures of the tail pond last night and Joe hasn't seen him since."

"Oh no."

"If that's where he went, I know where we can start looking." He reached out and took hold of her shoulders. "Don't worry, Kate. We'll find him. We won't give up until we do." He turned to leave.

"Wait a minute—I'm going with you."

He stopped before he had gone two paces. "No way."

"Chief is my friend," David put in. "Me and Chris are going, too." The boys moved closer, their determination clear.

Chance set his jaw. "You can't go—none of you. We'll have to go onto Consolidated land. That means we'll be trespassing. I don't want any of you involved in something like that."

Kate squared her shoulders. "I said I'm going, Chance, and that's all there is to it."

"Me, too," David said stubbornly.

"If Dad's going, I'm going," said Chris.

Chance sighed. "All right. You can go as far as the fence line. Jeremy is meeting me there. We're going to walk the rest of the way in. If we can't find Chief, we'll have to call the sheriff, round up some men, and go in on horseback. For now, let's just hope we find him"

Kate changed out of the tennis shoes she had been wearing into a pair of Hi-Tec leather and canvas boots she had recently purchased and already fallen in love with. She grabbed her jacket, and they all trooped out to the truck, the boys climbing into the bed behind the cab, Kate climbing into the passenger seat next to Chance.

She hadn't been in the Dodge for weeks, but the familiar smell of gun oil, rope, and leather reminded her instantly of the man sitting beside her. Memories returned: the first time he had kissed her, dancing together at the Antlers, the night they'd made love on Lookout Mountain.

Chance must have been remembering, too. She could feel those piercing blue eyes on her, but when she looked at him, he glanced away. Kate forced the memories to the back of her mind and vowed not to think of them again.

They drove in silence along the road that followed Beaver Creek up into the Mission Mountains, Chance's jaw tight and grim, his hands gripping tightly the steering wheel. At a bend in the road, they turned down a gravel lane that led onto reservation land and soon deteriorated into a rutted dirt track.

Chance shifted into four-wheel drive and kept on going. "This winds its way up to the northern border of Consolidated's property," he told her as the big truck dipped and swayed in the deep, hard-crusted ruts. "If Chief wanted to get to the tail pond without being seen, this is likely the way he would come."

Kate said nothing, just clung precariously to the seat, each bump in the road jarring her teeth. She looked back through the window to be sure the boys were okay and gave up a sigh of relief when the truck finally pulled over to the side of the road, stopping next to Jeremy's battered blue Chevy pickup.

The boys jumped out of the truck bed and Kate used the running board Chance had installed to lever herself to the ground.

Jeremy walked toward them, a black look on his face. "What the devil are they doing here?" he said to Chance, jerking his thumb toward Kate and the boys.

"They were determined to come along. I told them I'd bring them this far, but they'd have to wait here."

Kate ignored the comment, just hauled her jacket out of the truck, slid her arms into the sleeves, and zipped it partway up. "The boys are staying here until we get back. I'm going with you."

"No way," Chance said. "This is tough terrain. You'll stay here with David and Chris."

Kate just smiled. "I walk a million miles a day in that cafe. I'm going with you." Little by little, she was becoming more and more of a mountain person and today she was glad. Ignoring the hard set to the two men's features, she marched toward the barbed-wire fence, propped one of her boots on the bottom wire, spread it open as she had learned to do, and ducked through to the opposite side.

"Coming?" she prodded, flashing them a confident smile. Chance just sighed and started walking toward the fence.

"We'll be back in a couple of hours," Jeremy called to the boys. "Keep an eye out for Chief and stay close to the trucks."

The boys nodded their understanding, and the three of them started climbing up the steep mountain trail leading into the forest.

"The Beavertail Mine is about two miles from here," Chance said. "We'll head in that direction and keep our eyes open along the way. Once we get there, we'll search the area around the tail pond. If we don't see any sign Chief's been there, we'll head back to the trucks, drive down the hill into cell phone range, and get on the horn to the sheriff."

Kate nodded and fell in line between Chance, who led the way, and Jeremy, who followed behind. The going was steep, and a cold, blustery wind swept down through the mountains, whistling eerily through the trees. It was nearly November. At this altitude, it was clear that winter was on its way.

The trail continued, a narrow winding path that penetrated more deeply into the forest. Chance settled into a brisk but bearable pace, probably slower than he would have traveled if Kate hadn't been along, but covering a lot of ground just the same. Kate managed to keep up with less effort than she had expected. Chance looked back a couple of times, seemed satisfied that she was able to stand the pace, and continued up the trail.

She watched his broad back ahead of her, shoulders stretching well beyond his canvas backpack, his lean frame moving with a comfortable stride that could only come from years of living in this beautiful, rugged country.

Her breath came hard by the time the trail leveled off at the top of the hill. Chance stopped for a moment to give them a breather, for which she and Jeremy both seemed grateful. When he turned in her direction, she couldn't miss the warm approval on his face.

"You're making this look far too easy," he teased. "You're supposed to be huffing and puffing by now."

Kate smiled, her breathing already back to normal. "Maybe I'm turning into a mountain girl."

His expression softened, lingered a moment on her face. "Maybe you are."

His eyes held hers, seemed to reach inside her. She wanted to touch him, run her finger over the hard planes of his face, the strong, lean sinews of his body.

"Anybody need a drink of water?" Jeremy held out his canteen, ending the moment, and both of them turned away. Kate accepted the metal flask just to have something to do, cranked off the cap, and took a welcome drink. She passed it to Chance, who must have tasted a hint of her lipstick on the rim, for when he looked at her again, his eyes seemed darker, more intense.

He put the cap back on with brisk efficiency and returned the canteen to Jeremy, careful to keep his eyes focused off toward the distant ridge. "Time's wasting. We'd better get back on the trail."

They set out again, heading inward, across the top of the mountain, then beginning a steep, short descent down the opposite side of the hill. When they reached the far edge of the forest, Chance lifted his hand, calling a silent halt to their progress.

"You can see the tail pond from here," he said softly, careful to stay back in the cover of the trees. "Jeremy—you circle left and I'll go right. I'll take Kate with me."

Jeremy nodded, the wind whipping the ends of his long black braid. He set out slowly, his footsteps nearly silent as he disappeared into the shadowy forest.

"Stay close," Chance said. "And try to be as quiet as you can. There'll be men working not far away."

She followed along behind him, walking as soundlessly as she could. She noticed him looking back several times to make sure that she was still there.

A little stream trickled out of the woods, swirling around mossy rocks and boulders as it ran off down the hill. Chance stepped over, took her hand, and helped her across, and they kept on going, traveling along the muddy bank on the opposite side. His nearly soundless footsteps, muffled by the moist, dark earth, turned toward the tail pond. That was the moment she spotted it—a small, bright flash of yellow at the bottom of the stream.

"Chance . . ." she whispered, halting him and bringing him back down the trail. Crouching beside the creek, she reached into the icy water and pulled out a small torn piece of yellow cardboard. It was the top off a box of film. She searched along the bank of the stream until she spotted several pieces of mangled gray plastic. She pulled them from where they lay half hidden in the rocks.

"It's a camera," Chance said darkly, recognizing the crushed and broken pieces as one of the inexpensive kind tourists bought at Dillon's Mercantile. "Chief must have been here."

"Yes, and after coming this far, he wouldn't have left without it."

"Let's fan out, see what we can find. Just don't get too far away."

She nodded and began to search the ground, looking for tracks or marks of any kind that might indicate where Chief had gone. They searched for at least twenty minutes before she heard Chance's urgent whisper, "Over here!"

Kate hurried in that direction, heading for the shallow ravine where he had disappeared. She found him down on one knee behind a thick stand of brush in the gully.

"What is it?" Before he could answer, she spotted the thin, jean-clad legs sticking out of the brush. "Oh God, no."

Chief was covered in dirt and blood, his face so swollen he was barely recognizable. Her hands shook as she quickly knelt beside him, her heart thumping at an agonizing rate.

"Is he . . . ?"

"He's still breathing, but barely." Chance slung his backpack off his shoulder, unzipped the center pouch, and hauled out a blanket and first aid kit. "It looks like they dragged him here. Probably figured the weather or the animals would finish him off." He carefully opened the old man's jacket to find the front of his plaid flannel shirt covered in blood. Chance unbuttoned and eased it open. Frothy blood leaked out a small ragged hole in his thin, gray-haired chest, and a sob welled up in Kate's throat. She bit hard on her lip to keep it firm.

"His cheekbone is broken. He's got a couple of busted ribs. One of them must have punctured a lung." He draped the blanket over the unconscious man on the ground in an effort to get him warm. "He probably has internal injuries as well. It's amazing he's still breathing."

Her throat closed up. She swallowed past the thick

lump swelling there. "We have to get help. We have to get him out of here."

She gasped at the strength of the gnarled old hand that reached out and gripped her wrist. Chief's ancient eyes slowly opened and came to rest on her face.

"Pictures ..." he whispered. "Pack. Under the bush."

"Take it easy, *say-laht,* Chance said, speaking to the old man in Salish as Kate hadn't even known he could. He said a lot of words she didn't understand, but the gist of it seemed to be that they had come to help him. *"Yo lu hom-kanu-le-hu,"* Chance said to him gently. "We'll take you to a place where it's safe."

Chief gave the faintest shake of his head. *"Chiks imsh lu ch'en-ku dtu-leewh."* His eyes slowly closed. For a moment Kate thought he had slipped away. Then his frail chest rose on another shallow breath of air.

Chance's face looked grim. "He says today is the day he journeys to the other world."

"No!" She caught hold of Chief's weathered hand. "You aren't going to die. We won't let you!"

At the edge of her vision, she saw Jeremy standing like a statue in the brush. She hadn't even noticed his arrival.

"I'll go down to the mine and get help."

"He'll need a chopper," Chance said. "It's the only chance he has."

Jeremy nodded. "I'll be back as quick as I can." He disappeared as quietly as he had arrived and Kate's worried gaze swung to Chance.

"Isn't it dangerous for him to go down there? Look what they did to Chief."

"Chief was a harmless old man. Jeremy is well known in the community. Besides, he'll go directly into the main office, tell them we're here and what we've found. They'll be forced to help—they won't have any other choice."

Her hand trembled as she laced it with Chief's. "Just hold on," she whispered, looking down into his swollen, battered face. The tears she had been fighting welled in her eyes and began to slide down her cheeks.

"Do not cry, *I-huk-spu-us*. Friends are here. It is good to die with friends."

The lump in her throat grew so large she could barely speak. She squeezed his icy fingers, then looked up at Chance, whose own eyes looked suspiciously moist. "What did he call me?"

"The nearest translation is 'pure heart'."

Kate bit down on her lip. *Pure heart.* He had once said something like that to her, that she had a very good heart. She had come to love this old man who had befriended her and her son and now lingered on the very edge of death. He had lost so much blood and he was so weak. Beneath her fingers, she could barely feel his feeble, erratic pulse. She said a silent prayer but she thought that God's will might very well be to carry him on his journey homeward, just as he had said.

Chief's icy, brittle fingers tightened faintly around hand. "I have . . . heard . . . that you have been there . . . that you have seen . . . *Schi-mas-ket.*"

She didn't need Chance to translate what he said or the question that was clear in his pain-filled eyes. She brushed at the tears on her cheeks. "Yes, I've been there. It's the most beautiful place. Greener even than the mountains here. The sky is so blue it hurts your eyes, and the light . . . the light is like a fine mist of gold that shimmers all around you. It warms you from inside, fills you with a joy unlike anything you've known on earth. All of your friends will be there. And your family, Chief. Your mother and your father. They'll be there to welcome you home. They'll be so happy to see you after all of these years."

She looked down at his face, barely able to see for the thick film of tears. "It's everything you ever believed it would be and more."

She felt a faint squeezing of her hand. The edges of his mouth lifted up in the faintest, briefest of smiles, then his eyes slowly closed. The hand that held hers went limp and slack, and she knew that he was gone.

Oh dear God! Part of her wanted to call him back, to beseech him to stay, to let the doctors have a chance to heal him. But another part knew the peace he had already found, knew the pain was now gone and joy replaced it, and she could not summon the words.

She felt Chance's hand on her shoulder, just the gentlest of touches, and yet she could feel his strength. It began to flow into her even as the tears rained down and she clung to the old man's ancient, weathered hand.

"He's gone, Katie. There's nothing more we can do."

She shook with silent sobs but still she did not move. She felt Chance's hand on her elbow, helping her to her feet, then he pulled her into his arms.

"Oh, Chance," she sobbed, unable to stop the tears.

"It's all right, darlin'. He heard your words and it gave him peace."

She looked up at him through the wetness. "Do you think he believed me?"

The edge of his thumb brushed over her trembling lips. "I know he did."

She buried her face against his chest and cried until her tears soaked the front of his jacket. Chance just held her, whispering soothing words, telling her how glad he was that she had been there, how much of a comfort she had been to Chief.

"How could someone do this?" she asked between ragged breaths. "How could they hurt that dear, sweet old man?"

She felt his hand gently smoothing over her back. "I don't know what drives people to do something like this. I don't know who it was, but I promise you, Kate, I'll find out."

Chance didn't say anymore and Kate just stood there, grateful for his comforting presence. In what seemed like hours, but must have been less than thirty minutes, the whop, whop, whop of a chopper pressed down from overhead.

The helicopter landed in a clearing not far from the ravine and two men in white uniforms leaped out. They pulled out a stretcher, ducked beneath the whirling blades, and ran toward where she and Chance stood at the top of the ravine.

Kate stood forlornly, the wind whipping her hair, as Chance led them over to where Chief lay beneath the blanket and they loaded his body onto the stretcher. The helicopter hadn't yet lifted off when Jeremy arrived, a worried look on his face.

Chance just shook his head.

They made one final stop before they left—to retrieve the pack and the roll of film that had been important enough for Chief to die for. Then they started back toward the trucks.

It was a grim trio who arrived at the base of the mountain. One look at Kate's tear-stained face and David knew the worst had happened.

"They killed him, didn't they? Those dirty bastards murdered him!"

Jeremy led Chris a little way away and Chance clamped a steadying hand on David's shoulder. "We'll find out who did it, son. We'll make them pay for what they did."

David tried not to cry, but his eyes were wet and his hands were shaking. Chance drew him hard against his chest and wrapped his arms around the boy's shoulders.

"It's all right to cry, Davy. Sometimes that's what it takes to get rid of the pain."

David clung to him for several long seconds, then he stepped away. When they drove up in front of the house, he jumped out of the truck and ran inside, letting the screen door slam behind him.

Kate started to climb down from the pickup and go after him, but Chance caught her arm. "Let him go, Kate. He needs a little time to sort things out."

He was right and she knew it. She sighed and leaned back against the seat. Chance bent over her, caught her chin between his fingers, and turned her to face him.

"I want you to know how proud I am of you, Kate. I'm glad you were there today. I've never known another woman like you."

Kate blinked and fresh tears rolled down her cheeks. "Thank you."

"There's something else. Something I'll say just this once and never again." She saw the emotion in face he didn't try to hide. "I love you, Katie. It doesn't change anything. Nothing can change what I have to do. I just wanted you to know."

She wanted to tell him she loved him too, wanted to say it so badly she ached. But he was marrying someone else. He would never be hers, and she just couldn't say the words. She swallowed past the thick lump in her throat.

"I have to go in," she said.

Chance nodded, looked away. "I know."

With a last painful glance at his dear, beloved face, Kate jumped down from the pickup and raced up the front porch steps. She was sick inside, sick with pain and grief for Chief.

And aching with a bitter, agonizing despair for herself, she knew it would not go away anytime soon.

Chapter Twenty-seven

Lon Barton hung up the telephone in his office and leaned back in his chair. His hands were shaking. He was thirty-seven years old and when his father called, he trembled like a kid.

He slammed a fist down on the top of the desk, sending a paper clip flying into the air. Sonofabitch! Forcing himself to take a calming breath, he reached over and pressed the intercom button.

His secretary answered immediately. "Yes, Mr. Barton?"

"Find Mullens. Get him in here ASAP."

"Yes, sir. Right away."

Twenty minutes later, Duke knocked lightly on the door and sauntered in. "What's up, boss?"

Lon leaned back in his expensive black-leather swivel chair. "My father called from his place up in Whitefish." It was just one of the houses he owned from Beverly

Hills to West Palm Beach. "He got word today from that lady friend of his in the sheriff's office. You know the one—Barbara what's-her-name." An attractive woman Lon had asked out a few times himself. Barbara had said no to him, but not to his father. At fifty-seven, William Barton was lean, fit and handsome, one of the wealthiest and most powerful men in the country. Women had always found him attractive and he never took no for an answer. Though he was married to his fourth and presumably final wife, he'd been seeing Barbara in secret for nearly a year.

Lon looked over at Duke, whose big body lounged against the closed door, his arms crossed over his chest.

"Barbara says the sheriff's being pressured to exhume Nell Hart's body."

"Shit."

"If that happens, and it turns out her death wasn't an accident like Silas Marshall claims, if the sonofabitch actually murdered her, that property we bought could wind up in court, just like I said. My father doesn't want that to happen. He wants this matter settled, once and for all."

I'm tired of your incompetence, his father had said in his usual disapproving tone. *I want this over and done with— you hear me? I don't care how it happens.*

Duke straightened, came away from the door. "You want me to handle it?"

Lon nodded, feeling slightly sick. "That ought to make your day."

"Let me make sure I got this right. You want Kate Rollins out of the picture. You figure, once she's gone, the whole thing will eventually blow over."

"That's about it."

"When do you want it done?"

"I figured maybe Halloween. That's tomorrow night. Her kid will probably be out trick-or-treating. There are always troublemakers out and about, and the cops will be busy."

"Sounds like a good idea to me." Duke turned toward the door.

"One more thing. This has to look like an accident. If it appears to be anything else, we'll be stirring up more trouble than we've got already."

Duke seemed to mull that over, then he nodded. "I'll take care of it. It's amazing what happens to a house when someone accidentally leaves the propane on."

Lon grimaced. He didn't want to hear the gory details, but this time he needed to know. He needed to be sure the matter was handled correctly. Too much was at stake if anything went wrong. "All right, if that's what it takes. Do it."

Duke flashed him a look he couldn't quite read and turned to leave. Maybe he wasn't as happy about the job as Lon would have guessed. Cruelty was one thing, murder was another. Still, whatever it took, Lon could count on him to get the job done.

Swearing silently at his father, who always seemed to demand more than his son could possibly give, Lon returned to the paperwork piling up on his desk.

"Have a good time!" Standing on the front porch, Kate smiled and waved goodbye to David, who jumped into the back seat of Willow's minivan next to Chris.

"I'll have him home no later than eleven," Willow promised. She and Jeremy were taking the boys to the Halloween carnival at Chris's school, then to visit the "haunted house" in Ronan put on by the local 4-H Club.

"Are you sure you don't want to come with us?" Willow asked.

Kate shook her head. "Sounds like you're going to have fun, but tonight's the coalition's weekly online chat group. Since I'm not running things anymore, I try to be there to answer questions and help them come up with new ideas."

"That's important stuff." Willow jerked open the passenger door and slid into the seat next to her husband, who sat behind the wheel. All of them waved as Jeremy turned the minivan around, headed down the driveway, and turned onto the road, disappearing seconds later into the thickening darkness.

The wind was blowing tonight, whining through the branches of the pine trees, stirring up grass and dead leaves. A dense layer of heavy black clouds smothered the moon and stars and warned of a coming storm.

As she walked back into the house, Kate ignored a faint uneasiness and remembered instead the smile on David's face when he climbed in the car, the first she had seen since the day Chief had died. The funeral had been just yesterday. A simple graveside service at the little cemetery on the reservation, but most of the townspeople were there, as well as those from the surrounding area, including Ed and Chance. Chief would surely be missed.

Kate and David had gone with Willow and Jeremy. Knowing the grief David suffered, Kate had spent every spare moment with him, which was why she hadn't gone tonight. She thought it might be good for him to go without her.

With a last look into the darkness outside the house,

Kate checked to be sure the front door was locked—a habit she had acquired living in the city—went into the kitchen, made herself a cup of tea, and carried it upstairs to her office.

She could hear the wind whistling, rattling the windows, an eerie sound in the creaky old wooden house, a perfect night for Halloween. Sitting behind her desk, she flipped on the computer and it started humming away, dispelling some of the Halloween chill.

She typed in the proper commands and pulled up her e-mail, read a message from Sally, an update on life in LA and what was happening at Menger and Menger. She answered with the latest on the anti-mining campaign, telling Sally she had resigned her position and wishing her a happy Halloween. She replied to an e-mail from a friend in Chicago she had met on a business trip and still kept in touch with. Then, at eight o'clock, it was time to go into the AOL chat room where members of the coalition met once a week.

Usually no more than five or six people attended. Ed Fontaine was the moderator, great at keeping everyone on track. Jake Dillon typically made at least a brief appearance. Kate had mentioned the meeting once to Aida Whittaker and, using her son-in-law's PC, she had dropped in for a visit last week. Diane Stevens, the television anchor, had joined the group once, and that lawyer up in Polson, Frank Mills, who had represented the Salish in their bid for an injunction, was a guest at one of the group's recent meetings. Sometimes, Chance dropped in.

Kate put that thought out of her mind as she tuned in to the group, reading comments from Ed as to what had occurred since the previous meeting.

Half an hour into the chat, her thoughts began to

wander. Something tugged at the back of her mind, drawing her attention away. Sliding her chair back from the screen, she listened to the rattle of the wind, the scrape of the branches against the windowpanes, and another, indistinct sound that seemed to be coming from downstairs.

Her heart kicked up a little. Kate left the computer running, went across the room, eased open the door, and leaned out into the hallway.

Nothing but silence greeted her. She shook her head at her runaway imagination. *What did you expect—it's Halloween.*

She started to close the door when she heard a faint scraping sound in the kitchen, as if one of the breakfast table chairs was being moved.

This is silly, she told herself, but she couldn't go back to work until she knew. Better to face the unknown than to let it grow into phantoms inside her head. She pulled open the door and headed downstairs. She reached the bottom step, flipped on another light switch, marched through the dining room and into the kitchen. Terror streaked through her. A scream erupted at the unexpected sight of the man in the ski mask standing in front of the stove.

Kate turned and started running.

"Oh no you don't!" He was behind her in a heartbeat, catching her before she could reach the front door, his arm snaking around her waist, slamming her up against his chest. "I think we've done this little dance before, haven't we, sweetheart?"

"Let me go!"

"Sorry. Not this time." Dragging her away from the door, he pulled a roll of duct tape out from inside his shirt, jerked her wrists in front of her, and wrapped them with the tape. "I warned you, but no—you wouldn't listen. Now you'll have to pay."

"I did what you asked," she told him desperately. "I resigned from the campaign."

"But you couldn't quit stirring up trouble, could you? You just couldn't let things alone."

"I don't . . . I don't know what you mean."

"Yeah, well it doesn't matter whether you know or not."

Kate tried to twist her hands free but the tape wouldn't budge. All she succeeded in doing was hurting her wrist. She looked up, saw him standing with his feet splayed, a big brawny man that somehow looked familiar. An image arose of that same bulky frame brawling with Chance in the parking lot. Good Lord, it was Duke Mullens! She should have figured it out the first time he was there. Not that it would have mattered, since she didn't have even a shred of proof.

"What are you going to do?"

Through the opening of the ski mask, she could see his big teeth flash and his thick lips move. "If you mean am I going to get between those pretty little legs of yours—sorry, sweetheart, I don't have time." Gripping her arm, he started dragging her toward the closet, and fear bloomed inside her.

Kate had no idea what he meant to do, but she wasn't going to let him do it without a fight. She could scream, but she was too far from the cafe for anyone to hear her. Instead, as they neared the closet, she twisted, kicked him hard in the shin with her sturdy Hi-Tec boot, and started running.

Duke grunted and swore. "Sonofabitch!"

The front door was locked. She would never have time to get it open. Whirling to the left, she raced up the stairs, her heart pounding as hard as her feet. There was a phone in her office. She slammed the door, wedged a stout oak chair beneath the knob, and raced for the phone on her desk.

Her bound hands were shaking as she jerked up the receiver, jammed it against her ear, and punched in 911. She could hear Duke Mullens outside the door, turning the knob, swearing when it didn't open, ramming his shoulder against the thick slab of wood.

"Come on," she whispered, dialing the number again. Nothing. It took a moment for her to realize the wires had been cut. The phone line was dead.

Oh, dear God. A wave of fear rolled through her and her mind went numb. For a moment, she couldn't seem to think. Kate whirled toward the computer, the screen glowing with its usual warmth. When she had accepted the job heading up the anti-mining campaign, she'd had a separate phone line installed for the computer. It came into the house from a different location than the older telephone lines Nell had installed years earlier. She was still hooked into the chat room!

With her wrists bound tightly in front of her, her hands were beginning to go to numb. Her fingers felt stiff and unresponsive as she twisted her arm a little and was finally able to rest one hand on the keyboard. Forcing herself to go slow, she typed in: *Man in the house. Trying to kill me. Dial 911. Kate.*

Wood cracked. Any second Mullens would burst through the door. "You're dead, you hear me, you little bitch? First I'm gonna fuck you, then I'm gonna turn the gas on and blow you to kingdom come!"

Oh, God! She was shaking now, terrified of what would happen once he got into the room. She needed a weapon, something that— For God's sake—the gun

Chance had lent her! It was lying right there on the credenza behind her desk. She'd been using it as a paperweight to glue some photos into an album she was making.

She whirled in that direction, fumbled for a moment, fighting to pick it up with the duct tape so tight around her wrists, jerked open the top drawer of her desk, and fumbled for the box of shells. The cardboard cut one of her fingers. Her hands were shaking so badly she nearly dropped the box. Eventually, she shoved two bullets in, closed the cylinder, and aimed it toward the door.

"Get away from the door! I've got a gun in here and it's pointed right at you! Get away or I swear I'll pull the trigger!"

"No one fucks with the Duke—you hear me? I'm gonna kill you! And I'm gonna do it real slow!" He threw his heavy weight against the door one last time, splintering the wood, and Kate fired the pistol.

The shot was deafening in the small, closed up room. Her ears rang as she pulled the trigger a second time, heard it rip through the wood, then the door gave completely away and crashed forward into the office.

Duke Mullens sprawled on top of it, arms and legs bent in unnatural positions, blood pooling beneath him, a bright red puddle that spread like a growing tide all over the door, pumping out of Mullens's chest with every heartbeat. He was breathing hard, sucking in great gulps of air.

"I should have . . . killed you the first time."

Kate pointed the empty revolver in his direction as he clumsily levered himself to his feet. She was shaking so hard she could barely hold onto her useless weapon. Instead of coming toward her, Mullens turned and staggered back toward the stairs, smearing blood on the wall as he leaned against it for support. He made it to the top of the landing, took the first step, and pitched forward, rolling headlong, then crashing in a bloody heap at the bottom of the staircase.

Kate let go of the gun and it hit the floor with a clatter. Racing down the stairs, she stopped a few feet from Mullens's body.

"Why?" she asked, desperate to know. "Why did you want to kill me?" But Mullens didn't answer. His chest no longer moved. Duke Mullens was dead.

Kate slumped against the wall, trembling all over, her stomach rolling with nausea. She didn't understand what had happened. Why had Duke Mullens wanted her dead?

She had to get up, go back to her computer, make sure her message was received and the sheriff was on his way, but her legs felt like cotton and her lungs burned like fire with each breath.

"Why?" she whispered, wondering if she would ever find out. "Are you the one who murdered Nell?"

"Duke didn't kill her. I did."

Kate jerked toward the sound of the voice coming from below the stairs. Lon Barton, dressed in black from head to foot, stood with an automatic pistol in a black-gloved hand. It was obvious he had been watching through the window and equally obvious he wasn't pleased that Duke's mission had failed.

"You . . . you were the one?"

"I didn't intend to. I only came to the house that day to convince her to sell the well."

"But . . . but surely—"

"My father was adamant about owning it. Nell refused to see reason. I had to do something."

"Silas Marshall said that he was the one who killed her."

Lon shook his head. The ends of his curly blond hair stuck out from beneath his black knit cap. "He must have shoved her, like he told the police. I guess he thought he killed her—he drove out of here like a madman. When I went into the house, Nell was lying there in the dining room."

"But she was still alive."

"She was breathing, but just barely. When I realized how close she was to death, I figured—why not? I pressed a pillow over her face. I figured if anyone found out, Silas would get the blame."

Chills raced up and down Kate's arms. Lon Barton had killed Nell. That was the reason he had sent Duke Mullens to kill her. She had to keep him talking, give the sheriff time to get there. God knew how long that would take—especially since tonight was Halloween. And she wasn't even sure her message got through.

"Surely Nell fought you."

"Only a little; she was too weak. It only took a few seconds and she was dead." Barton raised the pistol, aimed it straight at her heart. "Just like you're going to be."

"The sheriff is coming," Kate said hastily, inching backward up the stairs. "Even if you kill me, they'll catch you."

Barton shook his head. "I don't think so. I think Duke Mullens killed you . . . just like you killed him." He moved closer. "He was always overzealous. That's why he killed Nell. He knew Consolidated wanted to buy that well and that Silas Marshall would sell it, once Nell was out of the way. Then you started digging and Duke got scared. He had to shut you up. Unfortunately, he died in the process." He slid the action back on the deadly-looking pistol.

"I'm sorry, Kate, I really am. I never wanted any of this to happen. Somehow it just did."

Kate turned and bolted up the stairs. Barton fired the pistol and the shot slammed into the wall behind her. A second shot splintered the handrail, but Kate kept running. She had almost reached the upstairs hall when she heard the back door crash open and the thunder of a man's heavy boots. Chance tackled Lon Barton like a champion bulldogger going for the rodeo record.

The pistol went flying, sailing across the hardwood floor and cracking against the wall. Kate raced after it, bolting down the stairs in time to see Chance roll on top of Barton and began to slam one hard punch after another into his face.

Someone started pounding on the door. Kate spotted Ed Fontaine's van out in front, the driver's door open, the tailgate down, Ed wheeling himself up the path toward the steps. Randy Wiggins stood on the porch, hammering madly away.

Kate hurried to let him in and he raced past her into the entry, stopping next to where Chance continued to batter an unconscious Lon Barton.

"He's had enough," Randy said. "You'll kill him, Chance."

Chance pulled his next punch but the effort it took left his fist shaking. He climbed off Lon Barton, and walked straight toward her, stopping only long enough to pull a folding knife out of the pocket of his jeans and cut through the duct tape, then she was securely in his arms.

"God, Katie." He gathered her closer, buried his face in her hair, and she clung to him, her arms sliding up around his neck. "I've never been so scared in my life. Are you all right?"

She nodded against his shoulder, felt the tremors running through his lean frame. "I shot him, Chance. I killed Duke Mullens."

He looked over the top of her head to the body sprawled like a broken toy at the foot of the stairs. "I'm just glad I gave you that gun."

"How did . . . how did you know?"

"I was with you in the chat room. I knew you'd be uncomfortable if you knew I was there, so I just kept quiet. When I read what you wrote, I thought I was going to be sick."

"Barton killed Nell, Chance. He said his father wanted the well she and Silas owned."

Chance released a weary sigh. One of his hands slid over her hair to cup the back of her head and he cradled her cheek against his shoulder. "I suppose that makes sense. William Barton has been pulling Lon's string for years. Lon was completely dependent on him. His position with the company, his high-paying salary. All the wealth he had accumulated over the years was a direct result of his father's good will. If he lost it, he lost everything."

"I wonder how his father is going to feel now."

Ed Fontaine spoke up from the doorway, where Randy had managed to wheel his chair. "I know how I'd feel if I drove my son to do something like that." For an instant, his gaze flicked to Chance, who still held onto Kate. "But William Barton? I don't think we'll ever really know."

Colored lights flashed on the walls of the living room as the sheriff's car finally drove up. Halloween was a busy night, the perfect time to commit a murder. Another car arrived and Lon Barton was taken into custody. Ed and Chance both stayed until one of the deputies had taken Kate's statement, then she was finally done.

"You can't stay here." Chance cast a glance toward the body being photographed at the bottom of the stairs. "As soon as David gets home, I'll drive the two of you down to that little motel on the way to Ronan. In the meantime, we'll wait for David over in the cafe." He caught one of the deputies' eyes and he nodded, understanding where to send the boy when he got home.

"I—I have to pack a bag." She moistened her lips, wishing she didn't have to pass Mullens's body to get upstairs.

Reading her thoughts, Chance took her hand. "Come on. I'll take you up."

"Be careful what you touch," one of the deputies called out. "Remember this is a crime scene."

Again. Kate shivered, thinking of Nell's murder and wondering how she would handle living in the house with so many bad memories.

They made their way up to her bedroom, being careful not to disturb anything along the way. Kate packed a bag for herself and one for David and they headed back downstairs. They were sitting in the cafe, drinking decaf coffee when a pale-faced David walked in with Jeremy, Willow, and Chris.

"Mom!" he raced toward her and she opened her arms, felt his thin frame shaking against her as she closed them around him. "Are you all right?" David asked. "The cop said a man tried to kill you and you shot him."

"I'm fine, honey. And it's all over now. We're going to stay in a motel for a couple of days, until they get the house cleaned up. Chance is going to drive us."

It would be easier if she just drove the rental car she had been using, but she was still so shaky she didn't trust herself behind the wheel.

"Why don't you stay with us?" Willow offered.

"Good idea," Jeremy agreed. "We might be a little bit crowded but—"

"I appreciate it, but I'd really rather not. You've both been wonderful friends. But to tell you the truth, I think David and I need a little time to ourselves."

"Are you sure you'll be all right?" Willow asked worriedly, while Myra hovered protectively a few feet away.

"I'll be fine. I'm just glad this whole thing is finally over."

At the Night's Rest Motel, a little row of faux-log cabins on the road down to Ronan, Chance checked them in and carried her bag inside. David carried his own in, turned on the TV, and flopped down in front of it as Kate walked Chance to the door.

"Thank you for coming when you did. You saved my life, Chance."

Chance ran a finger along her jaw and a thread of heat filtered through her. "Even if I hadn't gotten there, I think you would have outsmarted Barton, just the way you did Duke. You're an amazing woman, Kate."

Kate said nothing. She was looking at Chance and wishing he were staying there with her, wishing she could convince him not to marry a woman he didn't love.

Knowing that he wouldn't listen.

"I thought Rachael would be back by now," she said, just to put some distance between them. Chance stiffened, drew away, as she had known he would.

He sighed into the frosty darkness. "She'll be back the end of the week."

Kate ignored a stab of pain. "I appreciate everything you've done, Chance. But after tonight, I don't want . . . I don't want to see you again. Not even as a friend."

"What about your car? At least let me take you back to get it in the morning."

"Myra can come and get me."

He looked away, off into the silent world around them. Somewhere in the night, an owl hooted, a forlorn, empty sound. Kate stared at Chance's hard, implacable features, thought how much she loved him, and a hollow ache rose in her chest.

"You're right," he said. "It's better if we stay away from each other. At least now I won't have to worry about you. With Duke Mullens dead and Nell's murder out in the open, you'll be safe."

Knowing she shouldn't, Kate laid a hand against his cheek. She could feel the roughness of his late-night beard and the warmth of his skin. For a moment his eyes slid closed and he leaned his face into her palm. Then her hand fell away. When he looked at her again, his features were dark with pain.

Kate swallowed past the lump in her throat. "I love you, Chance," she told him, her chest aching, fighting to hold back tears. "I had to tell you, just once."

"Katie . . ."

She only shook her head, unable to hear him say more. Turning away, she left him standing on the porch in front of the little cabin. Her heart felt like it weighed a thousand pounds as she walked back into the room and quietly closed the door.

Chapter Twenty-eight

Sitting in his wheelchair behind the big mahogany desk in his study, Ed Fontaine waited while Chance walked in an closed the door.

"You wanted to see me?"

Ed wheeled his chair out from behind the desk and motioned Chance to take a seat in one of the leather chairs in front of it. He hated looking up to people, especially a man as tall as Chance.

"My daughter's flying in tomorrow night. I imagine she called to tell you."

Chance nodded. "She phoned a couple of days ago. Said she was finished with her job in the city." He jackknifed one long leg across the other then settled his dusty black Stetson on his knee, turning it absently with his hand. "She says she's got things pretty much all lined out for the wedding."

Ed didn't respond to that. "Tell me something, Chance. Are you in love with my daughter?"

Chance's wide shoulders went a little bit straighter. He sat up taller in his chair. "I love Rachael. You know that. I can hardly remember a time I didn't know her. The two us have been friends for years."

"I know you love her. You two were practically raised together. I want to know if you're *in* love with her."

For an instant, Chance looked away. Ed watched him fiddle with the crease in his hat, outlining the folds with his index finger. Then he looked Ed straight in the eye.

"I'll make her a damned good husband. I'll take care of her, see she gets anything she wants. She won't lack for a thing."

"But you aren't in love with her."

Fierce blue eyes fixed on his face. There was so much emotion there it made Ed's chest feel tight. "Rachael and I both know where we stand. She wants the same things I want. Neither of us is going into this marriage with our eyes closed."

"So you're saying she isn't in love with you, either."

Chance came to his feet. "Dammit, Ed, you're turning this all around. What do you want me to say? Rachael and I have been planning to marry for years. We've both agreed. Now that's just what we're gonna do."

"Even if it means losing the woman you're in love with?"

Chance stared over Ed's head, his gaze fixed on a spot on the wall. The muscles in his throat moved up and down, but no words came out.

"You do love her, don't you? I've known you for years, Chance, and you've never looked at a woman the way you look at Kaitlin Rollins."

When Chance finally spoke, his voice came out deep and rusty. "It doesn't matter. My future is set. I'm marrying Rachael. I give you my word I'll make her happy."

"Sit down, son. You know I how I hate looking up at you."

Chance sank like a stone in the chair, the muscles in his neck and shoulders rigid with tension.

"You're marrying Rachael because of me, aren't you, son? You think it's what I want. You think you owe it to me because of what happened that day on the mountain. Because you blame yourself for the accident that put me in this chair."

Chance's jaw looked rigid. "It was my fault. If I had listened to my father—"

"If you'd listened to half of what that hardheaded old SOB said, you wouldn't be the man you are today. What happened in that storm could have happened any time, any place, anywhere. Life's hard here. You know that. My luck just ran bad that day."

Chance said nothing. Twenty-one years of guilt wasn't that easy to wash away. Ed had hoped that by now it would have faded.

"Listen to me, son. I know you're doing this for me. There was a time I wanted you to marry Rachael more than anything on this earth. I wanted you to be the father of her children. I wanted that strong blood of yours to run through my grandchildren's veins. Now that I know you're in love with someone else, it isn't what I want anymore."

Chance swallowed, his fingers gripping the hat so hard he was putting a new crease in it. "What about the ranch? What about the legacy you wanted your grandchildren to have? You've talked about it for years."

"When the time comes, my grandkids will inherit the

Circle Bar F. That's as fine a legacy as any man could ask.''

"What about Rachael? I made her a promise. I can't just—"

"Yes, you can. We both know Rachael isn't any more in love with you than you are with her. Maybe I was doing as big a disservice to her as I was to you. We'll let Rachael save face and call the engagement off. That'll take some of the sting out of it. She's a beautiful girl. She'll find someone else, hopefully a man she can love the way I loved her mother. In the meantime, I'll leave it to you to give me those grandkids. After all, you're as close to me as any son I might have had. And more than anything in the world, I want you to be happy."

Chance sat forward in his chair. "Are you sure, Ed?"

"Last night I saw what happened when a man put his own selfish interests ahead of what was best for his son. I'm sure, Chance. More sure than I've ever been of anything in my life."

Chance came to his feet. Reaching out, he clasped Ed's hand in his, leaned over, and hugged him. He was smiling, but his eyes looked moist. "Thanks, Ed. You'll never know how much this means to me."

Ed just smiled. "I think I got a pretty good notion. You give Kate my best, will you?"

Chance grinned. Ed realized he hadn't seen the boy do that in weeks.

"I'll tell her." Long strides carried him out of the study and down the hall, and Ed's smile widened. He had done the right thing. Rachael would be fit to be tied, but in the long run, she would agree it was the right thing for both of them. She cared for Chance, the same way he cared for her, and she would want him to be happy.

Besides there were other good men in Silver County. Take that big, strappin' Ned Cummings. He was a damned fine rancher and he'd always had a secret yen for Rachael. Now that he thought of it, the two of them might just get along.

Ed chuckled to himself as he wheeled himself over to the desk. Maybe he'd throw a nice little dinner party on Saturday night to celebrate Rachael's return and her broken engagement.

He picked up the phone. And maybe he would just invite Ned Cummings.

Kate tied an apron on over her jeans and went to work. The best way to put the ugliness of the past few days behind her was to keep herself busy and get on with her life.

Since they were still living in the little motel on the road to Ronan, she'd had to take David to school, so she had missed the morning shift. Lunch was in full swing by the time she got there. Bonnie was working, but she could always use a hand. Kate busied herself serving a platter of chicken-fried steak, country gravy, and mashed potatoes. Then the bell rang over the door and Chance walked in.

He looked so good in his butter-soft jeans and white Western shirt that for a moment she found herself staring, drinking in the sight of him. She quickly turned her eyes away and set the platter of chicken-fried steak down on the table. Harvey Michaelson thanked her and dug right in.

Chance took a seat in one of the booths in front of the window. He was studying the menu, his eyes carefully trained there, but there was something different about him, something she couldn't exactly pin down. His eyes looked different, less guarded, even bluer than they usually did, and his posture seemed more relaxed.

He was handsome as sin, and incredibly appealing—and he belonged to someone else. Dammit, he wasn't supposed to be there, Kate recalled with a shot of anger. He was supposed to leave her alone. Tomorrow night, his fiancée would be arriving, for heaven's sake.

She clamped her jaw. Maybe seeing Rachael was the reason he looked so damned pleased with himself.

Fighting to hold onto her temper, Kate walked briskly over to his booth. "Are you ready to order, cowboy?"

Chance looked up at her and smiled so sweetly her heart turned completely over. "Yeah. But first I was wondering . . . you know that coconut cake you served last week?"

"What about it?" Kate snapped.

"I was thinking . . . if you could make a coconut cake as good as that, maybe you could whip up a wedding cake."

For a minute she just stood there, her temper so hot she wondered if flames might be shooting out of her head. She clamped her hands on her hips and leaned toward him.

"If you think for one minute I'm gonna bake you and that anorexic blonde you're engaged to a wedding cake, you have gone completely—"

Chance actually grinned. She couldn't remember the last time she had seen him grin like that.

"It's not for Rachael and me," he said. "It's for you and me. How about it, Katie? Will you marry me?"

For a moment, the room seemed to spin. She had to

grab hold of a chair steady herself. When she looked around, she saw that everyone in the restaurant was staring at her, waiting for her to answer.

"What . . . what about Rachael?"

White teeth flashed. "Rachael threw me over. I'm a free man again. What do you say, Kate?"

Rachael threw him over? Kate didn't think that was anywhere near the truth. No woman—not even one who looked like Rachael Fontaine—would ever be that insane. "You'd better be serious, Chance McLain."

Chance slid out of the booth and took hold of her hand. "I'm dead serious, darlin'." The cocky grin slipped from his face. "Say yes, Katie. Put me out of my misery. I don't want to live another day without you."

Her heart expanded, felt as if it would burst through the walls of her chest. "Well, when you put it that way, I guess I've got no choice. I'll marry you, cowboy."

Everyone cheered as he wrapped her in his arms, lifted her off her feet, and whirled her around in the center of the room.

Kate hugged his neck, laughing and crying at the very same time. She didn't know how it had happened, but she was marrying Chance McLain. What had started out as a miserable day of trying to forget the past and get on with a very lonely future had turned into the happiest day of her life.

"Let's get out of here," Chance whispered. Sliding an arm beneath her knees, he hoisted her up and carried her out the door. She didn't know where he was taking her and she didn't care. She loved him and he loved her. At far as Kate was concerned, that was all that mattered.

She waved goodbye to Myra, who had followed them

out of the cafe and now stood wiping away happy tears with the corner of her apron.

Smiling up at Chance, Kate slid her arms around his neck, pulled his mouth down to hers for a deep, sexy kiss. She didn't stop till she heard him groan.

Epilogue

Kate padded out of the bathroom and quietly returned to bed. Sliding beneath the covers, she rolled over on her stomach and plumped the soft down pillow, using it to prop herself up.

It was dark outside, not yet daylight, but the bedroom was cozy and warm. The big king-sized bed was rumpled, quilted comforter askew, the sheets in disarray and smelling pleasantly of last night's lovemaking.

Chance was busy getting dressed, preparing to go out and join his men. Today was the last day of spring roundup. There was still lots to do and Kate was planning to help, but she had always hated getting up early, and this morning Chance had insisted she sleep in.

"Hannah will have breakfast ready for the men," he'd argued when she had groggily, halfheartedly insisted.

"You can come down and join us whenever you're ready."

Kate smiled to think of the way he pampered her. And Hannah watched out for her, too. To Kate's surprise, the two of them had bonded almost instantly. Hannah liked her job at the ranch and Kate had no intention of taking it away from her. Kate loved having someone to help her manage such a big place, especially since she still had a restaurant to run.

And David already loved her. Hannah had taken to the boy like a hen to a chick, mothering him the same way she had always mothered Chance. David, of course, basked in the older woman's attention, seeing her as the grandmother that he had never had.

Hannah had clearly accepted Kate as part of the family, mostly because she knew how much Kate loved Chance.

Watching him now, his back turned toward her, lean and muscled in the soft light of the lamp, as he pulled on his jeans and boots, she wished she had awakened earlier. Chance enjoyed making love in the mornings and so did she. This morning she had simply been too sleepy.

Fighting down an annoying jolt of lust, Kate shoved her curly red hair back over her shoulder. It was longer now, since Chance seemed to like it that way. He particularly loved her breasts, she knew, and thinking about the way he had kissed them last night made them feel swollen and achey.

She watched him pull his Western shirt on and pop the snaps closed on the front. He tucked in his shirttail and tightened his leather belt. Reaching for the chaps he wore when he was working, he buckled them around his waist, picked up his hat, and turned toward the bed, meaning to kiss her goodbye, the way he always did.

"I thought you were going back to sleep," he said, striding toward her, making the wide leather at the bottom of his chaps flip out over his boots.

"I've been watching you get dressed."

He smiled, reached down and sifted a hand through her curly mop of hair. "Lady, you look good enough to eat."

Kate returned the smile. "So do you." Lord, did he. There was something about a man in chaps—particularly her man. The way they cradled his slim hips. The way the opening at the front neatly cupped his sex. As his hand ran over her bare shoulder and gently stroked a breast, the fit of his jeans grew snug and it was obvious she had aroused more than his interest.

Kate looked up at him from beneath her lashes. "Did you know I have a secret fantasy about making love to a man in chaps?"

Chance cocked a black eyebrow. "Is that so?"

"Too bad you have to leave."

"Isn't it, though?" But he didn't seem to be in all that much of a hurry. Instead he bent down and kissed her full on the mouth, running his tongue inside and making her heart set up a clatter. Long dark fingers teased her nipple and it tightened almost painfully.

"I don't have much time," he said softly, kissing the side of her neck, nibbling on an earlobe.

"Maybe we can improvise."

"Yeah ... maybe we can." Reaching down, he unzipped his fly and Kate reached out to touch him. He was big and hard, pulsing as her fingers closed around him. Tossing back the covers, she came up on her knees and before he realized her intention, took him fully into her mouth.

Chance hissed in a breath and a shudder went through him. "God, Katie."

Ignoring the feel of his hands sliding into her hair, she teased him a while, enjoying the taste of him, enjoying the fantasy. She squeaked in surprise as he pulled her away, lifted her up, and wrapped her legs around his waist.

"All right, darlin'—now it's my turn." Stroking her gently, he kissed her hard, then drove himself fully inside. Pleasure tore through her like a bolt of white lightning, and she heard Chance groan.

Kate gasped at the feel of his smooth leather chaps against her bottom. She clung to his neck and closed her eyes, savoring the feel of him, thinking how much she loved him. Chance drove into her again and again, heightening the pleasure, sending little shafts of heat roaring into her stomach.

Her body throbbed, ached for release. Something hot and sweet burst open inside her. She reached a powerful climax that left her trembling from head to foot, and softly moaned his name. A few more driving thrusts and Chance came, too, his lean body shaking, the muscles across his shoulders as rigid as bands of steel.

He held her for several sweet moments, bent his head and gently kissed her, then he settled her back down on the bed. Kate yawned as he adjusted himself, zipped his fly, and pulled the sheet up over her breasts.

"Go back to sleep, darlin'. I'll see you a little while later."

Kate just nodded, a drowsy smile on her face, her eyes already drifting closed. When she woke up two hours later, she felt pleasantly sated and deliciously content.

By the time she walked into the kitchen, David had left to join Chance out at the corral. Her son had finally adjusted to life on the ranch, though it hadn't been easy in the beginning. He didn't know the first thing about cattle or ranching, but the hands respected his determination and eagerness to learn and helped him any way they could. And Chance was always there for him, as his real father never had been.

David was a good rider now. He could fish like a native, and even shoot a rifle, though she wasn't sure he would ever want to hunt.

The deaths that had touched him so young, his grandmother and Chief, even Duke Mullens, had destroyed a portion of his youth. He often seemed more man than boy, and though she missed the child he once was, she was proud of the adult he was becoming.

Interest in Nell's murder had finally faded. The charges against Silas Marshall had been dropped the day after Lon Barton's arrest. William Barton had, of course, hired the country's most expensive attorneys. Lon had pled innocent at first, but the evidence continued to mount against him.

Along with his attempt on Kate's life, Nell's body was exhumed and traces of skin were found under her fingernails. The DNA perfectly matched Lon Barton's. Then an itinerant Indian named Bobby Red Elk showed up, claiming he had seen Barton's car parked near Nell's house the day of the murder.

Bobby had been headed south, to panhandle in a warmer climate, but on his return to the reservation, he had heard about Nell and Barton's upcoming trial. Apparently, Bobby had stopped by to see Nell on his way out of town, since she was always good for a handout. He'd seen Silas drive away and a white Jeep Cherokee pull up on the side of the road. Since Nell had visitors, he had decided not to stop.

Bobby wasn't much of a witness, as witnesses went, but the evidence was becoming harder and harder to refute. On his attorney's advice, Lon had accepted a deal. He'd pled guilty to manslaughter, accepted a fifteen-year sentence at a minimum-security prison, and hoped to be out in ten. It didn't seem like a high enough price for murder, but with the courts the way they were, they were lucky he hadn't walked away.

And to sweeten the deal, he had given up the men responsible for killing Harold Ironstone—Joe Saugus, Ben Weeks, Fred Thompson, and Duke Mullens, all employees of the Beavertail mine.

Which meant there was even better news. Consolidated Metals had dropped their attempt to overthrow the cyanide ban and build a new heap-leach mine in Silver County. With all that had happened, the public was simply too solidly entrenched against them. The Beavertail mine was closing—thanks to Chief's photos of the leaks in the tail pond and the gigantic fines the court had finally imposed.

There would be no new mine on Silver Fox Creek.

Kate reached the big pine kitchen and shoved open the door.

Holding a cup of hot coffee, Hannah turned at her approach and padded toward her across the wood plank floor. "Here. This'll warm you up."

"Thanks, Hannah. Maybe now I'll finally be able to wake up. I don't know what's the matter with me this morning."

Hannah cast her a look that said she knew very well

what the matter was, and what exactly had gone on upstairs. Fighting down her embarrassment, Kate shoved open the back door and stepped out into the brisk spring morning.

Dressed in jeans, the cowboy boots Chance had bought her, and a sweatshirt with a picture of a moose on the front, she walked down the gentle slope to the corral. A dozen cowboys, some horseback, others on foot, were busy branding calves.

She wrinkled her nose at the smell of burnt hair and tried to ignore the little calves' bawling as they were branded, vaccinated, and neutered, but she wasn't worried about them anymore. The first time she had watched the men working, she had been surprised and pleased to see the calves treated with so much care.

Chance spotted her walking toward him, jumped down from the fence, and strode toward her. Unconsciously, her glance strayed to the front of his chaps where the leather cupped his sex, and her face heated up again.

Chance grinned, reading her thoughts exactly. "You know what I love about you, Katie?"

Her blush deepened, sure he was going to say something embarrassing about how much she liked making love. "What?"

Chance leaned down and kissed her. "Everything." His expression turned serious. "Marrying you was the best thing I've ever done, Kate. You've made me the happiest man on earth."

Kate smiled, her eyes misting with tears. God, how she loved him. "How are things going?"

He looked back toward the corral. Little puffs of dust rose beneath the horses' hooves as the men lassoed each calf and brought it down. "We'll be done by the end of the day, just like we planned."

The customary steak barbecue was scheduled for late afternoon and a number of friends, and everyone who helped, was invited. Kate had been working with Hannah for the last two days, getting everything ready.

"Anything I can do to help?"

"How 'bout keeping me company for a while?"

She grinned. "My pleasure, cowboy." She walked with him back to the corral and he helped her climb up on the fence. On the opposite side, David sat on the little buckskin gelding Chance had given him as what he termed "a wedding present." Kate had her own horse, too, a pretty little palomino quarter horse that she had fallen instantly in love with.

Life on the Running Moon was good, had been since the day she and David moved in. They had never lived in Nell's old house again, not since the night she'd shot Duke Mullens. As soon as Chance had settled things with Rachael—which went better than either of them had expected, thanks to Ed, and perhaps Ned Cummings—Kate and Chance had been married.

It was a small church ceremony with only a few close friends, but it was what both of them wanted.

Chance cast her a teasing, slightly wicked glance. "You get any more sleep after I left?"

Kate just smiled. "Actually, I did. It was strange, though. I had a dream about Nell. She was thanking me for proving Silas wasn't to blame for her death." Kate stared up at him. "You don't suppose that was her real message, do you? That Silas wasn't the man who killed her and she didn't want him to go on blaming himself?"

Chance just shrugged. "Maybe. It would be just like

her. She always used to worry about him. I guess you'll never know for sure."

But Kate thought that maybe she would know ... someday in the far distant future. The day she left her earthly body and made the journey home. When she joined friends and family who had gone before.

And she saw her grandmother again.

Books by Bestselling Author
Fern Michaels

Available Wherever Books Are Sold!
Check out our website at **www.kensingtonbooks.com**

Romantic Suspense from
Lisa Jackson

See How She Dies	0-8217-7605-3	$6.99US/$9.99CAN
Final Scream	0-8217-7712-2	$7.99US/$10.99CAN
Wishes	0-8217-6309-1	$5.99US/$7.99CAN
Whispers	0-8217-7603-7	$6.99US/$9.99CAN
Twice Kissed	0-8217-6038-6	$5.99US/$7.99CAN
Unspoken	0-8217-6402-0	$6.50US/$8.50CAN
If She Only Knew	0-8217-6708-9	$6.50US/$8.50CAN
Hot Blooded	0-8217-6841-7	$6.99US/$9.99CAN
Cold Blooded	0-8217-6934-0	$6.99US/$9.99CAN
The Night Before	0-8217-6936-7	$6.99US/$9.99CAN
The Morning After	0-8217-7295-3	$6.99US/$9.99CAN
Deep Freeze	0-8217-7296-1	$7.99US/$10.99CAN
Fatal Burn	0-8217-7577-4	$7.99US/$10.99CAN
Shiver	0-8217-7578-2	$7.99US/$10.99CAN
Most Likely to Die	0-8217-7576-6	$7.99US/$10.99CAN
Absolute Fear	0-8217-7936-2	$7.99US/$9.49CAN
Almost Dead	0-8217-7579-0	$7.99US/$10.99CAN
Lost Souls	0-8217-7938-9	$7.99US/$10.99CAN
Left to Die	1-4201-0276-1	$7.99US/$10.99CAN
Wicked Game	1-4201-0338-5	$7.99US/$9.99CAN
Malice	0-8217-7940-0	$7.99US/$9.49CAN

Available Wherever Books Are Sold!
Visit our website at **www.kensingtonbooks.com**

Praise for Marta Perry

"With her crisp storytelling, strong suspense and unique, complex characters—both Amish and Englisch—Perry is sure to hook readers in. Add to that combination an intricately woven plot, with several twists, and fans won't be able to put *Search the Dark* down."

—*RT Book Reviews*

"Perry's story hooks you immediately. Her uncanny ability to seamlessly blend the mystery element with contemporary themes makes this one intriguing read."

—*RT Book Reviews* on *Home by Dark*

"Perry skillfully continues her chilling, deceptively charming romantic suspense series with a dark, puzzling mystery that features a sweet romance and a nice sprinkling of Amish culture."

—*Library Journal* on *Vanish in Plain Sight*

"Marta Perry illuminates the differences between the Amish community and the larger society with an obvious care and respect for ways and beliefs…. She weaves these differences into the story with a deft hand, drawing the reader into a suspenseful, continually moving plot."

—*Fresh Fiction* on *Murder in Plain Sight*

"*Leah's Choice*, by Marta Perry, is a knowing and careful look into Amish culture and faith. A truly enjoyable reading experience."

—Angela Hunt, *New York Times* bestselling author of *Let Darkness Come*

"*Leah's Choice* is a story of grace and servitude as well as a story of difficult choices and heartbreaking realities. It touched my heart. I think the world of Amish fiction has found a new champion."

—Lenora Worth, author of *Code of Honor*

MARTA PERRY
WHERE Secrets SLEEP

HQN™

ISBN-13: 978-0-373-77960-4

Recycling programs
for this product may
not exist in your area.

Where Secrets Sleep

This edition published by arrangement with Harlequin Books S.A.

For questions and comments about the quality of this book,
please contact us at CustomerService@Harlequin.com.

® and TM are trademarks of Harlequin Enterprises Limited or its
corporate affiliates. Trademarks indicated with ® are registered in the
United States Patent and Trademark Office, the Canadian Intellectual
Property Office and in other countries.

www.HQNBooks.com

Printed in U.S.A.

Dear Reader,

Welcome to the first book in my latest Amish suspense series. Since so many readers of Amish fiction write to me about quilts, I decided that an Amish quilt shop would be an ideal centerpiece for the new books. But where would I put the quilt shop? Once again, my own experiences gave me the answer. Blackburn House, a lumber baron's mansion turned into a building housing small shops and businesses, is based upon a similar mansion in a town in northern Pennsylvania that is now a delightful bed-and-breakfast inn. So if you ever happen to find yourself in Ridgway, Pennsylvania, be sure to stop at The Towers to see the original.

As always, my imaginary town has become very real to me in the course of the writing, and I'm already excited about the next story in the series. I'll enjoy revisiting familiar places, browsing in the quilt shop and catching up on the characters from this first book.

Please let me know how you feel about my story. I'd be happy to send you a signed bookmark and my brochure of Pennsylvania Dutch recipes. You can email me at marta@martaperry.com, visit me at facebook.com/martaperrybooks or martaperry.com, or write to me at HQN Books, 233 Broadway, Suite 1001, New York, NY 10279.

Blessings,

Marta Perry

This story is dedicated to my granddaughter, Estella.
And, as always, to Brian, with much love.

He who has no money is poor;
he who has nothing but money is even poorer.
—Amish proverb

CHAPTER ONE

ALLISON STANDISH WAS swept with an overpowering urge to throw the nearest heavy object or scream at the top of her lungs or, at the very least, slam the door. She did none of those things, clinging instead to the maxim she'd hammered out for herself years ago: if they see you lose control, they win.

She actually managed to pin a stiff smile on her face. "Sorry I interrupted." She turned and walked steadily toward the door of Greg's loft.

It was Diane, her boss, who rushed after her from the bedroom, wrapping a sheet around her abundant curves. "Allison, wait. This isn't what it looks like."

Allison's temper nearly slipped its leash at the trite remark. "It's exactly what it looks like. No wonder you were so eager to see me get on the road."

"Now, Allison." Diane reached for her with one hand while she grabbed the wandering sheet with the other.

The sheet was one of those Allison had picked out to go with the bedroom furniture she'd helped Greg choose. She'd even gotten him her professional designer's discount.

"Let's be adult about this," Diane continued. "There's no reason why we can't continue working together."

"Listen to her, baby." Greg appeared in the bedroom doorway, wearing a hastily donned T-shirt and shorts.

"Shut up." Diane tossed the words back over her shoulder.

Greg ran a hand through the shoulder-length black hair that inevitably attracted female attention. If he'd said something to her then...

But he didn't. He subsided, looking sulky. Diane had that effect on a lot of people.

"Come on, Ally." Di's voice turned coaxing. "These things happen. Take your week off. By the time you come back to the office, this will just be a memory. You have a good thing going. Don't ruin it."

For a man. Di didn't say the words, but they were implied. Di wouldn't dream of sacrificing one single step of her career for a man. That was how she'd become manager of the most prestigious interior design firm in Philadelphia.

Allison found she actually could manage a smile at that. "Sorry. I guess I'm not really that adult." This time she did slam the door.

She'd gotten all the way to the car before reaction set in. It took her three tries to unlock the car door, and she slid behind the wheel, relieved that she didn't have to trust her legs to hold her up any longer. She clutched the steering wheel, willing herself not to be sick.

A rusty meow from the backseat demanded attention. If Hector had to be confined to the cat carrier, he considered the least she could do was keep the vehicle moving.

"In a minute," she muttered. If cats were supposed to sense one's mood, Hector was deficient in that ability.

Diane had been similarly concerned to get her moving this afternoon, suggesting Allison leave the office early so she could beat Philadelphia's rush-hour traffic. Clearly she hadn't anticipated that Allison would stop by Greg's loft to say goodbye before setting off for Amish country.

She nearly hadn't. Hector had been recalcitrant about getting into the cat carrier, wedging his fat orange-striped body under the dresser just out of her reach the instant he'd seen the carrier. She'd finally had to resort to a can of tuna to snag him.

Then, with cat carrier and suitcase stowed in her compact, she'd had, she thought, just enough time to give Greg a goodbye kiss before heading for the wilds of Lancaster County and the property she'd so surprisingly been left in her grandmother's will.

She'd probably known the truth when she'd spotted Diane's Volvo parked in front of Greg's building. Her head just hadn't been able to convince her heart. She'd had to see for herself.

Well, she'd seen, all right. Now she just had to figure out what she was going to do with her life.

Hector complained again. Loudly.

"All right, all right." She started the engine and pulled onto the street as cautiously as a sixteen-year-old learning to drive.

At least she had a breathing space before making any tough decisions. She'd already planned to spend a week in Laurel Ridge arranging to rid herself of the white elephant her birth father's mother had so surprisingly left her. But now she didn't have any reason to rush back.

Allison joined the steady stream of traffic heading out of the city. There would be other jobs. One thing she could say about Di: her code, whatever it was, might allow her to poach a friend's man, but she wouldn't stoop to withhold a glowing reference, even if it meant Allison would be decorating multimillion-dollar homes for one of her competitors.

As for Greg—well, apparently he didn't live by any code at all except the whim of expediency. Allison must have had blinders on not to see that. Still, it was easy to be dazzled in the early stages of love, or whatever had passed for love between them.

Several hours later, Allison had begun to think she'd also had blinders on when she'd read the map and decided she could reach Laurel Ridge before dark. The April evening had quickly faded, and only the faintest glow on the western horizon remained. She seemed to have been wandering past fields and forests on a two-lane county route for hours, and the sole vehicle she'd passed in miles had been an Amish buggy.

The GPS she relied on was not helpful. Its metallic voice hadn't contributed anything in the past half hour but a persistent "Recalculating" that was nearly as annoying as Hector's raucous complaints. When the cat started sounding like a rusty hinge, it meant the situation was getting desperate.

Her tired brain played with the idea that Laurel Ridge didn't exist, that her legacy was one last spiteful act on the part of the grandmother who'd never acknowledged Allison's existence while she was alive.

Pondering the possibility, Allison nearly missed the sign. She stopped, backed up and read the words she'd been looking for. Laurel Ridge, 2 Miles. Relief swept over her, and she put the car in gear.

"Cheer up, Hector. The end is in sight."

A doubtful scratch at the carrier's door was his only response.

A few minutes later she was driving down Laurel

Ridge's main, and maybe only, business street. Store-fronts were dark and foot traffic nonexistent. Apparently Laurel Ridge shut down early. The only sign of life was a café and, across the street, a bed-and-breakfast with a porch light left on. Probably for her, since she'd booked a room there for the week.

As she pulled to the curb, Allison's gaze was caught by the building next to the bed-and-breakfast. In contrast to the homey Victorian charm of the white clapboard inn, this building loomed over the street, three stories of Italianate classic architecture dwarfing the smaller buildings around it. She could just make out the brass plate attached to the wrought-iron gate. Blackburn House. So this was her inheritance.

An Italianate mansion dating from the 1850s. The attorney's voice, dry and pedantic, sounded in her mind. *It belonged to Laurel Ridge's founding family. Your late grandfather purchased it from the Blackburn family fifty years ago. He had it zoned commercial and divided to form several shops and offices.*

The attorney's voice had sounded disapproving, either of the property or, more likely, of her.

Allison had mentally translated his description into old and dilapidated, with the architectural integrity of the original house compromised by ill-conceived renovations. But from the outside, at least, the building looked well kept, its paint flawless, small lawn smooth and green, and early spring daffodils in bloom along the front walk. A porch wrapped around the sides of the building, and a round tower anchored each end of the front.

Allison slid out and hauled the cat carrier from the backseat. "There it is, Hector. What do you think of it?"

Hector's snarl was probably meant to express his displeasure with his confinement, but it echoed her feelings quite well.

At least she ought to be able to realize some profit from the place when she put it on the market. Aside from a few random gifts that had been totally unsuited to either her age or interests, her father hadn't contributed much but a name and an accumulation of genes to her life. Maybe his mother had decided to make a last gesture toward rectifying his failure with her bequest.

"We may as well have a look. Don't you think so?" Talking to the cat was becoming a habit. Was that a sign that she'd eventually turn into an old maid with no one in her life but cats? At least Hector didn't betray her or smash her dreams to bits.

Holding the cat carrier in one hand and fishing for the keys the lawyer had sent her with the other, Allison advanced on the door of Blackburn House.

NICK WHITING STEPPED OUT into the cool April evening, the lock clicking behind him on the door to the old Blackburn carriage house, now the workshop of Whiting and Whiting Cabinetry. The only way he'd convinced his father to go home in time for supper was to assure Dad he'd stop back later to check on the shipment of brushed pewter cabinet knobs that had been guaranteed delivery today.

It was important for Nick to be home for supper with Jamie, important to supervise his son's first-grade homework and to go through the bedtime rituals with him. When you were six, that sort of thing mattered.

Not that Mom or Dad wouldn't have been happy to take over, but where his son was concerned, Nick didn't take shortcuts. Jamie might have lost out in the mother department, but he'd always know he could rely on his dad.

So he'd settled Jamie in the twin bed in the room Nick and his brother had shared as kids, tucking him under the tractor quilt that was Jamie's favorite. And then he'd driven the mile back into town to the shop.

The package had been leaning against the door, probably having arrived soon after they'd left. He stowed it away in the workshop, pleased the supplier had come through. This meant they could finish Mrs. Phelps's new kitchen cabinets tomorrow, unless she changed her mind yet again. He'd lingered in the shop for a few minutes, looking over the finished cabinets one last time. He liked checking the progress of the work on hand, enjoyed running his palm over the warm maple and the elegant curves of their custom cabinets.

Nick grinned into the dark. He'd seen his dad do the same thing often enough. It must be a Whiting family trait, one that had somehow skipped his brother, Mac. Double-checking the door, Nick headed for his car, thinking about the wedge of cherry pie Mom would have saved for him.

A light from one of the windows of Blackburn House caught his eye as he rounded the corner of the building, and he paused. First floor—it was in the bookstore. Ralph or his clerk must be working late, maybe unpacking a new shipment of books. Even as he thought it, the light switched off. Five steps later the light reappeared, in the quilt shop this time.

He stopped, frowning. Sarah Bitler wasn't likely to be in her shop at this hour. Sarah was Amish, and she didn't like driving her buggy along the country roads after dark. Apprehension slid along Nick's skin like a touch, and he reached into his pocket for his keys.

The light went out and the pattern repeated as another came on, this time in his showroom. Someone was getting into the businesses on the first floor of Blackburn House. Yanking his keys out, Nick ran for the back door.

A prowler? It could be the custodian, he supposed, but Fred Glick was usually gone by this hour, and making a final pass through the building wasn't characteristic of his lackadaisical approach to his job.

The rumors that had been making the rounds in town popped into his mind. Laurel Ridge couldn't seem to decide whether it was being plagued by a prowler, a Peeping Tom or a sneak thief. Maybe now he'd get the answer to that question.

Nick held the knob firmly as he unlocked the back door, wary of any betraying creak as he eased it open. Stepping inside, he considered his brother Mac's reaction if Nick actually caught the prowler. Mac, Laurel Ridge's police chief, had been skeptical from the start about the rumors, saying it was probably a manifestation of cabin fever after the long winter.

Nick slipped past the storerooms at the back of the building and slowly opened the door that led to the front part of the house. The wide hallway that ran from this point to the front of the building was deserted, but a patch of light lay on the marble floor. Staying in the shadow cast by the wide center staircase, Nick moved silently forward. To judge by the location of the light, the intruder was in their showroom. He heard the sound of movement, as if something brushed against a cabinet.

If he went to the showroom door, he'd be seen instantly. But he could slip in the door that led from the

hallway to the office behind the showroom, and he might be able to get close enough to see without being seen. Pulse racing, Nick crossed to the office door and fumbled for the key. He realized he was enjoying this small adventure, and he had to laugh at himself. Maybe a guy never outgrew all those cops versus bad guys scenarios of childhood.

Holding his breath, Nick pushed open the door and sidled into the office. No one was here, but a stream of light spilled from the open door into the showroom. He worked his way around the desk and groped the wall next to the door. He paused there for a moment and then cautiously peered into the showroom.

The rows of cabinet doors on display made an effective screen. He couldn't see the guy from here, but he could hear footsteps, followed by a soft thud as something bumped one of the cabinets.

Nick held his breath and moved soundlessly farther into the showroom, taking cover behind a Peg-Board displaying hardware styles. The footsteps came nearer. Frowning in concentration, Nick counted the steps, estimating the prowler's location. One step, two—he must be within a foot now, so close Nick imagined he could hear a breath.

Muscles tense, he waited. The instant he saw movement, he lunged, grabbing the form. Several things happened at once. He realized he was clutching a female, he felt her swing something and he heard the crack as it hit his leg with numbing force. Another crack, a banshee shriek and an orange ball of fur plummeted toward the floor.

The cat turned on a dime, hissed and spat at him, spine arching. The woman, yanking free of his grasp, looked as if she'd like to do the same. Nick had a quick image of shining auburn hair, pale creamy skin and bright green eyes that seemed to shoot sparks of rage.

"What are you doing? Are you insane?" She held what he now realized was a cat carrier, its door hanging by one hinge. She raised it threateningly, and he had no doubt she'd hit him again at an unwary movement.

He raised both hands, palms out, and took a step out of range. "Take it easy. I could ask you the same thing. What are you doing in my shop?"

"Your shop?" she echoed.

Nick saw the doubt enter her face, and a delicate pink stained her cheeks. The green eyes were framed by uncompromising brows, and her heart-shaped face had a stubborn cast along the line of her jaw. As for her lips... for a moment he was distracted, and he forced himself to focus.

"That's right, my shop. I'm Nick Whiting. This is the office and showroom of Whiting and Whiting Cabinetry. I repeat, who are you? How did you get in? Or maybe I should just call the police." He sketched a gesture toward the pocket that held his cell phone.

"That's not necessary." Her chin lifted. "You're Mr. Whiting? I'm Allison Standish." She said it as if it should mean something to him.

It did. "*You're* Ms. Standish? The long-lost granddaughter Evelyn left this place to?"

"I haven't been lost, Mr. Whiting." Her tone was cool. "But, yes. I'm the new owner of this building, so I have every right to be here."

He raised an eyebrow, wondering if it would infuriate her. "You may or may not be the owner of Blackburn House, but this is my shop. According to my lease, I'm supposed to be notified in advance if the owner wants access."

Nick had no idea if the lease actually said that, since it had been negotiated by his father years ago, but if it didn't, it should.

"I see." Her tone was icy. "I suppose I should have a look at all the leases, shouldn't I?"

Naturally she would, possibly to his sorrow. Maybe he shouldn't have mentioned it. He took the opportunity for a long look at her. Sleek chin-length hair the color of polished mahogany, earrings a delicate tangle of silver and jet, jacket of butter-soft leather and a silk shirt that molded full breasts, a skirt that flirted with her legs and a pair of high-heeled boots that looked capable of kicking if necessary.

Well. With this woman taking over Blackburn House, there might be a lot of changes coming

ALLISON MADE A concentrated effort to collect herself. Her nerves, already shredded by the events of the day, hadn't been up to this additional assault. It was taking every bit of control she had to keep her courage up with this obnoxious character. If he was typical of the tenants she'd have to deal with, the sooner she sold this place, the better.

She bent to pick up the cat, smoothing her hand over Hector's ruffled fur. Poor thing. He'd had a bad day, as well. It was a shame he hadn't managed to run his claws into Whiting's leg.

Glancing up under her lashes, she assessed the man. Light brown hair, cut in a short, almost military style, and tanned skin. He had a jaw that proclaimed his stubbornness, and at the moment it was set like granite.

He met her gaze, and his eyes were a shade somewhere between gold and brown that reminded her of
topaz. His gaze seemed to grow intent as he realized she
was assessing him, and she looked down, trying to ease
an affronted Hector into the cat carrier. He snagged the
dangling door with one paw.

"Look at this. You've broken my cat carrier." Tears
stung her eyes. Ridiculous, but this really was the last
straw. "How can I walk into the bed-and-breakfast carrying a cat in my arms? I can't expect the owner to accept that. She wasn't eager to have a cat on the premises
as it is."

Whiting knelt next to her, and a flicker of alarm went
through her at the quick movement and his unexpected
closeness. She caught her breath. How did she know he
was really who he said he was? She shouldn't be lingering in an empty building in a strange town alone with a
man she didn't know.

"You hold the cat. I'll deal with the door." His tone
warmed, filled with amusement, as if he'd guessed what
she was thinking.

Speechless, Allison gathered Hector into her arms
and eased a little away from him. She watched Whiting's
hands as he worked on the carrier. They were square,
strong, workman's hands, a little scarred but deft and capable. In a moment he'd popped the door back into place.

"That should do it." His hand moved toward Hector,
who reacted with a hiss. Whiting retreated prudently and
held the cage door instead while she stooped to bundle
Hector inside. "I don't think that cat likes me." He rose,
putting a hand under Allison's elbow to help her up.

"It's the traveling he doesn't like. He's had a rough
day." As she had.

"Looks like he's not the only one."

It was all she could do not to wince. "If that's your idea of a compliment, I don't think much of it."

Whiting grinned, the sun lines at the corners of his eyes crinkling. "My mother says I have all the finesse of a bulldozer. I just meant— Well, you've had a long drive from Philadelphia, and it's late to be inspecting a building, besides being assaulted by a stranger who breaks your cat carrier with his leg. I'll help carry your stuff over to Mrs. Anderson's place."

"How did you know that's where I'm going? Or that I've come from Philadelphia?"

Allison was instantly suspicious, but the gaze that met hers was guileless.

"You said you were staying at a B and B. There's only one in town. And everyone has been buzzing about the unexpected relative scooping a piece of the pie."

"Oh." She felt foolish, which was probably what he'd intended. "Thanks, but I can manage my own things." She straightened, grasping the carrier and her bag. "Good night."

He nodded. Waiting until she'd left the showroom, he switched off the light, locked the door and strode off toward the rear of the building.

That was that, she thought, rather surprised that he'd given in so easily. He looked like the kind of person who'd keep pushing, as if being female meant she couldn't manage to carry anything heavier than a feather fan. She made her way to the front door, paused a moment to admire the frosted patterned glass that must have surely been original to the building and let herself out, locking the door behind her.

By the time she reached her car, Nick Whiting was

waiting there for her. She glared at him. "I thought we'd already established that I can manage my own bags."

"You can, but you don't have to." He leaned against the car, blocking her entry, seeming immovable.

Allison wasn't going to stand here all night arguing. She shoved past him unceremoniously, pulled out her suitcase and laptop bag, and clung to the handle when he attempted to take the suitcase from her.

"I can manage," she repeated.

He raised one eyebrow, a trick she found annoying. "Come on, give me a break. It would reflect badly on my parents if I didn't help you."

"No one will know," she snapped.

The grin transformed his face. "You're not used to small towns, are you? Somebody always knows." Before she could react, he seized the bag from her hand and strode off toward the bed-and-breakfast.

Allison had to hurry to keep up with his long, lithe stride, and she scolded herself for noticing how he walked or anything else about him. Hadn't she just learned a painful lesson about the chasm between looks and character in a man?

When they reached the door, Whiting put the bag down and pressed the doorbell before she could reach it.

Allison fixed a smile on her face. "Thank you. You're actually right about one thing. I don't know anything about small towns, and I don't intend to find out. I plan to sell Blackburn House as soon as possible."

Thoughts of financial security, maybe starting her own business, flickered through her mind.

Nick Whiting seemed to withdraw, even though he didn't move. "Sell? I don't think that's what Evelyn would have wanted."

She was startled to hear his familiar reference to the grandmother who was little more than a name to her, and annoyed that he presumed to speak for the woman.

"Since I never knew Evelyn Standish, you can hardly expect her wishes to be important to me."

Allison turned away, trying to ignore his frowning disapproval, and marched into the bed-and-breakfast when the door opened. But even though she didn't look, she could sense him standing there, frowning after her.

CHAPTER TWO

SHE SHOULD HAVE known there would be strings attached, Allison told herself the next morning as she stared across the polished mahogany desk at Jonas Litwhiler, her grandmother's attorney. She knew perfectly well that no one gave you something for nothing. So why was she feeling oddly hurt at this reinforcement of her preconceptions about her grandmother?

Litwhiler, perhaps made uncomfortable by her silence, cleared his throat. "You understand, Ms.…er…Ms. Standish? The bequest from Mrs. Standish is conditional on certain requirements being fulfilled."

"I understand." She leaned back, trying to demonstrate an unconcern she didn't feel. "I'm waiting to hear what those requirements are."

"Yes, I see." Litwhiler fiddled with the delicate china cup and saucer that sat on a small, doily-covered tray at the side of his desk. Coffee, by the smell of it. As if reminded, he gestured toward the cup. "Would you care for coffee? It won't take a moment."

"No. Thank you." *Let's just get on with it.*

Jonas Litwhiler was the image of an old-fashioned small-town attorney—white hair, white shirt, conservative tie, dark suit. The only surprise to his appearance was the white carnation in his lapel. Even his offices were a masterpiece of dark paneling and Oriental carpets, located in another of the Victorian houses in which Laurel Ridge seemed to specialize. He looked as if he'd strayed into the contemporary scene from a 1930s black-and-white movie.

"According to the trust set up by Mrs. Standish, the ownership of Blackburn House passes to you completely if you run it successfully on your own for a period of one year."

So many questions crowded Allison's mind that she didn't know which one to spit out first. "Can I sell it?"

An expression of profound disapproval settled on the attorney's face. "Not until you've completed the year satisfactorily."

It was all very well for him to be disapproving. He hadn't had his entire life turned upside down in the past twenty-four hours. "And who decides if I've been successful? You, I suppose?" If he was acting for the other heirs as well, that struck her as a conflict of interest.

"No." The answer was short, and he looked as if he'd just sucked on something sour. "If Mrs. Standish's accountants declare that Blackburn House has been run at a profit for one year, the matter has been decided."

She suspected his reaction meant that he'd been offended to have that decision taken out of his hands. Still, it seemed to indicate that Evelyn Standish had tried to be fair, according to her definition of fairness.

"And if I fail or choose not to accept the challenge?"

"Ownership passes to Brenda Standish Conner, your father's cousin," he said promptly.

She nodded, vaguely aware he'd mentioned the cousin in their telephone conversation. Apparently she and her daughter had lived with Mrs. Standish. They'd probably expected to scoop the lot. Well, they might still do so.

"Didn't it occur to Mrs. Standish that I'd have a career and a life elsewhere?" Even as she asked the question, Allison realized it wasn't true in the sense that it had been the previous day, though she did still have an apartment and friends in Philadelphia. And nothing could reconcile her to uprooting her life to a place like Laurel Ridge.

"I don't believe Mrs. Standish was concerned about your career. In any event, I don't feel comfortable discussing Mrs. Standish's reasons for her actions."

Something about his acid tone suggested to Allison that her grandmother hadn't seen fit to ask his advice.

Allison took a steadying breath, trying to compose her thoughts. She'd come into this meeting unprepared, it seemed to her. She eyed the attorney, wondering how much of the truth he'd care to share.

"Is it actually legal to attach such conditions to a bequest?"

His grip tightened on the pen he held, and he put it down precisely on the desk blotter. "You can contest the will if you like, of course. It will be expensive, and in my opinion, you will lose."

Allison wasn't sure she'd like to take his word for that. Maybe she should consult another attorney. But it would take time, and meanwhile she'd be stuck in Laurel Ridge. Maybe she'd been right in her first assessment, and this was just a final insult on the part of the grandmother who'd ignored her existence. Evelyn Standish didn't fit anyone's idea of the doting grandmother.

"Didn't you say there was a partnership in a quilt shop in the bequest?" That was the shop she'd seen briefly the previous night, before her run-in with Nick Whiting.

"That comes under the same one-year provision, except that in the case of the quilt shop, ownership will pass to Sarah Bitler, the current owner."

It had begun to sound as if there were a lot of people who'd be happy to see her leave town.

Litwhiler riffled through a sheaf of papers. "I think that about covers it. You'll find the business accounts in Mrs. Standish's office in Blackburn House. Funds for operating expenses and any necessary repairs are provided." He hesitated. "You'll also find that an apartment adjoins the office. A separate account has been set up for any renovations you'd care to do. Mrs. Standish thought you might want to live there, should you decide to stay."

If there was a question in that comment, Allison ignored it. She wouldn't commit herself to anything until she'd had a chance to consider the options.

As for the apartment— She thought again of her apartment in Philadelphia, of the time and care she'd put into making it the perfect home. "Could I rent this apartment?" she asked abruptly. "Or is it tied up with conditions, as well?"

"No, no conditions." He looked surprised, as if that hadn't occurred to him. "If you stay, you can do as you like with it."

"I'll give it some thought." She slipped the strap of her bag onto her shoulder and slid to the edge of her chair.

"You…you don't want to give me an answer now?" He seemed disconcerted, as if this interview hadn't gone as he expected.

"Not without considering all my options." She rose, looking down at him across the massive stretch of mahogany.

Litwhiler stood abruptly. "There's another option I've been asked to put before you." He seemed to be picking his words carefully, wearing a faint expression of distaste.

"Yes?" She raised her eyebrows, feeling as if the balance of power had shifted slightly in her favor.

"Brenda…Mrs. Standish Conner, I mean, feels perhaps…" He let that die out, as if it hadn't been the right approach. "Mrs. Standish Conner asked me to say that in the event you did not care to accept the terms of the bequest, she would be willing to make the sum of over one hundred thousand dollars to you."

Allison fought to keep her face expressionless, while her mind raced. One hundred thousand. She could do a lot with that amount. On the other hand, she'd guess that was a fraction of the actual value of the building. Even in a town the size of Laurel Ridge, a fully occupied commercial building had to be worth far more.

She adjusted her bag deliberately and turned away. No wonder Litwhiler looked uncomfortable, quite aside from the fact that he seemed to be representing one heir against another. The offer was an insult to her intelligence.

"Shall I tell Ms. Standish Conner you'll consider her offer?"

Allison took a couple of steps toward the door and turned to smile back over her shoulder at him. "I'll consider it," she said. "But first, I believe I'd better take some legal advice of my own."

It wasn't a bad exit line, she decided. She walked quickly out of the office.

NICK WOULD ALWAYS rather be working in the shop than the office. On this April morning, with sunshine pouring through the big windows in the front of the show-room, it was almost bearable to be stuck in the office.

The sunlight showed a faint rim of dust on one of the display cabinets, and he wiped a cloth over it. One of the disadvantages of an old building—the dust must seep through the walls or drift down the chimney.

One aspect of his partnership deal with Dad, made when he'd come home after the disastrous end to his marriage, was that he'd take care of the sales and paperwork, letting Dad concentrate on what he loved best—working on the cabinets. At the moment, Dad was focused on the pine jelly cupboard he was making for Mom's birthday. It was only fair that Dad should have his choice, and Nick didn't resent taking on the book work.

But today he was having trouble getting down to the tax records that waited for him in the office. His mind was too preoccupied with Allison Standish and the changes that were undoubtedly coming to Blackburn House. How difficult was she likely to be? It wasn't that they couldn't move the business elsewhere if they had to, but it would be inconvenient and expensive, most likely.

Nick glanced across the wide center hallway and spotted Sarah Bitler pausing in the door of her quilt shop. Seeing him, she smiled and raised her hand.

Taking that for an invitation to talk, Nick seized the chance to delay the taxes a bit longer. He crossed the marble hallway to join her.

"Morning, Sarah. Quiet today?"

"So far." Sarah brushed an invisible bit of thread from the blue apron that matched her dress as well as her eyes. Her normally serene face was alive with excitement. "Have you heard? The new owner is in town. She checked into the bed-and-breakfast last night."

"Yes, I know." He hesitated, not sure he wanted to discuss the woman with Sarah when his own impressions were so negative.

"I hope she comes in today," Sarah hurried on, oblivious to his discomfort. "I'm so excited to meet her."

Well, he could hardly keep it from Sarah. "You won't be the first. I met her last night."

"You did? But how? Why? I assumed she went straight to the bed-and-breakfast, and Mrs. Anderson said it was nearly nine when she checked in. Mrs. Anderson thought she must have gotten lost."

"I don't know about that, but I spotted her wandering around Blackburn House when I came back to the shop to take care of a delivery. I suppose she wanted to have a look at her new acquisition."

What had Allison Standish made of Blackburn House? Apparently not much, since she was so eager to get rid of it.

"And you came in to tell her *Wilkom*," Sarah said.

He had to grin. "Not exactly. I saw the lights going on and off in the bookstore and this place and our showroom, and I figured it was the prowler everyone has been talking about."

"Nick, you didn't!" Sarah shook her head. "A prowler wouldn't be turning on the lights, knowing he could be seen from the street."

"You're too practical, Sarah. I didn't even think of that. Just got caught up in the moment, I guess. I thought I'd catch him in the act. So I slipped in, hiding in the shadows like we used to when we were kids playing hide-and-search." He could laugh at his actions now. "Then I jumped out and grabbed her."

"No— Nick, how could you? Did you hurt her?"

"It was the other way around. She rammed the case she was carrying into my leg."

"Serves you right," Sarah said severely. "I hope you didn't give her the wrong impression of us."

He shrugged. As far as he could tell, Ms. Standish had already had a negative impression of Laurel Ridge and all its inhabitants before she arrived.

"Poor thing. Coming all this way alone to be greeted like that." Sarah's tender heart asserted itself.

"She wasn't exactly alone," Nick said with a vivid memory of the cat hissing at him. The animal would have been happy to sink its claws into his flesh. "She had a cat in the case she hit me with."

"Well, I'm not one to believe in keeping animals in the house, but after all, I live on a farm. A woman on her own in a city apartment might be lonely, poor thing."

That was Sarah all over, always seeing the best in everyone. He was afraid she was going to be disappointed in Allison Standish, and he wasn't sure how to warn her. It was annoying that so many people had to depend on the whims of this stranger.

"Evelyn loved the quilt shop." Sarah was obviously following her own train of thought. "But she was always content to be a silent partner. *Ach*, I couldn't expect anything else, she was such a busy woman. Maybe Allison will want to be more involved. I hope so."

"I hope you won't regret what you wished for." There was no point in trying to sugarcoat the facts for Sarah. At least he ought to try and prepare her for the woman who was now her partner. "Look, Sarah, I wouldn't count too much on Allison Standish if I were you. I can't picture the woman I met working in a quilt shop. She struck me as a snobbish yuppie who can't wait to shake the dust of Laurel Ridge from her feet."

He realized that Sarah was staring past him, a horrified expression on her face. He swung around. Allison Standish stood not more than five feet behind him, well within earshot. She'd undoubtedly heard him.

Well, what difference did it make? She'd told him herself that she was eager to sell up and leave.

"And here she is," he said. "Good morning, Ms. Standish. What did you do with the cat?"

She blinked, apparently not expecting that question. "As it happens, Mrs. Anderson turned out to be a cat person. As soon as her tabby established her dominance over Hector, they settled down together."

"She likes to be the boss, I take it." He felt a momentary sympathy for Hector. "Well, you'll be wanting to meet your new partner. Sarah, this is Allison Standish. Allison, Sarah Bitler."

Allison's eyes widened as she took in the fact that Sarah was Amish. Then she extended her hand. "It's nice to meet you, Sarah. I saw a bit of the shop last night." Her glance swept back to Nick. "Speaking of last night, you must have thought it was amusing when I told you I planned to sell the building as soon as possible."

Nick realized he was staring at her blankly. "Why would I find it funny? A sale could have serious consequences for all of us."

"So you don't know." There was an edge to her voice. "I'm surprised. I thought you knew all about everything having to do with my inheritance."

"Listen, I'm sorry. I gave you the wrong impression last night."

She seemed to ignore what he said, preoccupied with

some issue of her own that had her fuming. "You may as well know. I'm sure it will be all over town shortly. It turns out my inheritance has strings attached. I can't sell or do anything else except run the building for an entire year."

The Amish woman was staring at Allison with a puzzled expression.

"I don't understand," she said. "We were told you inherited Blackburn House and Evelyn's share of the quilt shop."

Apparently everyone in town had known her grandmother better than she had. Allison pushed aside the sense that she'd lost something of value. How could she mourn a relationship that had never existed?

Sarah turned to Nick Whiting. "Did you know about this, Nick?"

He shook his head, frowning a little. He seemed honestly confused, although Allison wasn't inclined to take anything at face value where Nick was concerned.

Seen in daylight, her impression of his rough-hewn good looks was confirmed. Attractive enough to cause a quiver in the stomach, if you went for men who wore jeans and flannel shirts to work. She didn't.

"Evelyn always was wily about keeping her secrets." His frown dissolved in a reluctant smile. "She certainly put one over on all of us this time. Including you, I guess." His smile included Allison, but she thought she detected an edge of malice in the curve of his lips. "Evelyn tied your hands, did she?"

Sarah gave him a quelling look. "That's enough, Nick. This is no way to get acquainted with the new owner."

Somewhat to Allison's surprise, he took the reproof

with a nod. "Right you are. Guess I'll get to work and let you two sort it out between you."

Before she could deny there was anything to sort out, he had turned and crossed the hall to his showroom.

And little though Allison wanted to admit it, she was trapped in a situation she hadn't foreseen, with no knowledge of who she could trust. She needed information before she could attempt any decisions, and Sarah might be able to supply it.

At the moment, Sarah was watching her with a slightly anxious expression. "Will you come into the shop?" She gestured to the quilt store. "*Ach*, it seems strange to invite you in when it's half yours, anyway."

Allison responded with a smile. She'd already broken her cardinal rule several times with Nick Whiting by letting him see her reaction to him. There was no point in compounding the problem by letting Sarah see her as anything but pleasant and professional. She'd realized when her father walked out on her and her mother that there was a lot to be said for being independent, and a big part of independence for her had meant hiding her emotions, especially the negative ones.

"I'd love to have you show me around the shop. There's so much I don't know."

"*Komm.*" Sarah led the way, a tiny bell jingling as they opened the door. They moved into an aura of bright colors and soft textures that seemed to envelop and comfort at the same time.

The shop was in what must have been a parlor in the original mansion. The front windows were angled to form a bay with a bench under them. Sarah must have been responsible for the quilted cushions that turned it into an inviting seating area. The wallpaper, if not original, was a good copy of the flowered style so common in Victorian homes. Allison hadn't had much occasion to decorate homes of this period, since most of Diane's business had been with the busy young corporate execs who moved into a house, decorated in the latest style, then sold and moved on when they reached the next step of the corporate ladder.

But she knew something good when she saw it, and the fireplace was a masterpiece of High Victorian with its intricately carved and mirrored mantelpiece that dwarfed everything else in the room. Sarah had wisely not tried to change the intrinsic charm of the room but allowed her quilts to make their own statement.

"Didn't you know that your grandmother intended for you to have this?" Sarah's gesture took in the quilt shop and beyond it, the whole building.

"I hadn't the slightest idea until her attorney called me." It was pointless to hide the fact, since probably everyone in town would know the details before long. Evelyn Standish had apparently been someone important in Laurel Ridge. "As far as I know, she never saw me or attempted to make contact."

Sarah's blue eyes darkened with sympathy. "I'm so sorry. I can't understand any *grossmammi* doing that." She flushed slightly. "*Ach*, I'm sorry. Sometimes the *Deutsch* word just comes out when I'm talking *Englisch*. And the other way around, too."

That little tidbit caught Allison's imagination. "You mean you use *Englisch* words when you're speaking dialect?" The instant she'd asked the question she wondered if Sarah would take offense, but Sarah responded with a quick smile that showed a dimple in each cheek.

"For sure. I guess you could say Pennsylvania Dutch

is an old dialect. Dates from when the Amish came here
in the 1700s. So when new things come along and we
don't have words for them, we just use the *Englisch*
words."

Allison nodded, relaxing in the face of the other
woman's friendly attitude. It would be foolish to let
herself be put off by the fact that Sarah's clothes were
old-fashioned and her hair pulled severely from a center part and confined under a white covering at the back
of her head. Those externals didn't affect the warmth
of her smile.

"You haven't seen much of the Amish, ain't so?"
Sarah's tone was matter-of-fact.

"Am I being obvious? To be honest, you're the first
Amish person I've ever talked to."

Sarah's dimples showed. "You're not the first *En-
glischer* I've talked to, that's certain sure. Mostly around
here the *Englisch* and Amish know each other pretty well."

"I could see that you and Nick Whiting know each
other." She hoped her tone didn't give away her impression of him.

Sarah paused, her hand on a double bed in the front
of the shop. It was completely covered by colorful quilts
laid one on top of another. "Nick's family lives on the
property next to my parents' farm, so we've been friends
since we were small."

So naturally her sympathy would be with Nick. She'd
spoken to him as she would to a brother.

Well, that was enough of betraying an interest in Nick
Whiting. He'd already made his attitude toward her presence plain.

"These quilts are all for sale?" she asked, touching
the blue-and-white one on top.

"*Ja*, this is what we have in stock now." Sarah seemed happy to turn her attention to the quilts. "I always display them this way so folks can see how they look on a bed." She flipped the top quilt back to display the next, an intricately designed one that glowed in jewel tones. "The maker's name and the price are on a numbered tag in the corner of the quilt, and I keep a card file with all the information about it."

It seemed a simplistic method of keeping track of stock in the twenty-first century, but maybe that was what Sarah was comfortable with. "They are beautiful." Genuine admiration filled Allison's voice. "Works of art." She stroked the detailed quilting on the border, each stitch put in perfectly by hand.

"You have that in common with your grandmother, then," Sarah said. "Even though she didn't do much in the shop, she really loved the quilts."

Somehow she was surprised that they'd had anything at all in common. "How did the two of you become partners?"

Sarah's smile became reminiscent. "I worked for Mrs. Standish when I was a teenager—cleaning the house and such. When I didn't marry…" She shrugged. "Well, most Amish are pairing off by the time they hit their twenties. Evelyn was…" Again she hesitated. "Evelyn asked me what I wanted to do, and I told her my hope was to start a shop to sell the things Amish quilters made." Sarah lost her hesitancy, her blue eyes sparkling. "Women like my *mamm*, who didn't have a *gut* place to market their quilts. And she offered me this." A sweep of her arm encompassed the shop.

"So you became partners." That argued a generosity on the part of her grandmother that surprised her. Ev-

elyn Standish might have been more complicated than
Allison's impression of her.

"She put up the money to get started, and I paid her
back out of the profits." Sarah sounded more knowledge-
able than Allison would have expected. "I have my copies of our agreements if you want to see them, but I'm
sure Evelyn's will be in her office upstairs."

Allison nodded. "The attorney mentioned the office
to me. I suppose I'll have to go through it before I can
make any decisions."

"Decisions," Sarah repeated. "But didn't you say that
you can't sell for a year?"

"Meaning there's no decision to make?" Allison
shrugged. "I can always walk away. Go back to my life
in Philadelphia and let Blackburn House go to Brenda
Conner."

Sarah actually looked disappointed. She'd have
thought the woman would be only too happy to see the
last of her.

"I hope you don't. I've always wanted to have an ac-
tive partner in the business."

"Me? I don't know anything about quilts."

"You appreciate them," Sarah said. "I saw your expression when you touched them." She smiled. "It's like
mine."

"I know what goes into them. I'm an interior designer
by profession, so naturally I have an appreciation. But—"
Before she could add that she had no desire to spend the
next year of her life in Laurel Ridge, they were interrupted.

"Hey, Sarah, do me a favor, will you?" Nick stood
in the doorway, holding a large dog of indeterminate
breed by a piece of rope that looked inadequate. Even

as Allison watched, the dog made a dive for the nearest display rack, which was hung with an assortment of baby crib quilts.

"No!" Allison's instinctive cry was echoed by Nick, and he hauled the dog back by the rope. The animal didn't seem to show any resentment of the handling. It sat on Nick's foot and looked up at him with an adoring doggie expression, tongue lolling.

"Is this bring-your-dog-to-work day?" she asked tartly.

"Not my dog," Nick replied, his face relaxing in a grin that invited her to share his amusement. "A beauty, isn't he?"

Her expression must have spoken for her, because he chuckled.

Sarah hurried to interpose herself between them with the air of one who was used to being a buffer between fractious personalities. "I see Ruffy showed up again. Mr. Sheldon must have let him slip out of the house."

"Who is Mr. Sheldon, and why is his dog here?" Surely, as what she supposed was provisional owner of the building, she had the right to ask.

"Randall Sheldon had an office upstairs before he retired," Nick said.

"And Ruffy used to come to work with him every day," Sarah contributed. "Ruffy doesn't seem to understand retirement. He keeps trying to come to work."

By this time the dog was sniffing at Allison's boots, probably smelling Hector on them. She stepped back. "Wouldn't it be a good idea to call this Mr. Sheldon to pick him up?"

"No need." Nick hauled the animal to him, forestalling an effort to pursue Allison and the interesting smell of cat. "I'll take him home. Sarah, I'm expecting Mr. and Mrs. Pierce in to look at cabinets. Will you tell them to start looking around? I'll be back as soon as I can."

"Of course," Sarah said. "Give my best to Mr. Sheldon."

Nick nodded. "Heel, Ruffy." The dog promptly sat down. "Come. Walk." No response. Nick finally had to drag the animal across the polished marble to the front door.

Sarah had already turned back into the shop, and Allison followed her, unable to resist a comment.

"With that casual attitude toward his customers, I'm surprised Whiting has any business at all. Why didn't he make the owner come and get the dog?"

Sarah seemed surprised. "Because that's not the kind of person Nick is. He knows Mr. Sheldon regrets retiring, and he doesn't want him to have to come in for the dog." She smiled a little. "You might not know it to look at him, but Nick has a tender heart."

Allison felt as if she'd been put in the wrong, no matter how gently. And the incident just emphasized her feeling that she'd wandered into a world she didn't understand.

"Still, you wouldn't leave your shop unattended, would you?"

Sarah seemed to consider. "Well, usually there would be someone else around. Sometimes my mother is here, sometimes members of the quilting group. But if I had to, I could trust Nick to keep an eye on things."

It was a different attitude—that was all she could think. She would no more walk off and leave a shop full of valuable merchandise than she'd take flight.

"Of course, if I had a partner here, it wouldn't be a problem." Sarah's smile teased her.

"I...I'm not sure that's possible," Allison muttered, feeling ill-equipped to cope. She'd assumed knowing more would help her decision become clear. Instead, everything she learned just seemed to make it more difficult.

CHAPTER THREE

SHE REALLY OUGHT to go through the building and introduce herself to the other renters, but Allison decided she needed a break from other people's expectations. Lunch and a little time to decompress—that was the solution.

Telling Sarah goodbye and trying to ignore the trace of disappointment in her blue eyes, Allison headed across the street toward the café she'd noticed the previous night.

The Buttercup Café lived up to its name, painted inside with a yellow so sunny it made Allison blink. In that instant, she realized something else. The room had fallen completely silent at her entrance, and every single person in the café, with the exception of a toddler banging on a high chair tray, stared at her.

Feeling her cheeks warm, Allison moved forward. The middle-aged woman behind the counter, seeming to rouse herself, hurried to greet her. Amish, Allison noted. Like Sarah. There must be a lot of them in the area.

"Table for one, Ms. Standish? Right over here." Somehow Allison wasn't surprised that the woman knew her. Apparently, from what she'd heard so far, anonymity wasn't an option in Laurel Ridge.

At Allison's nod, the woman gestured to an open table and then pulled the chair out, her ample cheeks bunching with her smile. Her eyes seemed to take in every detail of Allison's appearance from behind the wire-rimmed glasses she wore. With her white hair, rosy cheeks and round figure, she reminded Allison of a china figure of Mrs. Santa she'd once had. But the woman's gaze was both curious and cautious, unlike the loving expression of her Mrs. Santa.

"I'm Anna Schmidt, owner, chief cook and just about everything else at the Buttercup. I'd recommend the chicken potpie. It's the special today, and I made it fresh this morning."

Allison had intended to order a salad, but she sensed it might be more diplomatic to agree. "That sounds lovely." She handed the menu back. "Just water to drink." She'd resolved to cut down on caffeine, although possibly this stressful time wasn't the best for healthy changes.

Allison glanced up, caught an elderly man staring at her and fished in her bag for her cell phone. Maybe she'd have to resign herself to being a subject of curiosity for a time—not that she'd intended to stay long enough to become familiar to the denizens of Laurel Ridge.

Propping her arm on the bright yellow-and-white tablecloth, she checked her messages. Nothing from either Di or Greg. Maybe that was just as well. She opened a text from Leslie, her closest friend. An attorney, Leslie's reaction to news of an unexpected legacy had been to advise caution.

Don't sign anything without reading it thoroughly. That was the gist of it.

The text was brief. Call and tell me all about it.

Smiling, she responded. Nothing ever as it seems. Talk later, okay?

She couldn't expect Leslie to rush to Laurel Ridge to represent her, but Leslie would be generous with legal advice. If there was a way out of this tangle, Leslie would find it.

Anna Schmidt returned a few minutes later, bearing a steaming bowl of what appeared to be a chicken stew rich with square noodles whose uneven sides declared that they were homemade. The woman lingered until Allison took a cautious first bite. At Allison's involuntary exclamation of pleasure, she beamed.

"Never had real homemade chicken potpie, ain't so?"

"No, I haven't. It's delicious."

"Your *daadi* love my chicken potpie. I was certain sure you would, too." Still smiling, Anna turned away to attend to another customer, leaving Allison bemused.

Odd, that she hadn't even thought of her father since arriving in Laurel Ridge. The more she considered it, the stranger it seemed. Hugh Standish had walked out of her life when she was six. She'd trained herself not to dwell on him, because doing so inevitably led to pain. That was yet another good reason for not taking up a new life in this place.

Allison had just about succeeded in dismissing her father from her thoughts by the time she returned to Blackburn House later that afternoon. She'd brought Hector along in the carrier, deciding she'd relieve the innkeeper of his presence.

Before she talked with Leslie this evening, she really needed to have a better grasp on the economics of the situation. She couldn't expect advice if she didn't have the facts, and Leslie was a glutton for details. She'd want to know the assessed value of the property, the taxes, the expenses and the amount of rent that came in each month before venturing an opinion as to the best course of action for Allison. The logical place to look for those answers was in the office her grandmother had maintained upstairs.

Early spring daffodils curtsied in the cool breeze that swept across the lawn in front of Blackburn House. Care of the grounds was undoubtedly her responsibility. She could only hope her grandmother had a service in place to deal with such things.

The stained-glass detail in the transom pane above the front door glowed as a slant of sunlight hit it, and the brass door handle echoed with a gleam of its own. The meticulous care that had been taken of the building seemed to indicate that Evelyn Standish had been fond of the place. Odd, surely, that it didn't bear her family's name.

Allison went inside, the cat carrier dangling from one hand, and nearly ran into Nick, who was just turning away from the door to his showroom, keys in his hand.

He smiled, eyes crinkling, and nodded toward the cat carrier. "You're not going to attack me with that again, are you?"

She couldn't seem to stop herself from responding to that smile. "I was just defending myself, remember?"

"True enough." He reached out to test the cat carrier door, earning a hiss from Hector. "Is it holding together all right?"

"Fine, thanks." She glanced at the door to his showroom. It bore a hand-lettered placard. *Out now. Leave a note or try the workshop in back.* That reminded her of her disapproval.

"Closing early today?"

Nick blinked, as if not understanding her for a moment. Then he shrugged. "I can't waste time sitting there hoping someone will come in. If anybody does, they know to look for us back in the shop."

She couldn't help frowning a little as she glanced at the shop door. "Wouldn't you get more business if you kept the showroom open?"

His brow lifted in that infuriating manner. "Know a lot about cabinetmaking, do you?"

"No, but—"

"Then maybe you ought to let me run my own business while you tend to yours." He strode off toward the back of the building, obviously having had enough of her.

She clutched the cat carrier and stalked to the stairs. All right, fine. She'd take care of her own business. That's what she planned to do right now. Avoiding the gaze of the bookstore proprietor, who had come hopefully to the entrance to his shop, Allison hurried upstairs toward her grandmother's office, heels clicking on the marble stairs.

NICK, PROPELLED BY what he considered righteous indignation, stormed to the back door, but before he could reach it Ralph Mitchell darted out of the bookstore and intercepted him. Ralph's thin pale face was anxious, his nose twitching so that he looked like an elderly rabbit.

"You were talking to her. What's she like? What's she going to do? Did she tell you?"

Nick curbed his annoyance with Allison and tried to look reassuring. "I don't know. I don't think she's decided yet what her plans are for the building."

It was on the tip of his tongue to tell Ralph about the restrictions to Allison's ownership, but he held back. Ralph's reputation as a gossip was well deserved. He talked to everyone who visited Blackburn House, to say nothing of all the people he encountered on his daily trips to the post office and the bank. He collected tidbits of information everywhere he went, sometimes sewing them into a fantastic array of speculation, but more often than not into something very close to the truth.

Ralph would undoubtedly find out about Allison's provisional ownership from someone, but it didn't have to be him.

"But how can you be sure? If she sells, what's going to happen to us?" Ralph was close to wringing his hands. "You know Evelyn hasn't raised our rents in years. How could we find comparable places for our businesses at those prices?"

"We probably couldn't." That was the truth, and Ralph knew it as well as he did, but it was hardly reassuring. "Look, we don't know anything yet. For all I've heard, Ms. Standish may intend to just turn the business over to a property manager to handle and head back to her job in the city. That would be the easiest thing she could do."

"True." Ralph pushed his glasses back up on his nose with a characteristic gesture. Usually they clung to the end of his nose and he peered over them nearsightedly. "Still, I don't understand why she hasn't come to talk to me yet. It makes me nervous."

That was a good question. As far as Nick could tell, Allison seemed inclined to avoid her responsibilities here.

"I'm sure she'll be around to see you soon." He patted Ralph's slumped shoulder. "No need to start worrying before you have to, right?"

"I suppose you're right." Ralph sounded reluctant. "But do you think—"

"Gotta go. Dad's expecting me, and I'm late." He

moved as he spoke, knowing if he didn't, Ralph was capable of keeping him there talking and speculating all afternoon.

In a couple of minutes he was clear of the building, and he blew out a breath of exasperation. He felt sorry for Ralph, but the man's timidity and gossipy nature about drove him crazy.

Dad, on the other hand, was so calm that Nick sometimes wondered if he caught all that was going on around him. When he reached the workshop he found his father already well into the next job they had on hand, humming tunelessly while he worked. He was what Nick would be in another thirty years, he supposed—lean, leathery, with tanned skin, wrinkles around his eyes, going a little gray at the temples.

Nick tossed his jacket in the general direction of the hook on the wall and joined him. The new cabinets were cherry, and the wood a challenge but a joy to work with. He smoothed his hand down the fine grain.

"Sorry I'm late."

Dad shrugged. "No problem. Somebody come in the showroom?"

"Nothing like that. I had another little run-in with Allison Standish."

"Was that a good idea?" His father's voice was mild.

"I didn't start it." Nick wished the words back the minute they were out of his mouth. It sounded like what he and Mac used to say when they'd been squabbling. "Anyway, the woman is being unreasonable. She hasn't even talked to the rest of the tenants in the building yet. Ralph is in a state about it."

"Ralph's always in a state."

True enough. "I couldn't blame him this time. Seems

to me she's trying to impose her big-city standards on Laurel Ridge, and that's not how things are done here. The least she could do is to talk to everyone and let them know what's happening instead of standing back looking down her nose at us." He frowned down at the screwdriver in his hand and wondered what he'd picked it up for.

"Hmm." Dad took a careful measurement, wrote it down and then measured again. Only then did he glance at Nick. "So, besides being obnoxious and superior, what's Allison Standish like?"

He shrugged, for all the world as if he hadn't paid attention. "Red hair. Well, more coppery-colored, I guess you'd say. Green eyes. Sort of a heart-shaped face and fair skin. She's got a way of looking up at you that..." Never mind about his reactions. He certainly didn't want to discuss them with his father. "Not much like her grandmother, that's for sure."

"You hardly noticed her, right?" Dad's eyes were twinkling.

"It's not like that," he said with as much dignity as he could manage. "I'm just concerned about all of us. She could do a lot of damage through not understanding how small towns work."

Dad didn't respond. He just kept on working, but Nick felt sure there was something more. As the silence stretched, he had to speak.

"Well?"

Dad gave him a considering look before turning back to the piece of cherry work he was shaping. "Seems to me you might be jumping to some conclusions based on appearances." He paused, probably to let that sink in. "The way I see it, the woman's been thrown into a stressful situation she probably never expected. Maybe we have to give her a chance to find her balance."

He didn't say anything more. He didn't have to. Nick knew exactly what Dad was hinting at. He thought Nick had an unfavorable opinion of Allison because she reminded him of Sheila.

His first impulse was to deny it. Loudly. But he had too much respect for his father's judgment to reject it out of hand. Maybe there was a fragment of truth to the idea. He couldn't deny that Allison seemed to be everything that Sheila had wanted to be.

He and Dad worked side by side in silence for a few more minutes. The feel of the cherry wood beneath his hands soothed him.

When he finally spoke, much of his irritation had disappeared. "Why do you suppose Evelyn left Blackburn House to a stranger?"

Dad shrugged. "That stranger is her granddaughter, you know."

"The way I heard it, Evelyn never showed the least interest in Allison, so it doesn't sound as if she cared whether she had a granddaughter or not."

"Evelyn Standish was never one to show her feelings," Dad commented, holding the piece he'd been working on up to the light. "I doubt anyone knew what she thought of her son's child."

"Not even Brenda?"

"Especially not Brenda." Dad's tone was dry.

"From what I've heard, Brenda expected her aunt to leave everything to her. I imagine she's none too happy about this turn of events."

Dad shrugged. "Allison's her own blood. Her son's child."

"Hugh Standish, you mean." Nick frowned, trying to remember what he'd heard about the man. "He had left town before I was old enough to know much of anything about him. From what I've heard, he wasn't much missed."

"Funny thing, that was." Dad paused, staring absently at the window that looked toward Blackburn House. "Old Mr. Standish was the soul of honor. Evelyn, too. And Hugh was as twisty as they come, even as a child. Long on charm and short on character."

"So he left."

Dad nodded. "He left. Married, had a child, then left them, too. Seems he spent his life leaving people. I'd guess that's why Evelyn bequeathed Blackburn House to Allison. Kind of making up for Hugh."

The resentment Nick had been feeling toward Allison seeped slowly away. He still didn't like her behavior. But maybe her family story was enough of a reason for him to give her a break.

ALLISON ENDED UP spending the afternoon in her grandmother's office, becoming more and more engrossed in what she found there. The office itself was something of a surprise—stripped down, businesslike, with none of the frills one might expect from a wealthy woman.

Hector had his own opinion of the office. When she'd put him down, he'd prowled the room eagerly at first, intent on his search for any sign of his hereditary enemy, the mouse. Finally, disappointed, he'd leaped on top of the file cabinet. He established himself there, sphinx-style, his paws tucked in front of his white bib. The only sign of life was the occasional blink of his eyes.

Allison's first task had been to get a grasp on the financial situation. Evelyn's records were clear and organized, and it didn't take long for Allison to discover that her supposition had been correct. Blackburn House was worth considerably more than her cousin was offering, even though the rents Evelyn had charged seemed ridiculously low.

Still, Allison had to admit that she had no idea what typical rents might be in a town like Laurel Ridge. Something else she ought to find out.

Once she had jotted down every detail she thought Leslie might need to give her an informed opinion on how to proceed, Allison leaned back in the leather swivel chair, considering.

Searching through the office had given her a guilty sensation. She didn't belong here, but by her actions, Evelyn had grafted her on to the family tree.

Maybe that was an apt expression. She'd felt grafted on to another family tree when her mother had married Dennis Goldman. Dennis was a dear, of course, and he'd always done his best to treat her exactly as he did the two half brothers he and Mom had produced. She loved them all. She knew they loved her. Still, she'd always felt like the odd man out. The cuckoo in the nest, in a way.

Unfair, to feel that way, but she'd figured out a long time ago that a person couldn't argue with her feelings. One just had to accept them and move on.

And speaking of feelings, what was she to think of the grandmother who'd appeared so suddenly, reaching out from the grave, it seemed? She'd formed an opinion of Evelyn Standish long ago—imperious, proud and strong-willed. Nothing she'd learned since she'd arrived in Laurel Ridge had changed that opinion.

But being privy to the woman's business life had certainly added to the picture she'd formed. Evelyn had been a good businesswoman, meticulous if a bit old-fashioned in her methods.

She had been capable of surprising generosity. There was the partnership with Sarah for one thing. And apparently Evelyn had also carried the bookstore through a couple of dry periods, carefully noting the dates on which she'd been paid back. Without interest, it seemed. Generous, yes. So how did a woman who was so giving to others justify ignoring her only grandchild?

Sighing, Allison brushed her hair behind her ears and massaged the back of her neck. That was a riddle to which she'd probably never know the answer.

A glance at the window showed her that it was getting dark already. Allison checked the time and began gathering papers together. Get a bite to eat first, and then go back to the inn. By the time she'd done that, Leslie should be home from the office and ready to talk.

The building had grown dark and quiet around her while she worked. She'd been vaguely aware of the occupants of the other offices leaving, hearing the sound of voices and the clatter of heels as they went down the stairs. She ought to be alone in the building, but she could hear the distinct sound of movement.

Puzzled but not alarmed, she went to the door and opened it. For a moment all was silent. Then there was the sharp sound of a footstep, and then another.

Allison couldn't seem to prevent the frisson of alarm that rippled along her nerves. If every office and shop in the building was closed, who was here?

The custodian, of course. She nearly laughed out loud. She'd just been looking at the building records. There was a custodian, even though she hadn't met him yet.

Well, no time like the present. Leaving the office open and the lights on, she moved quickly down the hall toward the stairs. "Hello?" Her voice echoed as if she'd called into a canyon.

Nothing. No one answered.

"Mr. Glick? Is that you? It's Allison Standish."

Still nothing, but the footsteps were clearer and more hurried now, coming from the hall below. Allison hustled to the top of the stairs and looked down.

From this vantage point she could see the entire front half of the hallway that bisected the building, with the quilt shop on her left and the cabinet showroom on the right. Nothing moved there.

Annoyed now, she hurried down the steps. How rude, not to answer when she called out. Surely anyone who belonged in the building would know who she was, even if they hadn't met yet.

Anyone who belonged. She stopped three-quarters of the way down, clinging to the bannister. Someone, maybe Nick, had said something about a prowler.

Allison reached for the pocket of her jacket and found it empty. Her cell phone was lying on the desk upstairs.

She should go back to the office and call the police. But then she'd look remarkably silly if her prowler turned out to be someone who had every right to be here.

Allison took another tentative step down, undecided, and heard a rush of footsteps followed by the bang of the back door. The noise galvanized her into action. She ran down the stairs, swung around the newel post at the bottom and raced for the back exit. She couldn't possibly catch the person, but maybe she could get a glimpse of him.

The back door was closed but not locked. She yanked

it open, charged forward and nearly ran into Nick Whiting, who grasped her by the elbows.

The tinge of fear transformed into anger. "What do you mean by sneaking around the building that way? Were you trying to alarm me?"

Nick's open face tightened. "Is fighting mad always your first response? I wasn't in the building. I was just coming out of the workshop when I thought I heard someone call out. I came to see what was wrong."

That sounded logical. Besides, the person she'd heard was going out. He or she wouldn't turn around and come back in, would they?

Only if they wanted to make you think they were just arriving on the scene, a little voice commented at the back of her mind.

Allison pulled away from Nick's warm grasp, aware of his strength. "What are you doing here this late, anyway?"

"Working," he said briefly. "I went home to put my son to bed, and then I came back to work for an hour or so."

"Son?" She wasn't sure why she was so startled. Of course someone like Nick would be married. He ought to wear a wedding ring. "I didn't know you were married."

His strong features tightened again. "I'm not. My son, Jamie, is six. We live with my folks."

Allison's mind seethed with questions, none of which she dared ask. Better stick to the point. "I heard someone in the building. Whoever it was, he didn't answer when I called. You had mentioned something about a prowler."

"So you decided to go after him alone?" His eyebrow rose in that gesture she was beginning to dislike.

"Certainly not. I heard him go out of the building.

I was just hoping to get a look at him." A shiver went through her. "Did you see anyone?"

"Not a glimpse, but anyone could have gone around the corner before I got to where I'd see him." He gave her a measuring look, as if assessing how much she was to be trusted.

She did her best to ignore it. "Do you suppose he broke into any of the offices?"

"I'll have a look," Nick said. "You stay here."

That sounded tempting, but her pride intervened. "I'll go with you."

Exasperation was written clearly on his face, but he didn't argue. Together they moved through the ground floor, checking doors. She hated admitting that she wanted to stick close to him. Somehow that rough-hewn appearance of his was very appealing right now. He looked as if he could handle anything.

The shops were all locked, dark and, she supposed, normal.

"My keys are upstairs in Evelyn's office. We could look inside," she offered.

"I don't think there's much point. If someone had broken in, it would be obvious." Nick flicked a light switch, bathing the back part of the hallway in its glow. The storerooms were locked and dark, as well.

Allison eyed Nick's face as they went up the stairs side by side. His jaw was set, and his gaze was intent. He looked tough and determined, and she would definitely stack him up against any prowler.

There was that word again. "Why did you think there might be a prowler?"

He looked startled for an instant. "You mean when I saw you last night?" He shrugged. "There have been rumors making the rounds about a prowler in town, but no one seems to have seen anything definite."

"If that's the case, this should be reported to the authorities. I'll call 911—"

"No need," Nick said. "Consider it reported. As it happens, my brother, Mac, is the police chief. And oddly enough, I'm the mayor."

"You? The mayor?"

Nick grinned at the doubt she made obvious. "Yes, me. Don't be impressed, though. In a town of eight thousand people, being the mayor is as much a popularity contest as anything else."

"I see." She studied his face, wondering just how serious he was. "What, exactly, does the mayor of Laurel Ridge do?"

Nick shrugged. "Goes to a town council meeting once a month. Declares it Safety Week or Blueberry Day. Serves as a judge for the annual Pet and Toy Parade."

Was he serious? Apparently so. "I'm sure you're well suited to judging the Pet and Toy Parade, whatever that is."

"Hey, that's a serious event here." He assumed an injured look as he checked office doors and rattled handles on the second floor. "And judging isn't a piece of cake, especially when the contestants might cry if they don't win. Or bite the judge."

Her lips quirked as she thought of Hector's reaction to him. "As I said, well suited."

"The owners of last year's contestants in the most colorful pet competition nearly came to blows." He shook his head. "It wasn't a pretty sight, believe me."

His gaze met hers, his golden-brown eyes bright with

amusement, and Allison felt an unexpected lurch in the area of her heart.

No, she told herself firmly.

"Since everything seems secure, I'd better pack up and get over to the—" She opened the office door, and Hector streaked out, moving so fast he was nothing more than an orange blur.

Nick jumped back, then gave an unsteady laugh. "I think that cat's out to get me. What's he so upset about now?"

Allison's hand froze on the knob. "Look." In the far corner of the room was a door that she'd assumed led to a closet. It had been closed and she'd thought locked when she left.

Now it stood wide-open, revealing a flight of wooden stairs that led up into darkness.

Nick's hand closed on hers, and he drew her back from the door. "I take it you didn't have the attic door open?"

"I didn't even know that's what it was." She shivered. "We'd better call the police."

Nick took a cell phone from his pocket and pressed it into her hand. "I'm going to have a look. If you hear anything odd, press 9-1-1."

She clutched his arm. "What do you mean, odd? Like you being knocked over the head? Let the police do it. You don't need to be macho about it."

"I'm not." He took both her hands in his. "Look, if I call in, that means whoever's on duty will rush over here in the patrol car, siren wailing. It would probably be Johnny Foster—eighteen, eager and inclined to trip over his own feet. Let me see if there's any sign up there first, and then I'll talk to Mac quietly. No point in setting the whole town gossiping about you your second night here."

Much as she hated to admit it, his words made a certain amount of sense. "All right. But be careful." She frowned. "I thought the sound I heard came from the other end of the building."

"Could have," he said. "The attic stretches clear across, and there's a stairway in each corner. Whoever was up there, he might have heard you go out of the room and slid down this way, then on downstairs by the back stairway."

She blinked. "I didn't even know there was a back stairway."

He grinned. "You'd best explore your new property. But not now." He squeezed her hands, crossed the room quickly and disappeared up the dark stairway.

Allison stood where she was, clutching the cell phone. If he didn't come back in a few minutes, she was calling, no matter how much fuss it made.

But Nick reappeared, dusting himself off, before panic had her pushing the buttons. "He left the door open onto the stairway at the other end of the building. That must be how he got in. But there's nothing upstairs but a lot of junk people have left there over the years. What was the point?"

She shivered, rubbing her arms. "If it was to scare me, he succeeded." She scooped together the notes she'd made and stuffed them into her bag. "Right now all I want is to find Hector and get out of here. Do I need to stay around and talk to your brother?"

"Not tonight." His attention seemed to be elsewhere, and she suspected his mind was busy with something he didn't intend to share. "I'll get Mac, and we'll have a quiet look around. He can stop by casually tomorrow to have a word with you."

Hands full of papers, she looked at him. "You're going to a lot of trouble for me."

He smiled, eyes focusing on her for a moment. "Just doing my duty to the voters, that's all. Come on. I'll help you find that dratted cat."

CHAPTER FOUR

By MIDMORNING THE next day Allison had met, as if by accident, with McKinley Whiting, Laurel Ridge's police chief. Mac, as Nick had referred to him, was a slightly younger, slightly darker version of Nick, with the same straight nose and regular features but dark brown hair and dark eyes.

He'd been polite, he'd looked around, and he'd left Allison with the impression that he didn't take the situation seriously, despite his assurance that he'd keep an eye on the building.

Following his visit she'd made the rounds of the upstairs offices, meeting in turn a Realtor, an investment adviser and an attorney. By the time they'd all exchanged pleasantries and each one had asked about her plans for the building, Allison had felt the need for escape, so she'd slipped downstairs to the quilt shop.

Once again, the warmth and color of the place enveloped her, and Sarah's smile was the friendliest thing she'd seen yet today.

"Allison, *wilkom.* I'm glad you stopped in." Sarah was sorting a stack of quilted place mats, apparently rearranging her display.

"Those are lovely." Allison touched the tiny, intricate blocks that made up the pattern, each of them not more than an inch square.

"That's postage-stamp quilting, worked in a Sunlight and Shadows pattern." Sarah moved her hand over the design, which almost seemed to ripple. "My mother made these."

"She must be a very accomplished quilter to do such fine work." Each tiny piece was joined to the next by stitches so small and even that they were almost invisible.

"*Denke.* Thank you, I mean." Sarah's fair skin seemed sun-kissed today, as if she'd been doing something in the spring sunshine that had brought out a faint dusting of freckles. "*Mamm* will be in one day this week to set up a quilting frame in the corner. Once the weather is fine, we start getting more visitors from out of town, and they like to see a quilt in progress."

"And it encourages them to buy," Allison said, appreciating the marketing angle.

"*Ja,* that, too." Sarah smiled on the words, her eyes sparkling. "Never underestimate the craftiness of a Pennsylvania Dutchman in making money, that's what folks say."

"I guess it applies to the Pennsylvania Dutch woman, as well." Allison, feeling relaxed for the first time that day, picked up one of the place mats. "Let me help you arrange these."

"*Denke,*" Sarah said again, and Allison stored the word away, realizing it meant thanks.

They worked in silence for a few minutes. Allison glanced at the other woman's face. Sarah had an air of calm and stillness about her that seemed to say she could be relied upon, and Allison longed to talk to someone about what had happened the previous night. But she didn't know how Sarah might react. Would she be frightened at the thought that someone had been in the building? Or disapproving of the action Allison had taken?

"Are you feeling as if you know your grandmother any better now?" Sarah shot her a questioning glance. "I thought her office might answer some of your questions."

"Well, it cast a new light on her in some ways," Allison admitted. "I hadn't realized she was such a businesswoman, for one thing."

Sarah nodded. "She was, that's so. After her husband passed and your…your father left, I suppose she didn't have much else to occupy her. Evelyn never was one to be idle. She just dug in and started handling the business herself."

Allison eyed her. "You wouldn't remember my father, I suppose." Sarah probably hadn't been born when Hugh Standish had said goodbye to Laurel Ridge.

"No, but you know how folks talk." There was something a little apologetic in her tone.

"I don't imagine they had anything good to say about him," Allison said.

"*Ach*, I didn't mean—"

"It's all right. I know better than most people how unreliable he was."

Sarah nodded, blue eyes softening. "I'm sorry."

She shrugged. "It's been a long time. I don't think about him much anymore." Except for the occasional bad dream. "I'm glad to get a better picture of what his mother was like." At least, she thought she was.

"I wish…" Sarah began and stopped abruptly at the sound of someone entering the shop. She looked up, a welcoming smile on her face that seemed to stiffen.

"I see you're making yourself right at home." The voice belonged to a fortyish woman who stared at Al-

lison as if memorizing every detail of her appearance.
"That is…well, I suppose half of the shop does belong
to you and…" She seemed to lose herself in a welter of
words, the challenge that had sounded in her first statement sagging under the weight of her qualifications.

Sarah came to the rescue. "Allison, this is Brenda
Conner, your cousin."

"Brenda Standish Conner," the woman corrected,
straightening the shoulders that had begun to droop.
She stared at Allison again, her smile flickering nervously on and off and on. "I was your father's cousin.
You wouldn't know, I suppose."

The truth of the matter was that she'd never heard of
a cousin until the business of Evelyn's will came up, but
it didn't seem polite to say so. Brenda could never have
been beautiful, but she might have had a fresh-faced
charm before her round face had settled into those lines
of discontent. She seemed somehow faded, as if life had
drained her, and the classic gray suit might have looked
stylish if it hadn't turned her complexion a similar shade
of gray. It hung from her sloping shoulders as if it had
been made for a larger woman, or at least one who stood
up straight.

"Mr. Litwhiler mentioned your name to me." *And re-
layed your not-so-generous offer.* "It's nice to meet you.
I'm afraid I know very little about my father's family."

That admission seemed to please Brenda, for some
reason. She stood up a little straighter and fingered
the rope of pearls that hung around her neck. "No, you
wouldn't. Your father never valued his family heritage,
so he wouldn't be likely to pass it on to you."

Allison's response was a noncommittal sound. Did
Brenda know that Hugh had walked out on Allison and

her mother when Allison was six? Or was that just a strike in the dark? She probably wouldn't believe it if Allison told her that she didn't remotely care about the Standish family heritage, whatever that might be.

"Speaking of Jonas Litwhiler, I believe he passed on to you a certain offer I made." She cast a glance at Sarah, as if expecting her to disappear. Sarah went on stacking place mats on the shelf.

"He did, yes." Allison tried to keep her voice neutral.

"He tells me you didn't have an answer yet, but now that you've had a chance to think about it, I'm sure you'll agree that accepting is the best solution for everyone." Brenda reeled that off as blandly as if she'd memorized the words. "If you'd just give me your approval, we can get on with the paperwork."

"I'm afraid I can't do that." Allison felt a certain amount of pleasure in saying the words. Brenda needn't think it was going to be as easy as she'd undoubtedly hoped. "I'm consulting with an expert as to the value of the building, and I can't give you an answer until I receive that information." The expert in question happened to be a college sorority sister of Leslie's whose family owned a real estate office somewhere in central Pennsylvania.

"Well, but—" Brenda hadn't expected that answer. "Of course, you might find someone who would say the building is worth more, but the amount I mentioned is all I can afford at the moment. Besides, you have to consider the cost to you of staying here in Laurel Ridge for an entire year."

"I'll take all of that into consideration." She produced the smooth, professional tone she used when an estimate for vertical blinds came in unexpectedly high. "I'll let you know my decision as soon as possible."

"Yes, well, that's... I guess that's all right." Brenda cleared her throat, seeming to brighten a little. "Meanwhile, I thought you should meet some people in Laurel Ridge while you're here, so I've arranged a little get-together this evening at seven. Perhaps you'll be interested to see the Standish house. Anyone can give you directions. And you'll meet my daughter, Krysta." She held that out as if it were an irresistible lure. "I'll see you then, shall I?"

Allison was tempted to say no, just to see her reaction. But the truth was that she was curious about the place where her father grew up. Surprising, since she'd thought she didn't care.

"Thank you," she said. "I'll see you then."

When the woman had left, Allison glanced at Sarah, who seemed to be pretending she hadn't overheard anything.

"I wonder if I'm making a mistake in attending her party? It's pretty obvious what Brenda wants."

"What do you want?" Sarah said, with an air of facing up to facts.

Allison folded another place mat and put it on the shelf, considering the question. "I don't know," she said finally. "But I admit, I'm curious about the place where my father grew up."

"Then you should go. Family is more important than just about anything, don't you think?"

"I guess so." Even when you felt like the odd man out. "My father left when I was six."

"I'm sorry." Sarah reached out to clasp her hand in an impulsive grip. "That must have been hard."

She nodded. Funny, that she was talking to a stranger about something she seldom mentioned to anyone. But Laurel Ridge seemed to have that effect on her. Maybe small-town living did have something to recommend it.

"Seeing the Standish house might help you understand him better, ain't so?" Sarah hesitated. "But Brenda… well, I think you should be careful. She's not like your grandmother."

Allison nodded. Sarah had obviously admired Evelyn, and Brenda…well, even she could see that Brenda was trying to emulate Evelyn Standish and only coming off as a pale copy.

"Do you have any homework to do tonight?" Nick glanced at Jamie as they walked down the street from the elementary school to the workshop, where Mom was going to pick him up after her dentist appointment. The backpack his son wore looked too heavy for him, but Nick knew better than to offer to carry it. He'd already made that mistake, and Jamie had been offended.

"One page of number problems." Jamie hopped, two-footed, over a crack in the sidewalk. "And spelling words to practice."

"Sounds good." He ruffled his son's wheat-colored hair, and Jamie grinned up at him. "I'll be home in time to help you, right?"

"Right." Jamie shifted the backpack slightly. "Race you to the workshop."

He was off and running before he'd finished saying the words, giggling. Nick let him get several yards ahead and then jogged after him.

Mac was headed for the shop from the other direction, and Jamie ran straight at him, confident his uncle would catch him. Mac grabbed him and tossed him into the air, caught him and set him down again.

"What are you up to, sport?" Mac plopped his police officer's cap on Jamie's head.

"Racing my dad. I beat him. I won!" He grinned at Nick.

"You're too fast for me," Nick said, feeling a little lurch in his heart as he looked at his son. One day that really would be true. Jamie would go on to do things Nick couldn't even imagine.

"Gotta see Grandpa," Jamie declared, giving back the hat, and fled into the shop, letting the door bang behind him.

"I'm thinking we come in well behind Dad in the pecking order as far as Jamie is concerned," Mac said, grinning.

"No doubt. Grandpa's helping him make a birdhouse. We can't compete with that." Nick clapped his brother on the shoulder. "You coming in?"

"Just for a minute," Mac said. "And I'll have you know I put together that model plane with Jamie last week. I was king of the walk then."

"How the mighty have fallen," Nick teased. "He told me that Grandpa is a champion carpenter. He knows because Grandpa told him."

"Hey, I let him wear the police chief's hat," Mac protested. "That should count for something."

"Not in a burg like Laurel Ridge. Now, if you were hunting down bank robbers, he might be impressed." He followed his brother into the shop. Much as he loved riding his little brother, he was conscious of gratitude. Jamie had a good man to idolize in Mac. Mac was a lot like Dad—solid, dependable, honorable. When he and

Jamie had come home to live, they'd been absorbed into the family as if they'd never been anywhere else.

"So, what brings the police chief here this afternoon? Looking for bad guys?" He leaned against the work-bench, studying Mac's strong-boned, impassive face.

"I talked to Allison Standish this morning," Mac said, his straight brows lowering slightly. "She told me her version of what happened last night."

"I don't suppose it was much different from what I told you," Nick observed.

The frown didn't lift. "Look, how seriously should I take this woman? Do you think she really heard anything or was it just an overactive imagination?"

That wasn't an option that had occurred to him. He'd taken it for granted that Allison's account was accurate. "I doubt it," he said slowly. "Mainly because she was really scared and angry when she ran into me. She wasn't faking it."

"If you say so, I'll buy that she was scared. But what are the odds on overactive imagination? Did you actually hear anyone?"

Nick frowned, considering. "Didn't hear anything, no. But I did find that door to the attic standing open, so it looked as if someone had been in there."

"No reason why she couldn't have opened it herself, is there?"

"No, but the one at the other corner of the building had been left open, too. And why would she say it if it wasn't true?" Far be it for him to support the woman who might put him out of business, but he didn't see any reason for Allison to make up that story.

"Imagination," Mac said. "Not being used to the

sounds an old building makes. Trying to draw attention to herself. Take your pick."

Nick pushed down the voice that wanted to deny it heatedly. "Could be, I guess, but that doesn't seem sufficient reason. I'd say she's not the hysterical type. Or easily scared."

"What about the way the building was left in Mrs. Standish's will? I've been hearing rumors around town. What happens if Allison doesn't claim the building?"

"From what I understand, it goes to Brenda Conner. That might give Brenda a reason for trying to scare Allison away, but no reason that I can see for Allison to invent such a story." Was he really defending her?

Mac mulled that over for a couple of minutes. "Seems like there might be a lot of people with a reason to want Ms. Standish gone."

"True. Maybe even me."

"You? Why you?"

Nick shrugged. "I guess I might figure Brenda would be easier to deal with."

"Pretty vague, don't you think?" Mac spread his hands out, palms open. "The story doesn't amount to much of anything, even so. A bunch of solid citizens aren't likely to be prowling around to scare her, even if they aren't happy about her ownership. But I'll keep an eye on the place, anyway."

Nick nodded. It might be just as well if he did the same.

ALLISON PAUSED AT the entrance to the bookshop, glancing around, caught as always by the sheer pleasure of being surrounded by books. Though she had to confess that she bought most of her books online in recent years, there was still nothing like a visit to an actual bookstore to get the juices flowing.

A display of regional history books and pamphlets attracted her attention, but before she could reach the rack she was intercepted.

"Ms. Standish!" A man came hurrying from the back between the racks of books, his white hair ruffled and his expression both eager and apprehensive. "I've been expecting you to stop by. I'm Ralph Mitchell."

"Of course." She extended her hand. "It's nice to meet you, Mr. Mitchell. I'm sorry I didn't get in sooner. There's so much to deal with…" She let that trail off, hoping it was an acceptable excuse.

"Naturally, naturally. And you must call me Ralph. Everyone does." He pumped her hand, his eager eyes seeming to take in every detail of her appearance so intently that it was as if he memorized it.

Allison did a little noticing of her own. Mitchell looked so much like the popular concept of a bookshop owner that he was almost a caricature. Wire-rimmed glasses slid down a pink nose, and he peered anxiously over the top of them. His white hair was worn a little long, and it stood up as if his head was lost in a cloud.

"It was such a shock to all of us to lose our dear Evelyn." His voice actually shook a little, and his hands trembled. "She was very good to us."

"I'm sure she was." Allison's thoughts flickered to that loan her grandmother had made to the bookshop owner. Perhaps they had been close friends, and he was genuinely mourning her.

"You have my deepest sympathy in your loss," he added.

She nodded, not sure what to say. The truth was that

her grandmother had never been anything to her but a name, so how could she be expected to mourn her? There probably wasn't a soul in Laurel Ridge who hadn't known Evelyn Standish better than she had.

"You have a lovely shop here," she said, feeling a change of subject might be the best response. "You seem to be well stocked for a small-town store."

"We try, we try," he said, glancing around with satisfaction. "Evelyn was a great reader, you know, and she encouraged me to branch out a little in what I carried."

The quilt shop, the bookstore—her grandmother seemed to have had a variety of interests and had been willing to back up those interests financially.

"I hope you plan to continue as Evelyn would have wanted," he said, his tone wistful. "It's not easy for an independent bookshop to compete with the chains and the online stores, but Evelyn felt a bookshop was important to the community."

"Yes, I'm sure she did."

Mitchell was putting her on the spot, and she didn't like it. "I really haven't had time to gather all the information I need to make plans yet. My grandmother's bequest came as a surprise to me, you understand."

"Ms. Standish." A peremptory male voice sounded from behind her. She was certainly in demand today. Allison turned.

"I'm Thomas Blackburn. I'd like to speak with you." The man was probably about the same age as Ralph Mitchell and his hair was just as white. But there the resemblance ended. Mitchell looked like nothing so much as a slightly anxious rabbit, while Blackburn—tall, erect, faultlessly dressed—had hawk-like features with eyes that pierced and judged.

"Mr. Blackburn." She acknowledged his words with a nod. "I'm sorry, but I was talking with Mr. Mitchell—"

"Oh, no, no," Ralph said quickly. He stepped back, as if longing to efface himself. "We can chat another time. Really. I must…must get back to…to my inventory."

She could have insisted, but it was obvious Mitchell preferred to slip away in the face of Blackburn's commanding air.

"Fine." She smiled at him and then gestured Blackburn to the stairs. "Shall we go up to my office?" It was the first time she'd referred to the office as hers, but she decided she needed a bit of bolstering with Blackburn staring at her so disapprovingly.

They went up the steps in silence. Blackburn seemed to know the way to the office as well as she did. She unlocked the door, crossed the room and sat down behind her grandmother's desk. Blackburn took the visitor's chair, planted his elbows on its arms and leaned forward.

"I don't believe in mincing words, Ms. Standish. Blackburn House is Blackburn by rights. Blackburns built it, Blackburns lived in it. I want it in Blackburn family hands, where it belongs."

Allison leaned back in the chair, feeling as if she needed to be a bit farther from the power of that commanding presence. "I understand that the building was purchased by my grandfather a number of years ago."

"Selling was a foolish action on the part of my father." Blackburn dismissed the sale with a wave of a large hand. "He was under a certain amount of financial stress at the time, and frankly, your grandfather took advantage of him."

Despite the fact that she had no reason to defend the grandfather who was completely unknown to her, Allison found the comment annoying. "The sale was obviously perfectly legal. I'm not sure why you're bringing it up now."

Blackburn's face twitched in an unconvincing smile. "I merely wanted to show you that I'm serious in my desire to buy Blackburn House. My son and grandson carry the Blackburn name, and it should be their legacy."

Not yours. He didn't say the words, but they were implied by his tone.

"Did you discuss this subject with my grandmother?" Allison wasn't quite sure where the question came from—maybe from the fact that she was sitting in her grandmother's chair.

Blackburn's face tightened until it looked as if it might be carved on a monument. "I made repeated offers to Evelyn Standish. She seemed to take pleasure in thwarting my wishes." His face reddened. "She even talked about changing the name to Standish House."

Allison struggled to hide her amusement at this example of small-town rivalry. Somehow she could imagine her grandmother doing just that. She'd probably enjoyed clashing with Blackburn. But Allison just found the old man's insistence disturbing, particularly when she had no choice but to say no to him.

"I'm afraid selling is not possible right now, to you or to anyone else," she said quickly. "The terms of my grandmother's will—"

"I know all about the will." Blackburn looked as if he were gritting his teeth. "Evelyn enjoyed making things as difficult as possible for people. However, that's not insurmountable."

"I'm not going to contest the will—" she began, but he shook his head.

"No, not litigation." He smiled slightly. "That benefits no one but the attorneys, I find. I have already spoken with Brenda Standish Conner. She is willing to sell to me."

The arrogance of that took her breath away. "Brenda is not the owner of Blackburn House, provisional or otherwise."

He didn't seem impressed by the statement. "I understand that she has already made you an offer to relinquish your claim." He held up a large hand to quell her protest. "A ridiculous offer, as I'm sure you agree, but that's Brenda all over. Always looking for a bargain, and perfectly willing to cut off her nose to spite her face. However, I'm sure you'll agree that staying in Laurel Ridge for a year is an onerous requirement for an ambitious young professional like yourself. As for seeking to run the place at a profit for a year—well, so many things can go wrong in managing a building like this one. Unexpected repairs could eat up your profits very quickly."

Allison was beginning to feel her back stiffen at the automatic assumption everyone seemed to make that she didn't belong here. And how did he know she was an ambitious young professional, anyway? "What exactly are you proposing, Mr. Blackburn?"

He didn't hesitate. "Naturally you'd like to gain a tangible profit from your inheritance and get back to your own life. In return for your agreement to Brenda's offer, I will increase the offer. Shall we say double?" He drew a checkbook from his breast pocket, clearly prepared to write a check here and now.

Allison had the sensation that she was being pushed toward a precipice. She shoved her chair back, rising. "I'm afraid not, Mr. Blackburn."

"Not?" His face reddened. "Do you understand what I'm offering you, young woman?"

"I understand you're trying to pressure me into a decision before I'm ready. As a businessman, you should understand that I need to investigate all the possibilities before taking any action."

Blackburn stood, towering over her and looking even more like a bird of prey. "Suppose I tell you that my offer will not remain on the table indefinitely?"

Since he'd already betrayed how much he wanted to regain the property, his argument wasn't as convincing as he might have thought.

She smiled. "I'll pass your offer on to my attorney. You'll be hearing from us in due course."

He glared at her for a long moment, his face so red that she wondered just how high his blood pressure might be. "You'll regret this, Ms. Standish." He stalked to the door.

The best word to describe his exit was *stormy*, Allison decided. Once the door had slammed behind him, she took a long look at her actions.

Was she burning bridges by her refusal to act before she was ready? She didn't think so. If Blackburn wanted the building as much as he seemed to, he wouldn't give up that easily. Probably he'd hoped to push her into a decision before she had a chance to think it through.

She wouldn't be pushed, but she would have to make plans for her future and the future of Blackburn House. Soon.

CHAPTER FIVE

It WASN'T MORE than a few minutes later that Allison saw the door of her office slowly begin to open. If Blackburn had returned for another round—

But the face that peered around the corner of the door was a small one, topped by a shock of wheat-colored hair. Brown eyes surveyed her with curiosity.

She smiled. "Come in. Did you want to see me?"

The answering smile identified him beyond any doubt, since it bore an uncanny resemblance to Nick's. This had to be Nick's son.

"Hi. I'm Jamie." He sidled in, darting a look around the room.

"I thought you must be." She pushed her chair away from the desk. "I'm Allison. It's nice to meet you."

He nodded, as if to say he already knew that. "I'm called Jamie because my grandpa is Jim, and Grammy says it would be too confusing if I was Jimmy, 'cause sometimes she calls him that when she's being silly."

Allison nodded, engaged by his artless chatter. "That makes good sense. And Jamie's a nice name."

"It's okay. I'm the only Jamie in first grade, anyway. Do you have a nickname?"

"My brothers always called me Ally." She had a quick memory of Luke and Chad at that age, always exploding with energy.

Jamie's gaze flickered around the office again. "My daddy says you have a cat. He said you hit him with it."

She had to repress a smile at this artless confession. "I bumped him with the cat's carrier. I didn't mean to." That wasn't exactly true, but she hadn't meant to hit Nick in particular. Just whoever had grabbed her.

Jamie stooped to look under the desk. "I thought maybe your cat would be here."

Clearly it was Hector who was the attraction. "Hector is over at Mrs. Anderson's house. He was taking a nap with her cat when I left, so I let him stay."

She expected Jamie to be disappointed, but he grinned.

"He's having a sleepover. My friend Kevin had a sleepover at my house once, but he had a bad dream in the night, and Daddy had to take him home. Daddy said he should have known better than to say yes, but Grammy said they shouldn't say no just because it was incon...incon..."

"Inconvenient?" she supplied.

"Yeah, that's it." Jamie was swinging on the edge of her desk by this time, seeming sure of his welcome. "And Daddy said he was the one who had to drive back to town at one o'clock and she said it wouldn't hurt him. And Uncle Mac said—"

Allison began to feel a bit guilty listening to all this. "Maybe the sleepover will work better the next time you try."

"Maybe," he said, sounding doubtful.

"So you live with your grammy and grandpa, do you?" she asked, trying to change the subject but having little idea what interested a six-year-old.

"Grammy, Grandpa, Daddy, Uncle Mac and me. And Shep, that's the dog."

"Sounds like a full house." And it sounded as if Jamie was surrounded by people he loved. His parents were divorced, according to Sarah, but wasn't his mother in the picture?

"Yep." He came closer, leaning confidingly on the arm of her chair. "My mommy lives in Los Angeles. Sometimes she sends me presents."

That was said very matter-of-factly, but it caused a twinge in Allison's heart. "When I was little, my daddy lived far away, but he used to send me presents sometimes, too."

He nodded, fixing a pair of big brown eyes on her face. "Did he sometimes send things that were too baby-ish for you?"

"Sometimes," she admitted. "I guess he just didn't know how much I'd grown."

"Yeah, that must be it. Can I see your cat sometime?"

"Sure you can. Anytime." There must be a kind of universal pattern for children who had a parent leave them behind. But Jamie seemed to be well provided for with people who cared for him, and he had plenty of confidence.

"Jamie!" The voice floated up from below. "Jamie, where are you?"

"Sounds as if we'd better tell your daddy where you are, right?" She rose, thinking she'd walk him to the door.

"Sure thing." He grabbed her hand. "You come, too, okay?"

Since he was tugging her along, she didn't have much choice. They reached the head of the stairs, and she glanced down, seeing Nick staring up at them, his eyes widening slightly at the sight of her with his son.

Jamie pulled her hand. "Come on, Ally."

They started down the steps, with Jamie's hand confidently in hers. It felt nice. He was the first person she'd met since she'd arrived in town who hadn't wanted something from her.

Jamie seemed to feel her watching him. He looked up as they neared the bottom of the stairs. "Were you scared last night?"

"Scared?" Her mind spun. "What makes you think that?"

"I heard Uncle Mac and Daddy talking, and Daddy said somebody might be trying to scare you. And Uncle Mac said maybe you were imagining it."

"So that's what Uncle Mac thinks, is it?" It sounded as if her little chat with the police chief hadn't gotten her anywhere.

"That's what he says when I say there's something under my bed."

"Well, I'm sure there's not really anything under your bed." That had to be the right response, didn't it? As for the Whiting brothers...

She met Nick's eyes and realized he'd overheard.

His gaze slid away from hers, and color came up under his tan. "Jamie, it's not polite to listen to what other people are saying."

"But, Daddy, you're always telling me to listen when grown-ups talk."

Allison's lips twitched. "I think he has you there."

Nick's embarrassment dissolved in a smile. "Sorry. Mac was just, well, trying to figure out the possibilities."

"I'm sure." She longed to ask him if he'd meant it

when he said someone might be trying to scare her away, but she couldn't say that in front of the child.

"Daddy, Ally says I can come see her cat anytime." Jamie was tugging on Nick's sleeve.

"She does, does she?" Nick looked down at his son, and there was suddenly so much love in his expression that her heart turned over. Nick gave her a questioning glance. "Ally?"

"That's her nickname," Jamie said, sounding important. "Her little brothers used to call her that."

Nick's brows went up. "I didn't know you had brothers."

There was no reason why he should. "Two of them. Half brothers, to be exact. They're ten years younger than I am. Twins."

"Wish I was a twin. It would be fun to have someone look just like me."

"Two of you?" Nick ruffled his hair. "I think one is enough. Look, here's Grammy."

Jamie went running to the woman who'd just come in the front door. He hurled himself at her legs. "Grammy, Grammy! I got a star on my spelling homework, and Ally says I can come see her cat anytime I want."

The woman bent to hug him. "That's great, Jamie. Do you want to introduce me to your new friend?"

He took her hand and pulled her over. "Ally, this is Grammy."

"Allison Standish," Nick murmured.

"I'm Ellen Whiting." She held out her hand to Allison with a wide smile. "Welcome to Laurel Ridge. I've been looking forward to meeting you."

They were unmistakable, Allison thought, for three

generations of one family. Nick had his mother's eyes, and Jamie her wide, happy smile.

"It's nice to meet you, Ellen. Jamie has been telling me about his family."

"Telling you all the family secrets, no doubt." She smiled. "Not that any of them are very secret. Jamie loves to chatter, don't you, sweetheart?"

Jamie's grin echoed hers, and he nodded.

"Now, Allison, we have to get better acquainted. Goodness, I remember your father from when we were in elementary school together. You must come and have supper with us one night."

"That…that's very nice of you." But she wasn't sure she wanted to get any further involved with the Whiting family. They, like everyone else, had a vested interest in any decisions she made about Blackburn House.

"Good." Ellen seemed to take that as an acceptance, though she hadn't meant it that way. "What about tonight?"

"I'm afraid I have something else going on this evening." She wasn't particularly looking forward to Brenda's cocktail party, but it was a valid excuse.

"Tomorrow night, then," Ellen said, her tone brisk and decided. "Nick will pick you up at five o'clock. We eat early with a little guy in the house."

"I don't…" She wasn't sure which to tackle first. "There's no reason for Nick to drive me. Just give me your address and I'll set the GPS."

"Nonsense, it's no trouble at all. Nick will be delighted, won't you, Nick?"

The expression on Nick's face didn't speak of delight, but his mother didn't seem to notice. "You're being bossy, Mom," he pointed out. "Maybe she'd rather drive herself."

So she can leave early. The words were unspoken but clear to Allison.

"Don't be silly. We don't want her getting lost on those back roads." She clasped Allison's hand. "We're glad you've come home to Laurel Ridge at last, Allison."

Allison wanted to deny that Laurel Ridge was home to her in any sense. But she couldn't deny the warmth of Ellen Whiting's welcome.

TWO SOCIAL INVITATIONS in such a short period of time ought to be gratifying, Allison told herself. Would be, if not for the fact that she wanted to stay detached from the residents of Laurel Ridge, given the decisions she had to make.

She stood in the center hallway of the home her father had grown up in that evening, wondering what she was doing here. Mrs. Anderson hadn't been able to mask her surprise when Allison mentioned where she was headed, but Allison hadn't been able to tell whether the surprise was at Allison being asked to the Standish house or at Brenda for hosting a party.

Laurel Ridge seemed to have more than its share of large Victorian homes—relics, so Sarah had told her, of the days when the town was founded and lumber barons grew rich on the virgin timber of the ridges.

The Standish place was more modest than Blackburn House, making her wonder if that was part of the obvious rivalry between the families. But her father's home had a grace and charm of its own. Pocket doors on either side of the central hallway led on the right to a dining room where an oval cherry table carried an array of finger sandwiches and hors d'oeuvres and on the left to a formal living room. Several well-dressed women were cruising the table, while a few men gathered around a sideboard bearing wine bottles and glasses.

Allison accepted a cup of punch from a white-aproned server and moved toward the living room. She'd greet her hostess, make the rounds and slip away early, before anyone could try to persuade her—

She stopped, staring at the silver-framed photograph that stood on the ornate Victorian mantel. This, then, was her grandmother. Allison moved closer, studying the features of the woman who'd been such a mystery to her.

Evelyn Standish must have been in her seventies when the photograph was taken, but she sat with her shoulders erect and her head held high. The face was austere and fine-boned, but with a hint of softness in the eyes. Or was Allison just hoping she read there some regret? Nonsense. Evelyn Standish had made her choice clear when she'd wiped her granddaughter out of her life. It was too late to go back now.

"Allison. You're here." Brenda, turning away from the fireplace, sounded as if she didn't know quite what to do with Allison now that she'd invited her. "I'm sure there are people who'd be delighted to talk with you." She looked around as if hoping to spot someone.

A hefty male figure loomed up behind her. "Well, this must be the long-lost granddaughter." He nudged Brenda as he ran an obviously experienced eye over Allison. "Introduce me."

"Yes, of course." Brenda's relief was visible. "Allison, this is Thomas—"

"Tommy Blackburn," he said, seizing Allison's hand and holding it a bit too long. "Don't call me Thomas or

I'll think you mean my father. Glad to meet you. Nice of Brenda to arrange this little shindig so we can get acquainted."

Allison freed her hand from his. "It was thoughtful of her." But exactly what Brenda's thought had been, she couldn't say.

"What do you think of Laurel Ridge now that you've had a chance to see it?" He grinned and nudged her. "Don't blink or you'll miss it, right?"

Tommy Blackburn was as much a contrast to his father as she could imagine. He had to be in his forties, at least, and what man that age still wanted to be known as "Tommy"? Ruddy, jovial, with thinning hair and an incipient paunch, he looked as if he'd spent the afternoon on a golf course.

"I've met your father," she said, taking a step back as he invaded her comfort zone.

"I heard." He rolled his eyes. "You have my sympathy. The old man is obsessed about getting Blackburn House back in the family."

Allison lifted her eyebrows. "You don't share his eagerness?"

"Who wants to be burdened with more property? The way the economy is going, the only sensible thing to do with money is enjoy it. You can guess he doesn't agree with that idea."

"No, I can see that he wouldn't." Apparently Blackburn's son had no desire to be an empire builder.

"Now here's the Blackburn that will see us into the future." Tommy reached out a long arm and caught a passing teenager by the shoulder. "T.J., say hello to Ms. Standish. Allison, this is my boy, Thomas Jeffers Blackburn."

"It's a pleasure to meet you, Ms. Standish." The boy, who couldn't be much over seventeen or eighteen, had a prep school blazer and prep school manners, but his gaze swept over her figure much as his father's had done. With his dark curly hair and that bold gaze, he probably had the teenage girls lining up for dates.

"Do you go to school here in Laurel Ridge, T.J.?" she asked, nodding to the prep school crest.

"St. Francis." He shrugged gracefully. "Old family tradition, and all that." He glanced from her to his father. "If you'll excuse me, I'm supposed to be getting some punch for Mrs. Conner."

"Sure, go on, then, before she thinks you've forgotten." His father waved him away. "He's a good kid. Closer to my father than I am, I think sometimes." Tommy leaned in a bit. "I'll bet you'd like to see something of the place where your dad grew up. Let me show you around. There's a sunroom on the back that has a nice view of the gardens. This way." He put his hand on her waist, as if to steer her toward the hall, and let it drift down over her hip.

"Thank you, but I think I'll let my cousin show me around if she cares to." She slid away from his grasp. Did he find that approach actually worked on women? Or maybe he expected the Blackburn name to awe her.

With a polite nod, she crossed the room to where Brenda stood, gesturing with a glass dessert plate as she talked to a tall redhead with overly made-up eyes and a sulky smile.

Brenda swung toward her, arranging her face in a smile that seemed to argue with her anxious eyes. "Are you enjoying yourself, Allison? Tommy especially wanted to meet you."

"I noticed," she said, and the redhead gave her a surprised, involuntary smile. Up close, the girl was not as old as she wanted people to think, plainly still in her teens.

"This…this is my daughter. Krysta." Brenda touched the girl's arm lightly. "We were just…" She let the sentence die out, as if she didn't want to finish it.

Disagreeing about something, Allison would guess, judging by the sulky look that settled back on to Krysta's face.

"I don't see any reason why I have to hang around," she muttered. "It's just a bunch of old people making stupid conversation."

Allison had to suppress a smile. Krysta would probably class her with the old people and be surprised to learn Allison felt very much the same.

"Don't talk like that." The words should have been a reprimand, but instead they sounded like a plea. "You know I wanted you here to meet your cousin Allison and make her feel welcome."

"Welcome!" Krysta threw off her mother's hand with an impatient gesture. "Like anybody welcomes her. Why don't you tell her the truth?" Her voice had risen, and Allison felt the embarrassment anyone experiences when someone else's child is acting out in public.

She took a step back, and the movement seemed to draw Krysta's fulminating gaze to her. The girl's blue eyes narrowed. "You want to know why Evelyn left Blackburn House to you? I'll tell you. She wanted to humiliate us, that's why."

Krysta's voice had risen above the chatter of the crowd, and she seemed suddenly aware that people were staring at her.

"You are behaving like a child, Krysta Conner. Perhaps you'd better go to your room until you can manage to act like an adult."

The woman who spoke had gray hair cut mannishly, a forbidding expression and a commanding voice. She stared Krysta down without apparent effort, and the girl turned and ran from the room, face flaming.

Forced chatter resumed as people cast sidelong glances at Brenda, whose face was nearly as scarlet as that of her daughter's.

"Really, Julia, you didn't need to speak to her that way." Brenda's protest was muted.

"Someone had to. It should have come from you. You're her mother. I'd suggest you develop some backbone before that headstrong daughter of yours does something you'll both regret."

For an instant Allison thought Brenda would flare out. Then she shook her head and carried her plate over to a side table.

The woman flashed a glance at Allison. "I always think one of the privileges of getting to be an ugly old woman is being able to say what you really think. I'm Julia Everly. I was a friend of your grandmother's." Her smile showed patently false teeth and gave her a shark-like look. "Well, sometimes we were friends and sometimes enemies. At least we were never boring."

Allison couldn't help laughing. "I can readily believe that."

Julia gave an unrepentant grin. "You're wondering why your grandmother left Blackburn House to you. Trust me, it wasn't because of anything Brenda and Krysta said or did."

Allison studied her. Despite what she'd said, Julia

wasn't exactly ugly. With her round, wrinkled face and bright eyes she resembled an intelligent monkey. She would never have had the kind of classic beauty that Evelyn must have possessed, but she was instantly likeable.

"Is this a guessing game or do you know why my grandmother left it to me?" she demanded, suspecting Julia preferred people to be as direct as she was.

The woman shrugged. "Can't say I knew everything she was thinking. Evelyn had a way of keeping her own counsel when she wanted. But I do know that she'd always planned to make provision for you. When your mother remarried, she said to me, 'Julia, that little girl will be all right now, so I won't rock the boat. But when I go, I'll see that she's taken care of.'"

That didn't answer all of her questions, but it was more helpful than anything else she'd learned since she came to Laurel Ridge. So, her grandmother had known about her life, even without contacting her. And she'd at least considered her.

She realized Julia was studying her face and spoke quickly. "Thank you. I appreciate your telling me."

Julia squeezed her hand, and Allison felt the woman's cluster of rings bite into her fingers. "Don't you let anybody rush you into any decisions. That's my advice, for what it's worth. Come to lunch one day, and we'll talk. I'll call you."

"Thank you," she said, before it occurred to her that she'd planned to be gone in a week's time. But nothing seemed as clear-cut now as it had when she'd made that plan.

By the time an hour had passed, Allison had been introduced to so many people and had made so much meaningless chatter that her head felt about to split. She caught a passing server and asked directions to a powder room, thinking to escape the noise for a few minutes.

The girl pointed vaguely to the back of the center hallway, and Allison walked quickly in that direction. Surely she'd been here long enough to satisfy the demands of courtesy. She'd find Brenda and make her excuses.

She opened the door at the end of the hall, took one step forward and froze. She'd wandered into the sunroom Tommy had spoken of, and she wasn't alone. T.J. and Krysta were sprawled on a wicker sofa, with the girl's dress pulled up nearly to her waist.

The door swung shut behind her, and they both turned at the sound. T.J., eyes heavy-lidded and mouth swollen, looked both older and more dangerous than the prep-school image he'd projected earlier, while Krysta, paradoxically, looked younger and more vulnerable. She scrambled to her feet, smoothing her dress down.

"I told you we shouldn't." Krysta's voice quavered.

"Didn't figure on somebody spying on us." T.J. got to his feet and took a swaggering step toward Allison. "What is it to you, anyway?"

"It's nothing to me what you do, T.J." Allison kept her voice even. "But Krysta is my cousin."

Krysta seemed to regain her persona now that she was decently covered. "I don't need a cousin like you." She practically spat the words.

"I'm not thrilled with the relationship myself," Allison said. "Get back to the party, and I won't say anything to your mother."

Krysta glared at her for a moment. Allison didn't move. It would take more than a couple of spoiled teenagers to make her back down.

Finally, muttering a vulgarity that Allison chose to ignore, Krysta ran out of the sunroom. T.J. gave her a head start, then strolled toward the door, brushing against Allison deliberately. Then he was gone.

Allison let out a long breath. It had begun to seem that for every friend she made in this place, she racked up twice as many enemies. But Krysta, no matter how sulky and spoiled, was her cousin, and she couldn't pretend that didn't mean something to her, no matter how inconvenient.

IT HAD BEEN a mistake to let his mother anywhere near Allison Standish, Nick decided as he drove to the bed-and-breakfast to pick up Allison for supper the next evening. Not that he could have prevented it.

He might have known Mom couldn't resist the temptation to start mothering Allison. Ellen Whiting collected strays the way some women collected shoes. It never seemed to occur to her that some of them might not want to be gathered up in her motherly embrace.

He hadn't missed the expression on Allison's face when his mother insisted he'd come for her. It had probably mirrored his own. Well, they were both stuck.

He'd be polite to Allison, of course. He just didn't want to be entangled with the woman. She might very easily prove to be bad news for all of them. If she found some way of selling Blackburn House, he didn't doubt that Thomas Blackburn would be waiting to snatch it up. He'd made no secret of the fact that he intended to buy the place as soon as probate was settled. He just hadn't known that Allison would be the one to inherit. Heaven only knew what plans he might have for the place.

And if Allison herself decided to run it, he could hardly think the situation would be much better. She had no knowledge of how things functioned in a town like Laurel Ridge, and obviously no desire to learn.

He'd presented his role as mayor lightly when Allison had asked about it, but it wasn't as simple as he'd made it sound. He'd run for office because he thought Laurel Ridge needed protection from those who advocated change at any cost. Not that he was a reactionary, but Laurel Ridge was a good place to live and to raise a child. It deserved people in power who appreciated its positive qualities and took thought for its future instead of running after short-term profits.

All things considered, the inhabitants of Blackburn House might be better off with Brenda Conner in charge. She was so obsessed with turning herself into the social leader her aunt had been that she'd be unlikely to rock the boat.

He stopped in front of the bed-and-breakfast, got out and took a deep breath, feeling like someone who'd been coerced into a blind date with a buddy's visiting cousin. That sort of thing never worked out well.

By the time he reached the porch, Allison was coming to meet him. At least she hadn't kept him waiting. He'd give her points for punctuality.

She stepped forward to face him, and his breath caught. He'd have to change the comparison. This wasn't in the least like going out with someone's ugly duckling cousin. Allison wore a dress of sea green that matched her eyes and swirled around her legs with every movement. Her hair swirled as well, swinging glossy and smooth as silk, and the heels she wore made her legs seem to go on forever. With an effort, he tore his gaze from those legs—a little late, judging by her expression.

"Is there something wrong with the way I'm dressed?"

"Trust me, there's nothing at all wrong." She might be a bit overdressed for a simple supper at the Whiting household, but that didn't mean her appearance wouldn't be appreciated.

When they reached the car, he opened the door for her and raised an eyebrow when she slid in without comment.

"Aren't you going to tell me you can open car doors by yourself?" He leaned against the frame of the door, looking down at her.

She smiled sweetly. "I wouldn't want you to get in trouble with your mother."

Touché, he supposed. He got in without further comment.

By the time they reached the end of town, which didn't take long no matter which way one was going, he knew he'd better start a conversation if he didn't want to ride in silence all the way home.

"How was the party at Brenda's?" His smile flickered. "Boring?"

"Not really."

A glance at her face told him she was thinking of something in particular. A not very happy something, by the look of it.

"What's up? Was she chintzy on the refreshments? Evelyn didn't entertain much, but when she did, there was a lavish spread."

She shrugged. "The food was fine. Catered, I suppose. I met some people who were…interesting. Do you know a woman called Julia Everly?"

"Everyone knows Julia." He relaxed into a grin. "She prides herself on being a character. Was she outrageous?"

"Not to me. She was actually very friendly. I gathered she and my grandmother were good friends."

"Friends, enemies, sparring partners, you name it. She was probably the only person in Laurel Ridge who'd tell Evelyn what's what. If you've talked to her, you'll have realized that she doesn't have a filter. If she thinks it, it comes out her mouth."

Allison's face relaxed its watchful expression. "I did notice that she seemed to take pride in her bluntness." She smiled. "She reminded me of Jamie, in a way."

"Right you are. Someone else without a filter. Still, that's more normal when you're six than when you're seventy-six." He shrugged. "I try to keep him from blurting out everything he thinks to strangers, but—"

"Don't discourage him," she said quickly. "It's delightful." She shot a sidelong, smiling glance at him. "Especially what he repeated you had said about me."

"I'm sure." He returned her smile, and their gazes tangled for heated seconds before he yanked his eyes back to the road.

He could feel her intent gaze still on his face.

"He mentioned his mother."

"Yes." He clamped his lips shut on the word.

"He said he doesn't see her, but sometimes she sends him presents. At a guess, things that are inappropriate for his age and interests."

That startled him into looking at her again. "How did you know?"

"Because that's what my father did, too."

"I didn't realize…" He did some reorganizing of the life he'd thought she'd lived. "How old were you when he left?"

"Six. The age Jamie is now." Her lips trembled a little,

and she pressed them together for a moment. "I suppose you make excuses for her."

He shrugged. "What else can I do?"

"Nothing, I guess. But he probably knows the truth. I always did."

He slowed, turning the car into the lane that led to the farmhouse, and she swung to face him. "I know it's none of my business. But I wanted to say that it's obvious that Jamie is very well loved and very confident. You don't need to worry about his mother's attitude affecting him. Not when he has all that love to rely on."

He stopped the car so that he could face her. "Thanks." His voice had turned husky, and he was annoyed with himself for revealing so much to her. But it seemed she'd guessed it, anyway.

He clasped her hand for a moment. There was more to Allison Standish than that polished, beautiful exterior. He might have to rethink the opinions he'd been forming about her.

CHAPTER SIX

THERE HAD BEEN a moment of discomfort for Allison when she'd first entered the rambling old farmhouse, so different from the polished, static perfection of the house where her father had grown up. She was, she'd realized, overdressed for the casual country supper her hosts had planned. But by the time she'd held Jamie's guinea pig, suffered through wet kisses from Shep, the collie, and helped set the long pine table for supper, she'd forgotten what she was wearing.

Ellen, her pleasant face flushed from the heat of the stove, was so honestly happy to see her that Allison couldn't doubt her welcome. Jamie bubbled with enthusiasm, wanting to show her everything at once and only deterred from dragging her to the barn by a quiet shake of the head from his grandfather. The elder James Whiting had a look of Nick in the strong bones of his face, along with an air of quiet dignity that she found appealing. Even Mac seemed to shed his law-enforcement persona while being scolded by his mother for coming in without wiping his shoes on the mat.

As for Nick…well, it was fascinating to see what he was like in his own setting. He seemed to relax, all the tension gone from his face, and his laughter came easily.

By the time the platter of roast beef was passed, Allison felt as if she were home again, with her two half brothers squabbling over who'd received the bigger portion.

Nick reached across her to take the meat platter from his brother's hands. "You don't need to act as if you haven't eaten in a week," he said. "Give our guest a chance first."

"You mean you want her to pass it to you. If you'd had the workday I've had—" Mac began, winking at Allison.

"Workday? Very funny. We all know you spend the day sitting behind the wheel of a patrol car. When you're not wandering into the bakery for a handout."

"I'll have you know I never accept bribes, even when they're jelly donuts. It's not my fault if Anna always gives me an extra-large serving."

"That extra-large serving will give you an extra-large waist if you don't watch it," his mother said tartly. "Now, you boys stop squabbling in front of Allison."

"That's okay," she said. "Reminds me of my twin brothers when they were about ten or so."

"Ouch." Nick's eyes were laughing as he took the bowl of mashed potatoes from her. "How old are they now?"

"Eighteen, and both of them driving. My mother says they've given her a whole crop of gray hairs."

"I know exactly what she's feeling," Ellen said. "Your mother remarried then, after your father..." She let that trail off, flushing a little.

Allison nodded, ignoring the pause. "She and Dennis are great together."

"What are your brothers' names?" Jamie slipped half a biscuit to Shep under the table. "Do they have any pets?"

"Luke and Chad. We've always had cats and dogs. No guinea pigs, though."

Jamie grinned. "Sometimes girls don't like to hold guinea pigs, but you did, didn't you, Allison?"

She evaded Nick's gaze, knowing she'd see laughter there. "I sure did."

"And we have chickens, and ducks, and a milk cow, and two horses. We had a goat one year, but Grammy said it was too much trouble."

"Mac talked me into that one." Ellen shot him a mock wrathful look. "He didn't tell me it was a billy goat. Or that it would eat its way through any restraint and consume a whole row of tomato plants and half my dahlias."

"Guess that wasn't the best idea I ever had," Mac admitted.

"It wasn't the worst, either," Nick retorted. "If Mom and Dad knew…"

"Enough of your misdeeds," his father said. "We probably already know. The two of you were never as sneaky as you thought you were." He turned to Allison. "I understand you were invited to the Standish place."

Apparently everyone in town knew about her movements. Were other people talking about her supper with the Whiting family right now?

Ellen made an impulsive movement toward her. "Now, don't think we're being nosy. It's just that having you here is one of the most interesting things that's happened in Laurel Ridge in a long time."

Allison smiled. "Not much must happen here, then."

"We have the usual small-town things to talk about," Ellen said. "Who's getting married, who's breaking up, who must have had a good year because they're going on a cruise. In a small place, you're naturally interested in your neighbors."

"I guess so." She glanced down at her plate. "I know a lot of people have a stake in whatever decision I make about the property," she said carefully. "But everything about the inheritance came as a complete surprise to me. I need time to figure out my course of action."

"Of course you do." Ellen's voice was warm. "And if any of my family are pushing you for a decision, you just tell me and I'll deal with them."

She smiled. "I'll do that." She had the satisfaction of seeing Nick look uncomfortable. But maybe it was time to slip away from the subject of her plans.

"I was glad to have a chance to see the house where my father grew up," she said, handing her plate to Ellen as the woman rose to clear the table. "And to see a photo of my grandmother. She had an interesting face."

"You mean you'd never seen a photo of her before?" Ellen set the plates on the counter with a clatter.

Allison shook her head. "We never had any contact at all."

"Evelyn could be a stubborn woman," Jim observed.

"How she could do such a thing, I don't know." Ellen seized Jamie in a fierce hug. "Her own grandchild."

"Ouch, Grammy, don't squeeze my tummy."

Ellen released him and dropped a kiss on his hair.

"If you're that full, maybe you want to wait awhile before you have dessert. What do you think?"

Jamie nodded and spurted off his chair as if he were on springs. "Please, may I be excused? I'll get my ball and glove. Do you want to play catch with me, Allison?"

"Allison's not dressed for ball today," Nick said firmly.

Jamie's face fell.

"Another time, okay?" Allison said. "I had to pitch to my brothers a lot when they started playing baseball, so I'm not too bad."

"Okay." He slapped his leg to summon the dog. "Come on, Shep." Boy and dog raced out the back door, with Ellen calling to him to take a jacket.

"Boys," she said. "Never do anything quietly. Allison, will you have vanilla ice cream on your cherry pie?"

She felt about as full as Jamie, but Ellen would probably be hurt if she didn't have dessert. "Just a small piece, please. And a little ice cream."

"I'll eat her extra," Mac said. "So, who all did Brenda invite to meet you? Not us, obviously."

"We're not grand enough for her," Nick said, grinning. "Allison met Julia Everly."

"Oh, dear." Ellen set what seemed a mammoth wedge of pie in front of Allison. "I hope she didn't say anything too outrageous."

"Not to me," Allison said. "But she did scold Krysta about her manners and, by implication, Brenda for not correcting her."

"Krysta was rude, I suppose." Ellen slid into her chair. "She's been through a difficult time. It can't have been easy for a teenager, losing her father and having to move in with a great-aunt."

"You always find excuses for people." Jim glanced fondly at his wife. "The girl's spoiled, that's all, like too many teenagers these days."

"You're starting to sound like an old grump," his wife informed him. "Who else did you meet, Allison?"

"Tommy Blackburn. The elder Mr. Blackburn wasn't there, but I met Tommy and his son."

"Don't bother telling me Tommy didn't make a pass

at you, because I wouldn't believe it," Nick said, eyes challenging hers above a forkful of ruby-red pie cherries.

"Minor-league pass," she said. Apparently these people really did know each other well.

"T.J.'s the one I feel sorry for," Ellen said. "His father doesn't set much of an example for him, and his grandfather expects too much, I've always thought."

"His mother isn't in the picture?" Allison asked, remembering T.J.'s reaction when she'd inadvertently walked in on him and Krysta. That certainly hadn't made her feel sorry for him. As Jim said, Ellen seemed to have plenty of sympathy to go around.

"Poor Nina." Ellen shook her head. "She passed away two years ago. Accidental overdose of sleeping pills or some such thing. Goodness knows what Dr. Walker was thinking to prescribe so much medication for her."

"Walker's getting past it," Jim observed. "And he never was all that bright. A man should know when to retire."

His sons exchanged glances at that sentiment.

"And you don't need to look that way, either," Jim said tartly. "I'm still sharp enough to outwork the two of you any day of the week."

Allison suppressed a smile. "I'll bet you are."

"Welcome to family supper at the Whiting house," Nick said. "You can't say we put on any airs for you." He gave her a smile of such amazing sweetness that her heart seemed to turn over in her chest.

Careful, she told herself, panicky. *Careful*. Unfortunately neither her emotions nor her body seemed to be listening.

DUSK HAD FALLEN by the time Allison slid into the passenger seat of Nick's car. She'd said her goodbyes and her thanks, and she smiled as Jamie, sitting on his uncle's shoulders, waved an energetic farewell.

She turned back, aware of how quiet it was alone in the car with Nick. To say nothing of how close he was. His hands were lean and capable on the wheel as he turned from the farm lane onto the blacktop.

She forced herself to look away. *Keep it cool, light, superficial.*

"That's Sarah's family farm," Nick said, nodding to the white farmhouse set well back from the road. Maybe he was equally determined not to recognize the attraction that sparked between them. If so, it should be easier to do as she intended.

"You said you were neighbors. I guess I expected the houses to be closer."

"Not out here in the country." Nick grinned at her. "City girl," he teased.

"That's me. The closest to country I ever got was the suburbs of Chicago." She glanced at the farms that lined either side of the road. Fields sloped gently up at the far edges, like a very shallow bowl. The slopes led upward to the ridges on either side. For the most part the trees were still brown and bare, but pale green touched a few here and there.

Nick followed the direction of her gaze. "In a few more weeks, the valley will be filled with color. The Amish are already plowing. That farm belongs to Sarah's uncle."

"You're surrounded by the Amish," she said. "No wonder you seem so comfortable with Sarah."

Nick shrugged. "Amish aren't much different from anyone else. You looked like you were getting along pretty well with Sarah yourself."

"She's a good person." Allison stared blankly at the

two-lane road unrolling in front of them. She didn't want to disappoint Sarah, but she couldn't determine her whole future on that fact.

"Yes, she is." Nick's lips quirked. "As someone who's known her since she was four, I'm in a position to say."

"I guess you are. I can understand why Sarah grew up on a farm. That's a very Amish thing to do. But why you? What do your parents want with a farm when your dad's business is in town?"

Nick's smiling glance caught hers. "Blame it on the era they grew up in. I wouldn't go so far as to say they were hippies, but they had a lot of ideas about living close to the land and being self-sufficient. Mix that up with a determination to raise their kids to respect the value of work, and you've got our life."

"You like it." She hoped that wasn't wonderment in her voice.

"I do, yeah. Oh, Mac and I both did our share of complaining when we were teens. Why couldn't we live in town like everybody else? None of our friends had to get up early to milk the cows or miss playing a game to help get the hay in before it rained." He paused, shaking his head. "I'm not sure we meant it all even then. Now... well, I can't imagine a better life for my son."

He seemed to mean it. It must be nice, to be so sure of what you wanted from life. But where did ambition come in?

"I can see that you're satisfied," she said slowly. "But you're obviously smart and educated. So, why are you content to make a living working with your hands in a place like this when you could be doing something more, well, important?"

His lips twisted. "Maybe I think what I do is important. I figure I have two jobs, and raising my son is the most important one. I don't want to settle for less than the best in quality in each of them." He darted a look at her. "You don't get it, do you? I guess we value different things."

"I suppose so." She felt somehow disappointed. He might have tried to sway her, but he probably didn't think it was worthwhile.

They were approaching the bed-and-breakfast, and Allison gave herself a mental shake. She was trying not to get involved, remember? So why was she disappointed?

Nick pulled up at the curb and got out. "I'll see you to the door."

"Not necessary," Allison said firmly. "Thank you for driving me. And thanks again for supper. I enjoyed it."

She glanced at Blackburn House to assure herself that all was well. The windows of the various businesses were dark, but a glow came from the pole lamp in the front lawn, illuminating a patch of grass and shining on the sidewalk. It was set on a timer so that it stayed on all night. The bushes on either side cast a pool of shadow where the lamplight didn't reach.

"Thanks for accepting Mom's invitation. She'd have been disappointed if you hadn't." Nick stood very close as she reached the sidewalk, looking down at her. "And I'm glad you came, too." His voice lowered on the words, and her breath caught. "You—"

He stopped, his attention apparently captured by something he saw over her shoulder.

"Now what is going on?" he muttered.

Allison spun around. Blackburn House lay in the

deepest darkness. The lamp she'd noticed only a moment ago had gone out.

"I don't understand. I thought that pole lamp was supposed to stay on until dawn."

"It is." He took a step toward the building. "I'd better see what's going on. Maybe a circuit blew."

Or maybe someone flipped it. That was what he was thinking, she realized. "I'll go with you."

"No, you won't."

Her temper flared, as he must have expected. "Give me one good reason why not."

"I'll give you two," he said. "I know where the circuit breakers are. You don't. And in those shoes, you'd probably break an ankle trying to get down the stone steps to the cellar."

It was a great thing to know when you were outflanked. Allison leaned against the car with as much dignity as she could muster.

"If you're not back in five minutes, I'm calling the police."

"Make it ten." His smile flashed. "It'll take a little time." He was gone before she could argue the point.

Allison checked the time on her cell phone and kept it in her hand. It was probably foolish to think there was anything wrong, but she hadn't forgotten the presence of someone in Blackburn House or the open door that led to the attics. Someone had certainly been prowling around the place then, whether Mac thought she was imagining things or not. Still, she didn't see any good reason for anyone to shut off the lights.

Waiting in the dark wasn't conducive to happy thoughts. She checked the time again. Only four minutes had passed.

The chill April air crept up her legs, but at least she didn't feel trapped in the car. If anything frightened her, she could call out and someone would hear.

The seconds ticked by. Her eyes grew accustomed to the dimness, and she could make out the line of the porch railing and the walk that skirted the building and ran back toward the workshop. That was the direction Nick had gone. Presumably he'd come back the same way.

But wouldn't the lamp come on first? Well, only if it really was just a flipped circuit breaker. If it was something more complicated, Nick wouldn't try to fix it, would he? He'd come back to report the issue, and she'd have to call an electrician tomorrow. Was there money set aside for repairs of that sort? She should have found out more specifically what the fund the attorney mentioned would cover.

Another check of her cell phone told her seven minutes had passed. She stared into the dense shadows cast by the porch. Movement. Yes, that was definitely movement. Relief swept through her. Nick was coming. Apparently he—

No, it wasn't Nick. She didn't know why she was so sure, but she was. The figure wasn't the right size or shape, somehow. Holding her breath, she shrank back against the car.

Whoever he was, he didn't seem to be headed out the walk. Instead, the silhouette crossed the lawn, stepping over the daffodils, and jumped the low wrought-iron fence at the side. A moment later he emerged on to the sidewalk farther down the street. His stride took him directly under the next streetlight, and she knew him. It was T. J. Blackburn.

T.J. She pressed against the car, thoughts focused on

the threat that had been in his eyes when she'd interrupted him with Krysta. Was this some kind of payback?

And where was Nick? If Nick had encountered T.J....

Not stopping to think any further, she pushed open the gate and hurried the way Nick had gone, using her cell as a flashlight. She rounded the corner, her steps hurrying. A shadow loomed in front of her, and someone grabbed her hands.

Nick. She recognized him before she lifted the light to his face.

"I thought you were going to wait by the car," he said, his voice resigned. His fingers clasped her wrists lightly.

"I saw someone coming from this direction." The words spilled out in her relief. "It was T. J. Blackburn. I thought he might have been in the house, and if you surprised him—"

"He would have attacked me? Your imagination is getting ahead of you. Why would T.J. want to vandalize Blackburn House, given the way his grandfather feels about it?"

"I didn't think of that," she admitted. "But it could have been payback against me." She caught his questioning look. "I walked in on a petting party between him and Krysta. He didn't like it."

"I can imagine." Nick's face was a frowning mask in the dim light, all lines and shadows. "Well, the circuit breaker was tripped, but I couldn't get it to go back into the on position. I guess you'd better have an electrician take a look at it. Do you want me to call someone?"

"Thanks." A breeze hit her, and she shivered. "And thanks for checking it out for me."

"No problem. As for T.J...." He hesitated. "He could have been taking a shortcut from the alley to the street.

I didn't see any obvious signs of break-in. I'll mention it to Mac."

"Maybe you'd better wait until I see what the electrician says." She could imagine that no one would be eager to accuse Thomas Blackburn's grandson without proof.

Nick nodded, looking dissatisfied. He was probably wishing she'd never shown up to complicate life in Laurel Ridge.

She shivered again. "I should go in."

"Right." He put his arm around her shoulders, as if to warm her. But he didn't move toward the inn. Instead, he stood, looking into her face.

There it was again—that hitch in her breath, the thump of her heart in her chest, as if something important had just happened. Or was going to happen.

His face lowered to hers. Slowly, giving her time to pull back. She should. But she didn't.

His lips found hers, and the chill she'd felt was replaced by heat that spread through her. She wasn't going to respond, but she couldn't seem to keep herself from clutching the front of his jacket, from leaning into him. His arms tightened around her, pressing her against his chest, and she didn't know whether it was her own heartbeat she heard or his.

Nick yanked away from her, and the cool air struck her like a splash of cold water.

"Sorry," he muttered. Grabbing her elbow as if she were an old lady he was helping across the street, he piloted her toward the bed-and-breakfast.

When they reached the porch steps she pulled her arm free. "I can make it from here." She gave him a meaningless smile, not sure whether she was gratified, humiliated or just embarrassed. "Good night."

"Nope, not as simple as flipping a circuit breaker, that's for sure." The electrician Nick had contacted was probably about Nick's age, with faded jeans, a Penn State T-shirt and a baseball cap worn backward.

"I appreciate your getting here so early. Can you fix it before the offices open?" Allison stood on the bottom cellar step, careful not to touch anything. Nick had been right—she'd never have made it down these uneven stone stairs in the dark wearing heels. Ahead of her, a corridor stretched dimly into the distance, fading from view as it went. It was intersected every few yards by massive stone pillars that presumably held up the rest of Blackburn House.

"Sure, I can do a temporary fix." Tim Elliott of Elliott's Electric shone his work light on a section of wire leading from the circuit box. "You can see where the insulation is worn away from the wires. I'll get you back in business in half an hour or so."

She studied the cable. It looked as if something had been chewing at it. "Did it just break through? Or could something or someone cause it?"

He shot her a quick, intelligent glance. "Vandalism? Nick asked me to keep a lookout for anything like that."

Nick seemed to have been sharing a bit too much. Still, how else would she know the cause?

"And what do you think?"

He shrugged. "It's almost impossible to say. The cable was in bad shape, anyway, and there's no obvious sign of tampering. But it could be done. Stick something under the cable where it's attached to the wall and give a good yank, and you'd get the same effect."

So it could have been a nasty trick played by someone

who wanted to mess with her, but there was no proof. Allison shifted her focus to another problem.

"You said you could do a temporary fix. Why not permanent?"

"Take a look around." He swung his lamp in a circular movement, illuminating one dank, dusty wall after another. "No electricity when this place was built. It was put in later and tinkered with over the years. I took a quick look at the records before I came over, and the last time we did any substantial work here was close to thirty years ago. With all the electronic gadgets in use upstairs, what the system needs is a complete overhaul, not more tinkering."

"That sounds expensive." Allison seemed to feel the weight of the building pressing down on her.

He shrugged. "You can get a couple estimates before you decide. Meantime, I'll get you up and running."

That sounded like an invitation to her to get out of his way. She went gladly enough, edging her way up the steps and out into a cool, cloudy April morning. She stood for a moment, eyeing Blackburn House as it loomed over her. An overhaul of the electrical system would be a major expense. Litwhiler had mentioned funds available for repairs and maintenance. She'd have to talk with him about exactly what that would cover.

White elephant. The words came unbidden to her mind. The house could so easily become a money pit. That's what she'd thought from the beginning.

A car pulled into the parking area beside the workshop. Nick's car. Allison spun and headed around the building for the front door. She had no intention of running into Nick until she was sure she could do it without last night's kiss foremost in her mind. And that could take a while.

The power was back on in less than the promised half hour, and Blackburn House returned to business as usual. Allison settled down to peruse the contents of the next file drawer in Evelyn's office.

It was midmorning when she came up for air, aware that her stomach was complaining. She'd stinted on breakfast because she'd been meeting the electrician so early. Maybe Sarah would like to join her for a coffee and a snack from the bakery.

Allison skirted around a middle-aged couple making their way up the stairs, probably to call at one of the offices. She nodded, and they both stared at her, the woman turning her head to watch as Allison went down the steps. Obviously her celebrity or notoriety, whichever it was, hadn't worn off yet.

Sarah greeted her with a smile. "I hoped you'd stop in soon. Did you have a nice time last night?"

"Last night?" Allison felt her cheeks warm. Sarah couldn't know about that kiss, could she?

"Having supper at Jim and Ellen Whiting's." Sarah brushed off a bit of the fabric fluff that inevitably was attracted to her dress. "My little brother saw you go by."

"Yes, right." She tried to close the door of her thoughts on Nick. It didn't work. "Nick pointed out where you live. I had a lovely time with them." And nobody needed to know about the lovely time she'd had outside in the dark. "I thought I'd bring back a coffee or tea from the bakery. Do you want anything?"

"I'll save you the trip." Sarah beckoned her toward the back room. "I brought a shoofly pie from home, and it won't take a minute to put the teakettle on the gas ring."

"Sounds great if you're sure I'm not interrupting you."

Sarah shook her head. "I'll get the kettle on. By the way, there's some mail for you. I put it beside the cash register."

Allison detoured to pick up the mail tucked under the edge of the cash register. That was one of the oddities of Amish life she'd noticed—Sarah used a modern phone and an electric cash register in the shop, but the small fridge and tabletop burners in the back room were gas. She had yet to figure out how the rules for being Amish worked. Sarah probably wouldn't be offended if she asked, but Allison hated to admit her ignorance.

She picked up the single envelope, frowning at it. Her name, in care of the quilt shop, was typed, not computer generated, which seemed odd. Who used a typewriter any longer? She ripped open the envelope to find a single page written in a small, tight hand. Glancing at the bottom, she checked the signature line. *Your grandmother, Evelyn Standish.*

Allison took a startled step back, bumped into the counter, and stayed there, staring at the handwriting.

Dear Allison,
You will be surprised to hear from me after so many years of silence.

That was putting it mildly. Allison's immediate reaction was to rip up the letter and toss it in the wastepaper basket.

She didn't, of course. She smoothed out the page and began to read.

I'm sure you're also surprised that I have decided to leave you something in my will, after having ignored you for so many years. Having ascertained that your stepfather is well-off, I had not intended to, but I've begun to feel that would be unfair to you. You are hardly responsible for the fact that Hugh was such an unsatisfactory son. I put up with his foolishness for as long as I could, but when his actions bordered on the criminal, I had to draw the line. I'm sure anyone would agree that my actions were justified, and I could hardly be expected to welcome his subsequent marriage or the arrival of a granddaughter I'd never see.

Allison's fingers tightened on the fine, monogrammed stationery. So Hugh had been an unsatisfactory son. He'd been an unsatisfactory father, too, but that didn't mean she wanted to hear anyone else condemn him. She nearly tossed the letter aside, but she couldn't quite do that.

As I look back on my life, I realize that my greatest regret was never having put my pride aside in order to have a relationship with my only granddaughter. I hope this bequest may help to make up for my actions in some small way.

It was signed formally. *Your grandmother, Evelyn Standish*. Well, at least she'd been wise enough not to presume on a relationship that had never existed by signing it Grandmother.

She'd been wondering what made Evelyn Standish decide to leave something to her. Now she knew. The tone of the letter was that of an old woman looking back at her life and attempting to justify her choices. But there was also an underlying sorrow that wouldn't allow Allison to dismiss it too readily.

Odd, that Evelyn hadn't left the letter with her attorney for delivery to her. Instead, she'd apparently entrusted it to someone with instructions to post it after Allison had arrived in Laurel Ridge.

What if she hadn't come? Would she ever have seen it?

Shaking her head, Allison started to slide the letter back into the envelope, but she noticed something written on the back.

She unfolded it again. The pen strokes were uneven and sprawled, as if the postscript had been added hurriedly. The addition was dated, and she realized with a sense of shock that it had been added just a few days before Evelyn's death.

My dear Allison,
It is only fair to mention that some things about Blackburn House have disturbed me in recent days. Perhaps *worried* would be a better word. I'm not sure what is going on, but I expect to find out shortly. I only hope I can resolve this, so that your inheritance won't cause you more trouble than pleasure.

So something had bothered Evelyn, presumably during the last weeks of her life. Something to do with prowlers in the building? Or something else entirely that Allison couldn't begin to guess at?

Carrying the letter, she hurried to the back room, where Sarah had a kettle boiling, sending up gentle puffs of steam. Sarah was cutting wedges from the golden-brown, crumbly shoofly pie. She looked up, and something in Allison's face seemed to arrest her attention.

"Allison? Is something wrong?"

Allison fluttered the page in her hand. "This letter is from my grandmother. Did she ask you to mail it for her?"

Sarah's lips formed an *oh* of surprise. "No. I had no idea she wrote to you." Her face seemed to clear. "I'm glad that she wanted to communicate with you, even if it was only in a letter. Does it answer any of your questions?"

Allison frowned, wondering how much to say. But that was silly. She could trust Sarah, and if she expected to learn anything from her, she'd have to.

"I suppose, in a way. She talks about regretting that she'd never gotten to know me."

"*Ach*, that's good. I'm glad."

"But that's not all." Allison frowned down at the paper. "She's added a postscript. I'd like for you to read it and see if it means anything to you." She held it out to Sarah.

Sarah, seeming perplexed, took the letter. Her head bent as she read it.

When she looked up again, Sarah's expression struck Allison like a blow. Sarah's face had gone white, and her eyes darkened. The paper quivered in her hand.

"Sarah?" Allison grabbed her arm. "What is it? You know something, don't you?"

"I…I thought it was nothing. But if she wrote that to you…" Sarah stopped, took a deep breath and nodded. "The last day, when she came into the shop, I could see your *grossmammi* was worried. I asked her if I could help. She said no. She said there was something wrong here, in Blackburn House, and that she meant to get to the bottom of it. She said that by the next day, she'd know what she ought to do."

Allison felt as if she couldn't breathe. "What did she say? That next day? What did she tell you?"

"Nothing." Sarah shook her head, her eyes wide. "The next morning, when the custodian came to open the building, he found her. She was lying at the bottom of the stairs." Her gaze flickered toward the central staircase. "She was dead."

Allison grabbed the counter to steady herself. "But I was told she died from a stroke." That was what the attorney had said, what the obituary had said.

"The doctors said she probably had a stroke while she was on the stairs and fell. No one ever hinted at anything different. But I...I wondered."

An elderly woman, a stroke, a fall. No one would question it.

But clearly Sarah did. And she did.

She had to talk this through with Sarah. Had to find out exactly what the coroner had thought. Had to find out what it was that worried her grandmother about Blackburn House. Because if it had something to do with her grandmother's death, she couldn't just walk away. Maybe they hadn't had a relationship, but however much she might resent her grandmother's actions, she wouldn't think much of herself if she didn't do what she could.

One thing became obvious. She wouldn't be leaving Laurel Ridge anytime soon.

CHAPTER SEVEN

ALLISON'S THOUGHTS HAD stopped their useless spinning by the time she sat opposite Sarah at the table in the small back room of the quilt shop, a mug of tea cradled in her hands. Sarah pushed the plate of shoofly pie toward her.

"You should eat something. You've had a shock."

Allison managed a smile. "Is food the universal remedy among the Amish?"

"That's certain sure." Sarah's concerned expression eased a little. "But it only makes sense, ain't so? You can always face trouble better if you're not hungry or tired."

If that was the case, she should have been eating steadily since she arrived in Laurel Ridge. But Allison took a bite of the molasses-rich pie, figuring it was easier than arguing. Besides, she wanted Sarah relaxed enough to answer her questions. The need to know, to do something, pounded at her, but she suspected that rushing Sarah would accomplish nothing. She had yet to see Sarah hurry at anything, but she accomplished a great deal. Did all the Amish take such a steady approach to life? Or were some of them like her, propelled forward by the need to act?

As Allison took a sip of the fragrant tea, some of her tension eased. The room behind the shop was small to begin with, and seemed even smaller with the sheer amount of stuff it held. In addition to the table and tiny kitchen area, the room was lined with shelves holding, she'd guess, everything that Sarah didn't have room for in the shop—a sewing machine, bolts of fabric, spools of binding, boxes of quilt batting. An entire shelf was taken up by books on quilting.

Sarah saw the direction of her gaze. "My *grossmammi* taught me to quilt the traditional Amish patterns, but with all the *Englisch* customers we have, I decided I needed to educate myself about different kinds of quilting." She smiled. "Besides, it fascinates me."

"I can see why." Allison took another sip, letting its warmth soothe her. "Did my grandmother have an interest in actually making quilts?"

Sarah shook her head. "She always said she didn't have the patience." She hesitated, seeming to steel herself. "It's all right. I know you want to ask me questions about Evelyn's dying. You'd best go ahead."

Allison nodded. Sarah seemed more shaken about discussing her grandmother's death than Allison did. But that was hardly surprising. She had actually known and liked Evelyn Standish.

"Did my grandmother give you any hint of how she thought she was going to get an explanation for whatever was troubling her? She must have had some specific plan, if she said that she expected to have answers by the next day."

"That's so. Evelyn always had a plan." Worry lines appeared between Sarah's eyebrows, marring the usual serenity of her face. "She didn't really say so, but I had the impression she was going to talk to someone. But I suppose she might have been getting information some other way, ain't so?"

"True, but let's assume for the moment that she did

plan to talk to someone. Did anything about her words or attitude hint at whether it might be a man or a woman?"

"No, no. Nothing so definite." Sarah pushed the idea away with her hands. "But she was here. In Blackburn House, I mean. Here when she told me, and here when she died." Sarah's gesture took in the building around them.

"She might have planned to talk to someone in the building, then. Or she might have asked someone to meet her here after hours for a private talk." Someone who might not want to be seen having a private conversation with Evelyn? That was possible, but it didn't seem to lead anywhere.

"If it was someone in the building," Sarah began, her voice hesitant, "well, couldn't she talk to them anytime? She wouldn't have to come back late in the evening for it."

Actually, the same logic applied. "If they wanted privacy, meeting after hours might be the best solution." She frowned. This didn't seem to be going anywhere. "It could be something other than meeting someone here, I suppose," she said, thinking aloud. "She might have intended to do some research on the computer, or go through her files." She stopped, a spark striking. "Or go through someone else's files. She'd have had keys to all the businesses, right?"

"But Evelyn wouldn't go through someone else's things." Sarah looked horrified at the thought.

"She might if she thought someone was doing something illegal in Blackburn House. Or even something unethical," Allison said. "She apparently had pretty high standards." High enough that she'd broken the bonds with her only son when she'd caught him doing something wrong. Or maybe because he wouldn't stop acting in a way that ran counter to her ethics.

Her mother had never spoken of her father's rift with his family, except to say that there'd probably been wrong on both sides. Allison suspected it hadn't been easy for her mother to maintain that attitude, but just as she'd never criticized her father to Allison, she'd never complained about his mother. It had frustrated Allison when she was young, but as an adult, she had to admire it.

"I suppose," Sarah said, doubt in her voice. "But I don't see how you'll be able to find out."

"I haven't figured that part out yet," Allison admitted. "Tell me something. If you were as upset as you say, why didn't you talk to the police about your feelings?"

Sarah's frown deepened, and she traced a circle on the tabletop with her finger. "I don't know if you can understand. It's something engrained in the Amish, maybe because our people were persecuted for so many years. We obey the laws, but we don't seek out *Englisch* justice. For an Amish woman to go to the police..." She held out her hands, palms up. "It's just not done."

Sarah was right. She didn't understand it. "But to withhold information from the police is wrong."

Sarah shook her head. "I wouldn't do that. If Mac had asked me anything, I'd have told the truth. But it seemed so clear to everyone what had happened, and the doctor said it was an accident. The police were satisfied."

The police, in this case, meaning Mac Whiting. She was used to thinking of police in terms of investigation teams, forensic specialists and all the paraphernalia she assumed accompanied a death in an urban area. Police work was clearly different in a place like Laurel Ridge.

She studied the serene oval that was Sarah's face, not-

ing the steadfast quality of the blue eyes that met hers
calmly, waiting. Sarah believed what she believed, and
arguments wouldn't change her.

"I can see why you wouldn't want to speak to the police with nothing to back you up," she said carefully. "But
now there's the letter my grandmother sent. If I were to
show it to Mac Whiting, may I tell him that Evelyn also
spoke to you?"

Sarah considered for a moment. Then she nodded.
"If Mac comes to me with questions, it's only right that
I answer them."

"Good." Allison was aware of a wave of relief. She
wasn't going to be the only one rocking the boat. "I can't
ignore it. Maybe I never had a relationship with her, but
she was my grandmother. I have to do something." That
letter, harsh as it was in places, had made her understand
the woman, at least a little.

Sarah nodded. "I understand." She hesitated a second.
"Does this mean that you are going to stay?"

Allison struggled with the answer to that question.
Was she going to stay? There was so much involved—
her career, her apartment in Philadelphia, her friends
there, the future she envisioned for herself. How could
she just walk away from all of it?

"I'm not saying I'll stay for the whole year," she said.
"Brenda and Blackburn may still get what they want.
But as long as I don't know if they were involved in
my grandmother's death, I can't just walk away and let
them have the place." Maybe she'd inherited a bit of her
grandmother's stubborn will.

Sarah's gaze widened. "But you can't suspect either
of them of having something to do with Evelyn's death."

"Can't I?" Allison's hands clenched into fists. "You're

forgetting—I don't really know anyone in Laurel Ridge. I can't begin to guess what my grandmother found out. But I'm not going anywhere until I know the truth."

NICK FIGURED THE roar of the saw as he cut cabinet shelves ought to be loud enough to drown out his thoughts. Unfortunately, that didn't seem to be working. No matter what he did, his mind kept drifting back to the moment last night when he'd kissed Allison.

What had he been thinking? She was the last person on earth he had any business being attracted to. A woman like that, so like Sheila, would be trouble even if it weren't for the complication of her ownership of the building.

The trouble was that he hadn't been thinking at all—or at least not with his brain. She'd been so close, the dim light playing on her features, turning her into someone soft and mysterious and desirable—

Well, in the cool light of day he knew better. It was a mistake to get anywhere close to Allison Standish.

It shouldn't be too difficult to stay clear of her. After all, she probably regretted what had happened just as much as he did.

Now that his mother had discharged her duty to welcome Allison to Laurel Ridge, he could probably steer her away from any further invitations. Allison would make her decisions, clear up her business in Laurel Ridge and go back to that other life of hers.

Feeling satisfied, he switched off the saw, ran a cloth down the length of the shelf to remove the clinging sawdust and set it aside. Pulling off his safety glasses, he shook them free of dust and glanced across the shop.

And saw Allison, standing there talking to his father.

Nothing about his reaction to the sight of her gave him any hope that he was going to be able to ignore her. Dad gestured, waving him over.

He went, running a hand through his hair to get rid of the coating of sawdust. What difference did it make how he looked? He asked himself the question irritably, frowning at his father.

"Morning, Allison." He gave her the briefest of nods. "Listen, Dad, I want to finish up those cabinet doors—"

"Never mind that." Dad was smiling at Allison as if she were an old friend. First his son, now his father, acting as if Allison was the best thing they'd seen in a long while. "Allison's decided to renovate the apartment on the second floor. She wants our advice on who to hire." Dad's eyes twinkled. "Naturally I told her we were the best people for the job."

Allison's glance at him wasn't nearly as warm as the one she turned on his father. "I thought perhaps it wasn't the kind of job you do," she said.

Giving him an out, maybe? Or herself?

"We can do it, okay." He certainly wasn't going to say they couldn't, just to get out of working with her. "We can set up the work with electricians and plumbers. But it depends on what all you want done."

"The kitchen and bath will have to be completely redone," she said, with what he thought was a little shudder. "And a decent-size closet put in the bedroom. Other than that, it'll be a matter of painting and possibly refinishing floors."

"I hope this means you're planning to stay." Dad's face warmed. "We'd be pleased to hear that."

"You'd probably be in a minority." Allison's gaze flickered to him for a brief second. "I'm not sure of anything yet, but I can't get away as soon as I'd thought, since…well, since the situation is so complicated." She looked as if that wasn't the way that sentence was supposed to end, and Nick's curiosity was piqued. He'd expected her to grab the money and run. What had changed?

"Renovation can be an expensive job." Dad's tone was doubtful. "If you're not going to live there, you might not want to sink that much into it."

"According to my grandmother's attorney, she left a substantial fund available to renovate the apartment. So it may as well be done. Even if I don't stay, it will increase the value of the building."

"That's so." His father was still gazing at her with a speculating look, but he didn't ask any more about it. "Why don't you make up a detailed list of what you want done, and then Nick can go over the place with you."

"Me?" He couldn't help the way that sounded. The last thing he needed was to be pushed into any tête-à-têtes with Allison.

"Of course you." Dad raised an eyebrow. "That's our deal, remember? You take over the business end."

"Yes, but—"

Before he could marshal any arguments, his father had turned away and grabbed his windbreaker off the hook. "I ordered hoagies for our lunch, so I better get over there and pick them up. Back in a few minutes."

He was gone, well beyond the reach of argument.

Not that it would have done any good, Nick knew. They had made a deal. He just hadn't anticipated it turning out this way.

Nick turned to Allison, fishing for a topic of conversation that avoided things like kissing in the moonlight. "The circuit breaker box is fixed, I take it?"

"Your friend took care of everything. Thanks for calling him." She hesitated, not meeting his eyes. "I asked him if someone could have caused the problem."

"I figured you would." He propped his hip against the side of a workbench and watched her face. Plenty of light in here, but she still looked just as appealing, with that creamy skin and the curving lips that begged to be kissed.

Allison frowned. "He said it was possible, but there was no way to be sure. So I guess I won't pursue it. I suppose that makes you happy."

"Not happy, no. If T.J. is causing trouble, I want to see him stopped. That boy is a little too smug for my tastes. But I'd hate to see you stir up a hornet's nest with Thomas Blackburn. I don't know what he feels for his grandson, but the Blackburn name is everything to him."

"I certainly won't do anything without proof." Her gaze seemed to lose focus for an instant, as if she were thinking of something else.

"Something wrong?"

"What?" She jerked her attention back to him. "No, not at all." Her face relaxed in a smile. "Well, not more than usual, anyway."

For a moment she hesitated, and he thought she was on the verge of saying something more.

But then she turned away. "I'll make up that list, and then we can go over the apartment."

"Right." Something was wrong, he could feel it. But if she didn't want to tell him, he couldn't force it. Besides, he didn't want to get involved, remember?

Allison took a step toward the door and then paused,

reaching out to touch the child-size combination desk and bookcase that stood waiting for the finishing touches.

"This is lovely. Is it for Jamie?"

He nodded, no more immune than anyone else to feeling pleasure at hearing his work praised. "His birthday is coming up, and he thinks he needs some 'big boy' furniture in his room." He stroked the curving edge of a shelf. "Lots of boy furniture available, decorated with every cartoon character and superhero you could imagine, but none of it very well made. I wanted something of quality for my son."

"Even though he'll outgrow it?"

He couldn't see anything but honest curiosity in her face as she looked at him, the desk between them. "Quality's important in a piece of furniture, no matter who it's for." It was important in other things, too, but he didn't think he wanted to discuss that with her. Talking to Allison seemed to end with him revealing more than he'd intended.

But judging by the way she looked at him, she'd already guessed what he meant.

ALLISON WENT BACK to Blackburn House after a visit to the police station that afternoon, wondering what good, if any, she'd done. Mac had been polite, professional and had promised to talk to Sarah. And all the while she'd had the feeling he thought she was making a fuss over nothing.

She'd had a nice walk, in any event. Her exercise routine had suffered since she'd been here, and there was really no excuse. Laurel Ridge might not have a fitness club, but she could always take a morning run.

There was the little fact that she didn't have running

clothes or shoes with her, among other things. Since her stay had been extended indefinitely, she really needed to return to Philadelphia, pack properly and deal with things there.

Allison mounted the steps to the porch. Someone, maybe the custodian but more likely Sarah, had planted pansies in the massive urns on either side of the steps. Their cheerful faces seemed to turn toward Allison as she went up.

She reached to the door handle and paused, because Sarah stood on the other side of the door, taping a poster advertising something called Spring Fest. Sarah smiled, stuck down the last bit of tape and pushed the door open.

"Sorry. The posters were just delivered, and I wanted to get them up right away." Sarah held several more posters over her arm, and the door to the quilt shop already bore one. "Spring Fest is next Saturday, so these should go up right away."

"What's Spring Fest?" Should she warn Sarah that Mac didn't seem to be taking seriously their concerns about Evelyn's death?

"*Ach*, it's a big celebration." Sarah's blue eyes sparkled. "They close down Main Street to traffic, and all the clubs and organizations have booths. There are craft stands and food stands. You can get your weight guessed or shoot baskets for a prize or—"

"I don't think I want my weight guessed." Allison found it impossible to resist Sarah's enthusiasm. "I take it Spring Fest is a big deal in Laurel Ridge."

"Sounds silly to you, I guess," Sarah said, her good nature not impaired. "You're used to the city, where things are happening all the time. Here, folks get to feeling trapped at the end of a long winter. They love cutting loose a bit at Spring Fest."

"Do we... Does Blackburn House, that is, have a part in all the festivities?" She asked the question with some trepidation, wondering what she might be getting into. "Not a dunking booth or a pie-eating contest or anything, is it?"

Sarah actually giggled at the thought. "No, we save those for the Harvest Fest. We sponsor the Jumble Sale to benefit the Volunteer Fire Department." Her face sobered all at once. "At least, we always have. Your grandmother thought it important, but if you don't want to..."

"I wouldn't change a thing," Allison assured her. At least not about a Jumble Sale, whatever that might be. Probably like the yard sales that blossomed in the suburbs on warm Saturdays.

"Good." Relief showed on Sarah's face. "I wouldn't want to disappoint the fire volunteers."

"I guess we'd better stay on their good side," Allison said. She hesitated, but Sarah should be prepared for a visit from the police. "I talked to Mac Whiting about..." She hesitated. A public hall was probably not the best place for this conversation. "Well, you know. He'll want to ask you some questions."

Sarah nodded, her eyes seeming to darken at the thought.

"He was polite, but I don't think he took it very seriously. Still, I'm not going to let it drop."

Sarah eyed her face, as if measuring her determination. "But if he says there's nothing in it, what can you do?"

"I don't know," she admitted. "But I'll have to do something."

Her voice had risen a bit in emphasis, and she realized too late that Nick was coming down the stairs.

"Do something about what?" he asked.

Sarah looked instantly guilty, and Allison spoke quickly.

"About those doors into the attic. I don't like the idea that anyone can get up there."

"You need dead bolts," Nick said. "I'll put them up for you."

His automatic assumption that he would take charge annoyed her. "That's not necessary. I can get someone—"

"You don't need to," he said with exaggerated patience. "That's the kind of thing neighbors do. Right, Sarah?"

Sarah, looking alarmed at being drawn in, nodded. With a murmured excuse, she vanished into the quilt shop.

"Anyway, you're hiring us to do the work on the apartment, aren't you? We'll throw that in. I was just looking for you about that, in fact." He held up a clipboard. "If you have time to show me what you want done in the apartment, we'll get an estimate ready."

Allison took a breath and counted to ten. "Yes. Right. We can do that now." She spun and started up the stairs, waving at Ralph, who had come to the door of the bookshop and was undoubtedly listening. "I hope he heard enough," she muttered under her breath.

"Don't mind Ralph," Nick said, keeping pace with her on the stairs. "I never do. If it makes him feel important to know what we're working on, that's fine with me."

They'd nearly reached the top of the stairs. Allison glanced down, but the curve of the stairwell cut off her view of the bookshop. "Well, he's also heard all about Sarah's plans for the Jumble Sale," she said. Ralph couldn't have heard what she'd said about seeing the police, could he?

Nick chuckled low in his throat. "Poor Ralph. He has to pretend to support it, but he hates the Jumble Sale."

"Hates it? Why?" She made the mistake of looking into Nick's face. With laughter lines radiating from his eyes and that amused quirk to his lips, he was just a bit too attractive. She focused on getting out her keys, hoping he hadn't noticed.

"Ralph hates the Jumble Sale because so many people bring in books. Basically all the readers in town pass them around through the sale. They could just give them to each other, but this way the fire company benefits. Anyway, Ralph figures it cuts into his sales, because nobody will be looking for something new to read for a few weeks."

"I can understand that, I suppose." She found the right key and inserted it in the lock. "Independent booksellers don't have an easy time of it with all the online stores, as well as the chains, competing for their business. I'm surprised he's as successful as he is."

"People are used to Ralph." Nick seemed to check out the fit of the door as he opened it. "He knows everyone's tastes, so he can order in books he knows will sell. And he's always willing to deliver for those who can't get out. People here appreciate that, so they support him even when they might buy cheaper elsewhere." They stepped into the living room of the apartment, and Nick sent a quick look around the room, probably assessing what he had to deal with. "It's not in bad shape, considering."

"Wait until you've seen the kitchen."

But Allison had to agree with him on the apartment

in general terms. The high-ceilinged rooms were well proportioned, and the tall windows let in plenty of light. The woodwork throughout was the same fine quality as in the rest of the building, and the living room boasted a small fireplace with an elegantly carved mantel. She might seldom decorate anything in this Victorian style, but that didn't mean she couldn't appreciate it.

Evelyn apparently hadn't chosen to rent the apartment in some time, but it had received the same thoughtful attention as the rest of Blackburn House.

"Any changes to be made in this room?" Nick held a pen poised over the clipboard.

"Just painting. I'd love to see it papered in a period style, but most renters prefer neutral paint."

Nick shrugged. "There's a team of Amish painters who could do either for you, and Nelson's Hardware has a wallpaper and paint selection. Why don't you suit yourself?"

"Because this is business, not personal." She could understand his view, after having seen the comfortable old farmhouse filled with the objects his family had loved over the years, but she didn't intend to settle down for life at Blackburn House. "Isn't there a chain home improvement store anywhere in the area? I could probably get a better deal there."

Nick held the pen in abeyance, frowning. "You could drive to Lancaster, but you'd be better off buying local."

"Why? If I can get a better deal—"

"Ever hear of goodwill?" He interrupted her, exasperation in his tone. "Look, this is a small town, and Blackburn House is an institution here. People will be offended if you take your business elsewhere."

Allison had to bite her tongue to keep from snapping back at him. The trouble was that he made a certain amount of sense. Her position here was precarious at best. There was little point in making enemies if she could make friends, and Mr. Litwhiler would release the funds no matter where she bought.

"Okay." She managed a smile. "I see your point. Do you make a habit of being right?"

Nick grinned. "When I can. Now, what about this kitchen?"

He listened to her complaints about the outdated kitchen, making notes and not venturing an opinion. Allison stopped in the middle of a lecture on the proper distance between the appliances.

"Are you humoring me, by any chance?" she asked.

"My dad gave me a valuable piece of advice when he took me into the business. Never argue with a woman about a kitchen." His eyes laughed at her. "I plan to pass that on to my son, as well."

"Do you expect Jamie to come into business with you?" She couldn't help the tinge of criticism in her voice. If he didn't want more for himself, she'd think he'd want more for his son.

"Jamie will do whatever he wants," Nick said. "If he'd rather fly a plane or argue a case in court than build a kitchen, I'll back him all the way." He paused, his face growing serious, and she realized he wasn't finished. "As far as what he'll be—I can't say better than what my parents said to me and to Mac. Be kind, be honorable, always do what's right, no matter the cost."

She discovered quite suddenly that there was a lump in her throat. "That sounds like something my stepfather would say."

Nick studied her face, as if searching for a clue to her feelings. "Are you close to him?"

"I suppose so." But not as close as her parents would have wanted. If she could have satisfied them about that, taken Dennis's name as they'd wanted her to, would that have made a difference? Maybe then she'd have stopped feeling like a "step" instead of a member of the family.

But at eleven, when the subject had come up, she hadn't seen it that way. All she'd been able to feel was that she ought to stand up for her real father, because no one else would.

Her cell rang, cutting off anything else she might have said. "My mother," she said. "She must have known I was thinking about them."

"Go ahead." Nick pulled out a metal tape measure. "I'll take these measurements while you're talking."

She pressed the phone button. "I just have a minute, Mom. I'm with someone. Can I call you back this evening?"

"As long as you promise to do it." Her mother's voice came as warmly over the phone as if she were here instead of in Denver. "I want to tell you about our spring break ski trip. And hear about—" there was a faint hesitation in her mother's voice "—about your visit to Laurel Ridge. Are you back home yet?"

"Not yet. Some things came up. I'll tell you all about it tonight, I promise." But it would be a carefully censored version. There was no point in opening old wounds for her mother.

"Okay. Love you, sweetheart. And love from Dennis and the boys."

"Same to them. I hope you had a great trip."

"Wonderful, but we missed you. I'm sending a picture," her mother added.

She clicked off and brought up the photo. The four of them, skis propped up beside them, leaning their heads together and laughing with a snowy mountain in the background. A happy family.

It was no one's fault but hers that she'd always felt like that odd man out. Everyone said how lucky she was to have a great guy like Dennis for her stepdad. And he was a great guy. But when she looked at Mom and Dennis and the twins, all she could think was that they were a whole family without her.

Allison slipped the phone back in her pocket. Nick seemed intent on his measurements, pretending he hadn't heard her side of the call.

Had he thought about what it would be like for Jamie if he remarried? The thought made her uncomfortable. It certainly wasn't any of her business, was it?

Nick straightened, snapping the tape closed. "If we can go through the rest of the apartment now, I can get an estimate to you in an hour or so. We'll want to apply for the permit right away so we can get started next week."

"That's fine." She was restless suddenly, eager to get moving. She seized on the idea that popped into her mind. "I'll be leaving early tomorrow, anyway. I'm going back to Philadelphia for a day or two."

She saw the surprise in Nick's face. Well, she'd surprised herself, too. But she had to go sometime to pack up what she needed and make a decision about her apartment in the city. And maybe putting a few miles between herself and Laurel Ridge, with all its problems, would settle her.

CHAPTER EIGHT

"DID YOU GET everything done that you wanted to in Philadelphia over the weekend?" Sarah asked Allison Tuesday morning. She shifted the box she was carrying so that she could unlock the door to the storage area. "I was worried when you weren't here yesterday."

"I couldn't complete subletting my apartment until Monday." Allison followed Sarah into the storeroom and stacked the box she was carrying on top of an existing pile. "Where did all this stuff come from?" She glanced around at the boxes and bags that cluttered the storage area.

"Things for the Jumble Sale." Sarah balanced her box carefully on the top of a teetering stack. "They'll likely overflow into the hall before the week is out." Maybe seeing the distaste in Allison's face, she hurried on. "It will just be for a few days. Spring Fest is Saturday, and afterward volunteers will pack up the leftovers and haul them to the Salvation Army store."

Allison bent and picked up the item on top of an opened box. "People will buy this? Seriously?" She gestured with a dented saucepan.

"For sure." Sarah's eyes sparkled with laughter. "People can't resist the idea of getting a bargain. And if you need an extra saucepan, even just to dip oats for the horses, you don't care if it has a dent."

"I'll take your word for it." Allison followed her out of the storeroom and watched while Sarah locked it again. "I brought so much back from Philly that poor Mrs. Anderson probably thinks I'm planning to have a jumble sale in my room."

"I'm sure she doesn't mind. She's glad enough to have a guest at all this time of year." Sarah smoothed down the green apron that matched her dress. "And you—did you get a good tenant for your place in the city?"

"I hope so. It's a young woman from my friend Leslie's office, so Leslie will keep an eye on things." She'd been fortunate to have the sublet fall into place so easily.

"Sehr gut." Sarah smiled. "Very good, I mean."

Allison responded absently. There'd been an envelope waiting for her at her apartment, containing a check and a note from her former boss. Former friend, as well.

Your salary for the rest of the month, as well as the bonus you earned on the Naismith job. When you decide to return, there's always a place for you. Don't mess up your career for a guy. He's not worth it.

Di had been generous. And maybe a bit guilty. But her comment about Greg had been on target, Allison realized. She certainly hadn't spent much of the past week mourning his loss, maybe because she'd never risked caring that much for him. Was that a reflection on his inability to inspire love or her own failure to trust it?

Running footsteps interrupted a futile train of thought as Jamie scurried toward them from the cabinetry showroom.

"Hi, Ally. I'm glad you're back." He flung his arms around her in an impetuous hug.

"I am, too." She returned the hug, irrationally gratified. "But what are you doing here? Don't you have school today?"

Jamie rubbed the front of his cartoon character T-shirt. "I had a tummy ache this morning, and Grammy had to go somewhere, so I came to work with Daddy."

"If you're well enough to pester Sarah and Allison, you must be well enough to go back to school this afternoon." Nick emerged from the showroom, regarding his son with mock severity.

"If I have to eat in the lunchroom I'll be sick again," Jamie announced, eyeing his father to see how that went.

"*Ach*, he's no bother at all," Sarah said. "And I know just what you need, Jamie. I have some of my *mamm*'s homemade chicken noodle soup in my little refrigerator. When you feel like eating something, I'll heat it up for you. All right?"

Jamie nodded with enthusiasm, while Nick shook his head.

"Spoiling him, that's what you're doing."

"Seems to me I remember you liking *Mamm*'s chicken soup pretty well yourself when you were his age." Sarah spoke with the comfortable certainty of one who'd known Nick too long to be impressed.

Nick grinned, as if conceding the point. He turned to Allison. "Have a good weekend?"

"Fine." She assumed that was just a polite way of getting down to business. "Will you be able to start work on the renovations this week?"

"Should be. And I finished securing the attic accesses." He pulled a ring of keys from his pocket and handed them to her. "There are four, one in each corner of the building. And you'll need to keep the keys some-place where the tenants can get to them. Most of us have things stored up there."

"Repair people need to go up sometimes, too," Sarah added. "What about in the storeroom on the board with the other keys? No one can get in the storeroom but the tenants, so they should be safe."

Allison nodded, remembering the board just inside the storeroom where marked keys dangled from hooks. "Fine. I'll put them there and let everyone know." She was actually beginning to feel like a landlord when she said things like that.

"We can't start tearing out the old kitchen until we have the permit," Nick continued. "My father went down to the clerk's office to get it. He should be back soon."

"I thought Daniel was picking it up yesterday," Sarah put in.

Daniel. That would be the Amish youth Allison had seen helping Nick's father in the workshop.

Nick frowned. "He went by, but the clerk said there had been some delay. That's why Dad went himself. He hates bureaucratic paperwork with a passion, so he's probably blowing off steam right now."

"I'm sure he'll straighten it out," Sarah said.

Nick nodded. "Anyway, Ally, you can come to the showroom anytime and pick out what you want for the kitchen cabinets."

Allison blinked at the familiar nickname, not sure she wanted to hear it from Nick. Wouldn't it be better to stay on more formal terms with her tenants? She caught Jamie's smile and returned it. On the other hand, it was probably way too late for that.

Jamie's small face lit as he looked past her toward the stairwell. "You brought your cat! Cool!" He darted toward Hector, who paused on the third step from the bottom as if waiting for applause.

"I hope no one's allergic." Besides, having Hector here made the place feel a bit more hers.

"Careful," Nick warned his son. "He doesn't like people."

Hector carefully sniffed the hand Jamie held out for inspection. Then he rubbed his head against Jamie's hand in a clear invitation. A moment later he was seated in Jamie's lap.

Nick surveyed them. "Okay, maybe it's just me that he doesn't like."

"Actually he doesn't usually respond so well to strangers." Allison smiled at Jamie. "Jamie must be a very special person."

"Must be," Nick said, sending her a meaningful glance. "Or maybe it's because he hasn't been used as a battering ram against Jamie."

She smiled, refusing to be drawn.

"Here comes Jim now." Sarah nodded to the door as Jim Whiting came in.

"Everything go okay?" Nick asked.

His father gave a grunt of assent and waved a piece of pink paper. "Got it, anyway. But not without a struggle. Clerk was determined to be obstructive."

"Inefficient, more likely," Nick said. "He didn't want to admit he'd been lax."

"Nope." Jim turned to affix the pink certificate to the front window. "It wasn't that at all. I can see as far as the next man. He'd been told to slow it down. So I just told him to speed it up instead if he wanted to keep his job."

"Told to slow it down?" Allison echoed the words, trying to make sense of them. "But I don't understand. Why? Who?"

Jim exchanged glances with his son. "He wouldn't say, but I can guess. There's only one person who wants Blackburn House badly enough to throw roadblocks in front of anyone who wants to make changes. Thomas Blackburn."

To Allison's surprise, Nick and Sarah both nodded as if it were a foregone conclusion.

"But...he can't do that, can he?"

"He can't succeed," Jim said with satisfaction. "That doesn't mean he won't try."

Thomas Blackburn. It made sense. She could easily imagine him intimidating a clerk to do his bidding.

If he would do that, what else might he have done? How much did he want Blackburn House? And how deep had the enmity between him and Evelyn Standish gone?

"TELL ME THE style you want for the kitchen, and I'll show you the cabinets that best fit." Nick had always found that the simplest method of cutting down on the practically endless choices available.

Allison, seated next to him at the round table in the showroom the next day, frowned at the loose-leaf notebook filled with images of kitchens. Nick thought he could guess what she'd want—a modern, sleek kitchen with gray granite countertops and stainless-steel appliances. Eighty percent of the people who sat here talking about kitchens did—influenced by television shows and glossy magazines. And since she decorated houses for a living, she'd probably want the latest of everything for herself.

Still frowning, Allison flipped over a page, then another. "It's important that the kitchen fit in with the style of the building. I don't see anything here—"

Suppressing his astonishment, Nick closed the book. "Forget this, then. Just talk to me about what you want. If you're really going back to the 1880s, the kitchen might not be too functional. Unless you have a maid, butler and cook, of course."

He'd surprised her into a smile that made her eyes sparkle, reminding him of sunlight dancing on the surface of a rippling stream.

"I don't think we need to go that far. No need for washstands and kerosene lamps. I'd settle for a style that doesn't scream reproduction but that can exist harmoniously with the high ceilings and window moldings."

"No stainless steel and granite?" he asked. "That's what most people request."

"I guess I'm not most people, then." Her lips quirked in amusement. "Actually, if this were a gated community in a city suburb, I'd have to go with the expected."

"No room for something different there?"

Allison seemed to take the question seriously. "Those places are occupied for the most part by rising young professionals who don't expect to stay in one place for long. That's the pattern—stay for a couple of years, accept a transfer or a promotion and move. That means the house they buy has to be readily salable, so they decorate with that in mind."

"Makes sense for them, I guess." He'd never really thought of it that way. When people settled in Laurel Ridge, they expected to stay for a generation or two or three.

He reached out a long arm and pulled another sample book from the shelf. "Have a look at these, then. They're some kitchens we've done over the years in older houses."

Even as she opened the book, he plopped something else down in front of her. "And what about something like this for the countertops? This is quartz, so it has a lot of the same qualities as granite, but it's a lot warmer-looking."

Allison ran her hand over the smooth stone. "Nice. I've actually suggested it a few times, but people always want granite."

"Influence of television remodeling shows," he suggested.

"Most likely." She flipped through the book. "Let's make a decision on cabinet styles first, then I can decide about the quartz. Glass-fronted cabinets would be in keeping with the period of the house, wouldn't they?"

He nodded, putting his hand over hers to turn to the right page. "You're taking a lot of care over this, aren't you?"

"Of course." She glared at him. "You don't need to sound so surprised. As it happens, I value quality in my work, too."

"I don't doubt it," he said quickly, holding up his hands to defuse any argument. "I'm just here to take orders. It's your kitchen, and you're the boss."

She gave him a skeptical look. "Am I supposed to believe that?"

He grinned. "You can try."

Allison laughed with him, but then she seemed to sober, looking at him as if she measured him against some standard of her own. "Can I ask you something?"

He nodded, not sure where this was going.

"Do you think your father was right, and it was Thomas Blackburn who tried to throw a monkey wrench into the permit process?"

The sudden change of tone silenced him for a moment as he considered it. "Actually, my dad is usually right about things like that. The only other person who'd have a reason to want to disrupt your plans is Brenda, and I don't think she'd have the nerve. She's been making a valiant effort to replace Evelyn, but she knows she can't match Evelyn's influence."

Allison was studying his face. "If it was done to encourage me to give up and leave, it couldn't be any of the tenants, could it? Or do they want me to leave, too?"

He blinked. "Not us. After all, we're doing the renovation. We wouldn't be likely to torpedo it."

"I suppose not." She didn't sound totally convinced.

He looked at her, exasperated and not sure what would convince her. "Look, we wouldn't, that's all. And I don't think any of the other tenants would, either. What would be the point? To try and avoid an increase in rent?"

Allison's eyebrows lifted. "As I recall, you seemed to think Brenda would be easier to deal with than I would."

He smiled, trying to cover his embarrassment. He had said something like that. "I was just needling you. Anyway, it wouldn't be Brenda, would it? It would be Blackburn, and who knows what his plans for the building might be? He's so obsessed with the family name, he might do anything."

"How obsessed?" Her eyes seemed to darken, and he realized she was serious. "How far would he go to get hold of Blackburn House?"

"I don't know. That's the honest truth." He hesitated. "Look, it's obvious that you have something on your mind. If I can help…" He let that trail off, not sure what he was offering.

Allison was silent for a moment, staring down at her hands on the table. Then she lifted her gaze to his face.

"Sarah says you can be trusted."

"Sarah always tells the truth, but she might look at her friends through rose-colored glasses." And if Allison kept looking at him that way, he wasn't so sure he could trust himself.

She turned suddenly to take an envelope from her bag, hanging on the back of the chair. "I think I'd like you to read this, especially the postscript."

It was a letter from Evelyn. Whatever he'd expected, it wasn't that. "Where did this come from?"

She shook her head. "It just came in the mail. Obviously my grandmother gave it to someone to mail for her. I thought perhaps Sarah, but she says no."

He considered. "I would guess Julia Everly. She's probably the only person Evelyn would trust with it."

"I wondered about her. I think I'll talk to her. See if she knows anything. Assuming she's willing to tell me."

Nick couldn't help smiling. "I'd guess if she knows, she'll talk. Give you her opinion, as well."

He read the letter through slowly. It displayed all the qualities Evelyn had in such abundance—imperiousness, self-assurance, rigidity. But it also showed a willingness to confess regret and what might have been a longing to repair the past. Unfortunately one could never go back and do that.

Finally he read the postscript, frowning over it.

"Do you have any idea what she meant by that?" Allison sounded as if she needed an answer, but it was one he didn't have.

"Not a clue. If something was troubling her about Blackburn House, she didn't confide in me. Did she talk to Sarah?"

Allison nodded, her hair brushing her cheek. "She told Sarah that she'd uncovered something very troubling about someone in Blackburn House. Something that upset her. But she expected to get answers that evening, and by the next day, she'd know what to do." Allison's clasped hands tightened, her fingers straining against each other. "That was the night she died."

He could read what she was thinking in her face. "You think there was something malicious in what happened to her? But how could there be? She had a stroke." Another thought hit him. "Does Sarah think that?"

"It worried Sarah," Allison said, seeming to choose her words carefully. "She didn't feel she could talk to the police about it, but she wasn't satisfied."

"But the stroke—"

"If my grandmother had an altercation with someone on the stairs, if she was pushed or even if she fell on her own, the stroke could have been the result, not the cause."

He wanted to dismiss it. He wanted to say it couldn't have happened that way. But a small sliver of doubt in his mind wouldn't let him.

"I don't know, Allison. I really don't know." Without planning to, he put his hand over her wrist and felt her pulse hammering against his palm. "But you… If there's any chance, you have to be careful. You know that, don't you?"

She nodded, her gaze never moving from his. They seemed to be locked into that moment, linked by the touch of their hands and the depth of their gaze. He could feel thoughts, emotions, swirling through him. Through them.

The outside door banged shut as his father came in. They pulled apart, and Nick could get his breath. And he didn't know if he was glad or sorry for the interruption.

ALLISON WASN'T SURE whether she was feeling disappointment or relief when she hurried back to the quilt shop. Nick's father had walked in just in time—or a moment too soon, depending upon your point of view. In any event, whatever had almost happened, she needed time to think before she let it happen again.

Somehow the quilt shop worked its usual magic when she walked through the door, soothing and comforting her, stilling her tumbling thoughts. She moved between the racks of quilt fabrics, pausing to touch the rich blue-green of a pattern here and the jewel-like ruby of a solid piece there.

"You have a feeling for the cloth, ain't so?"

Startled, Allison glanced up. An older Amish woman sat in the rocking chair by the window, a basket overflowing with fabric pieces by her feet. Beyond her, Hector lay comfortably curled on the windowsill, sleeping. He opened one eye at Allison's approach and then closed it again.

"I hope Hector's not bothering you."

Smiling, the woman shook her head. "I like having a cat around." With her hair pulled severely back from a center part under the snowy *kapp* and the dark gray of her dress, she looked for an instant like the painting of Whistler's mother. Then Allison saw the resemblance in the clear blue eyes and the serene oval of her face.

"You must be Sarah's mother. She said you come

in sometimes to demonstrate quilting. I'm Allison Standish."

This woman's smile was just like Sarah's, lighting her eyes and making it clear that the wrinkles on her fine skin were the result of living and laughter. "*Ja*, I'm Hannah Bitler. Our Sarah has told us about you, but I didn't know you had a love for working with fabric."

Allison had to shake her head. "I appreciate the quilts, but I don't know a thing about making them."

"But you sew, *ja*?"

"My step-grandmother taught me when I was young." Dennis's mother had always treated Allison as if she were just as much a grandchild as the twins. Memory presented her with an image of herself sitting next to Grammy Rose, trying to copy the tiny stitches she was putting into a piece of embroidery. "But I haven't done much in years. Too busy, I guess."

"You could start again, ain't so? It's wonderful soothing to sit down to after a busy day."

She could do with a little soothing. Allison moved a folding chair closer so that she could see the handwork in the woman's lap. She was stitching tiny scraps together in a pattern so intricate that Allison could make no sense of it.

"You're making a postage-stamp quilt, aren't you?" She'd learned a good deal about different types of quilting from Sarah in the short time she'd been here. In a postage-stamp design, the individual pieces were no bigger than the stamps for which the method was named. Somehow, the quilter was able to piece them together to make a coherent whole, but she couldn't imagine how.

"I could do the piecing on the machine." Mrs. Bitler

smoothed out the square she was making. "But Sarah says the *Englisch* like to see someone doing it by hand."

Allison nodded, applauding Sarah's wisdom. Those relatively unfamiliar with quilting would be doubly impressed at the sight of someone doing it by hand. "I think Sarah's right about it, but I probably wouldn't have the patience."

"Patience grows with practice." Sarah's mother said the words as if they were self-evident. "If you pick out a pattern and the material, I'll help you get started."

"It would have to be something very, very simple." She smiled, not wanting to commit herself. She'd almost said she didn't have time, but maybe she did now that she wasn't working into the evening or rushing out the door for a dinner or one of the innumerable art shows Greg had dragged her to.

"Your *grossmammi*...did she quilt?" The woman's needle flashed in an out of the fabric as she talked, her stitches so tiny they were nearly invisible.

Allison frowned, trying to remember. "I don't think so. She did needlework and cross-stitch, and she tried to teach me how to crochet." She chuckled, remembering. "I think that mostly involved her tearing out my mistakes and getting me started again."

"It's *gut* you had her, since Evelyn..." Hannah stopped, shaking her head, her face distressed. "*Ach*, I shouldn't say that."

"It's all right. Everyone seems to know that Evelyn Standish didn't play any part in my life. Since I never knew her, I can't miss her."

The woman shook her head slowly. "That was a bad business, that's certain sure. Evelyn was a *gut* woman, but proud." She darted a look at Allison. "Pride can cause such pain. Maybe that is why God calls us to be humble."

Allison nodded, turning that over in her mind. She'd never given much thought to humility, maybe because it wasn't a virtue that was especially prized in a competitive world. But to the Amish, it seemed to be a way of life. "Did you know my grandmother well?"

Sarah's mother paused, thinking over the question. "As well as anyone, maybe. I worked in the house for years, and then Sarah after me. Evelyn wasn't one to show her feelings. Kind, *ja*, and wonderful generous if anyone was in need. But not forgiving if someone did wrong. She wouldn't rest until the wrong was put right, no matter who it was."

"That must have made her some enemies," Allison said slowly. Including her own son, it seemed. What had Hugh done that had caused his own mother to cast him off? That might be something else she could ask Julia Everly about. Brenda might know, but she instinctively rejected the thought of asking her.

"That's true." Hannah took a few more delicate stitches. "Evelyn...*ach*, sometimes she didn't see what the results would be of her insistence on exposing the wrong." Her gaze touched Allison's face. "Like losing her only grandchild."

Or like creating an enemy who would strike back? It sounded as if Evelyn had never realized that insistence on the right could be dangerous.

The bell on the door jingled as someone came into the shop. Standing, Allison spotted two women, arms laded with packages, headed for the quilt displays.

"Looks like customers. Is Sarah here?"

"She took some things back to the storeroom. I'll get

her." Sarah's mother started to rise, and Allison shook her head. "I'll do it. You'll be better able to answer any questions they have."

Allison went quickly back to the hallway, unable to prevent a glance into the cabinetry business, but it seemed to be empty. Perhaps Nick and his father were already at work upstairs.

The door stood open to the storeroom, and she found Sarah vainly trying to make another box stay on top of an untidy heap. Allison grabbed it before it could fall on their heads.

"You have customers. I'll take care of this."

"Fred Glick was supposed to clean up in here to make more room, and I don't believe he's done a thing." Sarah sounded as exasperated as Allison had ever heard her. "He's probably down in the cellar taking a nap."

"I'll get him." She pushed Sarah gently toward the door, ire rising at the thought of the custodian. "I think it's time he realized he's not getting paid to nap."

Allison's annoyance carried her out the side door and halfway down the stone steps to the cellar before she realized that coming down might not be the smartest move. The sparse sunlight filtered down the steps, revealing dust motes dancing. Beyond, the space stretched dark and echoing. She fumbled for the switch she knew was close to the circuit box, collecting what felt like a cobweb on her hand. She touched the switch and flipped it.

The bare bulbs that hung at intervals from the ceiling looked as if they were the lowest wattage possible, creating as many shadows as illumination.

"Fred? Are you down here?" It seemed an unlikely place for anyone to take a nap, but for all she knew, the custodian had a cozy little den for himself somewhere under the building. "Fred?"

Her voice echoed, sending whispers back from the dark. Quite suddenly she seemed to hear Nick's voice again in her mind. *Be careful*, it murmured. *Be careful*.

Her foot hovered over another step. Then she drew it back and turned. She'd make more space in the storeroom herself rather than go on. But as soon as possible, she and Fred Glick were going to have a reckoning.

Glad to shut the cellar doors behind her, Allison hurried back to the storeroom. Come to think of it, there had to be access to the cellar from somewhere inside the building. The exterior hatchway couldn't be the only entrance. She ought to find the building plans and familiarize herself a bit better with her inheritance.

Things weren't quite as bad in the storeroom as she'd anticipated, once she started at the back. The problem was that everyone who'd come in had probably dumped things as close to the door as possible. She pulled boxes back toward the shelving that lined the walls, wondering at some of the things people had decided to donate.

Surely no one would buy a box of used candles, would they? Or a stack of yellowed sheets? Maybe someone had a use for them, but she couldn't think what it would be. On the other hand, there were boxes of books that lured her to explore them.

She pulled herself away. Just because there was what seemed to be a complete set of Louisa May Alcott books that she remembered from her childhood, that didn't mean she should give them room in her already crowded bedroom at Mrs. Anderson's. But she began to see the temptation of the Jumble Sale.

Something sounded from the other side of a teetering stack of boxes. She stopped, listening. Maybe Fred, overcome with an attack of conscience?

Something brushed against a box, setting it rocking slightly. "Fred? Is that you?"

No answer. A tiny flicker of alarm shivered down her spine. But that was foolish. It was broad daylight.

Broad daylight outside, maybe. Feeling as if she were whistling in the dark, Allison walked toward the door, hearing her own footsteps on the wooden floor. She rounded a rack of coats and stopped, her heart jolting before she saw who it was. Tommy Blackburn stared at her over an armload of yet more boxes.

"Allison! You startled me. I didn't know anybody was here." He hefted the boxes. "I cleaned off some bookshelves. Where do you want these?"

She'd had time to catch her breath by then. "At the end of this row you'll find some space." She pointed. Was Tommy aware of his father's machinations with the permits? Or didn't the elder Blackburn confide in his son?

Tommy headed in the direction she'd indicated and then stopped, balancing his burden on the edge of a battered file cabinet. "Allison, I just wanted to say…" His ruddy face flushed a deeper hue. "Well, I heard about my dad leaning on the town clerk over your permit. I wanted to apologize." He gave her a hangdog look. "I don't suppose he'll apologize, and someone should."

"It's not your fault," she said quickly. "And it all worked out, in any event."

"Good, good." He made an attempt at his usual hearty tone, shaking his head. "Sometimes I think the old man's getting a bit senile. Imagine acting like that. If people knew, the whole family would be embarrassed. Lord knows I can't control him."

"I won't say anything." Tommy seemed both pitiable and harassed, caught between his formidable father and a son she suspected was also out of his control. "You don't need to worry about that."

"Thanks, Allison. I appreciate it." He eyed her with something of his former appreciation. "Maybe we could—"

The box he was balancing slipped out of his hands, sending a cascade of books toward the floor. Allison was just moving to help him when she heard someone calling her name.

"I'll clean this up," Tommy said hastily. "You go ahead. Somebody wants you."

Nodding, she headed for the door. Just as she reached it, Jamie rushed toward her, grabbing her hand.

"Ally, where's my daddy?" Panic threaded his voice. "I thought I could find my daddy here, but he's not any-where!"

The words ended in a choked sob that went straight to her heart and set up a reverberation there. She knew what Jamie was feeling. She ought to. She'd felt that panic and loss herself when she was his age, and she'd never quite shaken it off.

CHAPTER NINE

LEAVING TOMMY BEHIND picking up books, Allison led Jamie out into the hall, her hand on his shoulder. She could feel him tremble as he obviously tried to control tears.

"Jamie, it's okay. There's been some mix-up, that's all." And what kind of mix-up let a six-year-old in for such a fright? Anger boiled along her veins, and she fought to suppress it. "We'll find your father."

"It's my fault." Jamie's lips trembled, and he pressed them together. He was six—too grown-up to cry, he'd be thinking.

"Listen, I'm sure it's not your fault." She knelt so that they were face-to-face. "It isn't." How she'd once wanted to hear someone say those words.

Jamie shook his head. "I was s'posed to take the bus home today, but I forgot. So I thought I'm come to the workshop and Daddy would take me home."

She brushed the silky hair out of his eyes. It was doing him good to talk. He was calmer already.

"Wasn't there someone who was supposed to get you on the right bus?" Surely the school had some system in place.

"The bus lady was new today. She didn't know." He looked down at his shoes. "Guess I should have told her, but I forgot."

"Everybody forgets sometimes. So you came to the workshop—"

"But it was locked! Nobody was there. So I came inside 'cause I thought they'd be in the office, but it's locked up, too. And I thought I'd go to Sarah's and she would call my grammy for me, but I saw she had customers, so then I found you." He gave her an anxious look. "Do you think Daddy will be mad?"

"I'm sure he won't." He'd better not be, or she'd have a few things to say to him. And maybe she'd say them, anyway.

"But it's my fault," he repeated.

Allison took him by the shoulders, holding him gently and meeting his gaze. "Listen to me, Jamie. I know. It's not your fault. Okay?"

The faintest smile teased at his lips. "Okay." He grew solemn again. "But I still don't know where Daddy is, and Grammy will be worried when I don't get off the bus."

"I guess we'd better do something about that, then." She stood. "I'll bet your daddy and grandpa are upstairs working on the new project. Let's go see. And if not, we'll call your grandmother, and then I'll drive you home."

They started up the stairs, with Jamie clutching her hand. At the top, she pointed toward the apartment. "They're doing some work for me up here, so maybe they started already."

As they reached the door, he carefully detached his hand. She had to smile. Male pride was coming to the fore.

Allison opened the door. Nick was kneeling, holding a tape measure as his father ran it to the wall. He looked up at the sound of the door, his eyes widening when he saw his son.

"Daddy!" Jamie rushed to throw his arms around his father, nearly knocking him over. "I'm sorry. I missed the bus, and I couldn't find you, but Ally took care of me."

"Hey, it's okay." Nick held his son between his work-hardened hands. "You're safe now. But why did you miss the bus?"

Jamie hung his head. "I forgot."

"Apparently the bus lady is new and didn't know what she was doing." Allison thought it was time she intervened. If she could prevent it, Nick wasn't going to scold the boy. After all, this was the fault of the adults in Jamie's life.

"But didn't Grammy remind you when you left that you were supposed to go home on the bus?"

Jamie nodded. "I forgot," he said again.

"Your mother's going to be scared to death," Jim put in, pulling a cell phone from his pocket. "I'd better call her."

"Tell her I'm sorry," Jamie piped up.

His grandfather gave him a reassuring smile. "I'm sure she knows that." He turned away, and in a moment he was talking in soothing terms to an obviously upset Ellen.

Nick tilted his son's face toward his. "What should you have done when you realized you'd missed the bus?"

"Told the bus lady. Or the teacher." Jamie hung his head.

"That's right. You—"

"Can I speak to you, Nick?" Allison could hear the edge of anger in her voice, and she hoped Jamie didn't recognize it. As for Nick—well, she really didn't care if he knew she was angry or not.

"Sure thing." Nick rose to his feet, eyeing her warily.

"Out in the hall." She yanked the door open.

Jamie seemed engrossed in talking to his grandmother on the phone. She doubted that he even noticed them leaving.

Once the door had closed, she swung on Nick. "What do you mean by scolding the boy? It wasn't his fault."

He might have said it was none of her business, but he didn't. "I wasn't scolding him, exactly. But Jamie needs to know what to do when things don't go as expected. He should have told an adult, not walked down here on his own."

That probably made sense, but she was too worked up to admit it. "He's a six-year-old. It's not his fault. The adults in his life are supposed to be looking after him."

Answering anger flared in Nick's face. "Look, I'm not sure what makes you an expert on raising a child, but Jamie is my concern. I take care of him."

"Is it taking care of him to put him in a situation where he goes looking for his father and can't find him? Do you know how frightening that is for a child?"

"Sure I do. And I'll keep reassuring him. But I'm also going to reinforce what he should have done. That's my responsibility. What do you know about it, anyway?"

The angry question struck too near home. *Everything,* she wanted to say. *I know everything about having your father let you down.*

She didn't speak, but maybe some of what she was feeling showed in her face.

"Allison?" He grasped her wrists, holding her when she would have turned away. "What do you know about it?"

"Nothing," she snapped. She pulled her hands free, charged into her office and slammed the door.

ALLISON LEANED AGAINST the door, shaking. What had she done? Righteous indignation was one thing, but she had lost control.

She knew why. Jamie's fear had stirred her own long-hidden feelings. It was humiliating, knowing that a scared, devastated six-year-old child still lurked within the capable adult exterior she prized. And fearing, too, that she'd shown it to Nick.

He couldn't have known. Could he?

Hugging herself, she crossed the room to the desk. Hector had followed her upstairs, and he was curled atop a stack of ledgers like a furry paperweight. He opened one eye, looked at her and closed it again.

Work, that was what she needed. Something to occupy her mind while the memories sank beneath the surface again. Sitting down in the swivel chair, she opened her email account and began flipping through the contents of her inbox.

Nothing important, it seemed. A few business-related messages that she forwarded back to the office. Let Diane explain why Allison wouldn't be available to work with her clients any longer. The usual number of deals on everything from computers to books to spring fashions. Another email...she stopped, frowning at the sender, and then clicked on it.

The name was familiar to her—a headhunter who specialized in upper-echelon design jobs. But she'd never registered with the firm, so why were they contacting her?

A job, it seemed. Her name had been mentioned, there

happened to be an opportunity in San Francisco that she might fit, was she interested in pursuing it? If so, contact the agency as soon as possible.

Her fingers hovered over the keys. San Francisco… home of craftsman bungalows, elegant row houses and an eclectic art scene. And no snowy Philadelphia winters.

Tempting, definitely tempting. What harm would it do to pursue it a little? Her fingers hovered on the brink of hitting reply, but she pushed herself away abruptly. If the opportunity was real, it could wait until she could approach it with a calm mind.

Hector, apparently disturbed by her movement, rose, stretching his back into an arc, and jumped down from the desk, leaving flecks of orange-and-white fur floating in the shaft of light from the window. He stalked to the door, pawed it once and looked over his shoulder at her with an expectant gaze.

"Yes, all right." She should go back downstairs anyway. Sarah could no doubt use some help with the stream of donations coming in.

Allison opened the door cautiously and peered out. She didn't particularly want to run into Nick again at the moment.

The door to the apartment was ajar, and from beyond it she could hear the murmur of male voices. She went quickly to the stairs and started down, the cat bounding ahead of her.

Glancing down the hallway as she reached the bottom, Allison realized that the storeroom door was open. She'd probably left it that way when she'd hurried to help Jamie, unless one of the tenants was there. She'd better check.

She stepped inside the storeroom. The lights were

on, but Tommy might have left them that way when he'd dropped off the things he'd brought.

"Hello? Anyone here?"

There was a momentary silence. A box scraped, and Ralph appeared at the end of the row, several books in his hands. "Allison." He seemed almost relieved to see her. He rubbed the tip of his nose. "You'd think people would dust things before they bring them in, wouldn't you?"

"They're probably too eager to get them out of the house." She joined him, eyeing the boxes he'd obviously been investigating. "Tommy Blackburn brought those books in today."

Ralph seemed to feel his actions required some explanation. He peered at her over his glasses, shrugging nervously. "I...I was just planning to check on some things I have stored on the shelves. Wouldn't want them mixed in with the sale items, would I?"

Since tenants' supplies were clearly labeled on the steel shelves that lined the walls, that chance seemed unlikely.

"I suppose as a bookseller you're interested in what people have donated," she commented.

"Yes, well..." Ralph hesitated, clearly on the verge of telling her something. His lips twitched, increasing his resemblance to a white rabbit. "I've had a bit of petty pilfering in the shop, so I thought I'd have a look at what's come in."

Did he realize how little sense that made? "I'm surprised that anyone would shoplift books, of all things. And how would you know if a given book had been taken from your store?"

"Well, I...I guess I wouldn't." He seemed to become aware that he was still holding books in his hands and shoved them back into the nearest box with a nervous laugh. "Silly of me, I guess. More likely a mistake in our inventory than anything else, anyway."

He headed toward the door, and Allison followed him, intending to be sure the storeroom was locked.

"Laurel Ridge seems like a fairly law-abiding place, but I suppose there's a certain amount of shoplifting wherever you are."

Ralph watched as she locked the storeroom. His glasses slid down his nose, and he pushed them up. "There's just as much evil in a small town as a big city," he said. "Per capita, of course." He tittered. "Malice is everywhere. Especially here." He glanced over his shoulder, as if checking to see that they weren't overheard. "You must realize that," he whispered. "After all, you put locks on all the attic doors."

She hadn't realized her actions would be the subject of conversation. "Only because I found one of the doors standing open. If someone went up without permission and was injured in some way, we might be considered liable."

"I suppose, I suppose," he repeated the words. "I must get back to the shop." He scurried away.

"Ally, my grammy is here," Jamie called from the stairwell as he jumped down the last two steps and stood waiting for Ellen, who descended more decorously and approached Allison with outstretched hands.

"I can't tell you how glad I am that you found Jamie." She put her arms around Allison in a quick hug and then stepped back, smiling. "Such a mix-up. You should have seen me running down the road after the school bus, shouting at them to stop. Of course, the driver didn't hear a thing with all those children making noise."

"I'm sorry, Grammy." Jamie pressed against her for a moment. "Next time I'll go right to my teacher."

"That's always the smart thing to do." Ellen ruffled his hair. "And I know you're a smart boy, right?"

"Right." He grinned.

Had Nick told his mother about her little explosion? If so, she couldn't tell by the way Ellen reacted to her. She was beginning to think she'd made a fool of herself.

Ralph's comment about malice slid into her mind. Maybe it wasn't just Jamie's predicament that had precipitated her loss of control. Maybe there was something in the atmosphere of Blackburn House.

FORCING HIMSELF TO CONCENTRATE, Nick unscrewed the hinges of the old cabinet doors in the apartment kitchen that evening. He wasn't paid to work overtime, but it was a fact of life when you ran a business.

Anyway, he'd been restless and irritable after he'd put Jamie to bed—so much so that his mother, after watching him change the channels on the show she was trying to watch several times, took the remote from him and suggested in a firm voice that he find something to do with himself.

Did Mom know what was bugging him? She seemed to know most things by some sort of instinct, whether a person told her or not.

The sun was doing its vanishing act behind the ridge, and Blackburn House was quiet around him. If he made a head start tonight, they'd be that much further along tomorrow.

Allison hadn't been in the building when he'd arrived. Just as well. He was in no mood for another dressing-down about his parenting skills.

He lifted the cabinet door down and moved on to the next. There'd been something more behind that outburst of Allison's. He felt sure of it. Something personal. But he doubted she'd ever confide in him, and he wasn't sure he wanted her to.

It would be a mistake, he reminded himself, to get too close. She would leave here, sooner or later. And he would stay, because this was the life he wanted for himself and his son.

The door to the apartment rattled, and someone stepped inside. He heard her steps approaching the kitchen, and in another moment, Allison appeared in the doorway.

Nick focused intently on the hinge. If she wanted a fight, she'd have to do it without him.

"You're working late tonight," she said.

Allison didn't sound as if she were spoiling for a fight. In fact, she seemed subdued, pale in the artificial glare of the work light.

"Just thought I'd do a little more of the clearing away since I had time." The screw jammed, and he forced himself to take it easy as he worked it loose. Dad wouldn't thank him if he split the old door.

"I guess there's a lot to do before you can start on putting in the new kitchen." She moved a little closer, coming to stand with her elbow on the counter as she watched him.

"Right." The hinge came free, and he lifted the door and set it on the floor. "We always save as much as we can of the old stuff. You can never tell when it might come in handy."

She tapped on the old door. "I can't imagine what anyone would want with these cabinets."

"You'd be surprised. One of the guys just asked me today if he could buy some old cabinets cheap. Said they were just the thing to put in the cellar for his wife's canned goods."

"As far as I'm concerned, he can have them free. I thought you'd probably just take a sledgehammer to them."

Nick grinned, moving the step stool over to the next set of doors. "That's not how we work."

Her gaze slid away from his, and she grimaced. "I'm beginning to think that's what I did earlier today—used a sledgehammer to swat a fly."

He considered. "Not sure I like being compared to a fly."

"You know what I mean." She shook her head and gave him a smile that seemed to wobble around the edges. "I'm trying to apologize, you know."

"Oh, is that what you're doing?" Nick leaned against the counter, studying her face. "I wasn't sure."

She took a deep breath. "I overreacted. I'm sorry." She turned as if to leave, and Nick discovered he didn't want her to go.

"Why?" he asked.

She glanced back at him. "Why what?"

"Why did you overreact?" He kept his tone calm. Patient. "I appreciate your concern for Jamie. But that wasn't just about Jamie."

For an instant it seemed she'd walk out without answering. Then she turned back to him. "No. It wasn't just about Jamie."

She met his gaze, and the remembered pain in her deep green eyes shocked him. There was something more. This was something important, and if she told him, that would change things between them.

"What is it?" he asked gently.

She shook her head.

"What happened to you, Ally?" he persisted.

Maybe it was the use of the nickname. Maybe she just needed to talk. Whatever it was, he could see the decision in her face.

Allison rubbed her hands along her upper arms as if she was cold. "Jamie was so frightened when he couldn't find you. It just…reminded me."

"Reminded you of something similar that happened to you." He put the pieces together. "How old were you?"

"Six." Her lips trembled. "Six, like Jamie. I suppose that's why I…overreacted. That's all."

"It's not all. Who was it? Your mother?"

She shook her head.

"Your father, then?" Everyone said Hugh Standish had been selfish and self-centered. Had he proved that to his daughter?

Allison nodded. For a moment it hung in the balance, and then she seemed to cave in all at once.

"My parents were separated. My dad wanted to see me, so on Fridays I was supposed to ride a different bus from school, one that stopped near his apartment. He'd be there to meet me, I'd stay overnight and then he'd take me back to my mother's on Saturday afternoon." She shook her head. "Now it seems so crazy to me that they expected that of a six-year-old, but at the time I just accepted it."

She sucked in a breath, and he could see her stiffen, as if to face something unpleasant.

His own heart was bleak. How much damage might

he and Sheila have done to Jamie when a marriage became a battleground?

"Anyway, one Friday I got off the bus, clutching my school papers with the stars to show him. But Daddy wasn't there." She rubbed her palms on her arms. "I waited for a while. It seemed like ages, but it probably wasn't all that long. And he didn't come. I didn't know what to do. People were looking at me, I thought. One woman asked if I was lost, but I said I was waiting for my father." She shrugged. "Anyway, I remembered how to get to my dad's apartment, so I decided to walk there."

"Like Jamie," he said. No wonder she'd been hit by what happened today. But he suspected her story didn't have a happy ending.

She nodded. "I found the building, and I went up to his door. I knocked, but no one answered. So finally I just sat down on the floor and waited." She managed a feeble smile. "I wasn't as smart as Jamie, I guess. At least he came up with some ideas."

"He had people around that he knew. People he could come to." Nick leaned against the counter next to her, not quite touching but close enough to feel her warmth and smell the fragrance of her hair. "It sounds as if you didn't."

"If I'd thought to find the manager...but I'm not sure I knew there was such a thing. In any event, someone must have called her eventually, because she came to see what was going on. When I told her why i was there, she kept shaking her head. She said Hugh Standish had moved out days earlier, not telling anyone where he was going.

"I didn't believe her, of course. Finally she opened the apartment and let me see for myself. All the closets and drawers were empty. It was as if he'd never been there."

He didn't know what to say to her. Rage shook him like a dog with a bone between his teeth. If he could get his hands on Hugh Standish—but Hugh had gone beyond the reach of retribution.

"I'm sorry," he said finally. There didn't seem to be anything else that fit. To say that he understood would be an insult, because he didn't. He couldn't understand how any father could do that to his child.

She shook her head. "Stupid, I know, to feel it still. I'd have said I'd forgotten it entirely, but when I saw Jamie this afternoon..." She shrugged again. "Well, I guess it wasn't buried as deeply as I thought."

"Someone got in touch with your mother, I assume. She must have been furious with him."

"Right. There were no cell phones then, so it wasn't a simple matter. Since I was, she thought, safely with my dad, she'd decided to go shopping and then have dinner with some friends. The apartment manager was very nice, though. She insisted I have supper with her family, and her teenage daughter played games with me that must have driven her crazy with boredom."

"I am sorry." He touched her wrist lightly. When she didn't pull away, he encircled it with his fingers, feeling the pulse throb against his skin. "Every parent makes mistakes, of course. Sometimes there isn't any best answer, and you just have to pick the least hurtful. But that—well, people around here always did say how selfish Hugh was. It sounds as if he didn't improve with age."

Allison's eyes seemed glazed with remembered pain. "It's hard for a child to admit that about a parent. You always want to believe that your mother and father love you, no matter what."

"Yeah." He looked down at their linked hands. "I've

made it a rule never to bad-mouth Sheila in front of Jamie, no matter what she does. But it's tough to keep that promise when I hear him talking about how pretty she is, and how if she were here, she'd pick him up from school and all the kids would see her."

Allison turned toward him, putting her other hand on his arm. The bars between them were gone for the moment, at least, and he could read the concern shining in her eyes.

"He needs that now," she said. "Believe me, I know. One day he won't need it any longer, and it will fade away. But for now…"

"For now," he said, and the words carried the gravity of a promise. "Thank you, Allison. Thank you for trusting me with your story. It helped me understand."

A smile trembled on her lips. "Maybe that's the purpose of painful things."

"Maybe so." He raised his hand, letting his fingers trace the line of her cheek. Her skin was warm and soft and alive to the touch.

Allison didn't move. She looked almost dazed. Slowly, very slowly, she lifted her face to his.

Nick smothered the voice that was crying this was a bad idea, it would lead to trouble, he'd be sorry. His lips found hers, gently at first and then surer, claiming them. No point in saying this shouldn't happen between them, not when it already was, not when it had been happening since the first moment he saw her.

CHAPTER TEN

BY THE NEXT AFTERNOON, Allison had still not shaken off her guilt over her deepening relationship with Nick. Her rational mind was telling her one thing, and even as she listened to it she was doing the opposite.

And when she could manage to wrench her thoughts away from Nick, there was the possibility of a job in San Francisco to tempt her. She'd have to respond to the email soon if she was ever going to. But pursuing the position would just confuse her already mixed-up life even more.

"Here you are." Sarah's voice was a welcome disruption. She propped a plastic bin on the quilt shop counter. "If you're going to make a nine-patch place mat or wall hanging, you won't need anything larger than these cuts of fabric. Except for the backing, of course."

Allison blinked. "Am I making a nine-patch?"

"*Mamm* says you are." Sarah's eyes sparkled. "If you don't want to…"

"No, no, I don't want to disappoint her. Anyway, I'd like to try it. I suspect it's going to give me a whole new respect for quilters."

"You'll do fine." Sarah took the lid off the bin, revealing stacks of fabric pieces, obviously left over from other projects, all neatly pressed and stored away for possible use. "You'll want to pick nine colors. Then you can use something contrasting or a matching one for the binding and reverse."

"How do I begin to choose?" She picked up a stack of pieces and fanned them out on the counter, attracted as always by the texture and color.

"A nine-patch has nine small square patches joined together to make a bigger square. Then those squares are joined together to make a larger square and on and on, depending on how big a piece you're making."

"Small," she said quickly. "Place mat–size sounds about right." She riffled through the pieces again, automatically beginning to sort them into color groups. Solids, prints, maybe a stripe...

"You must work a lot with fabric and color when you're designing people's houses," Sarah said, watching her.

Allison nodded. "I love it, but it's frustrating when people just want what's fashionable at the moment or what they've seen in a decorating magazine." She darted a look at Sarah. "That idea must sound odd to an Amish person."

"*Ach*, I know about it, that's certain sure. People come in and buy a quilt because it's made with certain colors, not because it's beautifully crafted and useful. Can you imagine?"

Allison had to laugh at Sarah's expression. "They probably don't even know what their favorite colors are. Only what's in style."

Sarah laughed with her. "But it doesn't stop me from selling quilts to them, and I suppose it doesn't stop you from decorating their houses."

"True enough. You have to work, and it's satisfying enough of the time to keep me happy." Her mind flickered to the job in San Francisco and back again. "And I think you're even happier with the quilt shop, aren't you?"

Sarah nodded, looking around with a smile. "When Evelyn talked to me about a shop, I had no idea it would bring me such satisfaction."

Allison studied the peaceful expression. Sarah would never have her today spoiled by worrying about tomorrow. It was a rare gift to take life that way. Still...

"When you told me about it, you said Evelyn approached you when she realized you weren't going to marry. But you're young. You could fall in love—"

Sarah shook her head, lips setting in a firm line. "Evelyn knew, you see. I...I loved someone, but he didn't love me back." She shrugged. "Funny how Evelyn understood even better than my *mamm* and *daad.* They thought I could get over him, marry someone else and be happy. Evelyn saw that I couldn't."

An argument was on the tip of Allison's tongue, but she held it back. Sarah had the right to her own feelings. If she felt there was only one person she could love, it wasn't Allison's place to argue the point. Besides, she didn't have all that strong a case for happiness herself. She'd never really loved anyone.

She suddenly seemed to hear herself telling Nick the story about her father. How much had that early betrayal had to do with her inability to dismantle the barricades that protected her heart?

"*Ach*, what are we doing, making each other sad?" Sarah shook her head, as if to shake off a dark cloud. "I'm nearly forgetting. *Mamm* wants you to come home with me for supper tonight. Is it okay?"

"It's very kind of her." Allison hesitated. "Is there

anything special I should know about visiting an Amish home? I don't want to make a mistake."

Sarah's laugh bubbled over. "You couldn't make a mistake with us. We're friends. *Daad* will have silent prayer first, but then we eat just like anyone else. Except that my little brothers will bicker about who got the biggest piece."

"That will seem just like home, then. The twins are always doing that. My mother used to try and reason with them, but my stepfather finally said the next time he heard it, neither of them would get any dessert. They—" She stopped, because someone was coming into the shop.

Not just someone. Brenda entered, followed by Krysta, looking bored and carrying a shopping bag.

Sarah, with a glance at Allison, hurried forward. "Brenda, Krysta, *wilkom*. Are you shopping or bringing things for the sale on Saturday?"

Brenda gave a dismissive glance around the shop. "Krysta has a bag for the sale. I'd like to speak to Allison."

Her tone came close to outright rudeness, and Allison stiffened. But Sarah was already moving toward the door.

"*Komm*, Krysta. I'll show you where to put things for the sale."

In a moment the two of them were gone, leaving Allison alone with Brenda, except for two Amish women who had been browsing among the quilt fabrics for a good half hour and didn't seem near a decision yet.

"What can I do for you, Brenda?" Allison kept her tone cool. She should have expected a visit from the woman. It was hardly likely she'd give up on gaining control of the building so easily.

Brenda didn't waste any time. "Have you reconsidered my offer?"

"Your offer or Thomas Blackburn's?" she asked.

Brenda's sallow skin flushed. "Mr. Blackburn told me that he had increased the offer. I don't think the place is worth that much, but it's an old man's dearest wish, after all."

If Brenda was making a bid for pity for Blackburn, Allison wasn't buying it.

"Blackburn House is worth every bit of it and more. I'm quite sure you both know it as well as I do."

"Your sense of property value has been distorted by city prices," Brenda snapped.

Allison shook her head, smiling slightly. "I've seen the valuation for taxes, you know."

"Yes, but you have to stay here in Laurel Ridge for a year to realize anything on the property." Brenda pressed what she obviously saw as her advantage.

And maybe it was. Allison thought again of the position in San Francisco. If she pursued it, if it worked out, she'd have no choice but to walk away from Blackburn House.

That was a lot of ifs, but it only made sense not to burn any bridges behind her. If Brenda discovered that Allison actually needed to sell in order to take another job, she'd control all the cards.

"I honestly haven't made a decision about staying." It was a good thing Sarah wasn't within earshot. "I'll think it over."

"Very well, then." Brenda's smile was stiff. "I'll wait for your answer, but the offer won't be good indefinitely."

Allison just smiled. From what she'd seen of Thomas

Blackburn, she suspected the offer would be open as long as it took.

They stood there awkwardly until Sarah and Krysta reappeared from the direction of the storeroom. "Krysta has some more bags in the car," Sarah called. "I'm going to help her with them."

"I'll do that," Allison said quickly, skirting the counter. She'd had enough of skirmishing with Brenda. "You have customers ready." The two Amish women had picked up some bolts of fabric, apparently having finally decided.

Without waiting for any goodbyes, she hurried out, following Krysta to a late-model hatchback that was parked at the curb.

Krysta handed out bags, filling Allison's arms, and took another full load herself, balancing them on her knee as she closed the hatchback.

"Thanks," she muttered.

"No problem." They went up the walk, one behind the other. Allison propped the front door open with her shoulder and followed Krysta back to the storeroom.

Inside the storeroom door she paused, trying to pick the best spot for the bags she carried. Krysta propped hers on top of a box that was turned on its side, spilling its contents on the floor.

"Where to?" she asked.

"Farther back." Allison nodded toward the end of the row. "This looks as if someone was hunting for early bargains. I'll have to clean it up."

"Most of it looks like junk, but I guess some people will buy anything." She plunked down her bags where Allison indicated and turned to face her. "Look, I guess I need to thank you for not telling... Well, you know." Her fair skin flushed, making her look younger.

"No problem," Allison said, wondering if T.J. shared Krysta's attitude.

"Are you going to take this offer my mother and Mr. Blackburn cooked up between them?" Krysta asked abruptly.

"I haven't really decided." Allison was surprised the teenager cared in the least.

"Well, I just want you to know that I think the two of them are nuts. I mean, who cares who owned a building thirty or forty years ago?"

"Apparently Thomas Blackburn cares," she said, her tone dry.

"Nutty," Krysta said. "And T.J. says the same thing, too. Who cares about that dead and gone family history, anyway? T.J. says his grandfather is obsessed with getting the building back, and he thinks it's ridiculous."

"Does he?" Allison's memory presented her with a picture of T.J. walking quickly away from the scene the night the power went out. "Are you sure T.J. wouldn't do something to make me want to sell, if just to please his grandfather?"

"You're talking about somebody vandalizing the building, aren't you?" Krysta's eyes sparked fire. "I heard about that."

"Not necessarily. I just wondered—"

"You can't go around saying things like that! T.J. would never—" She stamped her feet, looking as if anger had taken away her ability to express herself. "I should have known I couldn't talk to you!"

Krysta whirled and darted out of the room. By the time Allison reached the hallway, Krysta was disappearing out the front door.

APRIL WEATHER HAD turned fickle, and a brisk wind swept clouds across the sky amid a shower of rain. Allison was relieved that Sarah hadn't insisted on transporting her by horse and buggy, and instead they both went to the Bitler farm in Allison's car.

"I'll take you for a buggy ride another time," Sarah said, seeming to assume that Allison would consider it a treat. "There's the lane, coming up on the right."

Allison made the turn, passing between a mailbox on one side and a willow tree, already turning green, on the other. The farm lane was a long gravel stretch, much like the lane at the home of Nick's parents. Glancing across the intervening field, she could see the farmhouse Nick and his family called home.

The Bitler house was actually very similar from the outside—white frame with a long porch across the front. Beyond it were several outbuildings—a large barn, twin silos and a number of smaller buildings whose purpose she couldn't guess.

As they neared the house, Allison found herself tensing. She'd never been in an Amish home before. What if she unintentionally insulted someone? Sarah had laughed at the idea, but Allison couldn't rid herself of the feeling that she was stepping into unfamiliar territory.

"You can park right by the back porch," Sarah said, pointing to a gravel pull-off bordered by a long hitching rail.

Allison followed instructions. "Your place is very similar to Nick's," she commented.

"I'd guess most of the houses along this road were built in the same time period. Some are Amish, some are *Englisch*."

"So, you can't tell the difference." That was oddly reassuring.

"Well, the sure way to tell is to look for an electric line running into the house. If there isn't one, it's Amish." Sarah settled her bonnet in place. It was practical wear on a day like this. It would protect her from the rain.

"You don't have any electricity in the house?" Allison couldn't imagine living without electricity.

"It's not as bad as it sounds." Sarah seemed used to the attitude on the part of outsiders. "We have gas appliances and lighting, and an oil furnace. Of course, we can use things run on batteries or even a generator for something like a dairy operation. To keep the milk safe, you see. We couldn't sell it otherwise."

"I see, but I don't understand. If you can use electricity in that way, why not from the lines?" Sarah seemed to imagine she'd understand all of these rules. People who lived in the area probably did.

Sarah turned toward her, hand on the door handle. "Well, it's because the Scripture tells us to live separate from the world. We Amish try to work out what that means in today's world. So we use modern appliances, but we don't connect with the power grid because then we wouldn't be separate." She smiled. "It sounds silly to you, most likely, but it's what we feel is right. And the other side of it is that we're not going to be running televisions or computers off bottled gas."

"Televisions are bad?" Allison slid out, buttoning her jacket against the chill wind.

"Not bad in themselves," Sarah said, following suit. "Just bad in that they isolate families. If everyone's watching a screen, they're not talking to each other."

Now, that did make sense, she supposed. "My mother

would probably agree with you. She always put a tight control on how much television the twins could watch. She said it hypnotized them."

Sarah linked arms with her and led her toward the house. "Your *mamm* sounds like a very caring mother."

"Yes. She is." More so with the twins than with her? But that probably wasn't a fair question. When Allison was small, her mother had worked two jobs just to pay the bills. Everything had changed after she'd remarried, of course. But then there were the twins...

Sarah opened the back door of the house and swept Allison into the farmhouse kitchen—into warmth, light, laughter and wonderful smells. For an instant it confused her, and then Sarah's mother was greeting her with a warm hug.

"*Wilkom, wilkom.* We are so glad you're here, Allison. You must *komm* often, ain't so?" With her arm still around Allison's waist, Hannah Bitler turned to the rest of her family. "Here is Sarah's *grossmammi*, Elizabeth Bitler."

"We are *sehr* glad you're here, Allison." The elderly woman said her name carefully, as if it was unfamiliar. Snow-white hair was pulled back under her *kapp*, and the severity of the black dress and apron she wore was mitigated by her beaming smile. Her skin creased into a web of fine lines, as delicate as a fading rose petal.

"This is my husband, Eli," Hannah went on, "and our younger boys, Jonah, Thomas and Noah."

Allison hesitated, not sure whether it was proper for an Amish man to shake hands with an *Englisch* woman, but Eli resolved the dilemma by seizing her hand. He shook it, beaming, his ruddy face filled with pleasure. *"Wilkom, wilkom."* He wore the usual male Amish clothing of black pants, a plain blue shirt and suspenders, and his beard was brown and curly. Blue eyes surveyed her with a twinkle. "Our Sarah's partner is always *wilkom* in our home." He tapped the nearest boy—Jonah, she thought—on the head. "Greet our guest."

He grinned. "We're *sehr* glad you're here."

The other two boys gave echoing murmurs, surveying her with round blue eyes that looked identical. In fact, all three were like stair steps, almost exactly alike with their pale blond hair and fair skin, with only a couple of inches of height to distinguish them.

"*Komm*, sit down, everyone." Hannah shooed them toward the table. "Sarah, you sit by our guest. Jonah, help me get the *schnitz und knepp* to the table."

Allison tried to remember her high school German, but Sarah leaned over and whispered in her ear.

"Apples, dumplings and ham. You'll like it," she added, as if sure no one could fail to enjoy it. And the dish, served in an immense pottery bowl, smelled wonderful.

More dishes were whisked on to the table by Hannah and her helper...applesauce, pickles, baked corn, lima beans...were they really going to eat all of these? But judging by the expressions on the boys' faces, they couldn't wait to dig in, and she remembered her brothers' appetites. Teenage boys were bottomless pits, she guessed.

When everyone was seated, Eli glanced around the table and then bowed his head. Silent prayer, she remembered, following suit. But if it was silent, how did they know when it was ended? She peeked from beneath her lashes and saw every head raised again almost simultaneously, as if they had an internal timer.

A cheerful babble of voices broke out as the dishes were passed, the argument between two of the boys as to who had the bigger serving so familiar it made her smile.

"*Ach*, what will Allison think of you?" Eli reached out to tap his nearest son on the hand. "Don't be greedy."

"They sound like my little brothers," Allison said quickly. "They're twins, and they never could get through a meal without arguing about who got more. And I heard the same teasing between Nick and his brother when I went there for supper. Brothers just seem to do that."

"There's plenty for all," Hannah intervened firmly. "How old are your brothers, Allison?"

"They're eighteen now, so they don't argue as much." She smiled at the three boys lined up on the opposite side of the table.

"These three might grow out of it sometime," Eli said, with what they obviously recognized as mock severity.

The platters and bowls of food kept coming. Allison tried to take a little of everything, not sure she could possibly eat it all. She took a cautious bite of the apple and pork mixture and gave an involuntary sigh. "This is wonderful."

Hannah flushed with pleasure. "*Denke*, Allison. Sarah thought you would like to try the traditional dishes."

"Sometimes we have pizza," Noah, the youngest one, put in. "Is that trad—whatever?"

Eli chuckled. "Only for Italians. But your *mamm* makes *gut* pizza, ain't so?"

"Everything *Mamm* makes is *gut*," Noah said, as if surprised there could be any doubt, making the adults smile.

Allison studied him. Probably about eight, she'd

guess, a little older than Jamie. "Do you go to school with Jamie Whiting, Noah?"

The boy shook his head. "He goes to the school in town. We go to Pine Creek School, down the road." He waved his hand vaguely. "We play together, and sometimes we go fishing."

"That must be fun."

"The Amish *kinder* go to Amish school here," Eli said. "Some places they might go to school with the *Englisch*, I've heard, but here we have our own school."

"We go through eight grades," Sarah explained. "Then we might learn a trade or work in a family business."

It was on the tip of her tongue to ask what happened if a child wanted more education than that, but she reminded herself that she didn't want to risk offending anyone.

Eli smiled at her. "Seems strange to you, ain't so? The *Englisch* keep their *kinder* in school much longer. But we believe eight grades teaches Amish children enough to fit them for the lives God wants for them. Whatever else they need, they learn from their parents or by an apprenticeship."

"Or by taking trade school classes," Sarah added. "Sometimes they might need that for a particular job."

Allison nodded, determined not to argue. Was that really satisfying? It seemed to be for Sarah, at least. Despite having only eight years of education, she was running a successful business. Clearly the Amish had different ideas about what constituted a good life than most Americans.

And they seemed satisfied. Happy. She glanced around the table at the cheerful faces. They didn't have the things most people would consider essential to their happiness, but they seemed content.

Could she be content if she gave up her busy urban lifestyle, the advantages of city living, the possibility of advancing in her career? If she decided to stay in Laurel Ridge, that's what the cost would be.

Odd that she was even considering such a thing. But she didn't know if she wanted to or even if she could. And until she did, she'd be sitting on the fence.

IT WAS NEARLY dark by the time Allison drove back into town, still feeling so full she couldn't think about eating again anytime soon. After supper, she and Sarah had washed the dishes while her mother put away the food and Eli and the boys had headed out to do the evening chores. There always seemed plenty of work to do on a farm.

Once they were all back in the house, the boys had talked her and Sarah into a board game. Judging by the battered condition of the box, it must have been one they played often, sort of a farmyard version of a game her brothers had played before they were lured into electronic games. She had to confess it was more fun to be actively playing around a table, watching the exultation of the boys when they made a good move and listening to their laughter and teasing. Allison was still smiling when she pulled to the curb in front of the bed-and-breakfast.

She grabbed her handbag and reached for her computer case, only to realize that it wasn't there. She paused for a moment, mind scrambling, before she realized where it was. She'd left it on the counter of the quilt shop when they'd locked up and headed out for supper.

It would be safe enough there, but there were some

emails she'd intended to answer tonight, and that would be much easier on the computer than on her phone.

Hesitating on the sidewalk, Allison glanced at her watch. Only eight o'clock, and the clouds had been replaced by a nearly full moon. Voices and laughter spilled out from the café across the street when someone opened the door.

How childish, to be afraid to enter a building she owned just because it was dark. It would only take a moment to run into the quilt shop, and she wasn't going to let herself start imagining things. It was Ralph's talk of feeling malice in the air that had her spooked, and that was ridiculous. Ralph had a malicious streak of his own, for that matter, and he'd probably done it deliberately, just to see her reaction.

Somehow that decided her. She marched briskly toward the door, pulling out her keys and fumbling for the right one.

She finally found it, reflecting that there should be a brighter light on the pole lamp. Still, for the most part, people weren't coming in after dark. She stepped inside and let the door swing closed behind her.

The dark, echoing space seemed to press on her, as if the very air was heavy. Shaking off the feeling, she slid her hand along the wall until it met the switches and flicked the nearest one, which turned on the fixture directly over the door.

In the instant that the light came on, she glanced back down the hallway. The door to the bookshop was ajar, and the window reflected a faint sliver of light. She stopped, frowning. A reflection from the hall light? She took a step to the side, but the light was still visible. She felt for her cell phone, pulling it out of her bag. If there was an intruder, the sensible thing was to slip back outside and call 911.

Allison held her breath, taking a step back, and heard a faint scraping sound, as if a box had been pushed along the floor. In an instant she realized what was happening, and her tension vanished, leaving her feeling rather foolish.

Ralph had received a new shipment of books that afternoon, and he'd been rather testy over the fact that he couldn't fit them in the storeroom to his satisfaction. He'd finally declared, with a martyred air, that he'd have to put them in the tiny back room of the bookstore and stay late to unpack them. The slant of light must be coming from the back room of the bookshop. If she'd called the police over something like this, they'd have every right thinking her a hysterical woman intent on dramatizing herself.

She paused, keys in one hand, cell phone in the other, tempted to retrieve her laptop and slip out before Ralph realized she was there. Sarah would think that less than neighborly, she felt sure. Maybe, in the interest of good relationships with her tenants, she should at least ask if he needed help.

She walked quickly back down the hallway and pushed the door open, stepping inside. "Ralph? It's Allison. Do you—"

The light in the back room went off. She froze, the words caught in her throat. For an instant her mind didn't work, and then she knew. It wasn't Ralph. He wouldn't switch off the light at the sound of her voice.

She had to get out. Get clear of the building. Call the police. With only the dim light that reached it from the bulb in the front of the hall, the bookstore was a place of

looming shapes and dark shadows. Her heart thumped.
Turn back toward the door, then she'd be able to see
enough to get out. But she'd be seen, as well. If she were
between an intruder and his only way out...

Anyway, she couldn't. Some atavistic trait demanded
that she not turn her back to an enemy. She took another
step back, fumbling for the buttons on the cell phone.

The phone light came on, allowing her to press the
buttons. Pinpointing her position to someone there in
the dark.

She took a step to the side as she raised the phone to
her ear. If he came toward her she'd hear the footsteps,
she was closer to the door, she could run—

A sharp crack, something looming over her, plummeting toward her. She raised her arms in a defensive
gesture. And then it hit her, knocking her to the floor,
books raining down on her head. She crouched, curling herself together and waited for another blow to fall.

CHAPTER ELEVEN

NICK'S PULSE THUNDERED in his ears as he burst through the front door of Blackburn House and ran toward the bookshop. He could hear his brother's young patrolman behind him, telling him to wait, and ignored the warning. Allison— Mac's call had been brief, saying only it appeared Allison had been attacked. He hadn't waited to hear more.

He shoved through the partially open door, groping for a light switch. "Allison! Where are you?"

"Here." Her voice sounded blessedly strong. "I'm okay."

He finally connected with the switch. He flipped it, flooding the room with light, and looked at chaos. One of the freestanding bookcases had been knocked over, scattering books across the floor. And over Allison. She half sat, half lay under the heavy fallen bookcase. He was next to her in a second.

"Are you all right?" He grabbed the bookcase, trying to ease it off her.

"I'm okay." Her face was pale, and there was a streak of dust across her cheek, but otherwise she seemed in one piece. "I just can't get out."

"We'll have it off you in a minute." He gestured to the patrolman, who was returning his phone to his hip. "Give me a hand with this."

The kid nodded, looking a little pale himself. He'd probably never been first at the scene before. "Chief's on his way. He'll be here in a second. You sure we should move it?"

Nick choked back a sharp retort and knelt next to Allison. "Will you be all right if we lift it up? We don't want to hurt you trying to free you."

"I'm fine. Just get it off me."

"Okay." He seized one end while the patrolman grabbed the other. "One, two, three."

They lifted. The bookcase came reluctantly, a few last books spilling out as they set it back in place.

"Wait. Let us help you get up."

It was probably a measure of how shaken Allison was that she didn't argue. He and the kid, Johnny Foster, eased her on to one of the upholstered chairs Ralph had placed around the shop to encourage people to linger.

Foster seemed to be gaining confidence. He leaned over Allison, his young face concerned. "Do you hurt anywhere, Ms...."

"Standish," Nick supplied the name. "Did you call for EMTs?"

Foster nodded. "Chief did. Should be here in a couple minutes."

"I'm all right. Really." Allison propped her head on her hand. "I think I'd just better sit for a moment."

"You take all the time you need." Foster straightened. "I should take a look around for the intruder. Probably long gone, though. You'll stay with her?" He made it a question.

Nick nodded, his pulse slowly returning to normal. "I'll be here." He knelt next to Allison, taking a firm clasp on her hand. "I'm not going anywhere."

"Thanks." Allison's voice held a slight wobble. She seemed to hear it, because she straightened, meeting his eyes. "You always seem to be around in emergencies."

"I could do with fewer of those," he said, relieved that the color was returning to her cheeks. "Don't I remember asking you to be careful?"

She rubbed between her eyebrows with two fingers. "I've been giving myself that advice, too." She shook her head, then seemed to regret it. "Ouch. I thought it was Ralph, you see."

He opened his mouth to ask for details and changed his mind. "I hear Mac coming now. He'll want to hear the whole thing, so maybe you'd rather wait and tell it once."

"Right." She leaned back and closed her eyes, the lashes making dark shadows against her pallor.

The approaching footsteps stopped, and Nick heard the murmur of voices as Mac probably spoke to young Foster. When he came through the door, Nick greeted him with a frown.

"How come you're never on duty when you're needed?"

"I am on duty. Was out at a fender bender on Dillstown Road." After a quick glance around, he joined Nick in kneeling next to Allison. "Paramedics are right behind me. Don't try to move, okay?"

"I'm all right," Allison said for the third or fourth time. Her voice seemed to sound a little stronger each time she said it.

Mac studied her face for a moment and seemed to accept it. "You feel okay enough to tell me what happened?"

She nodded, then winced as if the movement hurt. "I'd been out at Sarah's for supper. When I got back, I realized I'd left my laptop in the quilt shop, and I came into the building to get it. I saw the bookstore door was ajar, and there was a light on in here."

"This light?" Mac pointed to the overhead fixture with the pen in his hand.

"No, the one in the back room. I thought it was Ralph." She rubbed her forehead again. "He'd had a shipment this afternoon, and he was upset because he claimed there wasn't space in the storeroom. There was, but he seemed to want to make an issue of it. So anyway, I thought he was unpacking, so I came to see if he needed help." She managed a faint smile. "Trying to soothe his ruffled feathers, I guess."

"Ralph doesn't like all the stuff piling up for the Jumble Sale," Nick explained.

"I see. So you came in. What happened next?"

Allison frowned. "I called his name, and when I did, the light went out. So I knew it wasn't Ralph."

"You should have run out then." Nick tightened his grip on her hand.

"Of course, but it wasn't so easy in the dark. I knew someone was there, but I couldn't see where he was…" Her eyes had widened, and now she was grasping him. "I didn't want to get between him and the exit. I had my cell in my hand, so I pressed 911. About then the roof caved in." She shot a glance at the scattered books. "I guess he ran out."

"You didn't get a look at him?"

"No." She clearly wasn't going to make the mistake of shaking her head again. "I had my hands over my head in case anything else came down."

The tramp of feet announced the arrival of the paramedics. Nick stood, stepping back to surrender his place to them. His brother moved to his side.

"Other than this—" Mac's gesture took in the area around Allison "—nothing out here seems to have been touched. I'll have a look at the cash register."

He moved behind the sales counter, and Nick, after a glance back at Allison and the paramedics, followed him. But here, too, everything seemed secure.

"Allison said the light came from the back room," Nick said. "So apparently the intruder was back there."

"Not your average break-in artist, then." Mac frowned, meeting his gaze. "Let's have a look."

Giving a wide berth to the bookshelf, standing now at an angle where he and Foster had shoved it, they headed for the back room. Mac pushed up the light switch with the end of his flashlight.

The room couldn't have been much more than twelve by fourteen feet, with a desk and chair taking up most of the space. The walls were lined with shelves, loaded with a miscellany of objects from books to cleaning supplies to a coffeemaker. Every drawer of the desk had been pulled out, its contents dumped on the floor.

"Looks as if Ralph uses this primarily as an office," Mac said. "Maybe the perp thought he kept cash back here."

"Why would he, when the cash register is sitting in plain sight?" Nick stepped over a litter of what looked like invoices on the floor. "I'd say it looks more like someone was searching for something."

"What?" Mac's tone was filled with frustration.

"I don't know, but maybe the same thing that took somebody up in the attic."

Mac eyed him skeptically. "You're assuming there really was someone in the attic."

"The door didn't open itself."

Mac grunted. Nick could read him only too easily. He wasn't satisfied with a quick answer, but he didn't like making things complicated, either.

"Chief?" Foster's face appeared around the door. "The owner's here. He's pretty upset. I think you better see him."

"Okay, Foster. You go on back to the door and make sure no one else comes in. Good job," he added.

"Thank you, sir." The boy flushed to the tips of his ears as he hurried off.

They found Ralph standing in the middle of the bookstore. His face twitched, and he was literally wringing his hands. "This is awful, awful." He burst into speech as soon as he saw Mac. "What is this world coming to? And poor Allison. I'll just never forgive myself."

"Why? It's not your fault, is it?" Nick asked before his brother could speak.

Ralph goggled at him. "Well, no. I mean, I don't know why anyone would break in here. But naturally I feel bad if someone's hurt on my property."

Ralph's attitude of assuming everything was about him had never been more annoying. Nick opened his mouth to speak, but his brother elbowed him.

"We'd like you to take a look around and tell us what's missing, if you would. Especially anything of value."

"Of course, of course." Ralph gave an uncertain glance around and then headed for the cash register.

Nick, seeing the paramedics starting to pack up, went back to Allison.

"What's the verdict? Should she go to the hospital to get checked out, instead of assuming you guys know what you're doing?"

The EMT in charge, Mike Callahan, had been in

school with Nick. He grinned, unfazed. "Not unless Ms. Standish wants to, and she says no."

"I don't want to spend an hour or two in an emergency room," Allison said, her voice firm. "A couple of aspirins and a warm bath are all I need."

"You'll have some dandy bruises where the shelves hit you by tomorrow." Mike handed her a form. "If you get a headache or start to feel dizzy, you make sure you call us, okay? And it would be best to check with your own doctor."

"I will. Thank you." She smiled up at him.

Mike propped an elbow on the back of her chair and put on an expression Nick remembered from high school. "Now, I mean that. You can call me personally anytime. My number is on the form."

"Yeah, she already thanked you." Nick elbowed him out of the way. "Stop flirting and go home to your wife and baby, Callahan."

Mike grinned, raising one hand. "Okay, okay. I'm going. One of you walk the lady home, though. No letting her wander off on her own."

"No fear." He looked down at Allison. "We'll take care of her."

Before he could say anything else, Ralph tripped over to Allison, tiptoeing around the books on the floor. "Are you sure you're all right, Allison? I just feel so terrible about this. Interrupting a vandal the way you did—you could have been badly hurt."

"You think it was a vandal, do you?" Nick asked before she could speak.

Ralph raised his hands. "What else could it be? They didn't touch the cash register, and there's nothing else of value here. Except books, and you can't expect people like that to care about books."

"It seems funny that they'd think of vandalizing your shop," he pointed out.

"We've had all those people in and out of the building getting ready for the sale," he said. "That probably explains it."

Nick didn't see that it explained anything. "The back room looks as if it's been searched," he said.

Mac, coming up to them just as Nick spoke, glared at him. No doubt he was thinking that Nick should leave the investigation to the pros.

"What about it, Ralph?" he asked. "Anything in the back room anyone might want?"

Ralph looked even paler than he normally did. "No. Well, I do sometimes leave a locked cash box in there. If I'm not going to the bank, you see."

"And did you do that tonight?" Mac looked as if someone had given him a present.

"No, no, I didn't. I just left the cash in the register. I was so busy…" He let that trail off, maybe deciding that his busyness wasn't relevant.

"Still, someone could have thought you had. Comes to the same thing, in the end."

Ralph got paler, if that was possible. "Oh, dear, I just can't believe it. I've never been robbed, not in all my years in business."

"I'm so sorry," Allison began.

"Are you finished with Allison?" Nick interrupted ruthlessly, frowning at his brother. She could be here for hours comforting Ralph, if he didn't intervene.

Mac seemed to get the message. "Sure. You go on

home, Allison, and try to get a decent night's sleep. I'll touch base with you sometime tomorrow."

Allison started to rise, and Nick slipped his hand under her elbow.

"I'll take you."

She gave a slight smile of agreement. Holding her close, he walked with her out the door and down the hall.

When they'd stepped out onto the front porch, he paused. "I think you ought to come home with me," he said. "To my folks, I mean. My mother would like nothing better than to fuss over you."

"Suppose I don't want any fussing," she said, gripping the railing.

"I could tell her to go easy on it," he offered.

"No, thanks. Mrs. Anderson will take care of me."

"Are you sure? I don't like the idea of you being on your own tonight."

"I'm sure." They went slowly down the steps and out the sidewalk. He held the gate open for her.

"I'm worried about you, that's all." He couldn't seem to keep himself from saying it.

"I know. Thank you." Her voice was soft. "I'll be fine." There was a finality to her tone that told him there was no use arguing.

Nick nodded his agreement, but he didn't let go of her arm until he'd safely delivered her to a clucking and dismayed Mrs. Anderson.

SHE SHOULD BE seeking out Mac to learn if anything new had been discovered, Allison told herself the next day. And she should be checking on Ralph's bookshop, to say nothing of that email from the headhunter.

Instead, she walked straight into the quilt shop, longing for its undemanding comfort. Sarah came scurrying toward her the instant she entered.

"Allison, I made certain sure you wouldn't come in today. How are you?" She took Allison's hands in a warm clasp.

"Sore," Allison admitted. "I keep finding new bruises every time I move. You wouldn't think books could be so hard. But I'm in one piece."

"*Ach*, what a thing to happen to you. Do the police know anything yet? Did you get any hint of who it was?"

"Not a glimpse," she admitted. "Frustrating, isn't it?"

"I'm just wonderful glad you're not worse hurt. Let Mac figure out who did it." Sarah put her arm around Allison's waist and led her toward the rocking chair by the window. "You sit and rest for a bit. You probably should have stayed in bed. Do you want something? A cup of tea, or a cinnamon roll?"

"No, thanks." Allison sank into the padded rocker where Sarah's mother usually sat. "Mrs. Anderson has already stuffed me full. Everybody here seems to think food cures all ills."

Sarah smiled, pulling a straight chair over to sit close to her. "It's comforting, anyway, ain't so?"

"Just being here in the shop is comforting." Allison leaned her head back against the cushion. "This place is very…well, restful, I guess." Her thoughts flickered briefly to the office in Philadelphia. There had been nothing restful about it. Di's frenetic personality had imbued the whole place with an air of turbulent energy.

"Have you told your family about what happened to you last night?" Sarah's gaze clouded. "They'll want to help."

"There's nothing they can do, living so far away." She

suspected Sarah wouldn't understand. All of her family seemed to be gathered in and around Laurel Ridge. "Anyway, I don't want to worry them."

"*Mamm* always says worrying is a mother's job." Sarah looked troubled, but she didn't press the matter. "I checked on Ralph this morning already. He's so nervous he's jumping at the least sound. You'd think he was the one who was hurt."

"That shop is his baby, I think." She set the rocking chair moving gently. "You'd feel that way if it was the quilt shop that was broken into, wouldn't you?"

Sarah sent a quick, possessive glance around her. "For sure." She shivered a little. "I guess they could have broken in here as easily."

Allison frowned. "Why the bookshop, I wonder? It seems such an odd choice." She broke off at the sounds of the door opening, and Sarah quickly rose.

"More things for the sale," she said. "I've had to start putting a few of the lighter things up in the attic." She shrugged. "The more we have, the more money we'll make for the volunteer fire company."

Sarah moved away to deal with the new contributions. Maybe she ought to get up and help, Allison thought, but Sarah would probably chase her right back to the chair.

She frowned, mind returning to the question that had been revolving in her thoughts. Why the bookshop? And was this connected to the other things that had happened? Or was it all a series of random coincidences?

The postage-stamp quilt top that Hannah had been working on lay on top of a basket at Allison's feet. Hannah had contrived to sew the tiny pieces together in such a way that each piece blended with or complemented the surrounding ones, something that seemed a nearly impossible task.

Too bad that the pieces of Allison's life didn't fit together in the same way. Her grandmother's death, her unexpected legacy, the breach with both her lover and her boss—everything had combined to bring her here. But here, she'd been faced with still more odd pieces to a puzzle that wouldn't fit together.

Julia Everly had come through with her promised invitation to lunch. If she could just ask the right questions, Julia might have a few of the puzzle pieces she needed.

"What are you doing out already? You should be resting."

She hadn't heard Nick come in, and his voice startled her. She looked up to find him frowning…a frown that didn't quite succeed in hiding the worry in his eyes.

"If you think it's restful to have Mrs. Anderson forcing food on you every fifteen minutes, all I can say is that I don't." She looked past him. "Good morning, Mac."

"Morning, Allison." Mac took the chair where Sarah had been sitting, leaving his brother standing. "I hope you don't mind going over things again in the light of day."

"You sure you're all right?" Nick's gaze held hers.

"Fine. I just have a colorful collection of bruises, that's all. Hard to believe paperback books could cause so much trouble."

"More likely the shelves," Mac put in. "Good thing one of those pine shelves didn't catch you on the head."

"Trust me, I'm very thankful for that." She was aware of Nick, his gaze so intent that even though a good eighteen inches separated them, they might as well be touching.

Mac flipped open a notebook. "Any idea what time it was when you came into the building last night?"

"It was somewhere around eight. I'd been out to Sarah's place, and I'd stayed after supper to help with the dishes and play a game with the boys. The drizzle had stopped by time I left, I know."

He made a note. "You said you saw a glow of light from the bookshop. What made you investigate it yourself? Why didn't you call us?"

Nick prowled around, staying within a few feet of her, for all the world like Hector when he was disturbed. She forced herself to concentrate on the question.

"I assumed it was Ralph. He'd been complaining earlier about not having any place to put a shipment of books because of all the things for the Jumble Sale, so I thought he was unpacking."

"You usually help him with that?" Mac's eyebrows lifted in a question.

"Of course she doesn't," Nick snapped. His hands came down on her shoulders from behind, and her breath caught at the unexpected touch. "Ralph had been carrying on about how inconvenienced he was. You know how he can be."

"As I told you last night, I thought it might soothe his ruffled feelings if I offered to help him," she added.

Mac grinned suddenly, seeming to drop his law officer's dignity. "He's ruffled now, all right. He's been carrying on as if he was personally attacked."

She remembered what she'd said about the shop being his baby. "The store is obviously very important to him. Was anything taken?"

Mac's eyes darkened as he frowned, and his expression seemed to emphasize his resemblance to Nick.

"Nothing, according to Ralph. The intruder didn't even touch the register, as far as we could tell. But Ralph seemed to think they were after the cash box he sometimes left in the back room."

Nick's fingers tightened on her shoulders. "I'm not sure I buy that idea. How would a casual thief know about it? If this is connected with the other things that have happened in Blackburn House—"

"There's no reason to think that," Mac said. He gave Allison an apologetic smile. "My brother's got the wind up about this whole thing."

"You can't deny it's odd," Nick snapped. "People prowling around the building, the power going off the way it did—something's been going on since Evelyn's death. And given what she said to Sarah…"

"That might not have anything to do with any of it," Mac said.

"But it might. I think Allison needs protection if she's going to stay here." His palms pressed firmly on her shoulders, as if willing her to agree.

"I don't…" she began.

"Nick, be reasonable," Mac protested. "The Laurel Ridge police force consists of me, a kid barely out of his teens, a patrolman on the verge of retirement and a couple of part-timers who can't do anything more challenging than direct traffic. How am I going to mount a guard on Allison?"

"You're not," she said forcefully, before Nick could speak. "If you did offer protection, I'd decline. I don't need it."

"You could have used it last night," Nick snapped. "You can't—"

"I shouldn't have come into the building after dark

by myself. I won't make that mistake again." She kept
her voice firm. She wasn't going to let the responsibility
for her own safety pass out of her control. She frowned
from Nick to his brother. "If you want to do something,
find out who's behind this…this harassment."

Behind my grandmother's death, she wanted to say,
but there was no proof that Evelyn's fall had been anything but an accident. A letter, a brief conversation—
they didn't amount to proof, just suspicion.

Nick and Mac exchanged looks, and she suspected
they were thinking the same thing. "All right," Nick
said. "No police protection. But that doesn't mean we
can't keep an eye on Allison. You, me, Dad, Sarah…we
all need to look out for her."

She didn't want to rely on other people, but it sounded
as if she wasn't being given a choice. And she couldn't
deny the reassurance she felt with Nick's hands on her
shoulders.

ALLISON HAD EXPECTED that Julia Everly's home would
be one of the traditional Victorian houses that seemed
so common in town. She'd been wrong. Julia lived in a
well-kept ranch-style house on a quiet residential street,
and she had served their chicken salad and croissants at
a glass-topped table in a small sunroom at the back of
the house, overlooking a pocket-size backyard.

"Not what you expected, right?" Julia refilled Allison's tall glass of iced tea, grinning.

"I have to confess, I assumed your home would be
more like…"

"The Blackburns', the Standishes' and every other
member of the old guard," Julia finished for her. "When
my husband died, I took a look at my life. What did I

want with that big mausoleum when I was on my own? I decided to simplify—a place I can take care of on my own, a little car to get around, a lawn service to tend the outside—that's all any widow needs."

"I don't think my grandmother agreed with you," Allison said, her mind on the elaborate Victorian which had to be expensive both to run and to keep in repair.

"Evelyn thought she had a standard to maintain. I'd rather have comfort." Julia sat down across from her and pushed her empty plate back with an air of clearing the decks for action. "What did you think about your letter from Evelyn?"

"So it was you who mailed it. I thought it must be." Julia was making it easy for her, going directly to the subject Allison wanted to discuss. Somehow that didn't surprise her.

Julia nodded. "I thought it a bit overly dramatic, waiting until you'd arrived in Laurel Ridge, but Evelyn was determined, so I kept my promise. Well?" Her eyes were bright, and it seemed clear she wasn't going to be satisfied with an evasion.

"I was surprised, obviously." Allison considered the possibilities. Her instinct was to trust Julia, and there was also the fact that if she opened up, Julia might do the same. "I wasn't sure what to think. Did she show it to you?"

Julia hesitated. "Well, yes, she did. Looking for confirmation that she was doing the right thing, maybe." She shrugged. "It wasn't what I'd have said in that situation, but if I've learned anything in a long life, it's that you have to take people as you find them. It was very Evelyn."

Allison's fingers tightened on the cold glass. "She

sounded as if she still hadn't forgiven my father." The old longing to defend him seemed to still exist, despite the fact that she knew his behavior had been indefensible.

"She was so proud of him, you see. Well, any mother would be, I guess. Hugh had a way about him that made you love him even when you suspected he was manipulating you." She frowned, seeming to look into the past. "Evelyn made excuses for him, always trying to believe he was the golden boy she imagined him. In the end, when she had to face the truth about him, she just couldn't go on."

"So she abandoned him, just like he abandoned me." The bitterness in her voice startled her. She'd thought she'd developed enough maturity to forget the past. But in Laurel Ridge, it seemed the past had been waiting for her.

Julia regarded her with an expression reminiscent of a teacher whose student has come up with a ridiculous excuse for being late. "Hugh was a grown man when he left here. You were a child when he left you."

She grappled with the unpalatable reality of the words. Maybe, like Evelyn, she'd been trying to find excuses for Hugh Standish. She took a deep breath. "Evelyn implied that he'd done something criminal. What was it?"

"Took money under false pretenses, I suppose you'd call it. He convinced people in the area that he represented an investment opportunity bearing his father's name, supposedly with his mother's backing."

Allison could only stare at her. "But he must have known it would be found out."

"Sure he did. But by then, he'd pocketed a tidy sum. The only difficulty was deciding when to do his vanishing act, but he managed it." Julia's voice had hardened.

After all this time, she'd obviously not forgotten. "Evelyn was devastated. She paid everyone back somehow. I don't suppose she'd have been liable in law, but she didn't care about that. She came pretty close to bankrupting herself, but somehow or other she pulled out of it eventually."

"He seemed to have a talent for leaving devastation behind him." Allison realized her hands were twisting together painfully. She pressed them flat on the tabletop.

Julia eyed her cautiously. "Are you okay?"

"Yes." She kept her tone firm. "I'm not six any longer. It's time I gave up trying to make excuses for my father." A weight she hadn't realized she'd been carrying slid from her at the words.

Julia nodded slowly. "It's not easy, this business of facing who people really are."

"No, it's not." She faced Julia squarely. "So I'm not making excuses for my grandmother, either. She could have helped us, but she acted as if my mother and I didn't exist."

"Because she didn't know you did exist." She nodded emphatically at Allison's startled look. "It's true. After about a year, she started trying to find Hugh. Wanted to know he was all right, I suppose. But she didn't have any luck. She finally hired a private investigator. Not sure how good he was, but he finally found out about you."

"So my grandmother could have gotten in touch with us."

"Yes, she could. But by then your mother was engaged to be married. Evelyn said she had to consider what would be best for you. She eventually decided it would do more harm than good to disrupt your life at that stage." Julia shrugged. "I don't know whether she was right or wrong, but she was trying to put you first."

Evelyn Standish had always been a distant, forbidding figure in the back of her mind. She'd known her grandmother existed, but when she'd asked once why they didn't visit her grandmother, her father had been so angry that she'd never asked again. Now she began to see Evelyn as a person, and she wasn't sure what to make of what she found. It sounded as if Evelyn had at least faced up to her mistakes and tried to do the right thing.

"She showed you the letter." Allison said abruptly. "Did you see the postscript?"

"Postscript?" Julia's eyebrows lifted. "No. What did it say?"

Allison pulled the letter from her bag. Wordlessly she handed the paper across the table and waited while Julia read it.

Julia frowned, shaking her head. "I never saw this, no. I knew something had been bothering Evelyn that last week or two, but she didn't tell me." The frown deepened. "One thing I know—if Evelyn uncovered something wrong going on in her building, she wouldn't have ignored it."

No. That was what Allison thought from the little she knew of the woman who'd been her grandmother. She'd have handled it, apparently on her own. If Evelyn Standish had relied on other people a little more, she might still be alive.

CHAPTER TWELVE

ALLISON HAD BEEN aware of people watching her all day, no matter what she was doing. Sarah, James…even Ellen made an excuse to stop by on her way to pick up Jamie from school. But by late afternoon, Blackburn House was like a pot slowly coming to a boil as people began setting up for the Spring Fest. Hammers sounded outside, and from the front window she could see booths springing up along Main Street like so many mushrooms. If she heard one anxious comment about the weather forecast for the next day, she heard a dozen.

Over Sarah's protests, Allison helped her pull out several boxes of small items for tomorrow's sale. "How soon do we actually set things up?" she asked. "And how on earth do you decide on prices?"

Sarah's eyes crinkled. "Pricing is an art, that's certain sure. It depends on so much, including who's doing the buying. Some folks will give you more than a thing is worth, just to make a donation. Others might really need whatever it is but not have much money to spare, so I usually ask for half what I might otherwise." She shrugged. "And late in the day, every price gets cut. After all, we don't want to pack it all up again."

"Sounds too complicated for me," Allison admitted. "Maybe you can find me something useful to do that doesn't involve making decisions."

"That won't—" Sarah stopped, her gaze fixed on several men who were coming in the building's front door. Five of them, mainly youngish, Allison thought, and two of them Amish.

She nudged Sarah. "Who's that?"

"Just some of the volunteer firemen. They'll put the tables up, and then we can start setting out the sale items."

Sarah made it sound very routine, but there was a faint color in her cheeks that hadn't been there before.

"What about the Amish?" She didn't think she was imagining the way Sarah's gaze clung to one particular Amish male—tall, with a curly chestnut beard and broad shoulders.

"That's Aaron King and his younger brother, Jonas." Sarah's tone flattened, and she busied herself sorting through the items in the box. "Plenty of Amish volunteer for the fire company. After all, Amish houses and barns burn the same as other people's do."

"I suppose so." Her thoughts were caught, remembering what Sarah had said about not marrying because she'd loved someone who didn't love her. Was Aaron King that someone? She couldn't ask. If Sarah wanted to share, she'd listen, but she couldn't ask.

A customer came in just then, waving a scrap of fabric she apparently wanted to match. Allison left Sarah to deal with the woman and slipped out, for the first time that day managing to do so without a question as to where she was going.

Not that her destination was any secret. She'd somehow managed to avoid Ralph's lamentations all day, but she really should check on him. She headed back down the central hallway, weaving her way around men carrying folding tables and a few giggling teenagers who'd apparently been pressed into service to carry donations from the storeroom. An impressive scene, now that she stopped to consider it. Everyone seemed to be happy about working together on a project for the community's good.

Nice, but Allison felt quite sure that Laurel Ridge, despite this current harmony, wasn't any utopia. Her grandmother's worries expressed in her letter, Ralph's mutterings about malice, her own fear when she saw that bookcase toppling toward her—all those things combined to convince her that behind all this small-town charm, something nasty lay concealed.

She was vaguely dissatisfied with herself. She'd stayed because she felt she had to know the truth behind her grandmother's death, or would feel she'd somehow failed herself by running away from the challenge, but what had she accomplished? Evelyn had seemed convinced that something was going on in Blackburn House, something unethical or illegal or both. But what? And more to the point, by whom?

Not Sarah, certainly. That was ridiculous on the face of it, and besides, Evelyn had confided in her. Nick? Her stomach clenched at the thought. Not Nick, unless he was a far better actor than she gave him credit for. But she wasn't sure that her judgment was altogether sound where Nick was concerned.

There was Ralph, of course, but Ralph seemed far more likely to be a victim than a villain. Still, her "accident" had taken place in his store.

Then there were the occupants of the upstairs offices. She hadn't gotten to know them very well yet, other than brief introductions and exchanges of greetings. The owner of the real estate office, Harvey Preston, was clear in her mind, maybe because real estate agents tended to be outgoing and chatty. He might have been sizing her up as a prospect.

The attorney, Richmond Willis, was barely thirty, with an eager, hopeful look each time his office door opened. Someone else looking for clients, she supposed. It couldn't be easy to establish a solo practice in a town like Laurel Ridge, where people had probably been dealing with the same firm for generations.

Then there was the financial adviser. She frowned slightly. It was a two-person firm, apparently, and the partners, Bart Gordon and Lena Oberlin, hadn't exactly welcomed her with open arms. Not that she'd expected anyone to do that, she told herself firmly. They probably preferred a businesslike relationship with the building's owner, and she'd been telling herself that was what she wanted, as well.

With Ralph, unfortunately, that desirable gap had been irrevocably bridged already. The bookshop door stood open, and Ralph was arranging a display of paperbacks on a folding table just outside. He seemed totally absorbed, and when she said his name, he jumped.

"Allison. It's just you." He blinked rapidly, running his hand over ruffled white hair.

"Sorry if I startled you." She wasn't sure what he had to be upset about. After all, she was the one who'd been attacked.

"Foolish of me." An unconvincing smile twitched his mouth. "I'm just unnerved. I mean, a break-in. Who would imagine it? Such a thing has never happened in all the time I've had my business in Blackburn House. Not until now."

Was the implication that she had somehow brought trouble with her? Well, it did seem that way, didn't it?

"Was anything taken? Or damaged?" She knew the answer from Mac, but she wanted to hear what he'd say.

"It was a mess, of course. But I can't say anything was really damaged. And as far as I can tell, nothing is missing." He said it with seeming reluctance, as if it would have been more satisfying to have an actual theft. "I suppose maybe you scared them off." He darted a glance at her and then looked away. "What—what brought you to my shop last night, anyway?"

"I thought I'd told you. I was going in the quilt shop to pick up my computer when I saw the light from the back room."

"Yes, yes, of course. I suppose you felt responsible, being the owner and all. Well, you won't have to worry about that much longer." He blinked repeatedly, turning away so that she nearly lost the final words.

It took a moment to register. She caught his arm, turning him to face her. "What do you mean? Why won't I have it to worry about much longer?"

"Why I...I thought I heard... Well, maybe it was just a rumor... But aren't you going away? I thought you were taking a position out west someplace."

The job in San Francisco, in other words. But how did Ralph know anything about it?

"Where did you hear about it?"

He tried to pull away, but she gripped him tightly.

"It's important, Ralph. Where?" she demanded.

He shrugged. "I don't know. You know how people talk. I just got the impression..."

"From whom?" She had a strong urge to shake him. Maybe then the truth would come spilling out.

"I don't know, exactly. Someone...it might have been Brenda, now that I think about it."

Brenda. How could she know? Had Brenda been in her office? Accessed her computer? That seemed impossible. But impossible things happened every day, and it seemed this might be one of them.

BLACKBURN HOUSE HAD been a storm of activity from the moment the doors had been unlocked at nine o'clock on Spring Fest day. But by midmorning the surge had mellowed to small waves of people who were shopping, chatting and nibbling on treats they'd picked up at the booths outside.

"It's going well, ain't so?" Sarah tucked a few more bills in the cash box. "I think we might be able to sit for a bit." She gestured to the folding chairs that had been set up behind the tables for workers.

"Good idea." But Allison leaned over the table so she could see down the center hall to the bookshop, glad to notice little more than a minor ache from her bruises. "Looks as if Ralph turned the sale over to his clerk."

"He's certain sure been nervous since the break-in," Sarah murmured, sympathy in her voice. "Poor man. He's easily upset, I think. And I'm sure Emily is enjoying being in charge."

Allison nodded, but her mind was preoccupied with Ralph's surprising knowledge of the contact from the recruiter about the job in California. When she'd been satisfied she wasn't going to get anything else out of Ralph, she'd gone so far as to call the headhunter, for all the good that had done.

"Allison?" Sarah eyed her quizzically. *"Was ist letz?* What's wrong?"

Allison hesitated, but there was no real reason to hold

back the information from Sarah. Sarah certainly knew the people involved far better than she did.

"Ralph said something odd to me yesterday. Something that indicated he had knowledge of an email I'd received about a job in California."

"But...you're not going, are you?" Sarah's gaze sought hers for reassurance.

"No. Not now." That at least she felt sure of. "But what bothered me was how Ralph could know anything about it. When I pressed him, he said he'd heard it from someone, possibly Brenda."

"How would Brenda know anything?" Sarah's reaction was the same as hers had been. "She hasn't been in your office, has she? I haven't seen her in the building for several days, not since she brought those things in for the sale."

"That's what I wondered. I finally called the recruiter who'd contacted me about the position. Asked him how he'd heard of me. He edged around the question, finally saying that was confidential. But when I mentioned Laurel Ridge, I thought I heard a reaction in his voice."

"So you think what?" Sarah's usually peaceful expression turned troubled.

"I think someone got in touch with the recruiter and urged him to offer me a job at a nice, safe distance from Blackburn House. If I accepted, that would suit Brenda, but somehow I don't see her doing such a thing. Does she have any business connections? Do you know what she was doing before she came here?"

"I wouldn't think so." Sarah answered the first question with a considering air. "Before she came to live with Evelyn, they lived in a small town upstate. Her husband ran a hardware store, and after he passed, she and Krysta came here."

Allison grimaced. "Doesn't sound likely she'd have much knowledge of specialized business recruiters."

"It sounds more like Thomas Blackburn," Sarah said, and then put her fingers to her lips. "I'm not meaning anything by that. It's just that he's run the mill for more than forty years, so he likely knows a lot about business."

Thomas Blackburn. Yes, the act certainly fit better with his position and his personality. There was a certain amount of subtlety to the notion that seemed unlike Brenda. Logically they might have linked forces in their efforts to dislodge her. Well, they were going to be disappointed. The more she was pushed, the more determined she was to stay.

Sarah looked about to ask another question, but her attention was diverted when her brothers popped up in front of her. Jonah and Thomas had been detailed to run errands for them, with little Noah tagging along behind. They looked expectant, and it seemed Jonah had been appointed spokesperson for them, because he stepped to the front.

"Do you want us to do anything chust now, Sarah?" Jonah spoke the best English of the three of them, she'd noticed, other than a few difficulties with the *j* sound.

Sarah's eyes twinkled. "Not right now. I wouldn't wonder but that you want to go and get a treat, ain't so?"

Three blond heads nodded in unison. "*Ja*, please."

"I guess we can do without you for a little while, ain't so, Allison?"

"I expect so." Allison fished a ten-dollar bill from her pocket and handed it to Jonah. "You get something to share, okay?"

"*Denke*, Allison." Jonah grinned. "It's wonderful kind of you."

"Just don't bring any cotton candy back in with you," Sarah warned as they sprinted toward the door. "*Ach*, you wouldn't believe the mess that makes."

Allison grinned. "You're forgetting I have two little brothers. They brought cotton candy in the car one time. Believe me, it was the last time. It took three washings to get it out of my hair."

Sarah chuckled. "Cotton candy aside, you should try some food from the stands. The Methodists have great barbecue sandwiches, and the Presbyterians are making fresh-cut French fries, I heard."

"What about the Amish?" she asked.

"Funnel cakes," Sarah said promptly. "And whoopie pies. *Mamm* is making funnel cakes this morning. *Sehr gut*."

"I'll try one," she promised.

Sarah rose as a couple of women approached the stand, and she was soon deep in conversation with one of them.

Allison tackled the other, who was scanning the table, obviously searching for something in particular.

"May I help you find something?" she asked, hoping she'd know how to respond.

"I was hoping to find some nice quilted table runners." The woman, middle-aged and rotund, seemed determined to touch every object on the table. "You had some last year," she added, sounding aggrieved.

"I'm sure we do. I remember seeing some." But a cursory search failed to turn up the desired item.

"Maybe somebody else will have them?" The woman started to turn away, her purse stubbornly closed.

Allison's competitive spirit rose. "Just one second." She turned to Sarah. "Sarah, didn't we have a couple of boxes of quilted place mats and table runners?"

"I'm sure we did." Sarah ran an experienced eye down the tables. "*Ach*, I think those were the boxes we put up on the attic steps, remember? I guess they were never brought back down."

She remembered perfectly, now that Sarah had reminded her. They'd carried a few boxes upstairs to store them when the storeroom started to overflow.

"I'll run up and get them." She smiled at the potential buyer. "If you'll just look around for a few minutes, I'll come right back."

"I should go—" Sarah began, but Allison was already out from behind the table.

"You can't leave," she said. "You're the only one who knows about the pricing. It will just take me a minute."

Actually, it would be good to get away from the buzz of noise for a few minutes. At first she'd been swept up in the excitement, but she had begun to long for a break.

Allison hurried down the hall, dodging shoppers. Their temporary lull seemed to be over, as a steady stream of people flowed through the door. She went up the stairs quickly, glad her stiffness had begun to pass away. Another few days and she probably wouldn't have any unpleasant reminders of her encounter in the bookshop.

She emerged into the upstairs hall, automatically noticing that a push broom had been left leaning against the wall next to the stairs. She'd really have to speak to the custodian. Somehow she doubted that Evelyn would have let him get away with such carelessness.

She hurried to her office, pulling the keys from her

pocket. Hector, snoozing on a stack of files on her desk, opened one eye, then jumped down to come and weave circles around her feet.

"I know." She stroked his back. "You don't like being shut in here, but there are too many people going in and out today. You're safer here."

Hector didn't appreciate her reasoning, she supposed. He'd already become used to having the run of the building, and he'd probably gained a pound from the snacks Ralph kept sneaking him.

She unlocked the attic door. If the boxes weren't here— But they were, and she bent to lift the two stacked boxes in her arms. Not heavy but bulky, they stuck out in front of her. She closed the door again with her foot, just in time to keep Hector from darting up to the attic in search of the mice he seemed to believe dwelt there.

"Sorry. You stay here." Fending him off, Allison slipped out of the office, balancing the boxes on her hip while she locked the door.

She headed back down the hall, hearing the rumble of voices from downstairs, louder now. Obviously foot traffic had increased. She'd better get downstairs and help Sarah.

At the top of the staircase she paused, feeling with her foot for the edge of the step. The noise was louder here, and she could see the people milling around the hall as they moved from table to table.

One of the volunteers glanced up and met her gaze, and she recognized him as the Amish firefighter Sarah had known. She took a step down, her elbow against the railing, and suddenly his face changed. He lunged toward the steps, shouting something, just as she stepped down. Something hit her ankle, her foot slipped, the boxes lurching. Then they were falling and she was falling, too, helplessly out of control, stumbling down the stairs and trying to grasp something, anything to hang on to—

She ran abruptly into a solid body, stopping her headlong plunge, and then others were there, everyone exclaiming at once, some in English, some in Pennsylvania Dutch.

Helping hands eased her to a sitting position on the stairs, and then Nick was there, touching her gently.

"Are you all right? Allison, tell me where you're hurt. Did you hit your head?"

She tried to shake her head, but a wave of dizziness swamped her, and she lowered it to her knees instead.

"Easy, just sit still." Nick's palm cradled her head.

"Some of the paramedics are right outside," a male voice said. "They're coming now."

She'd argue that she didn't need them, but she couldn't seem to form the words. She heard Sarah's voice, felt Sarah slide on to the step next to her and put an arm around her waist.

"What happened?" Nick sounded angry. "Did anyone see?"

"Ja." It was the same male voice, and Allison managed to peek up long enough to assure herself that it was indeed the man Sarah had identified as Aaron King.

"I saw her coming down with the boxes and was going to help her. Then I saw the broom—wedged across the stairs it was, a couple of steps down. Most likely she couldn't see it because of the boxes."

The broom. There was something about the broom...

"It wasn't on the steps when I went up." She glanced up and immediately regretted it and leaned her forehead against her hand. "It was against the wall, a couple of feet away."

"Somebody must have brushed against it," Aaron said slowly. "Careless, not stopping to move it again."

"Maybe so." Nick's hand clasped hers, holding it tightly. He knew, just as well as she did, that this was no accident.

"I DON'T NEED to go to the emergency room." Allison was still protesting when the EMTs loaded her into the ambulance.

Nick climbed in after her. "Give them a break," he said. "They don't have a chance to take someone to the hospital every day. And it's the least they can do when you've been raising money for them all day."

"That's right." Traci Elder, the newest member of the rescue squad, smiled at Allison and smoothed a blanket over her. "You let us do our job, okay?"

Nick knelt, taking Allison's hand and not caring whether somebody saw him or not. "Just listen to her." He pressed her fingers. "Here's poor Traci getting her first shot at treating somebody. You don't want to spoil it for her."

Allison lips relaxed into a slight smile. "All right, all right. But this better not cost me an arm and a leg."

"Everybody's volunteering their services today," he said, relieved at seeing the smile.

Almost immediately Allison's face darkened again. "That broom—"

"I know," he said quickly, darting a glance at Traci, who seemed preoccupied with filling out a chart. "Mac is taking care of it. Don't worry about it now."

"Okay." Her eyes closed as they hit a pothole turning into the hospital lot. "I won't."

He held her hand in both of his. *I'll do it for you*, he promised silently.

When they reached the emergency entrance, Allison was whisked away from him immediately, taken to a curtained cubicle to await the doctor, who'd apparently been busy with one chest pain, two upset stomachs and one shortness of breath already today. Nick stood in the hall waiting. Wondering.

The door swung open to admit his brother. "How is she?"

"Waiting for the doctor." He took Mac's elbow and guided him over to the window, hopefully out of earshot. "What about that broom?"

"Well, it didn't jump out and throw itself across the stairs," Mac said. "Either someone knocked it down or someone put it there."

"Who would knock it over and not pick it up again?" Nick demanded.

"I know, I know." Mac frowned. "That business in the bookshop wasn't necessarily aimed at her. In fact, it seems more likely that if anyone came in, it would be Ralph."

He had to agree. "Right. Whoever it was just wanted to get away without being seen, the way I figure it. But what happened today…"

"I talked to Sarah," Mac said. "According to her, Allison went upstairs to get a couple of boxes of things they'd forgotten to bring down. She says anyone could have heard them talking."

Nick nodded. "And anyone might have figured Allison would be coming back carrying things, maybe not able to see what was under her feet."

"Improvised, but serious. And pretty darn safe for the perp. He was probably downstairs mingling with the crowd by the time she fell. She might have managed to catch herself, but if she didn't, and if Aaron King hadn't happened to look up at just the right moment…well, it's a long way down to that marble floor."

"Far enough to kill Evelyn," Nick reminded him.

"The doc says Evelyn had a stroke," Mac said.

"But he couldn't say whether she fell because she had a stroke or whether she had a stroke because she fell."

Mac shrugged. "Amounted to the same thing in the end." He held up his hand to prevent the protest he clearly saw coming from Nick.

"Look, I'm not saying there aren't a few unanswered questions about Evelyn Standish's death. But it looks to me as if several people have an interest in chasing Allison out of town, regardless."

"Thomas Blackburn wants Blackburn House. He's not likely to get it if Allison stays her year and claims it." Nick ticked the names off on his fingers. "Brenda Standish Conner. She wants the money Blackburn House represents, I'd say. Then there's her daughter. Would Krysta be likely to seize a chance like this?"

"I don't know her well enough to say, but Allison did mention the repeated offers from Brenda and Blackburn." Mac frowned. He didn't like not knowing the people in his jurisdiction. He'd said more than once that a lot of small-town policing involved knowing who'd be likely to do what.

"There are the other Blackburns, as well," Nick pointed out. "I don't think Tommy's interested in much beyond his golf game, but young T.J. seems ripe for trouble."

Mac seemed to consider the list. "What about any of the current tenants? Anybody who'd rather take their chances on a known quantity like Brenda inheriting?"

Nick shook his head in frustration. "I don't know. On the face of it, I'd say it was unlikely, but it happened. Evelyn didn't foresee what trouble she was going to cause with her precious will."

"Trying to control things from beyond the grave like she did in life," Mac said. "Seems to me that's a recipe for disaster."

"Right." Nick's jaw set in a hard line. "And Allison's the one it's all going to land on."

CHAPTER THIRTEEN

THE LAUREL RIDGE ER seemed loath to let Allison go, but finally she'd talked them into discharging her. With a sprained ankle, a pair of crutches, a splitting headache and the probability of a colorful black eye in addition to the bruises she already possessed, she'd begun to conclude that Laurel Ridge wasn't exactly the safest place she'd ever been.

"Sure you're all right?" Nick asked. He eased her into his car as carefully as if she was made of glass. "Maybe you should have stayed at least until tomorrow."

"They didn't offer that as a possibility," she reminded him. "And I wouldn't have stayed, anyway. I can nurse my bruises at Mrs. Anderson's as easily as anywhere."

Looking doubtful, he closed the door gently, as if even a door slam might hurt her, and rounded the car to slide into the driver's seat. "You don't have to go to the B and B, you know. Mom would make up the spare room for you in a minute. She'd be delighted."

"I appreciate it." Allison gripped the armrest as he made the turn out of the parking lot. Amazing, how it hurt to move even in a car. "But honestly, going someplace else just seems too much effort. All I want right now is to go to bed. The pain med the doctor gave me seems to be acting like a sleeping pill."

He flashed her a grin. "It might well be." He sobered

a bit, studying the tree-lined street as if it were a strange moonscape. "Best thing you can do is rest. I know Mac wants to talk to you again, but he'll wait until you're ready."

"Did he say that, or are you putting words in his mouth?"

"He's still my little brother, even if he is the police chief. He'll wait until you feel well enough to talk to him."

Given the implied threat in his tone, she suspected Mac would do as he was told.

"Is he at least taking it seriously?" If anyone else mentioned accident to her, she might scream.

"He is." Nick sounded grim. "We'll all blaming ourselves right now. We should have kept a better eye on you. I guess none of us expected an attack in broad daylight."

"Not an attack, exactly." She tried to be fair. "More like a trap, which I was obliging enough to fall into. If I hadn't been carrying those boxes, I'd have seen the broom."

"If someone was watching, he could make a pretty good guess that you were going upstairs to fetch something." Nick turned down the alley that ran parallel to the blocked-off main street.

"It could have been someone close enough to hear, for that matter. There were people around." Frowning made her headache worse, and she tried to smooth the wrinkles away with her fingertips. "If we could find out who was in the building at the time…"

"Leave that part of it to Mac," he said, pulling into the rear driveway at the B and B. "He's working on it now." He stopped the car close to the back door. "Let's get you settled so you can rest."

With Nick's strong arm supporting her, Allison made

it into the hall without incident. Mrs. Anderson and Sarah rushed to meet her.

"You'll get right into bed," Mrs. Anderson scolded. "And I'll bring you a tray with some hot soup. Nothing like chicken noodle soup to comfort you when you're feeling bad."

"You're right on target, Mrs. A." Nick leaned over to kiss her cheek. "I can't convince Allison to go home and let my mom take care of her, but I know you'll do just as well."

Sarah clasped Allison's hand. "We'd love to have you come to us. *Mamm* said that first thing, but I thought you'd be missing your electric and your computer in an Amish household, ain't so?"

Allison managed a smile. "I guess I would, at that. Really, nobody needs to fuss over me. I just want to rest."

"We won't fuss," Sarah said. "But Mrs. Anderson is giving me the room adjoining yours for tonight, so I can take care of you."

"You don't have to—"

"It's all settled, so there's no purpose in arguing." Sarah sounded remarkably firm for someone who was usually so gentle.

"Well, at least go back to the sale now." It was surprising how wearing it was to fend off people who wanted to take care of you. Wearing, but nice, too.

"*Mamm* and my cousin are looking out for things until I get back," Sarah said. "I can stay and help you get settled…"

"No need. I'm just going to get into bed, eat my soup and take a nap. I'll talk to you later, all right?" She was beginning to sag. If everyone would just go away and let her rest, she'd be fine.

Maybe Sarah realized that, because she nodded. "I'll go, then. I'll see you later." With a light touch on her arm, Sarah left.

"Well, now, I'll go and dish up that soup I've been keeping hot. Nick, you'd best help Allison up the stairs with those crutches."

"I'll do that," Nick assured her. The instant Mrs. Anderson disappeared, he lifted Allison off her feet and strode to the stairs.

Bereft of breath, she clutched the crutches to keep from hitting them against the wall. "Nick, put me down. She said help me, not carry me."

"If you don't stop wiggling, I'm likely to drop you." His teasing smile was aggravatingly close as he mounted the stairs, cradling her against his chest. "Just hold still and enjoy the ride."

She'd say something smart, but she was suddenly afraid that if she did, he might guess what she was feeling. All of her exhaustion had dropped away, and she had an almost irresistible urge to snuggle her head against his shoulder. The flannel shirt was soft against her cheek, and his warmth and strength seemed to permeate it.

Weakening, she pressed her face closer and heard his breath catch. The pulse in his neck was beating a mile a minute, and she suspected her own was just as fast.

He reached the top. "Which room?" The words were a husky rumble.

She nodded toward the door to her room, felt him fumble for the knob. He shoved it open and carried her straight to the bed. He put her down, and for a dizzying moment he leaned over her. Close, so very close. His hands were braced on either side of her, his lips no more than a heartbeat away.

"Ally," he murmured, closing the gap.

With a thump, something landed on the bed. Meowing harshly, Hector pushed his fat furry self between them.

Nick's lips curved in a reluctant smile. "Foiled again. And by a cat."

She could breathe once more. "Better the cat than Mrs. Anderson, I suppose. How did he get here? Poor baby—I left him shut in the office, didn't I?"

"I'd guess Sarah realized he was there and brought him over." Nick ran a strong hand along the silky fur. Hector decided to be pleased, arching his back in response to the touch. Sort of how she felt, Allison decided.

A rattle of china announced the approach of Mrs. Anderson. Nick straightened. "I'd better—" He stopped, muttered something under his breath, and bent to give her a quick, hard kiss. "Stay safe this time, will you? Mac and I will be here later."

She nodded, a little dazed from the kiss. "We'll talk later." And maybe it was a good thing Mac would be coming with him, because she wasn't quite sure what would happen if they were alone.

BY THE TIME Nick reached Blackburn House, he'd managed to get himself under control. Tricky thing, this attraction. He hadn't felt anything like this in a long time, and he'd be just as happy to do without it now. Sexual attraction was one thing, but the complicated mix of emotions that seemed to be attached to it where Allison was concerned was something else again.

His son had to be his first consideration. Always. He couldn't let himself get seriously involved with a woman without thinking about how it might affect Jamie. And Allison...to say the least, she seemed to want a com-

pletely different life than the one he'd carved out for
himself and his son. If something didn't have a chance
of working out, it was way better not to start it.

The crowd in Blackburn House was larger than he'd
expect this time of day, and he was pretty good at estimating the ebb and flow of people at Spring Fest after
all these years. He hadn't taken two steps before he knew
why—every second or third person stopped him to ask
if the story was true, if Allison was in the hospital, if he
knew how it had happened.

Evading the questions as best he could, he went in
search of his brother. He finally ran Mac to ground in
the small room in the basement that was officially called
the custodian's closet. Fred Glick had turned it into a
little home away from home with a well-worn recliner
and a tiny refrigerator. At the moment, Fred was glaring
at Mac, shoulders hunched as if prepared for an attack.

"Hey, it's not my fault if somebody knocked over a
broom on the stairs. I didn't do it. Ms. Standish probably did it herself, and now she's trying to blame me."

Nick found his hands curling into fists and forcibly relaxed them. Fred was just being Fred—according to him,
he was never responsible for anything that went wrong.

Mac's expression said he wasn't buying it. "Why was
the broom left up there to begin with? Are you saying
that wasn't you?"

"Not my fault," Fred repeated, his tone turning whiny.
He rubbed his nose with what looked like a cleaning rag.
"You don't know how much extra work this Spring Fest
makes for me. Nobody appreciates it, I can tell you. I'd
no sooner get started on one thing than somebody called
me to do something else. I had to go help set up tables,
and I forgot, that's all. Can't blame a man for that."

"So, that means you were around all morning, does it?" Mac changed course.

Fred eyed him suspiciously. "Well, yeah, mostly. Like I say, there was a lot to do."

"Who went upstairs while you were so busy? You must have been able to see the stairs if you were working in the hall."

"See them, yeah, but I didn't have time to go noticing who went where. Seemed like half the town was there at one time or another. Not my job to watch who goes where."

Mac barely suppressed a sigh. "Did you notice anyone go upstairs?"

"I s'pose. Nobody who didn't have a reason for being there. No strangers, I mean. Your brother here went up and came down carrying a couple of boxes, I know."

In answer to Mac's questioning look, Nick nodded. "I brought down stuff for the sale, but that was pretty early. Before nine, anyway. I didn't notice the broom then, but that doesn't mean it wasn't there. I was in a hurry."

Mac nodded and turned back to Fred. "All right, Fred. That's all I need for now. You can get back to work." When Fred didn't move, he added, "They'll be starting to tear down soon. Go see if anyone needs help."

Mumbling something under his breath, Fred shambled off.

"Let's get out in the air." Mac headed for the nearest door. "This place smells too strongly of Glick."

Nick followed him out. "I don't know why Evelyn kept him on here all those years. He certainly doesn't earn whatever she paid him."

"She probably figured he couldn't do much else," Mac said. "How's Allison?"

"Feeling pretty rocky, I'd say." His treacherous brain produced an image of Allison on the bed looking up at him, half longing, half startled. "I told her you'd be back to talk to her after she'd rested."

Mac nodded. "I will, but I'm not sure what else she'll be able to tell us. It was a neat plan. By the time she fell, whoever put the broom there could be safely mingling with the crowd or could have come and gone by the back stairs."

"That door's usually kept locked," Nick said. "Someone could go out, but—" He stopped, because Mac was shaking his head.

"Apparently it was left unlocked all day. Glick again. According to him, he figured he might as well leave it open because they'd use that door to carry boxes out to the truck after the sale was over."

True enough. At the end of the sale, everything left was loaded up and taken to the Salvation Army store for donation. "That wouldn't happen until after four," he said. "Fred had no call to leave it open all day."

"Anything to save him an extra step, I suppose." Mac shrugged. "The point is, was this deliberate? And if so, who wants to get rid of Allison Standish that much?"

"I don't see how it can't have been deliberate." There he was, clenching his fists again. "The broom was leaning against the wall when she went up. From what she said, she must have been upstairs no more than five to ten minutes at most, and when she came back down, the broom was lying across the stairs."

Mac shook his head. "Not just lying. I found the marks where it had been pushed between the uprights. I don't see how that could have happened accidentally."

Nick's stomach churned. "No. It was no accident." He

sucked in a breath. "Whoever it was took an awful risk, though. If anyone looked up—"

"I tried it," Mac said. "You could stay behind the corner of the stairs and slide the broom out, wedging it between the bars, without ever coming into the open at all." He frowned. "Seems like whoever it was must have left by the back stairs, though. Or waited until after Allison fell to go out in all the turmoil. Nobody thought of checking around upstairs."

"Yeah." He gave himself a mental kick. "I should have, but I didn't."

"Don't beat yourself up over it," Mac advised. "There are plenty of places to hide upstairs, especially if one of the attic doors was left unlocked."

"So what next?" Nick glared at his brother, needing to blame someone. He was behaving just like Fred Glick, it seemed. "Have you found out if any of the people concerned in the ownership of Blackburn House were inside this morning?"

"Believe it or not, I did think of that." Sarcasm laced Mac's voice. "All of them were, at one time or another. The entire Blackburn family made an appearance, and Brenda Conner and her daughter were both there for a time." Mac shook his head. "Are we seriously imagining one of those solid citizens was upstairs setting a trap in order to get Allison out of the way? That's hardly their style."

It was hard to envision, Nick had to admit. But someone had done it. "As far as solid citizens go, I wouldn't exactly describe T.J. as that. He's been skirting the edges of serious trouble for the past year. And Krysta's the type who never seems to see the consequences of her actions."

"True. But I've never noticed either of them going to

any trouble to oblige their elders." Mac grinned. "Not like you and me. I wouldn't expect them to move a finger to try and regain Blackburn House."

They'd rounded the building as they talked. A few people stood on the sidewalk, clustered around the hot dog stand. As they approached, Tommy Blackburn turned, hesitated and then came toward them carrying a foam coffee cup and wearing a suitably solemn expression.

"I was just hearing about Allison's accident," he said. "Is she all right? Is there anything I can do?"

"She's doing fine," Nick said quickly, before Mac could respond. "Luckily Aaron King spotted her when she tripped and was able to break her fall." He watched Tommy's reaction but couldn't read anything more than concern and relief.

"Good thing he was there. I've always thought those stairs were dangerous. Slippery, and it's a long way down to that marble floor."

He was getting tired of that particular cliché. "Allison didn't slip. She tripped on a broom someone had left across the stairs."

"Still a dangerous spot, no matter what caused it," Tommy said. "My father says that stairway is a masterpiece, but I don't see it myself. Give me a comfortable modern place all on one floor any day."

"No desire to get back the family homestead, then?" Nick asked, trying to keep his voice light.

Tommy grimaced. "That's a fool notion of the old man's. Waste of money, as far as I can see, but of course, he wouldn't take my advice." He shrugged. "Well, give Allison my best. I'm glad she wasn't seriously hurt." He turned away and was absorbed by the crowd again.

"There's one person who doesn't have any reason to get rid of Allison, according to him," Mac said quietly.

"According to him," Nick repeated as they went back into Blackburn House. "Still, he might want to please his father more than he lets on. It's Blackburn Senior who holds the purse strings, and rumor has it he's getting tired of funding Tommy's lifestyle."

Mac nodded, seeming distracted. "I didn't have a chance to talk to Ralph Mitchell yet. There's not much chance he'd see anything since the stairway faces the other direction, but I'd better try." He glanced at his brother. "Don't you have work of your own to do?"

"Is that a hint that you could do without my company? Too bad, because I'm not vanishing. I'll tag along while you talk to Ralph. After all, it was his shop that was broken into. If the two things are connected—"

"I don't see how," Mac said, but he didn't offer any objections when Nick walked back to the bookshop with him.

But it seemed they were destined to disappointment. Emily, Ralph's clerk, shook her head when Mac asked for him.

"He's gone on home," she said, her porcelain-blue eyes distressed. "He was just so upset after Ms. Standish's accident that he couldn't settle down. Why, he was shaking so badly he couldn't even drink the nice cup of tea I made for him."

Nick exchanged glances with his brother. "It seems odd that he'd be that upset," he said. "Ms. Standish wasn't badly hurt, you know."

"Oh, I know, and I'm just so thankful. When I think of how bad it might have been..." She let that trail off, shuddering. "But Ralph is just so sensitive. I don't think he's really recovered from the trauma of having the store broken into, you know."

"He must be sensitive, as you say." Mac kept a straight face. "I'm sorry he was so upset."

"Well, it was a shock, you must admit, but we just have to carry on." Emily nodded, patting her soft curls in satisfaction, as if priding herself for not laying claim to nerves. "Why, after Ms. Standish fell, he was in such a state. I remember his very words. He said, 'It could have been any of us that was intended to fall into that trap. Any of us.'"

Any of us, Nick repeated silently. Was that just an example of Ralph's timid nature? Or did he actually mean something by it?

"So you really don't have any idea who did this." Allison gestured toward her bandaged ankle, propped up on a footstool Mrs. Anderson had brought to her room.

Mac and Nick exchanged glances, and Sarah reached out to pat Allison's shoulder. "I'm sure Mac is doing everything possible," she said.

Allison shook her head impatiently. "I know. I'm not blaming anyone." Her fingers tightened on the arms of the rocking chair. "I'm just frustrated, that's all."

"Yeah, me, too." Mac paced to the window, shoulders hunched. "Trust me, I don't want things like this happening in my town."

"It's not Allison's fault," Nick snapped, apparently taking offense at his brother's tone.

"It's nobody's fault," she said quickly. The frilly Victorian bedroom seemed about to burst with the presence of so much male testosterone. She certainly didn't want to be the cause of a fight between the brothers. "Except the person who planted that blasted broom. I don't suppose fingerprints are of any use?"

"Might be if he or she had touched the handle," Mac said. "It looks to me as if it was just pushed over across the steps and into place. They wouldn't have had to touch anything more than the bristles. Maybe even nudging it into place with a shoe would have worked."

Threading her fingers through her hair, Allison shoved it behind her ears. "It can't have been planned, it seems to me."

"No." Nick had a weight of irritation in his voice. "We thought you were safe enough in broad daylight. Whoever it was had to have seen you go upstairs, noticed the broom and just seized the opportunity."

"But anyone might have come along." Sarah sounded horrified. "An old person, a child."

"Could be, but it wasn't likely," Nick said. "The offices were closed, so there was no reason for anyone to go upstairs other than people working the sale, and very few of them had occasion to leave their tables." He looked as if he'd like to pace the floor, but unfortunately the bedroom didn't really provide pacing space.

"You're sure you didn't glimpse anyone upstairs? Or maybe hear anything odd while you were there?" Mac was grasping at straws, she suspected.

She shook her head, tired of saying it.

"Look at it another way," Nick suggested. "Who did you see in the crowd before it happened? Anyone you know?" His gaze softened. "I know you're tired. Just try to visualize the people down in the hall, if you can."

Allison closed her eyes, wishing she could just climb into bed and go to sleep. She forced herself to picture the wide downstairs hall at Blackburn House, the marble floor, the stairwell soaring upward. She furnished the image with tables along each side, filled it with people looking, people manning the stands, people talking.

She opened her eyes. "I'm sure I saw Brenda and Krysta at some point, but I don't know when."

"I did, too," Sarah exclaimed. "I didn't think of it before, but I remember being a little surprised. Krysta looked like she didn't want to be there, ain't so?"

"She probably didn't." Allison visualized the bored expression on the teenager's face, then saw it lighten when she glimpsed someone. "She noticed someone or something back near the bookshop that made her smile, so I'm guessing it was probably T.J."

Mac nodded, picking up his uniform cap. "That fits with what we've heard from other people. The only one I haven't been able to talk with is Ralph."

"Why not Ralph? He might have noticed if T.J. was actually there." Maybe she was jumping to conclusions about it, but she didn't know who else would make Krysta light up that way.

"Ralph went home early." Nick seemed to suppress a smile. "Emily told us he was devastated by what happened, because he's so sensitive, you know." His grin broke through.

"According to Emily, Ralph said it could have been anybody in the building who fell into the trap. Even him, I guess." Mac jerked a nod toward the door. "Come on, Nick. Let's give Allison a break."

Nick stood, but instead of heading for the door he came to her. He leaned over, taking her hand and holding it between both of his. "You look awful. Get some rest." His gaze clung to hers for a moment, and then he dropped her hand and stepped away. "Good night."

He followed Mac out. "Lock this," he said briefly, and closed the door.

Sarah flipped the lock. "I'm not afraid, but it's wise to talk precautions, ain't so?"

"I guess." She reached for the crutches, and Sarah was there instantly, supporting her.

"You just sit on the bed, and I'll help you with your nightgown. Where is it?"

Allison yawned. "Top drawer. But it's pajamas. I haven't worn a nightgown since I was about six."

"They're comfy to snuggle up in," Sarah said, pulling open the drawer.

Before Sarah had a chance to bring the pajamas, Allison's cell phone announced a call. She checked. It was Diane.

"I'd better take this, or she'll keep calling back. You don't need to leave," she added when Sarah made a move toward the door between the rooms. "It's going to be brief."

She pressed the button. "Hello, Diane."

"Tired of the boonies yet?" As usual, Diane didn't waste time or politeness. "Ready to come back to work?"

"That's not going to happen." Maybe if she said it firmly enough, Di would get the message.

"Now, don't be so quick. You haven't heard my offer yet." Diane sounded pleased with herself.

"Offer?" She was mildly intrigued. What incentive was Diane willing to offer to avoid trying to replace her?

Hector, who had retired under the bed while the men were in the room, jumped on her lap, distracting her. She petted him absently.

"How does partner sound to you?"

"Partner?" She had to repeat the word to be certain she'd heard it.

"That's right. Partner." Diane sounded very sure of herself. She obviously thought this was an offer Allison couldn't refuse. "I like you, Allison. We work well together, and it's time I had somebody to share the responsibility. So, what do you say? Are you in?"

Allison's brain started working again. "You haven't been in touch with anyone else from Laurel Ridge lately, by any chance?"

"Laurel Ridge?" Diane sounded blank. "What's that? Oh, you mean that hick town you ran off to? Of course not."

Diane could lie and do it very convincingly. Allison had heard her do it. But she actually sounded sincere, so maybe this wasn't another ploy like the position in San Francisco.

"I don't—" she began.

"Don't answer me now," Diane said quickly. "I'll email you the partnership proposal. Look it over carefully, think about it and let me know. Talk to you later." She ended the connection before Allison could say another word.

Staring blankly at the phone, Allison put it on the bedside table. A partnership. Diane must really want her back. She realized that Sarah was staring at her.

When she met her gaze, Sarah flushed and averted her face. "I'm sorry. I couldn't help but hear. You… Are you going away?"

"I don't know." But even as she said the words, she realized she did know. "No. No, I'm not."

Sarah smiled. "I'm wonderful glad of that. It was a *gut* offer, though?"

"It was a very good offer." Allison pictured it with a little regret. "But if I took it now, it would be running away." Her fingers clenched. "I don't run away. I'll be darned if I'll let somebody scare me away from having what's mine."

CHAPTER FOURTEEN

BY MONDAY, ALLISON really couldn't stand being alone in the bedroom any longer, no matter how cozy it was. So she moved to the quilt shop, negotiating the sidewalk carefully with her crutches, with Sarah dogging her steps and opening doors. Finally she was ensconced in the rocking chair next to Sarah's mother.

"I'm *sehr* happy to see you moving around." Hannah paused in her stitching. "It's *gut* to be back out again, ain't so?"

"I was getting a little stir-crazy." Allison smiled, watching Hector smell the crutches she'd propped up against the wall. "They haven't changed," she assured him, and Hannah chuckled.

"He must be sure they're not dangerous. Or something to eat."

Seemingly convinced that the crutches were neither, he leaped onto his favorite windowsill, turned around a few times and settled down, paws tucked beneath him so that he resembled a sphinx.

Allison leaned back in the chair, her head cushioned against the pad that lined it. "I haven't used crutches since I broke a bone in my foot when I was fifteen. It seems a lot harder now."

"Maybe you'll be able to get rid of them soon." Hannah paused, studying her face. "Do your parents know about the…accident?"

"I called my mother yesterday. I had no intention of telling her, but she knew something was wrong the minute I spoke. I had trouble convincing her she didn't need to hop on a plane and come to help me."

"You told her you had good friends here to help, *ja*?"

Allison smiled. "As a matter of fact, I did." Strange, that she should feel that about Laurel Ridge so quickly. Or at all, for that matter. It seemed odd now that she'd initially come with the idea that she'd only be here for a few days. The place was growing on her.

Still, what would she do if she stayed here? Run the building? Help out in the quilt shop? She liked being a designer, and she doubted there was enough business in a town like Laurel Ridge to support an interior designer.

Hannah smoothed a completed quilt square out on her apron, where it made a bright patch of color against the black.

"That's lovely. You're working so fast."

"In a few weeks I'll be getting busy with the garden, so I'd best get as much done on it as I can now. I want to have a sizable area pieced by the time Sarah starts getting *Englisch* tourists on the weekend."

She nodded. "That's a good way of marketing the quilts. Does business pick up much in the summer?"

"Quite a bit, I'd say. On the weekends, mostly. The areas near Lancaster get the most visitors, that's certain sure."

"Yes, I've seen the tour buses." Allison studied Hannah's face. Sarah must have gotten her serenity from her mother. It was hard to picture Hannah perturbed about anything. "Some of the quilts aren't traditional Amish ones, are they?"

Hannah's eyes twinkled. "You guessed it. If I'm making a quilt to sell to the *Englisch*, I might use a lot of white for the background, with lighter colors like yellow. But if I'm making something for a gift, or for the family, I use the traditional colors, like this one. All solid, deep colors—the pieces that are left from making clothing. Or maybe saved when a garment is discarded."

The deep colors Hannah mentioned were saturated shades of burgundy, purple, blue and green—the shades one typically saw in an Amish man's shirt or a woman's dress. When pieced together, the deep colors seemed to glow like jewels.

"Are you making this one for something special?"

"You might say so." Hannah smiled, then glanced up as Sarah, finished with a customer, came over to them.

"You two look as if you're having a fine chat," Sarah said. "You're not getting too tired, Allison?"

"I rested enough yesterday," she said firmly, before Sarah could express the suggestion that she go and lie down. "We were talking about the quilts, and I was wondering if you do any advertising."

Sarah nodded. "I buy an ad in the magazine they give away to all the tourists. That brings people into the shop."

"I'm sure it does, but I was thinking of something not so dependent on tourism. What about internet sales?"

"*Ach*, I wouldn't even know how to begin to do something like that. Besides——" Sarah stopped, looking troubled.

"What?"

"People might think I was being prideful," she said.

Allison bit back the suggestion that she not care what

people thought. Obviously, if you were Amish, you did care. "I wouldn't want to suggest anything that would get you into trouble with the church."

"Nonsense," Hannah said robustly. "Sarah, you know perfectly well that many Amish businesses have websites, or whatever they call them. You wouldn't be advertising yourself, just the quilts."

Allison was delighted with the support, all the more so because she'd thought Sarah's parents might object.

"I don't know…"

"Why don't you let me look into it?" Allison said. "It will give me something to do while I'm laid up. You don't have to commit to anything."

"It's a fine idea," Hannah said.

"And honestly, someone in the city would expect to pay far more for a handmade quilt than you charge in the shop. It's a way to reach those customers."

Sarah smiled. "All right. But just look into it, mind. I haven't said I'd do it yet."

"Good." Allison reached for the crutches, and Sarah looked alarmed.

"I didn't mean right this minute," she said quickly.

"Relax," Allison said. "I just want to get a little exercise. I think I'll go and check on Ralph. Is he back in the shop again today?"

"I think so." Sarah steadied the rocker while she rose and put the crutches under her arms. "Don't get too adventurous, now. And if you decide to go upstairs, you'd better take the elevator."

Allison grimaced. "That rickety old thing sounds as if it's about to die. I'm not sure it's any safer than the stairs."

"Promise me," Sarah insisted. "Or else I'll have to come with you."

"All right, I promise. You're turning into a nag, you know."

Sarah grinned. "That's what friends do, ain't so? Nag you for your own good."

Allison hadn't thought about it that way, but she supposed it was true. In any event, it was good to have people here who cared for her to balance out those who wished she'd go away. And perhaps did more than wish.

She made her way back the hall, noticing that every trace of the Jumble Sale had been cleared away. The floor was spotless. No one would guess that hundreds of people had been through here on Saturday. She'd congratulate Fred on a good job, if not for the fact that she suspected the volunteers had done most of it.

When she reached the bookshop, she stopped and glanced back at the stairwell. As she'd thought, the angle of the steps made it unlikely Ralph had noticed anything on Saturday. Still, it wouldn't hurt to talk to him. If someone had come in from the back of the building, he would have been likely to notice that.

Ralph stood behind the counter, his gaze fixed on the computer monitor. As she clattered through the doorway, managing to bang a crutch against the frame, his head jerked around, eyes widening. "Allison! It's you."

"As you see." She made her way to the counter. "How are you, Ralph? I understand you were upset by the accident." She couldn't imagine why. After all, he wasn't the one who'd plunged down the stairs.

Perhaps some of that feeling showed in her voice, because a flush brightened his pale cheeks. "I just couldn't stand listening to everyone talking about it and specu-

lating about whether you were going to be all right."
He shuddered. "People can be such ghouls, can't they?"

"Some people do seem to stare at accidents, don't
they?"

"Disgusting habit."

Ralph was silent for a moment, but his mouth worked
as if there was more to say. He was afraid, she realized.

"It could have been any of us." The words burst out
of him. "Who would do such a thing, not knowing who
might be hurt? It could have been me. I went upstairs
Saturday morning, too."

She blinked. This was something worth exploring.
"What time was that, do you know?"

"I'm not sure." He grimaced. "I happened to think of
something I'd forgotten, so I went up. Before you fell,
obviously."

"The stairs were clear when you came down?"

He blinked. "I—I didn't come down the stairs. I used
the elevator."

Did that narrow it down any? Perhaps not. If Ralph's
trip had been earlier than hers, it didn't really matter.
"Did you see anyone else upstairs?"

"I think someone was in the real estate office. There
was a light on. But no one was in the hallway as far as I
remember." Ralph shivered. "You mean the person who
did it might have been hiding up there? That's terrible.
Frightening."

He looked afraid at just the thought, and she took
pity on him.

"Well, we're both back in action today, anyway." She
gave him a reassuring smile.

"I almost wish I'd stayed home again." Ralph fussed
with the cash register, opening and closing the drawer.

"As it is, I had Mac Whiting in here the minute I opened up, asking questions and making me think about it all over again."

"I'm sure he was just doing his job," she soothed. "After all, he had to ask whether you'd seen anyone behaving suspiciously."

"As if I'd notice that with the crowd of people who were in here. Anyway, I can barely see the steps from here. I did hear the fuss when you fell——" He stopped, rolling his eyes a bit as the elevator trundled its way upstairs with a lot of creaking and groaning. "Nick and his father have been up and down a dozen times today if they've done it once." He glared at the wall beyond which was the elevator shaft and the back stairway. "And if they're not using that creaky old elevator, they're banging against the wall of the stairs carrying things up and done."

"They're putting in the new kitchen in the apartment," she said. She eyed the wall, speculating. "I didn't realize you could hear the elevator so clearly from here. And people using the back stairs, as well."

"It's a disadvantage to this space, let me tell you. I always felt I should get a bit more of a break on my rent because of the inconvenience." It was Ralph's turn to study her, as if wondering how likely she was to be influenced in that way.

"You were in the shop most of the time on Saturday, weren't you? I mean, I noticed that you weren't out working the tables."

"I don't like crowds," he said. "And Emily loves to do it."

She really didn't care why they'd split the work that

way on Saturday. She just wanted to know what Ralph had heard.

"So I suppose if anyone had gone up the elevator or the back stairs on Saturday morning, you would have heard them." Allison made an effort to sound as if it were of no particular consequence.

Ralph tilted his head to one side, looking like an inquisitive rabbit. "Well, the elevator I would. And I didn't, I'm sure of that. Now, the stairs—let me think."

She realized she was holding her breath and let it out. After all, even if he'd heard someone going up or down, he wouldn't necessarily know who it was unless that person had passed the bookshop on the way.

"I'm just not sure." Ralph shook his head regretfully. "I don't pay particular attention, not unless someone's making a lot of noise." He hesitated, gaze still on her face. "You're thinking the person who set that trap might have gone up and down the back stairs, aren't you?"

Ralph, at least, seemed to accept that it had been a trap, rather than a somewhat peculiar accident.

"Well, if I were trying to avoid being seen, that's what I'd do. What about someone going to or coming away from the stairwell? They'd have to pass the shop, wouldn't they?"

"That's what Mac said, but as I told him, why would anyone do that if they didn't want to be seen? They could just go in and out the side door. I heard Fred left it open all day."

Something seemed vaguely wrong about his response, but she couldn't think what. Then she realized. He hadn't really answered her question. "Did you see anyone?"

Ralph's gaze slid away from hers. He waved a hand toward the computer. "I was far too busy to be noticing who was passing by. Spring Fest threw us behind on everything, and as for the amount of business it brought me, I might as well have closed for the day." He turned rather obviously back to the computer.

What had Mac thought of Ralph's responses to his questions? No doubt he knew the man better than she did. Was Ralph just naturally evasive, or was he hiding something?

EMERGING ONTO THE ground floor from the back stairs, Nick spotted Allison ahead of him in the hallway. He couldn't miss her in any event, but was there another woman who could manage to look both vulnerable and sexy on crutches, with that silky hair swinging forward as she moved and the sway of her hips in the sleek-fitting pants?

Shaking his head at his own wayward thoughts, he hurried to catch up with her. "Shouldn't you be resting? Or at least sitting down?"

She looked up with a quick smile at the sound of his voice. "Thanks, but if I rest anymore I just might start shrieking."

"Are you exercising? Or going somewhere?"

"I stopped in to see Ralph." Her clear eyes seemed to cloud. "I can't quite make him out."

"Welcome to the club. I've known him for fifteen years or so and I still don't know what makes him tick." He studied her face and knew that was more than a casual comment. "Does something in particular about Ralph have you puzzled?"

Allison paused for a moment before apparently deciding to speak. "Were you with your brother when he talked to Ralph about what happened on Saturday?"

He nodded, then glanced around. "If we're going to talk about this, it shouldn't be here. How would you like to come upstairs and check the progress on the apartment?"

"Sounds like a good idea. I'll take the elevator."

He grinned. "I could carry you up the steps, if you like."

"But would we remember why we were going upstairs?" Her green eyes teased him, and again he had that vivid image of Allison on the bed, looking up at him.

"True," he conceded. "Guess it had better be the elevator." He moved ahead of her to press the call button. The elevator creaked its way down to them, and he held the door.

Allison's glance took in the small enclosure as she negotiated the uneven gap into the elevator. "You guarantee this thing is safe?"

"Absolutely." He smiled, closing the door and pressing the button that would take them up. "It may be noisy, but it's thoroughly inspected on a regular basis. Evelyn was always particular about that."

She nodded. "I saw the records in her files. She was very meticulous, wasn't she?"

"She was, yes." As always, he sensed something cautious, something hidden and wary, when Allison spoke of her grandmother. "But you wanted to know about Mac's interview with Ralph. Something in particular bugging you about Ralph?"

"Did he say anything that was at all helpful?" She leaned against the wall of the elevator, easing the crutches away from her shoulders.

"Not that I recall." He frowned. "Complained mostly, about how inconvenient Spring Fest was. And he demanded to know how he could be expected to watch the stairs with all the turmoil going on."

Allison's lips quirked. "Yes, I heard that lecture, as well. But did you realize that from the counter in the bookshop, you can hear the noise each time the elevator goes up or down?" The elevator shuddered to a stop with a protesting squeal. "That noise," she said.

Frowning, he opened the door and stood aside to let her get off. They were in the rear of the building here, near the doors to Allison's office and the apartment, so no one was close enough to hear them talk.

"So he'd have heard if anyone used the elevator on Saturday morning. Did you ask him?"

Allison nodded. "He waffled a bit, but finally he said he didn't think so."

Nick wasn't sure where she was going with this. "Granted, the person who rigged the trap might have come up the back. That would be the sensible thing to do, I guess. But if Ralph didn't hear the elevator—"

"You can also hear people in the stairway." She said it with a note of triumph, but then she sobered. "Well, you can if people are making much noise. Ralph complained about all the racket you made getting cabinets up and down the stairs."

Nick grinned. "I hope he didn't hear Dad when one of the cabinets got stuck. But did he notice anyone going up or down on Saturday morning?"

"He caught on right away what I was after. But he said he wouldn't have noticed."

"Well, then…"

"I asked about people passing the shop. There's a window that looks straight out at that hall, and it would be in his line of sight if he was working at the computer."

"Mac asked him that, as well."

"Did he give Mac a direct answer? Because when I asked him, he evaded the question, going off into a complaint about Spring Fest instead."

Nick paused at the apartment door, pulling the keys from his jeans pocket. "Now that you mention it, he did the same with Mac. I guess it didn't register at the time because it was so typical of Ralph. He never wants to give a direct answer to a question, and he's usually obsessed with whatever complaint he has at the moment."

"Maybe that's true." She looked at him, her green eyes dark and serious. "Or maybe he did see or hear something and doesn't want to be involved. Or is afraid to be involved."

"Afraid is the most likely scenario, if so." He pushed the door open. "And if that's the case, I'm not sure how we can get the truth out of him."

"If he's pushed, surely he'd see that it's safer to talk to the police than to be implicated in an attack by keeping silent."

"Fear has a way of trumping logic. Haven't you noticed?" He waved a hand toward the apartment. "So? What do you think?"

Allison made her way inside, watching her step with the crutches, before she looked up. "Wow. You've made a lot of progress in the past few days."

"It's coming together," he said. "Luckily the people we need to work with have been available. You have to make a final decision on the paint colors, and then the paint crew can get going on the living room."

Her expression suggested she was busy decorating the space in her thoughts. "A pale cream in here, I think. It'll make this beautiful woodwork show up so well."

Nick grinned. "I'm glad to hear you're not one of those people who call the woodwork old-fashioned and want to cover it with paint."

"That would be criminal." She reached out to stroke the eight-inch-wide beveled strip that surrounded the door.

"Come and see the kitchen. We're almost ready for the countertop." He couldn't help the pride in his voice. They'd all worked overtime to get the cabinets done so the rest of the work could progress, but they hadn't skimped on the effort.

He led the way to the kitchen and went in first, wanting to see her expression when she viewed the work. "You'll just have to visualize it with the hardware installed. That'll be done this afternoon."

"Nick, it's wonderful." Allison's face glowed with pleasure. "The cabinets are a masterpiece. I'm so glad we went with your father's suggestion. They're perfect." Again she reached out with that characteristic gesture to stroke the cabinets, as if she could appreciate it better with her fingertips, and his own hands tingled.

"Dad has a good eye for what things will look like when they're in," he said, trying to downplay his pleasure at her response. "I hope I'm developing it, but I'm not there yet."

"I can see exactly what the kitchen will look like when it's finished. Minimal window treatments, to let all that light in, I think. And the tile is going to be perfect for the floor. You want a kitchen in a building like this to be light and warm and welcoming, not cold and sterile. I can't tell you—"

Enthusiasm and pleasure lit her eyes and warmed her voice. She turned toward him with one of her quick movements, maybe forgetting the crutches in her excitement. One slipped out of her control. She stumbled, gasping a little, and he caught her, holding her steady against his chest.

"Easy." His voice had turned husky despite an effort to keep it light. "The last thing you need is another tumble."

She put her hands on his chest to steady herself, and the second crutch slid to the floor. He could feel the warmth of her palms through the worn flannel of his shirt, the touch more sensual than the way she had touched the cabinet he'd crafted. Her breath caught, and she looked up at him, eyes darkening.

He swore silently. He hadn't meant to do this again. But with her eyes meeting his and her body pressed against his chest, what was a man to do?

With a repressed groan, he bent his head and kissed her. She tasted of warmth, and longing, and challenge all at once, and he knew it to be a dangerous combination, but he brushed the voice of caution away. He deepened the kiss, feeling her arms go around him, tentative at first and then pulling him even closer. The world had narrowed to the two of them, to this time and this moment.

He wasn't sure which of them drew back first. Her eyes were dazed, her cheeks flushed. She seemed to make an effort to regain control.

"I wasn't quite expecting that." Her voice caught on something that might have been a suppressed laugh. "Or maybe I should say I expected it but didn't quite realize…" She let that die out.

"I know." He grinned, suddenly feeling as if he could leap tall buildings. "Me, either."

"Yes, well…" She drew back, then seemed to realize

she'd lost her support and clutched his forearms. "Maybe you'd better give me back my crutches."

"Yes, ma'am." He managed to suppress the thought that crutches weren't necessary for everything. He held her steady with one hand while he collected the crutches with the other.

Once they were safely detached from each other, Allison ran a hand through her tousled hair. "I ought to get downstairs before Sarah sends out a search party for me."

He nodded. "Come back later. You can see how the cabinets look with the handles in place. And don't forget to check over those paint chips we left for you."

"I will." She headed for the door, and he followed her, stopping when she did for a last look around the living room. "It really is going to be perfect," she said. "I can see it."

"Picturing it filled with your own furniture? You could live here instead of renting it, you know."

He said the words lightly, giving voice to what he'd assumed all along—that Allison was fixing up the apartment for herself.

And then he saw her expression. Saw the doubt in her face at the idea.

It was like having a barrel of cold water dumped over him. What had he been thinking? That just because she was here for now she'd be staying?

"I...I don't know," she murmured, and she went as quickly as the crutches would take her to the exit.

CHAPTER FIFTEEN

ALLISON WAS IN the back room at the quilt shop, her foot propped up on a padded stool, when Sarah popped her head in.

"You have company. Don't move," she added as Allison began to rise. "She'll come in." She ushered Krysta Conner into the room and slipped away.

Allison's nerves tensed. After the way they'd parted the last time they'd talked, she wasn't sure she wanted a visit from her young cousin. But Krysta carried a bouquet of daisies and carnations and wore a tentative smile.

"Hi." She gestured with the paper-wrapped flowers. "These are for you." She put them on the table next to the mug of chamomile tea Sarah had insisted Allison needed. "I just stopped by to see how you are."

She stood awkwardly, swinging a small backpack from one hand, and Allison realized she must have come straight from school.

Today Krysta looked much more her age, showing so clearly the uncertainty that Allison remembered only too well from her own teens. "I'm doing much better." She gestured to a chair. "Please, sit down and talk to me. Sarah is busy, and I'm beginning to bore myself."

"Thanks." Krysta visibly relaxed. She slung the bag on the back of the chair and sat. "I was on crutches one time when I sprained my ankle. It's a pain. You can't carry a thing, can you?"

"Not unless I sling it around my neck. The doctor says I can graduate to a cane in a couple of days. Then I'll just look like an old lady."

Krysta studied her face for a minute and then shook her head. "No way."

Allison couldn't help but feel pleased, knowing that to a teenager, nearing thirty was probably aged. She pushed a plate of cookies toward her. "Have a snicker-doodle, at least."

"Thanks." Krysta snagged one and munched on it with obvious pleasure. "Do they... Do the police know yet how it happened?" She nodded toward the crutches.

Careful, she told herself. If Brenda was behind the things that had been happening, it wouldn't be wise to confide in her daughter. In fact, Krysta might be here for that very reason. It was hardly a question Brenda would feel comfortable asking herself.

"They're still investigating, apparently. The trouble is that anyone could have done it. Anyone who was in Blackburn House that morning, that is." *Like you. And your mother.* But somehow she didn't think Krysta was a good enough actress to carry this visit off if she'd been the one to set the trap. She touched the petals of a white daisy lightly. "I'll drop a note to your mother thanking her for the flowers."

Krysta looked startled, and then she grinned. "That would surprise her."

"What— Oh, you mean she doesn't know about this." Somehow she'd assumed that Brenda was behind this visit. "Well, thank you doubly, Krysta."

"My mother—" Krysta began and stopped. She

looked down at the table and picked up a cookie crumb with her forefinger. "It's embarrassing, that's all. I mean, after all she got from Aunt Evelyn..." She let that die out.

Allison considered. Teenagers were often embarrassed by their parents—it was part of growing up. "I don't know. I suppose it's natural enough that I came as a surprise to her. After all, she must have given up her own life when she moved here to look after Evelyn. Naturally she'd feel entitled—"

"Is that what she told you?" Krysta pursed her lips. "She would. It was the other way around, if you want to know. My dad's business was on the rocks, and when he passed away, all he left for us was debt." Her face softened. "Poor Dad. He never was meant to be a businessman."

"I'm sorry." She knew what it was to be disappointed by a parent and yet go on loving him, regardless.

"Yeah, well, Aunt Evelyn came to the rescue. I don't think she especially wanted to have us living with her, but she didn't complain."

Allison could hear the hurt in Krysta's voice. Embarrassment, as well, that they'd thrown themselves on the rich relative.

"You know, Krysta, Evelyn didn't have to leave you anything, but she did. She split things between us, so that proves she loved you, even if she didn't say it."

Krysta seemed to weigh her words. "You should have gotten it all. You were her granddaughter."

"The granddaughter she'd never seen." Allison grimaced. "It's a pretty tangled family we've got, that's for sure. Maybe it's best to just accept the way things are and move on."

"T.J. says—" Krysta stopped.

"Go on. What does T.J. say?"

Krysta shrugged slim shoulders. "I know you don't like him. I shouldn't have mentioned him."

"I don't dislike him, Krysta." Allison hesitated. It seemed to her that her young cousin needed someone to talk to, but she didn't think she was suited for the role of counselor. "I just didn't have a great first impression of him." Her thoughts flashed to that scene in the sunroom.

Krysta's color deepened. "T.J. takes some knowing. He's had a rough time, but he's really a sweet guy underneath. Just sort of…impetuous, I guess you'd say."

Allison flashed onto an image of Krysta glancing toward the rear of the first floor, her face lighting up at whatever she saw. "T.J. was here in the building on Saturday morning, wasn't he?"

"I… What makes you think that?" She was stalling, obviously.

"I saw you looking back down the hallway just before I started down the stairs. Your expression spoke for you."

Krysta hung her head and nodded, looking very young all of a sudden. "But he wouldn't do anything to you. He's not mean."

"Impulsive, maybe? Whoever set that trap did it on the spur of the moment."

"Not T.J.—he wouldn't." She sounded as if she were trying to convince herself. "I mean, he tries to act tough, but it's, like…just a cover. He doesn't have anybody to hold on to."

"His father, his grandfather—" Allison began.

"You don't know." Krysta's head came up, and indignation flamed in her face. "T.J. was devoted to his mother. He never actually says this, but I think she was probably mentally ill. Or maybe bipolar or something."

She flung the terms around loosely. "People say all kinds of things. They say she drank, but T.J. says that's not true. He says his dad never did anything to help her."

"It's true I only know what I've heard, and that hasn't been much," she said carefully. "But it's possible that T.J. didn't know the whole story of his parents' relationship."

"Kids always know," Krysta said firmly. "Anyway, when she took an overdose, some people said it was suicide, but T.J. says it had to be an accident. He says if his dad had helped her instead of running around on her, it wouldn't have happened."

"I'm sorry," she said, conscious of how lame that sounded. "His grandfather—"

"His grandfather doesn't approve of him. He's always telling him he's got to act like a Blackburn, whatever that means. Anyway, T.J. doesn't have anybody, but he trusts me, and I know he couldn't do anything so mean as to hurt you." She leaned across the table, her young face passionate. "You have to believe me."

Allison wasn't sure she could go that far, but Krysta obviously believed in what she was saying. "He has a good friend in you."

"Yeah, well...he counts on me." Her gaze evaded Allison's. "It's just...well...sometimes he wants more than..." She let the words die out. "He says if I loved him, I would."

So, boys were still using that line, were they? Allison felt a longing to have T.J. here so she could shake him until his teeth rattled.

But that wouldn't help Krysta. And Krysta wouldn't be saying this to her if she didn't want help, whether she recognized it or not. There was a certain wry irony in

Krysta wanting advice from her, of all people, on her love life.

"I haven't always been smart about my relationships with guys," she said slowly. "But one thing I do know is that someone who really loves you wouldn't press you to do something you're not ready for. Love isn't…" She paused, trying to find the word. "Demanding."

Krysta nodded, but her gaze didn't meet Allison's.

She was failing this kid, she suspected, and she didn't know how to make it any better. "You'll be heading off to college before too long, won't you?"

"In the fall." Krysta's face lit up, and her eyes sparkled. "University of Maryland. Mom wanted me closer, but I think that's close enough."

Allison had to smile at that. "I know exactly how you feel. Well, the thing is that going away to college is a chance to start all over for most people. You don't have to go on being the person you've been. And you don't want to be carrying a lot of emotional baggage with you."

Krysta nodded slowly. "I get it. You're right." She jumped to her feet, all her energy restored. "Thanks, Allison. You've been really nice, especially after…well, everything." She swooped over to press her cheek against Allison's. "It's good to have a cousin who knows what's what." She grabbed another snickerdoodle and darted out the door, leaving Allison to stare at a tableful of crumbs.

So, she knew what was what, did she? Then why did she spend so much time trying to figure out what to do with herself?

"HAVE THE DISHWASHER here by tomorrow morning, or I'll get it from someone else." Nick hung up the phone with a decided click. He preferred to deal with a local business, but Tom Walker's empty promises were starting to get old. The countertop couldn't be installed until the appliances were in, and Tom had promised the dishwasher would be here two days ago.

Closing the office door behind him, Nick reached the hall in time to see Krysta Conner emerge from the quilt shop, sling her backpack on and head out the front door. Frowning, he looked after her. He didn't actually suspect Krysta of any complicity, but someone seemed intent on driving Allison away from Laurel Ridge, and Brenda Conner had the most to gain, he'd think.

Making a quick decision, he strode across the wide hall to the quilt shop. He ought to find out what Krysta had wanted. That was all. His visit had nothing to do with wanting to see Allison again.

Inside, he gave a quick glance around. Sarah was putting some bolts of fabric back in their racks, and her mother sat by the window with a quilt patch on her lap. Allison was nowhere to be seen.

"Nick." Sarah greeted him with amusement crinkling her eyes. "Allison is in the back room." She exchanged glances with Hannah, who seemed equally amused. Apparently he was being obvious.

"Okay, quit it, both of you."

"Quit what?" Sarah was all innocence.

"You know what I mean. I just want to ask Allison something, that's all."

Sarah nodded, a smile tugging at her lips. "*Ja*, I'm sure."

He gave up. Sarah had known him all his life, and there was no point in trying to convince her she was wrong in her reading of him. Especially when she wasn't.

"I'll just…" He headed for the back room, skirting the

long aisles of quilt fabrics and hearing a soft chuckle behind him. Women liked to match-make, and Sarah was as bad as any of them. She meant well, but she couldn't understand how complicated it was for him.

He found Allison balancing on her crutches while trying to wipe off the table. "Here, let me do that."

She seemed to go still for an instant at the sound of his voice, and then she looked up and smiled. "Thanks." She surrendered the cloth, his hand brushing hers in the process.

Reminding himself to rein in his response didn't seem to help. "Snickerdoodles make a lot of crumbs, but they're worth it." He brushed the crumbs into the trash can and then proceeded to make some more by grabbing a cookie from the plate. "How can you stand there and resist them?"

"Because I don't have the metabolism of a teenager any longer," she said. "Apparently you do," she added as he took another cookie.

"Hey, I do a lot of physical labor," he said, grinning.

"Thanks to these things, I can't do any." Allison slapped the crutches irritably.

"It won't be for long," he said. "I saw Krysta leaving. What was she doing here?" He didn't succeed in quashing the edge of suspicion in his voice.

"She brought me these." Allison picked up a spray of flowers that lay on the table. "I was about to put them in a vase, but I can't reach it. Do you mind?" She pointed to an upper shelf.

"Got it." He pulled a milk glass vase from the shelf and took it to the sink. "I'll take care of these. Sit down and tell me about Krysta's visit. I thought she had a hate on for you."

Allison handed him the daisies and carnations without argument and sat in the padded rocker with a little sigh. She'd been doing too much, obviously.

"Let me." Nick pulled over the stool she was reaching for and gently lifted her bandaged foot onto it. "This ankle is pretty swollen. You've been on it too much."

"Stop sounding like my mother and stick those flowers in some water." She shook her head. "Sorry. Not being able to do what I need to is making me irritable."

"You should have heard me barking at one of the suppliers," he said. "You don't have a corner on irritability." He filled the vase with water and stuffed the flowers into it. "So, what did Krysta want, besides being an errand girl?"

"You're assuming the flowers were from her mother, aren't you? I did, too. Turns out Brenda had nothing to do with it. According to Krysta, her mother is being unreasonable."

"Well, I can't argue the point." Yanking a chair from the table, he pulled it around so that he could sit facing Allison, carefully avoiding the bandaged ankle. "It beats me why Brenda cares about Blackburn House so much. After all, she scooped the rest of the pie, and she's only a niece."

He studied Allison's face, or as much of it as he could see. She'd averted it, staring down at her hands.

"Hey, what are you brooding about? You're not thinking she deserved Blackburn House, too, are you?"

"No, no, not that." She looked up, seemingly startled by the question. "I just don't like having someone really dislike me. I've run into professional jealousy before, but this is personal."

Nick frowned, considering it. "Yeah, it is personal,

but it's Brenda's problem. Evelyn was very good to her, you know. If she hadn't stepped in when Brenda was left high and dry after her husband died, Brenda would have had a rough time of it."

"That's what Krysta said. I hadn't realized. I suppose I thought that Brenda had come here to take care of Evelyn, not the other way around."

He snorted. "Evelyn never wanted anyone to take care of her. She was a law unto herself, believe me. I keep forgetting that you don't know all about the family."

"No, I don't."

He wasn't sure what those three words expressed. Anger? Regret?

"Well, at least don't start thinking you've deprived Brenda and Krysta of anything by coming here. They're well-off, and Evelyn wanted you to have Blackburn House."

Allison nodded and leaned her head against the tall, padded back of the rocker. "I know. And I've given up trying to understand Brenda. If she was behind that job offer, she might have—"

"Wait a second." He stopped her. "What job offer?"

Allison looked confused for an instant. "I guess I didn't tell you or Mac about that, did I? I received a job inquiry from a recruiter on the West Coast, completely unsolicited. It struck me as odd, so I called the man to ask how he'd gotten my name. He insisted he couldn't divulge that information, but when I asked about Laurel Ridge, I'm sure he reacted."

"Why do you connect Brenda with it?"

"Because Ralph said he'd heard I was relocating to San Francisco. When I pressed him about it, he said he'd heard Brenda mention it."

Nick tried to imagine Brenda pulling those sorts of strings and failed. "It doesn't sound like her. Far more the kind of thing Thomas Blackburn would do."

"That's what Sarah said. But how would Brenda know about it, in that case?"

"They both have an interest in seeing you give up your inheritance. They could have concocted it together, although I wouldn't expect Blackburn to confide in Brenda." Nick studied Allison's face. "What did you say?"

She gave him a blank look. "What?"

"What did you tell the recruiter?" He shouldn't feel so upset at the thought of Allison leaving. She was bound to, sooner or later.

"I told him no." She shrugged. "I'm not going away, at least not until everything is resolved here."

"Brenda." He repeated the name slowly, and then shook his head. He couldn't quite imagine it. "We know she was here on Saturday morning."

"Yes, but when I glanced down from the top of the stairs, I saw her. I don't think she could have planted the broom and made it to where she was in the time available."

"Maybe not, but she might have had someone do it for her."

"If you're thinking of Krysta, that's ridiculous." Allison's tone was sharp. Apparently Krysta had made an impression on her.

"Why?" He kept his voice mild. "From what I know about her, she's a spoiled kid with a grudge against you—"

"No. Well, maybe Krysta is spoiled, but she's come around where I'm concerned. She doesn't understand why her mother is holding on to a grudge about my inheritance." Allison looked as if she defied him to say otherwise. "Anyway, she couldn't have done that business with the broom for the same reason Brenda couldn't. She was standing with her mother, and I don't see how either of them could have managed it. The only way they could have made it to where they were standing would have been to come down the front stairs, and surely they wouldn't risk that."

Nick had to agree, although he wasn't entirely convinced of Krysta's change of heart. Still, Allison was right. The person who planted the broom couldn't have come down the front stairs without raising immediate suspicion when Allison fell.

"That's a valid point." He leaned toward her, hands planted on his knees. He wasn't going to risk touching her. "I just wish you'd be careful. Our efforts to keep an eye on you don't seem to be meeting with much success."

Her gaze met his, and the moment seemed to flow into slow motion. She caught her breath. Blinked. "I'll be careful. Krysta did admit one thing to me when I asked her. T.J. was back by the bookshop when I fell. Within easy reach of the back stairs."

"T.J. Now, that I can easily imagine. That kid is nothing but trouble."

"Krysta believes in him."

"How many seventeen-year-old girls have good judgment about guys?" He let his skepticism show. "T.J. has had brushes with the law more than once, and he always skates out with a little help from his grandfather."

"Krysta says he's troubled. He blames his father for his mother's suicide, and his grandfather is constantly putting pressure on him." Her face was flushed. "You can hardly blame him for acting out with a family situation like that."

"He's old enough to be responsible for his own actions." He clung to his opinion.

"I suppose you were a model citizen at seventeen. You can't assume—"

He grinned suddenly, hearing them as if he listened to two other people. "I can't believe we're arguing about T. J. Blackburn, of all people."

Her expression eased, as the battle lines disappeared. "You're right. Believe me, I've no particular love for T.J." Allison's lips tightened, making him wonder what she knew about the kid that put that expression on her face. "But why would he do it? It doesn't sound as if he'd go out of his way to oblige his grandfather."

"Who knows? Sheer cussedness, maybe. The point is that he could have done it. He was in the right place. And Brenda and Krysta couldn't. So we've narrowed it down a little."

"I guess so." She frowned slightly. "We're assuming the trap was intended for me. But what if it was meant for someone else?"

Against his better judgment, he reached out and touched her hand. It turned in immediate response, clasping his. "I'd like to think that, but honestly, who else? You're the one whose presence here is a threat."

"I suppose." Her fingers tightened on his, and she stared down at their linked hands. "It's uncomfortable, thinking that someone wants me out of the way that much. But Brenda? She's so…well, ineffectual."

"I know. And Thomas Blackburn is a pillar of the community. But even people like that can act irrationally when something they want is threatened. And if we grant that your grandmother uncovered something wrong here in Blackburn House, it opens up a whole field of possibilities."

Allison rubbed her forehead with her free hand. "It's making me dizzy, as the song goes. I don't know what to think about anyone." Her gaze met his. "Except Sarah, of course. And you."

The heat was starting to sizzle between them again, and it wasn't safe. He put her hand down carefully. "You know, maybe you ought to leave—"

"I won't." Anger flared in her face. "Are you seriously suggesting that I give up? Let Brenda have my inheritance? Never find out what really happened to my grandmother or why I was attacked?"

"That's not what I'm saying at all." He clung to the sudden enmity between them, because it was better than the alternative if he expected to keep his heart whole. "I just meant you could leave for a short time. Surely the will doesn't mean that you have to stay put every day for a year. It would be reasonable to take a short break. Tell everyone you want to see your own doctor about your injuries. Tell them you have to go back to Philadelphia to settle things there. Tell them anything, just get out of reach of whoever this nut is."

"No." She held up her hand to cut off any protests. "Going away now would be an admission that I'm afraid of whoever is doing this, and I won't do it."

"If you aren't afraid, you should be." His fear for her was fraying his temper.

"I'm afraid, all right. But I'm not giving anyone the satisfaction of knowing it."

"Afraid and stubborn," he said. "And the stubbornness is winning. Sometimes it's best to be cautious."

She shook her head. "I'm not trying to be reckless. Or brave. But tell me this—why would my going away for a week or two solve anything? When I came back, the problem would still be here."

"I suppose you're right." Little though he wanted to admit it. "I just thought…"

"You wanted to protect me. That's sweet, but it's my problem, isn't it?"

It wasn't just that he wanted to protect her, but there was no point in saying so. He rose and stood looking down at her for a moment. Stubborn woman. And the feelings she aroused in him were equally stubborn. Well, he'd just have to try harder to resist, because he couldn't risk his son's happiness on someone who might leave, just like his mother had.

CHAPTER SIXTEEN

A COUPLE OF quiet days did wonders for Allison's state of mind, to say nothing of her ankle. It was still strapped and tended to swell when she'd been on her feet for a time, but at least she'd been able to give up the crutches.

Life seemed to have returned to normal at Blackburn House. If Mac was still investigating, she saw little evidence of it. People came and went with only the occasional wary glance at the staircase. And Nick Whiting avoided her.

She couldn't mistake it. Ever since that moment when the attraction had flared so strongly, he'd been careful not to be alone with her. Irritation prickled. Did he think she was going to throw herself at him?

Well, fine. She could take a hint. Besides, she had enough to concentrate on at the moment. If Sarah would cooperate...

The camera she had slung around her neck bumped against her breastbone as she navigated the doors, cautious not to move too fast.

"Allison! You're walking without the crutches." Sarah's mother came toward her, beaming. "That's wonderful *gut.*"

Sarah hurried out from behind the counter. "I'm so glad you're better. But you mustn't try to do too much."

"I won't," she promised. "Believe me, the ankle reminds me if I get too ambitious." To say nothing of the assorted bruises that were turning graphic shades of yellow.

"You brought a camera." Sarah's expression was wary. "You know that Amish don't want their pictures taken, ain't so?"

"That's all right." Allison realized she had heard that at some point, but she'd forgotten. "It's the quilts I want to take photos of, not people."

Relief washed over Sarah's face. It seemed there were unanticipated pitfalls in a partnership between English and Amish.

"Why pictures of the quilts?" Hannah's blue eyes brightened with curiosity.

Allison sucked in a breath, hoping she wasn't going to run up against another Amish prohibition. "If we're going to put something about the shop on the internet, we should post photos of the various quilts. You said I could try, remember?"

"I said we'd talk about it." Sarah was hesitant. "What will people think?"

"*Ach*, don't be foolish, Sarah." Hannah was brisk. "We've already been through this. Plenty of Amish businesses advertise on the internet—some of them in our own church district. Besides, it will be Allison doing it, not you."

"That's right, Sarah." Allison took quick advantage of the support. "I can take care of the whole effort. And think how good it would be to have another outlet for sales."

Sarah looked from her mother to Allison and nodded. "All right, if you think so. But I'd be surprised if someone would buy a quilt without touching it and seeing it up close."

"You'd be astonished if you knew how much internet shopping goes on," Allison told her. "Some of my friends don't even go to the store for their groceries."

Sarah shook her head. She was probably just humoring Allison by agreeing. She'd clearly be astonished if this project worked out as well as Allison hoped.

"I'll get started, then." Allison moved to the double bed display area. "I'll just do a few to start with, and I'd like to post some information about the pattern and maybe even about the quilter, if that would be allowed."

Hannah, who seemed to have appointed herself the backer of the plan, nodded. "I can tell you all that, for sure. And maybe if you chust used the first names, that would be best. No one would mind that way."

"I'll get something to make notes on," Sarah said, seeming to get interested in spite of her doubts. "We can write things down while you take the pictures."

The morning light pouring through the windows allowed Allison to avoid the use of the flash. She took several photos of each quilt, marveling again at the intricate details and careful craftsmanship of each.

Sarah flipped to a quilt done in blue, yellow and rose in which a pattern of stars seemed to explode from the center, and Allison's breath caught. "That is amazing. Tell me about it."

"It is, ain't so?" Sarah looked at her mother and smiled. "*Mamm* won't tell you so, but this is one of hers."

"Really? It's… I'm at a loss for words. The pattern is so different from any I've seen."

Hannah ducked her head, probably embarrassed at the praise. "It's not typical Lancaster County Amish," she muttered, almost in apology. "A cousin of mine in Ohio made a similar one. That's where I got the idea. I used the brighter colors to appeal to the *Englisch* customers."

Allison snapped picture after picture. The colors ranged from a deep yellow star at the center to surrounding fragmentary stars in green, blue, rose and yellow on a solid blue background. The colors and pattern combined to create an effect that made her think of a stellar explosion.

"It's called Broken Star, ain't so, *Mamm*?" Sarah was making notes.

Hannah nodded. "Maybe I was wrong to do it." Her voice expressed doubt. "It hasn't sold."

"It will," Allison said fervently. She glanced at the price tag affixed to the quilt and shook her head. "And it will probably bring double that amount."

Hannah and Sarah were still exclaiming over that when Allison moved back to the doorway, hoping to get a shot of the interior of the shop. A voice in her ear startled her.

"Tell Hannah and Sarah to turn away," Nick murmured. "They won't want their faces shown."

"Right. Thanks." She hoped she didn't flush at his nearness. "Sarah, why don't you and your mother turn around so I can take a couple of photos of the shop?"

Sarah nodded, backing up, and Allison shot the pictures quickly. She should have thought of that herself. Hadn't they just been talking about the Amish aversion to being photographed?

When she put the camera down, Nick was still there. This was different—Nick seeking her out after avoiding her so intentionally. She glanced up at him, and he took a step back, irritating her.

"I wanted to remind you of the picnic supper tonight.

We keep telling Mom she's rushing the season, but she insists the good weather is going to hold long enough." He looked doubtful. "I'd say plan to bring a jacket or sweater, just in case."

"I will." Ellen had stopped by yesterday with the invitation, and apparently all of Sarah's family was attending what Ellen had called the first cookout of the year.

"We can always move indoors if we have to." He sounded philosophical about it. He paused for a moment, looking past her instead of at her. "Do you want me to pick you up?"

"No, thanks," she said quickly. "I'll drive and bring Sarah." Now it was her turn to hesitate. "Look, would you rather I made some excuse and bailed on tonight?"

"No." Nick looked genuinely startled. "Why would I?"

She glanced around, but no one was within earshot. "You've been making an effort to avoid me for the last couple of days. I'm just trying to make it easy." She couldn't seem to erase the edge in her voice.

His color deepened, but he met her gaze squarely. "It's not—" He stopped, then started over. "Look, it's just that I have to be careful when it comes to relationships. I have Jamie to consider, and I don't want him to be hurt by anything I do."

Allison's temper flared. "You're assuming a lot, aren't you? Maybe I'm not interested, either."

She felt his anger even as his hands shot out and grasped her wrists. Her breath caught in her throat, and her pulse pounded against his palms. There was no mistaking the desire in his eyes.

"Aren't you?" His voice was low and tight. "You're feeling the same thing I am, aren't you?"

She couldn't deny it, but at least she didn't have to affirm it, either.

Nick didn't seem to need words. He dropped her hands. "I'll see you tonight." He turned and walked quickly toward the back door.

NICK POLISHED OFF the last bite of Hannah's peanut butter iced chocolate cake, staring moodily across the backyard. Despite the chill of the May evening, everyone seemed to be having a good time, including Allison. Jamie was leaning against her lawn chair now that he'd finally been persuaded to stop showing her all of his favorite things on the farm so they could eat. The fact that he'd already given her the tour the last time she was here hadn't deterred him, and Allison had seemed happy to go wherever Jamie wanted.

Nick didn't like the bond that was developing between them, but what could he do about it? He couldn't very well tell his mother to stop inviting her. At least, he couldn't do that without telling her why, and he cringed at the thought. That subject wasn't something a man wanted to discuss with his mother.

Mac, helping himself to a large slice of rhubarb pie, nudged him with his elbow. "Why are you standing there looking like a thundercloud? Somebody steal your favorite toy?"

"I'm not." He met his brother's challenging gaze and shrugged. "I just don't think it's a good idea for Jamie to get so attached to Allison."

Mac glanced from Nick to Jamie, who was being lured away from Allison's chair, apparently to play catch with Sarah's brother. "So the kid likes her. What's not to like?"

Trying to put his worries into words was more than a

little difficult, even with Mac. "She's... Well, who knows how long she'll actually stay here? She says she's going to be here for a year, but she could change her mind tomorrow. It's not as if she belongs in a place like Laurel Ridge."

"She seems to be fitting in at the moment," Mac pointed out. "Anyway, I don't see how you can keep Jamie from liking her. Or yourself, for that matter. Do you expect to live like a monk forever, just because you got burned once by making the wrong choice?"

"Who said anything about living like a monk?" Nick aimed a mock punch at his brother's midsection. "I'm not crazy. But before I let myself fall for a woman, I have to be sure she wants the kind of life I do."

Mac snorted. "Not that I have much experience with it, but from what I can see, love doesn't work that way."

"You're right about that," Nick told him. "You're no expert. You hop from woman to woman like you're afraid to hold still long enough for anyone to catch you."

"Yeah, well, it's worked so far, hasn't it?" Mac grinned. "Anyway, that's not the point. I have eyes in my head, and anyone can see the sizzle when the two of you are together."

"You're dreaming," he scoffed. Was he really being that obvious? He must be, if Mac of all people had noticed it. He was as oblivious as most guys his age when it came to feelings.

"Keep telling yourself that," Mac said, and he wandered off to join the ball players.

His mother motioned him over to where the women sat in a circle of lawn chairs. "Nicky, is the Memorial Day parade on Saturday or Sunday this year?"

"Sunday." He smiled down at her, knowing it was

useless to ask her not to call him Nicky. She'd promise and forget the next minute. "The council decided to
leave Saturday free for the craft fair and the kids' game
day at the park."

"It's coming up fast, that's certain sure," Sarah's
grandmother said. "I'd like to get a few more quilted
pot holders ready for the craft fair. They're usually good
sellers."

Mom nodded. "They sure are. I'm doing some straw
wreaths, but I don't have enough dried flowers to finish,
so I'm at a standstill until I get can some more. Sarah,
what are you making?"

"Just machine-sewn place mats is all." Sarah shook
her head regretfully. "I haven't had time to make anything more ambitious."

"So does everyone in town make things for the craft
fair?" Allison asked.

"Not everyone, no. After all, some people prefer to
buy. Either way, they're supporting the sale. The money
is going for new playground equipment this year." His
mother leaned forward impetuously to touch Allison's
hand. "Why don't you make something, Allison? We'd
love to have you take part."

"Maybe Allison's not interested in that sort of thing,"
he said quickly, with some vague thought of not wanting
his mother to be hurt by a turndown.

Allison darted a frowning glance at him. "I don't
know if anyone would buy them, but I've knitted a few
scarves in my time. I'm not nearly as inept with knitting
needles as I am with sewing needles, and those infinity
scarves are popular and quick to make."

"That's wonderful," his mother said quickly. "We'll
take any you want to contribute." She rose, gesturing

with her cup. "I'm getting some coffee. Anyone want anything?"

There was a general shaking of heads. As his mother turned from the group, she caught Nick's arm, pulling him a few steps away as the conversation resumed behind them. She stopped at a safe distance and gave his arm a shake. "What was that all about?"

"What?" He pulled his arm free.

"Jumping to the conclusion that Allison wouldn't want to help. That wasn't very nice."

He and Mac both knew those words were the equivalent of Mom saying, "I'm ashamed of you."

"Sorry," he muttered. "I'm just not sure it's a good idea to get too close to Allison."

His mother surveyed his face for a long moment. Then she shook her head. "I can understand why you might feel that, Nicky." She spoke softly, and he suspected that was pity in her eyes. "But I don't think your dad and I raised you boys to be afraid of caring for people, no matter how long they're in your lives."

It was a good thing she didn't wait around for an answer, because Nick didn't have one.

His attention was caught by the sound of Mac's cell phone. He watched his brother's face grow steadily more serious as he listened. Mac said a few words and ended the call, then glanced around and caught Nick's gaze.

"What is it?" Nick crossed the space between them, feeling his brother's tension as surely as if it were his own.

Allison stood, seeming to pick up the change in mood in an instant. "Is something wrong?"

"Ralph's house has been broken into," Mac said. "I have to go."

"Is he all right?" Allison had paled.

"He wasn't there," Mac said quickly. "He came home and found things a mess and called in. Apparently he's pretty shaken."

"Poor thing." Mom was instantly sympathetic, and Elizabeth nodded. "If there's anything we can do…"

"I'll let you know." Mac glanced from Nick to Allison, frowning. "You know, maybe we were wrong about who the target is." He turned and jogged toward his car, leaving Nick and Allison staring at each other.

"Do you think he's right?" Allison wrapped her arms around herself as if cold.

Nick guided her to the table where the coffee thermos sat and poured her a cup. "Here, this will warm you up." He frowned down at the cup as she took it in both hands. "I don't know. It could be a coincidence, I guess."

"It was Ralph's store that was broken into." Allison seemed to turn the thought over in her mind. "But the business with the broom—"

"Ralph was upstairs that morning, remember? But he came down in the elevator. Maybe it was a miscalculation on someone's part, and they got you instead of Ralph."

"If so…" Allison broke off to give him a tentative smile. "I'd be happy to think none of this harassment was aimed at me, but I'm not sure. I am sure that Ralph hasn't said everything he knows."

"Maybe he'll be a little more forthcoming now if he's scared enough." He paused, not satisfied. "Do me a favor. Don't let down your guard, okay?"

She nodded. "You don't need to worry about that. I'm spooked enough already."

AFTER A FEW moments of charged silence between them, Allison set the coffee cup back on the table. She could sense the struggle going on in Nick, and she didn't quite understand it—at least, not entirely. They were both adults. If they were attracted to each other, what was so wrong? His excuse about considering Jamie had sounded like just that, an excuse to avoid involvement.

She turned away, thinking she'd rejoin the women, when Jamie came rushing at her and flung his arms around her legs.

"Did you see me catch the ball? I caught it three times in a row." He looked up at her, his face flushed, beaming.

"That was terrific." She bent to hug him, inhaling the scent of cut grass and small boy. It was surprisingly touching to feel his arms around her neck. "Wasn't it, Nick?"

She glanced up and caught the expression on Nick's face—a mingling of longing and disapproval combined, and it seemed to strike her in the heart. Nick wasn't just determined to be careful of emotional involvement for Jamie's sake. He actually disapproved of her in the role.

Allison's temper flared. She hadn't asked to be involved with him. If he couldn't imagine her as a potential stepmother for his son...

The train of thought came to a screeching halt. *Stepmother.* Was she really thinking that? If this attraction between them became serious, if they decided they were meant to be together, then what?

Suppose they married? That would make Jamie her stepson. If they had children of their own, would Jamie end up feeling as she so often had—that they were a complete family without him? A cold hand grabbed her heart and squeezed.

She took a cautious step away from Jamie, and Nick grabbed him, swung him upside down and then set him on his shoulders. Giggling, Jamie grabbed his hair. "I'm the tallest one here," he boasted.

"You sure are." She managed a smile, trying to stop her mind from spinning. "It's starting to get dark. I think I'd better head for home."

Jamie objected vociferously. Nick didn't. Clearly the best thing she could do was to leave.

It couldn't be accomplished that fast, of course. By the time she'd said her goodbyes and her thanks and avoided Ellen's efforts to pack up an entire picnic of leftovers for her, another fifteen minutes had passed, and the sun had slipped behind the ridge. It really was getting dark fast, and she'd rather not drive that lonely, winding road alone at night.

She set the piece of apple crumb pie Ellen had forced on her on the seat beside her and started the car. Nick leaned down and tapped on the window, and she opened it.

"Maybe I should follow you home. Just to be on the safe side."

Her heart gave a little jolt at his nearness. "Not necessary," she said quickly. "I'll be fine. I'll see you tomorrow." She closed the window before he could argue and drove out the farm lane.

Once she'd made the turn onto the two-lane blacktop road, she was impressed anew with how dark it was in the country. Some outside lights had come on at one or two farmhouses, but the others she passed were either dark or showed only the faint glow of lights from their windows. Those were the Amish ones, she'd guess.

Allison was honest enough to recognize that she was concentrating on trivialities to avoid thinking of the insight that had shaken her. Her rational mind had all sorts of reasons why she was being silly. Unfortunately it was arguing against something deep in her heart, and her heart was winning.

If she felt that way about a potential relationship with Nick, she should back off, shouldn't she? And after all, she and Nick were at the very beginning of whatever it was they felt for each other. Maybe it was best to stop now, while it wouldn't hurt so much to end it.

Wouldn't it? Something in her denied that idea.

Headlights reflected in her rearview mirror, blinding her for a moment. Annoyed, she flicked the mirror angle, but it didn't seem to help. The idiot had his high beams on. Didn't he know that was dangerous?

Then she realized it was probably Nick. She ought to be annoyed that he had disregarded her words, but she couldn't help being pleased that he—

The car hit her bumper, jolting her head back. What on earth…? That wasn't Nick. Her heart thudded into overdrive, and her hands gripped the wheel.

If she'd been hit on her usual drive to and from work in Philadelphia she'd stop, check for damage, exchange insurance information. But not on a dark, lonely road. She slowed a little, peering into the rearview mirror, trying to get a glimpse of the car and driver.

Useless. All she could see was the glare of the headlights, approaching fast. A big car, she thought, dark color. She was ready for the hit to the bumper this time. Braced herself, mind racing. Turn into one of the farm lanes? But that would be a dead end if no one was home.

The blow wasn't as bad as she'd half expected. He was trying not to damage his car—that was it. But another hit could easily send her careening off the road, to be stuck and vulnerable.

Her mind raced, searching for options. Try to get her cell phone from her bag? But that would involve taking one hand off the steering wheel, and how could she? Fingers gripping the wheel, knuckles white, she accelerated, increasing the distance between them, but a curve was coming up, and if she didn't slow down she'd go out of control.

That might be his plan. An innocent car accident, with nothing to prove that she'd been forced off the road. Hands tight on the wheel, she wrestled the car around the bend, staying on the road by what seemed sheer force of will.

All right. She managed a breath. Her success gave her a small measure of courage. She just had to stay ahead of him until she got to town where there were lights and people. That was all.

But how far was it? Surely not too far now, *please, God*. Her heart was thumping, her breath short. If she didn't reach town soon she'd lose control, and there could be no good ending to that.

He was speeding toward her again, his headlights taking over the mirrors, closing in, blinding her. All she could do was cling to the steering wheel…

And then he was gone, disappearing from the mirrors as suddenly as he'd appeared. She had a quick glimpse of a dark vehicle turning off on to a side road, and then nothing.

Allison sucked in a breath. A car was heading toward her, driving sedately on the right side of the road. Ahead of her she could see the lights of the gas station at the end of town.

She exhaled, feeling limp. Now what? Drive to the police station to report it?

But Mac wouldn't be there, most likely. He was probably still investigating the break-in at Ralph's. She really didn't want to try explaining all of this to a dispatcher or whoever was on duty at this time of night.

Driving as carefully as if she were ninety-five, she made her way back to the bed-and-breakfast. It would be better to call Mac and let him know what had happened. Or maybe wait until morning. He apparently had enough on his hands at the moment.

One thing seemed clear—their assumption had been wrong. The break-in at Ralph's didn't mean she was out of the woods.

CHAPTER SEVENTEEN

NICK WAS STILL trying to figure out what had happened between him and Allison the previous night when he walked toward the office to retrieve some measurements needed by the flooring supplier. One minute she'd been responding to Jamie and the next she'd withdrawn into herself and made an excuse to leave.

He should be relieved. If she pulled back from any possibility of a relationship between them, whether it was because of Jamie or not, he'd have an easier time keeping a distance between them. Trouble was he didn't feel relieved in the least. Annoyed, irritable, attracted—all of those, certainly. But not relieved.

As he passed the quilt shop, Nick couldn't stop himself from taking a quick look inside. He stopped in midstride. Mac was deep in conversation with Allison. Disregarding the voice of reason saying that it wasn't any of his business, he changed direction and approached them.

"What's going on? Did you figure out what happened with Ralph's break-in?" He focused on Mac, although a quick glance at Allison had taken in every detail of her appearance, including the fact that she looked pale and heavy-eyed.

Mac shrugged. "Like I was just saying to Allison, it looks more like vandalism than a serious attempt at burglary. Nothing was missing but a watch from the top of the bureau. The computer hadn't been touched, or that silver Ralph collects."

Anyone who visited Ralph had been shown his collection of antique silver. It was probably the most valuable thing he owned.

"I suppose it could have been someone who had no idea how to get rid of the silver," Nick said. "A watch would be small and portable and easily hocked."

"Right. I'd chalk it up to a petty thief or a druggie looking for cash if it weren't for the break-in at the shop." Mac sounded as if the events were a personal insult. Or maybe it was more likely that he felt offended that he hadn't figured it out yet. "That makes it look more like a personal grudge against Ralph."

"Seriously?" He raised an eyebrow. "I suppose that's the best explanation, but it's hard to imagine anyone having that big a grudge against somebody like Ralph. He's irritating at times, but he doesn't have enough force of personality to be disliked."

"Then give me another explanation," Mac challenged. "Because I'm sure not coming up with one on my own."

"People do take offense at the oddest things," Allison said. "Vandalism is usually done by teenagers, isn't it?"

"Any teenagers in particular?" Mac asked.

She shook her head, but Nick suspected she was thinking of T. J. Blackburn.

"At least this makes it look as if Ralph is the target." Nick couldn't deny the relief he felt. "Probably Allison just happened to be in the wrong place at the wrong time."

Mac looked as surprised as he ever did. He shot a look at Allison. "Didn't you tell him?"

"I haven't seen him," she said. "I assumed you had."

"Tell me what?" His tone reflected the tension that seized him. "What's going on?"

"Don't overreact," Mac said. "After Allison left the picnic last night, someone followed her and apparently tried to run her off the road."

"What do you mean, apparently?" Allison sounded indignant. "You can look at my bumper if you don't believe me."

"I already—" Mac began, but Nick spoke over him.

"Why didn't you tell me about this? What exactly happened?"

Mac and Allison exchanged glances again, and Mac seemed to accept the responsibility for telling him. "Allison was followed by another car. It hit her bumper several times, but she managed to stay on the road. When they got close to town, the other vehicle veered off, apparently on Foster Creek Road."

A pulse was pounding in Nick's forehead. It was all he could do to control himself. He zeroed in on Allison's face, and she stared back at him. "Why didn't you tell me? Are you sure you're not hurt?"

"I'm fine," she said, her voice crisp. "The air bag didn't even go off. There's no need to overreact."

It was the second time in five minutes someone had told him not to overreact. It wasn't helping. "You could have been hurt. You should have let me follow you home the way I wanted to."

"I didn't need a bodyguard. Or a nanny." Allison wielded the words like weapons to keep him at bay.

Mac cleared his throat. "Guess I'll let you two argue it out," he said. Lips twitching, he left.

From the corner of his eye, Nick saw Sarah emerge from the back room, take one look at them and retreat.

Good. He could stand some privacy to say what he wanted. "Maybe you need just that. When will you get it through your head…" He let that trail off and counted to ten. It didn't seem to help. "Could you identify the driver or the car?"

"No. All I could see was the light glaring in my rear-view mirrors. The car was dark in color. Big, I think, not a compact. Other than that, nothing." She made as if to turn away. "If there's nothing else…"

He started to grasp her hands and prevented himself. That never seemed to end well. "You should have called me at the first sign of trouble."

"I was a little busy trying to keep the car on the road. Stop telling me what I should have done. If I could have used the phone, I'd have dialed 911."

"I was a lot closer than the police." He was starting to sound like a stubborn idiot, even to himself, and he shook his head. "Sorry. You're right. I just wish I'd followed my instincts and gone after you."

The determined facade Allison was wearing seemed to shiver at his words. "When I first saw the car, I thought it was you." Her voice had softened. "Then it hit me."

He could see the remembered fear in her eyes. "You must have had a job to keep the car on the road."

She nodded. "The first time was the worst, because I didn't expect it. I was prepared the next time I saw the headlights getting close."

Maybe it was good for Allison to relive the experience. The tension seemed to be going out of her as she talked.

"How many times did he hit you, or couldn't you tell?"

She actually managed a shaky smile. "I wasn't counting, but three or four, I think." She frowned. "It seemed to me that he was trying not to connect too hard. Mac said he might have wanted to avoid leaving too much evidence if he did succeed in making me crash."

"You didn't," he said. "You're safe, and we're going to make sure you stay that way." Where had it come from so quickly, this feeling he had that it was his job to protect her?

Allison rubbed her forehead tiredly. "I stayed awake most of the night trying to figure this out, and I'm no closer to an answer than I was days ago. Who? And how does it tie into this business with Ralph? That makes even less sense."

"If Ralph knows something about the person who's been attacking you…" He stopped, frowning. "But in that case, why go after his property? You're right—it doesn't make sense."

"Maybe it's two separate campaigns." She had the air of someone grabbing at straws.

"Two different bad guys, both embarking on vendettas against people connected with Blackburn House at the same time?" Nick's doubt showed in his voice. "In a place like Laurel Ridge, that's next to impossible."

"Because the people here are saints?" The edge was back in her tone.

"No, because there just aren't enough of them," he shot back. "I mean, what are the odds that out of eight thousand residents, two of them would be inspired to such strange behavior at the same time?"

"I suppose you have a point." Allison leaned back

against the counter, as if too tired to hold herself upright any longer.

Nick studied her face. Stubborn. Determined to hold him at arm's length. And vulnerable. "Look, I know I don't have any right to tell you what to do—"

"Why do I think there's a *but* coming?"

"But, please, don't do anything alone until this is resolved. It's just not safe."

For a moment he thought she'd flare out at him. But then she nodded. "I'm not that stubborn." Her smile trembled. "I won't go anywhere on my own. I promise."

WORKING IN HER office later, Allison remembered that promise. "I just said I wouldn't go anywhere on my own," she told Hector, who was curled in her lap, getting between her and the computer. "Being alone in my office is perfectly safe."

Hector kneaded his paws on her lap, blinked and dozed off again.

Not that she was really alone. She could hear a murmur of voices from the apartment and smell the aroma of paint. The Amish painting crew had been hard at work all day, and they were certainly within shouting distance, as were the inhabitants of the other offices on this floor.

Returning her attention to the computer, Allison clicked through the various links of the quilt shop website she'd been setting up. As far as she could tell, everything was working fine. She'd give it a final check later, and tomorrow it could go live.

Something accomplished, at least, she thought as she saved and closed her work. She'd half expected more interruptions from the police, but Mac had apparently been occupied elsewhere. He'd left the shop so abruptly this morning—clearly he hadn't wanted to get entangled in whatever was going on between her and his brother.

Nothing was going on, wasn't that the point? The whole situation had become very simple. Nick didn't want to be involved with her because he didn't think she'd be good for his son. She didn't want to be involved with him because knowing the risks, she didn't want to be a stepmother. Fine. They'd stay away from each other. End of story.

Hector swiveled his head and looked up at her, as if he'd heard her thoughts and doubted them. Then he stared fixedly at the door. His ears pricked up, hearing something she didn't.

A frisson of fear slid along her spine, and Allison forced it away as a knock sounded at the door. An attacker wouldn't knock.

"Just a moment." She rose, displacing Hector, and went to unlock and open the door. Ralph stood waiting, blinking rapidly when he met her gaze.

"Ralph, please, come in."

He bobbed his head, his gaze sliding away from hers, and sidled through the door. Judging by his pallor and the tremor in his hands, he felt even worse than she did.

"Come and sit down." She took his arm and guided him to a chair. "How are you? It must have been so upsetting to have your home broken into that way."

Ralph shivered all over like a frightened horse. "You can't imagine. It was terrible. I'll never get over it. Never." His pupils dilated, and he shot a look around the office.

"I know it's frightening, but you shouldn't let it get

you down so." Saying things like that never helped, but they seemed to come readily to a person's lips. "I'm sure the police will find the vandals and make sure they never bother you again."

"They won't." He shook his head and went on shaking it as if he couldn't stop. "The police will never identify anyone. He... They wore gloves, and nobody saw anything."

Allison's gaze sharpened, and she studied Ralph's face. He, he'd said, before he'd corrected himself. As if he knew there had been only one intruder. But how could he, unless he knew what this mysterious 'he' was after?

"You suspect someone, don't you? Who was it, Ralph? And why?"

"No!" His voice rose, eyes widening. Ralph gripped the arms of the chair. "How would I know?"

In an instant he'd bolt, and she'd have lost the chance to learn what frightened him.

"It's all right." She leaned over to pat his shoulder, and then she dragged a chair over so she could sit down close to him. "You have friends here, Ralph. Everyone wants to help you. Just tell me what you're afraid of, and I'll make sure you're protected."

For an instant she saw in his face the longing to speak. And saw, too, the moment when fear drove the words from his tongue.

"You're wrong. I don't know anything." He darted another suspicious glance around the room, lingering for a moment at the door to the attic as if expecting something from a nightmare to burst through it.

"But it was your shop. Your house. Surely—"

"It's this place!" His voice grew shrill, and he seemed

to teeter on the edge of hysteria. "Don't you feel it? You should. It's unlucky. Bad things happen here."

That jolted her, with its reminder of her grandmother's letter about something going on in Blackburn House. "What do you mean? What bad things?"

He shook his head, putting one hand to his lips. "I don't know. I'm upset. I don't mean anything."

"My grandmother died here." She kept her gaze firmly on his. "She left a letter for me, saying she'd learned that something was going on here. You know what that something was, don't you?"

"No!" He jumped to his feet, nearly knocking over the chair in his haste. "I don't know anything except that I can't stay here any longer. I want out of my lease."

The words stunned her, and she struggled to grasp their meaning. "You mean you want to close the store?"

"I have to. My nerves won't stand it here another day. Let me out of my lease, and I'll clear out."

Appalled, she shook her head. How could she do that? According to the terms of the bequest, she had to make a success of running Blackburn House. If she started losing tenants, where would she be?

"You can't refuse! It…it's a matter of my health. I can't stay here." Ralph twisted his hands together, and she thought he was on the verge of tears.

"Ralph, calm down, please. You must see that I can't make a decision like that without time to consider. I'd have to speak to the attorney for the estate as well as the accounting firm. It's not that easy—"

"I have to go now. I can't wait. You can't make me." He fled to the door and flung it open. "You're killing me by keeping me here."

She hurried after him, appalled, hoping to calm him. "You don't mean that—"

"You're just like your grandmother," he cried. "Self-righteous and stubborn. You won't be happy until I'm dead!"

He surged into the hallway and scurried toward the stairs, clinging to the wall all the way like a mouse running along the baseboard. He grasped the handrail and hurried down, disappearing from view.

Allison turned away, shaken and breathless. The door to the apartment was open. Nick and his father stood there, staring. Behind them she caught a glimpse of the painting crew, looking shocked. Obviously they had all overheard. As piercing as Ralph's voice had been, the whole upstairs had probably heard.

Nick took a few steps toward her. "Is everything okay?"

She threw out her hands, palms up. "Ralph's afraid. He wants out of his lease."

"He really has the wind up." Nick, crossing the short distance between them, shook his head. "Ralph has always been the nervy sort, but I've never seen him like this."

"I'm sorry for him, but I can't just agree to let him out of his lease, not without looking into what that will mean. I have to run this place at a profit, remember?"

He nodded. "I'm not blaming you. I'm just wondering what has him so terrified."

"I saw that, too." Her defensiveness slipped away. "It's almost as if he knows why someone was in his shop and his house, but he wouldn't admit it."

"Too scared to."

She could almost hear the wheels turning in Nick's brain.

"I'll talk to Mac about it." With a glance back at the

apartment, he lowered his voice. "Maybe a little quiet investigation of Ralph would pay off."

ALLISON PROPPED HER ankle on to a pillow and leaned back against the headboard with a sigh. It had been a long day, and she was more than ready for it to be over.

She drew her laptop toward her and then pushed it away again. Sarah had approved the website, and it would go live in the morning. Any other work could wait.

Her thoughts slid back to that odd encounter with Ralph that afternoon. Surely there had to be more going on with him than he admitted to. Nick had said they'd look into it, and she suspected he wouldn't let Mac rest until he'd agreed.

If Ralph had been involved in some wrongdoing…

The cell phone chimed. Glancing automatically to see who was calling, she abruptly sat upright. The bookstore. No one would be calling her from the bookstore phone but Ralph.

Connecting cautiously, Allison prepared herself to be calm but firm. "Hello?"

"Allison?" Ralph's voice shook on her name. "I have to talk to you."

She leaned back against the pillows. "If this is about your lease—"

"No, no. It's not, I promise." His voice faded, then grew stronger again, as if he'd turned away from the phone briefly. "I…I'm sorry. About how I acted today."

"You were upset," she said. Far more upset than was called for, she'd think. "We'll talk it over after I have more information about the lease."

"No. I mean—" He broke off, then started again, speaking quickly, the words tumbling over one another.

"I could see what you thought, and you were right." His voice dropped to a harsh whisper. "I've been hiding something. But I can't take it any longer. I can't!"

"I'm sure it will be all right." Her voice soothed while her thoughts raced. So Ralph did know something more than he'd told about what was going on. "If you just tell the police—"

"Not the police!" His voice rose, panic-stricken. "You. I'll tell you."

"It really would be better to talk to Mac. You know you can trust him."

"I can't." It came out on a sob. "Please, Allison. I'll tell you, and then you can do whatever you think is best. Please. Just come to the shop now, so we can talk with no one hearing."

Red flags went up all over the place. "I can't. You come over to the bed-and-breakfast. We'll have privacy."

"That's no good. You have to come here. I can't explain unless you come." He was crying in earnest now, sobs breaking into his words.

He was hysterical, and she shouldn't attempt to deal with him alone. Or to set foot in Blackburn House at night without someone with her.

"All right." She broke into his sobbing. "I'll come. It will take a few minutes. I have to dress." She didn't, but it would give her time to call Mac.

"Thank you." He whispered the words, and then the receiver seemed to clonk down on the counter. She imagined him dropping it and burying his face in his arms.

Swinging herself off the bed, Allison pressed Nick's number. No point in calling the police station at this hour.

She wouldn't get anyone but the patrolman on duty. Nick would know where Mac was.

Nick answered on the first ring. "Allison? Is everything all right?"

"It's Ralph. I just had a hysterical call from him, insisting that I meet him over at the shop right now. He's been hiding something, but he says he won't tell anyone but me."

"Mac and I will be there in a few minutes. We'll handle it. You stay put."

"I can't." She shoved her feet into sneakers as she spoke. "He insists he won't talk to anyone but me."

"Don't—" he began.

"I'll wait for you," she said quickly. "I won't see him alone."

She could almost feel the argument humming through the air toward her, but Nick must have realized it would be useless.

He let out an exasperated breath. "Stay outside until we get there. Don't go in without us."

"I know. I'll wait on the porch."

"See you in ten minutes."

Allison pulled on a jacket and stuffed her keys into the pocket. Clutching her cell in her hand like the lifeline it was, she headed downstairs. The faint sounds of a television show drifted in from Mrs. Anderson's private quarters in the rear. She probably wouldn't even realize Allison had gone out. Just as well, since she'd developed alarming mother-hen tendencies lately.

It was nearly full dark already. Allison gave a nervous glance around but saw no one. She hurried to the gate to the Blackburn House property and then up the

walk, slowing as she approached the shadows around
the porch.

Nothing moved. She couldn't stand there staring.
She'd said she'd wait on the porch, and that was what
she'd do. Trying not to imagine someone springing from
the dark, she hurried up to the porch and approached
the door.

And realized instantly that something was wrong.
There should be several lights on in the building, and
one on the porch. All of them were dark.

Allison stood for a moment, frowning. Ralph knew
she was coming. He wanted to see her. Therefore he
wouldn't turn off the lights.

Not unless he'd planned a trap, some cautious part of
her mind suggested.

Unlikely. That had been genuine fear in his voice…
fear for himself. All the more likely, then, that he'd seek
the safety provided by having the lights on.

Feeling foolish, she pressed her ear against the glass
in the front door. Nothing. Her fingers closed on her
keys. She had to unlock the door, anyway. Perhaps, if
she eased it open an inch or so, she'd be able to hear any
sounds from inside.

The lock slid back noiselessly. A quick glance down
the street told her that Nick wasn't in sight yet. Heart
pounding, she eased the door open a couple of inches
and listened.

When it came, the sound startled her so badly she
nearly banged the door shut. Soft, barely reaching her
ears, it was a breathy moan, followed by another.

Her heart thudded so loudly in her ears that it was a
wonder she could hear anything. She pushed the door

open another couple of inches and held her breath, listening.

A groan. Then a scrabbling sound. It produced an image of fingers clutching at the marble floor.

Probably a mouse, she told herself. Except that mice didn't groan. Someone was in there. Someone was hurt.

The light switches were just inside the door. Without giving herself time to think, she slipped inside and began flipping switches, one after another. Nothing. No lights came on. And from the darkness came another groan, a faint sound that might have been a cry for help.

She should go back outside. She'd said she'd wait on the porch. But someone was hurt. She had to do something.

Allison took a cautious step, then another. The darkness was intense, pressing down on her, taking her breath away. If she pressed a button on her cell phone, she might be able to see a little in its glow.

But that meant that anyone lurking in the dark would know exactly where she was. Her finger froze.

The harsh sound of labored breathing seemed to assault her ears, demanding that she do something. Cautiously, the cell in one hand, she reached out with the other to feel her way along the wall.

She reached the door to the quilt shop. A faint glow came from the window opposite the door, and she took comfort from the interruption of the velvety blackness. Further on. Her mind provided her with an image of the hallway, but distances were deceptive in the dark. Was she nearly at the stairwell or not? Surely Nick and Mac would come soon. They'd see that the door was open and rush inside. She should have waited for them—

Her foot hit something soft and yielding. Off balance, she fell to her knees, her outstretched palm hitting the floor and coming away sticky. She caught back a cry, and her finger involuntarily hit the cell phone. The screen light came on, and she turned it toward what lay on the floor.

It was Ralph, crumpled at the bottom of the stairs. He was on his side, the whites of his eyes showing. Around his head...she recoiled. The marble floor around his head held a pool of blood, and blood stained her hand.

Shuddering, she tried instinctively to wipe it off, even as she bent over him. "Ralph? Can you hear me?" She put a hand gingerly on his chest and felt the faintest movement.

"Ralph!" Why didn't they come? Should she call and tell them to get an emergency squad here? Even as she thought it, Ralph's eyelids blinked.

"Ralph, I'm here. It's Allison. Help is on the way."

His hand moved convulsively, scratching the floor. "Sorry," he whispered.

She clasped his hand firmly in hers. His already felt cold, as if the warmth and life ebbed out of him. "I'll call the emergency squad—" But even as she fumbled with the phone, his hand tightened on hers.

"Tell you," he murmured. "Sorry." He coughed, gasping for air.

"It's all right," she said quickly. "Don't try to talk now. Later."

"No...no later." His breath rattled. "Evelyn. Didn't mean...didn't mean..."

"What about Evelyn? Ralph, what about Evelyn?"

But his eyes flickered, losing any hint of recognition. His head sagged to the side.

Allison fumbled, trying to feel a pulse in his neck. Unable to find one. He couldn't be gone. He couldn't—

Footsteps pounded. A powerful torch swept the hallway and then settled on them like a spotlight.

"It's Ralph," she said, her lips numb. "I think he's dead."

CHAPTER EIGHTEEN

NICK THOUGHT HIS heart would stop when he bolted through the door to Blackburn House and the light picked up Allison, kneeling next to a huddled form at the base of the stairs, her eyes wide and her hands stained with blood.

"Allison!" He rushed toward her, ignoring Mac's command to stay back. She was hurt, she needed him… "You're injured." He went down on his knees next to her. "What is it? Where are you hurt?"

She blinked. "I'm not." Following his gaze, she looked down at her hands. A shudder went through her. "Ralph—I was trying to help him, but I can't feel a pulse."

"Let me try." Mac eased her away from Ralph and pressed his fingers to Ralph's throat.

"Easy." Nick helped her slide a few feet away from the body and leaned her against the wall. Her face was ashen in the glare of the flashlight Mac held. "Do you feel faint?"

She shook her head and then rested it against the wall. He wasn't convinced. She looked as if she might pass out at any moment. "What happened? Why did you come in instead of waiting for us?"

Mac looked up from barking into his cell phone to frown at Nick. "Hold on. Wait until I get some help here."

He felt an intense desire to hit his brother, but maybe he was right. Allison looked as if she could use a respite from answering questions for a few minutes, at least.

He heard Mac ask for the emergency squad and looked a question at him as Mac ended the call. "Is he...?" He didn't finish but nodded toward Ralph.

Mac shrugged. "I think he's gone, but I'm no doctor. We have to do this by the book, and that means letting the medics have a look first."

Allison moved slightly, and Nick realized she was holding her hands away from her, looking at them with horror. He grasped her elbow.

"You don't have to stay here. Let me take you in the back room of the quilt shop, where you can wash your hands."

"Just a second." Mac stopped him as he began to lift Allison to her feet. "I'd better have a sample of the blood from her hands first."

Nick's fists clenched. "You don't need—"

"Until we know how Ralph died, this is a criminal investigation." Mac squared up to him, meeting him glare for glare. "It may be important."

"It's all right," Allison said, her voice weak. "What do you want me to do?"

"Just hold out your hands and let me wipe them. I don't have an evidence kit here, but we'll make do." Pulling out a handkerchief, he swiped it down Allison's palm and then folded it into itself. "I don't suppose you have such a thing as a plastic bag here?"

He was looking at Nick, but Allison answered. "There's a box of them in the back room of the quilt shop. The drawer to the left of the sink."

"I'll get it," he began, and then realized they only had

the one flashlight between them. "There's a flashlight in my glove compartment—"

"Right." Mac sounded frustrated. "Get that first, then the plastic bag. Then you can take care of Allison."

Leaving the flashlight with Mac, Nick hurried to the door, guided by the dim light washing in from outside. He snatched the flashlight and raced back. If Mac started badgering Allison with questions at this point—

But the two of them were still the way he'd left them, with Allison sagging against the wall and Mac watching her, frowning a little. Allison straightened when she saw him. "You'll need my keys. In my jacket pocket." Holding her hands away from her, she nodded to the pocket.

Nick reached in, pulled out the keys and went quickly to the quilt shop door. It was a matter of moments to fetch the plastic bag and hand it to his brother. "I'm taking Ally in the back room. She doesn't need to stay here and watch."

Mac nodded, looking harassed. "We don't have a big enough force to deal with a situation like this. Once backup arrives and we can get some lights on and check out the building, I'll have some questions."

"If you're lucky, it will just be a thrown switch on the circuit box." Nick took Allison's arm, nudging her gently away, trying to ignore Mac muttering under his breath.

By the time Nick had gotten her to the room behind the quilt shop, Allison seemed to have regained some of her strength. She moved steadily to the sink and washed her hands, scrubbing them over and over, as if she'd never get them clean. He watched as long as he could stand, and then he took her hands in his, rinsing them, and dried them on the dish towel that hung over the edge of the sink.

"They're clean now. It's all right."

She looked at him, her eyes wide and dark. "If I hadn't argued about coming over, if I hadn't waited to call you, I might have been in time to help him."

"You might have been lying there next to him." He made his voice firm with an effort. "We don't know yet what happened, but whatever it was, you're not to blame." When she continued to stare blankly, he grasped her arms and shook her lightly. "Snap out of it, Ally. It's terrible that you found him, but nothing you did or didn't do could change the result."

She blinked, and some life came back into her eyes. She sucked in a deep breath. "I'm sorry. You're right. It's just…shock, I guess."

"Come and sit down." He led her to the rocking chair, and she sank into it. Flashing the light around the small room, he found another chair and dragged it over to sit in front of her, knee to knee. He clasped her hands warmly in his and tried to focus his thought. "Why did you come in? You were going to wait for us. Did you see something?"

"I don't think so." She pressed her fingers to her forehead. "The outside light wasn't on. I noticed that, and then I thought I'd unlock the door so we could get inside right away. I heard a noise." Her voice trembled. "I thought…I thought it was someone moaning. Someone hurt."

A siren wailed outside, announcing the arrival of reinforcements. Mac would probably say he shouldn't have asked any questions until he was there, but Allison had clearly needed to talk, and Mac couldn't be everywhere at once.

They would have to call for help from the state police.

He faced that unpalatable fact. Mac wouldn't like it any more than he did, but there was no choice, at least when it came to the crime lab. A place like Laurel Ridge didn't have the personnel and equipment for a case like this.

"He was moaning when you came in? He was still alive, then."

His fingers tightened on hers. "Did he say anything? Did he tell you who—"

She shook her head before he could finish the question. "He said a few words, that's all. Nothing that made much sense."

The light came on in the hallway. He let out a breath and got up to switch on the light. Allison sat, blinking and pale in the sudden glare.

"That's better." He managed a smile. "Things always look better in the light, don't they?"

Allison shivered. "I'm not sure this does. Nick, none of this makes sense. Was it an accident? Surely no one could have wanted to kill Ralph."

"I don't know." He wished he had answers that would wipe the anxiety from her face, but he didn't. There weren't any.

The overhead lights in the shop area came on, and footsteps approached. Mac paused in the doorway, frowning. At the fact that he was holding Allison's hands? Maybe. If so, he could lump it.

"What do you think?" he asked before Mac could speak. "Accident?"

Mac's frown deepened as he came over to them. "It's too early to say. I suppose he could have fallen down the stairs."

"No," Allison said suddenly, and they both turned to stare at her. "I mean, I don't see how. He was in the office when he called me. Why would he rush upstairs when he knew I was coming to meet him in a few minutes?"

Mac nodded slowly. "Good point. But we can't be sure. If he thought of something he wanted to show you, something he had to get from upstairs, he could have been hurrying." His face tightened. "I've called in the state police crime scene team. And they'll have to handle the autopsy, as well. We don't have the facilities."

Nick could hear the irritation in his voice. Mac didn't like the idea of turning any part of the investigation over to someone else, but there was no choice. And if the state criminal investigation people got involved— His mind backed away from that idea. At least Mac knew the circumstances and the people, which was more than any strangers could.

"Now, Allison." Mac perched himself on the corner of the table and pulled out a notebook. "Tell me just what Ralph said."

"On the phone, you mean? Or when I found him?"

That jolted Mac off the table. "He spoke to you before he died?"

She nodded. "Not much. Just a few words." She frowned, as if determined to get it right. "He said, 'sorry.' He said it a couple of times. And then he said, 'Evelyn.' And he said he was sorry again. Something about how he didn't mean something." She shrugged. "It doesn't make a lot of sense. I tried to ask him about my grandmother, but he…" Her voice trailed off.

Mac stared at the words he'd written down, as if he could wrest meaning from them. "Okay." The whine of another siren, followed by the sound of tramping feet, had his head jerking around. "I'll have to get out there.

Look, I think the best thing would be for Nick to take you back over to Mrs. Anderson's. When I'm done here, I'll have to ask you some questions."

She nodded, seeming to understand that he didn't want an audience for this part of the investigation. "All right. I'll be ready whenever you need me."

"Okay." He took a step toward the door and turned back. "The building will have to be closed tomorrow, maybe longer. Depends on what we find. You'll have to come into the station tomorrow to make a formal statement and sign it." He hesitated. "You aren't planning to go anywhere in the near future, are you?"

"No." Allison's voice was firm enough, but Nick found it too easy to read the bleak fear in her eyes. She had just realized how bad this situation could be.

ALLISON HAD EXPECTED to be awake for what was left of the night after the questioning that went on until the early hours. Instead, she sank deep into slumber the instant her head hit the pillow, for all the world as if she'd been hit by a rock.

She didn't know how long she'd have slept if not for Hector.

He'd leaped on the bed, walking on her chest and meowing for his breakfast, forcing her awake. The instant her eyes opened memories came flooding back, and she swung herself off the bed. It was nearly nine. What had been happening while she'd been dead to the world?

Going barefoot to the window, Allison pulled the shade an inch or so aside and peered out at the building next door. Surrounded by orange tape, it had been transformed into an object of curiosity. Several people stood at the gate, peering at the building as if it could tell them something. A patrolman stood guard on the porch. Other than that, she could see no sign of activity. Did that mean the police had wrapped up their investigation of the property? She suspected that was a bit too optimistic.

Allison ran her fingers through her hair, glaring at her image in the mirror as she turned away from the window. A shower would help, but she doubted anything would hide the shadows like bruises under her eyes or the haunted expression.

Forty-five minutes later, showered, dressed and made up, she was sitting at the table in the sunroom at the rear of the house, trying to fend off Mrs. Anderson's curiosity as best she could without offending her. Presumably she thought food the best answer to an emergency, since she'd prepared enough breakfast for half the town.

"The police cautioned me not to talk about it," Allison said for the third time, removing Hector from her lap before he could snag a piece of bacon from her plate. "And it was so terrible to find Ralph that way…" She let that trail off, shuddering in the hope that would discourage the woman.

Before Mrs. Anderson could launch into more questions, the doorbell sounded. She made an exasperated noise. "Been ringing all morning. That Hardesty boy from the newspaper was here before I'd even had coffee, wanting a story from you for that paper of his. I gave him a piece of my mind, I can tell you that." She marched off, militant, apparently ready to repel anyone who had a similar idea.

But when she returned a moment later, it was to usher Sarah into the room. "Look, here's Sarah," she said unnecessarily. "I'll get another coffee cup." She disappeared kitchenward, and Sarah came to hug her, face worried.

"*Ach*, I couldn't believe it when I heard. Ralph dead, and you finding him that way. It must have been terrible." She gave another squeeze.

Allison nodded, her throat suddenly tight. "How did you find out?"

"Nick came by first thing this morning. Now *Mamm* wants you to come and stay with us, for a few days at least, until things get back to normal."

Somehow she doubted that was ever going to happen, but she tried to hide the feeling. "It's lovely of your family. But I'm not sure…"

"You don't have to decide now." Sarah slid into a chair. "Come anytime. The room will be ready for you."

"Thank you," she said again, quick tears springing to her eyes. "I appreciate it." So, Nick had stopped by Sarah's parents' place this morning. He hadn't come here. She tried to think what that meant, if anything.

Sarah glanced toward the window. "It seems strange not to be able to go into our own shop. What are they doing in there?"

Allison shrugged, unsure. "I guess trying to find something to tell them whether Ralph's death was an accident."

Sarah's eyes widened. "But what else could it be? Poor Ralph. He was so…so harmless."

"I know." She kept her voice even with an effort. "But he called me a few minutes before he died. He was upset. *Distraught* might be a better word. He kept saying that he had to see me, to tell me something. He wanted me to come over to the shop, but when I got there, he was dying."

Sarah nodded, eyes wide. "Nick said he was lying at the bottom of the steps. I thought he fell."

"Maybe he did. But the police have to be sure." Ironic, in a way, that they were now doing the investigation she'd thought they should have done when Evelyn died.

"I'm sorry." Sarah spoke softly, touching her hand. "You won't want to talk about it."

"It's not so much that, but the police told me not to discuss it with anyone." She smiled at Mrs. Anderson, who reappeared with another mug and a carafe of coffee. She had no doubt that the woman had been listening from the kitchen, but she hadn't said anything that probably wasn't general knowledge by now.

"Denke." Sarah held the mug while Mrs. Anderson filled it.

"Sarah, you'll have some apple walnut coffee cake, won't you? I'm sure it's not as good as your mother's, but it's not bad if I do say so myself."

"It's delicious," Allison said quickly. "Thank you so much. I'm sorry I've put you behind with everything. I guess no one's getting much work done today."

"That's certain sure, since we can't get into the shop. Nick has been calling people, making sure they know they can't get into the building. He put a sign up on the gate telling anyone who comes where to call for the offices."

So Nick had been busy, even if he hadn't been in touch with her. "That's good of him. I didn't even think of it."

"Ach, folks will understand. After all, nobody can argue with an emergency like this one," Sarah said.

"That's right," Mrs. Anderson chimed in loyally. She chased Hector and her tabby off one of the chairs. "Now just you stop it, you naughty cats. You think we're too busy to notice, but we're not."

"They were taking advantage of our distraction," Allison said, and then realized that Mrs. Anderson was staring past her, toward one of the large back windows of the sunroom. "What?" She turned to see someone peering through the window at her.

"That boy from the paper!" Mrs. Anderson marched to the closet, grabbed the broom and headed for the back door. "I'll show him I mean what I say."

Before Allison could say anything, Mrs. Anderson had charged out the door, brandishing the broom and advancing on the reporter like a fury. Well, like a short, pudgy, graying fury, she amended. As Mrs. Anderson charged, the tall, lanky young reporter backed up, holding up his hands in defense. His mouth moved, as if he were trying to argue, perhaps to cite the freedom of the press. The broom swung, and he turned and bolted, abandoning his dignity. Allison caught Sarah's eye, and they both dissolved in helpless laughter.

"Who would think she had so much fight in her?" Allison gasped the words out, trying to control herself before Mrs. Anderson came in.

"We don't believe in violence, but I have to admit, I want to clap for her." Sarah wiped her eyes.

Mrs. Anderson had disappeared around the side of the house, apparently in pursuit of the reporter. When she came back, through the front, she had company, since she was busy scolding whoever it was. They came through to the sunroom, and Allison saw that Mac was the object of her lecture.

"...what good are the police if you can't stop reporters from trespassing and bothering people in their own homes, tell me that."

Mac, wisely, chose the path of least resistance. "Sorry, Mrs. A. The officer next door should have noticed what was going on before you had to handle it yourself." If his lips quivered slightly, he managed to suppress it. "If you notice anyone around who doesn't belong, you give the officer a shout right away. He'll come and help you."

"I'm so sorry, Mrs. Anderson," Allison put in. "I'm sure I'm the one he wanted to see. I don't want to bring trouble on you."

"No trouble at all," Mrs. Anderson seemed mollified. She eyed Mac. "I suppose I'd better make some more coffee." She headed for the kitchen again.

"That is all the more reason you should come and stay with us for a couple of nights," Sarah said, her tone persuasive. "Just until things settle down."

"I don't want to bring reporters in on you, either. Besides…" She glanced at Mac. "I have to get permission from the police before I make any moves."

"What?" Sarah sounded as outraged as she was capable of being. "What are you going on about, Mac? Have you lost your senses?"

Mac raised both hands, palms out, much as the reporter had done. "Now, Sarah…"

"Ralph's death changes everything, you see." Allison spoke the truth she'd been realizing since the previous night. "I'm not a bystander or a victim any longer. I'm a suspect."

"A witness," Mac corrected quickly. "Look, we don't know yet if Ralph's death was an accident or…something else." He seemed reluctant to use the word *murder*. "Let's not get ahead of ourselves."

"Well, you don't need to treat Allison that way." Sarah was still not satisfied.

"I understand," Allison said, before the situation could become even more awkward. "Mac has to follow the rules." She managed a smile for him. "Do you have more questions? Should Sarah leave?"

"No, no." He sent Sarah a wary glance. "I just wanted to ask you to come by the station around two to make a formal statement."

Allison nodded, relieved that was all. "I'll be there."

Mac turned to leave, then glanced over his shoulder. "I'm sorry about this."

So am I, she thought, watching him stride out. *So am I.*

Sarah reached over to clasp her hand. "I don't understand it." Her voice was troubled, her forehead wrinkled. "All this wickedness coming out since…"

"Since I came?" Allison asked.

"I was going to say, since Evelyn died. That day she told me about finding something wrong—maybe I should have done more. If I'd asked her…" She hesitated, shaking her head. "She just wasn't a person you could question."

"I've gathered that." Would she have liked her grandmother, if they'd had a different start? Or would it have been better if Evelyn had never thought of her at all? She'd never have come here, never met Sarah, or Krysta, or Nick. Her heart stuttered at the thought of Nick.

She hadn't heard from him since he'd brought her to the bed-and-breakfast last night. He hadn't even come with Mac for that late-night questioning.

What had she expected, that he'd ride in to rescue her? If she needed rescuing, she'd do it herself. Besides, the mayor could hardly take sides in what might be a criminal case, especially not when his brother was the chief of police.

BY LATE AFTERNOON the next day, the reporter still sat in his car, parked at the curb in front of the bed-and-breakfast. Allison turned away from the downstairs window and set her overnight bag on the floor. She couldn't drive to Sarah's with a reporter on her tail. She might not know a great deal about the Amish, but she felt sure they wouldn't relish that type of publicity. No one would.

Allison glanced at her watch. Maybe he'd get hungry and leave long enough to pick up something to eat. And maybe not. Persistence was probably a good quality in a reporter, but at the moment it was simply annoying.

She considered the possibilities of speaking to him, but everything in her shrank from the idea. Besides, what could she tell him? Mac had cautioned her repeatedly not to reveal anything that had happened for fear of jeopardizing the investigation.

The door to Mrs. Anderson's quarters in the rear of the house opened, and she beckoned to Allison, her eyes wide with suppressed excitement. "Come along and bring your case. We have a way out for you."

We? Allison grabbed her bag and followed the woman into the kitchen. Nick was obviously waiting, glancing toward the backyard. His face lightened at the sight of her.

"Good, you have your bag. My car's parked in the next street. I'll drive you to Sarah's while our ambitious young reporter sits there watching your car."

She hesitated, her thoughts churning, remembering her vow of independence.

"Go on, dear," Mrs. Anderson urged. "Hector can stay here with us. He'll be fine. I'll go up and switch the light on in your room so that reporter will think you're there." Her lips twitched. "It's no more than he deserves, bothering people like he is."

When Allison still didn't move, Nick grasped her arm, took the bag and hustled her toward the door. "We have to go now. He paid a kid to keep an eye on the back, but the kid got bored and went home a few minutes ago. We need to leave before he comes back."

Who was she kidding? She might not want to accept help, but at the moment, she needed it. "All right. Thanks." She turned to give Mrs. Anderson a quick hug. "Thank you. And I'm sorry—"

Mrs. Anderson waved away the rest of that sentence. "Most excitement I've had in ages. You go along now. Come back when things have calmed down. Your room will be waiting."

If things calmed down, Allison amended. Surely once Mac had announced the preliminary results of his investigation, the interest in her would wane. She hoped.

Nick led her quickly across the back lawn and around the garage, careful to keep the house between them and the reporter. "This way." Skirting an arbor in the adjoining lawn, they hurried along in the shelter of a row of overgrown lilacs and emerged onto the street that ran parallel to Main Street.

Nick's car was parked at the curb. He ushered her inside, tossed her bag in the trunk and they were off. "Bend over and tie your shoe until we get farther down the block, so he can't see us through the gaps in the houses."

"My shoes don't tie," she pointed out, but she bent over, anyway. She glanced up at Nick, seeing his face foreshortened from below and noticing a quirk to his lips despite his frown of concentration. "You're enjoying this," she accused.

His face relaxed in a grin. "Maybe so. First time I ever had a chance to play James Bond."

"Whatever your motives, I appreciate the thought."

"Better thank Mac, then. It was his idea." The car stopped, presumably at the stop sign at the end of the block, and then moved on. "Apparently the reporter was nosing around the police station, as well. I think it's safe to sit up now."

"Mac?" Her face was warm from the effort of practically standing on her head. "Why would he care?" She couldn't help the slight edge to her voice. When she'd complained to Mac about the reporter following her to the station when she gave her statement, he'd said that he couldn't interfere as long as the man stayed on the public street.

"He felt bad about not being able to protect you from the press." Nick gave her a quick glance. "But the newspaper would jump all over him for bias in conducting the case if he interfered."

"I understand. His image as a public official—"

"Image!" He muttered something under his breath that she probably wasn't supposed to hear. "Look, let's get something straight. The reason Mac kept me from sitting in on his questioning, the reason he insisted that Mom not invite you to our place and the reason he couldn't help you with the reporter are all the same thing. He feels that the county district attorney is just itching to take over the case. If Mac makes the slightest slip in conducting an impartial investigation, he'll pounce." His face was grim. "Trust me, things would be a lot more unpleasant if someone else was running the case."

"I see." She clasped her hands in her lap. "Does that mean the district attorney thinks I killed Ralph?" She waited for an answer, holding on to her courage by a thread.

CHAPTER NINETEEN

"IF HE DOES, he's an idiot." Nick's voice was strong with confidence, and something that had been tight in her chest relaxed.

"Thank you." She forced the words out around the lump in her throat.

He nodded, then reached over and gave her hand a quick squeeze. "Don't forget, we know exactly when Ralph called you, and your call to me was just a few minutes later. The doctor is bound to confirm that Ralph's injury couldn't have taken place much earlier or later than we think, since we were on the scene almost immediately. You didn't have time. Or a motive."

"Well, then." She'd think that would be obvious to anyone.

"The district attorney is a politician, and he's up for reelection next year. I'd rather not rely on his common sense."

"You're a politician," she pointed out. "Can I rely on yours?"

He winced. "Please, don't call me that," he said. "I was drafted by people who thought I was the least objectionable candidate, that's all."

Allison had to smile. Nick could put on a facade of not caring about his status of mayor, but she'd seen how he cared about this town. It was important to him, just as his family was.

"How is Jamie?" she asked. "I haven't seen him lately."

"He's fine." Nick fumbled in the center console and pulled up a sheet of paper. "He made that for you."

"How sweet of him." She unfolded the paper to see a bright crayon drawing that showed what appeared to be several animals standing in a slightly tipsy line. Below was a row of *x*'s and *o*'s and a straggling, uneven word. *Jamie.*

"In case you can't tell, that's the dog, the goat, the chickens and Jamie's teddy bear. He says they make him feel happy when he's sad, so he thought they might cheer you up." Nick glanced at the paper with a smile, but Allison was blinking back tears.

"That's so sweet of him." She folded it and tucked it carefully in her bag. "Tell him I really appreciate it, and he was right. I do feel better."

"Good." Nick sent her a sidelong look. "Are you feeling well enough to talk about what Ralph said?"

"Of course, but didn't your brother tell you not to discuss the case?"

"He might be the police chief, but he's still my little brother. He won't speculate about what Ralph meant, but there's no reason why we can't. Have you been thinking about it?"

"I haven't been thinking of much else, but I don't really have any answers." She brushed her hair back with her fingers. "He just kept saying he was sorry. And my grandmother's name."

Nick nodded. "The more I consider it, the more I think it has to have something to do with her death. Was he there that night? Did he see her fall? Did he push her?

Was he the person she'd planned to confront, or did he know who that person was?"

"Those are the possibilities. Or of course, he might just have been wandering mentally last night."

"He was dying," Nick said bluntly. "I'd think whatever a person said in those circumstances was what was important to him. What do we know about Ralph's recent behavior?"

She considered. Going over it aloud seemed to clarify her thoughts, which had been spinning in reckless confusion. "We know that his shop was broken into and searched. And his house."

"That seems significant to me. An ordinary thief would have snatched the computer or the objects that were obviously valuable."

"True. And as far as we know, nothing was taken from the bookstore at all. If you were going to break into Blackburn House to steal something, there surely were more valuable targets than a bookshop." She wasn't sure what it amounted to, but it made sense.

"There was the trap you fell into. We assumed it was part of a campaign against you, but what if it was intended for Ralph?"

"It could be, I suppose. He was upstairs at some point, we know." She shook her head. "It seems to be such a haphazard way of attacking an individual. Anyone could have fallen into it."

"Yeah, but if it was intended for a warning, it might serve its purpose no matter who was hurt. And don't forget, Ralph was so upset he went home in the middle of the day."

Allison thought how little she actually knew about Ralph Mitchell. "If it was intended for Ralph, why? Are we really saying he knew something that made him a threat to someone? Is that likely?"

"Sounds odd, doesn't it?" Nick grimaced. "I'd say most people thought of Ralph as someone...well, negligible. He didn't have power or money. But he was insatiably curious. He always had to know the latest gossip. Maybe he stumbled upon something related to Evelyn's death."

"I suppose it's possible." She turned it over in her mind. "But don't forget that Evelyn talked about there being something wrong going on at Blackburn House. How does that fit with Ralph? Surely he wasn't the person she meant— I mean, what could he do?"

"True," Nick admitted. "He owned his own business, so he couldn't be robbing the till. And I seriously doubt that he was dealing drugs in the back room."

"If he had been, he'd have had a younger clientele," she said.

He grinned. "The blue-haired set doesn't usually go in for that sort of thing. But even considering what Evelyn said—isn't it possible that she was after someone else entirely, and Ralph just happened to see something that made him a danger to that person?"

"Wouldn't he have gone to the police?" She hadn't known Ralph well, but she'd have thought him too easily frightened to do anything else.

"He might not have been sure. Or the person might just suspect Ralph knew something. Or Ralph might have wanted to hug the information to himself for a time. He was like that, you know. He took pleasure in knowing what other people didn't."

"That makes more sense than anything else we've

come up with," Allison said. "But I don't see a way of proving any of it."

"Don't get discouraged." He clasped her hand again, his grip warm and comforting. "Something may turn up in the lab results that points to someone. And Mac has been going through Ralph's house with a fine-tooth comb. He may find some other indication."

It seemed unlikely to her that anything new was going to turn up, but she managed a smile. "I hope so."

Nick released her hand as he slowed to negotiate the turn into the lane at Sarah's place. "By the way, you can tell Sarah that we've been cleared to get back into Blackburn House as of nine tomorrow morning."

"Really? That's good." A thought hit her. "I suppose I should call everyone and let them know."

"Don't bother. Mac is having his office make the calls. Better, anyway—let him deal with the inevitable questions. That's what he gets paid for."

Thinking about the repeated conversations and questions, she could only be grateful. "That's a relief. It won't be an easy day, but at least we'll get it over with." Another thought hit her. "But what about the cleanup?" She seemed to see again blood on the marble floor. "I'll have to—"

"You don't have to do anything," Nick said firmly. "I'll stand over Fred Glick myself until everything looks like new." He nodded to the lane ahead. "It looks like a welcoming party."

Sarah, her parents, even her brothers stood beside the porch, smiling, and Allison's heart lifted. "It's so nice of them. I don't know why they're being so kind to me."

Nick captured her hand again. "You're pretty easy to be kind to, Allison Standish."

Her gaze met his, and she felt her cheeks warm at the look in his eyes.

"I guess I can't kiss you goodbye with all of them watching," he said softly. "But know that whatever happens, I'm glad you came to Laurel Ridge."

BEDTIME ON AN Amish farm came a bit earlier than Allison was used to, but she was exhausted enough that she had no desire to stay up later. She sat on the twin bed in Sarah's bedroom, smoothing her hand over the Sunshine and Shadows quilt that covered it. The room was plain, she supposed, with white walls and green shades on the windows. The only thing on the walls was a calendar with pictures of scenes from the Grand Canyon, but the space certainly wasn't bland. Colorful braided rugs glowed against the wide wooden floorboards, and each piece of furniture must have been made by hand.

And then there were the quilts on the two beds, each of which would probably bring in a thousand dollars or more at a high-end shop in the city. They were both Sunshine and Shadows, but done in different colors. The effect of the shades blending into each other from light to dark and back again was like sunlight moving across a field, casting alternating waves of sunshine and shadow.

She watched as Sarah took down her hair. Released from the *kapp* and the tightly pinned coil, it flowed to her waist, rippling like water.

"Your hair is so pretty, it seems a shame to keep it hidden," she said, hoping that wasn't treading on sacred territory.

"*Ach*, it's just hair." Sarah wielded a brush vigorously. "You're wondering why we keep our hair the way we do, ain't so?"

"I guess so. I realize it's the custom, but I don't know why." Fortunately Sarah never seemed to take offense at her questions.

"The scripture says that a woman should have her head covered when she prays, and I might want to pray anytime of the day." Sarah parted the shiny flaxen mass and began to put in a loose braid. "And it seems to us that the worst sin is being proud and looking down on others. So if we all wear the same clothes and do our hair the same way, it helps to keep us from being prideful." Her fingers slowed on the plait. "I think it must be very special for a man to see his wife with her hair down for the first time."

There was a tinge of sorrow in the words that touched Allison's heart. Perhaps a younger Sarah had dreamed of the night when Aaron would see her this way. "I'm sorry," she said softly. "About Aaron, I mean."

Sarah shrugged. "It wasn't his fault. He loved someone else. We can't control who we love, can we?"

"I guess not." She thought of Nick, and her heart clenched a bit. But that wasn't love, she assured herself quickly. Attraction, yes. Even caring and admiration. But surely not love, not so quickly.

Sarah fastened the braid and started on the second one. "I have a happy life, anyway. I have family, and good friends, and work that I love. Many people don't have all those things."

Could she adjust the way Sarah had, if her dreams had been shattered? Could she go on with living and find happiness in other things?

Sarah was watching her, a question in her eyes. "You have feelings for Nick, ain't so?"

"Does it show?" She managed a smile.

"When you look at him." Sarah's lips curved. "It's hard to conceal love."

Love. There was that word again. "I'm not sure I'm in love with him." She glanced down, tracing a quilt square with her fingertip. "I mean, I care about him, and I'm attracted to him. But love—" She shook her head. "You know about Jamie's mother?"

Sarah nodded. "I remember, not that we saw much of her around here. She didn't like it here."

"I gathered that she was someone with big-city dreams. I can see it sometimes in Nick's face, that he's comparing me to her. I don't know if he could get past it."

"She was a..." Sarah paused, her hands fluttering. "Like a butterfly. Or a moth, maybe, drawn to the light. She always had to have excitement. Nick knows you well enough to know you're not like that."

"I'm not sure. I think he'd like to believe it, but every once in a while, I can see it in his face. And then there's Jamie."

Sarah's eyes widened. "But you like Jamie, and you're so good with him. And he adores you, too."

"He's easy to love." She couldn't help but smile, thinking of the picture he'd drawn for her. "But I don't know if I could be a stepparent. What if I messed up? And even if I didn't, would Jamie really be ready to share his daddy? Or would he feel left out?"

She had a feeling Sarah understood the things she didn't say. "I don't know," Sarah said. "No one can know for sure." She hesitated. "But I think it can never be wrong to love, even if that love isn't returned or doesn't work out."

Allison considered the words. Was Sarah right? She'd always thought it was important to protect her heart. To keep her guard up, so she wouldn't be hurt. But if Sarah's way was better, she'd been missing out all along.

Her phone beeped. She reached for it automatically, then hesitated and gestured with it, looking at Sarah. "Is it all right if I check my phone? If you'd rather I didn't, I'll shut it off."

"It's fine," Sarah said quickly. "We don't try to control what other people do, just ourselves. And I'd hate to try and find out how many cell phones teenagers have among the Amish. Most parents turn a blind eye to that, until they're baptized."

Allison scrolled through her messages. "I suppose teenagers are all pretty much the same, whether they're English or Amish." Her thoughts flickered to Krysta, hovering on the edge of adulthood and not quite sure which way to jump. She hoped it wasn't into T.J.'s arms, even though it wasn't her business.

She stopped at a message and read it again. A grin spread over her face. She jumped up and plopped onto Sarah's bed next to her. "Look at this. Just look." She thrust the phone into Sarah's hand.

"What is it?" Sarah frowned at the tiny letters. "One of the quilts, *ja*?"

"The quilt your mother made that we put up for sale on the internet. It's sold—and look at the price. Twelve hundred dollars, and the buyer agreed without so much as a quibble!"

Sarah gasped. "Twelve hundred? I can't believe it. Who would pay so much for a quilt?"

"Not just a quilt," Allison corrected. "It's a work of art. I knew someone would appreciate it if we just got it out there." She tapped out a quick response to the buyer. "It's a good thing we can get back into the building tomorrow. We'll have to pack it up and get it ready to ship as soon as the payment clears." She grinned. "Your *mamm* is going to be happy."

"Happy!" Sarah still seemed disbelieving. "Even after our commission, that's more than she's ever received at once. She'll be wonderful glad to have the money. I bet she'll want to buy another calf to raise. I can't wait to tell her." She clasped her hands together. "This is *gut* news, that's certain sure."

A calf. Well, that was one way to spend money, she supposed, and Sarah seemed convinced that would make her mother happy. The Amish took such pleasure in simple, ordinary things, unaffected by the competitive consumer culture that had enveloped the rest of society. Even in the midst of being disappointed in love, Sarah had been able to find joy in her everyday life.

Would she be able to accept disappointment as well as Sarah? The question recurred, demanding an answer. She certainly hadn't so far in her life. She might resolve to do better, but could she? Her thoughts flickered to Nick. Actually, she might be in a place to find out.

WHEN ALLISON AND SARAH approached the building the next morning at nine, they found a cluster of people gathered on the porch, all apparently waiting for someone else to make the first move.

Allison forced herself to smile. "Good morning."

A muted murmur of greetings answered her. They were skittish, she thought, noticing how they avoided each other's eyes. If the residents were that bad, what would the reaction of their customers be?

"Time to be sure we're ready to open," she announced, and pushed her key into the lock. Snatching a deep breath and aware of Sarah just behind her, Allison opened the door and stepped inside. Apparently that broke the spell, because the others surged in behind her.

Allison's stomach lurched as she looked toward the spot where she'd stumbled into Ralph's body. The marble floor was spotless, and the stairs looked freshly polished. No one would have guessed that the area had been the center of a grim police investigation such a short time before.

Either the police had cleaned up after themselves, or Nick had forced Fred Glick into Herculean efforts. At any rate, Blackburn House looked just as it should, and for that she was grateful. There were no lingering reminders of what had happened here, except in her mind.

Sarah went ahead to unlock the shop, switching on lights as she did, but Allison lingered, watching as the inhabitants of the upstairs offices headed up the steps. They glanced nervously to the left and right, but at least they went.

Richie Willis, the young attorney, stopped next to her, flushing a little as she met his eyes. He had to be at least her age, but his curly red hair and boyish face made him look about eighteen, and the way his fair skin showed a blush must have been a disadvantage in his profession.

"Are you okay, Ms. Standish?" He seemed uncertain but determined to make an effort.

She nodded, trying to manage a smile. "It's a terrible situation. But probably the sooner we get back to normal, the better."

"Yeah, I guess so. When Mrs. Standish—your grandmother—well, when she passed away, it was sad. Upsetting, I guess. But this—" He stopped, shook his head. "Anyway, I wanted you to know if you need anything,

I'm here." He flushed again. "I'm not trying to drum up business. But I'd be glad to help."

"Thank you." Allison was unexpectedly touched. She hardly knew him, but he seemed to take it for granted that he should be on her side. "I appreciate it."

He nodded, obviously glad to have that off his chest. "Okay, then. Off to work." He strode to the stairs, moving with a springy step.

It would take a little time, she assured herself, but the brief encounter had raised her spirits. People would become used to what had happened, and Ralph's death would be just another incident in the long history of Blackburn House.

She became aware that someone was standing at her elbow. She spun, startled. It was Emily, Ralph's clerk, her eyes reddened with weeping. Here was someone who genuinely mourned Ralph.

Allison clasped her hand. "Emily. I'm so sorry for your loss. If you don't feel able to come in today, I'm sure that's not a problem. You should take what time you need."

"So kind," Emily murmured, blotting a tear away with a tissue. "But I'd rather be busy. Oh, Ms. Standish, you probably don't know. Ralph left the shop to me. Can you imagine? I never dreamed of such a thing, but that's what his attorney said."

It was a surprise, but really, it made sense. "He didn't have any family, did he? And you were as much a part of the bookshop as he was. I'm sure he did the right thing. And very glad you'll be taking over." A sudden thought chilled her. "You do plan to keep the bookshop open, don't you?"

"Yes, yes, I can't imagine anything else." There was a

gleam of pleasure in the woman's face, quickly masked by the decorum she probably considered necessary. "I wouldn't have tried to open today, but the attorney recommended I keep the shop open as usual, right through probate. He said it would lose value if I didn't."

"That's probably true. The sooner you open again, the sooner it will start to seem normal." She thought of adding that it was what Ralph would want, but she'd always thought that sort of claim about the deceased was presumptuous. But it seemed to spring naturally to the lips when trying to comfort someone. "If you need any help, you be sure to call on us." Allison patted her hand.

Emily grasped hers. "There is something you can do." She looked a little shamefaced. "Would you go in with me? Just this first time? It would feel so much better to have someone with me."

"Of course I will." Allison caught Sarah's eye, and Sarah nodded. "Let's do it now. If you're dreading something, it's always best to get it over with quickly."

Emily nodded, her white curls bouncing. "Yes. I'm sure you're right."

Still, Allison had to grasp Emily's arm to get her started toward the bookshop. The police would have searched the shop, she felt sure. Did they leave it in suitable shape? She could hardly have expected Fred to pay attention to the interior of the shop, since his job included only the common areas unless he'd made specific arrangements with the leaseholder. Should she warn Emily of the possibility?

Before she could decide, she spotted Nick coming in the side door, a tool belt slung around his waist. He veered from the direction of the stairs and came toward them.

"Good morning." The words were ostensibly addressed to both of them, but his gaze rested on Allison, and her heart did a little dance in her chest. "Emily, I'm so sorry about Ralph. If you don't feel like opening today—"

"Did you hear that Ralph has left the shop to Emily?" Allison interjected quickly, before Emily could start to weep again. "The attorney advises her to keep it open as usual."

Nick looked as if he considered congratulating her and rejected the thought. "Ralph made the right choice. No one could care more about the shop than you, Emily." He clasped her hand warmly.

"Thank you, Nicky." She patted his cheek. "You're so thoughtful." She turned to smile at Allison. "Everyone is being so kind. Allison came with me so I don't have to go in the shop alone the first time. Isn't that sweet?"

"It is," he added gravely, but his eyes danced when he glanced at Allison. "I'll come with you, too, all right?"

That flustered Emily so much that she dropped her keys, and Nick had to retrieve them and open the door. He stepped in ahead of them and switched on the lights. "There, now. Everything seems to be in order."

Following him in, Allison had to agree. The police searchers had left no trace behind them. She was impressed.

"Oh, dear." Emily put her bag on the counter, and her tears spilled over again. "I just have to glance at the computer, and I see him sitting there. How will I go on without him? What if I make a mistake?"

"I'm sure you know everything about running the shop," Allison said, feeling out of her depth at dealing with the woman. But from what she'd seen, Emily really

ran things here. "Even so, you might want to hire someone to help out."

"Yes, I could do that." She seemed to brighten. "It
will be lonely here without him, especially during the
slow times."

"I should probably mention that the police had to
search the shop," Nick said. "They did their best to clean
up, but it wouldn't surprise me if some of the books are
in the wrong places. I suppose you could just leave it…"

"Goodness, no." Emily was suddenly animated. She
stuffed her bag behind the counter without a glance toward the computer chair. "I'll do a thorough job of shelving everything properly. The key to running a bookshop
is knowing where every book is so you can advise customers." She snatched up a duster and headed for the
nearest bank of shelves. "I'd better get busy. Thank you."

In an instant it seemed she'd forgotten them as she
began taking books down from the shelves, clucking to
herself when she found something out of order.

Nick touched Allison's arm, and they slipped out of
the shop.

"That was brilliant," Allison said.

Nick grinned. "I knew all she needed was something
to occupy herself. What I said was true as far as it went,
although I think Mac and his searchers did try to put everything back where they found it."

They were standing very close to each other in the
hall, and Nick's hand still clasped her arm. She could
feel the warmth through the thin knit of her sweater,
and she could recognize her own response. She drew
away reluctantly.

"I'd better get back to the shop and see if Sarah needs
any help, and then I have some office work to do."

"I'll be up in the apartment. Stop by when you come upstairs." His fingers brushed hers again.

"I will," she said, although she probably shouldn't. *Play with fire and get burned*, she reminded herself as she hurried back to the quilt shop. Too bad she couldn't seem to take her own advice.

Sarah looked up from sorting fabric samples as soon as she came in. "I was afraid you got stuck there propping Emily up." She made a face. "*Ach*, I shouldn't talk so. I'm sure she really is missing Ralph."

"At the moment, she's restocking books she thinks the police disarranged, so that should keep her too busy to dwell on Ralph for a time," Allison said. "Do you need me for anything?"

"What about sending the quilt?" Sarah's eyes sparkled, reminding Allison of how her mother had looked that morning when they'd told her about the sale.

"That's true." Allison set her laptop on the counter. "I'll just check and be sure the payment went through. Do we have a box that's big enough?"

"One of the fabric cartons should do it. I have some in the back. Will we take it somewhere to send?"

"Let me check and see if one of the carrier services will pick it up. That would be simpler. We'll have to figure the cost of shipping into our prices in the future."

"It's a nice problem to have," Sarah said. "Things are going to be all right, ain't so?"

She obviously was thinking about more than selling quilts. But Allison told herself that if she could weather Ralph's death without losing the bookshop from the building, things just might be all right.

It was surprising, how much that seemed to mean to her. A month ago, the name of Laurel Ridge would barely have sounded a faint bell in her mind. Now—she didn't like to admit it, but it had begun to feel like home.

Working with Sarah was soothing, Allison found. They actually found themselves laughing a little as they boxed up the quilt for sale. Odd that she felt so much satisfaction from that small success. She'd handled far bigger deals in her time, but none that had brought her happiness as well as satisfaction.

For most of her career she hadn't done much where she was working cooperatively with someone else toward the same goal. There had always been a competitive edge to what she'd done in the past, with the sense that someone else would be waiting to grab her spot if she let down at all. Working with Sarah, running the building—could she really be content with that? Or would she soon become bored, looking for new challenges?

They were preparing to take some more quilt photos when the bell on the door jingled, and Emily hurried in. "Ms. Standish, I'm glad you'll still here. I just don't know what to do about this. Please—you'll come and help me, won't you?"

"What is it, Emily?" She was willing enough, but she couldn't quite interpret the expression on the woman's face. She seemed both excited and distraught, if such a combination was possible.

"I don't know what to do," she repeated, literally wringing her hands. "I don't... I mean, I'd rather you just came to see what I found. You don't mind, do you, Sarah?"

"Of course not." Sarah began to fold the baby quilt she'd just spread out. "Go on, Allison. We can finish this later."

Apparently she didn't have much choice. When she'd

thought about what running the building would entail, she certainly hadn't included this sort of thing, whatever it was.

They went back down the hallway yet again, with Emily almost trotting in her hurry.

"Emily, if you'd just tell me—"

"I can't. You have to see it, that's all." Emily stopped at the door and unlocked it, giving Allison the chance to wonder why she'd closed up the shop just to come after her. With a quick glance around that suggested they were fellow conspirators, Emily hurried inside. She relocked the door behind them.

"Don't you want to stay open?" Allison asked.

"Later. Not while this is here," she added cryptically. She led the way to the back room. Several boxes had been pulled out from the shelves, lids open to reveal books.

"I finished checking the shelves," Emily said. "I noticed we didn't have much in the way of local history on display, so I came back to look in some of the storage boxes." She hesitated. "Sometimes...well, sometimes I thought that Ralph held on to books he should have returned for credit, but maybe there'd be something in these boxes that should be on the shelf."

"I assume you found something more than books." Emily was taking her time in getting to the point.

Emily nodded. "I don't know when I've been so shocked. It was right down in the center of the stacks of books. If I hadn't knocked a few books out trying to reach them, I'd never have found it." She reached into the center of the box and pulled out a gray metal box about the size of a file box. She looked at Allison, blinking.

"I opened it. Maybe I shouldn't have, but I didn't know what else to do."

"Anything in the shop is now yours, surely," Allison said, trying to be reassuring. Was she never going to see this mysterious find?

"I don't know about this. It seems to me Ralph must have kept it hidden for a reason. Look." She flung open the box lid, revealing the contents. Money. Neatly bound stacks of bills, all wedged into a metal box and hidden.

For a moment, Allison could only stare. Then she picked up one of the bundles and riffled through it. "These are hundreds." She felt as if she'd been hit with a brick.

"I counted." The excitement was taking over now. "There's over a hundred thousand dollars there."

"A hundred thousand?" Maybe not that much in the world of high finance, but a lot of money for a small-town bookshop. "It's surely not from the till?"

"Goodness, no." Emily dismissed that notion quickly. "So, where did he get it? And what should I do about it?"

Allison ran her fingers through her hair, trying to think. Technically speaking, if the money had belonged to Ralph, it now belonged to Emily. But if the money had been unlawfully obtained— Her mind stopped functioning. The money might explain everything that had happened. Or it might complicate matters beyond belief. But whatever the result, there was only one possible course of action.

"You'll have to show this to the police," she said. "Right away."

CHAPTER TWENTY

NICK HAD EXPECTED Allison to appear upstairs long before this, but she hadn't. Well, no reason he couldn't take a break and stroll down to see how things were going, was there?

The back stairs led down to the hallway outside the bookshop. He was halfway down when he realized people were gathered there, and another two steps showed him why. Mac's patrolman was stretching orange crime scene tape across the front of the shop.

Allison. Nick's heart was suddenly thudding in his ears. Another crime? Another attack? He reached the bottom of the steps with no memory of how he got there and burst through the crowd of gawkers to seize Johnny Foster by the arm and turn him around.

"What happened? Is someone hurt?" He shook him, trying to force an answer.

"The chief said—"

Giving up, Nick shoved past him into the bookshop, hearing the crowd murmuring behind him. A quick glance told him that whatever was happening, it was in the back room. He bolted toward the door and nearly sagged with relief when he saw Allison standing there, her arm around Emily's waist. Mac looked up from a box he was examining, clearly annoyed at the sight of him.

"Nick, you don't—"

"What's going on? Allison, are you okay?"

She nodded. "We're fine. Emily wanted me to see what she found, and I called the police once I did. Nick, Ralph apparently had a whole file box of cash squirreled away, hidden inside a carton of books."

Mac's expression of annoyance intensified. "Nick, nobody needs you to come to the rescue. It's not a crime to hide money away, but we'll have to try and figure out how it came here and if it had any significance to what happened to Ralph."

"If it's not a crime, why is your patrolman out there putting crime scene tape all over the front of the store?" Nick asked.

"He's what?" Mac shoved himself to his feet and stalked out, muttering under his breath. "Stupid kid" was the only phrase audible, but in moments they could hear his roar. "What do you think you're doing? I told you to secure the door so we wouldn't be interrupted."

"But, Chief—"

"Get that tape down and get in here. All I expected you to do was lock the door and put the closed sign on it."

"Poor kid," Allison murmured.

"He deserves it." Nick didn't feel in the least sorry for him. "He nearly gave me a heart attack. I thought someone had been hurt." He'd thought Allison had been hurt, to be exact, but maybe he shouldn't say that with an audience, and Emily was watching them, her eyes bright with curiosity. "Any idea how much was in the box?"

"I counted it," Emily said. She flushed. "Well, not every note, but I looked through and got a rough idea. A hundred thousand, I think." A thought seemed to occur to her. "If it belonged to Ralph, does that mean it's mine?" Her voice went up an octave on the last word.

"That might depend on where it came from." His thoughts tumbled over and over. What was Ralph doing with that kind of money? And in cash. Nobody in their senses kept that kind of cash hidden in a box of books. At least, not if it was honestly come by.

Allison seemed to be listening to what was going on out front. "It sounds as if Mac is trying to reassure everyone. I'm not sure it's working."

"Don't worry about it. Things will calm down in a day or two."

"Will they?" She didn't seem to take much comfort in his words. "Or will it keep getting worse? People aren't going to want to do business in a place where the police are always popping up."

"Relax. Folks around here are more resilient than that." At least, he hoped so. "And everyone knows it's not your fault."

"Sorry about that." Mac reappeared, the chastened patrolman nowhere in sight. "Look, there's no reason for all of you to be here. I just want to have a thorough look through everything in the room myself, in case there's anything else my boys managed to overlook when they were supposed to be searching. Emily, once I've finished, you can get back in. The sooner you open, the sooner things get back to normal."

"That's right." Allison seemed to forget her worries in comforting Emily. "Why don't you come over to the quilt shop with me? I'll make you a cup of tea, and you can relax for a bit." She urged her toward the door.

They'd just reached it when Mac's voice halted them.

"Allison, I'll need to talk to you again later. Will you be in the quilt shop?"

Her gaze was questioning, but she nodded. "There, or upstairs in my office."

Nick waited until he heard the shop door close behind them before he turned to his brother. "What do you have to talk to Allison about? She can't have anything to do with Ralph's stash of money."

"Look, you don't know that, and neither do I. Just stay out of it." Mac glared at him.

"If you think that, your uniform collar must be cutting off the oxygen to your brain. Allison's been here a matter of weeks. She barely knew Ralph, and she's been in the bookshop a few times at most. She's only involved at all because Emily asked for help."

Mac's jaw set. "It's not as simple as that."

"Explain it to me, then," he demanded.

"I have to talk to everyone again—everyone who was in any way involved with what happened to Ralph. He didn't fall down the stairs. He was probably never on the stairs at all that night. Somebody hit him from behind with a heavy object. He was murdered."

Nick had known it was a possibility. But he hadn't realized how tough it would be to face the reality. Ralph had been struck minutes before Allison found him.

"The murderer could have still been here when Allison came in."

"That's one alternative," Mac said.

"If you're implying that Allison called us and then struck him down with a blunt instrument, you're crazy."

"Look, I know you want to protect her." Mac looked tired, as if weighed down with responsibility. "But face facts. You're the one who said she'd only been here a few weeks, so she couldn't have known Ralph very well. The same goes for you. How well do you really know Allison?"

"THE CROWD IS GROWING, not dissipating." Allison turned away from the front window of the quilt shop the next day, frustrated at the sight of people who'd gathered to gawk at the building.

"Maybe they'll come in and buy something." Sarah had the air of one trying to find something optimistic to say even in dire circumstances.

"I doubt it after these headlines," she said, slapping the current day's newspaper on to the counter. The front page carried a prominent photograph of Blackburn House. "The newspaper did everything but label it the 'Murder House.' Krysta called to say she wanted to come over to see me, but her mother wouldn't let her. Apparently Brenda professes herself mortified by what's happened. And blames me, I imagine."

Sarah's normally serene forehead wrinkled as she stared down at the paper. "It's not as bad as all that, is it? Not that I like to think it, but such a thing could happen anywhere. It only happened here because this was Ralph's place of business, ain't so?"

"I suppose." There was no point in taking her mood out on Sarah. "I don't really blame the newspaper editor. If a well-known citizen is murdered, naturally they're going to cover the story. It's their job."

"They could take a picture of those nosy people out front," Sarah suggested. "That might embarrass them enough to make them go away."

"There's an idea." Allison forced a cheerful note into

her voice. "They're taking pictures of the building, so I could go out on the porch and take pictures of them."

"Look, some of them are coming in." Sarah stepped away from the window and smoothed down her apron. "If they come into the shop, I'll sell them something, you see if I don't."

"If you can pull that off, I'll do all the cleaning up for the rest of the day." It was a constant aggravation to have to reshelve bolts of fabric and put thread back in its proper place in the rack after customers had pulled everything out.

Sarah smiled. "You'll see."

The first few brave souls wandered into the hallway from outside, looking around as if expecting to see bloodstains on the floor. A couple of them came over to peer through the display windows into the quilt shop. One woman raised a camera, and Allison glared at her. If she dared try to take a picture of Sarah—

Apparently the glare was enough. She slid the camera into her bag. Hector, apparently ruffled by the silent antagonism, leaped down from his usual perch and jumped onto the display window, arching and flattening his ears to express displeasure.

That group moved on, only to be replaced in a moment by another. "Turn your back and look busy," Allison said. "Maybe they'll go away." She pulled out a bolt of chintz and pretended to show it to Sarah.

The jingle of the bell announced the failure of her ploy. Two men and three women came in—none of them regular customers. Hector, with a reversion to his usual attitude, jumped down and darted under the quilt display bed. *My hero.*

None of them even made a pretense of being interested in buying. Instead, they stared around the shop and then seemed to zero in on Allison, clearly identifying her as the person who'd found the body.

With surprising poise, Sarah marched up to them with a version of her usual smile. "*Wilkom.* What may I help you find today?"

The two men, confronted, muttered something and disappeared back out the door, red-faced. After a moment's staring competition, two of the women followed.

The third was apparently made of sterner stuff. "I'd like to see some...um, some quilted pot holders."

The cheapest thing in the store, Allison thought. It figured. She began rolling up the chintz she'd spread out.

"Of course." Sarah led the woman over to the display rack where the quilted pot holders hung. "If you'll tell me what color your kitchen is, I'll help you find some to match."

"Blue and white."

The woman fingered the pot holders as Sarah pulled them from the rack, seeming to grow intrigued despite herself. She kept glancing toward Allison, but Allison resolutely kept from meeting her gaze. She only wanted an excuse to start talking to her, and Allison wasn't about to give her one.

Inspired by Hector's example, she knelt behind the counter and began sorting through the scraps of material they kept in a basket there. Since she was now at Hector's level, he came out from under the bed and joined her, purring as he leaned against her, so heavily she nearly lost her balance, and then jumping into the basket.

Above her head, the dickering over the pot holders began. Sarah named a price for three that was nearly double what they usually charged. Then she let the woman bargain her down to a price that was still twenty percent higher, on the condition that the woman take six.

Allison had to muffle a laugh as the deal was concluded. When she heard the door close she stood, shaking with laughter. "Honestly, Sarah. How you got away with that I'll never know."

Sarah smiled complacently. "I thought she owed us something for being so nosy. My *daad* always says that no one beats a Dutchman in a bargain."

"I remember." It was the first time she'd laughed in what seemed like days. She shook her head, guilty. "I'm sorry, Sarah. I feel as if I've brought all this trouble on you. It's not fair."

"Nonsense." Sarah reached out to squeeze her hand. "You didn't make any of this happen. We all have to go through trials in this life. We just pray they make us stronger."

Allison nodded, but she suspected she didn't have the kind of faith that would allow her to look at trouble in that light.

The door opened again, and Allison stiffened her spine as she prepared to face more of the curious. But it was Emily, and she looked nearly in tears.

"Emily, what is it?" Sarah went to her immediately. "What's happened to upset you?"

"You've been having people staring at the shop, haven't you?" Allison's anger flared. Didn't people have any sense? If Mac wanted to do something useful, he'd find a way to chase off the gawkers.

"Not just the stares. That's bad enough." Emily dabbed at her tears. "But the questions were even worse. One man even asked me how it felt to have my boss murdered. Imagine the nerve."

Allison's palm tingled with the urge to slap someone silly for doing such a thing. Still, she didn't suppose getting arrested for assault would help matters. "I'm so sorry. What can we do to help? Do you want me to take over the shop for the rest of the day?"

"No, no, you girls have your own business to deal with." Sniffling, Emily dabbed her nose and fished a key ring from her bag. "I'm closing for the day. No one's buying anything, anyway, so I might as well. Do you think it will be better tomorrow?"

"I don't know." Allison couldn't lie to her. "Let's hope so. If not, maybe we can find someone to clerk for a few days, just so you can keep the bookshop open."

Emily nodded, but she didn't look very hopeful. "I just wanted you to know. I'll slip out the back way and go home."

Once she'd gone, Allison's ire bubbled over. "How can people behave that way? Emily doesn't deserve it. No one would be that bold with us, but Emily must look like a soft target."

"Poor thing. But that was a good idea of yours about getting someone in to cover the bookshop for a few days. I know a couple of people who have helped out from time to time. Should I get in touch with them?"

"Yes, let's do that. I'll pay them myself if necessary." Maybe that would ease her conscience a little. "Meanwhile, I think I'll go up to the office and work. If I'm not here, the interest might die out." There probably wasn't much chance of that, but it was worth a try.

A few minutes later she headed up the stairs, avoiding the glances of several more gawkers who'd ventured up to the second floor. Who could guess what they'd expected to see there?

She'd reached the upstairs hall when she was stopped. Harvey Preston, who owned the real estate office on the second floor, hurried toward her, his normally ruddy face even more flushed. He had the air of a successful man, satisfied, maybe even a little smug, about his place in the scheme of things.

"Ms. Standish. I'm glad I caught you. If I might have a word?"

Her heart sank at the thought of yet another conversation about their current difficulties, but she managed to nod. "Of course."

"This is a bad business all around. Poor Ralph." He assumed a suitably grave expression.

"Yes." What else was there to say?

"I'm sure you've noticed the crowd of gawkers outside. I spoke with the police chief about the problem, but apparently as long as they stay on the public street, he can't do much about them." His heavy jowls swayed as he shook his head in disapproval. "What we pay the police for, I don't know. As it is, several of my clients have postponed appointments for today. They don't want to go through a mob to get here, and I can't say I blame them."

"I'm so sorry. It's affecting the quilt shop, as well, of course. Perhaps by tomorrow it will be better."

"Nothing will improve unless and until the police catch the person responsible for the crime," he declared.

No doubt true, unfortunately. "I'm sure they will. The police are busy working on the case now, and I understand the state crime lab is assisting them. They'll work it out."

"I suppose they're doing their best." He sounded doubtful. "But if they don't bring this to a conclusion…

well, I might have to consider whether to move my business if things don't improve."

Appalled, she couldn't speak for a moment. "You have a lease..." she began.

"The lease contains a clause that releases me from any obligation if conditions in the building adversely affect my business." He paused, eyeing her face as she absorbed the information. "I'd call murder an adverse effect, wouldn't you?"

Apparently satisfied he'd made his point, Preston marched down the stairs, leaving her with the ground suddenly shaky beneath her feet. If he carried through with his threat, if others followed him...then what would happen?

She knew the answer to that question, didn't she? If she didn't run Blackburn House at a profit for one year, she lost it, along with a year in her career and her life. At the moment, the chances of her success seemed pretty slim.

Beating a quick retreat before anyone else could give her bad news seemed like a wise move. Allison hurried into her office and closed the door. For a moment she leaned against it, resting her head on the smooth wooden surface. Things were falling apart so rapidly she could hardly keep up with them.

Even as she had the thought, she realized she hadn't spoken to Leslie in several days. Not since before Ralph's death, in fact. With a sharp-as-a-whip attorney for a friend, she's been ignoring an obvious resource.

Pulling out her cell phone as she crossed to her desk, she called, fully expecting to be sent to voice mail and rehearsing a brief message in her mind. But Leslie answered immediately.

"Girl, where have you been?" Leslie's voice was tart. "Don't you check your messages? I called you a couple of days ago."

Allison leaned back in her chair. "I know, I know. But things have been a bit...crazy here." She took a breath. "There's been a murder."

"Murder," Leslie repeated. "Someone you know?"

"One of the tenants in the building—the bookshop owner. And I found the body."

Leslie's response was a sharp hiss of breath. "This is the one you said you thought was hiding something?"

"Yes." She'd been trying to keep Leslie updated, but she couldn't remember exactly what she'd told her and what she hadn't. "I was right about that, too. He said a few words while we were waiting for the police, and it was enough to convince me he was here the night my grandmother died."

"You told this to the police, didn't you?"

"Yes, but I'm not sure how seriously they're taking it." She hesitated, but Leslie could hardly help her if she wasn't honest. "The trouble is, I had a disagreement with Ralph the day he died—loud enough that other people heard."

"Are you saying they suspect you? That sounds like pretty flimsy evidence."

She could hear the scratch of Leslie's pen and knew she was making notes.

"I don't think the local police chief really suspects me, but with the district attorney putting pressure on him..." She let that sentence fade and rubbed her forehead. "I don't know, Les. Maybe I'm overreacting to the whole thing."

"You need a good criminal attorney to advise you," Leslie said briskly. "Who have you got?"

"You mean besides you? Nobody." She thought of the lawyer who handled her grandmother's estate. "There's a young attorney who rents space in the building. He's offered to help, but I don't think he's prepared to handle a criminal case. I'm not sure there's anyone here in Laurel Ridge I'd want to trust with this."

"Okay, give me a couple of hours. I'll do some checking and call you back with a recommendation. In any event, be careful of what you say."

"You mean to the police?"

"I mean at all." Leslie hesitated. "Look, you've been sounding as if you're feeling at home there. As if you've started to trust some people."

Sarah, Nick… "Yes, I have."

"It doesn't pay to be too trusting where murder is concerned." Leslie's voice was dry. "Just be careful. I'll get back to you as soon as I find someone."

As usual when she was in the office, Leslie clicked off without bothering to say goodbye. Allison put the phone on her desk and sat, staring blankly. Leslie was taking the possibility of an accusation seriously. Maybe it was time she did, too.

The sound of voices in the apartment next door drew her attention. She recognized Nick's voice, becoming clearer as he must have stepped into the hall, and she was swept by a longing to see him, to tell him…what? Hadn't Leslie just cautioned her about watching what she said to people here?

She could trust Nick, her heart argued, but Leslie's warning kept her pinned to her chair until she heard the door to the back stairway open and close.

He'd gone out, so she couldn't speak to him. Unfortunately, that didn't seem to end the longing.

A sharp knock on the door put an end to her internal argument. She answered, finding herself staring at the imposing figure of Thomas Blackburn. Something about that aristocratic, disapproving face put her instantly on the defensive, but she managed to preserve a calm exterior.

"Mr. Blackburn. Would you like to come in?"

She stepped back, and he strode past her as if she weren't even there. The man had a talent for making others feel insignificant, and she thought briefly of his son and grandson. It didn't seem to have done them too much good.

"What can I do for you?" Allison returned to her desk and gestured toward the visitor's chair, but he ignored the invitation, planting himself in front of the desk.

"I'm not going to mince words with you, Ms. Standish. You must see now that accepting my offer is the only option left for you."

Oddly enough, Sarah's words about not besting a Dutchman in bargaining came into her mind. Blackburn was bargaining—trying to convince her that she had no choice.

She put on a look of innocent surprise. "The only option? I'm not sure why I should think that."

"Let's not play games." His jaw tightened. "You've seen the curious crowds outside, keeping real customers away. You've seen the bad publicity in the newspaper." He actually winced. "To think I'd ever see the Blackburn name used in connection with a murder case—it's unbearable."

"I'm sure the interest will die down eventually." She

hoped. "It's inconvenient for the businesses at the moment, yes, but that's hardly my responsibility."

His face flushed, and she recognized the signs of rising temper. "Of course it's your responsibility." He planted his fists on the desk and leaned toward her. "If you'd accepted my offer to begin with, none of this would have happened."

She could only stare at him. Did he realize what he was saying?

"How can you think that? If Ralph became involved in something that caused him to be murdered, it would have happened no matter who owned the building. It was nothing to do with me."

Blackburn seemed to get himself under control. He pulled back, raising his eyebrows. "Really? I hope you can convince the police of that."

"The police—" she began, but he swept on as if she hadn't spoken.

"I'll hold the offer open as is for another day. But the longer this goes on, the less the building will be worth, to me or anyone else. Just bear that in mind as you make your decision."

He turned and slammed his way out of the office, leaving her wondering if she was behaving like a fool. Little though she wanted to believe it, accepting Blackburn's offer might be the only way to salvage anything from her time in Laurel Ridge.

CHAPTER TWENTY-ONE

NICK HAD GONE OUT to pick up a box of finishing nails and run into his brother. Mac, surprisingly, hadn't waited to be questioned before sharing the status of the investigation. It seemed the discovery of the money had changed everything. The DA had agreed that it would be premature to focus on Allison with so many unanswered questions.

Mac's relief hadn't been up to Nick's, but still, it was good to see that Mac's instincts told him Allison was innocent. He'd do his job regardless of instincts, of course. At least now there was a good reason for searching out other options.

Nick headed toward the quilt shop, his step lighter than it had been all day. Allison needed to hear this news. He opened the shop door, hearing the bell jingle, and Hector jumped down from the display window to weave around his legs, no doubt depositing orange fur on his jeans.

"What's this? Did you finally decide you like me?" He bent to run his hand down the cat's back, feeling it arch against his palm. "Not that I'm not happy to see you, but where's Allison?"

"She's not here just now." The voice belonged to Sarah, of course, not the cat. She came out from behind the counter, her forehead wrinkled. "It's been a trying morning with all the nosy gawkers, and then Emily came in crying, saying she couldn't take it and was going home. I think Allison needed a break, so she went up to the office."

"That was probably a smart idea. If she's not here, they can't stare at her." He hesitated, wondering at the degree of worry in Sarah's blue eyes. "Look, if it's bothering you, I'll see if Mac won't send a patrolman over to warn people off."

"No, don't do that. It might make things worse." Sarah rubbed her forehead. "Anyway, I'm more concerned about Thomas Blackburn. He went up to see Allison a while ago. I'm sure he was putting pressure on her to agree to his deal."

"She wouldn't." He tried to sound confident, but doubt reared its head. Could he be sure what Allison would do?

"I hope not. But you know what Thomas is like. He came down just a few minutes ago, looking around as if he owned the place and didn't like what he saw."

"He always looks like that. Anyway, even if worse came to worst, the quilt shop would still be yours. That's how Evelyn left it, right?"

She nodded. "I'd rather have Allison for my partner. And anyway, that's just the shop, not the property. If Blackburn owned the building, he could still put me out, ain't so?"

Nick wanted to comfort her, but he wasn't sure how to go about it. He'd like to say that everything would be all right, but would it?

"Look, I'm on my way to see Allison. I have some news I think will encourage her." And he'd sound her out on Blackburn. People were depending on Allison. She couldn't let them down.

And then there was the fact that he wanted her to stay for reasons that had nothing to do with the business. He wasn't sure he was ready to bring that factor into the equation yet.

Nick went up the stairs quickly, trying to deny that he was eager to see her. He'd be cautious about bringing anyone into his and Jamie's lives in any event, but the current circumstances made it even more important to move slowly. His brain was logical, but his heart and his body seemed to be out of sync with it.

He'd nearly reached the office when his phone buzzed. Mom was calling. He answered, leaning against the wall, his back to the office door. "What's up, Mom?"

"Okay if I drop Jamie off with you for about an hour while I run some errands? I can swing by and drop him—"

"No, don't do that." His reaction was immediate and instinctive. "I have to be here a while longer, and I think it's best if Jamie's not here."

He could almost hear his mother's surprise. "Why? Surely you don't think Blackburn House is dangerous? I thought you were more sensible than that."

"Well, maybe I'm not," he said, irritated that she seemed to see right through him. "I just don't want Jamie anywhere near Blackburn House right now, okay?"

"Right, okay." Now she sounded as if she were indulging his whim. "I'll take him with me. Talk later. Bye." She rang off before he could respond.

Maybe his feeling wasn't logical, but he had a right… He turned and saw Allison standing in the office doorway, watching him.

Nick made an effort to ignore the probability that she'd overheard him. "Allison, good. I was just coming to see you. I've seen Mac." He glanced around, aware that someone could come out of one of the offices at any moment. "Let's go in the apartment."

"Fine." But she didn't sound fine. She sounded frozen, almost, as if the word were an ice cube dropped from her lips.

The apartment door was locked, which meant Dad had left. Probably just as well. This ought to be a private conversation. He opened the door, and they stepped inside.

He'd expected her to look around in appreciation at the nearly finished remodel, but she didn't. She zeroed in on him. "You said you had some news."

"Right. I spoke to Mac, and he said the DA now agrees with him that it's too soon to limit the investigation in any way. There's the money to be explained, and the fact that they haven't yet found the murder weapon." He paused, expecting a response, and got none. "You understand, don't you? This takes the focus off you."

"For how long?" Her jaw tightened, and she shook her head. "I'm glad, don't get me wrong. But this has been such a roller coaster that it's hard to feel any relief when I know other people are looking at me and wondering."

"You mean like Thomas Blackburn?" He was fishing, trying to get at the reason behind her attitude. "Sarah told me he'd been up to see you. What did he want?"

Allison shrugged. "To renew his offer. What else?"

"You're not seriously thinking of taking it, are you? It's a fraction of what the building is worth." *And besides, I don't want you to leave.*

"Maybe I should. Business is off—you've seen that, haven't you? People are complaining and threatening to move out." She flung out her hands. "And what about this apartment? What chance will I have of renting it with the shadow of murder hanging over the building?"

He stared at her, not liking what he was hearing. "I thought you were happy here. You're not going to let Blackburn scare you away, are you? You have friends here, people who care about you."

The anger flared in her face as she swung on him, but he could see pain there, as well. "Do I? I heard you on the phone. You don't want your son anywhere near this place. Anywhere near me, in other words."

"That's not true. I don't—" He stopped, not sure where the line was between the truth and his feelings for her. "Look, you don't understand. Jamie's my son. It's my job to protect him—"

"From a woman who might be involved in a murder." She finished for him.

"That's not what I was going to say."

"Isn't it?" Her eyes were stormy. "That's not all, is it? You want to protect him from a woman you think is too much like your ex-wife to be safe. That's what's been going on all along with you."

Nick stared at her. He wanted to deny it. But before he could find the words, she spun and stalked out.

ALLISON HAD REACHED the bottom of the stairs before she realized she didn't know where she was going. Anywhere, so long as it was away from Nick Whiting.

She headed for the outside door but stopped in the act of pushing it open. Much as she'd love to walk as fast as possible with her sore ankle until her ire had burned itself out, she'd have to go through the cluster of people at the gate to do so.

Glaring at them didn't seem to help. What on earth

did they think they were going to see? Blackburn House looked the same as it always did. Still, observing Thomas Blackburn arrive and depart had no doubt given them something to chatter about.

Blackburn had made his desire to acquire the building clear. What did he expect to do with the place if and when it belonged to him? The quilt shop, the bookstore, the cabinetry—would they still be here if Thomas Blackburn were in charge?

Allison had no idea whether his wealth was large enough to permit him to buy the building and turn it back to the home it had once been. If he was obsessed enough, it could probably be done. The bones of the building were still there, and the renovation had been carried out with consideration to preserving the original charm as much as possible.

If that was Blackburn's intent— Her train of thought made an abrupt halt at the sound of footsteps in the upstairs hallway. Panic ripped through her at the idea that it was Nick coming after her. Refusing to glance in the direction of the footsteps, she darted into the quilt shop. Sarah was measuring a bolt of cloth at the cutting table, and she looked up, startled.

"If Nick asks for me, you don't know where I am." Flinging out the words, she dashed into the back room and closed the door, leaning against it, her breath coming as if she'd been running.

Pressing her ear to the door, she listened, aware all the time of how foolish she must appear if anyone watched. Nothing. No heavy male footsteps, no jangle of the bell over the door. Breathing a little easier, she moved to the rocker and sat down, trying to focus her thoughts and control her anger.

A tap on the door, and then it opened and Sarah came in. She studied Allison's face for a moment before she spoke. "Nick didn't come near the shop. Didn't even look. He marched straight out the door with a face like a black cloud with a storm coming on."

She could breathe again. "Thanks, Sarah." Realizing she'd actually asked Sarah to lie to an old and valued friend for her, she considered apologizing but decided the least said, the better.

Closing her eyes, Allison rested her head against the padded chair. When she opened them a moment later, Sarah was sitting opposite her, wearing a look of expectation.

"Well?" she said.

"Well what?" Allison attempted a smile.

"*Was ist letz?* And in case you've forgotten, that means what's wrong?" Sarah settled herself, looking prepared to stay there all day if necessary.

"Nothing." Allison's heart winced at the word. "I'm fine."

Sarah's eyebrows lifted. "So, this nothing happened in the past hour or so since I've seen you. That means it wasn't Ralph's death or the trouble with the property."

"Why not? Isn't that enough to upset anyone?" It occurred to her that she sounded like a petulant child.

"That's certain sure. But you wouldn't be hiding from Nick because of that. You had words with him, ain't so?"

It was no use trying to hide the facts from Sarah. She knew too much to be fooled. "'Had words' is putting it mildly." The hurtful thing burst out of her before she could contain it. "He doesn't think I'm a suitable person to be around his son."

Sarah looked aghast. "Nick never said such a thing."

"He did." Honesty compelled her to add a qualifier. "Well, not in so many words."

"Just because he said something stupid—" Sarah began.

"I heard him," Allison said, fingers gripping the curved wooden arms of the rocker. "He was talking to his mother on the phone. She must have wanted to bring Jamie over, because he said he didn't want his son anywhere near this place. In other words, near me."

"Maybe he didn't mean you, exactly." Sarah, expression troubled, seemed to try to be fair.

"Didn't he? I haven't seen Jamie since all this trouble started. That speaks for itself, doesn't it?"

"*Ach*, Allison, you have to understand. Nick is like a hen with one chick. He's always overreacting where that boy is concerned. It doesn't mean anything about you."

Allison shook her head. She knew better. It meant everything about her. "When he looks at me, it's like all he can think of is how much I'm like his ex-wife. When he forgets for a minute, he kisses me, and then he jumps away like a scalded cat."

"Did he actually say that to you?" Sarah would obviously like to cling to the belief that it was a simple misunderstanding.

"I said it to him." Her throat tightened at the memory. "He didn't deny it."

"Nicolas Whiting is an idiot where women are concerned, and I'll tell him so the first chance I get." Sarah was actually angry, and that was something Allison had never seen. "The idea of thinking you're anything like that flighty creature is ridiculous, and anyone with half a brain could see it. Maybe on the outside, you're all the things she wanted to be, but anyone who knows you

surely has to figure out the woman you really are—
strong and steadfast and a *gut* friend."

Allison's throat was now so tight she couldn't even try
to speak with the risk of ending up blubbering.

Sarah came to her, put her arms around her. "If Nick
is so *ferhoodled* that he doesn't know what you're really
like, then he deserves to be alone."

She gave Allison a fierce hug, and the tears Allison
had thought to restrain spilled over.

THE BUILDING HAD begun to get quiet around her, and Allison surfaced from the files she'd been going through
and glanced at her watch. It was after five. She'd been
hiding up here most of the afternoon, determined not
to see Nick.

But he must have been just as eager to avoid her, because from what she could see, he'd spent the rest of the
day in the workshop.

Aware of her promise to Sarah that she wouldn't stay
in the building alone, Allison stood, stretching her back.
Hector, who'd been sleeping on a stack of papers on
her desk, seemed to take that as a signal. He rose and
stretched his back as well, although he managed to do a
much more impressive arch than she had.

"Ready to go home? I am, too, but I'd better box up
the files that haven't been sorted yet, so they don't get
mixed up." She frowned, trying to think where she'd seen
some empty cardboard boxes recently. Just beyond the
top of the attic stairs, wasn't it? They'd left some extra
ones there in case they needed them for the Jumble Sale,
and it seemed doubtful that Fred had disposed of them.

Allison unlocked the door to the attic, and then realized how foolish it would be to open that door with Hec-

tor sitting there, his eyes pinned on it, his tail swishing. If he got up to the attic, she could be chasing him for hours.

"Time to go home," she said cheerfully, moving away from the door. She picked up the cat carrier, set it next to him and opened it. "Home," she repeated. "Supper."

That was one word Hector definitely knew. He climbed into the carrier, turned around and settled himself in his favorite sphinx posture, ready for the trip to his favorite cat food.

"Good boy." She checked the latch. "I just have to do one more thing, and I definitely don't want your company." She pulled open the attic door, switched on the light and started up, leaving the door open for ease in negotiating the stairs while carrying a box. Behind her, Hector complained loudly. She could only hope he was wrong in his obvious assessment that there were mice up here.

The attic stretched out around her when she reached the top, dim and shadowy beyond the reach of the single bulb at the top of the stairs. Dust motes drifted in the shaft of sunlight from the closest window. It she went to that window, she could look down at the workshop and see if Nick's truck was still parked there.

Wrong thing to think of doing. She'd actually felt better after a bout of crying, and Sarah's indignation at Nick had soothed her, as well. There were times when no one would do but a girlfriend.

That reminded her of Leslie, and the attorney she'd recommended. His offices were in the nearest larger town, and Leslie had said he was highly recommended by someone she knew.

But if what Nick had said was true, and the investigation no longer focused on her, maybe it wasn't necessary.

Even aside from the complicating factor of Ralph's hidden money, which clearly had nothing to do with her, if the police hadn't found the murder weapon after all their searching, didn't that mean the killer had taken it away with him? Mac and Nick could both swear that she hadn't taken anything away from the scene of Ralph's death.

Yanking her thoughts back to her purpose for being in the dusty attic, she peered around for the boxes. They weren't where she'd thought. Could that mean that Fred had actually taken care of a chore without being reminded? But, no, there they were in an untidy pile, behind a stack of what seemed to be boxes of books from the bookstore.

Putting one hand on a full carton for balance and praying there weren't any spiders, she stretched out, reaching for the box she wanted. Her fingertips barely brushed it when the box that was supporting her slid, tilting off its fellows. Off balance, Allison grabbed for it, trying to keep the books from spilling out.

One slid out, landing on her foot, and then another. She tried to right the box, shoving it back into place. Muttering, she bent to retrieve the books that had landed on the floor. They looked new, their glossy jackets unmarred, and she wiped them off carefully. Odd. They didn't appear to be used books, but judging by the titles she recognized, they were several years old. Had Ralph intended to box them up and return them, and then forgotten about it? She should remember to tell Emily... The thought trailed off as another layer of books slid to the side, revealing an open space right in the center of the stacks of books. For an instant, Allison just stared at it. A cache, just like the spot in the box of books where Emily had discovered the box of cash. Apparently Ralph had thought he'd found a secure method of hiding things he didn't want anyone to see.

Gingerly, Allison reached inside, her groping fingers finding a rolled-up plastic bag. She pulled it out. Not cash this time. She unrolled the bag so she could see what it contained. The only thing in the bag was a plastic pill vial, containing three or four capsules. The pharmacy prescription label carried a date three years earlier. She recognized the name of the medication—a popular brand of tranquilizer. And there was the name of the patient. She recognized that, too. Nina Blackburn. Tommy Blackburn's late wife.

What was a bottle of Nina Blackburn's prescription medication doing hidden in a box of books from Ralph's bookshop? Allison straightened, holding the bag up to the light to see if she'd missed anything on the label. To try to think what it meant.

"So, you found it." Allison spun at the sound of the voice. Tommy Blackburn emerged at the top of the attic stairs, looking at her, his face calm, his voice dispassionate. "After all the time I spent looking, you walk up here and find it. I always did have the worst luck in the world. But it looks like today, yours is even worse."

CHAPTER TWENTY-TWO

"Tommy." She tried to pin a smile on her face, tried to act as if everything was fine even as her mind twisted and turned, searching for answers. "You startled me. Were you looking for me?"

"Nice try." Tommy had reached the top of the stairs, and he stood between her and the way out. "It won't work. You're too smart. Too independent. You'll figure it out, if you haven't already."

It was pointless to try to convince him she didn't understand. He'd killed Ralph to keep his secret. He wouldn't stop now.

"You've been looking for this." She held up the plastic bag. "Why? What did Ralph have to do with your wife's tranquilizers?" Thoughts shifted like the changing patterns of a kaleidoscope. "Did you tamper with her medication? Is this the proof?"

She shook the bag, the capsules rattling, and saw his gaze fix on it with almost passionate eagerness.

"Give it to me." He held out his hand. "Just toss it over to me. I'll let you go if you do."

Let her go? Not likely. Not when a word from her could unravel the whole net. She took a cautious step backward. *Think*, she commanded. He was between her and the stairs she'd come up, but there were three other stairwells. If she could get to one of those... Hope leaped, and with it a fierce determination to live.

She couldn't just bolt, not without figuring out a path to the nearest stairwell. The attic was a warren of storage spaces, the hall that should lead to the next set of stairs might easily be blocked by boxes or odd pieces of furniture.

"Tell me first." She put the bag behind her back, determined not to let go. "You tampered with your wife's medicine. You wanted to be rid of her."

She could almost see his thought processes. The urge to tell, maybe even to brag about his success, was strong. That was the key, she realized. Tommy had to feel successful, even at murder.

"I don't believe it," she said, risking a cautious glance behind her. "How could you get away with something like that? Murder takes brains. Planning."

His ruddy face went even darker beneath his tan from all those hours on the golf course. "I planned it all. It was simple. Open a few of the capsules and insert triple the amount of medication. Then leave them in her room with a bottle of whiskey. I knew her. She wouldn't be able to resist taking more than she should have and washing them down with the whiskey she wasn't supposed to have. All I had to do was make sure I was with other people all day until I came in and found her, dead of an overdose."

"But for all your planning, something went wrong." Another glance gave her a mental map to take her toward the next exit.

"Ralph." His face twisted. "Interfering old... No one should have come in the house that day. I had the normal pill bottle in my pocket. All I had to do was switch it for the tampered one when I found her."

"Not such good planning, if Ralph could mess it up." She edged sideways toward a clear space.

"When I got there, the bottle was gone. All I could do was leave the regular one and hope for the best. Once the verdict of accidental death came in, I thought I was in the clear."

Ralph's cache of money. It had come from Tommy. "Until Ralph started blackmailing you."

Tommy muttered a few obscenities. "I couldn't find out who it was. I had a couple of ideas, but they didn't pan out. Then the day I brought the books in for the sale, the box spilled and a sales slip fell out, dated the day she died. Ralph, always catering to her because she had money, dropping books off for her as if he was some kind of traveling library. He'd taken the pills."

"So you started getting into the building, looking for the bottle." She frowned. "But some of the incidents with prowlers happened before you could have known about Ralph."

He shrugged. "That was T.J., trying to please the old man. Good idea, too. If he'd bought the building, I'd have had a free hand to look for the bottle. So I figured I'd help it along."

"You set the trap on the stairs the day of the sale."

"Clever, wasn't it? I was pretty sure I'd get either you or Ralph, and either way, I won."

"What about my grandmother? Why did she have to die?"

Tommy looked surprised. "You can't hang that on me. That was Ralph. I don't suppose he intended her to die. He didn't have the guts for that. But she found out he was blackmailing someone. Wanted him to come clean about it. Do the right thing. That was always Evelyn Standish's motto. He claimed that they were arguing about it on the stairs when she got sick, dizzy. She fell, and he ran away. He was too much of a coward to finish her off."

Do the right thing. Evelyn had tried, according to her beliefs, even when it had separated her from her only child. And only grandchild.

"If Ralph was such a coward, how did you get him into the building with you the night you killed him?"

"Offered him a big payoff." Tommy moved toward her. She'd have to run for it, trust she could get far enough ahead to make it to the door. "Too bad that won't work with you."

She saw the change in his face, saw him lunge toward her as she spun. Caught a glimpse of shiny metal as he swung something. It connected with her head even as she dodged, and she tripped, fell, lay helpless, putting up her arms in a futile attempt to block another strike.

It didn't come. Allison fought to focus, to find her balance, but she couldn't. Tommy was little more than a blur as he tossed the golf club aside. He started toward her. The evidence, he'd get it—

Heard his steps going away, then nearly choked on the acrid smell of kerosene. She struggled to her hands and knees to see him strike a match and throw it. A tiny spark landed, then sprang up in a roar of flame. He wasn't going to come after the pill bottle. He was going to burn it, and her with it.

"No." She coughed, choking on the word. The flames caught, feasting greedily on the dry wood of the floor. Tommy's footsteps, running back down the stairs.

Flames, smoke—no one would see, no one would know she was here until it was too late.

No. Please, God, no.

The light from the window was feeble in comparison to the hot glare of the flames—the window that looked down on the workshop. If she could get to the window— She crawled a few precious feet before the smoke got her, choking her, keeping her from breathing. Her hand brushed the golf club, laying where Tommy had thrown it.

Fingers closed on the smooth shaft, already hot to the touch. *Drag it, inch forward, head spinning, she wasn't going to make it...*

She had to. Had to break the window. Nick would see. Nick would help. *Lift the club, aim for the window, swing. Hear the satisfying crash of glass.*

The flames roared, consuming the added oxygen. But above the roar she heard voices shouting. Thankfulness swept through her. They'd get her out.

NICK FOLLOWED HIS father out of the workshop and locked the door behind them.

"Time we were getting home——" His words were interrupted by the crash of breaking glass. Startled, he looked up, following the sound, and his heart lurched into overdrive. One of the attic windows had broken, and smoke poured out.

He thrust his cell phone toward his father. "Call. I'll check to see if everyone's out."

Racing toward the closest door, Nick yanked his keys out as he ran. Allison, Sarah— No, not Sarah. He'd heard the sound of her buggy wheels when she'd pulled out.

Emily had gone earlier—that left the upstairs. And Allison.

Thundering through the downstairs hall to the center stairs, he shouted, "Fire, fire! Get out!"

No response, and a glance showed him the quilt shop was dark and locked. Saving his breath for running, he charged up the steps. The offices were dark; everyone had left at five. But where was Allison?

Running toward her office, he shouted again. "Fire! Allison, where are you? Are you here?"

The door was unlocked. He charged in and was sent reeling back by the smoke billowing out of the open attic door. Open, and Allison nowhere in sight—was she up there?

Slashing furiously at his shirt with his penknife, he pulled a piece free and tied it over his mouth and nose, finally identifying the sound he heard above the crackle of flames and the pounding of his heart. The cat, shut in the carrier—Allison would never have left it behind. She must be upstairs, trapped.

Nick sucked in a deep breath and headed for the attic stairs just as his father ran into the room, a fire extinguisher under each arm. He thrust one at Nick.

"I'll get her." Nick swung the fire extinguisher into position. "Get that blasted cat of hers out of here or she won't forgive either of us."

Dad snorted and reached for the carrier gate. "Cat knows enough to get out." He swung the gate wide, and an orange blur streaked toward the hall. "Let's go."

No point in arguing. It might take both of them. Nick advanced up the stairs, spraying the foam ahead of him. No need to ask about the fire company, either. They'd be on their way, along with half the town, most likely.

The smoke was thicker at the top. Coughing, he peered into it, trying to identify something, anything. "Allison!" He managed to shout her name, strained his ears for an answer. Behind him, Dad sprayed the flames furiously.

The window. She must have broken the window. She had to be in that direction, through the worst of the flames. He tapped his father's shoulder and pointed. Dad nodded. They advanced together. If the extinguishers failed... They wouldn't. They couldn't.

Coughing, choking, stumbling now, he pushed on, eyes watering. Stumbled again, and knew it was Allison. He dropped to his knees, pulling her against him. Staggered to his feet again, holding her. Dad grabbed his extinguisher, trying to spray both of them at the same time as he beat his way back toward the stairs. Nick caught the back of his shirt and stumbled blindly after him.

Two firemen in gear emerged from the stairwell, grabbed them and bundled them all down the steps. He could hear someone shouting orders as they were helped out of the office into the clearer air of the hall. Allison— he let himself look at her. Beneath the black soot her skin was deathly pale, and his heart stopped. If he lost her...

She moved. Turned her face into his shoulder, murmuring something, and began to cough.

"It's all right." Strength poured back into him, and he headed down the stairs. "Don't try to talk. The paramedics will take care of you."

"Nick." Her lips moved against his shirt. "I knew you'd come."

Her eyes closed, but it was all right. She was breathing. He headed for the front door, met by the paramedic team who hustled them both outside.

A few minutes later they were both on the grass next to the emergency truck. Oxygen was bringing the color back to Allison's face, and Mike Callahan was dressing his hands. Funny that he hadn't even noticed the burns until it was all over. He propped his arms on his knees, submitting to the bandaging and a certain amount of ribbing—man's protection from showing his feelings at the danger to an old buddy.

Allison pushed herself to her elbows. "Hector. What about Hector?"

A passing firefighter pulled off his mask, revealing Aaron King's face. "Is that the orange cat? Mrs. Anderson has him. He came shooting out of the building raising a ruckus just as we pulled up."

"There, he's okay." Nick patted Allison's shoulder awkwardly with his bandaged hand. "Just relax."

She shook her head. "It was Tommy. You have to tell Mac. It was Tommy. He killed Ralph because Ralph was blackmailing him." She reached into her shirt and pulled out a small plastic bag. "Over this." She paused for a cough. "Proof he doctored his wife's medicine."

"Tommy Blackburn." For a moment he couldn't believe it, but then it all started to click into place. Tommy, with his constant womanizing and his desire for money. "He started the fire?"

"He thought the evidence was in the building, and he was getting panicky, I think. He was going to burn it, and the evidence with it."

"And you." He took her hand clumsily in his.

"I got in his way." Allison looked down at his hand, and tears spilled on to her cheeks. "Your poor hands."

"It's nothing. Mike just wanted to practice his bandaging."

Mike, who'd been eavesdropping shamelessly, broke in. "I think it's time we took the both of you to the hospital to be checked out."

"Not until we tell Mac," Allison rasped. "He can't let Tommy get away."

"It's okay," Nick said, soothing her. "You go on to the ER and get checked out. I'll speak to Mac, and I'll meet you there."

Her eyes searched his face for a moment, and then she nodded.

Mike grabbed his elbow and hauled him to his feet. "You're even worse than your dad," he grumbled. "I thought we'd never get him transported. I finally had to threaten to put him on the phone with your mother. She was on her way to the hospital, and she said if he wasn't there when she arrived, she'd come down and haul him in herself. She said to say she'd see you and Allison there."

"Guess we know where we rank on the totem pole," he said. He jostled Mike's elbow. "Get Allison taken in. I'll be back in a minute. Do you know where Mac is?"

Mike gestured. "Other side of the building."

Nick set off, a little surprised that his legs seemed to be obeying his orders, maybe propelled by the fury that pumped through him. Tommy had tried to kill Allison. He wasn't going to walk away from this, no matter how important the Blackburns thought they were.

He got a jolt when he rounded the building. Mac was there, all right. He was listening to Tommy, who was waving his arms emphatically. Nick moved closer, silent on the grass.

"...tried to reach her, but the flames were just too bad. Goodness knows what she thought she was doing up there. I'm just as sorry as can be I couldn't save her."

Mac's eyes met Nick's over Tommy's shoulder. "I think you're mistaken, Tommy." Mac rested his hand on his holstered weapon. "Allison didn't die in the fire."

"Didn't——" Tommy goggled at him.

"No thanks to you." Nick grabbed his shoulder, spinning him around. It took all the control he could muster to keep from planting his fist, burned or not, in the man's face. "We got her out. She's okay, and she's talking. We know you started the fire."

Tommy paled, but he glared back at Nick. "That's crazy. If she said that, she must be delirious from smoke inhalation. She probably started it herself, hoping to collect something on the insurance."

Gritting his teeth, Nick managed not to swing. Instead, he held out the plastic bag to Mac. "There's the motive for it all. Ralph was blackmailing him over that medicine bottle of his wife's. I don't know what it all means yet, but an analysis of those pills will probably tell you."

Mac took the bag, looking down at the pill vial. In that instant he was distracted. Tommy bolted. Nick, reading the intent in his eyes, threw a punch that landed him on the ground. Nearly landed Nick on the ground, too, with the pain in his burned hand, but it was worth it. Mac leaned over Tommy, snapping handcuffs on him with scant ceremony, and hauled him to his feet.

"You couldn't let me do it," Mac complained. Then he began to read Tommy his rights in front of an interested group of onlookers.

ALLISON LEANED BACK against the pillow, mustering her strength for another argument. "There's no reason for

me to stay in the hospital." A spasm of coughing interrupted, weakening her argument.

"Hush, now." Sarah smoothed the covers over her as
if she were a child. "You're better off here, just in case
you need something in the night."

"That's right." Ellen proffered a glass of water, bending the straw so she didn't have to raise her head. "You
just take it easy. Tomorrow is time enough to face the
world."

"You don't want photographers snapping a picture of
you the way you look right now," Mac said, with a lam-
entable want of tact. His father elbowed him. "I mean..."

Nick gave him a shove. "You mean you're an idiot."
He looked around, frowning. "And there's way too many
people in this room."

Allison was aware of Ellen and Sarah exchanging
glances. "Come along now." Ellen's tone was brisk. "Go
get some coffee or do something useful, why don't you?"
She smiled at Allison, touching her hand. "Jamie is in the
waiting room. He wants to tell you good-night. I'll bring
him in a bit, if I can get the nurse to look the other way."

Before Allison could speak, Ellen had shooed her
husband and younger son out the door, with Sarah following, leaving her alone with Nick.

"I didn't get to thank your dad." She raised herself
up on her elbows.

Nick pushed her back gently. "You'll have time for
that later. Anyway, he doesn't want any thanks."

Her mind seemed to be getting back into gear. "But
what about Blackburn House? And what happened with
Tommy? Did Mac arrest him?" A thought struck with
force enough to knock her flat. "His prosecution won't
all depend on me, will it?"

Her heart was suddenly pounding, and she felt as if she couldn't get her breath. If she was the only witness against him, what were the chances Tommy could be convicted in a town used to thinking the Blackburns could do no wrong?

"Easy. Don't forget you took in a lot more smoke than the rest of us." Nick held her hands in a warm, reassuring clasp. "If you'll concentrate on breathing, I'll tell you everything. Without interruptions, please."

She nodded. It wasn't as if she had a choice.

"The building is fine, thanks to getting the alarm out so quickly. Only damage was to the attic, and the carpenters will start repairs as soon as the police and fire inspector clear it. Tommy is under arrest, and he's been moved to the county lockup. So far he's withstood the questioning, and his father has hired the best attorney money can buy."

Allison moved slightly, wanting to speak, but a frown kept her silent.

"T.J.'s another story, though. As soon as he found out about his father and the pills, he was only too willing to talk. It turns out he was the one who tried to run you off the road and tampered with the circuit box." A shadow crossed his face. "Poor kid. He doesn't have any doubt that his father was responsible for his mother's death. Says he thought that all along. Mac says he came up with a lot of details that made sense once you know what was behind it all."

She didn't like T.J.'s influence on Krysta, but she couldn't help pitying him. Considering his parents, he could be a lot worse off.

"And then there's the forensic evidence. Thanks to you for saving the pill bottle, the DA has lots of lovely evidence as to how the pills were tampered with, to say nothing of Tommy's fingerprints all over the vial and one clear set of Ralph's, probably where he picked it up initially."

He held her hand between both of his, and she realized that the bandaging had been reduced to a more basic level.

"So you don't need to start worrying that it's you against the world. It's not. You're not alone in this or anything else."

Allison blinked, trying to hold back tears, but one slipped away and rolled down her cheek. Nick's face worked at the sight. He wiped the tear away with one finger.

"I thought I'd lost you." His voice thickened. "When I found you there on the floor in all that smoke and fire, I thought you were gone."

"I'm pretty hard to get rid of," she murmured. Was he really saying what she thought he was?

He lifted her hand to his lips. "You were right. I knew it already, but I couldn't seem to admit it. All those excuses I kept putting up about protecting Jamie—I was protecting myself, too. Afraid to risk loving for fear I'd get hurt. How did you know?"

"Because I was doing the same thing. Afraid to get hurt. Afraid of hurting someone else." She stopped for breath. "Nearly getting killed seems to be a great method for taking a serious look at yourself. I don't want to live that way. I want a real life, with someone I love who loves me back."

She couldn't say more. She could only look at him and hope he knew what she was saying. *Are you that someone?*

"It's a good thing you feel that way." His lips moved against her skin. "Because I love you, Allison Standish."

Her smile trembled. "I love you." Three simple words, but they carried a wealth of promise.

All of her concerns about the future, about her career, slid away. Who was to say she couldn't build a satisfying interiors business right here? With the building to manage, and the shop to help run, and the prospect of a family of her own, a small business would be just fine.

Nick bent over the bed carefully, obviously not able to prop himself on his hands any more than she could sit up to meet him. They'd barely managed to get their lips together when there was a knock on the door, immediately followed by the eruption of a small boy hurling himself toward Allison.

"Easy, son." Nick grabbed him, wincing. "No jumping on Allison right now."

Ellen, following her grandson, took him by the shoulders, giving Nick a worried glance. "Be careful of your hands, Nick."

"I won't jump, I promise." Jamie's eyes were solemn. "But I have to kiss her good-night. You need a goodnight kiss when you sleep in a new place."

"My sentiments exactly," Nick said, his lips twitching. "Okay." He boosted Jamie up to sit on the edge of the bed.

"You'll be okay, won't you?" Jamie stared into Allison's eyes. "Grammy says you will."

"I'll be fine," Allison assured him.

"She'll be out of here tomorrow," Nick said. "Her mom and dad will be here then to take care of her."

"What?" She stared at him. "Who called them? I

was going to tell them about it myself so they wouldn't worry."

He shook his head. "Sorry, that ship has sailed. Mac figured they had to know before it hit the television news, so I called them. Now, don't get all excited. I talked to your dad, and he said he'd break the news to your mom, but they'd both have to see you before they were satisfied. So they're taking the first flight tomorrow." He hesitated. "Come on, admit it. You want to see them."

"And we want to meet them," Ellen added. "After all, we should be getting acquainted, shouldn't we?"

Allison looked at Nick, who shrugged. "I didn't say anything. Mom, do you think you could let me handle that part myself? We could use a little time."

She knew what he was saying—that Jamie had to be given time to get used to the idea; that they all had to figure out how they were going to fit together. But even while she was telling herself that, Jamie was snuggling up against her as if he'd been there all his life, and she hugged him close.

"Maybe not too much time," she murmured. Her fingers found the bed control, and she pressed it so that she and Jamie tilted upward. "Jamie is right," she said, looking into Nick's eyes. "I need a good-night kiss."

And since it seemed family was going to be such a big part of their lives, maybe it was appropriate that they were there when he leaned over for a kiss to seal the promise.

* * * * *